More praise for Sara Donati's

INTO THE WILDERNESS

"My favorite kind of book is the sort you live in, rather than read. *Into the Wilderness* is one of those rare stories that let you breathe the air of another time, and leave your footprints on the snow of a wild, strange place. I can think of no better adventure than to explore the wilderness in the company of such engaging and independent lovers as Elizabeth and her Nathaniel."
—Diana Gabaldon

"The author builds a powerful adventure story, animating everyone—German villagers, slaves and Scottish trappers alike—in a gorgeous, vividly described American landscape. The erotic passages aren't bad, either."—*People*

"Donati's captivating saga is much like the books in Diana Gabaldon's bestselling Outlander series, and it is definitely the romance of the year when it comes to transcending genre boundaries and appealing to readers who love lush historical epics or thrilling backwoods adventure."—*Booklist*

"A lushly written first novel. . . . Donati, a skillful storyteller, easily weaves historical fact with romantic ambience to create a dense, complex design. . . . Exemplary historical fiction, boasting a heroine with a real and tangible presence."
—*Kirkus Reviews*

"Remarkable . . . A vibrant tapestry . . . Sara Donati is a skilled storyteller who weaves historical facts into a grand adventure of love, mystery and intrigue. She takes us to an unfamiliar place and allows us to breathe the air of another time. This is exemplary historical fiction. . . . From page one, the action is nonstop. The more you read, the better it gets. No doubt we can look forward to a sequel."—*Tulsa World*

"An elegant, eloquent word journey . . . The author has [a] gift for capturing the history and the lives of the people of that time and place."—*The Tampa Tribune*

"Epic in scope, emotionally intense, *Into the Wilderness* . . . is an enrapturing, grand adventure."—*Bookpage*

"Memorable. . . . Draws the reader into the story from page one. . . . A powerfully good read."—*Toronto Sun*

"A splendid read. . . . Wonderful reading, suited for a cold winter's night."—*The Rocky Mountain News*

"Better buy some midnight oil, for this hugely satisfying novel is a page-turner."—*The Orlando Sentinel*

INTO THE
WILDERNESS

Sara Donati

BANTAM BOOKS

New York Toronto London Sydney Auckland

INTO THE WILDERNESS

A Bantam Book

PUBLISHING HISTORY
Bantam hardcover edition published August 1998
Bantam paperback edition / August 1999

ISBN: 0-553-57852-9

Published simultaneously in the United States and Canada

Bantam Books are published by Bantam Books, a division of Random
House, Inc. Its trademark, consisting of the words "Bantam Books" and
the portrayal of a rooster, is Registered in U.S. Patent and Trademark
Office and in other countries. Marca Registrada. Bantam Books, 1540
Broadway, New York, New York 10036.

PRINTED IN THE UNITED STATES OF AMERICA

OPM 10 9 8 7 6 5 4 3 2 1

For Emmy,
and (as always)
for Bill and Elisabeth

Author's Notes and Acknowledgments

In the past few years I have learned that writers of historical fiction must hang together or go aground. Without the support, advice, insight, finger-wagging, ranting, and the tons of factual information others have shared with me, this book would not exist in a form worthy of consideration. In particular, I am thankful to:

J. F. Cooper for inspiration, and S. Clemens, for perspective;

Diana Gabaldon for constant and consistent encouragement, for contacts of enormous value, for her generosity in matters small and large, and for long discussions about this strange and compelling undertaking of writing historical fiction;

Kaera Hallahan for reading the entire manuscript at a difficult juncture, for providing priceless commentary and badly needed, no-nonsense encouragement, for giving me the skinny on horses, and for bookmarks that tell tales;

Michelle LaFrance for help with things historical and Gaelic, for finally falling in love with Nathaniel, and for her companionship and friendship along the way;

Doctors Jim and Janet Gilsdorf for medical details—Janet on infectious disease; Jim on the nature and treatment of wounds. Jim in particular for invaluable technical and historical detail on hunting and trapping and canoeing in the bush;

Marty Calvert for listening, as she always does, with skill, and for putting her finger on holes with gentle insistence; Margaret Nesse, for careful readings and entertaining discussions;

The writers who grace the Research and Craft section of the CompuServe Writers' Forum, for sharing their experience and expertise in a wide variety of subjects, from the nature of black-fly bites, rifle slings, and left hooks to eighteenth-century terms for hard candy and pregnancy. I am indebted to Mac Beckett, Merrill Cornish, Susie Crandall, Hall Elliott, Rob Frank, Karl Hagen, Walter Hawn, Ed Huntress, Janet Kaufmann, Janet Kieffer, Rosina Lippi-Green, Susan Martin, Janet McConnaughey, Don H. Meredith, Susan Lynn Peterson, Bonnee Pierson, Michelle Powell, Barbara Schnell, Beth Shope, Elise Skidmore, Phyllis Tarbell, Arnold Wagner, and Karen S. White for their time, interest, and generosity. In particular, I am thankful to Dr. Ellen Mandell for providing a wealth of material on eighteenth-century medical practices, and for many encouraging words and useful discussions. In the Collectibles Forum, Michael Crowder, Chuck Huber, and Neil Rothschild were helpful with details on late-eighteenth-century currency and coins;

David Karraker for telling me that I could write all those years ago, and for his faith in me regardless of such trivial matters as differences in taste. If I could have fit his Ben and Janie into this tale, I would have done it, just to see the look on his face;

My agent, Jill Grinberg, for her enthusiasm, energy, endless hard work, and for those uplifting answering-machine messages;

At Bantam, Nita Taublib and Wendy McCurdy for loving this story and treating it so well;

Wendy Fisher House for careful listening; Pat Rosenmeyer for enthusiastic reading; Moni Dressler for feeding me chocolate and sympathy; Scott Spector for taking me to the movies;

My family for their patience and faith in me; Bill for his support in the face of crises of all kinds; Elisabeth, for her first breath and for every one she has ever taken since and for the billions yet to come. I thank her especially for not expecting me to mend her socks;

Now there's only Emmy. Emmy Liston provided calm when I needed it, enthusiasm when I was down, realism when I was off the ground, mysticism when I was too firmly anchored, faith in me at times I could spare myself not one shred. She gave me something I was missing in a greater writing community with an aesthetic that made me claustrophobic: permission to write this story. She is a writer's writer, and she is my friend, and this one is for her.

INTO THE
WILDERNESS

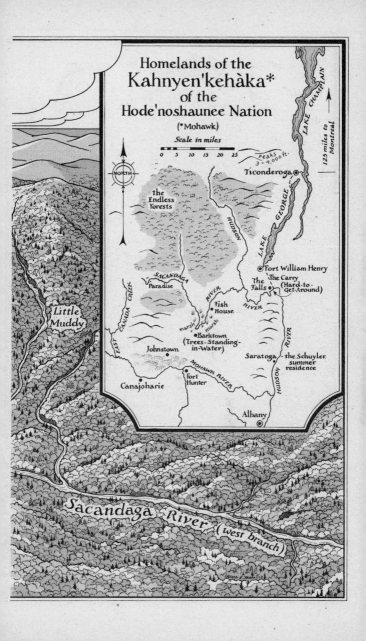

Major Characters

Residents of Paradise

The Middletons

Judge Alfred Middleton, landowner
Elizabeth, his daughter
Julian, his son
Curiosity Freeman, a freed slave, his housekeeper
Galileo Freeman, a freed slave, the manager of his farm and holdings, and Curiosity's husband
Daisy, Polly, and Almanzo Freeman, their grown children, in Judge Middleton's employ

The Bonners

Dan'l Bonner (known also as Hawkeye), a hunter and trapper
Chingachgook (known also as Great-Snake or Indian John), his adoptive father, a sachem of the Mahican people
Cora Bonner, Dan'l's wife, a native of Scotland (deceased)
Nathaniel Bonner (also known as Wolf-Running-Fast or Between-Two-Lives), their son, a hunter and trapper
Hannah (also known as Squirrel or Used-to-Be-Two), Nathaniel's daughter
Sarah (also known as Sings-from-Books), Nathaniel's wife (deceased)

The Kahnyen'kehàka (Mohawk)

Falling-Day, of the Wolf clan, Nathaniel's mother-in-law
Many-Doves (also known as Abigail), her daughter
Otter (also known as Benjamin), her son
Runs-from-Bears, of the Turtle clan

Villagers

Richard Todd, doctor and landowner
The Reverend Josiah Witherspoon, a widower
Katherine (Kitty) Witherspoon, his daughter

Anna Hauptmann, widow, owner and proprieter of the trading post, and her children, Ephraim and Henrietta

Axel Metzler, Anna's father, a widower and proprietor of the tavern

Billy Kirby, trapper, carpenter, lumberjack

Liam Kirby, Billy's young brother

Jed McGarrity, his wife, Nancy, and sons, Ian and Rudy, and infant daughter, Jane

Moses Southern, a trapper and hunter

Martha Southern, his wife, and their children, Jemima, Adam, and Jeremiah

Asa Pierce, blacksmith

John Glove, owner of a mill. His wife, Agatha, his children, Hepzibah and Ruth; and his slaves, Benjamin and George

Claude Dubonnet (known also as Dirty-Knife), his wife, Gertrude, and his children, Marie and Peter

Charlie LeBlanc, farmer and trapper

Isaac Cameron and his grown daughter, Hitty, and his sons, Benjamin, Obadiah, and Elijah

Jack MacGregor, hunter and trapper

Archie Cunningham and his wife, Goody, and their son Praise-Be and grown son Noah

Jan Kaes, and Matilda, his wife, and their grown daughters, Molly and Becca

Henry Smythe, his wife, Constance, and his daughter, Dolly

SARATOGA

Major General Philip Schuyler and his wife, Catherine; some of their children, Philip, Catherine, Cornelia, Rensselaer, and three of their grandchildren

Anton Meerschaum, their overseer

Sally Gerlach, their housekeeper

The Reverend Lyddeker

ALBANY

Judge van der Poole

Simon Desjardins, French aristocrat and merchant

Pierre Pharoux, French aristocrat and merchant

Samuel Hench, a Quaker from Baltimore, Elizabeth Middleton's second cousin

Leendert Beekman, a Dutch merchant

Baldwin O'Brien, a treasury agent

JOHNSTOWN

Mr. Bennett, an attorney
Mrs. Bennett, his wife

IN THE BUSH

Robbie MacLachlan, Scot,
    former soldier, a hunter
    and trapper
Jack Lingo, hunter and trapper
Dutch Ton, hunter
    and trapper
Joe, an escaped slave

GOOD PASTURE
    (KAHEN'TIYO)

Stone-Splitter, sachem
He-Who-Dreams,
    faith keeper
Sturdy-Heart, a maker of
    canoes
Spotted-Fox, a warrior and fur
    runner
Throws-Far (also known as
    Samuel Todd)

Made-of-Bones, clan mother
    of the Wolf
Splitting-Moon,
    granddaughter of
    Made-of-Bones
Two-Suns, clan mother of
    the Turtle
She-Remembers, clan mother
    of the Bear

TREES-STANDING-IN-WATER
    (BARKTOWN)

Sky-Wound-Round, sachem
Bitter-Words, faith keeper

AT OAKMERE, IN ENGLAND

Augusta Merriweather, Lady
    Crofton, Elizabeth
    Middleton's aunt and Judge
    Middleton's sister
Cousin Amanda Spencer and
    her husband, William
    Spencer, Viscount
    Durbeyfield

PART I

Discovering Paradise

I

December, 1792

Elizabeth Middleton, twenty-nine years old and unmarried, overly educated and excessively rational, knowing right from wrong and fancy from fact, woke in a nest of marten and fox pelts to the sight of an eagle circling overhead, and saw at once that it could not be far to Paradise. All around her was a world of intense green and severe white mountains, a wilderness of deep and bountiful silence, magnificent beyond all imagining. This was not England, that was clear enough. Nor was it the port at New-York where she had waited for months for the long trip north to begin, nor any of the settlements between New-York and Albany. Her journey was nearing its end.

They had set out early from Johnstown, leaving the Mohawk Valley behind to follow the Sacandaga River north and then west. At midday they had eaten a cold lunch in the sleigh while the horses rested and watered, and now, finally, Elizabeth found herself within only a few miles of a new home, and a new life.

Across from Elizabeth, her father and brother napped fitfully under piles of quilts, counterpanes, and pelts, their presence given away only by the shock of Julian's unruly hair, and warm clouds of breath which hovered over it. The only other person awake was her father's driver, Galileo, who perched on the box wrapped in many layers of patchwork mantle, pipe smoke trailing behind him in tendrils. Essentially alone, Elizabeth allowed herself to smile idiotically at her surroundings, struggling with her wraps until she could sit up straight. Then she drew in her breath both at the cold—she had never known such temperatures in England—and at the beauty of it. In the many years since her father had last visited England, he had often written of his holdings in upper New-York State, but his descriptions were limited to resources: so much timber, game, arable land, water. Although she had never said so, Elizabeth had thought it capricious and perhaps even imprudent of him to name the settlement Paradise. She saw now that she had been wrong.

Trees of more kinds than she could recognize covered the rolling landscape and moved up the hills and over the higher peaks without pause. The farther they traveled, the fewer the clearings: the track snaked back and forth, narrowed, approached the river and fell back again. Through birches and white pines, Elizabeth caught a glimpse of the frozen river now and again, the ice reflecting the forest and sky in a revolving blur of blues and greens. The woods cleared unexpectedly, revealing a sharp bend in the river backed by bluffs. A waterfall erupted from the cliff face, half frozen in mid-arch, half still falling in a crystalline rainbow to a break in the ice. Beyond the sounds of the river, the creaking of the harness, the rhythmic beat of the horses' hooves, and the rush of metal runners in the snow, the world was silent.

Then, in the woods between the sleigh track and the river Elizabeth saw movement. In the deep shadows a large deer was stepping gracefully through the snow, moving down toward the water.

At the same instant, there was a rustling in the underbrush just a few feet from the sleigh on its opposite side; Elizabeth turned, startled, to see a brace of hunting dogs emerge from a thicket, and close behind them, two men running quickly and silently. They were only in her line of sight for a moment, but Elizabeth took in the fact that they wore buckskins and fur, that they were both tall and straight, although one considerably older than the other, and that they bore long rifles held at a purposeful angle.

The team became unsettled and Galileo spoke to them sharply as they broke stride and slowed; this roused Elizabeth's father immediately.

"Galileo!" he called out, half-asleep. "Galileo! What is the matter!" Judge Middleton rose as the sleigh drew to a halt.

Elizabeth stood as well, stretching to follow the progress of the hunters, who had melted into the woods which lined the riverbed.

From beneath his rugs and furs, Julian stretched and yawned expansively and finally stood up to observe, peering over the driver's box. Just then the hunters, doubling back, emerged from the trees not far from the sleigh. Julian followed their progress with sleepy amusement.

"Highwaymen in New-York State?" he laughed. "I thought we left that kind of thing behind us on the London Road!"

Elizabeth gave her brother a half smile. "Will you be serious, please. Surely you can see that those men are hunters. Natives, I suppose."

Her father was holding a staccato conversation with Galileo as he rumbled around in the front of the sleigh, and then he turned to face his children with his own gun over his arm.

"Come on, Lizzie," Julian said, making ready to leave the sleigh. "There are bandits at hand. We might as well join in the fun."

"You will have to learn to look more closely, my boy," said the judge. "Don't you see anything worth your attention except hunters? Look where they're heading. There! At the next bend in the river. That's the biggest doe I've seen in two winters. And I've got a new musket, which I intend to put to good use."

"Lizzie!" urged Julian again, gesturing toward her, but the judge shook his head.

"Stay with the sleigh," he called to his daughter as he leapt down and sped off with Julian close behind. Julian sent her a look over his shoulder which she knew well: he was sympathetic, but unwilling to champion Elizabeth in her less ladylike pursuits.

Elizabeth was not surprised to be left behind; that was a woman's lot. Then she remembered that this was not England, and that she might ask for—and do—things considered bold at home.

"Galileo," she called up. "Can we move forward a bit so I can see what's happening?"

"Might be dangerous, miss," the man answered from the depths of his mufflers and wraps. "The judge don't have a feel for that musket yet."

"What!" Elizabeth laughed out loud. "Do you think he would shoot us?"

"Not on purpose, no, miss." Galileo sat down again on the box. "But I don't put much faith in that smoothbore of his."

When it was clear that the man meant what he said and did not intend to move into firing range, Elizabeth began to gather her skirts together. "Well, then, I'll go on foot," she said firmly. Balanced on the side of the sleigh for the jump down, she paused as a double gunshot burst and then echoed over the valley, chased by the baying of the dogs.

"Did they get the deer?"

Galileo was standing again to calm the horses and he squinted in the direction of the shots. "Somebody got something," he said slowly.

Elizabeth set off as quickly as she was able, but the deep snow reached over the tops of her boots, and her skirts were heavy. By the time she came within a few feet of the men she was flushed and overheated; pushing her hood of flannel and silk back onto her shoulders to feel the cold air on her scalp, she distinguished her brother's voice over the rush of the waterfall. She recognized the tone he reserved for servants and she groaned inwardly. At the same time, although she did not know exactly why, she feared for his well-being.

The men fell silent as she approached. Even the dogs settled down immediately beside the hunters.

"Elizabeth, my dear," said the judge. "I believe you would be more comfortable in the sleigh."

Elizabeth glanced uneasily from her father's friendly but distracted expression to her brother's angry one, and then at the hunters, who did not turn to greet her. This discourtesy she took as a sign of their disapproval, but Elizabeth was determined not to be sent off like a child.

"Did you get the deer, Father?"

The judge shook his head. "No, I'm afraid I didn't. Hawkeye—Mr. Bonner—got the doe, and I—well, I should have listened to Galileo. Most of my shot went wild but I'm afraid one ball did find a target—"

At that the two strangers turned toward Elizabeth. Surprised, she saw that neither of them—although dressed like natives, and wearing feathers in their unbound hair—were Indian. Then, with a wave of distress that left her unsteady, Elizabeth saw what her father had done.

A flower of blood blossomed freely on the younger man's right shoulder. Elizabeth stepped toward him, but he stepped back just as quickly, to avoid her; surprised, she looked from his wound to his face. She saw lines and planes so strong that she was reminded of a stone sculpture, straight dark brows over hazel eyes, and a high forehead creased in—pain? Anger? And Elizabeth took in the fact that this stranger, this man, was both furious and in complete control, and that his attention was focused, exclusively, absolutely, on her.

A half hour later, once again on their way, Elizabeth found herself seated across from two men to whom she had just been introduced in the briefest and most unusual manner. Dan'l Bonner—the one the judge called Hawkeye—was the focus of her brother's attention. His son, Nathaniel, was utterly silent.

At the back of the sleigh, strapped quickly across the piles of luggage, was the deer; Nathaniel Bonner had only agreed to come into the village for medical treatment once the judge—over Julian's protests—had acknowledged the Bonners' rightful claim to the animal. Now Julian fumed, arguing in turns with Hawkeye and his own father. Nathaniel took no part in the argument, but neither did he miss a word; Elizabeth was sure of it.

Elizabeth found herself glancing up at Nathaniel far more often than she knew she should, and without fail she found him looking at her. Each time this happened, Elizabeth looked away and vowed not to look up again, but she could not curb her curiosity: this was a white man, dressed like an Indian, with a long earring of beaten silver dangling from one ear; she had heard him speaking to his father in a language which must be native; he was tall and lean and as menacing as a whipcord; one broad hand held the barrel of the long rifle in a manner which was both casual and deliberate. There was a serious wound in his shoulder which had been hastily stanched with her father's handkerchief and Elizabeth's own scarf, but it seemed to concern him not at all; and he was determined to look at her, and only her, without pause. This behavior—impertinent, and distinctly unseemly—so unnerved her that Elizabeth could not think of anything suitable to say to him in reproach.

"Father, I simply do not understand. The land on which the animal fell belongs to you," Julian was saying.

The judge nodded. "It does. Right now we are just about in the middle of the original patent, which was about a thousand acres. Backs right onto the wilderness on the other side of Hidden Wolf Mountain."

Elizabeth, who at that moment was glancing up at Nathaniel, saw a slight tremor in his face.

"Are you in pain, Mr. Bonner?"

Her brother turned toward her irritably. "My God, Elizabeth. It's a minor wound. He won't die of it."

"No one has ever died of good manners, either, Julian," Elizabeth said dryly. "You might try some for yourself and find out."

This brought out a surprised grunt of amusement from Hawkeye, who shifted his attention from Julian for a moment to appraise Elizabeth.

"Then give him the doe as payment for his pain and suffering," Julian continued. "But do not call it his. You cannot countenance poaching."

"I have given Hawkeye and his son permission to hunt on my land, in perpetuity. In season, of course. That means that the animal is theirs. I wish they would sell me the saddle to roast for our dinner tomorrow—"

From the corner of her eye, Elizabeth noted how Nathaniel's face grew still at this.

"—but if they will not, I cannot force them."

"Mr. Bonner—Hawkeye," Julian said, turning to the older man. "Will you at least concede that my father has a right to a portion of the meat—"

The judge began to protest, but his son insisted on finishing. "—as a token of goodwill?"

Julian's behavior was shameful; Elizabeth could not deny this. But it was one thing to see all her brother's worst faults come to light, and quite another to see him do it in the company of strangers. If her brother could not feel the mortification which should be his, Elizabeth would. She tried to catch his eye, but instead she got the attention of Dan'l Bonner.

He was a man of about seventy years, with white hair touched with hints of his earlier black, and a deeply weathered face, but with a calm dignity and intelligence. His voice was deep and had a strange cadence, an intonation Elizabeth had not heard from any other American so far. He was, in short, intimidating in a way she had not anticipated from a backwoodsman. With a little regret for her brother, Elizabeth conceded Hawkeye Bonner's superiority.

She glanced up, found Nathaniel looking at her again, and blushed as if he had read her thoughts.

Hawkeye finished his perusal of Julian and then spoke to the point. "First off," he began, in his low, steady voice, "I was hunting in these woods long before your father set claim to them—"

He held up a large and callused hand to ward off Julian's interruption.

"You want to tell me what I already know, that the judge paid good gold for this land when it was took away from the Loyalists and auctioned. I won't argue that with you—now. Not right now. You want me to sell your father the doe as a gesture of goodwill, but this ain't a matter of goodwill," Hawkeye finished.

"What is it a matter of, then?" Julian asked with one brow raised.

"Hunger," said Nathaniel, speaking for the first time since he stepped into the sleigh.

At that moment, they came to a halt in front of a house built of timber and stone and Elizabeth looked up in surprise. They had driven through the settlement of Paradise and arrived without her taking in even the smallest detail of her new home.

The judge took the opportunity to interrupt the argument at

hand. "Well, there is a meal waiting for us now, and no one will leave this house hungry today. But first we need Richard to look after Nathaniel's wound. Galileo! Have Manny see to the luggage, and go after the doctor yourself. We need him straightaway." The judge helped his daughter from the sleigh, and then he turned to the hunters and smiled. "We'll have your needs addressed immediately," he said, and started for the house, with Hawkeye and her brother close behind.

Elizabeth was left alone with Nathaniel Bonner. She hesitated, searching for something to say.

"Never mind if you're going to make excuses for your brother, miss. Don't bother yourself."

"I was going to ask you if you have a large family to feed, Mr. Bonner."

For the first time, Nathaniel smiled at her. "I've got no wife, if that's what you mean."

It was the smile that set her temper flaring and her heart beating unevenly, Elizabeth told herself. She must forgive him his uncivil manner, and his forwardness, but the smile was more than she could rationalize.

"It makes little difference to me whether or not you are married, Mr. Bonner."

"We don't stand on such ceremony here. Call me Nathaniel. You're a spinster woman, no?"

Elizabeth's mouth fell open in surprise, but then she nodded. "I am unmarried, and content to remain so."

Nathaniel raised an eyebrow. "Are you now? And is your father as content to have a spinster daughter as you are to be one?"

This was too much. "Mr. Bonner, you are too familiar—"

"Am I?" he said, and smiled again, this time with something akin to kindness. "Or just too honest?"

"Not that it's any of your concern, Mr. Bonner, but my father respects my wishes and would never try to force a husband on—a spinster daughter—when I have no need or desire for one." Satisfied with this speech and her own logic, Elizabeth thought that Nathaniel Bonner must now desist.

"And what do you desire?"

The question took Elizabeth by surprise. *I don't think anyone has ever asked me that,* she thought, and then in an attempt to hide her confusion, she turned toward the house.

"We should go in," she said. "My father has called for a surgeon. He truly wants to put things right with you."

Just as suddenly as Nathaniel Bonner's smile had come, it left.

"We'll see how much your father wishes to put right, miss," he said, and he started for the house.

Her father's housekeeper was a long and very wiry black woman with a thin face framed by layers of calico. She took one look at Nathaniel's bloody shoulder and disappeared into the far end of the house, a loud and pointed monologue trailing along behind her. Elizabeth was left to find her own way to her room.

When she had located it and closed the door behind her, she found herself suddenly exhausted. There was a fire in the small hearth, and she gratefully fell into the chair before it, barely looking around herself at the furnishings. She noted that the windows faced east, but for the moment she could not rouse herself to go look out, although she had wondered for months what kind of view she might hope for. With trembling hands she removed her traveling cloak and hood.

Self-pity and whimpering, Elizabeth observed with a frown. *This is a fine start you're off to, my girl.*

She drew three deep breaths and with a suppressed sigh she rose from her warm spot before the hearth to walk to the dresser.

"You may be a spinster," she told her image in the mirror over the washbasin, "but you needn't be unkempt. You will start by making yourself presentable and finding your own way to the dinner table."

Quickly, Elizabeth washed her face and neck in cool water and then in rapid movements took out the pins which held her hair in place to shake her hair free. Uncoiled, it flew around her like an unruly veil, as deep as the night and rippling to her waist, falling from a widow's peak to frame a heart-shaped face, a strong, dimpled chin, an overgenerous mouth, and widely spaced light gray eyes ringed with darker gray, the same gray as the linen of her dress. Quaker eyes, her mother had always called them, affectionately. Now this thought of her mother helped Elizabeth, and she looked around herself. Perhaps her mother had brushed her hair before this very mirror in the cabin on the mountain the judge had built for her when they were first married.

With a start Elizabeth realized that her bags were not yet in her room, and that there were no brushes or combs on the dresser. She opened the door, hoping that Galileo's son might have been too shy to knock when they brought up the trunks, but the hall was empty. There was nothing to do but go and find her things.

Smoothing her rumpled traveling dress as best she could and praying that she would run into no one, Elizabeth made her way downstairs but found that the foyer was empty of people and luggage. She was confronted with a half circle of closed doors, the far one of which, she reasoned, led to the kitchens.

Finally, irritated at herself for her hesitance, she knocked and then opened a door, and found her father's empty study. The next door opened into the dining room, with a table set for an expansive midday meal, but also empty.

Growing impatient, Elizabeth opened the third door and found herself in the parlor.

Nathaniel Bonner was sitting directly before her on a low stool in the light of the window, stripped to the waist. Another man, tall and very broad, hovered behind Nathaniel's shoulder with a bloodstained rag in one hand and a scalpel in the other. At the far wall, on a stool next to the fire, the housekeeper worked over a mortar and pestle while Hawkeye watched with a critical eye. All four looked up at Elizabeth in surprise.

Even in her mortification, Elizabeth had to notice how different the two men were: one fair, with great masses of red-gold beard, and dressed expensively in linen and wool; the other dark and lean, dressed only in leather breechclout and leggings, his naked chest smooth and muscled. Then Elizabeth realized that she was looking at a stranger—a grown man—without a shirt, when she had never seen even her brother in such a natural state. She felt herself flooding with color.

Surprise crossed Nathaniel's face; he sat up and opened his

mouth to speak but Elizabeth had already begun to spin away, sending her hair around her into a whirl. She slammed the door shut behind her, her face burning, and ran back toward the stair, where she bumped full force into her father and brother.

"Elizabeth!" the judge said, startled. "Are you quite well?"

"Really, Lizzie," her brother chimed in, straightening the lace stock at his neck. "Look at you. What a sight you are."

Elizabeth scowled. "If I knew where my things were, Julian, I would not be here in the hall offending your sensibilities."

The judge put an arm around her shoulders. "Go back to your rooms, my dear. I'll send someone along with your bags right away so that you can change for dinner. Richard is here, and he's anxious to meet you, so put on something pretty."

The tone of this request, coaxing and unfamiliar, made Elizabeth pause in her flight up the stairs. "Richard?"

Her father smiled. "Richard Todd—I've written to you of him. You must have seen him just now, tending to Nathaniel. He is anxious to be introduced to you."

And Elizabeth remembered, suddenly, those words she had heard just minutes before: *Is your father as content to have a spinster daughter as you are to be one?*

"It seems the sights of the sickroom were such that she didn't notice the doctor," Julian was saying as Elizabeth disappeared up the stairs. At any other time, she would have responded to her brother's impertinence, but now, suddenly uneasy, she wanted nothing more than to get away.

II

The housekeeper was called Curiosity Freeman, and Elizabeth
soon understood how she had earned her first name. When
Galileo brought up her trunks and valise, Curiosity came along
—to help Elizabeth get settled, she said, but it was clear that
there was more than baggage on her mind.

"How many times the judge will get himself into mischief
with that smoothbore, I hate to think," she began without preamble. Over Elizabeth's protests, Curiosity lifted and moved the
trunks without catching her breath or losing her train of
thought.

"Never you mind, I suppose I can manage these few valises
of yours. I've lifted heavier things in my life."

Elizabeth noted Curiosity's broad hands and muscled forearms and had to agree that she was capable.

"Don't you worry about me, miss. Not much short of a
musketball could put me off my feet." This put her in mind of
the recent drama, and she took up the topic again. "Nathaniel
would be crossing to the other side this very moment if he
didn't have somebody watching over him, that's for sure. But
that little bullet certainly did push your homecoming out of the
way, didn't it?"

"Mrs. Freeman—" Elizabeth began.

"No, miss, you must call me Curiosity. It's the name my
mama give me, and I go by it."

Elizabeth smiled. "It seems everyone here goes by their first name."

"All except the judge."

"Well, then, please call me Elizabeth." This was a social breach which never would have been countenanced at home; Elizabeth knew that Julian would complain to her that she was too familiar with the servants. This train of thought was interrupted by Curiosity, who had her own questions to ask.

"You a Quaker, like your mama was?"

"No, we were raised by my aunt Merriweather, Father's sister. But I admire very much the Quaker teachings—"

"Well, you won't get no argument from me, as Quakers bought me and my Galileo free. It was your mama's daddy who done that for us, but I expect you heard that story. We been working for your folks ever since."

Elizabeth smiled at this good report of her family. "I hope my father's done well by you?"

Curiosity stood up suddenly. She gave Elizabeth a long, steady look, her dark eyes hooded. Then she smiled. "Time to get to table. The menfolk will be waiting." She turned toward the door, her wide skirts rustling around her.

"Has my father done well by you, by you and yours?" Elizabeth repeated, uneasy at the woman's sudden reticence.

Curiosity spoke with her back to Elizabeth. "He done pretty well by me and mine, miss. But there's others who ain't as satisfied." She turned and saw the questions forming on Elizabeth's face, and held up her palm.

"Time to get to table," she said, and then she was gone, before Elizabeth could remind Curiosity to call her by her Christian name.

When Elizabeth had changed into a simple gray dress with a lawn shawl tucked into the bodice and tamed her hair into a roll along the back of her head, she stood looking at herself in the mirror. The vision of Nathaniel Bonner, bare chested, rose up before her and she scowled fiercely at herself. Nathaniel was waiting downstairs, as was the mysterious Dr. Todd, and she would have to go and deal with both of them. This was not what she had expected for the first day in her new home. In England she had not been much in society; she had preferred the company of her books, and the few close friends she had left behind.

When she could wait no longer, Elizabeth found her way down to the dining room where the meal and the men waited for her. With great enthusiasm, her father took her by the arm and presented her to Dr. Todd; Elizabeth smiled politely and answered his inquiries as to her trip and health, all the while too aware of Nathaniel, who stood with his back against the wall, his arms crossed, and his gaze fixed on her.

Richard Todd did his best to capture all her attention for himself: he was solicitous and amusing, and the look in his blue eyes set below a mane of red-blond hair was friendly and seemed sincere. She judged him to be just over thirty, with hair thinning high on his temples. Elizabeth saw that while his coat and waistcoat were well cut and suited him well, they could not hide a propensity for fleshiness.

Seated at one end of the table opposite her father, Elizabeth found herself too near Nathaniel Bonner for comfort. He was on her left; Richard Todd sat to her right. At the table's head the judge was flanked by Hawkeye and Julian. Elizabeth noted with some relief that the three of them had immediately taken up a previous conversation on the war in France and that she would not have to entertain five men.

I can certainly manage this, she said to herself firmly, and she turned to Nathaniel, suddenly determined to make a new start with this strange man. He wore his own clothing again, the dressing on his wounded shoulder showing through the rent in his shirt, still stained with blood.

"Are you in pain, Mr. Bonner?" she asked. "Is your wound distressing you?"

"Nathaniel," he corrected her. Then: "I am comfortable enough, miss. Thank you most kindly for your concern and interest."

"You are most kindly welcome," she said, matching Nathaniel's tone of mild impertinence.

The dining room was small and somewhat dark, but it provided a profusion of serving tables and odd pieces of furniture for Elizabeth to concentrate on while she considered her predicament. She was at a loss on how to start a conversation which would engage both Richard Todd and Nathaniel Bonner; subjects which were the staples of polite dinner conversation at home would not do here, and she did not know them well enough to bring up more controversial political topics, although she would have liked to hear their opinions on President Washington's Proclamation of Neutrality, or the French defeat of Austrian and Prussian troops at the battle of Valmy. Neither could she ask them about their work without opening up many subjects which would be unseemly, although this topic interested her greatly. Elizabeth glanced around the room again and noted that there were a number of oil paintings, landscapes all of them, some quite awkward and naïve in their execution, but a few very appealing.

"I see my father has been collecting the work of local painters," Elizabeth said to both Nathaniel and Richard Todd. "Interesting, some of them. I like the mountain glade."

"That's a lopsided contrivance," Hawkeye volunteered from the other side of the table. "Nothing in nature to match it."

"Is that so?" Elizabeth asked. "Well, perhaps I haven't seen enough mountains to know. But I do like it."

"You are very generous," Richard Todd said, and Elizabeth turned to him. "Hawkeye is right."

"I agree that not all of the paintings are equally well done, but certainly there is some merit here—aren't you being rather hard on the artist?" Elizabeth asked.

"It seems I must be," Richard Todd said calmly. "As the artist, it falls to me to be my own sternest critic. The judge is too kind to be honest. He hangs everything I produce."

Elizabeth was surprised to learn that the doctor had painted these landscapes; at home, young women were sent to drawing masters to learn to make pretty sketches of mountains and children, but young men rarely showed an active interest in art.

"Are you interested in painting?" Richard Todd asked her.

She laughed. "I have no talent for it," she said. "But with such landscapes around me, perhaps I will try my hand.

"Don't you find it interesting," she continued, addressing her remark to Nathaniel Bonner, who fixed his attention on her willingly, "that such beauty and bounty has been left untouched and unappreciated for so long?"

"This land was not empty before the Europeans came," he said in clipped tones.

"Nathaniel," began Richard, but Nathaniel cut him off.

"It was not unclaimed," he continued. "And it was anything but unappreciated." With a glance toward Richard Todd, and then toward the judge, who was deeply involved in his own conversation and who had not followed this exchange, Nathaniel stopped himself.

Elizabeth was astonished and intrigued all at once; she wanted to hear the rest of what Nathaniel had to say. But before she could think of some way to make this clear to him, Richard Todd claimed her attention.

"You will want to have a look around the village, Miss Elizabeth," the doctor said to her with a friendly smile, helping himself to venison from the platter which Curiosity offered for the second time. "You must be very curious about your new home. I know Mr. Witherspoon—our minister—and his daughter are very anxious to make your acquaintance."

Thankfully, Elizabeth turned to him. "Yes, I am looking forward to my first trip to the village. I am especially curious to meet the children."

"Children?" Richard Todd smiled politely.

Elizabeth looked toward her father, who was arguing once more with Julian. "Yes, the children," she said. "It would be hard to teach school without them."

"You mean to teach school?" Nathaniel Bonner asked. All of his agitation had disappeared. His gaze was cool, but engaged.

"Why, yes," she said. "I do. That *is* why I came here."

"The judge hasn't said anything about that," said Richard.

For a moment Elizabeth was truly speechless. She had spent six months in England preparing to teach school, her first school. Buying books, consulting educators, reading. It had consumed her completely, and now she found out that her father had never even mentioned her plans to his closest companions. She was struck with a terrible thought: her father had brought her here on false pretenses. Everything Nathaniel Bonner had said to her in the sleigh was true.

She saw Curiosity observing her from the sideboard, she felt Richard Todd's eyes on her, and she knew the only way to rescue the new life she had thought to claim for herself was to speak up as she had never spoken up for herself before.

"Father?" said Elizabeth. "There seems to be some confusion. How is it that Dr. Todd and Mr. Bonner haven't heard that I will be teaching school?"

The judge's eyes darted from Elizabeth to Richard and back again.

"My dear," he began slowly. "All good things in their time, eh? You'll need a few weeks at least to settle in and learn your way around."

Elizabeth struggled to keep her growing surprise and distress hidden. With great deliberation she put down her fork and folded her hands in her lap. "I can at least make a list of the children and learn a little about them and their families, Father. And the schoolhouse itself will need to be got in order."

"What schoolhouse?" asked Hawkeye. "There's no schoolhouse in Paradise that I know of, miss."

Julian put down his fork and knife and turned to the judge. "You don't mean to say there is really no schoolhouse?" He cast a glance at Elizabeth, whose brow was drawn together in a threat he recognized too well. Then he shrugged his shoulders. "Well, sister," said Julian. "I guess you'll have your work cut out for you."

This was a shock, but Elizabeth took it well. She lifted an eyebrow toward her father and waited.

The judge cleared his throat expansively. "Well, maybe not technically, not yet, but there will be."

"Father," she began slowly. "You wrote to me that you would provide me with everything necessary to hold school here for any children willing to attend—"

"So I did," he interrupted, glancing at the doctor. "So I did. And I will see to it you have what you need. A schoolhouse will be built."

"And right smart, too, by the look of it," said Hawkeye.

"Or Lizzie will have something to say," added Julian.

"In the meantime perhaps there is some other building which can be of use," Elizabeth said. "Perhaps the church. On weekdays, of course."

"It's difficult to heat," said the judge. "It would be very uncomfortable."

"Well, then, there must be some other solution," Elizabeth said. "One way or another there will be school on the first day of the new year." She turned to Dr. Todd.

"How many children are there in the village, aged fourteen or less?"

He thought for a moment. "I would say there are a dozen or more. Not all of them will come to school, though."

"And why not?"

"Some of them ain't free," he said, not meeting her eyes.

"Surely their parents can spare them for a few hours in the winter when there is little farm work," Elizabeth said. She looked around the table with growing irritation. "Surely the parents want their children to learn to read and write," she continued.

She felt Nathaniel's gaze intensify and she glanced up at him; on his face Elizabeth saw something unexpected: revelation, and some astonishment. She addressed him.

"Mr. Bonner," she began.

"Nathaniel," he corrected her once again.

She looked around the table once again. "Surely the parents would like to have a school for their children?"

He nodded. "The parents might," he said. "But some of the owners ain't about to allow it."

"Come now, don't upset yourself," the judge said, pursing his lips. "I can't think of more than three slave children who would be of the right age anyway."

Richard Todd shifted uneasily in his seat as she drew herself up and turned her attention to her father, incredulous.

He anticipated her question. "Elizabeth, I have never owned slaves."

"But you allow men in the village to hold slaves?"

Agitated, the judge flushed. "That is not something that I can determine personally," he said. "Because I own land does not mean I control the legislature. And beyond that, Elizabeth, you must know that some slave owners are fair-minded people, good people," he said feebly.

"How do you know that?" she demanded. "How can you know that? How can you find anything fair or good in slavery?"

Richard Todd spoke up. "Because your father knows me, and I have two slaves," he said. "But they have no children to send to your school," he added.

Elizabeth's face drained of color; she addressed her father without acknowledging Dr. Todd.

"I will approach each of the slave owners, then, and ask for permission."

"No slave owner in Paradise is going to send his slaves to your school, Elizabeth," Nathaniel said quietly. She turned to him, and saw that he did not mean to offend her, but that he also was unwilling to spare her the truth.

"And if he did, then he wouldn't send his own children."

She squared her shoulders. "Then I will offer to teach them individually. In their homes."

The men looked at each other.

"I must try, at any rate," Elizabeth said. "In my school, any child is welcome." She felt suddenly deflated, and very tired.

"Now if you will excuse me, gentlemen, I beg your leave to retire."

"But Elizabeth," her father protested. "You have hardly eaten anything."

She stood, smoothing her skirt as she did so, sent her father one long but silent look, and took her leave of the party.

"Welcome to Paradise!" her brother called after her, and his laughter followed her up the stairs.

III

Nathaniel watched Elizabeth leave the room with conflicting emotions. She was not at all what he had anticipated.

He had expected her to be her father's daughter: oblivious and arrogant, with an outer but fragile coating of friendly condescension. Instead, he had found her to be alert and courteous, sensitive where her brother and father were insensitive, and keenly curious. She had wanted to hear what he had to say; she herself had things to say that surprised him. Nathaniel had expected a well-educated young Englishwoman of property to be haughty and distant; he saw little of that in her, either.

Nathaniel had expected a spinster who would sit in the corner by the fire reading and doing needlework, who would leave her warm spot only to venture among those she saw as less fortunate to bestow her gifts of learning and Christianity. There were others like that in this country who had done considerable damage, and Nathaniel had no patience with them. But he had not found her to be a missionary; instead, he acknowledged, she was a woman of considerable strength of character, and admirable goals for herself rather than for others.

Finally, too honest with himself to avoid the issue, Nathaniel admitted with a grim smile that he had expected the judge's spinster daughter to be thin and plain and sour; that wasn't the case at all.

Nathaniel realized that he was staring at the door where

Elizabeth had last stood and that her brother was watching him. He let his face relax and met Julian's chilly blue glare with complete equanimity. In the brother, at any rate, he had not been surprised; Julian was everything that Nathaniel had feared he would be.

Julian turned to Nathaniel as if he had heard the progression of his thoughts. "Listen," he said. "I am sorry about your shoulder. Must hurt like the devil. But it was an accident, after all. Now, what are we going to do about you?"

The judge looked up, still clearly disconcerted by Elizabeth's departure. "What do you mean?"

"What do we owe this man for his . . . inconvenience?" Julian asked his father. "Is there some set price to pay him so that he can be on his way?"

The judge looked between his son and Nathaniel blankly and then his face cleared. "Nathaniel. Of course. I mean to offer you employment; you are skilled with numbers and you could keep my books for me, couldn't you? You would be well recompensed. I couldn't offer you lodging in the house, however—"

"I had a monetary settlement in mind," said Julian. "That would seem to be sufficient in this case, don't you think?"

Hawkeye had been following this exchange silently but now he spoke up. "You won't get Nathaniel to sit inside over your books, Judge," he said with a grin. "He must needs be out of doors. His mother managed to get his letters and numbers into him, but he's not overfond of sitting down with 'em."

Nathaniel turned his attention to the judge.

"I won't keep your books, and I have a home of my own," he said. "But if you feel there's something you owe me, there's something I'll ask of you."

The judge nodded. "If it's in my power."

"Good Lord, Father," muttered Julian.

Nathaniel ignored Julian. "You can hire me to build the schoolhouse your daughter wants," he said. "For a fair wage. I'll start tomorrow."

"Tomorrow—" the judge said, bewildered.

"Even you can't build a cabin in the middle of winter," Richard pointed out.

"No, but I can cut the logs and lay the foundation and the chimney. I'll roll the logs after the first thaw. I'll need to borrow a team, when it gets that far. And I'll take half the wage up front."

"That's a very good offer, Judge," remarked Richard Todd. "I would take him up on it, otherwise you'll be dependent on Billy Kirby to build for you, and you know what a poor job he'll make of it." Richard looked pointedly at the crooked doorsills and window sashes.

"Done and done," said the judge with a sigh. "If costs can be kept to a minimum." He was relieved to have two sticky matters resolved at once. Elizabeth would have her school; his debt to Hawkeye's son would be eased.

"You've got your eye on that woman," Hawkeye said to Nathaniel when they were finally on their way.

Nathaniel shrugged. "And if I do, what's to come of it?"

His father laughed softly. "She's fine to look at, sure enough. And smart. Smarter than her father and brother put together, I'd wager."

They were making their way up Hidden Wolf, walking the horse the judge had lent them. The doe was strapped over the mare's back, and the dogs trotted along behind wearily, glad to be headed for home, but still, with short bursts of enthusiasm, setting off after any sign of a rabbit.

Nathaniel took his time answering. He knew his father approved of Elizabeth; he wouldn't be bothered talking to anybody he didn't like, and he had found plenty to discuss with her. He had a weakness for women with tongues quick enough to match his own.

"She's content to remain a spinster, she says."

Hawkeye grunted. "Well, look at her menfolk. If those are the only husbands she's ever seen at their work, who could blame her?" Then, with a sideways glance: "Todd will have her if he can get her."

Nathaniel's shoulder was aching; he rubbed it with the heel of one hand. "If she brings the land along with her, he will," he agreed. "But it don't look as though she'll be easily got. She calls herself a spinster, and proud of it."

"You had a conversation with her about her spinsterhood right quick, I'd say."

"She's the kind that provokes me, I won't deny that." The mare threatened to lose her footing and Nathaniel chirped to her calmly. "Maybe I scairt her off."

"Or got her interested."

Nathaniel nodded. "There's that possibility."

They walked in silence for a few minutes.

"It would solve some problems," Hawkeye pointed out.

"If she brought Hidden Wolf into the match, it would."

Hawkeye grunted. "I saw you looking at her, and it ain't the land that got your attention. You looked at her like you looked at Sarah, once upon a time. Now don't get that face on you. Sarah's been dead five years. She wouldn't have begrudged you a new woman."

"You trying to marry me off to the judge's daughter? Right now, with Chingachgook on his way here with a proposition that's going to make every white man in this valley howl?"

Hawkeye shrugged. "I don't deny the timing's bad. But there's some things can't be ignored, and that woman is one of them. You best keep your wits about you, or Todd will beat you to it."

They were silent for a while as they scrambled up a steep slope, urging the horse along behind.

"Can't see a woman like that scraping hide and hoeing corn," Nathaniel said.

"True enough. But there's others to do that work. She's a schoolteacher." Hawkeye said this last in a respectful tone. It was something Nathaniel had never understood about his father, his willingness to believe absolute good of any schoolteacher—until evidence to the contrary came to the front.

"Well, say for a minute she decides she's interested and I make her an offer. The judge wouldn't like it. Nor her brother," said Nathaniel.

Pausing to catch his breath, Hawkeye turned to look out over the village tucked into the elbow of the mountain. The evening was coming fast; long shadows of deepening dark blue moved down over the forest, reaching over the snowy fields to curl fingers around the scattered cabins and barns. Half Moon Lake glittered softly in the last of the evening light like a silver hand mirror thrown down carelessly on a rumpled white coverlet.

"Her daddy is white," Hawkeye said quietly, as if he and his son were not; as if they were of a different universe. "He thinks he owns the sky. The sky won't give him much of an argument, but that daughter of his will. He don't know what's coming his way." He shook his head and grinned. "That's a strong-willed woman, Nathaniel, and some men would run in the other direction. Richard Todd will, when he figures her out."

"Not if she brings the mountain to the match, he wouldn't run. Not if she had two heads and a tail."

Hawkeye drew up suddenly, a hand to his chin. "Aye, you're right. But if she's half as smart as I think she is—and set against marriage to boot—she won't let herself be auctioned off like that. And"—Hawkeye grinned now, his face a mass of wrinkles—"it weren't Richard Todd she was starin' at with her eyes all shiny, every opportunity."

Nathaniel inclined his head but said nothing.

"Your ma was strong-willed like her . . ." Hawkeye paused again, and when he spoke there was a loss in his voice that Nathaniel knew well. "You won't be sorry for it, in the long run. Although she'll tire you out in the chase."

"I haven't made up my mind to take up the chase."

"You tell yourself that," Hawkeye said, laughing softly. "See if you can make it stick. I don't think you can."

IV

Although she went to bed dispirited and unhappy about the possibility that her plans might be met with her father's reluctance rather than his help and goodwill, Elizabeth awoke on Christmas Eve morning refreshed and with her resolve restored. It was very early, the sun just coming up over the mountains, and the deep cold of the night had not yet begun to loosen; nevertheless Elizabeth could not stay in her bed, so she washed and shivered her way into her clothes, and ran down the steps to the kitchen.

Standing in the doorway, she was greeted by a blast of warm air from the hearth where a crowd of pots hung from a complex assortment of cranes and trivets. The whole room glowed with the reflected firelight in copper and pewter swaying from hooks in the ceiling beams. Against the far wall, baskets of flax and carded wool waited by a spinning wheel, and next to that a young girl worked a loom with the quick and automatic motions of the practiced weaver.

Another young woman stood at a rough wooden table peeling potatoes while Curiosity kneaded dough, her dark skin dusty with flour to the elbows. She looked up to see Elizabeth standing there and grinned.

"An early riser! Yes, I knew it, an early riser. You must be hungry. Breakfast won't be for a while yet but come sit down and Daisy here will do her best. Daisy is my second oldest.

Daisy! Say g'd day to Miss Elizabeth. Over there that's my Polly on the loom. And that there is Manny, just on his way out now to see to the firewood, weren't you, sweet thing?"

Manny was a strapping youth with a wide grin, but Elizabeth barely got a good look at him before he disappeared at his mother's bidding. She turned her attention to Daisy, who smiled at Elizabeth without a bit of shyness. She was slightly built but wiry, not quite so dark as her mother, but with a great abundance of hair tucked up into her cap. On one cheek there was a red birthmark in the shape of a flower, and Elizabeth realized that this must be the source of her name.

Daisy wiped her hands on her apron while she considered Elizabeth.

"Biscuits and honey, that should tide you over. And fresh milk."

"That sounds lovely," Elizabeth said, "but I would like to take a walk first—"

"A walk in this cold weather before you have good food in you?" Curiosity shook her head.

Uncertain, Elizabeth glanced out the window. It had begun to snow, and the sky was leaden.

"Paradise ain't going no place, before you have some break-fast," Curiosity stated, and in response Daisy began to butter biscuits.

There was a high stool at the table and Elizabeth took it, waiting for Curiosity to protest that she should eat in the dining room, but there was no such complaint; Curiosity went back to her bread dough and Daisy to her potatoes. The rhythmic thump of the loom made a nice counterpoint to the steady hiss of the fire in the hearth.

The biscuits were delicious and the milk was fresh; Elizabeth realized suddenly that she was very hungry indeed and she worked her way through the plate quickly. Her appetite and appreciation were not lost on Curiosity, who set her dough to rise and poured Elizabeth more milk. Elizabeth thought of ask-ing Curiosity to sit and eat with her, but she realized that the older woman had probably been up for hours and had eaten long ago, and that she had many hours of work ahead before she would find time to sit down again. Elizabeth was thinking

about Curiosity when a back door opened in a flurry of snow
and Galileo came in, stamping and whooshing with the cold.

"My Lord!" he said, dumping his load of firewood onto the
hearth. "But what a weather. Good morning, Miss Elizabeth!"

Elizabeth returned his greeting but he had already turned to
address his wife.

"And I suppose you still need those supplies, and I suppose I
still have to hitch the team and go down to the village in this
snow." He shook his head.

"And I suppose snow is nothing new and I suppose it's
Christmas Eve and I suppose you don't want me serving up
beans and pickled cabbage for dinner, do you?" Curiosity answered in staccato. But they were grinning at each other, and
Daisy did not seem in the least perturbed, so Elizabeth assumed
that this tone was an everyday one.

"Are you going into town?" she asked Galileo. "May I come
along?" She had already slipped down from her stool. "Please
do wait, it will only take me a minute."

It barely seemed worth the effort of hitching the team, for
the sleigh brought them into the village in just a few minutes.
Elizabeth wished that she had walked, for the village fairly flew
by: scattered cabins, the church of raw wood, its windows shuttered and the little steeple without a bell. The parsonage stood
off to the right, a somewhat finer building of board and shingle
rather than logs, but small and with only a few window sashes.
To the far left, a finer house of fieldstone and brick; no doubt it
belonged to the doctor. There were a smokehouse, stables, and
blacksmithy. She noted, although she tried not to, that each
cabin had a dooryard cluttered with stacked wood, farm tools,
and dark icy patches where dishwater had been tossed. Here
and there laundry had been hung out and shirts and trousers and
sheets seemed to be standing sentry, frozen into awkward con-
tortions. There were few people to see: outside a cabin of
squared logs a woman wrapped in shawls drew water at a stone
well, an old raccoon cap on her head and a baby strapped to her
chest with a leather belt. Down at the edge of Half Moon Lake,
surrounded with tree stumps like beard stubble, there were men
out on the ice fishing with nets. Boys pushed a ball with long
sticks, shouting and tussling.

Elizabeth was both relieved and disappointed: relieved to see people carrying on with normal lives such as she had known in England, and disappointed that everything was so familiar. The village was, if anything, shabby, and the buildings, while solid, were plain. The trading post was a log building like the rest but with a long, deep porch, empty now, and tiny glass windows on either side of the door. There was nothing picturesque about Paradise. It was hewn too rawly from the forest, it sat too awkwardly on the shores of the lake.

What a terrible prig you are, she sniffed at herself. *You'll have to do better than that, my girl, if you intend to teach school here.*

Watching Galileo tie the team to the hitching post, Elizabeth realized with a start that the people in this place would have children, and that she must convince them to send those children to her school. And more, there was no way to be introduced to them, except to do it herself. She had never in her life taken up a conversation with a person to whom she had not been properly and formally introduced, with the exception of servants and shop clerks. Almost paralyzed with worry, she watched as Galileo solved her problem by stepping into the room behind her and calling out: "Good morning. This here is Miss Elizabeth Middleton, the judge's girl."

Elizabeth tried hard to keep up with the hands that were thrust at her, the questions and good wishes. Confronted with the friendly curiosity of a roomful of people, Elizabeth was ashamed of herself for her less-than-generous thoughts about the village.

A woman of substantial height and breadth pushed easily through the small crowd to grasp Elizabeth by both shoulders and peer into her face. Elizabeth tried not to pull away from this unusual form of greeting, and focused instead on a pair of curious blue eyes on either side of a nose so small and dainty that it seemed it had somehow wandered onto the wrong face.

"Well, aren't we glad to see you!" she said for the fourth or fifth time, shaking Elizabeth a bit. "Aren't we all!"

Then she stood back and inclined her head hard to the right. "You'll have caught not a single name in all this commotion. I'm Anna Hauptmann. This was my husband's trading post until he took the putrid sore throat and died. Lost my three oldest,

too. That was four year ago and I been running things ever
since. Do some farming, as we all do here. D'you like cheese?
You'll want to try mine, it's worth the trouble, if I do say so
myself who shouldn't. My folks come over from the Palatinate
back during King George's war. That's my father over there.
Däta!" She shouted so loudly at an old man asleep in front of
the hearth that Elizabeth jumped.

"Däta, pass auf! No, don't you bother yourself about niceties, Miz Middleton, he's a solid sleeper, is Pa. Däta!"

This time the whole room jumped, but the bony shoulders
of the old man hunched over his clay pipe continued their
gentle rise and fall without a tremor.

"Miz Hauptmann—" Galileo called softly, and just as
quickly as she had claimed Elizabeth's attention, Anna turned
away and fought her way behind the counter between barrels
and boxes. With a little fold of concentration on her forehead
she began to gather things together in response to Galileo's
polite and low-voiced requests.

There was a lot to look at: the ceilings were hung with
hardware of every kind, from stirrups to a plow, barrels and
boxes piled everywhere. On one wall a profusion of hand-
painted signs crowded together, and Elizabeth looked them over
with great wonder and amusement. *Trust in the LORD your
GOD,* read a prominent one, surpassed in size only by *Wonder
Full is the MERCY of the Savior,* surrounded by more earthly
sentiments: *No Papper Notes but Pigs Took in Trade; 1£ = $3 & 50
NY; Good Strong Vinegar; No Cofee Til Spring; Turlington's Balsam of Life and Daffy's Elixer in Stock Permanent.* And a very large
one done in severest black letters: *NO spitting and that means
YOU!* In English, Dutch, German, and French. Elizabeth mar-
veled at the translation of both the meaning and the sentiment.

In the time it took her to read through the placards, Elizabeth felt the room fall silent around her. She knew that they
were looking at her, and so she straightened her shoulders and
turned to meet them. The group of men sat around the hearth
on makeshift stools, and in their center two young children
huddled by the fire, one with a corncob doll, the other with a
penknife and piece of wood. Anna was the only other woman;
the others were all men of various ages, clearly farmers here to

share news and the heat of the hearth on a snowy winter morning. She introduced herself to each of the adults, making a conscious effort to mark their names and faces: Henry Smythe, who had a tic; Isaac Cameron, who, while young, was losing his hair and who had a mouthful of poor teeth; Jed McGarrity, so tall he stooped and had the largest hands Elizabeth had ever seen on any human being; and Charlie LeBlanc, younger than the rest, who was missing both his upper front teeth and whistled when he talked. He avoided her gaze, blushing furiously as he shook her hand. Only Moses Southern seemed to give her his hand reluctantly, scowling at a point on the ceiling as he muttered his name. He was about sixty years old, his face crackled and roughened to the consistency of bark. The cold weather had turned his already substantial nose into a great red radish, and when she smiled at him he flushed a deeper shade.

Elizabeth turned to the children.

"And who have we here?"

"My two youngest!" said Anna. "Henrietta and Ephraim, they might tell you if they could find their tongues. Children! Come forward. A curtsy, please, Miss Henrietta. Ephraim, have you forgot your bow?"

"Have you had any schooling?" Elizabeth asked them in a kindly tone as she took their hands in turn. The children, both with sleek brown hair and placid eyes in pale faces, shook their heads, and then turned as one toward their mother.

"Nope, never had the opportunity," Anna answered for them. She laughed. "Too bad, ain't it, that you didn't bring a schoolmarm along with you from England."

"But I did," Elizabeth said, and smiled. "I am a teacher."

One of the farmers cleared his throat loudly, but had nothing to say in response to Elizabeth's statement. Even Anna Hauptmann seemed struck speechless.

"I am a teacher," she repeated, glancing around at them. "I plan to start a school as soon as space can be made ready."

"Well!" Anna said, her surprise ebbing to make room for enthusiasm. "Well, I never. The judge's daughter. A school in Paradise!"

"I suppose you expect folks to pay tuition," Moses Southern rumbled, not meeting her eye.

"I hadn't thought about that yet," Elizabeth said. "But of course the fee would be very small, and payable in goods—"

One of the men looked relieved at this, and Elizabeth went on, encouraged.

"I was hoping," she said, glancing at each of the farmers as she did. "I was hoping to get together a list of all the children who are of school age, so I have an idea of the supplies I'll need, and if I have enough books."

"Books!" Mr. Smythe exclaimed. "Did you bring books all the way from England?"

"I did," Elizabeth confirmed. "Or at least, they are coming with my trunks—as soon as Galileo has time to fetch them; they came after by iceboat. Primers and readers and arithmetic, some geometry and algebra, history—" She saw the faces around her begin to cloud and she continued, less sure of herself. "Geography, maps of course, literature, and Latin—"

"Latin!" Anna snapped the word. "What use would these children have for Latin?"

"Why, Latin is—" began Elizabeth, but she was interrupted.

"Reading and writing is fine," Mr. Cameron said. "Arithmetic and geometry are useful things. But Latin? And history, I don't know. My boys won't have much use for Romans and Greeks while they are trying to run a farm."

"Latin—" tried Elizabeth again.

"Latin will bring nothing but discontent! These are frontier children, they don't need ideas about philosophy! Next thing you'll want to send them off to university where their heads will be filled with poetry!" Moses Southern was working himself up to a high pitch, and Anna stepped in with a calmer tone.

"Our young folk don't need to know about lords and ladies and such-like."

But Moses wasn't to be calmed. "Royalty!" he fairly spat. "It took long enough to roust the Redcoats. Why would we want to study on them?" He seemed not to realize, or perhaps care, that Elizabeth was English.

"The girls will never look at another honest, hardworking farmer, if you fill their heads with royalty," Anna pointed out to Elizabeth, clearly torn between the wish to be an ally and the obvious truth of the situation.

Distraught, Elizabeth saw that she had taken the wrong strategy with the very people she needed to win over; without their support and the support of others just like them, she would never be able to start her school. She searched madly for an argument which would save her plans. They stood around her, their faces expectant, waiting for her to counter the logic they had served up. The Bible, thought Elizabeth, something from the Bible, but nothing came to mind. Frantic, she saw their expressions begin to close against her.

" 'Blessed are those wise in the ways of books,' " she said quickly, " 'for theirs is the kingdom of righteousness and fair play.' " Then she flushed. From the corner of her eye she saw Galileo, who had been silent throughout the entire exchange, raise a grizzled eyebrow in surprise. One of the farmers was looking at her doubtfully, but she lifted her chin.

"Matthew," she added, defiantly.

Suddenly her bravado left her and she wished for nothing so much as to walk away and come in to start over again. She was telling these people that she was worthy of teaching their children and the first example she had given them of her own education and worthiness of such a task was a completely fraudulent—and self-serving—Bible verse.

Elizabeth glanced over her shoulder to see if Galileo was ready to go, and she started.

Nathaniel Bonner stood at the door, and on his face, the certainty that he had overheard at least some of this conversation, and most certainly the part of which she was least proud.

Elizabeth had never been in such a situation in her entire life; she took in Nathaniel's cool but amused look, and she barely knew how to contain her embarrassment. He nodded to her, and wished her good day, but Elizabeth could barely nod in return. She took the very first opportunity to take her leave from Anna and her customers, who had returned to their places around the hearth.

Out on the porch Elizabeth was glad of the cold air which cooled her hot cheeks. For a moment she watched while Galileo loaded supplies into the sleigh, all the while sending her curious sidelong glances. Resolutely, Elizabeth avoided direct eye contact.

"I think I'll take a walk now, Galileo," she said as lightly as she could. "I'll be able to find my way back home."

And Elizabeth took off as fast as she could down a narrow but well-trodden path which led past a number of small cabins. Women came to doors to wave to her, but she pressed on, smiling politely. She needed to be alone for a while, to sort out her thoughts.

The path led through a stand of evergreens and then, beyond that, it took Elizabeth to the lakeside. She stopped suddenly within a foot of a little beach with its own dock, its supports all encased in ice, and saw that the fishermen were coming in now, dragging with them their heavy nets. There were six men and a number of boys, Elizabeth counted, and they were coming straight toward her with curious and expectant looks on their faces. She suppressed a little groan, and turned abruptly away back up the path, running as she did so directly into Nathaniel.

With a little cry Elizabeth slipped and would have lost her footing on the hard-packed snow if Nathaniel had not reached out to steady her, both his hands catching her upper arms just above the elbows, her own hands coming to rest on firmly muscled forearms. Dismayed at her own clumsiness and confused by his sudden appearance, Elizabeth looked up at Nathaniel, who stood calmly with his head inclined toward her. She felt the press of his fingers quite clearly through her cape and she was aware of his warm breath on her face; for a moment Elizabeth was strangely paralyzed, and then she pulled away with a little twist. Breathing heavily, she glanced back toward the lake at the approaching fishermen.

"Pardon me," she murmured to Nathaniel and she started up the path once again. "Excuse me, Mr. Bonner."

"Wait!" Nathaniel called after her, and Elizabeth walked all the faster. She picked up her skirts a little to increase her speed.

"Elizabeth, wait!" he called again, this time much closer. Realizing that she could not outpace him, Elizabeth stopped and tried to calm her breathing. Then she turned toward Nathaniel.

"Yes?" she asked as evenly as she was capable. He stood before her dressed as he had been the day before. Elizabeth noted that under his own lined mantle he wore a clean buckskin shirt, and this brought to mind his injury; her face fell.

"Pardon me, Mr. Bonner—" she began.

"Nathaniel."

Elizabeth drew in her breath and let it out. When she was calmer, she set her face in what she hoped were friendly but distant lines. "Please pardon me for bumping into you that way. I hope I did not disturb your wound."

Nathaniel glanced at his own shoulder and back again.

"I did not realize you were behind me," Elizabeth finished.

"I was coming after you," Nathaniel said. "I should have thought that was clear enough. I need to talk to you," he paused. "About your schoolhouse."

Elizabeth looked away and made an effort to control her breathing, to steady her voice. "I doubt that there will be a school," she said. "The people here don't seem particularly interested in one."

"You give up easily."

"I beg your pardon?"

"I wouldn't have thought it of you, that you give up so easy. That little bit of ribbing at the trading post couldn't change your mind, if it was really set."

"I haven't given up," she said. "It's just—" She paused, and seeing that Nathaniel was not laughing at her, she continued more slowly. "It's just more complicated than I anticipated. It's not what I expected," she finished.

"You're not what they expected, either," Nathaniel said.

"And what did they expect?" she asked, although she was a little afraid of what Nathaniel might offer in reply.

"Not a bluestocking," he said lightly.

The term was not familiar to Elizabeth, but she sensed that it was not complimentary. "I expect that unmarried women who care little for fashion are what you call bluestockings," said Elizabeth.

"A spinster who teaches school is a bluestocking, in these parts," corrected Nathaniel. Before Elizabeth could comment, he continued: "They thought that a princess was coming, you see, the judge's daughter. Dressed in silks and satins, on the lookout for a rich husband. The doctor, most likely. Which ain't what they got—if it weren't for those fancy boots you could be a Quaker, as simple as you dress. Since you won't be the spoiled princess they expected, they don't know what to do with you."

"I am so sorry to disappoint," Elizabeth snapped.

"On the contrary," Nathaniel said, producing a slow smile. "I ain't the least bit disappointed."

In a fluster, Elizabeth picked up her skirts in preparation for walking back uphill and caught sight of her boots: soft cordovan leather polished to a gleam, brass hooks, tassels, and delicate heels. Not sufficiently lined for the icy byroads of upper New-York State, her toes were informing her. Pretty boots: her one luxury and weakness.

"Don't go," he said behind her in a gentler tone. "I won't make light of your boots anymore."

Elizabeth came to a halt, wondering even as she did so why she should *not* go. Why she did not wish to go.

He said, "Folks will send their children to your school, but you got to have one first."

She had been ready to do battle, but Elizabeth found herself suddenly less angry than curious. She turned to him. "Do you think they'll come? I thought that I had ruined everything."

Nathaniel stepped back off the path to lean up against a tree trunk. Elizabeth noted, distracted, how big a man he was. There were many tall men in her family; uncle Merriweather dwarfed most in the neighborhood. She realized it was not so much his size but his gaze which truly disconcerted her, absolutely direct and without apology.

"Folks here're a little tougher than you might be used to, but they know an opportunity when they see one. Didn't the judge tell you that he hired me to build a schoolhouse for you?"

Elizabeth shook her head.

"Settled it at dinner last night."

She barely knew what to say. She had been truly afraid that her father would not honor his promise, that she would never get her school; but it seemed her father had arranged for its construction after all. A wave of reluctant appreciation overwhelmed her, along with the realization that she had Nathaniel to thank for this. Why he would want to be of help to her she could not imagine. There must be some other motivation, some good he saw in the idea of the school, to want to put himself in this position. She looked at him and tried to puzzle out what it was, but all she saw was Nathaniel's patient and somewhat amused look.

"I must say," she said with an uncertain smile, "I didn't expect—I had no idea. It is very kind of you—"

Nathaniel raised an eyebrow. "It's got little to do with kindness and more to do with cash money. He's paying me."

Elizabeth glanced down. "I see."

"But money wouldn't be enough to make the job to my liking if it weren't for other considerations," Nathaniel added.

When it was clear that Elizabeth did not know how to respond to this, Nathaniel found himself smiling. The woman had a quick wit, there was no doubt about that, but she was not in the habit of flirting. He found that this pleased him. He watched Elizabeth struggling to formulate some overly polite response and he was taken by the urge to tease her.

"I'm surprised your father didn't tell you himself."

"I haven't seen him yet this morning, I wanted to be up and about," Elizabeth said.

"Ah," Nathaniel said softly. "Couldn't wait to see the village, then. Looking for likely candidates."

She rose to this bait neatly. "Just what do you mean, sir?" she asked sharply.

"I meant you are on the lookout for students. What did you think I meant?" he asked, smiling even more broadly.

Elizabeth laid a hand on her hood to set it in place. Her hair had come loose and curls lay on her cheek; she brushed these back. Nathaniel resisted the urge to step up to her and pull them back out. He thought about doing it because he knew it would make her blush, and he found he was developing an appetite for her blushes. But he was patient, and she was not; he had the advantage, and he would use it. He admitted to himself that his father was right—he had plans for this woman.

"Have you made the acquaintance of the parson yet?" he asked in a kinder tone, not pushing for an answer to his previous question. "He's got a daughter, she'd be the person to talk to about the list you wanted. Of the children. Kitty Wither-spoon."

"Thank you," Elizabeth said. "That's very helpful." She looked about herself and saw they were hidden from both the lake and the settlement where they stood.

"I suppose I should be going, Mr.—" She paused. "If you are willing, we could speak this evening about the school-house."

"Are you asking me to call on you this evening?"

Elizabeth fought with an angry retort, realizing that she must learn new rules of engagement here that were, at present, be-yond her.

"It is Christmas Eve. I thought my father had invited all of his friends."

His gaze narrowed. "What makes you think I am a friend of your father's?"

"Whatever the quarrel between you and my father, it is Christmas Eve," Elizabeth repeated. "And if he has not invited you, then I shall invite you. And your family." She steadied her expression and looked him straight in the eye. "You may not be his friend, but—" She paused. "You will be mine, will you not?"

Nathaniel returned her gaze without a smile. "That I will, Boots," he said. "For a start."

V

Elizabeth arrived back at her father's home exhausted; the distance between the village and the house which had seemed so little in the sleigh had nearly undone her. She withdrew to her room after a brief conversation with her father, and although it was only mid-morning, she fell into a deep sleep without dreams.

Curiosity came to wake her in the mid-afternoon.

"I let you sleep through lunch but you must be half-starved by this time," she said, putting a tray on a small table by the bed. The aroma of chicken and gravy and potatoes rose from the covered dishes and made Elizabeth's stomach cramp with hunger. There were beans and relish and hot corn bread, as well. She thanked Curiosity and then fell to her food, noting out loud that the cold air and altitude were good for her appetite.

"It's running around the village in the snow," Curiosity pointed out. "But you've got your rest now. There's company waiting for you downstairs once you've had your fill."

Elizabeth looked up, startled.

"Calm yourself. Just Kitty Witherspoon, come to pay her respects. Your brother's entertaining her until you come down."

·   ·   ·

Katherine Witherspoon—she did not call herself Kitty to Elizabeth—waited in the sitting room on the edge of her chair. There was no sign of Julian, which was disappointing to Elizabeth: he was much better than she ever would be at the type of conversation required of such calls. But then, Elizabeth reminded herself, she had no idea how calls were made here.

Miss Witherspoon was a young woman in her early twenties, Elizabeth imagined. She was of medium height, quite mature in her form, with a narrow face below waves of pale blond hair. Her eyes, a watery blue, were surrounded with a fringe of the same pale blond. The younger woman came up from her chair quickly to greet Elizabeth, her hand damp with nervousness. She was so enthusiastic and eager that she stumbled a little over a speech Elizabeth thought was surely rehearsed, in which Miss Witherspoon listed all the reasons she was so very pleased to have Elizabeth and her brother in the neighborhood.

It had begun to snow in earnest and the two young women settled before the hearth in the sitting room, where Daisy brought them tea. Elizabeth sighed with relief to find herself in such peaceful surroundings after the last few days and the unsettling events of the morning. Thoughts of her conversation with Nathaniel distracted her for a moment away from the story Katherine was telling.

"I'm afraid I'm taxing you too much after your long journey," Katherine said, breaking off her narrative.

"Oh, no," Elizabeth assured her, wanting very much to set the young woman at ease. "Please pardon me. Everything is so new to me, I sometimes am distracted by little things."

"Were you thinking of yesterday's accident?"

Elizabeth considered her answer, realizing that everything that had passed between her family and Nathaniel yesterday was now common knowledge.

"Pardon me," Katherine went on, coloring slightly. "I shouldn't have presumed."

"No, that's quite all right," Elizabeth said, but she did not answer Katherine's question. An awkward silence fell between them, and Elizabeth roused herself.

"Miss Witherspoon—Katherine," she said. "Perhaps you

could be of assistance to me. You may have heard that I wish to start a school here for the younger children?"

Katherine nodded.

"The first step is for me to find out who my students will be, and to approach their parents: Since you must be acquainted with all the families in Paradise, would you be so kind?" And Elizabeth fetched paper and writing instruments and together the two women began a list.

Katherine listed eight families with school-age children, and was able to give Elizabeth names and directions to their cabins, as well as an approximate age of each child. Quite pleased to have this accomplished so easily, Elizabeth looked over the list and counted twelve names.

"These are all the children, then?" she asked, somewhat apprehensively. She was afraid she would have to directly inquire after the names of the children of slaves, but Katherine seemed to realize this.

"Those are all the children in the village, free or slave," Katherine said. "I expect that in some cases it will be hard for you to convince parents to let the children come to school. Billy Kirby, for instance."

"Billy Kirby?"

"He's a farmer, hunter, hauls timber, and he does some building. He built this house for your father. Billy is raising his younger brother since his parents passed on." Katherine hesitated. "He won't be very enthusiastic about the idea of sending Liam to school."

"Well, I can talk to him, can't I?" Elizabeth said.

"Those are all the children," Katherine repeated. "From the village," she added.

Elizabeth raised an eyebrow and waited, for it was clear that Katherine had something else to say.

"There is one more name I haven't given you, because that child doesn't live in the village; she lives with her family on the other side of Half Moon Lake, up on Hidden Wolf Mountain."

Elizabeth made ready to write. "I would like to have her name," she said. "I wouldn't want to exclude her if she would like to come."

Again Katherine hesitated. "I am surprised you don't know of her yet."

"Why would I know about this little girl?" Elizabeth asked, puzzled.

"Because she is Nathaniel Bonner's daughter," Katherine said.

Elizabeth smiled thinly. "His daughter?"

"Her name is Hannah. A bright little thing."

"Mr. Bonner is unmarried," Elizabeth said, and then wished she had not, because Katherine was looking at her with a kind of understanding that made Elizabeth uneasy. "Perhaps I misunderstood him. No matter."

"Everyone calls him Nathaniel," Katherine said easily. Then, without prompting: "She died in childbed," she said in a low tone. "In spite of everything Cora Bonner and Curiosity and Dr. Todd could do for her. Nathaniel has never recovered. She came down with a fever, you see—"

"How very sad," Elizabeth interrupted her gently.

Katherine dropped her eyes, perhaps to hide the eagerness there. *She knows it is unseemly to gossip,* thought Elizabeth, *but she can't help herself.*

"Nathaniel's mother-in-law keeps house for them since his mother passed on," Katherine volunteered, her voice trailing away reluctantly. With a nervous smile, she looked up at Elizabeth.

"Did my brother say where he was going?" Elizabeth asked suddenly.

There was a little sigh from the younger woman—relief? Disappointment? But Katherine followed Elizabeth's lead and put the subject of the Bonners aside. "An appointment in the village, he said. Let me tell you, Elizabeth, although I would not say it to him, that it is truly wonderful to have a young man of fashion and taste in Paradise."

Elizabeth smiled at this description of her brother. "What about Dr. Todd?" she asked. "He seems a very likely young man."

Katherine reddened and sat back to sip at her tea. Elizabeth saw clearly that she had disconcerted her visitor. *Now it is my turn to want more information than is seemly,* Elizabeth thought. *A good lesson.*

In the early evening her father came to find her where she read in the study, all excitement about the coming party and eager to share his enthusiasm with her.

"Well, Lizzie," he said, trying very hard to appear solemn. "What are you wearing this evening?"

Elizabeth put down her paper and quill and looked up at her father where he paced back and forth before the fire. At more than sixty he was still a very fine looking man, with an imposing figure, a high forehead, and a mane of gray hair bound at the nape of his neck with a simple black band. Powdered wigs were going out of fashion, and he had been quick to give them up; his full head of hair had always been a point of pride. Her father's color was very high, Elizabeth noted, and she wondered about his health, although she was pleased to see that he was in good spirits.

"Do I need to change, Father?" she asked, looking down at herself.

"What!" he cried out. "Gray for a party?"

Elizabeth smiled. "I usually wear gray, Father, but I have another gown which might please you better. I will wear that."

"Good!" he said, satisfied. "I want to show you off this evening."

She hesitated. "Father, I hope you will not think me forward, but I have invited Mr. Bonner and his son to the party. So that we can discuss the building of the schoolhouse." Her father had no objection to this, she could see, and so she continued.

"I am very much looking forward to meeting all your friends," she said. "But I would like to remind you that I have no intention of marrying."

The judge drew up, surprised, and turned to her with his hands clasped behind his back. His lips pursed, he considered his daughter for a long minute, until Elizabeth began to grow uncomfortable under his gaze.

"This cannot possibly surprise you," Elizabeth said finally. "I have been honest with you from the beginning."

"I would like you to marry," her father said shortly. "It would be a comfort to know you well provided for beyond my death."

"I have some money of my own," Elizabeth said. "You know that. I will never want for basic necessities. And when one day you are gone—I don't foresee that in the near future, but when that day comes, then I hope that my brother will be of assistance to me. He will not lack for material wealth."

The judge frowned. "You have more faith in your brother's ability to put his past behind him than I do," he said. "If he manages to reform, you may be right. But who knows what will happen? No, I would be remiss not to take your prospects and your best interests into consideration, my dear. And there is the matter of the land. The stewardship of this land is something I take very seriously indeed."

Elizabeth hesitated. "I do hope that Julian will keep his promise to you and to me," she said. "I think the repercussions of his actions are clear to him, finally, and I hope that the lesson will stay learned. He is capable of learning how best to manage the family holdings. He is certainly interested."

The judge gave a short wheeze of impatience. "You cannot build your future on your hopes for your brother. You need someone else to depend on, once I am gone."

"I trust that I shall always be able to depend upon myself," said Elizabeth with what she hoped was a disarming smile.

The judge walked up and down the room once, his hands crossed on his lower back. "Elizabeth, what kind of father would I be if I didn't make provision for you?" He seemed to consider, and then strode to his desk. From his waistcoat pocket the judge took a small key, and opening a drawer he took out a piece of paper. Squinting a bit, he looked it over, and then he came to Elizabeth and put it in her hand.

" 'Deed of Gift,' " Elizabeth read aloud.

The judge was looking very satisfied with himself. "The original patent," he said. "All of it, which includes Hidden Wolf. A thousand acres, my dear. For you. The rest of the property—another two thousand acres—is meant for your brother, of course. One day, when he has proven himself. It has been my life's work, and it is my primary concern to maintain the family holdings together and in trust for my children, and generations to come."

Confused, Elizabeth looked up at her father, and then down at the document again.

". . . said property and all leases and improvements upon it to the only use and behoof of my said daughter Elizabeth Middleton, her heirs and assigns . . ."

"But why?" Elizabeth said. "Why now, and in this manner? This is surely highly unusual."

"I thought you would be pleased," the judge said, a little affronted.

"Father," Elizabeth began. "Please do not think me ungrateful. I simply don't understand what would move you to do something like this."

"It is not so unusual," said the judge, "to want to see your property well disposed of, in the capable hands of trustworthy children."

Elizabeth wanted to take her father's words at their face value, to believe that she had his trust. But he would not meet her eye, and he began to gnaw on the stem of his pipe quite ferociously.

"It is unusual to pass valuable property into the hands of an unmarried daughter," she said. "I could do with it as I please, after all." Then she looked at the deed once again. A wave of understanding washed through her and left her feeling hollow.

"You haven't signed it yet," she said. "And it isn't witnessed."

The judge rocked back on his heels. "I will sign it before witnesses on the day you marry."

Startled, Elizabeth rose from her seat. "And whom do you have in mind for my husband?"

"Richard Todd," her father answered simply. "I thought that was obvious. It is an excellent match, Lizzie. Together you will have some five thousand acres. Not as large as some of the patents to the west, but sufficient. You shall be well provided for, no matter what foolery your brother gets up to with his lands once I am gone. Richard can be entrusted to look after Julian's interests as well as yours."

Elizabeth's knees were trembling. For a moment she thought she might be truly ill. How could she not be, with this bitter pill her father was asking her to swallow. She had come so far, and had such hopes of another life, only to find that he had been bartering away her freedom before she had ever had a chance to experience it. And for this he expected her admiration and gratitude. It was too much to bear, and yet she must, if anything was to be salvaged. She folded her hands tightly together and gave her father a look she had learned from her aunt Merriweather, the one reserved for the most outrageous of men's endless maneuverings. "I wonder that you think I am so dim-witted that I wouldn't see through this ploy."

"There is no ploy," the judge sputtered. "What have I done but to offer you almost half of my most valuable holdings?"

Elizabeth shook her head with such force that her hair began to slip from its pins.

"A married woman cannot possess land. If you sign that on the day I marry, the property goes almost directly to Richard Todd. It is not for me, but for yourself and for him that you are doing this. You must esteem him very highly. Or perhaps you fear him?"

"I am doing it for you," the judge fairly roared, waving the paper in her face. "A husband is someone who will look after your interests. If I die and all my property goes to your brother, he will gamble it into nothing in a year. I have spent my life building this village out of wilderness and it will all be for naught, and then where will you be?"

"Where I am right now, with a little money of my own and no property," said Elizabeth, raising her voice to speak over her father's blustering. "If you really wanted to show your concern for me and protect me from Julian's excesses, you would sign that deed today, and trust me to marry or not according to my own best interests."

There was a silence while Elizabeth watched her father stalk away to lock the deed in his desk.

"There is more at stake here than you are acknowledging," she said. "Is there some financial problem I don't know about?"

"None that concerns you," he said shortly.

"I would say that it concerns me if you are trying to marry me to a stranger in order to resolve your difficulties," Elizabeth responded.

He spun toward her, and she saw the ticking of a pulse in his cheek.

"Have I struck too close to the truth, Father?"

"I have had some bad luck with an investment," the judge said slowly. "That I will not discuss with you."

"Well, then," Elizabeth said. "If Richard Todd is so keen to have more land, sell the thousand acres to him. I would hope that would provide the liquidity that you lack, and there would still be two thousand acres for us, surely enough to live in comfort."

Her father flushed so deep a red that Elizabeth was alarmed.

"I have spent thirty years," he began, his voice wavering. "I have invested my life in this land. I will not sell it, not at any price. I am asking you to consider Richard's offer of marriage, because it would keep the property in the family, and resolve my difficulties. But I am also convinced that Richard would be a good husband to you and look after your best interests."

"It is very unfortunate," Elizabeth began in a tone that was calmer, but clear and resolved, "that we must argue on my first day here. But I hope you will do me the favor of believing me when I tell you that I will never consider marrying Dr. Todd. I could not marry someone who keeps slaves. Even if I loved him, I still could not marry him. My conscience would not allow it."

"He is the right husband for you," her father said. "If you were more sensible, you would see that."

There was a moment's silence as Elizabeth struggled with her temper. "Then I am not sensible," she said. "But I will not act against my conscience."

"There's no other man suited to you in station or property for many miles."

"You will not sell your property, but you will sell your daughter, have I understood you correctly?"

"You are impertinent!" he sputtered. "I would have expected that my sister might have done a better job with you—"

"Do you care, Father, about what I want?"

"I care about your welfare."

"Listen to me. What I want is independence. It is 'the grand blessing of life, the basis of every virtue; and independence I will never secure by contracting my wants, though I were to live on a barren heath.' Do you know who wrote that?"

"I haven't the slightest idea," the judge said, exasperated.

Elizabeth picked up the slim volume she had been reading when he found her and she handed it to him. "Mrs. Wollstonecraft. *A Vindication of the Rights of Women*."

The judge looked down at the volume in his hand and then shook his head. "You are being influenced by this, by this—"

"Yes," Elizabeth said. "I have been influenced by these writings. But no more than you have been by the writings of Thomas Paine."

The judge dropped the book on the table. "*The Rights of Man* cannot be compared to this drivel."

"You haven't read Mrs. Wollstonecraft, how can you know?" Elizabeth said impatiently. And then seeing that she was not going to sway her father, Elizabeth stopped and tried to gather her thoughts.

"Keep your property and your gift of deed. If you will sign it only on my marriage to Richard Todd, then it will never be signed. If you continue to attempt to force me into an alliance which I do not want, I will go back to England and take up my old place in the home of my aunt Merriweather."

The judge's jaw dropped. "You would not."

"I would. I came here to be free of the restrictions I lived under in England. If there is no freedom for me here, there is no reason to stay."

Elizabeth gathered her writing materials together and made her way to the study door.

"I'll leave the book with you," she said. "In case you care to read any of it. Now if you will excuse me," she said, "I have to make myself ready for your party."

• • •

The parlor was cleared of most of its furniture; only chairs remained in little groups of threes and fours, and a long table laid with gleaming linen and good plateware, onto which Curiosity and her daughters had piled food of every possible kind. The room was lit with beeswax and bayberry candles and a collection of pewter lamps. Although it was full dark outside, even at five, the room was as bright as midday.

Elizabeth went about her duties as hostess as she had been trained to do since her earliest girlhood, making sure that everyone was well supplied with food and drink, that no one was without a conversation partner for long. She smiled and nodded and answered questions as they came to her, but she was terribly distraught and sometimes felt that everyone must see this clearly on her face.

It was her father's duplicity which lay heaviest on her mind. Elizabeth could not look at Richard Todd, who smiled at her kindly and was helpful in every way, without thinking that he and her father had schemed together behind her back to plan a marriage she did not want and could not countenance. It was hard to be civil under such circumstances; it was harder to pretend that nothing was amiss. All of her plans were in peril.

And Nathaniel had not come. She was surprised, and a little hurt, and then distressed at her own reaction. She could not deny to herself that she was attracted to him, but she also knew that it was an inappropriate preference, one of which her father would not approve.

Unlike Elizabeth, Julian seemed to be completely amused by his surroundings; everything was to his liking, nothing could be improved on. There were pretty girls: Elizabeth watched him flirt outrageously with Katherine Witherspoon and with Molly Kaes, a young woman who ran her father's farm; there were games and dances and absurd behavior to make light of. There was very little to occupy him except the things he liked most; he did not take note of his sister's distress. Elizabeth knew her brother too well to expect anything else.

Every man in the room seemed to want to have a conversation, from the toothless Mr. Cunningham to Mr. Witherspoon, the minister. There were three or four young men who seemed to be unattached, and who followed Elizabeth with their eyes wherever she went. This was something unaccustomed for her, as she had grown up with three prettier cousins. Elizabeth had long resigned herself to spinsterhood; in fact, she found certain promises and comforts in the idea, and she was not pleasantly surprised or flattered by this unexpected and unwanted attention. She did not believe that these men were interested in anything but her father's holdings. But she managed to deflect their advances without hurting many feelings, by gesturing to the guests she must greet and look after. Only Richard Todd was truly persistent; he would not be put off and followed her around the room until she realized she must spend at least a few minutes talking with him.

Dr. Todd wore an expensively cut coat of deep blue with brass buttons, and a stock of linen and lace at his throat. His breeches were perfectly skintight and showed not a wrinkle from the floral waistcoat to the knee. He had trimmed his beard and cut his hair and his manners and address were everything polite and refined. He complimented Elizabeth on the brilliancy of her complexion, on the beautiful simplicity of her deep green gown, and on the wonderful table. She accepted some compliments graciously, disavowed any credit for preparations for the party—never letting him see that it was not a compliment to assume she had been busy in the kitchen. He worked very hard at presenting himself as a gentleman, and she did not want to embarrass him.

"You are an admirer of Mrs. Wollstonecraft," Richard Todd said when a lull had come once again into their conversation. "I saw your copy of *Vindication* and your father told me you had lent it to him."

Elizabeth glanced at him. "Yes. It is my book." She hesitated. "You are familiar with Mrs. Wollstonecraft's work?"

"I haven't read her volume," Richard Todd said. "But I would like to."

"Really," said Elizabeth, her face averted. "I am surprised that her writings interest you."

"Because I have slaves?"

"Because you have slaves."

They were silent for a long moment.

"I inherited my slaves from an uncle," Dr. Todd said finally. Elizabeth did not answer.

"There may be circumstances of which you can't be aware, which would make you less severe upon me in this matter," he added.

Elizabeth was a little engaged by his honesty; it was hard not to be. But she remained silent to see what else he might volunteer.

"When they are twenty-one, I will give them their freedom," he added, clearly discomfited.

"Not on my account," said Elizabeth.

"In part," he conceded.

Elizabeth wondered if he was sincere, and decided to test him.

"Then do it today," she said. "It would be a fitting thing to do on Christmas."

"Does Mrs. Wollstonecraft write about slavery as well as women's education?" he asked, changing the subject.

"She writes about liberty, which is relevant to all peoples." She caught his smile and stiffened.

"No!" he said, trying to catch her eye. "I was not laughing at you. I was just thinking how much like a schoolmistress you sound."

"Like a bluestocking," Elizabeth agreed. She stood and smoothed her skirt. "I am a bluestocking, Dr. Todd."

"You don't look anything like a spinster schoolteacher."

"You needn't make me compliments," she said. "I'm not used to them and they won't find an eager target." Elizabeth was shocked but pleased that she could find it in herself to be so blunt, as blunt as she wanted to be. As blunt as a man talking to another man. But Richard Todd was not put off.

"That is very unfortunate," he said calmly. "Because they are meant sincerely. You do not look like a schoolteacher."

"You are wrong," she said. "A schoolteacher is just what I am, and what I will always be."

Her father approached them and Elizabeth panicked at the idea of carrying on this conversation with her father in attendance. In a moment she had excused herself and disappeared into the hall and up the stairs to her room.

The sounds of the party rose up to Elizabeth where she stood at her window. The winter night was very clear: the moonlight reflecting on snow let her see almost to the village. In a moment Elizabeth had made up her mind to steal away for a walk, and she made her way back down to the hall, where she quickly found her heavy cloak and mittens, pushed her feet into her sturdiest boots, and hurried outside.

The night was as cold as it was clear; almost full, the moon hung low over the mountain, shimmering silver-white and gray, illuminating the snow. Elizabeth breathed in deeply and wrapped the cloak more tightly around herself, pulling the hood up. Taking note of her direction, she set off on a small path through the snow, thinking to walk only ten minutes, to clear her head of the party and Richard Todd.

She knew men like him in England. The only difference between Dr. Todd and them, she was forced to acknowledge, was that in England men like the doctor—in possession of fortune and good connections—did not need to bother with young ladies past their prime. He was a confusing man; she could not reconcile his manner, which was pleasing, with what she knew about him. She thought again of her earlier conversation with her father and she almost despaired.

She had been walking for just five minutes on the path when she entered the first woods, and there she saw a solitary figure ahead of her. Elizabeth stopped and looked about herself, wondering what to think of a stranger out at this time of the night, when she recognized that it was Nathaniel Bonner walking toward her. Surprise lodged in her throat and slid down slowly to rest in her chest.

He stopped before her and nodded. "Boots," he greeted her. She bit down on the urge to grin at his name for her.

"Good evening," she said. "I thought you would bring your father—and your daughter."

If he was surprised at her mention of his daughter, Nathaniel did not show it. "They're on their way to the party from our cabin, on the other side of the lake. I been out checking trap lines for hours."

Elizabeth glanced back over her shoulder toward the brightly lit house, just visible from where she stood.

"I didn't see them. Maybe I just missed them."

"The party didn't amuse you, then?"

She turned away so that he couldn't see her face; she thought she could not hide her unhappiness from him, and she was uneasy and shy.

"I should go back," she said. Then, suddenly resolute, she faced Nathaniel.

"Well, I must be honest enough to admit to you that you were right. About my father. About his plans for me."

"Richard Todd," said Nathaniel flatly.

"Yes, Richard Todd." Elizabeth drew in a shaky breath. "I don't know why I am telling you this. Two days ago you were a stranger to me."

He was silent.

"Yes, I do know," Elizabeth corrected herself. "You have been honest with me, and I find that honesty is as hard to come by here as it was in England."

Nathaniel looked toward the house and then back to Elizabeth, who stood with her face averted toward the woods.

"Are you too cold to walk for another few minutes?"

They set off down the path the way he had come. It wound through the woods for a quarter mile and then crossed a frozen stream. Here they sat on tree stumps in a small clearing. The night was very quiet, all the sound in the world seemingly drawn into the blanket of snow. Elizabeth heard her own breath and saw it in a hazy cloud before her.

"Todd is a smart man," Nathaniel said. "His uncle left him considerable money, and land. I have known him to deal straight with every white man who comes his way."

Startled, Elizabeth did what she had been studiously avoiding: she looked directly into Nathaniel's face and she saw that he was sincere. Why he should be promoting her connection to Richard Todd was unclear to her, and it caused her considerable distress to think she must take up this argument with him.

"I came to this country to live a life unavailable to me in England," Elizabeth said shortly. "I have no intention of marrying Richard Todd." She lifted up her chin and laughed, a trembling laugh. "There are many things I want to ask you, because somehow it seems to me that you are the only one who will tell me the truth of things." Her smiled faded away. "But none of it may matter, after all."

"Why is that?"

She stood and pulled her cloak more tightly around her. "Because I think I shall be going back to England."

Nathaniel looked up at her from his perch on the stump. "Why is that?" he asked again.

"Because," Elizabeth said. "Because I will not be bullied into a marriage I want no part of. I may as well go back, at least I know what to expect there."

"Is it just this marriage you want no part of," Nathaniel said, "or are you set against marriage altogether?"

"I don't see what difference that makes," Elizabeth whispered. And then: "Marriage would mean that other things—other things which are important to me—would no longer be possible," she said. "Married women have no control over their lives."

Nathaniel thought of pointing out to her that she had little control over her life, although she was not married, in spite of her money, but he stopped himself. Instead, he stood abruptly. "Let's go back," he said. "It's too cold for both of us."

He waited until Elizabeth had started down the path and then followed her. She walked firmly, taking quick but delicately placed steps; her back was straight. There was more about her to admire than he dared admit to himself. He wondered where things would go from here: she might not have any interest in Richard Todd, but her high color, her agitation, the way she spoke and looked at him, made him think that she was not as committed to a chaste life as she thought she was.

At the slope of the riverbed Nathaniel took the lead and waited on the other side. He watched while Elizabeth stepped carefully over the slippery wooden logs which served as a makeshift bridge. She started up the bank, holding her skirts up high. She was almost to the path when she lost her balance and began to slip.

Nathaniel leaned forward and caught her smoothly, his hands just above her elbows. He steadied her, and then pulled her gently up the bank. When they were on even ground, he released her, but he stayed where he was, with his head bowed over hers. They were so close that his hair brushed against her hood.

Elizabeth looked down at her feet. She wondered, confused, why she should be so disappointed that he had let her go. There was something strange happening to her, something completely unexpected, something tremendously exciting. She had thought herself immune to these feelings, and now she found that she was wrong.

"I have a question for you."

"Yes, Mr. Bonner?" She did not raise her head.

"Will you please say my name?" he said with an intensity which caused gooseflesh to rise on her arms.

She hesitated. "Nathaniel."

"Look at me and say my name."

Elizabeth looked up slowly.

Nathaniel saw in her face an overwhelming confusion. He saw that she had never stood like this with a man, that she had never imagined doing so, and that she was flustered and even a bit frightened, but not unhappy to be here with him.

"What did you want to ask me?"

"How old are you?"

Elizabeth blinked. "Twenty-nine."

"You've never been kissed, have you?" The white cloud of his breath reached out to touch her face. His hands jerked at his sides but he kept them where they were. Now she would tell him to mind his own business, and he could put this woman out of his head.

"Why?" said Elizabeth, raising her eyes to his with a critical but composed look. "Do you intend to kiss me?"

Nathaniel pulled up abruptly and laughed. "The thought crossed my mind."

Her eyes narrowed.

"*Why* do you want to kiss me?"

"Well," Nathaniel said, inclining his head. "You seem set on going back to England, and the Mahicans say that you should never return from a journey the same person."

"How very thoughtful of you," she said dryly. "How *benevo-*

lent. But please, do not discommode yourself, on my account."
She began to turn away, but Nathaniel caught her by the upper
arm.

"Now I for one hope you don't rush off," he said. "But I
want to kiss you, either way."

"Do you?" she said tersely. "Perhaps I don't want to kiss
you."

Elizabeth was afraid to look at Nathaniel directly, for how
could he not see the doubt on her face, and the curiosity? And
what would that mean, to let him know what she really
thought, how confusing this all was to her? To tell a man what
she was truly thinking—this was a thought more frightening
than any kiss could be.

"I didn't mean to get you mad," Nathaniel said softly.

"What did you mean to do, then? Have some fun at my
expense, but not so much that I would actually notice that you
were making a fool of me?"

"No," he said, and Elizabeth was relieved to see all trace of
teasing leave his face. "I'd like to see the man who could make
a fool of you. I meant to kiss you, because I wanted to. But if
you don't like the idea—"

She pulled away from him, her face blazing white. "I never
said that. You don't know what I want." Then, finally, she
blushed, all her frustration and anger pouring out in pools of
color which stained her cheeks bluish-gray in the faint light of
the winter moon.

"So," Nathaniel said, a hint of his smile returning. "You do
want to kiss me."

"I want you to stop talking the matter to death," Elizabeth
said irritably. "If you hadn't noticed, you are embarrassing me.
Perhaps you don't know much about England—I don't know
why you should, after all—but let me tell you that there's a
reason I am twenty-nine years of age and unkissed, and that is,
very simply, that well-bred ladies of good family don't let men
kiss them. Even if they want to be kissed, and women do want
to be kissed on occasion, you realize, although we aren't supposed to admit that. To be perfectly honest with you"—she
drew a shaky breath—"I can't claim that anyone has ever shown
an interest in me at home—at least, not enough interest that this

particular issue ever raised its head. Now." She looked up at him with her mouth firmly set. Her voice had lowered to a hoarse whisper, but still she looked about the little glen nervously, as if someone might overhear this strange and unseemly conversation. "You'll forgive me if I question why you would be thinking of kissing me."

"It's a wonder," Nathaniel said. "How purely stupid Englishmen can be. Scairt off from a pretty face—don't you scowl that way, maybe nobody ever thought to tell you before, but you are pretty—because there's a sharp mind and a quick tongue to go along with it. Well, I'm made of tougher stuff."

"Why—" Elizabeth began, sputtering.

"Christ, Boots, will you stop talking," said Nathaniel, lowering his mouth to hers; she stepped neatly away.

"I think not," she said. "Not tonight."

Nathaniel laughed out loud. "Tomorrow night? The night after?"

"Oh, no," Elizabeth said, trying halfheartedly to turn away. "I cannot—pardon me, I must get back."

"Back to England?" he asked, one hand moving down until he clasped a mittened hand. "Or just back to your father?"

Nathaniel saw Elizabeth jerk in surprise. She looked up at him sharply, her eyes sparkling. At first he thought she was angry again, then he saw that it was more complicated than that: she was furious, but not at him. Not at this. This almost-kiss, the idea of it, had released something in her.

"It isn't right that my father misrepresented things to me, that he brought me here under false pretenses, that he made plans for me that I want no part of."

"You don't want Richard Todd," Nathaniel prompted.

"No," Elizabeth said fiercely, and her eyes traveled down to focus on his mouth. "I don't want Richard Todd. I want my school."

"I will build you a school."

"I want to know why you're so angry at my father, what he's done to you."

"I'll tell you that if you really want to know," he said. "But someplace warmer."

"I don't want to get married."

He raised an eyebrow. "Then I won't marry you."

Her eyes kept darting over his face, between his mouth and his eyes, and back to his mouth, the curve of his lip. He saw this, and he knew she was thinking about kissing him. Nathaniel knew that this was a conflict for her, one not easily reconciled: she did not want marriage, and in her world—in this world—there could not be one without the other. This struggle was clear on her face, and as he expected, training and propriety won out: she was not quite bold enough to ask for the kisses she wanted. This disappointed him but he was also relieved. He didn't know how long he could keep his own wants firmly in hand. And this was not a woman who could be rushed.

"I want . . . I want . . ." She paused and looked down.

"Do you always get everything you want?" Nathaniel asked.

"No," she said. "But I intend to start."

Elizabeth let Nathaniel turn her back toward the house. Her hands and feet were icy, her cheeks chafed red with the cold, but she was strangely elated, her head rushing with possibilities. She felt that she could face her father now and that she must, she would, have her way. She had no intention of mentioning Nathaniel to him, of what had passed between them, although she recognized, she knew, that this was not over. She knew that it had just begun, and that it would take her places she could not yet imagine. It frightened her, how far she had come in just a few days, but it was also deeply exciting.

A strange thought came to Elizabeth: if her father would not give her what she wanted, Nathaniel might help her take it. He was a man such as she had never known before, and she wondered if he could be a part of her life and not an obstruction in it. She cast a wondering and speculative sideways glance at him, and shivered.

When Elizabeth stepped into the parlor with Nathaniel close behind her, she drew back in surprise, and her immediate plans for a private conference with her father were forgotten.

Most of the guests were gone. The few who remained were silent, their attention focused on the judge, who stood before the hearth with Hawkeye and two people Elizabeth had never before seen: a very old Indian and a young child. The judge was talking to the Indian, his head bent in a deferential and concerned manner. Elizabeth could not estimate the Indian's age: his form was still straight, but there was little flesh on him and a significant stoop to the wide shoulders. There was nothing fragile about the man, as was the case with most very old people; in contrast, it seemed that age had dried him to the toughest kind of leather.

Nathaniel drew in a surprised breath and then he moved past her to join this group. "Chingachgook," he said, and he bowed his head before the old man. "Muchómes."

The old man murmured in reply, reaching for Nathaniel's hands. His smile pleated his face into long folds that swallowed all the severity and distance in his expression.

Hawkeye spoke to the old man in the same language and Nathaniel replied to both of them as if they were alone in the room. Elizabeth realized that Richard Todd had come to stand next to her and she looked at him to see if he followed any of the conversation.

"Mahican," he said to her in a casual tone. "He calls Nathaniel his grandson."

Elizabeth was confused and a little shocked, but she could not ask for more details. Instead, she turned her attention to the child, who had stepped closer to Nathaniel. She was very striking, with hair like black walnut and eyes not quite so dark as those of the old man. But her skin was the glossy color of old honey, and her highly arched cheekbones left no question that she was Indian, in spite of her calico dress and the matching ribbon which secured the long braids which reached down her back.

She had moved up next to Nathaniel and stood close enough to touch him; in response he reached down without looking to cradle the child's head in one large hand. There was a sudden lull in the talking and the little girl's voice came clearly to Elizabeth, although she did not understand the language.

Richard Todd made a small sound and Elizabeth turned to him. "Mohawk," he said. "She calls Nathaniel *rake'niha*, 'my father.' Mohawk was her mother's language. The Kah-nyen'kehàka are matrilineal, you see."

"Kahnyen'kehàka?" Elizabeth's tongue stumbled on the strange word.

"Kahnyen'kehàka is what they call themselves, it means 'People of the Flint.' Mohawk is an outsider name for them. They don't like it, but it fits."

"What does it mean?"

The corner of his mouth jerked downward. "Man-Eaters."

Elizabeth focused, trying to absorb this information. She had heard the rumors of cannibalism; all of England had, but she lent them little credence. She was more interested in the role of women in the tribe, but of such things no one talked. But most of all, Elizabeth did not understand how Nathaniel could have a grandfather who was Indian. There was no doubt that his daughter was Mohawk—Kahnyen'kehàka, Elizabeth corrected herself. It followed quite logically from that fact that his wife, who had died in childbed, whom he still mourned, if Katherine Witherspoon was to be believed—must have been Indian. It was all very confusing. She had never known anyone who married outside his own race; in her world, to marry even a Frenchman or an Irishman was a social disaster of immense proportions. In England, a man of good family who married outside his own race would be ostracized and shunned for the rest of his life. The lady and her children would be invisible to any polite society, isolated and ignored.

"Sarah—Nathaniel's wife—was Mohawk. Her father was head of the Wolf clan," Richard Todd volunteered. She wondered if she really did hear something of distaste in his voice, or if that was her imagination.

"Who is the old man?" asked Elizabeth.

"Chingachgook—Great-Snake," Dr. Todd replied. "Some call him Indian John. He is Mahican. Hannah's great-grand-father."

Elizabeth was more and more confused. "I don't under-stand."

Dr. Todd looked down at her for a long moment. "No," he said finally. "It's not very clear. Chingachgook adopted Dan'l when he was orphaned as an infant, and raised him as a son. So he is by extension Nathaniel's adoptive grandfather. Although the natives would not recognize the validity of such terms. Once they accept a child into the family they no longer think of it as anything but their own."

"Elizabeth," the judge said, holding out one arm toward her to draw her closer. "I would like to introduce you."

For the first time Elizabeth noticed that her brother was nowhere in the room. She was glad that Julian was not present, for she was sure that the way Nathaniel looked at her as she moved toward her father would not go unnoticed by her brother. Elizabeth was very agitated and confused by all the things that had happened this evening, and she was suddenly shy of Nathaniel and a little frightened; how should she speak to this daughter of his? To his grandfather? She had never in her life spoken to an Indian, and she was nervous, and annoyed with herself for being nervous. The thought of Nathaniel's dead wife kept raising itself in her mind and she put it away resolutely. Elizabeth wanted nothing more than to escape to her room to consider all these strange happenings and feelings in solitude, but that possibility was not open to her.

With a tone which showed him to be deeply moved, her father made her acquainted with Chingachgook, whom he introduced as a chieftain of the Mahican people, a lifelong friend, and someone to whom the judge owed not only much of his good fortune, but his health and life. Elizabeth was very surprised by this introduction, and even more unsure of how to greet such a personage. She was in some danger of becoming truly flustered, but then she looked into the man's eyes. His intelligence lit up his face so that it shone like a copper farthing. He might be very old, but his wits were sharp, and while his look was critical, it was not unkind. She curtsied deeply with her head bowed and said nothing.

When she looked up her gaze went first to Nathaniel, and she saw that she had not offended him.

"Come," said the judge. "There is food and drink and you must be very tired— John has come very far, Elizabeth, he has been traveling for many weeks in the dead of winter. He honors us coming so directly to our home."

Elizabeth had thought to slip away to her own room, and she

began to make her excuses; then she caught sight of Nathaniel, who watched her closely. With a barely perceptible nod of the head she understood that he wanted her to come along with the men, that for some reason he thought it important to have her there. She nodded to her father and let herself be escorted from the room.

VI

They settled around the dining room table and let what was left of the party carry on in the other room without them. Curiosity saw to it that the visitors' plates and tankards were full, and the judge kept their conversation going. Elizabeth thought that she would have some time now to be quiet, to think over all that had happened, and to prepare herself for what might come, but she immediately felt herself observed, on more than one front. Julian had come into the room and taken a place at the table. His color was high, his manner extremely nervous. He tried to catch Elizabeth's eye. Nathaniel's observation of her was more subtle, but she felt it very clearly. Then Chingachgook addressed her.

"You remind me of my son's wife," he said to Elizabeth. His voice was deeply melodious and his English had an intonation which was unfamiliar to her. "She was one such as you. *Wìnganool, longochquen,* we say in my language."

" 'A keen-spirited woman,' " translated Nathaniel.

"Aye, that she was, my girl," murmured Hawkeye.

Elizabeth was flustered and gratified, but most of all she felt very much out of her depth, and was almost glad to have Julian interrupt, as he relieved her of the responsibility of a response.

"What brings you to these parts?" asked Julian, disrupting this easy exchange. He had found his pipe and puffed at it furiously.

"I come to be with my son and his people." The old man spoke quietly, but he addressed Julian without hesitation or a hint of apology.

"Chingachgook is always welcome in Paradise," said the judge.

"When I was a boy, these were Kahnyen'kehàka lands," said Chingachgook thoughtfully. He paused, and looked directly at Elizabeth. "Kahnyen'kehàka—the Mohawk—were a fierce people. They feared no tribe, they did not know hunger. But most of the Kahnyen'kehàka are gone." Chingachgook gestured to the northwest. "They fought with the British against the new government, and there is no place for them now in their homeland. Only a few of them are left here in the land of the Wolf, but those are very dear to us." He glanced at Hannah. "We must learn to live more closely together, we who are left behind."

"So you plan to take up residence in Paradise?" asked Julian in a deceptively even tone of voice. Elizabeth kept her eyes on her plate, and wished desperately that she had some way of removing her brother from this room.

The judge stepped into the conversation; there was a warning tone in his words that Elizabeth noted quite clearly, but that she feared Julian would miss. "Some years ago I incurred a great debt to Chingachgook," said the judge. "He and his people are free to live on my lands, for as long as they remain in my family's holdings."

All the men tensed at this formulation.

" 'His people' is very loosely framed, Father," Julian said.

The judge rose from his place. "Julian, I would speak with you in my study."

With a sigh, the younger man followed his father from the room. There was silence for a moment, as if a great storm had suddenly passed by without touching them. Elizabeth suspected that this tension which had grown in the room would return with her father. There was some unfinished business between the men, that was certain.

Chingachgook spoke to Elizabeth. "We have not always been dependent on the goodwill of friends. Once my people hunted to the east. There was game for everyone."

"Unfortunately, that's not the case anymore," said Richard Todd, who sat to Elizabeth's left. He had followed the conversation with close attention to this point.

"Well, that's true enough," said Hawkeye, with sudden great emotion; his anger sparked in his voice. "The legislature has been up to tricks," he explained to Chingachgook. "Those who never had to take a gun in hand to feed a family are forbidding woodsmen to hunt. As if they could keep track of the likes of us in the forest. You ask the judge, he'll tell you about how the rich men sit together and think up laws to vex common folk."

"Surely, Dan'l, but surely," said Reverend Witherspoon. "Surely you agree that we need laws to restrict the amount of timber that can be taken in a season, and to protect the spawning grounds in the rivers . . ."

"You don't get my point. Of course I can't deny that fools like Billy Kirby don't know when to stop and put down the axe. He would take down the whole forest if he could, and every animal in it. But a good hunter never shoots a doe with a fawn beside her, and he don't need laws written down to tell him so. Common sense is enough of a law, for those who don't let greed rule them."

"Common sense can't be legislated," said Elizabeth, and the men turned to her. Richard Todd raised an eyebrow in surprise, but the others did not seem surprised at the way she joined in the conversation.

"That is true," said Chingachgook. "And well spoken."

"It is true," said Richard, addressing Hawkeye rather than Elizabeth. "But Billy Kirby is a fact. There are too many like him. From that it follows that we need some greater authority to stop men who won't stop themselves. The citizens of Paradise will enforce the laws passed by the legislature. You know they will take pleasure in doing so."

"Aye, you're right." Disgusted, Hawkeye shook his head.

"There is a shortage of game," said Nathaniel, taking up the conversation. "We were out every day this week and didn't get any venison till yesterday."

Elizabeth looked down when she felt a hand on her own: the child Hannah, who sat to her right, was looking up at her with a shy smile. Elizabeth thought of bringing up the subject of school, when the door opened and her father came back in, without Julian.

"I apologize for my son," he said without preamble. "He has much to learn." He took his seat next to Chingachgook and clasped him firmly by the forearm.

"It is certainly good to see you here. It has been too long. You'll have to tell me about things down Genesee Valley way." The judge sought out Elizabeth and then smiled at her. "This man saved my life a total of three times, daughter. Twice during the wars, and once soon after, when I was traveling the Mohawk. I had every gold and silver coin to my name in the canoe, on my way to the auction where I bought the second patent, this very land."

The judge was a good storyteller, and most of his audience was attentive as he told of that last journey, of the run-in with thieves on the road, and how Hawkeye and Chingachgook had intervened when he believed all was lost. While he was telling this story, Elizabeth watched Nathaniel from the corner of her eye, seeing that he was distracted and that his attention wandered between herself and his adoptive grandfather.

"And there I made a vow to these two that they should have property rights on whatever land I owned, for themselves and their families. And now finally Chingachgook comes to take what I offered him."

The judge wound up with a great flourish, and lifted his tankard.

Nathaniel and Hawkeye exchanged glances. "Might as well make it clear now, Judge," said Hawkeye. "My father did not come up from Genesee on his own."

"Well, I hardly thought he traveled alone in the dead of winter," said the judge.

"Falling-Day's children came along, too," said Nathaniel.

"Otter," said Hannah, speaking out to the table for the first time. "And Many-Doves."

"Well, Hannah," said the judge kindly. "It must be good to have your aunt and uncle come to visit."

With a grin to his granddaughter, Hawkeye answered the

judge. "That ain't all of it," he said lightly. "She'll have to put up with them a sight longer. They come to stay."

The judge glanced at Richard, but before he could respond, Chingachgook held up one hand, much like a battered and seasoned split of oak. His wrists were ringed with faded tattoos in geometrical shapes.

"There is no peace in the Northwest Territory," he said. "Little-Turtle has unfinished business with Washington's troops, and I for one am too old to fight. I come to my friend the judge for myself, and for my family, and for my son's family. We will settle together on Hidden Wolf, and be good neighbors."

"You and your families are welcome for as long as you want to stay," said the judge, but he glanced uneasily at Richard Todd.

Chingachgook blinked slowly. "I come to ask something from the judge which is more than his hospitality."

There was a small silence.

"We are grateful for your friendship and your generosity. But we are a people who must fend for ourselves. It seems that the only way we can do that, and live as we must live, is if we own the land we live on, as the whites do."

While Elizabeth had been following the conversation closely, she still missed much of the meaning because the names of these people they discussed were new to her. But now she sensed Richard still suddenly: the tension rose in the room like a sudden blast of heat, and Elizabeth knew that something terribly important was happening. Her father was flushed and perspiring, and Richard sat with his hands in a fist on the table. But Hawkeye, Chingachgook, and Nathaniel were as calm and easy as they had been from the beginning.

"It is not our way to lay claim to land with pieces of paper. We have never understood this manner of the Europeans. But now it seems we must accept this practice if we are to have any chance of surviving."

Chingachgook paused and looked around the room, his dark eyes under their hoods of flesh sharp and observant.

"The judge has more land than he can use. I ask him as our friend, as a man who has always treated the Kahnyen'kehàka and the Mahicans fairly, I ask him as I would ask a brother who has hunted and fought with me for thirty years, to sell us the mountain called Hidden Wolf, where my son and his son's family live and hunt. So that we can sustain ourselves in these forests, not as his guests, but as his neighbors."

As tired as she was, when she finally had found refuge in her own room after the party, Elizabeth found that sleep eluded her for a long time. There was so much to consider that her thoughts collided and bumped together in a crazy quilt of images and colors: Anna Hauptmann's broad arms and the moon over the forest; the feel of Nathaniel's hands on her face and the shimmer of his daughter's smooth golden skin in the candlelight; the smell of burning sugar and spiced rum; the look on her father's face when Chingachgook had made his purpose known.

Uneasy, Elizabeth turned from side to side. She did not know what worried her more: her father's distant and uncommitted response to what had been a clearly presented and—it seemed to her—logical request; the cold look on Nathaniel's face at her father's lack of response; or the look Nathaniel had given her, as if to say: "You see, this is what you must understand about your father."

Before leaving England, Elizabeth had not thought much about the natives; generally people believed that they had been quiet for so long that they were no longer a threat, that they had become Christian and had settled into a new way of life. Elizabeth realized she knew nothing about them, about how or where they lived, now, or before the continent had been taken by the Europeans. She did not know her father very well, but she could see that he was torn between his debt to the Bonners and his terrible love of the land he had acquired with so much trouble, land he prized so highly that he was willing to sell her in marriage to keep it in his own family.

And there was the matter of Nathaniel's family, his Indian family. His wife, a Mohawk. She remembered Katherine Witherspoon's knowing look. She understood now that Katherine had wanted to tell Elizabeth about Nathaniel's Indian wife, but was unable to do so without seeming to gossip. To tell

Elizabeth that Nathaniel had married an Indian, that he had a daughter who was half Indian, this would be equal to telling her that he was unsuitable as even a casual acquaintance. To a white woman of good family, such as Elizabeth was. That was what Katherine Witherspoon must believe, Elizabeth realized. That was what she herself would have taken for granted just a week ago.

Elizabeth found in herself a deep curiosity, not just about Nathaniel and his family, but about how they had come to the place they found themselves now. He was like no one she had ever known, his life to this point beyond her imagination, his problems beyond her understanding. Elizabeth knew that she could not ask her father for explanations, and that whatever she needed or wanted to know about this new place, about the people here, and about her own future in it, she would have to learn from Nathaniel. That this man, as strange as it must seem, was her only ally here. That they could help each other: she would do what she could to advance his cause with her father, and he would introduce her to this new world.

She shifted uneasily in her new, unfamiliar bed, and thought of kissing Nathaniel.

VII

"Well, some things remain constant," remarked Julian on Christmas afternoon as he reclined full-length on the settee. "This may be the New World, but holiday afternoons are as boring here as they are in the old one."

Curiosity and her daughters had served a midday meal which had put them all to the test, and now the Middletons and their guests were gathered around the fire. Elizabeth had taken up her reading and was relieved to see Richard Todd do the same, hoping that it would spare her the necessity of another pointed conversation with him. Mr. Witherspoon and the judge were both drifting off to sleep, but Julian and Katherine Witherspoon were clearly eager for some activity.

Elizabeth looked up from her book to her brother's fidgeting.

"Don't suggest a walk, sister," Julian said, anticipating her recommendation. "My idea of entertainment doesn't include slogging around in two feet of snow after three servings of venison."

"Then maybe we should go down to the turkey shoot," suggested Richard Todd. He put down his book and walked to the fireplace where he stood with his hands behind his back, rocking on his heels.

"Oh, yes, the turkey shoot!" cried Katherine. She smiled at

Julian as if it had been his suggestion. "It's a Christmas tradition, we must all go along."

"Certainly this is a working day like any other?" asked Elizabeth.

The judge roused himself to join in the conversation, stifling a yawn. "Yes, of course. But we have a lot of Dutch and Germans here, and they have particular ideas about Christmas—"

Reverend Witherspoon cleared his throat in a disapproving way, and the judge shrugged as if to apologize for the less seemly habits of the villagers.

"The turkey shoot is a popular event. People take the time," he concluded.

"You must have three dozen birds in your coops, Father," said Julian. "Why would you want to go and pay for the privilege of shooting at somebody else's turkey?"

"I wouldn't," affirmed the judge, settling back down into his chair. "But it is good sport. Go on now, all of you young people, and see how Paradise amuses itself. Kitty and Richard will show you the way."

They set out in just a few minutes: Julian, Richard Todd, Katherine, and Elizabeth.

"Men come from all over to shoot," Katherine explained to Julian and Elizabeth. "Billy Kirby organizes it."

"At substantial profit to himself," added Richard Todd.

Katherine overheard this comment. It struck Elizabeth once again that her indifference toward Richard Todd was too studied, and too careful, to mean anything but the opposite of what it seemed to be.

They kept up a brisk pace so as to keep the cold from making too much headway, but still Katherine would talk.

"I wonder," she said to Julian, "if you should have brought out your gun. Should you like to try your hand at the competition?"

"I'll leave the shooting to the locals," said Julian shortly. Elizabeth observed him closely, but saw that he meant to say no more on this matter.

"Don't you care for hunting?" asked Katherine.

"On the contrary," Julian said with a smile. "But the game which interests me is a more civilized one."

Richard Todd's grimace was lost on Katherine and Julian, but Elizabeth noted it with dawning realization. She wondered whether Richard's distaste was for her brother, or for Katherine's flirtation. In either case, she found it difficult to listen any longer, and so Elizabeth stepped up her pace in hopes of outstripping the others. Soon enough she had left Julian and Katherine behind, but to her surprise Elizabeth found Richard Todd was unwilling to be shaken off.

"I think it is hard for young people who put high value on amusement and parties to live so far out," Richard said with an awkward smile.

Elizabeth looked up at him in surprise. Richard Todd was making excuses to her for Katherine, and she could not fathom why. Unless, of course, he had some tender feelings for her himself and her behavior distressed him. Elizabeth considered for a moment.

"I suppose that is true," she said. "It is a very small neighborhood, isn't it, and there cannot be much variety in the entertainment. I find that less of a burden. At home I was never so interested in the dances as I was in my uncle's library. But my cousins would not know what to do with themselves here."

Richard nodded. "Young ladies often have expectations which cannot be met by our little circle of friends."

"Well," said Elizabeth, feeling a little easier toward Richard now. "Young women have the habit of growing into older ladies, and giving up dancing for whist."

"But some young ladies seem to enjoy dancing more than others," said Richard. "Did you enjoy the party yesterday evening?"

"Yes, it was very pleasant," replied Elizabeth. She wondered if she dared raise the subject, and then decided that she might. "What did you think of Chingachgook's proposal to my father?"

Suddenly the easy feeling between them was gone, and Elizabeth thought that Dr. Todd would refuse to answer her. He cleared his throat.

"I think it will come to nothing."

"You fear it will come to nothing," asked Elizabeth, "or you hope it will come to nothing?"

"It is not an easy thing, what the old man asks," said Richard, slowly searching for words. "Peaceful times are precious in this part of the world, and I would be foolish to wish them gone."

"Why should a business transaction such as the one suggested last night mean the end of peace?" asked Elizabeth. "It seems a likely solution to the problem."

"No one wants to sell their land to the natives," said Richard Todd. "And the reasons for that are both so complicated and so simple that I cannot explain."

"But the lands once belonged to them, didn't they? Why shouldn't they buy them back?"

"With what? With what will they buy it back? Do you really think—" Richard Todd stopped and made a visible effort to calm his voice. "Miss Elizabeth, do you believe that they have the funds necessary to buy such a valuable tract of land from your father?"

Elizabeth considered for a moment, looking over the forests under their cloak of snow. "Well, they may have at least part of what they were paid for the land in the first place. How much were they paid?"

Dr. Todd stopped, the corner of his mouth twitching. One eyebrow raised, he looked like a schoolteacher who suspected a student of posing a question constructed to show him up. "Are you really ignorant of the history of this valley?"

They had come to the top of a little rise and the village was spread out below them, the lake covered with ice reflecting silvers and blues in the sunlight. The mountains reached up like fists into the sky, their shoulders cloaked with hardwood and conifers.

"Well, I know it was once theirs," said Elizabeth. "And that we now have it. I assume that was done lawfully, with appropriate compensation. But perhaps," she said thoughtfully, "perhaps I assume too much."

"You assume that they think and feel as you do," Richard said with a new edge to his voice.

"I assume that they think and feel as any human being must, who must live and eat."

He let out a small grunt, and Elizabeth realized that for all his careful reasoning, Richard's stance on this matter was based on a simple dislike of the natives. Although she sensed that if she were to confront him with this, he would deny it.

The conversation had slowed them down a bit and now Julian and Katherine caught up just as they came around one last bend and found themselves confronted with Paradise's annual turkey shoot.

Some thirty men and just as many women and children had gathered in the late afternoon. There were horses and dogs, and a great deal of talking and laughter. The women were feeding a great bonfire, most of them wrapped in a variety of shawls, with reddened noses and eyes watery with the cold.

Anna Hauptmann, directing the attention to the bonfire, was also engaged in a number of distinct conversations and called out cheerfully, more than willing to start another one. Her children dashed by Elizabeth in pursuit of an outsized puppy. Molly and Becca Kaes called to Katherine, and the younger girl set off in that direction on Julian's arm. Elizabeth continued toward the shooting stand with Richard Todd, stopping to greet the villagers as she went.

The men were dressed in raggedy furs, buckskin, and homespun in shades of butternut and brown. Their heads were covered with a variety of caps and hats, some of ancient vintage, many trailing frayed tails of animals Elizabeth could not identify. Young and old, chests were crisscrossed with leather straps supporting powder horns, and small leather bags sagging with shot. Several of them turned as Richard Todd approached with Elizabeth, and they called out cheerful greetings. At the foot of the tree stump which served as the shooting stand, Elizabeth saw Dan'l and Nathaniel Bonner. Nathaniel's long hair had been gathered together with a rawhide string and hung down his back in a thick tail. His head was uncovered and his ears were tinged red. Elizabeth realized that she was staring, and she turned away.

It's a small village, Elizabeth said to herself sternly. *You will have to learn to get along with others at close quarters. You cannot, you must not, act like a smitten schoolgirl.* The sound of Katherine's laughter rose from the crowd and Elizabeth focused on this, willing her heart to assume a more normal rhythm. *Leave flirtation to Katherine,* she told herself. *Nathaniel Bonner will speak to you, or he won't.*

The contestants were growing restless, and in response a man pushed his way through the crowd and leapt up on top of the tree stump.

"Billy Kirby," said Richard Todd, confirming Elizabeth's suspicion. She observed him with some interest. He was built like an overfull barrel, with a great breadth of chest and hamlike shoulders below a thick neck. Under a tricorn hat, odd twists of blond hair stuck out at all angles and blended into what must be at least three days' growth of reluctant blond beard. Between the bristles his skin was blotched red with cold, blemishes, scrapes. Thin lips bleached pale by the cold revealed tobacco-stained teeth. Elizabeth was surprised to see how young he was, perhaps eighteen or so.

Billy rested one foot on an empty fowl coop and surveyed the crowd. About a hundred yards farther on there was another stump, behind which a tremendously large tom turkey had been tethered by a short lead; it scratched in the snow, occasionally raising its spindly neck over the edge to observe the crowd with one bright black and mistrustful eye.

"It's a hard target, a skittery bird behind a stump," Richard Todd explained. "Billy will take in a nice profit."

Elizabeth answered without taking her eyes from the scene. "I see the Bonners are here. I expect Hawkeye came by his nickname with some reason?"

The doctor nodded. "He most certainly did. Even at his age he's a hard man to best with a long rifle. But I doubt whether he's got a spare shilling to place the necessary wager."

Elizabeth glanced at Richard, but his large, round face was completely serious. How could it be possible that Hawkeye and Nathaniel might not have a shilling between them? But before she could think of a way to put this question, Billy Kirby began calling out.

"Come on, then, come on, the finest bird you'll see this winter, I will put odds on it. A shilling a go, a shilling a go. A mere eighth of a Spanish dollar—why, he would cost you ten times that, and he'll feed the family for the week—two weeks, if your woman's the housekeeper she should be. Who'll be first?"

He cast his eyes over the crowd and then smiled.

"Hawkeye! Yes, the man himself, a shot like no other!"

Before Hawkeye could reply, Billy Kirby was at him again.

"But then maybe not, maybe not, you're not the youngest anymore—" There was a good-natured laugh at this, and Hawkeye turned to the crowd, his white hair lifting in the breeze.

"Don't doubt it," he called. "The boy tells the truth. Once I could of took the horn button off his mangy old tricorn at a dead run, but time creeps up on all of us. Though to be honest I am tempted—"

"Well, of course you are, it's a fine bird an' all," interrupted Billy.

"—by that button," finished Hawkeye.

Billy Kirby flushed at the crowd's laughter, and his watery blue eyes fell on Nathaniel. "Well, then, what about the son, then? What about you, Nathaniel? Got your father's sharp eye, now don't you, know a good thing when you see one. But then maybe you don't want to part with the price," he said with a nasty grin.

"He's got a bullet hole in his shootin' shoulder," called someone from the crowd.

"Well, this is bad news for a gamesman like myself," said Billy. "The two best shots in the area and neither willing to take the chance. If you won't try this bird, who will? You really going to let a little lead in your shoulder keep you from this bird?" Billy said with a wink to the crowd.

"I'll have a go," called Richard Todd, moving past Elizabeth. The crowd turned to him, and Elizabeth's eye met Nathaniel's. He nodded at her, smiling grimly, and then turned his attention to Richard, who was reaching inside his coat for the required shilling. At length he produced a handful of coins, and with a flourish he held one up so that it flashed in the sunlight.

The crowd was moving forward, and Elizabeth found herself propelled closer to the makeshift shooting stand.

Richard checked the load and the flash pan and made himself comfortable with the target, while the crowd gave him a good deal of advice. Elizabeth turned to her neighbor, remembering him from the difficult first encounter at the trading post.

"Mr. LeBlanc," she said. "Will you have a try at the bird?"

"Sure, Charlie will have a go, he contributes his shilling every Christmas, don't you, Charlie?" said Hawkeye good-naturedly.

Elizabeth was a little startled to find the Bonners so near, but she managed to greet them without drawing attention to herself. She wondered if she should expect Nathaniel to speak to her, and what he might have to say. Then, irritated with herself, she turned to watch Richard Todd adjust his sights.

"Well, maybe this year I'll have a chance," said Charlie. "As Nathaniel's got a sore shoulder. Although it's a damn skinny target to put my siller on, rare as it is."

"Waall," drawled Hawkeye, grinning. "A hundred yards is a short distance for a long rifle, after all. We may still give you a run for your shillin'. That turkey would be welcome with all the folks we got to feed these days."

"Is it true, then? Is Chingachgook come to stay?"

Nathaniel, who had kept his attention focused on Richard, now glanced up. "It's true enough," he answered for his father. "Falling-Day's two youngest along with him."

The crowd moved in even closer, bringing Elizabeth near enough to Nathaniel to touch him. She wondered if people were watching her, and if they were, what they might see on her face.

"Heads up! Heads up! Mr. Turkey, pay heed!" called Billy Kirby as Richard set his sights. And he let out a tremendous whoop just as the powder flashed in the pan, whether to upset the shooter's concentration or make the turkey jump was unclear.

The cloud of smoke rose away from the shooting stand. There was a sudden quiet and then another whoop when the turkey raised his head over the stump and glared.

"What a bird!" shouted Billy. "What a bird! Sorry, Doc, he's too fast for you. Unless you want another shot?"

But Richard Todd had opened the floodgates, and now other men crowded up to have their go, placing valuable coin in

Billy Kirby's grubby hand one by one, and one by one adding to his delight in the whole undertaking.

Elizabeth found herself surrounded now by Hawkeye, Nathaniel, Richard Todd, and Charlie LeBlanc, who seemed determined to keep her entertained throughout the process.

"Couldn't hit Half Moon if he fell out the boat," Hawkeye said of the skinny red-haired Cameron, who was just about as long as his musket. He rubbed one large, flat hand over the white stubble on his face and smiled.

"Now, old Jack MacGregor," said Hawkeye as a man about his own age came up to the shooting stand. "Jack once was a fine man with a rifle, but he's past his prime."

Nathaniel snorted. "He's two years younger than you at least."

"But he's got old eyes," Hawkeye replied, not put out at all. "My eyes are still good, better than most."

"Perhaps you'll tell me how you came to be called Hawkeye," Elizabeth suggested. "It must be an interesting story."

"Too bold a tale for young women of good family," Hawkeye agreed. "But I'll tell you anyway, lass, if you catch me in front of the fire one day and ask me nicely. Here's what we'll do," he continued, grinning broadly. "If I take that bird home to roast, you'll come up and eat it with us and listen to my stories. I could use a fresh audience. Folks around here don't appreciate my offerings much lately."

Elizabeth laughed. "Yes, I'll take you up on that," she said. "But there won't be any bird for you to roast if you don't take a chance."

"Well, me and the boy have still not come to a conclusion on how we should spend this one shilling we got between us," he said. "Nathaniel! How's that shoulder feel?"

Elizabeth wondered how she could offer them a shilling so that both could have a shot at the turkey, but nothing occurred to her which wouldn't embarrass them, and so she kept still, listening instead to their banter.

The cloud of gunsmoke had grown to considerable proportions and the crowd of shooters had dwindled. Billy did his best to keep a good thing going. "Now, I know some of you out there got the price of this bird," he called. "Step up and be counted. You, Nathaniel, you still leaning on that sore shoulder of yourn?"

There was a moment's silence, and then Nathaniel nodded. "I'll have a shot," he said calmly, and moved forward to hand Billy his entrance fee.

"Four quarter bits, four quarter bits, that's right, that's all it takes." Billy nodded, but his tone was much more subdued now, and it was clear that he thought the bird's life was about to come to a quick end.

Elizabeth wondered why she was so very agitated; it was only a bird, after all: she could see it very clearly, its very long, spindly neck and bobbing head, the wattle bright red against the background of snow. Not such a very hard shot, she thought, not for a good marksman with steady hands. The crowd was calling advice to Nathaniel as he stood up to the shooting stand and checked his rifle once more, the well-worn stock glinting in the sunlight.

"Come on, Nathaniel, we're depending on you!"

Yes, thought Elizabeth, *it seems that everybody does depend on you.*

There was silence as Nathaniel took aim. He was very much like his father, Elizabeth noted. He had the same long, straight back, and he held his head tilted just the same way, a blue vein pulsing lightly in the slight indentation of his temple where the dark hairs were drawn back. The line of his arm, the juncture of gun with shoulder, the very cloud of gunsmoke seemed to settle into stillness for a small moment. Elizabeth held her breath.

"Don't think about the shoulder," called Hawkeye gingerly. "You're made of stronger stuff than a little torn muscle."

"Think about Miss Elizabeth across the table from you instead!" called Charlie LeBlanc, just as the powder flashed in the pan.

"Well," said Hawkeye after a goodly pause. "He pulled too far to the left, ye see. Nicked the bloody bird's beak." He spoke to Nathaniel's back. "The shoulder's too wound, I told you so." And he set off down the snowy embankment toward the turkey with Billy Kirby and the other men in tow.

Nathaniel set to reloading his rifle straightaway. For the moment they were alone. Elizabeth watched as he removed the plug from his horn and poured a measure of powder into the barrel. From a pouch on his belt he took a greased cotton patch —Elizabeth noted with some surprise that it was brightly colored, the kind of fabric a woman would use for a skirt—and wrapped it around a lead ball which came out of his bullet bag. He detached the ramrod from its brackets and shoved this all down the rifle barrel with one firm push. Then he poured more powder into the priming pan. All of this took less than a minute's worth of quick and economical movements, and the whole time, Nathaniel seemed to be more focused on Elizabeth than he was on his job.

"I'm sorry," Elizabeth said, meaning that he had lost his shilling. Then she wished she had remained quiet.

Nathaniel grinned. "Well," he said. "I suppose I'll have to forgo your company at my table. At least for the time being."

Elizabeth looked away toward the men arguing over the state of the turkey. "I wouldn't have thought you would give up so easily."

He raised an eyebrow, amused. "There are other birds in the forest," he pointed out. "And as far as getting you to my table, I expect that won't be too difficult, either."

"Talk is easy," Elizabeth said lightly, causing Nathaniel to laugh out loud.

Down the embankment, Dr. Todd was called to officiate. The bird was pronounced scared half to death, but whole enough for the competition to continue.

"Maybe you'll get a taste of the bird anyway," Nathaniel was saying to Elizabeth, and she looked up with a start to see her brother at the shooting stand. She had been so involved with Nathaniel and the scene at hand that it had never occurred to Elizabeth that this was a sporting event—and that Julian's prom-ise to refrain from participating in such events was being tested for the first time since leaving England.

"Julian," she said. Then louder, calling to him: "Julian!"

Her brother turned, an eyebrow raised.

"You can't shoot," Elizabeth said.

Julian ignored her, but Katherine came up, flushed with cold and excitement. "Richard loaned him his rifle. Your brother's agreed to champion me," she said brightly. "Father would be very glad of the bird, and I thought it worth a shilling."

"Julian," Elizabeth said quietly to her brother's back. "You promised."

Rather than watch her brother check his gun and take sight, Elizabeth turned and walked away. She had just pushed her way free of the crowd around the shooting stand when Julian's first shot went afield. Clutching her skirt in her hands, she turned back to see her brother throwing another coin to Billy Kirby.

"Again," he said, and he traded the rifle for one freshly loaded and cocked. "He must tire of ducking soon, the bloody great monster."

"That's the spirit!" called Billy Kirby gleefully.

With a sense of dread, Elizabeth turned and caught Hawkeye's gaze. Nervously, she beckoned him toward her. Nathaniel and Hawkeye came away from the shooting stand to where Elizabeth stood near the bonfire.

"Please," Elizabeth said. "Won't one of you have another try?"

"Elizabeth, it's just sport," Nathaniel said kindly. "Let your brother have his fun."

Julian had missed again, and he turned to the crowd. "This next shot will be the one, I feel it. Anyone care to lay odds?"

Hawkeye and Nathaniel exchanged glances.

"I've got a shilling here for a gentleman who would be willing to champion me," she said in a voice as calm as she could manage. Elizabeth felt as though Hawkeye were looking straight through her, into the panic curling into a fist in her stomach.

"Why, that would be me," said Hawkeye. He turned toward the shooting stand, where Julian was in the process of negotiating the borrowing of yet another rifle. "Hold up there, Billy Kirby, letting one man have all the fun. I've got a shilling here and I claim a shot. I got a lady to champion myself."

The crowd closed around Hawkeye, who took up his place at the shooting stand and set to checking his rifle. Elizabeth felt Nathaniel's questioning gaze settle on her face.

"Can he make the shot?"

"Don't want your brother and this turkey on familiar terms, it seems," he said dryly.

"I'm determined to keep my brother solvent," she corrected him in a low voice. "But if he starts in again waging bets, I may not be able to."

Julian stood to Hawkeye's side, eyes narrowed, as the older man took aim. There were hectic splashes of color on his cheeks, his eyes narrow but flashing nonetheless.

"He has trouble staying away from the betting tables?"

"You could say that." Elizabeth nodded. "He had to be bought out of debtors' prison and put directly on the boat to New-York."

Nathaniel's frown put a crease between his eyes; Elizabeth was taken with a strong urge to run a finger down that crease to the point between his brows, to smooth it away. The urge to touch him was surprisingly strong, so she wound her fingers in her skirts once again, and she met his gaze as evenly as she could.

"But surely the judge can cope with your brother's gambling debts," he said quietly.

Elizabeth forced herself to look up into Nathaniel's face. "I'm sorry to disappoint you," she said. "But my father is cash poor. That's why there's this great hurry to marry me off. A better loan guarantee than a daughter with property is hard to come by." She knew she sounded bitter, and that she was telling too much, offering too much. She knew too that he would take what she offered. She wanted him to.

Hawkeye fired; the crowd was silent for a fraction of a second, and then began to shout in triumph.

VIII

In the weeks after Christmas, Elizabeth began to dream of Nathaniel, so that she grew both anxious before she fell asleep, and reluctant to wake in the morning. While the rising sun touched the frost on her windows and shattered into rainbows, she would lie half conscious in the warm nest of her covers and relive what she had dreamt, blushing and slightly breathless, confused and strangely discontent. She might pretend, in the day, that Nathaniel had not tried to kiss her, or that his interest was unimportant, an aberration, but at night her dreaming self took that almost-kiss and spawned from it a multitude of dream kisses, of growing warmth and intensity.

So Elizabeth began her days with a lecture. She would comb her hair out before the mirror and chide herself for a silly, weak, foolish creature. Every morning she was determined to make a new start in the name of reason and good sense. But still she caught herself staring at the curve of her lower lip. This lack of self-control soon began to wear on her usual placid good humor; Elizabeth went down to breakfast in a contrary mood.

The first of the new year came, and she was without a place to hold school. Her father refrained from pointing out to her that she had failed in the resolution she had put forth so forcefully at the first dinner in Paradise. Julian would not have been so sensitive as to spare her from teasing, if she had not had his behavior at the turkey shoot to hold over his head.

He had been avoiding Elizabeth since that event. At that moment when Hawkeye had killed the bird, Julian had sent her one sharp look and then stalked away toward home, leaving a surprised and worried Katherine Witherspoon behind. The other men had thought it was just bad sportsmanship on Julian's part, but Elizabeth had seen the old fever springing up in her brother, the compulsion which had cost him his fortune. She thanked Providence once again that they were so far from a real city where he might find other men as fond of cards and as careless with their resources.

To keep her mind off the delays in her plans and—although she did not voice it to herself so clearly—Nathaniel, Elizabeth spent her mornings organizing a work space in her room, putting her books in order, and writing teaching outlines. After lunch she would go for walks, if it wasn't snowing too hard; she made it her business to visit the children in the village and speak to their parents, hoping to get them used to her presence and accepting of the idea of her school before too long. She came to know many of the villagers well enough to talk to them comfortably. Martha Southern, a shy young woman married to a man old enough to be her father, especially sought out Elizabeth's friendship and encouraged her to come to the village. Martha had a daughter whom she wanted to send to Elizabeth's school, and a son who would soon be old enough.

Elizabeth found that she had most of her time to herself, and this was a great relief. Her father was often out on his errands, and Julian went down to the village where he had got into the habit of sitting with the farmers and other men who spent odd moments in the trading post or in the tavern that adjoined it.

In the third week of the new year, Galileo made a trip to pick up the trunks which had traveled up the Hudson behind them, and stopped in Johnstown for the post on his way home. Elizabeth came down to breakfast to find letters from her aunt Merriweather and her cousins, but more importantly, her school supplies. She immediately set to unpacking the texts and materials she had bought in such a spirit of hopefulness in England. There were grammars and composition books, volumes of essays and histories, philosophy and math. She was a little shocked now at how poorly she had anticipated the needs of the children of a place like Paradise, but Elizabeth refused to be shaken in her resolve. She spent a good part of the morning making plans and notes to herself, and constructing a letter to aunt Merriweather in which she requested another shipment of more basic texts, more writing materials, a large supply of ink, horn tablets, and after some consideration, storybooks, fairy tales, and mythologies.

She wanted to engage the children and not alienate their parents, and she spent a good amount of time pacing back and forth in the study while she chewed thoughtfully on the end of her quill. So deeply was she entrenched in her thoughts that she started at the knock on the door.

Hannah Bonner stood framed against the snowy landscape in her winter cloak. The fur-lined hood was pulled high over her dark hair, framing her glowing face, her teeth flashing white against the bronze skin flushed into deeper shades by the cold. She smiled brightly at Elizabeth and curtsied.

"I've come to fetch you home to eat turkey," she said by way of greeting. "Grandfather says it's high time."

Confronted with this logic, Elizabeth could see no recourse but to change her boots and go. She resolved firmly not to check her hair, or change anything about her appearance. Then she stopped in the kitchen to tell Curiosity where she was going, and she saw with some vexation that her agitation was not lost on the housekeeper.

Curiosity raised one eyebrow, pursed her lips, and set Daisy to wrapping things and putting them in a basket for the Bonners.

"Won't do to go up Hidden Wolf empty-handed," she said, and sent Elizabeth on her way without further commentary, but with a knowing look that made her feel Hannah's age instead of her own.

Elizabeth had seen Nathaniel, outside her dreams, exactly four times since the turkey shoot on Christmas Day. Twice he had been too far away to greet, driving the oxen he borrowed from her father to drag logs out of the forest. Once he had come to the house to speak with the judge about building supplies and she had not known he was in the house until she saw him on his way out.

It was at that point that it became clear to Elizabeth that the whole conversation in the dark woods had been a lark, a game: Nathaniel did not dwell on it, nor on her. Then she saw him, accidentally, for the fourth time.

She had been walking down to the village and heard the cry of a hawk; looking into the forest, she had seen Nathaniel standing in a grove of pine with his axe in his hands, and his eyes fixed on her. Startled, Elizabeth had stood very still. Then he just disappeared into the forest, as if he had never been there.

Elizabeth did not know what to make of it. He was watching her. Perhaps he had been watching her for days. For weeks. There was no good explanation for it; she pushed away impatiently the images and thoughts that worked their way to the surface, refusing to consider them. But they came to her unbidden, in her dreams.

And there was no escaping word of Nathaniel. Daily reports on how much timber he had hauled and the ongoing preparations for the building of her schoolhouse came to the dinner table. While she was tempted to retire before Richard Todd's evening visit, her curiosity always won out, and she ended up sitting with the men, a book in her lap, waiting for him to volunteer details about Nathaniel's progress without the necessity of asking.

Now Hannah walked quickly, glancing back once and again at Elizabeth as if to assess her endurance. She had her grandfather's easy way about her, talkative without being repetitive or tedious, and before they were even through the village and on the path up the first inclines of Hidden Wolf Mountain, Elizabeth had heard about every other child in the village who would be at her school.

"What about you, then?" she asked at the first opportunity. "Will you come and see what I can teach you?"

"I can read," Hannah offered. "And do sums, and write a fair hand, and I know how to sew, and I can spin and weave, and do some beadwork, though I ain't very good yet at it. And I know where things grow—" She stopped and pointed to a set of tracks in the snow. "Moose," she said, clearly surprised.

"And see." She pointed farther. "Otter and my father are track-ing him."

Elizabeth stared for a moment but couldn't make out much more than a jumble of footsteps in the snow.

"Who is Otter?"

"My uncle. His Kahnyen'kehàka name is Tawine—Otter, because of the way he swims. In the north, the Catholics call him Benjamin."

"What's your Indian name?"

"They call me Squirrel but my skin name is Used-to-Be-Two."

Elizabeth wondered about this strange name, but waited to see if the girl would supply an explanation without prompting.

Hannah pointed out the tracks of a fox, and spots where boneset and wild plum grew thick in the summer. Then she glanced at Elizabeth, and seemed to consider.

"My twin died at birth. So, my mother's people say that I am half of what I might have been."

It seemed to Elizabeth very important that she make the right response here, but what that might be was a mystery.

"I'm afraid I have a lot to learn," she started, slowly. "I don't really understand very much about the Kahnyen'kehàka—" She paused, not sure of the pronunciation but loath to use the term *Mohawk,* as the child seemed to avoid it. Hannah grinned at her attempt, and Elizabeth went on, somewhat more at ease. "Or the Mahicans, or how they are related—"

"The Mahicans ain't Six Nations," Hannah supplied, trying to be helpful, but making things all the more unclear. "They lived to the east, mostly below the lake."

"They live here now, with the Kahnyen'kehàka?"

"No," said Hannah simply. "They are all gone now, or most of them. In the wars."

"We have things to learn from each other, then," Elizabeth said. "We should have stories at school about your people, but I don't know enough to tell them."

Hannah smiled, but she was not to be drawn into a promise about coming to Elizabeth's school.

"Grandmother doesn't think much of your kind of schooling," the little girl said, perhaps a little apologetically. "She says the white men don't seem any the smarter for it."

Elizabeth digested this in silence, surprising herself. Even a week ago she thought she would have had much to say, and perhaps in anger, but even simple things were now so complicated that she saw the wisdom of holding back with her opinion. Soon the opportunity to ask more questions had passed: they were walking uphill, and breathing became an issue. Elizabeth began to think that her idea of exercise had been rather a tame one. The lanes and walks around Oakmere at their very worst were no more than wet and muddy; even the walking holidays she had taken with her aunt had been docile by comparison.

Off the track, the snow had drifted up to Elizabeth's hips in some places, but the path they walked was wind scoured and well enough broken. Still, it was rough going, and Elizabeth's admiration for Hannah was considerable: she moved lightly and quickly while Elizabeth struggled along behind her with the basket Curiosity had packed so thoroughly. The freezing air burned in her lungs, while her fingers and toes, well wrapped in wool and leather and fur, still grew wooden with the cold.

They had been walking uphill for what seemed like more than an hour when the wind picked up and began to blow, and just as suddenly, the sunlight flickered and faded, the clouds deepening in color to a deep gray-green. Hannah paused to look up, and then back toward Elizabeth.

"A storm," Elizabeth said. "I hope it's not much farther."

"Lake in the Clouds," Hannah responded and gestured with her chin.

"Lake in the Clouds?"

"This place," Hannah explained. "The Kahnyen'kehàka name for it."

The wooded ridge they had been following turned inward and then ended abruptly in a jumble of outcroppings, snowy evergreens, and granite slabs thrusting like splayed fingers out into the open air. This jutting shoulder of the mountain curved inward as if to protect the hidden glen Elizabeth now found before her.

A little breath of surprise and wonder left her in a warm

rush. Roughly triangular in shape, the glen was about half a mile in length, and perhaps half a mile in breadth at the widest point. On one side cliffs rose up in a flat sheet of marbled gray rock; on the other, the mountain's shoulder dropped away into the precipice. At the far end of the glen, a stream fell thirty feet from a fissure high on the rock face. It cascaded in an icy rush over a clutch of boulders and then fell again into a gorge that ran the length of the glen to narrow and disappear in the forest. From where they stood, Elizabeth could see the waters boiling lazily in a deep pool encased in ribbons of ice.

On one side, the banks of the gorge were built of layers of stone slabs like steps, which leveled into a series of terraces at the broadest point of the vale. There, in a grove of beech, pine, and blue spruce, a log cabin stood with its front porch facing the waterfall. It was low and solid, built in an L-shape, its deep roof scalloped with snow and dripping thick fingers of ice. Smoke curled above two massive fieldstone chimneys; lamplight glowed warmly from cracks in the shutters.

Snow began to fall in thick waves, large flakes twirling in the last of the light, disappearing into the trees and melting into the rushing water. As if in response, the door of the cabin opened and cast a slanted rectangle of butter-yellow light into the growing dark.

He wasn't there; she sensed his absence as clearly as she took in woodsmoke, tallow candles, dried apples, roasting turkey, and the strong smells of animal skins, bear grease, and human beings. Elizabeth blinked at the brightness of firelight reflected in wood and the glowing colors of the room.

Hawkeye seemed to be everywhere at once, setting Hannah a series of quick chores, calling out questions, and making Elizabeth reacquainted with Chingachgook. The old man greeted Elizabeth cheerfully from his chair by the fire. Around his shoulders was a blanket woven in geometric patterns in red, white, and gray. Still a little breathless, Elizabeth accepted the chair across from him.

"The storm came up fast," Chingachgook said.

Hawkeye nodded. "Good thing you two made tracks."

Elizabeth held her hands out toward the fire and smiled at him. "I expect your stories are worth a bit of a walk."

He laughed. "Well, I like to think they are. But if not, then Falling-Day will put a meal on the table that should make up for the trouble. Here she is, and Many-Doves with her."

Anyone would know them for mother and daughter. Identical in height, slender but wiry, Falling-Day was a sparser, more compact version of Many-Doves. There were twistings of gray in the long braids that hung over her shoulders, and fans of deep wrinkles at the corners of her eyes and mouth, but she moved like a younger woman, and there was a quickness in her that made her stand out; she reminded Elizabeth of her aunt Merriweather.

It was the smile that drew the final link: Falling-Day's resemblance to Hannah was unmistakable. Nathaniel's mother-in-law, then, and the younger woman—perhaps twenty years old —his wife's sister. Many-Doves' face was less guarded than her mother's; curiosity and wariness, hope and caution, were all there, in quick succession. Elizabeth could not remember ever seeing a young woman for whom nature had done more. There was an elegance to her bearing that was outdone only by the perfect proportions of her face, and the fine set of her eyes.

Elizabeth murmured things she thought she should say, and took their hands in turn, trying not to stare at the younger woman.

"You can call me Abigail, if you prefer," said Many-Doves. She took Elizabeth's hand firmly and met her eyes without flinching.

"Don't let Otter hear you do it, though," said Hannah, who had come up behind Elizabeth. "He won't like it."

"It's my name and not Otter's," said Many-Doves. "And it's none of your business, either." She added something in Kahnyen'kehàka that made Hannah wrinkle her nose in protest.

"Enough," said Chingachgook behind them in strong tones. "Speak English now, or you'll offend our guest." In the firelight Elizabeth noted how his tattoos seemed to flicker and move: a snake wound its way across the bony protrusions of his cheekbones, over the bridge of his nose, and around one eye to his forehead, where it disappeared into the sparse white hair at his temple. She wondered if Nathaniel was tattooed, as well, and then put this thought away.

It seemed for a moment as though Many-Doves would take offense: a flurry of irritation flitted across her face. But then she smiled reluctantly and turned to follow her mother into the next room, with Hannah in tow.

"Might I help?" Elizabeth called after her, but Many-Doves fluttered a hand behind her in a gesture of dismissal, and Elizabeth turned back to the men. Hawkeye had taken up a stool and was oiling a trap with a feather dipped in a strong-smelling grease; Chingachgook was braiding leather strips. Elizabeth looked around, self-conscious in her curiosity but unable to do otherwise. She found herself in a large common room, dominated by the hearth at one end, the other extreme lost in shadows. Every inch of space was dedicated to some purpose. On a large table stacked with all manner of equipment for the casting of bullets and gun-cleaning, a trap had been taken apart. Under a shuttered window, another table dominated by a large oil lamp was covered with papers and books. Bookcases stood to either side. The corners were lined with barrels of various sizes, a churn, stretching panels, a spinning wheel, and a small loom. Pelts were tacked on the walls and piled in the corners: Elizabeth recognized fox, and the great tawny fur of what she took to be a panther, and another, darker one of a small bear. Set up in a neat row, furs dried inside out stretched over individual boards. Hawkeye kept up a running commentary and told her what she wanted to know: the reddish-brown pelts were marten, the luxuriant dark ones, fisher.

In the center of the room there were rocking chairs and stools and a long board flanked by benches, set for a meal. From the rafters hung corn by braided husks, squashes strung together like outlandish necklaces, wild onions, apples, and great bundles of dried greenery and herbs Elizabeth could not begin to name.

On the mantelpiece there was a basket of sewing, and one of beadwork. Elizabeth picked up the volumes she found there one by one: Defoe's *A Journal of the Plague Year,* a thumbed newsprint copy of the *Declaration of the Rights of Man* in the original French, and even more surprising, a volume of poetry by Robert Burns.

"She was a great reader," Hawkeye said behind Elizabeth. He came up behind her to touch a small painting of a woman in an oval frame.

"I see that," Elizabeth said. "But I wonder how she managed to get this—" She picked up the Burns. "I wouldn't have thought that he could have come so far. Most people in England aren't familiar with this poet at all."

"Won't give him the time of day, you mean," Hawkeye corrected her, but with a smile. "The upstart, the scallywag. Ain't that what you're thinking?"

"Well . . ." Elizabeth put the volume back down again. "He is a bit . . . incendiary. How did your wife come by these volumes? And these others—"

"She was a Scot, and they stick together like their confounded porridge. Hardly a traveler ever came through Paradise from outwards without a parcel for Cora from somebody, and half the time it was books."

Elizabeth went up on tiptoe to look at the painting more closely. Hawkeye put the portrait into her hands. It was simply drawn, but a strong sense of the woman was caught in it. She had a clear, high brow, dark hair, and hazel eyes. "Nathaniel has his mother's coloring."

"And he's as quick as she was, and just as stubborn."

"With definite dislikes," agreed Elizabeth.

Chingachgook spoke up, his face creasing into a smile so thoroughly wrinkled that his eyes disappeared. "My daughter-in-law didn't like the English much."

"But she made an exception in your son's case," Elizabeth noted to him. Both men looked surprised at this, and then Hawkeye laughed, as if the idea of calling himself an Englishman was something that would never have occurred to him.

"Or are you Scots, too?" she amended. "I expect your name can be traced back to the Normans, in either case."

"I was born in these mountains."

"But your parents must have come from England?"

"I was given to understand they came from the far north of England," Hawkeye said slowly. "But I don't remember them. I'm a son of the Mahicans."

Elizabeth was suddenly aware of Chingachgook, and she realized her mistake. "Of course," she murmured.

"I never knew any other kin," Hawkeye continued. "I didn't have any English until I was ten, and I don't suppose I knew I was white, either. Still comes as a shock, sometimes."

Hawkeye dusted the carved frame with his shirtsleeve.

"How did you meet her?"

"Her da was a colonel assigned to Albany. She followed him to the Mohawk Valley. We helped her out of a fix or two, back in '57."

"That must have been the war with France."

Chingachgook had been silent, but he spoke up, his voice hoarse. "Most of our wars have been with the English or the French, or against them. We don't much have the energy to fight among ourselves anymore."

Elizabeth was beginning to see why these people would want to buy Hidden Wolf Mountain from her father. For all of their lives, and the lives of their parents and possibly their grandparents before them, they had known nothing but war and sorrow, and most of that at the hands of the English. A place of their own, the opportunity to live as they must, from the land, with a degree of security they had never known: it seemed very reasonable to her.

The door flew open with a bang, and two dogs galloped into the room, tongues lolling. Behind them, a young Indian materialized in a swirl of snow and cold air, blood trickling from a wound on his forehead. He stood in the door, legs spread, raised his rifle high, put back his head, and let out a whoop that echoed through the room and made Elizabeth jump.

"Otter!" Hawkeye strode across the room. "You'll scare Miz Elizabeth to death, she'll think you're after her scalp."

But Elizabeth had already collected herself and stood before the hearth with what she hoped was a calm air, although she could feel her heart racing. She had seen, almost immediately, that the high-pitched yip was one of satisfaction and pride.

"You got the moose!" Hannah had rushed in from the other room with Falling-Day and Many-Doves close behind.

Otter laughed and tugged at Hannah's braids. "Saw the tracks, did you? Nathaniel got him."

"Did you forget about your rifle and butt him with that hard head of yours?" asked Many-Doves.

Falling-Day made an attempt to examine Otter's wound, but he waved her away impatiently, muttering at her in Kahnyen'kehàka. Then he caught sight of Elizabeth, and stopped suddenly. A guarded look passed over his face, to be replaced, slowly, by a more open and friendly one as Hawkeye made his introduction.

Otter crossed the room, speaking in a low voice to the dogs, who were sniffing at Elizabeth's skirts distrustfully. They fell into a heap in front of the fire with a great show of sheepish yawns.

Otter's hand was chilled through, rough and not especially clean, but Elizabeth took it without hesitation and made a determined effort not to wipe it on her handkerchief once he had let it go. He was well grown; Elizabeth judged him as tall as Nathaniel, because she had to look up at him in the same way. His side hair was caught up in a plait secured with rawhide and studded with a single feather. Elizabeth remembered vaguely seeing drawings of young warriors, but Otter did not look at all like those representations: his head was not shaved in whole or part, and there was not a bit of paint on his face. He had the same deep bronze coloring as his sister and mother, but his dark eyes were much more animated, and less guarded.

Hannah tugged impatiently at Otter, pestering him for details of the hunt.

"You're the one Nathaniel is building the schoolhouse for," he said to Elizabeth, ignoring his niece. "Maybe you can teach this nosey one here some manners." And he laughed and dodged as Hannah swiped at his ear.

The adults stood laughing as Otter and Hannah wrestled. Their high spirits were infectious; Elizabeth began to feel more relaxed than she had since Hannah had come to fetch her. Then she looked up and saw Nathaniel standing across the room in the open door.

He smiled at her; her heart gave a sudden lurch, and then settled into a new rhythm.

.   .   .

Elizabeth found she had a ferocious appetite, and she concentrated on her food: there was the turkey, which had been roasted over the hearth, squash, onions and beans baked in molasses, and corn bread.

She was surprised to find that there was no pressure to converse at the table, and no awkward silences in the place of chatter. Otter told of trailing the moose through snowdrifts until it was exhausted enough to give up and stand still long enough to be shot. Elizabeth was very grateful that they did not expect her to talk; she knew that the thoughts that ran through her head like a chant were not things she could say out loud. Nathaniel sat across from her; she felt his eyes on her, although she could not meet his. *Why do you watch me from the woods?*

He broke bread; she watched his hands, the long fingers, the muscled forearms.

Then Many-Doves rose from the table to refill a bowl. Elizabeth looked up and saw her sleeve brush Nathaniel's shoulder as she set more beans in front of him; he murmured something and she laughed out loud. The look on Many-Doves' face was familiar to Elizabeth; if she looked in a mirror, she thought she would see the same flushed smile. Stricken, she looked down at her plate.

"I have plans for the school to show you," Nathaniel said to Elizabeth after some time.

"Good," she said. "Splendid."

"There's no hurry," Hawkeye said. "You've got all evening."

Elizabeth looked up, surprised. "But my father will be expecting me—"

"You're not going down the mountainside in this storm," said Nathaniel. "We'll take you home tomorrow." The howling of the wind picked up as if to agree with him.

"You look grieved," said Otter. "You worried about your reputation?"

As wretched and agitated as Elizabeth was, this still startled her. "Why should I worry about my reputation? It's not as though—" She looked up at Nathaniel and broke off.

Falling-Day rarely spoke, but now she sent her son a withering look. "Impudent," she said. "She's worried that the judge will be feared for her."

"You're safe here with us," Nathaniel said. "The judge knows that."

"She can read to us!" Hannah cried out. "Like Granny used to. Would you?"

"Why, that's a fine idea," said Hawkeye, clearly pleased.

Elizabeth looked around the table. Falling-Day, Many-Doves, and Chingachgook wore the same placid expression. Elizabeth wasn't sure how to interpret it, although she thought it wasn't directly disapproving.

Otter was grinning. "We'll make her sing for her supper yet."

She dared not seek out Nathaniel, and so Elizabeth began to gather the dishes together. "I'd be pleased to read."

"First there's apple grunt," said Falling-Day. "And then there's a moose to be hung. Then there's time for play." And she sent Elizabeth a rare smile.

When she could stand it no longer, Elizabeth lifted her head and found Nathaniel's calm gaze on her. She was relieved to see no pity there, but perhaps some sympathy, and a friendly openness that gave her great relief. Whatever his relationship to Many-Doves, there was some room for her here, she thought. If she could just stop dreaming of kisses that would never come.

"We'll sit down with those plans," he said. "After the apple grunt."

With a nod, Elizabeth busied herself with clearing the table. "Comfort me with apples," she muttered softly to herself.

"You are fond of quoting the Bible," Nathaniel noted dryly, and Elizabeth jumped so that the wooden dish in her hands clattered to the floor. She had not realized he was so close. Her heart was beating so that she thought at first she'd misunderstood him. Then she knew that she had not.

Bending down to retrieve the dish, his hair falling forward to brush the floor, Nathaniel had finished the verse for her in a soft voice: "For I am sick of love."

IX

Nathaniel made it his business to see that Otter went with the older men to the barn to skin and clean the moose and hoist the carcass into a tree, where it would be safe from scavengers. He sent Hannah into the kitchen with Falling-Day and Many-Doves to wipe dishes. When they finally had the great room to themselves, he cleared the table and spread out a large sheet of paper, using small stones to hold it down at the corners.

Elizabeth stood off to the side, her fingers working in the fabric of her skirt, her head inclined, considering him. He had the advantage, he knew that: everything she felt made itself known on her face, in the tension of her shoulders. When he gestured to the bench, she sidled over as if he were a dog known to bite.

But the plans intrigued her; once she had settled over them, she lost some of the terrible drawn look that had come over her face when he spoke to Many-Doves. She had no cause to be jealous of his wife's sister, but he didn't tell her that straight-away. Nathaniel liked the idea of her being jealous; it gave him some hope.

Nathaniel began to explain his drawings to her, hoping to put her at ease.

"Two main rooms," he said. "In between, a storage room and a hall, for wraps and such."

"Two rooms?"

Nathaniel nodded. "Eventually there will be enough children for two. And in the meantime, if you want a place of your own, away from your father, you'll have one."

She reached out and touched the plans. "Heat?"

"A double hearth on the center wall, facing either way. There's no shortage of wood; you can have the schoolboys chop and stack for you."

Elizabeth wrinkled her nose.

"What's wrong?"

"In England, woodsmoke is rare, but you can't get away from it here."

"Is it unpleasant to you?"

She shook her head. "No. It's much better than coal."

"Just one more thing to get used to."

There was a way she had of raising one eyebrow when she was surprised. "Yes."

They talked for a good time about the schoolhouse; she asked about practical things: coat hooks, washstands, bookshelves, desks, blackboards. She told him about schools she had visited in England, what was wrong with them, and what right. How important she thought fresh air and light were, and how many window sashes she thought she needed. Nathaniel listened to her voice grow more confident, encouraging her now and then but mostly happy to let her talk.

"So you're not headed back for England. Just yet," Nathaniel said, leaning back.

Elizabeth bent her head over the plans, the lamplight shining white on the part in her hair. "Well, no," she said. "Not just yet, at any rate."

Her hands were narrow and very white, the oval nails glowing pale pink. She held them flat on the table. Nathaniel resisted the urge to touch the delicate pulsing of a vein where it negotiated the curve of her wrist.

"Well, then," Nathaniel said. "Tell me what you meant about your father being cash poor."

Elizabeth looked up, surprised. "Oh, well, I thought that would be clear enough. He's overextended himself in his investments and he's thinking of taking a mortgage on the land itself.

If I marry Richard and bring my share of the property with me, Richard will settle his debts."

Nathaniel looked thoughtful.

"Richard would never sell you Hidden Wolf."

"No," Nathaniel agreed. "Richard has an uncommon appetite for land. And what about your brother?"

Her smile was sour. "Julian is part of the reason there's a shortage of cash. He had to be bought out of his debts, you see. He used up all his inheritance from our mother—and it wasn't an insignificant bequest, either. Then he started writing notes, and soon the damage was done. But hopefully he will have little opportunity to misbehave here. Although it's not his idea of Paradise."

Elizabeth hesitated. "This is a very comfortable house," she said, "but small, isn't it, for so many—". She stopped.

"You've never seen a longhouse," he said. "Whole families together, a couple of generations, sisters and all their young. The Hode'noshaunee don't think anything of it. The Iroquois, as the French call them," he added, when he saw her blank look. "Or sometimes you'll hear them called the Six Nations."

"But you didn't grow up in a longhouse," Elizabeth pointed out.

"No, I grew up right here. My father built this cabin when he married my mother. But I have spent some time in a longhouse. And you're right, it's feeling kind of small these days."

Elizabeth was tracing the outline of the schoolhouse with one finger, and refused to look up at him.

"Next summer, if things go as planned, we'll build another cabin. Many-Doves is full of plans for it." Nathaniel paused. "But her husband will build it."

She was not going to ask or comment, he could see that. Nathaniel began to regret teasing her.

"She's getting married in the spring."

"Oh?" Elizabeth blinked slowly. "How nice for her. In the spring?"

"Or maybe the summer," he confirmed, grinning.

"And when do you think the schoolhouse will be finished?"

"Well, I hope the snow lets up some soon, otherwise it will be longer than I thought. But I would guess, late April. You wanted to get started, I know. But there's this snow, and the need to be hunting."

She glanced at the pelts on the walls.

"Aye, well." He wondered how much of the truth she could stand. "We were well provisioned, in the fall, even for three or four more people. But that changed."

Elizabeth ran her hands over the school plans. He could see that she was intensely curious, but also that she had more self-control than most.

"Late November, we were down in the village and somebody broke in."

The eyebrow rose again.

"Shut the dogs in the smokehouse, took every bit of dried and smoked meat, and the few furs we had at that point. Mostly we spend the fall hunting for winter stores, and the winter trapping for pelts, so it weren't so much the fur they were after. I guess we're lucky they didn't take the corn or the beans, or it'd be much harder going."

Her mouth fell open. "Who would do such a thing?"

Nathaniel shook his head. "I've got my suspicions, but there's no way to prove it. *Why* is the more important question."

She turned her hand over on the table and wiggled her fingers. It was as close as she could come to hurrying him along.

"There's laws now against hunting out of season."

Elizabeth's back straightened. "If you can't hunt—" She paused. "And your provisions are gone—"

"There's nothing to do but go."

"Why the furs?" Then she held up a hand, not needing his answer. "So you couldn't buy what you needed. Somebody is trying to force you out."

He nodded, watching new emotions move on her face. Disbelief, and then, reluctantly, belief. And on its heels, outrage.

"That's why you want to buy the mountain. Can you hunt if you own it?"

"Not out of season, at least, not legal. But we can keep trespassers off, and maybe we can manage then."

She stood up suddenly, her lips pressed hard together. "My father?"

"No," Nathaniel said. "I'm sure of that much."

Elizabeth began to pace in the room, up and down, her skirts swirling, her boots clicking. Nathaniel could see the next question coming, but he waited for her to ask.

"Richard Todd doesn't believe you have enough cash to buy the mountain." She ran her knuckles over her brow. "Was it him, Richard?"

Nathaniel inclined his head. "Maybe."

"But you told me that Richard deals straight with people."

He got up to join her before the hearth. "I told you he deals straight with white men."

"But you are white."

"To you maybe."

Elizabeth looked up at him, her face tight with worry and guilt.

"You can't be responsible for what every man of your acquaintance does," he said easily.

"But what can I do to help?"

There were dark flecks in her gray eyes; her brows arched out, like wings. He inhaled. She smelled sweet, of dried summer flowers and talcum. Above the filmy fabric that was tucked into the neckline of her bodice, her skin was very white; there was a pulse in the hollow of her throat. He knew his nearness was making her uneasy, but he just didn't want to move away.

Elizabeth said: "I have some money. Is there anything at all I can give you that would help?"

Give me your mouth, he wanted to say to her. Maybe she saw this in his face, because she drew in her breath in a soft sound of surprise and froze, like a doe surrounded by torches in the night, her eyes burning furiously.

"This is dangerous business," Nathaniel said. He did not know himself exactly what business he meant.

"It's too late for that," she said with a calm that surprised him. "I'm already in it."

"So you are," Nathaniel murmured.

It was not the first glimpse he had had of the iron core in her, but it was the clearest. Of its own accord, one finger raised itself to touch her cheek. He wanted her to come to him of her own free will, but it was very hard to be here with her and not touch her.

Startled, Elizabeth opened her mouth to speak, and then closed it.

Hannah came streaking into the room suddenly, and they separated, moving to opposite sides of the hearth, as if they had been doing what they had both been thinking of doing. Nathaniel turned to catch his daughter, who threw herself at him and began to climb up one arm, dragging herself up by his hair until he cried out, half laughing, and managed to get a hold of her long enough to disentangle himself. "Finished with the chores," she panted. "That poor old moose is hanging in the beech, and I want to sit by Elizabeth before Otter comes and takes the best spot."

There was nothing more for it, and so Elizabeth allowed Hannah to pile books on her lap and took the seat she was offered by the corner of the hearth, where Hawkeye had set a pine knot burning on a slab of stone. Its light was clear and bright enough to read by.

"This is my favorite," she said. "And Grandfather is fond of this one, and this is Father's—"

"Enough," said Falling-Day, exasperated. Her hands were full of mending, but she paused to give Hannah a meaningful look. The child sighed, and sat at her grandmother's feet, accepting the bit of sewing that was passed into her hands.

They all had work to do: Many-Doves was piecing leather into a moccasin, Hawkeye picked up where he had left off with the traps, Otter set himself to making bullets. Nathaniel sat on a stool across from Elizabeth, and began to braid rawhide. Only Chingachgook had the leisure to both watch and listen to Elizabeth, but the look in his eyes was anything but critical or judging, and she did not mind him so much.

"Start with some of the *Poor Richard*," he suggested.

Elizabeth opened the volume and began to read at random:

"It would be thought a hard Government that should tax its people One-tenth part of their TIME, to be employed in its service. But Idleness taxes many of us much more; if we reckon all that is spent in absolute sloth, or doing of nothing; with that by bringing on diseases, absolutely shortens life . . ."

Chingachgook murmured in amusement each time Poor Richard's pronouncements were put forth. When Elizabeth stopped to turn the page, she looked up and saw Falling-Day's look of disbelief and scorn.

"A man who talks so much as that Poor Richard has little time to use his hands to work," she said, to which Chingachgook only smiled, but both Otter and Nathaniel laughed out loud.

Hannah was inching her way across the floor slowly as Elizabeth read, never raising her eyes from her needlework. Eventually she managed to come close enough to lean against Elizabeth's knee. Touched by this sign of the child's affection, Elizabeth was tempted to reach out and stroke her hair, but she felt Many-Doves' gaze on her and pulled back her hand.

After a while, Elizabeth put aside the *Almanac* and picked up *Gulliver's Travels,* a volume more familiar to her. She settled into the story, and read for a good time, the only other sound being the fire in the hearth, and the wind caught now and then in the chimney. When she thought to glance up at her audience, she sometimes caught one or the other looking at her: quite often it was Many-Doves, who seemed to be focused in a thoughtful and reserved way on Elizabeth herself, and less interested in the story. Most often it was Nathaniel's direct but guarded gaze. Twice Elizabeth became flustered, and lost her place, until she forced herself to keep her eyes on the page.

At one point, Falling-Day rose to put more wood on the fire. Elizabeth took this opportunity to take up the last volume. "Oh," she said, so that her audience looked up. "I'll do my best, but I'm afraid my Scots is lacking." And she opened the Burns.

Here Stewarts once in glory reign'd,
And laws for Scotland's weal ordain'd;
But now unroof'd their palace stands,

Their sceptre fallen to other hands;
Fallen indeed, and to the earth,
Whence grovelling reptiles take their birth.
The injured Stewart line is gone,
A race outlandish fills their throne:
An idiot race, to honour lost—
Who know them best despise them most.

"A man after my Cora's own heart," Hawkeye noted with a half smile, even as he winked at Elizabeth solemnly. She wondered at the strangeness of this: did he regard her as an exception to the "idiot race" his wife had so despised, or did he not see the insult in it? Elizabeth thought he must be testing her, and so she only raised a brow in reply.

Then she realized that Many-Doves was staring at the book in Elizabeth's hands, and it came to her with a shock that she had been given Many-Doves' place, and taken over a duty she held dear. Elizabeth leafed through the slim volume while she thought this through, and wondered how she might fix the slight without offending anyone else.

"This looks a likely poem," she said finally. "But I'm afraid the dialect is a bit beyond me. Do you know it?" she asked, extending the book toward Many-Doves.

Many-Doves accepted it with a glance at her mother. She cleared her throat and began not to read, but to sing in a clear voice:

Theniel Menzies' bonie Mary,
Theniel Menzies' bonie Mary,

Charlie Grigot tint his plaidie,
Kissin Theniel's bonie Mary.

In comin by the brig o Dye,
At Darlet we a blink did tarry;
As day was dawin in the sky,
We drank a health to bonie Mary.

Her een sae bright, her brow sae white,
her haffet locks as brown's a berry,

And ay they dinpl't wi' a smile
The rosy cheeks o' bonie Mary.

We lap an danc'd the lee-lang day,
Till piper-lads were wae and weary;
But Charlie gat the spring to pay,
For kissin Theniel's bonie Mary.

Many-Doves was already turning the pages in a familiar way. She paused and began to sing again softly, of "Peggy's Charms," and then in rapid succession, a series of songs, each with more energy than the one before. Finally, with a grin at her mother, she launched into a tune that set Hannah to laughing. She jumped up and joined Many-Doves, dancing as she sang along:

I'm o'er young, I'm o'er young,
I'm o'er young to marry yet!
I'm o'er young, 'twad be a sin
To tak me frae my mammie yet.

Hallowmass is come and gane,
The nights are lang in winter, Sir,
And you and I in ae bed,
In trowth, I dare na venture, Sir!

Fu loud an shrill the frosty wind
Blaws thro the leafless timmer, Sir;
But if ye come this gate again,
I'll aulder be gin simmer, Sir.

Elizabeth tried very hard not to be shocked, or show what an effort it was not to be, but Falling-Day put down her sewing to praise the girls, and Chingachgook spoke encouraging words. Nathaniel lifted up his daughter over his head as if she weighed nothing, and tossed her into the air while she screeched with laughter.

"I must say I didn't expect to find you fluent in Scots," Elizabeth said to Many-Doves. "But it's good fun that you are."

Hawkeye had been observing in silence, but he spoke up now and there was a bit of a hoarseness in his voice. "Cora never let the girls go to bed without some Scots to fall asleep by," he said. "They come by it honest."

Otter spoke up from the table where he had been pouring lead into bullet molds. "Many-Doves is good, it's true," he said. "But you should have heard Sings-from-Books. You would have thought she just got off the boat from Aberdeen."

"Sings-from-Books? Who is that?" Elizabeth asked, still laughing.

"Sarah," said Nathaniel. "Sarah was my wife." He let Hannah slide to the floor, leaned over her, whispered in her ear. With a few words and a curtsy to Elizabeth, she scooted away into the shadows.

Later that evening, Elizabeth climbed the ladder to the sleeping loft where the women slept. Many-Doves and Falling-Day followed her, and in quick motions they had undressed and slipped into the larger bed while Elizabeth still paused next to Hannah.

The child was curled under her covers, her head just a dark blur against the bedding. She never stirred when Elizabeth sat on the edge of the pallet to remove her shoes. Hannah had a damp, sweet smell about her, a little-girl smell. Elizabeth wondered if she looked very much like her mother. Like Sarah.

It was some time before she could put away the thought of Nathaniel's face when he had said her name. Finally, she slept deeply, and for the first time in a week, without dreaming.

X

Anna Hauptmann usually didn't hold much with men who wouldn't work, but Julian Middleton had a charming way about him. He spent a good deal of his time in her trading post warming his hands before the hearth, so she supposed it was a good thing he made pleasant company.

"So she didn't come down again?" Jed McGarrity asked Julian.

Moses Southern frowned. "You didn't go after her? Left her up there with them Indians?"

Julian sat before the hearth with his feet crossed on a barrel of molasses and the old tom in his lap. "Father thinks she's safe enough. And how would we get to her, anyway, with three feet of new snow on top of the old? Does it ever stop snowing in these mountains?"

The farmers exchanged glances.

"And I must say," Julian continued, when it was clear that they weren't going to make excuses for—or promises about—the weather. "I don't see what harm they could do her in such a short time."

"Don't tell me you're fool enough to think the Iroquois are no threat to a white woman," Moses barked. "There's plenty who had their women, and little girls too, stole away and never seen again. They have a way of 'doctrinatin' women, bringin' 'em over to their way, and they are good for nothing after that. Except to serve Indian bucks."

Anna shook her head. "Now stop, Moses. You're not talking about the Hurons on the warpath, and there's not enough Mohawk left to steal a three-legged cow. You know old Indian John, and Hawkeye—you been doin' business with them these many years. And if you have something bad to say about them, why then I know you're lying."

"Kidnapping?" asked Julian. "There were such rumors at home, but we thought they were exaggerated."

"Rumors!" Moses fumed, kneading a mangy cap between his fingers. "Rumors!"

"Moses had a sister took, when she was just ten years old," supplied Jed McGarrity.

The door opened and Richard Todd came in, shaking snow from his hat and his shoulders.

"Ask Todd here, he can tell you what they do to women. He knows about them. Why, if my sister walked in this room right now, you couldn't stand the smell, and you couldn't talk to her, either—she wasn't gone but three years and she didn't know her own tongue anymore, just the Abenaki gibberish. And she spent all her years putting out one Indian half-breed after another."

Richard greeted each of them. "Who got you started, Moses?" he asked dryly.

"Mr. Southern has a story to tell," said Julian. "I'm interested. After all, they live on my father's property."

Moses looked about himself as if he expected an Indian bent on murder and kidnapping to materialize. "I'll tell you, I wouldn't let my sister alone with them. There's that young buck, he's got a wild look to him. They got no business here in Paradise with decent folk. And you know that I ain't the only one to think so!"

"Folks are talking about Chingachgook wanting to buy Hidden Wolf from the judge," Jed said uneasily.

"Not bloody likely." Julian sat up abruptly, dumping the sleeping cat unceremoniously to the floor.

Moses nodded furiously. "We didn't rout the English—" He paused and sent a regretful look toward Julian. "Begging your pardon, but we fought hard to get out from under, and I for one won't stand by and watch the judge hand good land back to the red devils. They seem whupped, that's true; but let 'em think they got the upper hand and they'll start coming after our young'uns again, you watch."

"There hasn't been a kidnapping in these parts for twenty years," said Anna with an uneasy glance toward Richard Todd. "And I won't have talk like that here. Those people are good neighbors and good customers."

"Bah!" Moses scowled, and then jammed his cap on his head. With a nod to the men, he thumped the butt of his musket on the floor. "I'm going. But don't say I haven't warned you about your sister and them Indians." And without a word to Anna he left and slammed the door behind him.

"What's this about Elizabeth?" asked Richard.

"She went up to Lake in the Clouds yesterday afternoon and didn't come back," said Jed.

"Lake in the Clouds?" Richard asked. "But why?"

"To eat that confounded turkey, with the old man," Julian said. Then he grinned, one corner of his mouth drawn up. "She got caught up there in the storm. You worried about Nathaniel stealing your intended away?"

Anna perked up at this. "Intended? Is there some celebrating to be done, then?"

Richard looked annoyed. "Don't start rumors, Julian. There is no agreement between your sister and me."

"But there will be, if Father has anything to say about it," noted Julian. "And you seem set on it yourself, if I may make the observation. Unless you're worried that Nathaniel is too much of a threat."

"I'm not overworried about him," Richard said, irritated to be having this conversion within Anna's eager earshot, but still unable to keep quiet.

"Ha!" laughed Anna. "You don't know how many young women in these parts wish Nathaniel would come steal them away. Not that Dr. Todd don't have more than his share of eager eyes. Especially," she added with a wink, "of a Sunday at morning service. Especially in the front pew."

Richard looked at her darkly, and she withdrew with a nervous laugh.

"Hawkeye is probably on the way down with her now."

"Well, it's clear you want to go after her. Go on, then, old boy, if you can't manage to think of something better to do," said Julian. He stretched. "Mr. McGarrity," he said. "Do you by any chance play dice?"

Jed McGarrity started, his bony shoulders losing their perpetual slump for a brief moment to rise up around his ears and fall away again. "I was raised to think that dice and whiskey were the devil's instruments."

"Ah, well," Julian sighed. "Too bad, then."

Hawkeye suggested they leave straightaway after breakfast. He was afraid there would be another storm later in the day, and he wanted to get down to the village and back again before it hit.

"She probably doesn't have the first idea about snowshoes," said Otter. "She'll need a lesson."

Nathaniel had gone out before sunup and still had not returned, so Otter took Elizabeth outside to see to her instruction. Hannah came along, chattering, to provide assistance and encouragement. Elizabeth was anxious about what they were expecting of her, but she knew there was little choice, and so she stepped out into the morning with a little trepidation but considerable determination.

The first sun on the new snow reflected and reflected back again until it made her eyes water. Elizabeth blinked and squinted and wiped the tears from her cheeks. Finally she was able to look around her, and she stood stunned. "The cave of wonders," she said, mostly to herself, but Hannah grabbed her hand and yanked.

"What's that?"

Elizabeth glanced down at her. "From the stories called *A Thousand and One Nights*," she said. "The cave of wonders, where everything glittered of gold and jewels. Like this."

The glen was awash in snow, the branches of the trees woven thick with it, the boulders grown to strange proportions. And the sun struck what seemed to be every individual flake and set the glen shining in a kaleidoscope of colors.

Otter was strapping the snowshoes onto Elizabeth's boots, his hair falling forward to brush the snow into patterns.

"*A Thousand and One Nights?*" asked Hannah, awed. "Tell the story!"

"I'll save that one for school."

Hannah's face fell. "Then I may never hear it."

"I hope you will," Elizabeth said. "I'll do my best to see that you do."

Otter looked up. "You'll have some talking to do, then," he said. And, not waiting for Elizabeth to reply, he took her elbow and helped her up.

They made it around the corner of the house before Elizabeth got stuck. The snowshoes crossed, and unable to untangle them, she lost her balance and fell backward into a sitting position. They helped her up, and this time they got much farther: past the woodshed, and all the way to the barn, before she stopped again with her shoes crossed. But this time Elizabeth was able to get herself untangled on her own.

With great concentration she picked up her pace a bit and made it around another corner, moving deliberately in a steady rhythm, and watching her feet. They did two more rounds, and then diverted a little so that Elizabeth could have a try at going up and down an incline; she almost fell once, but after that was fairly steady. Then they returned to the porch, where Otter and Hannah hung back.

"Try it again," Otter said. "Show us what you can do."

Elizabeth grinned at them, and set off in a ducklike straddle. She liked the feeling of moving, suspended over the smooth surface of snow; she liked the cold on her face. She rounded the second corner in good stride and ran full force into Nathaniel.

"Umph!" He let out his breath as he caught her, and they fell backward through the crust of the snow.

Elizabeth looked down on Nathaniel in horror. For a brief second, their noses touched and her mouth hovered over his. His breath was warm on her face.

"You don't have to knock me down to get me to kiss you, you know," Nathaniel said with a grin.

With a strength she didn't know she possessed, Elizabeth leapt away from him and into a standing position. She stood breathing hard, wiping snow from her face.

Nathaniel got up, too. "I'm sorry," he said contritely, but his grin would not quite go away. "I shouldn't tease you."

"No," Elizabeth gasped. "You shouldn't."

Hannah came around the corner and almost sent Elizabeth colliding into Nathaniel again.

"Whoa!" he called, grabbing her. He turned to Elizabeth but she had already righted herself and was on her way.

"What did you do to her?" Hannah asked in Mahican.

"I gave her time to think about it," said her father. "My mistake."

It took all her energy and concentration, but Elizabeth focused on her snowshoes and moving over the surface of the snow; she would not think of what had just happened. She would not. She hoped Hawkeye was ready to go, because she didn't know how long she could continue not thinking of what she wanted and needed to think about.

Otter had gone off to the woodshed. Elizabeth fumbled the snowshoes off, and then stood for a moment trying to collect her thoughts. Finally, worried about Nathaniel's reappearance, she went into the cabin.

The common room was empty. Elizabeth passed through it and found Falling-Day scraping the moose hide, which had been stretched out on a frame. Many-Doves stood to one side with a bowl in the crook of her arm, mashing the contents with a pestle. The smells were very strong, and Elizabeth drew back a little.

Many-Doves caught her movement and looked up.

"I thought, if Hawkeye was ready—" Elizabeth said. The women didn't answer right away; she saw them taking in her color, and the fact that her breath still had not steadied completely.

"What's that?" Elizabeth asked, nodding to Many-Doves' bowl.

"The brains," Many-Doves said. "Every animal has just enough brains to cure its own hide."

"Ah. Well. Do you know where Hawkeye is? If he's ready to go?"

"Hawkeye went out to set traps," said Falling-Day. "Nathaniel will take you down to the village."

"Oh, I see." Elizabeth's smile felt brittle on her face. "Well, then, thank you for your kind hospitality. And the meal. I hope to see you again—" She had been about to invite them to visit her at home, when she realized how strange this might seem to them, and she paused.

"Goodbye," she said finally, and turned to go.

Nathaniel was waiting on the porch with Hannah. They were deep in an intense conversation, in Mohawk or Mahican; Elizabeth thought it might be Mahican. It sounded different from the language Falling-Day spoke to the children.

"Ready?" Nathaniel asked.

Hannah helped Elizabeth strap on the snowshoes once again.

"He'll take you down a different way," she said. "Better for the snowshoes." She smiled, and touched her fingers to Elizabeth's.

Elizabeth put her hand on the small, sleek head and nodded. Then she set off into the cave of wonders behind Nathaniel.

The trail through the woods accommodated only one person on snowshoes, compelling them to move in single file, for which Elizabeth was grateful. With Nathaniel in front of her, she could watch him as closely as she liked, without being observed or required to talk to him.

He moved purposefully, with a grace that made her own progress seem very awkward by comparison. The long line of his back was so straight that the rifle slung there barely swayed, although in the hush of the woods Elizabeth could just make out, above the sound of her own breathing, the soft sound of the gun's stock rubbing on his buckskin mantle. Nathaniel had not tied his hair back, and it fluttered behind him.

The branches bent low under their burden of snow, creating a roof over the narrow path like white arms of young girls crossed and crossed again. Elizabeth's pace flagged a bit so that Nathaniel pulled quite far ahead of her, walking through a tunnel of snow shot with sunlight. Then he stopped at a rise in the path where the forest fell away, and waited for her to catch up.

Elizabeth walked toward Nathaniel, drawn forward by his gaze, the force of his attention a magnet she could not resist. She joined him on the little rise and saw the valley and the village spread out below them. From here Half Moon Lake was an irregular bowl of the deepest frozen blue, and the world around it every shade of white. In front of them was an elongated clearing, framed by forest.

"Oh," she said. "Oh, how beautiful. You can't see this place from below, can you? What is it called?"

"The folks in the village call it the strawberry field. It's covered in fruit, in season. Children come up and eat themselves sick. Bears, too."

Nathaniel took Elizabeth's elbow and turned her to him. Her mouth hung open in a little circle of surprise, her lower lip full and blôodred, and he knew that his good intentions were worth nothing. He had tried for a month to stay away from her, but he remembered the promise of her mouth, as if no time had passed at all. This urgency in him was something he had forgotten about, something he thought gone forever; he had done so long without it. It was a surprise, and not an altogether welcome one, that there was something in the world, someone in the world, who could move him like this; it was shocking to *want* again. Here, in front of him now, her dark hair curling around her face, her skin so pale that he could trace the veins in her throat. So different from Sarah, but with the same core of flint, able to light the same fire in him. And he could see, in the brightness of Elizabeth's eyes, in the way she drew breath in at his touch, that she felt the same urgency, although she didn't have a name to put to it. Nathaniel stripped off his mitts and let his hands move up to push her hood back onto her shoulders.

"You look as if you've been eating strawberries," he said. "Your mouth is so red."

Elizabeth stared at him, her breath coming fast. Her blood rushed like a tide, and suddenly Nathaniel came into new focus: his eyes, which she had thought to be hazel but were shades of green and gold and brown, like sunlight in a summer forest; the high brow, furrowed, and the way his hair waved back from a widow's peak; the small cut healing high on his left cheek; the tiny white indentation on the bridge of his nose; the shadow of his beard.

"Tell me you don't want to kiss me," he said, his thumb stroking the curve of her cheekbone.

And his mouth, the clean lines of his lips, the blood pulsing there.

"I can't," Elizabeth said hoarsely. "I can't tell you that."

"Then do it," Nathaniel whispered. "Kiss me."

Startled, Elizabeth pulled away a little. Nathaniel was looking at her with an intensity that frightened her, and she saw that he meant it, that he was waiting for her to do this. His fingers threaded through her hair. He waited; she knew he would wait forever. She could do this, and take what she wanted, or walk away, and live without it. She felt flooded with heat; there was a tightness in her chest. Elizabeth leaned toward him and, reaching up, kissed Nathaniel.

His lips were surprisingly soft; Elizabeth hadn't imagined that a man's lips could be soft and firm all at once. Especially not this man, who seemed to be carved of wood. But his lips were very soft and gentle and moreover they were cold, while his mouth was not. This contrast was unexpected. His cheek was rough with beard stubble; his hair swept forward to touch her own cold cheek. His smells were strong, unidentifiable, overwhelming.

A little sigh escaped her as the angle of his mouth deepened and he tilted her head to meet him, kissing her lightly, a brushing; every nerve in her lips set to humming. They stood leaning toward each other across the awkward expanse of their snowshoes, joined like a wishbone by the soft suckling of mouths. Nathaniel slid an arm around Elizabeth's waist, and they crumpled into the deep snow together.

"Oh," she said, and he took her mouth, her warm mouth, and coaxed it open. Her whole consciousness was centered here where their mouths joined: the soft persistence, the way his head dipped as he changed the direction of the kiss. They sat in the snow, Elizabeth sprawled against Nathaniel's lap with her arms slung around his neck and snowshoes sticking up around them at odd angles. The cold was forgotten, all the snowy world around them was forgotten in the world of his callused hands, his rough, cold cheeks, his warm mouth on hers.

Finally she pulled away and stared at Nathaniel with her whole body trembling.

"Better comfort than apples, isn't it?" Nathaniel murmured, his thumb at the corner of her mouth.

"Oh, no," muttered Elizabeth. "Oh, no." She struggled to right herself, managing to situate herself on her snowshoes. She looked around wildly, brushing at her snow-clotted cape. Nathaniel got up to help her and she pushed him away. Then she grabbed both of his hands and squeezed them hard, looking at him with eyes gone suddenly severe.

"And where is this to go?" she asked. "What are we to do?"

Nathaniel looked down on her, at her gray eyes daring him to push her too far. On her face was the clear and desperate hope that he would give her an excuse to turn away for good.

"Where do you want it to go?" he said. "What do you want us to do?" A thought came to him that made him wonder. "Do you know what passes between a man and woman?"

"I'm a virgin," Elizabeth said grimly, dropping his hands. "Not an idiot. Of course I know what it means to—to mate." But she could not meet his gaze. With a surprising change of posture, her back straight and her shoulders set, she faced Nathaniel with a new stillness in her face, a terrible stillness.

"Is that what you want of me?"

"It's part of it," he conceded. "But it's only one part. I can't look at you and not think about touching you. How fine you feel to me, the warmth of you. What the rest of you must be like."

She drew in her breath audibly, her head falling back and all the harshness, all the anger, draining out of her face to be replaced by the drowsy and infinite pleasure of this, of hearing him say he wanted her. And Nathaniel saw something he had forgotten about women: that words can do the same work as hands and mouths and a man's body, that she was as undone by his admission of desire as she had been by his kiss.

"And the other part?" Elizabeth asked, her voice wobbling.

Nathaniel grinned. "Pretty women ain't so very rare," he said. "But a pretty woman who stands up to a room full of strange men and defends herself—that's something else. After all," he said softly. "'Blessed are those wise in the ways of books, for theirs is the kingdom of righteousness and fair play.'"

Elizabeth's head snapped forward. "So you want me because I misquote the Bible to serve my own purposes?" she asked. "That's not very convincing. Nor, may I add, is it very gentlemanly to remind me of that episode."

"Aye," said Nathaniel. "Here we are at the heart of it. I ain't a gentleman, but you don't want a gentleman, do you? You want somebody as set on their sights as you are, and willing to do what has to be done, and damn the consequences."

"Let me ask you this," Elizabeth said. "Will you let your daughter come to my school?"

Nathaniel laughed out loud. "That's what I mean. Well, tell me this: can I pay her tuition in kisses?" he asked, but Elizabeth's eyes narrowed and he saw his mistake. His face calmed.

"I can't let her come. I'm sorry, Elizabeth."

"I see." She turned and began to walk away, wobbling on her snowshoes.

"You don't see." Nathaniel came up next to her.

"I see that you want to put your hands on me and kiss me but that I'm not good enough to teach your daughter. I see that you admire my courage but that you don't value my convictions."

They walked for a moment in silence. "You don't understand about Hannah."

She swung around, and almost lost her balance, but caught herself quickly. "I understand you have a daughter whom you don't want to send to a school taught by a white woman."

A little shocked at herself, Elizabeth hesitated. She had let the words fall, though, and there was no calling them back.

"Is that what you think?" Nathaniel asked quietly. "That I don't trust you to treat her well, or teach her things of value? I don't want her in your school because you're white, and she's not?"

Elizabeth nodded. "Yes, well, that is my impression."

When they had gone on another ten minutes, they came to another bit of woods and they passed into it, and within a few feet they came to a small cabin.

"Come," Nathaniel said, and turned off the path. Elizabeth hesitated behind him, and then seeing him at the open door, and knowing that he would not concede, she stripped off her snowshoes and went in.

The cabin was a single room with a chair, a cot, a table, and a hearth. There was a lopsided betty lamp on the mantel, covered with dust. Nathaniel took a flint and steel from a pouch on his belt and set to the chore of laying a fire.

"We won't be here long enough to need that," Elizabeth said behind his back. She stood as far away from the cot as she could, with her arms crossed tightly across her chest. "Tell me what it is you want to tell me about Hannah and we'll be on our way. There's that storm coming, and I can't be caught here with you, alone."

Nathaniel went on with his work as if he had not heard her, coaxing the small and reluctant flame into something more substantial.

"Come over here and warm yourself," he said finally. "I promise not to touch you."

Elizabeth snorted. "We're talking about Hannah, and school," she said. "We'll talk about . . . kissing if and when we come to an agreement." She looked straight at him as she said this, although she could not control the color rising on her cheeks.

"Do you mean to blackmail me into sending my daughter to your school by withholding yourself from me?" asked Nathaniel, amused.

Elizabeth crossed the room with sharp taps of her boots, and held her hands out to the fire. "I'll not honor that with a reply," she said. "You know very well that's not what I meant."

There was a little pause as she collected her thoughts. "Your father was telling me yesterday that your mother was educated, and that her father thought it was right for girls to have schooling."

"True enough. My mother was well schooled, and she taught all of us."

"Well, then, your mother is no longer alive to teach your daughter, but I have things to offer her."

"I ain't disputing that, Boots."

"But you won't let her come."

"No."

She turned to him. "Why not?"

"Not because I fear what you'd teach her," Nathaniel said. "But because I'm afraid for her life."

Elizabeth's mouth fell open, and she stood there for a good long time just like that.

"You think . . . she's in danger?"

"I know she is," said Nathaniel. "We all are. Some in the village do fear us, and fear moves stupid men to recklessness."

"These are just children," protested Elizabeth.

"Oh, children ain't capable of meanness?" His tone bordered on bitterness. "Liam Kirby is coming, ain't he, and Peter Dubonnet and Praise-Be Cunningham, and maybe Jemima Southern?"

Elizabeth nodded.

"Well, now. There's a whole world of hurt and trouble in those names. Those are the children of the men who most probably broke in, last November. The men who would be glad to see us starve. The ones who killed livestock they couldn't carry with them just for the pleasure of it. They make no bones in public about wanting us gone off the judge's lands, and they ain't about to lose any sleep over a little half-breed girl. Especially not now."

"Not now?"

"Now that folks know about us wanting to buy Hidden Wolf." He paused. "They think the whole Kahnyen'kehàka nation is going to move in on them. And it don't help much that Falling-Day is Wolf clan—when they think of the Kahnyen'kehàka of the Wolf they think of warriors who fight like lions, and move quick as birds: gone with your scalp before you got a good look at them."

Sarah's clan, thought Elizabeth. Her fingers were tingling as they warmed, and she rubbed her hands together.

"Is there any reason to fear the Wolf clan?" Elizabeth asked in an even tone.

There was something like regret on Nathaniel's face. "There ain't a hundred Kahnyen'kehàka men of fighting age left in all of the territory," he said. "Most of them went to Canada and won't ever come back. There's only a few who tried to stay out of the war. And most of them have been beaten into the dust by liquor and humiliation."

Nathaniel's irritation and anger were suddenly deflated. Elizabeth wanted to ask a hundred questions, but she sensed that he had gone far beyond the things he had meant to say, and that the things he needed from her now were different.

"Well," she said simply. "I apologize for my outburst."

"As well you should," said Nathaniel, a bit calmer.

The fire crackled for a while without their talking.

"What about a trial?" Elizabeth asked. "To see if there is as much trouble as you anticipate?"

Exasperated, Nathaniel ran a hand through his hair. "You are stubborn, I'll say that for you."

"Now I'm stubborn," said Elizabeth, trying to smile. "Just a little while ago you were admiring my . . . persistence."

"We could talk about what I admire about you," Nathaniel said softly, but with such a focused look that Elizabeth stepped back.

"Your daughter wants to come to my school."

Nathaniel's look cleared. "She'd have to go down to the village every day on her own."

Elizabeth nodded. "That is true. But she came down yesterday to fetch me."

"Good God," replied Nathaniel. "I don't know what to do with you. Listen, now. If Hannah comes to your school she'd be traveling the same paths every day at the same times. Does that say anything to you at all? Can't you see what trouble that might be?"

"Oh," Elizabeth said. "You're afraid somebody might—lie in wait for her?"

The dim light in the cabin came from a window facing the path where a shutter had broken; Elizabeth looked about, realizing they were at an impasse and wondering where to go from here.

"Whose place is this?"

"Your father's."

She turned to him, her head inclined.

"Didn't they tell you? This was his first homestead on the patent. My father helped him build it."

All of her uneasiness forgotten, Elizabeth looked around herself with new amazement. "Then my mother must have lived here."

"She did," said Nathaniel. "Until the judge built the house down by the lake. The one that burned and had to be rebuilt."

Here was another story that Elizabeth had never heard, but her curiosity was pushed aside by a sudden awareness of the opportunity before her. She clapped her hands together suddenly in delight. Nathaniel looked up from the fire, startled.

"I could teach school right here! Until the new school is ready. It's not very big, but there's enough room if we economize carefully with the benches. There's a hearth that works, and—" She looked out the window. "A privy? No. Well, that could be managed without too much trouble, could it not?"

Nathaniel was leaning against the wall with his arms crossed, smiling and shaking his head.

"It's a good solution," insisted Elizabeth, as though he had disagreed. "And best of all, Hannah would be closer to home."

Before Nathaniel could object, Elizabeth's face lit up one more degree.

"I've got the feeling you've had another idea," he said dryly.

"Many-Doves," Elizabeth said.

"Many-Doves needs no schooling."

"No, but she could help me teach. And Hannah wouldn't be alone, coming and going."

Elizabeth began to pace the room again, looking at it more closely. "We need tables, but that's not hard, is it?" She whirled suddenly to find Nathaniel directly before her. Wound up in her new plans, she forgot to be nervous of him; presented with the possibility of her school opening very soon, she forgot, just for the moment, about kissing Nathaniel.

"Don't say no," she said. "Please, not right away. Think about it. It would be right to have her here. Little girls are kept away from the things that would make them strong, in the name of protection and propriety." She paused. "I came here hoping to change that, at least for one small place. Don't stop me before I've started, please, Nathaniel."

He nodded. "I promise to think about it."

Elizabeth's face, bright with excitement, suddenly shifted: her eyes drifted down to his mouth, and she looked away.

"Nathaniel." She raised her head and focused all her attention on him. "What began between us—out there. It is not a good idea."

"You're lying," he responded in a congenial tone, but his eyes were glittering, a feral gleaming. "You think it a very good idea."

Flustered, Elizabeth tried to draw her thoughts together. "I don't know what you want of me."

"You do know," he said calmly. "You know very well what I want of you. What you don't know is what you want of me."

Elizabeth stood shaken by the truth of it, unable at first to look at him. She could acknowledge that he was right and risk the discussion that would follow, or she could lie to him. She could force herself to meet his gaze; with enough willpower, she could steel her heart against him and tell him she knew what she wanted, and that it was not him. But it would be a lie, and she could not bear to lie to him. He deserved the truth, and she could give him no less. Elizabeth swallowed hard, and found that for once in her life words had deserted her.

"Don't tie yourself in knots," he said gently, and she flinched at this, at how easily he could read her thoughts and moods. He leaned toward her, touching her with nothing but his words. "I won't put a hand on you ever again unless you ask me to," he said. "But know this, Elizabeth. You will get what you ask for. So think hard about it first."

He opened the door and went out of the cabin ahead of her.

When Elizabeth emerged a few minutes later, Nathaniel was busy strapping on his snowshoes with economical and quick movements.

"I said more than I meant to," he said, gesturing for her boot so he could strap on her shoes. "I have to ask you not to talk about the thievery at Lake in the Clouds to anybody at all." For once when he looked at her, he was unguarded and she saw the full force of the rage generated by the threat to his home and family. The hope came to Elizabeth, in passing, never to see such fury directed toward herself.

They were coming down through the last wooded section before the outermost clearings when Nathaniel pulled up short and gestured to Elizabeth to be still. There was a crackling from the path ahead, and then Richard Todd came around the corner, with Billy Kirby just behind him. They were talking in low tones when Billy saw Nathaniel and stopped.

"Hail!" called Richard, looking up. "Hail, Elizabeth! G'd day, Nathaniel."

Nathaniel nodded. "You two out for a walk in the snow?"

"Another storm coming," said Billy. "We can see her home from here."

Elizabeth looked at Nathaniel and thought how strange it was that his face, so animated when he spoke to her, so capable of showing his feelings, could show nothing at all when he wished it, when he needed it so. *He might look at me like that someday,* she thought. And Elizabeth was stunned to find out something about herself, to recognize what she feared most of all: not Nathaniel's passion, or his anger, but his indifference. That he might take her at her word and believe the foolish things she had said to him in the cabin. *It's not a good idea.* Suddenly Elizabeth wished Richard Todd and Billy Kirby far away; if she could just talk to Nathaniel by herself, if she could just touch him, she thought, at this moment she could say things to him she had once—even this very day—thought herself incapable of.

He was turning toward her. She imagined a flicker at the corner of his eye.

"I'll say my farewells, then," he said. "Elizabeth, I'll be by in the next week or so, if you want to come along and see the foundations of the school. Weather permitting."

Richard was watching her closely over Nathaniel's shoulder.

"Yes, that would be very good. Thank you for your help, Nathaniel. And—you'll think about Hannah, won't you?"

"I'll do that. And do mark, if you've got a yearning for apples, you only need to ask."

Richard and Billy could not see Nathaniel's expression, but Elizabeth could, and she struggled not to let her face respond in kind.

With a murmur of thanks and farewell she brushed past Nathaniel and joined Richard Todd and Billy Kirby. When Elizabeth looked back, Nathaniel was already lost in the forest.

"Did the old woman make a crumble?" asked Billy.

She turned to him. "What?"

"Did Hawkeye's squaw make apple crumble?" he asked. "I'm mighty fond of it myself."

"No," said Elizabeth, taken by surprise and trying not to show it. *Hawkeye's squaw.* "They called it apple grunt."

"Ah, then," said Billy. As if he understood completely.

XI

Elizabeth was surprised to see her father waiting for her at the door when she came up with Richard Todd. The judge had been pacing the hall and watching out the window, and was out the front door to meet them before Elizabeth could get the borrowed snowshoes off and thank Richard for his help. With a calculating look at the judge's expression, Richard took his leave of them.

"I'm very sorry," Elizabeth said, when her father had made his displeasure known. "I had no idea you'd be so worried about my welfare. But there was no opportunity to send you word."

The judge stopped his pacing and turned his great head to look at her, incredulous. "It's not your welfare that worried me," he said. "I would hope that you yourself would see that it is your reputation at stake."

"I see," she said shortly, moving past him to dry the wet hem of her skirt before the fire. "You would rather I had gotten lost in the blizzard and perished than have the village gossip."

"If you hadn't gone up the mountain in the first place," her father said in clipped tones, "this dilemma would not have confronted you, and you would have been home, where you belong."

Elizabeth swirled to meet her father. All the force of her

morning's outing, all the emotion she had brought to Nathaniel, were close to the surface, and now they took another turn.

"I do not *belong* at home!" she said, struggling to maintain an even tone, and failing.

"The Bonners are good men," the judge said. "Chingachgook is as fine an Indian as ever lived." He stopped, more unsure of himself now. "But they are not suitable company for a young unmarried woman of good family."

"Why? Why exactly, Father?" Elizabeth watched her father squirm and redden. "What you are thinking but will not say is that they are the wrong color. That I should be spending my time with that insipid Katherine Witherspoon and Richard Todd, people of my own kind."

The judge's color rose another notch. "And I would have told you so, if you had bothered to ask me before running off to Lake in the Clouds!"

It was rare that Elizabeth truly lost her temper, but she felt all the blood in her body congregate in her hands, her fingers jerking with the need to pick up something and throw it. "Shall I infer from this that I may not accept an invitation without your approval?"

"You will ask my approval," her father said tightly, "or I'll lock you in your room!"

Elizabeth drew up to her full height. An awful calm came over her, and the room was silent but for the sound of the fire and her father's hoarse breathing.

"I will pack my bags this very day and set out for England, if you do not reconsider that position," she said in a voice so deadly calm that the judge swayed as if he had received a physical blow.

Elizabeth swept past him and shut the door quietly behind her.

In a blind rush, she began to pile her things together on her bed, pulling clothing out of the drawers, folding her dresses haphazardly, her hands shaking so that small objects fell to the floor and would not be picked up.

Curiosity appeared in short order, her smooth brown face creased with surprise and considerable irritation.

"Now what trouble have you got yourself in?" she asked with one brow raised, but in a kindly tone.

"As if the whole household didn't hear," Elizabeth responded, picking with great irritation at the hairpins which had scattered themselves over the comforter.

Curiosity shook her head. "I thought you had better hold of your temper than the judge."

"Ah, well." Elizabeth strode to her desk and began to pile books together. "There's only so much a person can bear."

"You *want* to go back to England?"

"No!" Elizabeth half turned. Her copy of *Inferno* slipped from the pile and suddenly the entire stack of books was sliding to the floor. She collapsed in a billow of skirts and began pulling them onto her lap. "I don't *want* to go. But what choice do I have?"

Curiosity was standing with her bony arms crossed, one toe tapping at the floorboards.

"Now who is this talking? Sound to me like some little girl don't know her own mind. Somebody who don't care about teaching school." Suddenly she leaned over and snapped up a book, held it out to Elizabeth.

"Of course I care," Elizabeth cried, taking the book from Curiosity. "But my father will stand in my way at every turn."

A smile from Curiosity was a rare thing, but she produced a grin.

"You listen here, Elizabeth," she said. "I been keeping house for your father for longer than you been pulling air, and my menfolk have run his farm for him just as long. We know him better than you do. Let me tell you—this ain't the worst idea ever come to you. Put a fright into him, see what good it bring. I'll have Galileo and Manny tote your trunks up here, and the judge'll be sweatin' so as he'll need to take off his hat or die of the heat."

Elizabeth laughed in spite of herself, a little bark of amusement.

Curiosity's eyes were narrowed, and she pursed her lips.

"You go on an' laugh. But you listen, too. Sit up here on them trunks and listen to your daddy pacin' up and down the house wondering what stars he could pull out of the heavens to keep you here. Wondering if there's a ladder long enough. Thinking about it hard."

"My father," said Elizabeth, "is made of the same fabric as my uncle Merriweather and every other Englishman I've ever come across. He cannot see my point, because he cannot see me. Do you realize that, Curiosity? He sees me as a—commodity. The person I am, that person is invisible to him."

"Lord, yes," Curiosity said. "But you come a long way, child. Don't stop now when the blind man just about ready to have his eyes opened for him."

"What is the use?" Elizabeth muttered. "He will never apologize."

Curiosity flapped her apron impatiently. "Is that what you want most in this world? Lord above. Tell me, are those few words more important to you than your schoolhouse, or your get-up-and-go, or the lock he threatenin' you with? Wake up, child. The man is at your mercy, don't you see that?" She sat down with a great thump, and began taking books out of Elizabeth's hands to stack them. "I forget sometime that you a maiden lady. But I got a feeling you ain't without some understandin' of how the menfolk think. You consider what your daddy wants from you, and what you want from him, and how you gonna come out on top."

"You make it sound like a horse trade."

"It's all a horse trade, when you got men to reckon with. White, black, or red. I expect even the yellow men ain't much different. All made by the same God." Curiosity stood and headed for the door.

Elizabeth got up to follow her but Curiosity shooed her back into her room. "Now, you sit there and read for the afternoon, and let him think you up here packin'. See if he don't come round to a boil by the time I put the ham on the table, ready to give you whatever you can think of to ask for."

And she disappeared down the stairs.

Elizabeth was still standing on the landing when Curiosity

called back up to her in a tone which would carry out to every room in the house.

"Yes, Miz Elizabeth," she called. "I'll send up them trunks directly."

When Julian found his way home for dinner the judge met him at the door in a frantic frame of mind. After listening to his father's story, Julian reluctantly agreed to try his hand at talking reason into Elizabeth. But she refused to admit her brother and would not answer a single one of his questions. Finally bored with the whole affair, Julian went down to table.

"Well, you've done it now," he said to the judge, helping himself to potatoes. "When she gets like this there's no moving her."

The judge picked distractedly at his food. He was truly unhappy about the idea of losing Elizabeth. He was very fond of her, in spite of her strange and sometimes dangerous ideas. And her absence would make many practical problems almost impossible to resolve.

From the sideboard, Curiosity watched the judge closely, which did not do anything to help his appetite. The judge and Curiosity were old adversaries: she ran the household the way she believed it must be run, and he thought it his duty to cross her on occasion. It was an ongoing irritation to him that she outmaneuvered him with so little effort, in ways he did not quite follow. The feeling of always being outthought, and by a Negro woman, no less, was vaguely unsettling, when he let himself dwell on it. But because the judge was so dependent on Curiosity's excellent care and skill, and particularly fond of her biscuits and gravy, he didn't allow himself to consider these things in any depth.

"What exactly did you say to Elizabeth?"

"I told her she shouldn't have gone up Hidden Wolf without my permission."

"Ah." Julian ate for a while in silence. His own appetite was excellent, and the ham was exactly to his taste. "That may be technically true, Father. But it is certainly not the way to endear yourself to Elizabeth."

"But she can't leave," the judge said miserably. "If she doesn't marry Richard, I shall have to sell the land to him outright."

Julian glanced at Curiosity. "Perhaps we should discuss this later."

The judge was slightly puzzled by Julian's unwillingness to talk in front of Curiosity. It had always been his fashion to discuss business in front of her, and sometimes with her: she was as closemouthed a creature as he had ever known, shrewd, but discreet. Thinking back, the judge would have been hard-pressed to recall an occasion on which he had ever seen her speak to a human being outside the family or guests at the table, or to give bad advice, when asked. He was about to pay her this compliment within his son's hearing when Curiosity herself spoke.

"Good afternoon, Miss Elizabeth," she said softly, and the men rose from their places with such suddenness that their serviettes dropped to the floor. There was silence for some minutes while Curiosity offered Elizabeth each of the dishes.

"All packed?" Julian asked.

Elizabeth cast him a cool look. "Almost."

She allowed Curiosity to fill her plate. "Curiosity," she said. "Would you kindly inquire of Galileo whether or not he would be free to take me as far as Johnstown tomorrow? I am sure I can hire someone to escort me to Albany from there."

"Before we get Galileo all in a lather," Julian said, leaning back in his chair to sip at his wine, "Father wonders if there is anything he can say or do to keep you here in Paradise."

Curiosity's excellent food all tasted exactly alike to Elizabeth: every biteful was dry and tasteless in her mouth. But she forced herself to eat, one steady forkful after another, a pause to cut her food, and onward. She felt her way cautiously, aware that she was walking an unknown and dangerous path, and that everything she wanted was at stake. When she thought she was enough in control, she raised her eyes to her brother.

"Father knows exactly what it would take to keep me here," she said. "But he is clearly unwilling to abide by the promises he made me before we came. Thus," she said, still not looking at her father, "I will go back to my aunt and uncle Merri-weather. Life may not be as exciting there as it is here, but at least the restrictions which I must live with are not misrepresented."

The judge's mouth fell open in astonishment. "What have I done to deserve this contempt?" he asked. "Except worry for the welfare of my daughter?"

"Your worry is not for me," Elizabeth said, finally addressing her father directly. "Or, more accurately, it is only indirectly for me. If you were truly concerned for me, it would matter to you what I want for myself. But it is only what you want for me—from me—that concerns you."

She put her hands in her lap to steady them. The thrill of telling her true feelings without considering good manners or the propriety of what she had to say was intoxicating. With more calm than she felt, she met her father's horrified gaze.

"But I am arranging for your schoolhouse! At considerable expense, I might add, when cash is at a premium!"

"Only after I questioned your good word in front of your friend," Elizabeth said calmly. "And in the meantime I have no place to begin my work."

"There is not a spare bit of space in the village which would suit your purposes," the judge said. "Is that not true? Ask anyone. Ask—ask Curiosity!" He turned to the woman, who stood in front of the sideboard with her hands crossed in front of her.

"Isn't it true, Curiosity, that there's no suitable space for Miss Elizabeth's school at the moment?"

"Not in the village," she answered, with a nod. "But," she added, causing the judge to tense and turn toward her. "Of course, there's the old homestead. That might do."

Elizabeth's head snapped up in surprise. Curiosity looked back at her impassively.

"The old homestead!" Julian turned to his father, astonished. "What old homestead is that?"

"Up Hidden Wolf, just before the strawberry glen," said Curiosity when the judge could do nothing more than sputter. "A cabin, just. But in good repair."

"My father clearly doesn't wish me to teach school," Elizabeth said. "Or he might have suggested the cabin before now."

The judge finally found his voice. "That's not true!" He was flushed, torn between outrage that Curiosity should betray him thus, and the need to pacify Elizabeth. "The cabin is too old and rough for Elizabeth's purposes, or I would have mentioned it."

"I see," Elizabeth said. "Are you saying that if the cabin meets my needs, and I am satisfied with it, you will give it to me until the schoolhouse is built?"

There was a silence as the judge struggled to find the right answer. He looked back and forth between his children, and then at Curiosity. "If that will keep you here," he said finally. "Yes."

"That, and one other thing," Elizabeth said, clasping her hands tightly together under the table.

The judge looked utterly beaten. Elizabeth almost took pity on him, and then she felt Curiosity's sharp eyes on her, and knew that she had to take advantage now.

"I will choose my own friends, and go my own way, on my own terms," she said. "Without interference from you. Of any kind."

Julian's ever-present grin had disappeared, and he glanced at his father uneasily, but the judge was focused on his daughter.

"What gives you such authority?" he asked, but in a weary tone.

"I give it to myself. I take it for myself," Elizabeth said. "Aren't you familiar with those words, Father? 'It is necessary to the happiness of man that he be mentally faithful to himself.' "

The judge glanced up, a spark of his old temper in his eye. "I will give you what you want, on the condition that you stop quoting that frightful woman to me!"

Elizabeth's level gaze met her father's.

"I am very pleased to hear that we can come to an agreement. I would be very sorry to leave your household."

"Then the deal is done," the judge said, his voice hoarse, turning to his plate for solace.

"But—" Elizabeth continued, and he froze, his knuckles clutching white on his fork and knife.

"—that was not Mrs. Wollstonecraft."

"It wasn't?"

"No," said Elizabeth with a smile. "It was Tom Paine. *The Rights of Man.*"

XII

"Miz Elizabeth, I think Washington could've made good use of your talents," wheezed Henry Smythe as he dropped a crate of books on the floor. "I'm sure you could have found some boots and blankets while we was freezin' on the Potomac back in '76." His tone was dry, but he smiled at her kindly, and Elizabeth understood that this was a compliment of the highest order.

"Well, then," she said, "perhaps you'd be willing to lend a hand with the firewood? We mustn't have your grandson's fingers too cold to hold a quill."

"It ain't cold in here now," observed Anna Hauptmann when Henry had closed the door behind him. She was hanging curtains and she looked over the cabin from her perch on the step stool. "Wouldn't have thought you could get so many bodies together in this little place."

Elizabeth looked around herself with a great deal of satisfaction. It was true: after just two weeks the cabin's transformation was almost complete. Jed McGarrity was making the final structural repairs with the help of his two boys. Isaac Cameron and his sons were putting the finishing touches on bookshelves and a blackboard while Charlie LeBlanc and two other men hammered boards into tables and benches. Martha Southern had come up to sweep the floors and cover them with an assortment of rag rugs.

Behind the cabin, another group of men were constructing an outhouse, chopping and stacking wood, and clearing a path to the stream which would provide water for the school.

"Now all you need is the children," observed Anna, casting a significant glance down at Martha Southern.

Martha handed Anna the next pair of curtains, coloring slightly. The younger woman touched her muslin cap with one rough hand. "I hope I will be sending my Jemima, Miz Elizabeth," she said. "I pray to the Lord that my good husband will see the value."

Anna grunted. "That *would* require some divine intervention."

Elizabeth knew the women expected her to take up a part of this conversation, and in fact that the men had quieted down in the hope of hearing her respond. But she turned away and set to unpacking the next crate of books. Elizabeth was resolved not to let herself be pulled into this debate; she knew she could not convince people like Martha's husband, Moses, and she was afraid that she might scare away the others in the process of trying to do so.

This small silence was disturbed by a deep double rumble from the stomachs of Ian and Rudy McGarrity, nine and ten years old but alike enough to pass as twins. They looked up from under shaggy blond hair to grin with something closer to pride than embarrassment.

"Why, Jed," said Anna, when the laughter had died down. "Your boys got innards you could set the clock by. Getting on toward midday."

"And dinner waiting on the table, if I know my women-folk." Jed unfolded his long frame from the window sash he had been sanding and reached for his hat. "We'll be back tomorrow in the early, Miz Elizabeth. Not much more to do."

The others began to put their work down and find their wraps.

"Can we see you home?" Charlie LeBlanc asked Elizabeth as he had every day he had come to work on the cabin. From the corner of her eye, Elizabeth saw the grin on Anna Hauptmann's face, which she steadfastly ignored. It still came hard to Elizabeth to find herself the object of so much attention from young men, although she was improving in her ability to respond graciously.

"Thank you very much," she said. "But I'd like to get these books unpacked."

She thanked each of the workers by name and stood on the porch with her shawl clutched around her until they had all disappeared down the path toward their midday meals and afternoon chores.

Martha had lagged behind the others. Her face, freckled even in the dead of winter, was serious. "You can't et books, you know," she said. Distracted, she patted the rounded form of her belly as if to send this message to the child sleeping there, blessedly unaware of the possibility of hunger. Martha had been keeping house since she was nine, first for her father, and then for her husband; she didn't seem to be able to put aside her basic function in life, which was to make sure that people were fed.

"Thank you most kindly for your concern," Elizabeth replied. "I just have a little more to do, but then I will go home and let Curiosity feed me properly."

Martha nodded, satisfied. But she still did not turn to go.

"I don't suppose my Moses will change his mind about the schooling," she said. "I hope you'll forgive me."

"I'm sorry to hear that," said Elizabeth. "But there's nothing to forgive, after all."

"Jemima will be sore disappointed. But maybe—could we maybe borrow a schoolbook, once in a while? I would like that, reading together of an evening."

"You are very welcome to borrow books whenever you like. Would you like to take one with you today?"

Martha flashed a shy smile. "I would, but I think I had best not, Miz Elizabeth. Not till I've asked Moses about it. You know how men can be at times."

Elizabeth nodded, biting back words she knew could not serve any good purpose.

When Martha was at the turning in the path, she turned back and raised an arm in farewell.

"Don't forget your dinner!" she called, and Elizabeth nodded in agreement.

She would have forgotten her dinner, because the next crate of books was one with many fond memories. One by one she pulled out the Roman and Greek myths, the stories of the Germanic gods, spending some time with feckless Peer Gynt. Then she took up the plays that had so occupied and fascinated her as an adolescent: silly, love-struck Juliet; *Henry V,* which had made her want to masquerade as a boy and go off to war. *Dr. Faustus,* which still could send shivers down her spine, and Mrs. Behn's *The Rover,* which made her smile.

"Lost in her books, as usual," said Julian at the door, and Elizabeth looked up with a start.

"We've brought your dinner!" called Katherine Witherspoon, coming up behind him. Her cheeks were reddened from the cold and she laughed, knocking the snow from her shoulders and hood.

Elizabeth jumped up to take the basket from Julian, who immediately began to prowl the cabin, sticking his nose into corners and sniffing indelicately at the smell of the betty lamp.

"I suppose it will do, Lizzie," he said. "For your little school. Although I can't imagine being shut up here for hours at a time with a crowd of runny noses."

"Will you stop," Elizabeth said, unpacking Curiosity's ham and cheese pie.

"I think it's very nice," Kitty said in a conspiratorial whisper to Elizabeth that was not meant to be missed by Julian. "I had my lessons at the table, from my father and from Richard, and this would have been much more jolly, I'm sure."

"Oh, very jolly." Julian snorted softly. "If they don't slit each other's throats."

"Julian."

"Sorry, Lizzie. I'll try to look on the bright side for your sake."

They sat down around the food, and ate. Conversation was handled primarily by Kitty and Julian, who laughed and talked of everything that was of no interest to Elizabeth at all. Kitty was very animated, and it occurred to Elizabeth that while she may have once had hopes of Richard Todd, she had now most obviously shifted her attentions to Julian. Which was a very sad thing, for Elizabeth knew her brother well, and was sure he would not attach himself to Kitty. If he ever married, it would be a move calculated to make him comfortable, something not possible with Kitty. She wondered if there was any way for her to make Julian aware of the dangerous game he was playing, and then she realized that he knew full well. It was only the danger that interested him, after all.

"When will you be starting up the school, then?" Kitty was asking.

"It is most kind of you to take an interest. I think I can call school to session on Monday next."

"Oh, good," said Katherine. "That's good news, isn't it, Julian? You see, your brother and I wanted to talk to you about going to Johnstown. It's been two months or more since I've been, and I would like to see my friends the Bennetts, and see about fabric—"

"I can't go away, not now," interrupted Elizabeth.

"Oh, come along," said Julian, waving a hand in dismissal. "You need a little holiday before you start in on teaching, don't you think? A few days away might be just the thing."

While she ate, Elizabeth considered, letting them talk about the trip without committing herself. It was clear that Julian considered this trip to Johnstown a necessity; he would go, whether or not she came along. If she did accompany him, she might be able to keep him from getting into trouble. When Julian had spent or lost his own funds, he would appeal to her, or write notes on his father's credit.

Without her company, Kitty Witherspoon could not go to Johnstown, either. It was not possible for her to travel with Julian unaccompanied.

"I gather Father does not fancy a trip to Johnstown," Elizabeth said. "Or you would not be asking me."

"Oh, now you have struck me to the heart." Julian grinned. "Of course I would ask you. Who else could keep me out of trouble? So you will come?"

There was a soft knock at the door, and thankful for this interruption, Elizabeth jumped up immediately as the door opened.

"Many-Doves," she said, surprised and a little flustered. "Abigail. How nice to see you. Do come in."

Julian rose as the young woman came into the room, but neither he nor Katherine came forward.

"May I—" began Elizabeth, and then stopped, wondering how best to introduce her.

Many-Doves pushed her hood from her head and stepped toward them of her own accord, offering her hand.

"Good day, Miz Katherine."

Kitty nodded primly, her mouth turned down at one corner. In vexation at this interruption, or dislike, Elizabeth could not tell.

"My name is Many-Doves," she said in her low voice, extending her hand to Julian. "But please do call me Abigail if you prefer."

Elizabeth tensed, waiting for Julian's reaction, and then looked into his face and was taken by surprise. Her brother was looking down at Many-Doves with a slightly puzzled expression. Absent from his face was any trace of hostility or amusement, two emotions which seemed to rule him at most times.

"Many-Doves suits you better," he said, and he smiled as Elizabeth had not seen him smile since he was a young boy.

When Many-Doves had accepted the seat offered to her as well as a bit of their lunch, a sudden and awkward silence followed. Uncharacteristically quiet, Julian let Katherine and Elizabeth tend to the conversation without his assistance. Many-Doves seemed to be content to sit and listen, although her attention shifted constantly to the bookshelves.

More nervous and agitated than usual, Katherine continued to look to Julian for confirmation and approval after every statement or question, but Julian himself was distracted. He kept his eyes on a piece of corn bread, which he slowly dismantled, grain by grain. Katherine was forced to carry on by herself; she addressed her comments primarily to Elizabeth, but then seemed to consider, and turned to Many-Doves.

"Julian and I were just talking to Elizabeth about a trip to Johnstown. We were hoping that she would join us for a few days. She seems to think that her school will suffer if she calls it to session later than she hoped."

"My family is going down the Sacandaga," said Many-Doves, causing both Elizabeth and Julian to look up suddenly. "Tomorrow."

"You are?" asked Katherine, amazed. "All of you?"

"No, not all." Many-Doves was suddenly uncomfortable, as if she had said too much. "Hawkeye and his father will stay behind to—" There was a slight pause in which Elizabeth imagined many things. "To look after the traps."

"What reason is there for all of you to travel so far in the winter?" asked Julian, speaking for the first time, but keeping his gaze fixed on his plate.

"The Uncle has come to announce the Midwinter Ceremony," Many-Doves said, although she did not explain what she meant by *the Uncle*. "We'll go to the longhouse of the Turtle on the Big Vly."

"How long will you be gone?" asked Elizabeth, feeling something strange and hollow when she thought of Nathaniel being away.

"Five days, I think, altogether." She turned to Elizabeth. "What I came to say was that Hannah will not be here if you plan to start school next week, but my mother gives me leave to say that we will come the week after."

Katherine was trying not to frown; the result was a strange half contortion of her face which Elizabeth might have found comical under other circumstances.

"Are you planning on coming to the school, as well?" she asked incredulously, looking between Many-Doves and Elizabeth.

Since her discussion with Nathaniel in this cabin two weeks before, Elizabeth had not mentioned to anyone the possible involvement of Hannah and Many-Doves in her school. But now it was clear that Nathaniel had not forgotten, that he had kept his promise and spoken to Falling-Day. He would send his daughter to her school. She was flooded with a range of feelings: satisfaction, relief, and thankfulness. And she realized that he had given her something valuable: his trust. That was the message Many-Doves brought with her.

"Abigail has agreed to be my assistant," Elizabeth said, confident that she would not be contradicted.

"Oh, really?" Katherine said coolly. "What do you think of that idea?" she asked Julian directly.

Julian's eyes flickered past Many-Doves toward Katherine and then to Elizabeth.

"Well, if it means that Elizabeth will come along to Johnstown because her assistant isn't available to begin school next week, I suppose that there are some significant advantages to the arrangement, however . . . unorthodox it may be otherwise," he said, sounding more like himself than he had since Many-Doves had arrived.

Elizabeth kept Many-Doves with her when Julian and Katherine left, in spite of Katherine's unhappiness with this arrangement. She wanted to ask her in more detail about the decision to let Hannah come to the school, but once they were alone she did not know how to broach the subject.

Instead she showed Many-Doves all that had been done to turn the cabin into a schoolhouse. The younger woman was so interested in the cabin and its improvements, in the books and maps and pictures, that they had much to discuss. She asked a number of very clear questions and paid close attention to Elizabeth's answers.

After some time, Many-Doves hesitated, and Elizabeth sensed a change in topic coming.

"Will you go to Johnstown, then?" Many-Doves asked.

"I don't really know," Elizabeth answered. "Why?"

Many-Doves shook her head, and then, in another change of direction, she looked at the window and her face broke into a smile. "Nathaniel," she said, just as there was a knock at the door. "And Runs-from-Bears."

XIII

"I promised to take you to see the foundation of your school-house," Nathaniel said by way of greeting.

"Hello to you, too," said Elizabeth dryly. She was determined not to let a silly smile compromise the friendly but detached air she was working so hard to present. Her pulse was racing, though, and she had to resist the urge to touch her handkerchief to her brow.

Nathaniel inclined his head toward his companion without taking his eyes off Elizabeth. "This is Runs-from-Bears."

"Many-Doves," said Elizabeth as Runs-from-Bears stepped forward and took the hand she offered. "Is this the Uncle you mentioned?"

"They call me Uncle because I come to call them to Mid-winter Ceremony. Next week I will be just Runs-from-Bears again."

He had a friendly smile, but Elizabeth saw that it was not so much for her as it was for Many-Doves, who was suddenly quite silent. It was hard to judge, but Elizabeth thought he was perhaps thirty years of age. He had Otter's dark, glossy skin and angular face, although he bore the evidence of a bout with the pox, as well as a line of tattoos which stretched over the bridge of his nose. Silver earrings dangled from both of his ears, and there were feathers braided into his hair. Even in his layers of deerskin and fur, it was clear that he was well built. On his person he carried an assortment of weapons: a long rifle, hatchet and knife, and something that looked like a war club. In spite of his easy manner and smile, the man looked as if he would be afraid of nothing in this world. Elizabeth wondered if she would ever get an explanation of his name.

"The Uncle is whoever comes to call the Kahnyen'kehàka to the Midwinter Ceremony," Nathaniel explained.

"I told her all about Midwinter," Many-Doves said impatiently. "So are we going to look at the schoolhouse or not?"

"You're not," said Nathaniel. "Falling-Day is waiting for you at home, best get on back." Then he glanced at Runs-from-Bears and grinned, the first time he had smiled since he came through the door. "You can show her the way," he said, and added something in Kahnyen'kehàka that made Many-Doves push him sharply as she left the cabin.

"You do like teasing people," Elizabeth noted to Nathaniel as they made their way down the mountainside. "It's a weakness, I think."

"Is that so? Well, Boots, it seems harmless enough to me."

"I don't know if I like you calling me that," Elizabeth said, a little peevishly. "Boots, I mean."

Nathaniel glanced at her over his shoulder. "It suits you."

"But I have a given name, and it's not Boots."

"A person can have more than one name."

She drew up short, surprised. "Is that so? How many names do you have?"

"Oh, a handful."

There was silence for a minute, and then Elizabeth could not resist asking.

"The Kahnyen'kehàka call me Wolf-Running-Fast," he said. "But my mother—she called me Nathaniel."

"Well," said Elizabeth. "Then you'll understand that my mother gave me a name, and it is not Boots."

"You're right," Nathaniel agreed easily. "You earned that name yourself. The Indians have names they bring with them into the world and names they earn. Chingachgook calls you Bone-in-Her-Back."

She stopped dead. "Bone-in-Her-Back?"

Nathaniel nodded. "It ain't an insult."

Elizabeth glanced up quickly but she could read nothing from his face.

"I suppose not," she said, strangely pleased. They started on their way once again. "And Boots is the best name you can find for me?"

"That's an unseemly question for a lady," Nathaniel said with a bit of a chuckle.

"Someday," Elizabeth said, "you may come to regret this unfortunate propensity you have for teasing. Have a care, you never know when you might find yourself on the other end of that particular blade."

Nathaniel stopped to hold aside a low-hanging branch for her. "And would that be you wanting to show me what I'm missing?" he asked as she passed by him.

"Perhaps sometime," she said, her chin tilted up, and then jumped as he let the branch snap and catch her on the back.

But it wasn't a day for irritations: the weather was beautifully clear, in a week's time she would be teaching her first school, and Nathaniel's daughter was going to be one of her pupils. Elizabeth wanted to talk to him about this, but she didn't know how to bring up the subject without opening others she thought she couldn't quite manage at the moment.

What do I want from Nathaniel? Since he had first asked her that question two weeks ago, it was never long out of her consciousness.

They were making their way down the mountain on a path she hadn't known about, moving through a large plantation of spruce and pine. Once again, Nathaniel was in the lead, which gave Elizabeth an opportunity to observe him closely without being watched in turn. At the moment, she thought, it was enough to be with Nathaniel and to learn one more thing about him: he was a man who kept his promises. It was enough to have him to talk to.

"Is Runs-from-Bears Many-Doves' intended?" Elizabeth asked.

Nathaniel answered without stopping. "You saw that straight off, I guess."

"She seemed . . . unsettled," Elizabeth said. "And that explains your teasing. What did you say to him in Kahnyen'kehàka?"

"I told him to watch out, snow can burn as hot as kisses."

"Oh. No wonder Many-Doves was put out. I take it that Runs-from-Bears is Wolf clan."

"No, Turtle," said Nathaniel. "And a good thing, too. It's against the Kahnyen'kehàka way to take a wife from your own longhouse. It would be like marrying a sister."

"Does that mean—"

"I wasn't adopted into the Wolf clan," Nathaniel said. "It wouldn't have stopped me if I had wanted her. But I didn't." He glanced over his shoulder at Elizabeth. "So there never was a need to be jealous."

"I wasn't jealous!" she sputtered unconvincingly.

"Don't tie yourself in a knot, Boots," Nathaniel said easily, moving on. "You can't pretend to me the way you do to the others."

Together with her father, Elizabeth had surveyed all of his property in the vicinity of the village. The judge had had a particular spot in mind on a piece of land too small to pact out to a farmsteader, but Elizabeth had immediately rejected it as too close to home. The site she wanted and had eventually persuaded the judge to relinquish for the school was on the side of the village opposite from home, about a half mile farther than the nearest farm. The path from the village wound through the woods along a stream which came down from the mountain, and then flowed into Half Moon Lake. At the juncture of the stream and the lake, a quarter acre of marsh spread out, reeds and grasses poking through the ice. On a rise between the marsh and the woods, in a natural clearing, Nathaniel had begun to build the schoolhouse.

"Yes," said Elizabeth softly as they came out of the trees. "This is exactly the right spot." And without hesitation, she strode to the foundation of her school.

"That elevation there gives you some shelter from the winds," Nathaniel pointed out as she walked around the shell of the building. He stopped near a great triangular stockpile of logs, their notched ends oozing sap.

"Water close by. It's a good walk home for you, though."

"That's the way I wanted it," Elizabeth said, distracted. Too pleased and excited to hold still, she leapt over the low beginnings of one wall and stood in the middle of what would soon be the main schoolroom.

She stood considering outlines of the rooms, one gloved hand against her cheek.

"Windows there, and there," she said suddenly, pointing. "And here," pivoting. "We need the early morning light."

"I ordered the sashes," Nathaniel said. "Although the judge ain't pleased at the cost."

Elizabeth smiled then. "I can imagine." She circled the second room with her arms crossed tightly around herself, and turned toward Nathaniel, her skirts swirling.

"This could be mine."

"Of course," Nathaniel said with one brow raised. "I thought that was the whole idea."

"No, no." She shook her head. "This—" She gestured around herself. "This could be mine. My home. Mine alone. This could be my hearth." She stopped in front of the foundation of the chimney. "My desk by the window. Bookshelves. A bed on that end—" She drew up short and laughed, a little self-consciously.

Nathaniel was leaning easily against the logs, but his eyes followed her every move. Elizabeth's hood had fallen back and stray hair clouded around her flushed face in damp tendrils. Her eyes snapped with energy and satisfaction, and Nathaniel wondered how long he could keep his word to her and not touch her without invitation.

"Well," he said. "Why not?"

She did laugh then, out loud. "A lady living alone?"

"If that's what you want most in the world, Boots."

She turned away suddenly, and spoke to him over her shoulder. "Can you imagine my father's reaction?" Suddenly she startled him: she crossed through the foundation and came up to stop in front of him and grasp both his hands in her own.

"This is enough for right now," she said. "And I have you to thank."

Nathaniel's earring twirled in the sunlight when he shook his head.

"No need to thank me," he said gruffly. "It's work I was hired to do."

"Thank you anyway, and thank you for Hannah," said Elizabeth. "I am so pleased that she'll be coming to school."

"That was Falling-Day's doing," said Nathaniel. "I left the decision up to her."

Elizabeth lifted her chin and grinned at him. "Is that so?" she said. "Is that what you want me to believe?" She dropped his hands and stepped back. "Well, let me tell you something, Mr. Bonner. You can't pretend to me like you do to the others."

Nathaniel reached out to grab her but she slipped away. "Oh, no," she said. "You promised."

"Not only are you teasing me," Nathaniel pointed out, "but you are flirting most outrageously. Hardly the behavior I'd expect from you."

Elizabeth drew up in surprise and the truth came to her with nothing more than a little glide of recognition. What she wanted from Nathaniel was simple: she wanted him near her, because she had fallen in love with him. She was looking up at him with all this showing clearly on her face, when there was the brief clap of igniting gunpowder from the forest. Elizabeth registered the flash at the corner of her eye and then a sudden surge of air against her cheek as the bullet flew past her to find another target.

Nathaniel let out a grunt of surprise, pitched forward to grab Elizabeth, and fell to the ground, pinning her underneath him. His solid weight pressed her into the snow from foot to shoulder; his blood was warm on her cheek.

The world went hazy for a moment. When her vision cleared Elizabeth realized that Nathaniel was looking at her. She closed her eyes, letting waves of relief and nausea wash over her. He rolled away, but stayed low to the ground.

"Are you all right?" she asked. "Are you shot?"

"Just a graze," he said, touching his face.

Elizabeth grabbed his hand to pull it away. There was a shallow red furrow bleeding freely, about an inch long. A few grains of powder were embedded around the wound like a scattering of pepper.

"Somebody shot at you," she said, stunned. Then she leapt to her feet and started toward the forest.

Nathaniel was so surprised that at first he could not credit what he was seeing: Elizabeth marching forward barehanded in pursuit of a man with a rifle. With a low curse he launched himself after her and caught her by the wrist to drag her down behind the partial wall of the schoolhouse.

"Stay down!" He scanned the trees warily, struggling all the while to keep her next to him.

"But somebody *shot* at you," she said finally, when she realized that he would not let her go.

"Ain't the first time," he said grimly. "Probably not the last, either. Although I will admit it was a bit close for comfort."

There was an awkward pause, and then Nathaniel smiled. "By God, Elizabeth, what did you mean to do? Grab him by the ear and drag him back to the judge?"

Elizabeth looked surprised. "I don't know what I was thinking," she said. "I didn't think anybody would shoot at me, I suppose."

"Well, you may be right about that," Nathaniel said dryly. "Whoever it was is long gone, at any rate." And he stood and pulled Elizabeth to her feet, brushing snow and debris from her overcoat. She reached up and touched his cheek again.

"Who would do such a thing? We have to find out."

"Elizabeth!" Nathaniel's hands rose to clench her shoulders. "Don't tell anybody about this. Not anybody."

Elizabeth blinked up at him.

"I ain't hurt," Nathaniel said, more gently. "And it's not time to bring things to a head yet."

She began to tremble then, and he slid an arm around her while he watched the riverbank over her head.

"It's all right," he said. "Everything is all right. They're long gone. Nothing more to fear."

Elizabeth was thankful for Nathaniel's solid presence and his calm: it was comforting to have his arms around her. Right at this moment, more frightened than she cared to admit to herself, Elizabeth found Nathaniel's gentle murmurings, the light touch of his hands on her hair, and his utter competence more seductive than any embrace could have been. She let herself relax against him, and soon stopped trembling.

Nathaniel pulled away a little, observing Elizabeth closely. He smoothed a hand over her hair one last time and managed a grim smile.

"There's blood on your cheek," he said, rubbing the spot softly with his thumb, his fingers threading into the hair above her ear. Then Nathaniel dipped his head and brushed her mouth with his lips.

"I promised not to do that," he said. "But maybe you'll make allowances, under the circumstances."

Elizabeth's face lost its stunned look, and she stepped away looking as if she had just woken up.

They walked away from the schoolhouse in silence. Glancing back, Elizabeth saw the outline of the foundation in the little clearing, the curve of the stream as it disappeared into Half Moon Lake. A beautiful spot, but she wondered if she could ever approach it again without thinking of what had almost happened today.

Nathaniel was walking along beside her silently, his attention shifting from side to side, his rifle cradled easily in his hands. For a few minutes they didn't talk at all.

"This must be about Hidden Wolf," Elizabeth said slowly.

Nathaniel shrugged. "Likely as not," he said. "But men have been known to take out after each other on account of a woman on occasion."

As shaken as she was, Elizabeth had to laugh out loud. "You don't think this was about me, do you? That seems very unlikely indeed." The idea that men could want her enough to shoot at each other was strange and upsetting, and she got no satisfaction from it at all. She was afraid to look at Nathaniel, afraid to see what might be on his face.

"I'll tell you what I think," Nathaniel said in a low voice. "I think that Richard Todd wants Hidden Wolf, and the quickest way to it is through you."

Then he stopped, and glancing around, Nathaniel took Eliz-

abeth by the arm and pulled her into the deep blue shadows of a
stand of pine.

Elizabeth looked up and found Nathaniel's face just inches
from her own, so that she started and dropped her gaze.

"Now," Nathaniel continued. "We need Hidden Wolf.
There's no denying that. Otherwise we'll have to move on up
into the wilderness where folks will let us be."

"So you are in the same position as Richard is," Elizabeth
said numbly.

Nathaniel's hands tightened on her upper arms until she gave
in and looked up, and then he held on to her gaze and refused
to let her look away. "Listen, now. Richard wants the mountain
and he'll take you to get it."

Elizabeth tried to drop her head but he put a finger under
her chin to lift it and looked her directly in the eye.

"I want you," he said.

A warm rush of breath left Elizabeth. She could smell him,
the oil on his skin. Leather and sweat and blood.

"I wake up wanting you and go to sleep wanting you,"
Nathaniel murmured, pulling her shoulders up to him so that
her head fell back and the arch of her neck rose to meet him.
"Elizabeth. I want you as much as I want to breathe, but I need
the mountain."

"Then the end result is the same."

"No." His eyes moved over her. "But the lack of you won't
kill me outright. If you decide you won't have me. That's in
your hands. But without Hidden Wolf we can't survive."

Elizabeth inhaled, and her voice sounded very small and
strange to her own ears.

"And my father won't sell it to you. How much did Chingachgook offer him?"

"One dollar seventy-five cents an acre."

Elizabeth's head snapped up and her mouth fell open in a
little circlet of surprise. "That's almost two thousand dollars.
Where in heaven's name—how—" She thought of the turkey
shoot, and the fact that there hadn't been an extra shilling between Nathaniel and Hawkeye.

"It's none of my business," she said finally.

Nathaniel inclined his head. "I can't tell you about that right now."

"But I can't believe my father would turn down such an offer!"

"Well, he did," Nathaniel said. "When Richard Todd offered him two dollars. You have to think, Elizabeth, that out near the big lakes, land is going for forty cents the acre."

Her head was down while she thought. "There's something else at stake here," she said. "If the prices are so high."

"You could say that," Nathaniel agreed.

She looked up, very businesslike. "You need another two hundred dollars, then." Elizabeth pulled away a little. "I could give you that much, or lend it to you if you prefer."

Nathaniel shook his head. "I don't think there's much use. Todd will just up his offer."

"How does Richard have so much cash at his disposal?" Elizabeth asked. "I don't understand."

"Well," Nathaniel said grimly. "It don't hurt to have a bachelor uncle who owns half of Albany leave you everything when he dies. And Todd is a clever man with a dollar."

The questions racing through Elizabeth's mind would not stand still long enough for her to give them voice.

"Something must be done to stop Richard," she said softly, mostly to herself.

The graze on Nathaniel's cheek had stopped bleeding, but a bruise was rising. Elizabeth registered the intensity of his level gaze, the slow flutter of his eyelids, the sheen of sweat on his brow, and it occurred to her that to have him so very close was to put aside all ability to reason clearly.

"Perhaps—" she began. "Perhaps there's some *other* way," she said. "If you give me a little time to think about it."

She turned away and started up the path again, and this time Nathaniel followed.

Just before the woods opened up to the Southerns' homestead, Nathaniel caught Elizabeth's hand to make her stop.

"Can you get on by yourself now?" he asked. "I don't want to be seen."

Without warning, a wave of homesickness for England washed over Elizabeth. It had never occurred to her that she would so soon yearn for the overprotective attentions of her aunt, who would not let her walk two miles to the village by herself if the weather was wet. She didn't want Nathaniel to leave her.

"I'll be fine," she said, but heard her voice shaking.

Nathaniel glanced around them and then touched her face.

"You're a brave one," he said. "My mother would have liked you, English or not."

"I'm all bluff," Elizabeth said, managing a sour grin. "Haven't you seen through me yet?"

"Oh, I see more than you think. I saw you run off after that shooter, didn't I?" But Nathaniel dropped his hand from her face. "Did Many-Doves tell you I'm going with the women to the Midwinter Ceremony?"

"She said you'd be gone a week."

"You think you might miss me a little?"

Elizabeth squinted up at him. He had undergone one of his transformations: now all trace of his fury and cautiousness were gone. It was an amazing talent he possessed, and she wondered if it could be learned.

"I don't see much of you as it is," she said, trying to match his tone. Elizabeth bit her lip, knowing how familiar this sounded, and what it gave away.

Nathaniel glanced around them again, and swung his rifle to its accustomed place across his back. "So maybe you will miss me a little."

"No," said Elizabeth. "I won't miss you at all, because I won't be here. Julian wants to go to Johnstown for a few days."

Nathaniel looked down at her in surprise. "Where did he come up with that idea? Did somebody tell him about Midwinter afternoons at Trees-Standing-in-Water?"

It was Elizabeth's turn to look puzzled.

"There's games played after the morning ceremonies," Nathaniel explained. "Some pretty serious wagering goes on, even the whites come to watch."

"But where is—Trees-Standing-in-Water?"

"The whites call it Barktown. Just about ten miles short of Johnstown, after you leave the Sacandaga. On the Big Vly."

"And there are games. I see," Elizabeth said thoughtfully. "Well, I wasn't sure about going along with Julian, but now I fear that I must. Nathaniel," she said, "you'll watch out for yourself?"

"I have no intention of getting myself killed, if that's what you mean." Nathaniel shifted his weight suddenly and stepped away.

"Moses Southern is coming this way," he said under his breath. "Don't be startled, now."

Elizabeth fixed her face in a friendly but neutral smile and turned as Moses approached. He had a fishing net draped over his shoulder, and he kept on walking, barely nodding to the two of them in response to Elizabeth's greeting.

"Got better things to do than stand and gab in the snow," he mumbled.

"So do we all." Nathaniel nodded. "I best be getting on home." Then, when Moses was well past, he lowered his head toward Elizabeth and whispered. "Remember, nothing about what happened at the schoolhouse."

"Will I see you in Johnstown?" she asked, trying not to let her voice creak with the effort it took to ask this question.

"I hope so," Nathaniel said. "But that would be up to you."

XIV

"What good luck!" Katherine called out suddenly over her breakfast, waving the newspaper in Elizabeth's direction.

At the start of the third full day in Katherine's company, Elizabeth's patience with the younger woman's sudden shifts of mood was wearing fragile, but now she put down her teacup and tried to look intrigued.

"What's that, then?"

From across the table, their hostess caught Elizabeth's eye and smiled kindly.

"You'll have to come visit with Kitty more often," Mrs. Bennett said. "She brings such enthusiasm with her, and you are the heart of serenity. You complement each other well. Don't you think so, Mr. Bennett?"

Caught unawares, Mr. Bennett looked up from his own newspaper with a puzzled expression. "Of course," he said. "I couldn't agree more."

Katherine jumped up from her place to put her arms around Mrs. Bennett. "What a dear friend you are," she said. "I would be here with you always if I could."

Elizabeth smiled her thanks for her portion of the compliment, but she made no promises about further visits. The Bennetts were kind people, hospitable and generous with the considerable comforts of their home, but Elizabeth was wishing herself back in Paradise. They had spent a full day in Johnstown and, in Elizabeth's opinion, exhausted its charms.

But as much as she would like to be away home, Elizabeth was not looking forward especially to the journey, as it would require another full day alone with Katherine. The trip to Johnstown had been difficult: it took some time for Katherine to come to accept the idea that Elizabeth had asked someone else—and an Indian woman no less—to assist at her school, and she had been distant and indignant for most of the journey, turning around constantly to see if Julian, who followed on horseback, was within hailing distance.

Elizabeth knew that they were once again on friendly speaking terms not because Katherine had come to some understanding or appreciation of Elizabeth's motives, but simply because she was so very pleased to be in town that she could not stay in a temper. She didn't even seem to mind Julian's absence, although he had spent not a half hour with them since they had arrived.

Mrs. Bennett patted Katherine affectionately and sent her back to finish her breakfast. Katherine went rather reluctantly and sat with her chin on her cupped palm. The sleeve of her morning gown showed faded and somewhat worn against Mrs. Bennett's good white linen, and Elizabeth felt suddenly sorry for Katherine, who so enjoyed beautiful things but had so few of them herself. Elizabeth caught sight of her own face in the silver of the teapot, the lace at her neck, and the fine gray silk of her own morning gown. She reached for the paper.

"Let's see," she said. Katherine brightened up immediately.

Elizabeth skimmed the advertisements for the one that had aroused Katherine's interest. "Ah," she said finally, and read out loud:

CLEMENTINA STOWE, Has just imported, and has
for SALE at her STORE on the Johnstown Main Street
a very neat assortment of MILLINERY GOODS
consisting of the following articles, caps, stomachers,
shoe-knots, Italian sprigs, lace, thread lace and edging,

spotted satin, crimson ditto, black peelongs, a great variety of sash and other ribbons, fashionable fans, all which she will dispose of on the lowest TERMS.

"You've been thinking of doing over your hat, I know," said Mrs. Bennett. "Mrs. Stowe has some lovely things."

"Then you must all go and satisfy your curiosity," said Mr. Bennett, folding his own paper and looking around the table as if he had just woken up. "And I must get to the office."

Elizabeth smiled. "May I come by and see your offices, Mr. Bennett?" she asked. "While we are in town?"

Mr. Bennett, about forty-five years of age, was a round, slightly soft-looking man, with a broad, good-natured face. Unless you looked at his eyes—which missed nothing at all in spite of their pallid blue—you might overlook Mr. Bennett completely. Elizabeth had felt him observing her more than once on her first evening as their guest. She had found him more than willing to discuss the turn of events in the French Revolution which had led—she learned with great unease—to the recent execution of the king. He had been the only one of the Bennetts to show any interest in her plans to teach school; they had even had a discussion about Mrs. Wollstonecraft, whose writings he had actually read, and thought about.

"Do you have a question of the law for me, Miss Middleton?" he asked now.

"Heavens," said Mrs. Bennett. "Why would Miss Middleton have need of the magistrate? I'm sure she would just like to see all of Johnstown while she is here."

"I thought we were going to the milliner's shop," said Katherine, saving Elizabeth the trouble of being more specific about her interest in Mr. Bennett's work.

"Yes, let's do that," Elizabeth said, rising from her place.

"I will detain you no longer, my dear," he said to his wife. "And please do bring the young ladies by the offices. I would be pleased to see you all there."

It took Elizabeth considerably less time to dress than it would take Katherine and Mrs. Bennett; she had learned this fact on the first morning of her visit, and now prepared herself for a half hour's wait by taking the paper with her to her room.

The Bennetts were quite wealthy, and their home was furnished in the latest style. The room they had given to Elizabeth was dominated by a large four-poster bed which was hung with a beautiful floral chintz and piled so high with feather comforters that the brass warming pan was almost unnecessary. Now Elizabeth sat by the window in a little bow-backed chair upholstered in a matching velvet and read the paper. She had gone through many notices of meetings of the local government and reports of legal disputes when her attention was claimed by the advertisements. There were ponies and land and bear traps for sale, but there were more personal matters as well. "Lydia Mathers," Elizabeth read,

the wife of the subscriber, has eloped from her lawful husband in the company of one Harrison Beauchamp, known gadabout and suspected thief, taking with her a good pewter jug, twenty pound in coin, three silver spoons, a snuff box, the slave girl Eliza and her husband's good underclothes. By this notice her much injured husband thinks it prudent to forewarn all persons from trusting her on his account, being determined, after such flagrant proof of her bad behavior, to pay no debts of her contracting. I treated her well.

Thy-Will-Be-Done Mathers of Canajoharee.

Elizabeth didn't know whether she should be more shocked at Mrs. Mathers' behavior or at her own first and abiding impulse to laugh out loud at another's misfortune. *I have been here not even two months,* she thought, *and my sense of propriety has been permanently undone.* She read the advertisement once again and wondered at a place in which a man would advertise so openly that his lawful wife had eloped with another man. At her aunt Merriweather's there was occasional talk of elopement, but the brides were always young women with more opportunity than good sense. Girls who ran off to Scotland to be married to men with too little money or who otherwise pleased their families too little. "Mark my words," aunt Merriweather had said without exception when these cases came to their attention. "Happy unions cannot take root under such a cloud of deception and artifice."

The next notice was much less amusing.

RUNAWAY SLAVE. Goes by Joe. Well grown field negro especially dark skinned, missing two toes on the left foot, run away from me Tuesday last. Thought to be headed into the Bush. Reward.

M. Depardieu, Pumpkin Hollow.

Mrs. Bennett was calling for Elizabeth, who rose and reluctantly put the paper aside on the chair. But as she was turning away, a word caught her eye and she picked up the paper again.

WANTED. Any word on the whereabouts of the old Indian Sachem Chingachgook, known also as Great-Snake or Indian John. To settle a debt.

Jack Lingo. Leave a message at the Trading Post, Stumptown.

Elizabeth stood reading this advertisement again and again until Katherine knocked at her door impatiently.

"Coming," she called, and with cold hands hid the paper among her things.

To Elizabeth's great surprise, Julian was waiting with the ladies at the foot of the stairs. He bowed to her most formally and then grinned.

"Good morning, sister," he called. "I understand we are to go to the shops. I could use your excellent advice, as I would like to have a new coat made."

Katherine was so pleased to have Julian along for this outing that she barely allowed Elizabeth time to answer her brother before she overwhelmed him with fragments of at least three different questions and requests. Once again Elizabeth realized that Katherine's single-mindedness was sometimes a boon: it provided her with time to think through awkward situations, and for that reason alone she should be thankful.

While Elizabeth's enthusiasm for the expedition into the town was even less than it had been before, she did not mind the walk at all and she managed to hold a polite conversation with Mrs. Bennett as they moved along, thinking most of the time about her brother, and managing to keep thoughts of Nathaniel at bay. Now that she was in Johnstown, she had no idea how she would ever make her way to Barktown to seek him out at the Midwinter Ceremony. Elizabeth was only a little disappointed, and she reasoned to herself that it would be only a few days before she returned to Paradise, to her school, and to Nathaniel. It all seemed very far away and strange now. But real. Nathaniel was real, and what she felt for him was real. She was here because of him, and what she might be able to do for him, and for herself in the process.

Katherine had taken the arm Julian offered, and the two of them were far ahead when Mrs. Bennett took up a new topic of conversation which demanded Elizabeth's entire attention.

"Your brother is kind to spend his morning with us," observed Mrs. Bennett. "When he must have other business to attend to."

There was a small pause, and then Mrs. Bennett surprised Elizabeth greatly.

"You must make allowances if Kitty seems sometimes overly . . . absorbed. She has suffered a quite crushing disappointment in the past year, and although she may seem to be insensitive, I assure she is just the opposite. She had hopes of Dr. Todd, until quite recently. Has she spoken to you of him?"

Elizabeth walked without answering for a moment, and then she began carefully.

"No," she said. "Katherine does not speak to me of her personal affairs."

"And Dr. Todd? Did he mention this to you?"

Elizabeth pulled up short, and found the older woman's brown eyes steady and unapologetically inquisitive.

"I wonder why you think that Dr. Todd would speak to me of such a personal matter," Elizabeth said. "I assure you there is no cause for him to do so, nor would I welcome such a cause."

"I see." There was a new tone in Mrs. Bennett's voice, whether of relief or disappointment, Elizabeth could not tell.

"You see the Grant mansion," Mrs. Bennett pointed out in passing. "What gardens they keep. You must come and see them in the summer. Mrs. Grant's roses are the envy of all of us." And then, with a small drop in tone, Mrs. Bennett took up her previous topic again: "Please forgive my forwardness," she said. "I forget you are here so recently from England, where things are perhaps not so direct. But I do worry excessively about Katherine. Her mother was my dearest friend."

Mrs. Bennett stopped suddenly and grasped Elizabeth's arm. "Look," she said with great animation, directing her attention across the road. "Mrs. Clinton is in town, do smile, do nod, Miss Elizabeth. The governor's wife. I wonder what the Clintons are doing in Johnstown. They must be visiting with the Dubonnets."

Katherine and Julian had turned back to join them, and Elizabeth had a moment to reflect on Mrs. Bennett's sudden switch of topic. She wondered whether the lady was as flighty as she seemed, or if this was a calculated attempt to distract Elizabeth and to disarm her. She thought ahead to her conversation with Mr. Bennett, and hoped that he would keep the topic of her visit to himself.

It wasn't until the contents of three shops had been inspected that Elizabeth was able to slip away and find her way to Mr. Bennett's offices. Julian and Katherine were so much enjoying themselves that they were best left to Mrs. Bennett's animated direction, and barely seemed to register her departure. She was let go once she promised to meet them at home for dinner, and with a great deal of relief Elizabeth made her way into the street.

Johnstown was a good-sized town with a great deal of business, and Elizabeth found it possible to lose herself in the foot traffic. This was the first time she had been on her own since leaving Paradise and she felt the pleasure of it. As they had spent very little time in any of the towns on their trip north from New-York, Elizabeth was interested in everything she passed, from the blacksmithy and tannery to the impressive homes of the town's first citizens.

Mr. Bennett's offices were in a street off the main business area. Elizabeth stood contemplating her errand when the door of a tobacconer's opened and Galileo emerged with his arms full of packages.

"Miz Elizabeth!" he greeted her solemnly with a deep bow of his head, and then broke into a grin.

"Where have you been keeping yourself?" Elizabeth asked. "I haven't seen you at all since we arrived."

"Errands to attend to for the judge," Galileo explained, holding out his packages as evidence of his industry. "The judge don't care for town, you see."

"Something I have in common with my father, then," Elizabeth noted dryly.

Galileo considered Elizabeth with one eye squeezed shut, the wiry salt-and-pepper twists of his eyebrows meeting in a tumble over the sharp blade of his nose. "Are you ready to head on home?" he asked. "I can have the horses ready first thing in the morning, just you say the word."

"That would be very good," Elizabeth said with a smile. "But do let me check with Miss Witherspoon, and with my brother."

"Huh!" Galileo's frown spread across his face and then disappeared as quickly as it came. "I don't think Mr. Julian ready to go just yet."

Elizabeth considered Galileo, wondering how much information he was willing to volunteer about Julian's whereabouts and his activities in the last two days. But it was getting late, and she cast a worried look toward Mr. Bennett's offices.

"I have an errand," she said. "But I would like to talk to you about . . . the trip home, later." She took her leave from Galileo and had turned away when across the road a weathered gray door flew open with a bang. From the dark interior a terrific bellowing erupted, followed by the form of a slight man dressed in ragged homespun who fairly flew through the air to land in a hump in the road.

"Come, Elizabeth," Galileo said briskly, taking her arm and trying to turn her away.

"But that man—" She pulled herself clear and looked more closely. Nothing had changed at all: people continued to make their way, ignoring the spectacle of a man lying in the road. The door he had come through was now shut. With an audible groan, the man raised his head from the snow and muck. He rose unsteadily to his feet and lurched off. His dark tangled hair covered most of his face, but not enough to disguise the copper gleam of his skin, the sharp bones, the sunken expression.

"Been drinkin', hard," said Galileo beside her. "Nothing you can do for him."

Reluctantly, Elizabeth turned away. Then she stopped and considered. "Who could?" she asked. "Who could do something for him?"

Galileo shrugged, his own dark face suddenly closed and protective. "God knows," he said.

Elizabeth's first urge was to go and tell Mr. Bennett about the Indian, but she knew she must be careful to restrict herself to topics which would not arouse his suspicion. It would not do to complicate the situation, she told herself, standing on the doorstep of his offices, trying to put the image of the man in the road out of her mind.

"What's the matter, Miz Elizabeth?" Galileo asked. He had insisted on walking her to her destination, and now waited on the curb. "Why you coming to see the magistrate?"

"There's nothing the matter," she said, trying to affect a calmer demeanor. "But I am worried about that man," she admitted. "I know what you told me," she said, before Galileo could list for her the reasons she should put the incident out of her head. "And I expect that you're right. He wouldn't welcome my interference in his affairs, either. I know that too without being told. Here," she said, reaching into her purse. "Perhaps he won't mind if it comes from you. Can you find him and make sure he has a warm dinner, today at least?"

"He'll drink it," Galileo said with a resigned look.

"Well, then, buy some cooked meat and give him that," Elizabeth said.

Galileo nodded. "All right," he said finally. "Can you find your way back to the Bennetts'?"

But Elizabeth had already turned away. She fluttered a hand

behind her in farewell to Galileo, composed her face, and entered the offices of John Bennett, attorney at law and magistrate for the northern counties in the state of New-York.

Mr. Bennett appeared to greet Elizabeth as soon as the door closed behind her. His clerk had relieved her of her coat and hat and she found herself with a cup of tea in a comfortable chair in Mr. Bennett's main office less than five minutes later.

"It's not often we get such company," he explained over her protests. "We must observe the amenities, or we may never see the like again."

When Elizabeth had seen and admired the fittings in the office, and had described for Mr. Bennett the morning's expedition to the shops and the hat his wife had bought, there was a moment's silence.

"Mr. Bennett," Elizabeth began. "Please do not think me disingenuous, but I do have a question of the law for you. I hope you will forgive me for not being more open with you earlier today, but it is quite a sensitive matter."

There was a slight flicker of interest in the pallid blue eyes, and then Mr. Bennett's face settled into a studied composure. He folded his hands on his desk in front of him. "I did suspect as much," he said. "And of course I am at your service."

Elizabeth glanced out the window into the road where the citizens of Johnstown moved about on their business. It could be a town almost anywhere, she thought. Midwinter snow trod into a gray muck, icy cobblestones, and spring so far off. With a shake of her head she focused her attention on the man before her.

"My father," began Elizabeth, "has expressed an intention to execute a deed of gift in my favor."

"Ah, yes," Mr. Bennett said. "I am familiar with the document. I reviewed it for him."

"Then perhaps I need not explain—" Elizabeth's eyes scanned Mr. Bennett's face. "I hope you will forgive my bluntness when I say that as I know no other person of the law to approach on this matter, I find myself compelled to trust you."

"Ha!" Mr. Bennett's laugh caught Elizabeth off guard, and she found herself smiling in return.

"You are an unusual young lady, if I may be so bold," he said, drawing a handkerchief from the cuff of his linen shirt and touching it to his mouth. "But I take your point. Please be assured of my discretion. You may ask what you like, and if it is within my power, I will answer."

Elizabeth stood up suddenly and walked to the bookcases which lined the wall. She ran a finger over the titles there.

"My father wishes me to marry."

"Dr. Todd," said Mr. Bennett.

Elizabeth's shoulders tensed, but she did not turn. "You are better informed than I would have guessed."

"I am sorry if I've offended you," Mr. Bennett said quietly.

There was something in his manner which caused Elizabeth to trust him. She was not sure exactly if it was his willingness to be amused, or his honesty.

"You haven't offended me. I'm not even greatly surprised, I must confess. Everyone seems to know more about this business than I do."

"This is a small society, after all," said Mr. Bennett. "We take as much interest in each other as any set of families in England."

"Yes, I am coming to see that," Elizabeth said. "Perhaps you will understand my meaning, then, when I say that I fear Dr. Todd's interest in me has more to do with the deed of gift than it does with myself."

There was a knock at the door, and the clerk came in with a bow to Elizabeth to put a note on the table in front of Mr. Bennett. Elizabeth was quite glad to have this interruption, for it gave her an opportunity to gather her thoughts.

"Let me ask you, Mr. Bennett. Is there any way to secure a woman's property for herself, once she is married? To keep her property for her own use, and independent of her husband?"

"No," Mr. Bennett said, with his head inclined. "Not really. There is the possibility of trusteeship, in which your property would be vested in a man other than your husband—but even that would not stand up in every court." There was a large volume on the table and he put one hand on it now. "Black-stone is quite clear on that matter."

Elizabeth nodded. "That is as I feared." She began to pace the room, her skirts swirling as she turned and then turned again.

"Very well, then," she said, stopping in front of the table. "Once the deed of gift is signed, the property is mine until I marry. Is that correct? Then it transfers to my husband?"

"That is correct."

"Could my father . . . change his mind? Ask the court to return the property to him?"

"Not unless there has been deception of some kind," said Mr. Bennett.

"Could you be more specific?"

Mr. Bennett settled back into his chair, and with his fingers tented under his chin, he summarized for Elizabeth the conditions under which a father might petition for the nullification of a deed of gift. "But," he concluded, "I have never heard of such a petition actually coming before the court in this part of the country. It would certainly be a scandal of the highest order."

"Between the time the deed is signed, and I marry, can I dispose of the property as I please?"

"Only with court approval," said Mr. Bennett. He picked up a small paperweight from his table and rolled it between his palms thoughtfully.

With her back to him as she looked out into the road, Elizabeth said: "I did not have the opportunity to read the deed closely. Is there any stipulation as to the identity of my husband?"

There was a small pause.

"There is no mention of marriage at all in the deed," Mr. Bennett said finally. "Any promises you make to your father—or to anyone else—are different contractual arrangements altogether, and have nothing to do with the deed. As long as it is signed and witnessed in my presence, it is valid. No matter whom you marry."

Elizabeth turned to find Mr. Bennett watching her very closely. "You are very perceptive," she said with a small smile.

"You mustn't give me credit for too much," Mr. Bennett said. "It is only that I am more familiar with Richard Todd's childhood than you might be. You haven't heard about his youth?"

Elizabeth wondered if she should allow Mr. Bennett to tell her this story.

"You have scruples, I see, about hearing this history. But I think you should hear it, as it may have a material effect on your own actions."

Mr. Bennett waited. When Elizabeth finally nodded, he sat forward in his chair with his hands flat on the table in front of him.

"The Mohawk kidnapped Richard along with his mother and brother during the border wars. He was about three at the time. The march north took them over Hidden Wolf."

The sunlight lay in great flat sheets across the table and illuminated Mr. Bennett's hands, the long fingers stained with ink, the pale nails glowing pink. Elizabeth found it hard to take her eyes off his hands.

"His mother was with child, she couldn't keep up the march. She died on the mountain. Richard was taken north to Canada. His uncle, Amos Foster, bought him out of captivity when he was eleven."

"I see," Elizabeth said hoarsely.

"So you understand his connection to Hidden Wolf is quite —personal in nature. He has been trying to buy it from the judge for years. I expect he will go to some lengths to secure his interests. He is tenacious, to say the least."

Mr. Bennett stood up with a little bow. "It is time we started home for dinner," he said briskly. "If I have answered all your questions?"

"Yes," Elizabeth said with an absent smile. "Thank you so much for your help."

"I'll get your things," he said, starting toward the door.

"Mr. Bennett?" Elizabeth asked, so that he paused with his hand on the knob.

"What happened to Richard's brother?"

"The uncle tried to ransom him, but he wouldn't leave. He stayed with the Mohawk and became a warrior."

"Is he still in Canada?" asked Elizabeth.

"No," Mr. Bennett said grimly. "He died in battle. Fighting for the English."

Elizabeth had been hoping for a quiet supper at the Bennetts', but she got both more and less than she expected. Just after dinner, a servant arrived from the Dubonnets' with an invitation to an evening party in honor of the visiting governor and his wife. Mrs. Bennett and Katherine were so very excited about this invitation that Elizabeth's own calmer reaction went unnoticed, until she asked Mrs. Bennett to decline her share of the privilege.

"I am very tired," Elizabeth excused herself. "I hope Mr. and Mrs. Dubonnet will understand."

"Lizzie doesn't care for such affairs," Julian pointed out needlessly. "She probably picked up some new book this afternoon and can't wait to get to it."

Mr. Bennett sighed. "A new book in front of the hearth sounds to me a much finer evening than listening to Ellen Clinton play the piano."

"Hush, John." Mrs. Bennett swatted at her husband impatiently, but grinned nonetheless. "What a thing to say." She turned her gaze to Elizabeth. "If it is a book, Elizabeth, won't it wait? You may never have another opportunity to meet Mrs. Clinton."

When Elizabeth had assured Mrs. Bennett that she preferred to stay home, Katherine spoke up. "It's our last evening," she said. "But if you really don't want to go out—"

"You are most welcome to borrow my cape," Elizabeth said with a smile.

She was served a late supper of soup and cold meat, which suited her perfectly; Elizabeth did have a new book—two, in fact—and many things to think about, but as she was finishing her meal the maid came to announce a visitor.

"Did you tell them that the Bennetts are out this evening?"

Elizabeth asked, trying hard to hide her irritation with this delay of her plans.

"Yes, miss, but the gentleman is asking for you."

"I see." Elizabeth touched a hand to her hair, began to rise, and then sat again abruptly, fighting with a sudden and quite explicable case of the jitters. Who could this possibly be but Nathaniel?

The maid was watching her closely. "Shall I just send him away, miss?"

"Oh, well. No, I think I shall just speak with him briefly—"

"You don't even know who it is, miss," the maid pointed out.

Startled, Elizabeth looked up. "Did you get a name?"

"We always ask for a name." There was a pause as the woman struggled to hide her peevishness. "This may not be England, miss, but we know how to answer a door."

"Of course you do," Elizabeth murmured, wishing very much that she did not have this disgruntled servant to deal with right at this moment.

"Since you don't ask, miss, then I'll just tell you. It's Dr. Richard Todd come to call."

The parlor was well lit, with braces of candelabra on the tables, so that as he paced, Richard threw his long shadow about the room. "I had some business to attend to in town," he told her. "And I thought I would pay the Bennetts my respects." He strode up and down Mrs. Bennett's good Turkey carpet with his hands crossed behind his back and his head bent forward as if his life depended on counting every cabbage rose he stepped on.

"I'm sure they will be sorry to have missed you," Elizabeth said.

"Hmmm." Richard stopped suddenly before the hearth and turned to face Elizabeth. "I really came to see you, you realize."

When Elizabeth refused to ask him to clarify this statement, he looked puzzled, and then dropped unceremoniously into a chair. His broad frame made the carved walnut back seem very fragile by comparison. He leaned toward Elizabeth with his hands on his knees and his elbows turned outward. *You are very good-looking,* Elizabeth thought to herself. *And very, very sure of yourself.*

"Do you realize this is the first time I've had the opportunity to talk to you alone for weeks? You avoid me in Paradise. You've never even been to my home."

Elizabeth raised an eyebrow. "I would say that you exaggerate, Dr. Todd. I see a great deal of you at my father's home. And I know you are sensitive to the delicacy of a single woman visiting an eligible bachelor."

"It's a very nice house," Richard said. "The only brick one in Paradise."

"It appears very nice, yes," Elizabeth said. "Did you come to talk about your housekeeping arrangements?"

Without further preamble, Richard jumped up and began his pacing again. Apparently Richard Todd was a man who needed physical movement to think clearly. It was quite irritating, really, and if it weren't for the story Mr. Bennett had told her earlier in the day, Elizabeth might have been more forward and asked him what he could mean by such strange behavior. She watched him sweep past the tables with their piles of books and collections of shells, round the armchair nearest the hearth so that his coattails brushed the firescreen, make a hook around the pianoforte, and sweep back again in her direction. There was a run in one of his silk hose, and a splash of dirt on the other, but otherwise he was dressed impeccably, as always.

Elizabeth could see no sign of his early trauma in him: he was nothing more than an ordinary man preoccupied with a goal, and insensible of his surroundings.

"Well," he said. "As a matter of fact, it does have something to do with my housekeeping." He paused, drew in a deep breath, and then turned to face her.

"You are aware that I own some three thousand acres of land bordering on your father's holdings. I own houses in Boston, Albany, and Paradise. I studied at medicine as an assistant to Dr. Adams and Dr. Littlefield of Albany. Since I left them I have been practicing medicine on my own with some considerable success. I have substantial resources and can be of assistance to your father in his current difficulties. I am thirty years of age, and in excellent health. Let me see—" He seemed to consider for a moment, and then his face lit up. "Oh, yes, on the first day of the new year I gave both my slaves their freedom."

Elizabeth had been following this narrative with carefully hidden amusement, but the last statement did take her by surprise.

"I am very glad to hear that," she said. "I mean, about your slaves. As to the rest of it—"

"Please allow me to finish. It comes to my attention that you are the kind of lady who would be able to take up a life where I live—on the edge of the wilderness, as you are aware—and flourish, in spite of the fact that you're English. Since I am in need of a wife, and you are unmarried, and there are material advantages to this match, I offer you my hand with your father's permission and approval."

She had been somewhat prepared for this event, but still Elizabeth was so surprised by the simple forcefulness of his application that she took a moment to collect her thoughts. Richard stood with one arm on the mantel watching her closely.

"You sound like a man with a business proposition," she said finally, "rather than one who wishes to marry."

She thought for a moment that he would smile, but the seriousness of the situation won out. Richard inclined his head.

"When you first came to Paradise I did try to court you in a more traditional manner, but you made it quite clear that you didn't appreciate those efforts. Now I do you the honor of presenting you with the truth of the matter," he said. "You are not a frivolous person, and I didn't think you would want loud protestations which you must yourself observe to be less than truthful."

Elizabeth was feeling a little more sure of herself, and she settled back into her chair. It was very strange to be receiving a marriage proposal, even as unusual a one as this, and while she would not wish for it, it was an interesting experience. Richard had clearly been practicing these speeches for some time, as awkward and silly as they were.

"Are you saying that you do not care for me, but that you wish to marry me anyway?"

"No!" He jerked up both hands as if to stop her. "I am

saying that I respect your intelligence and that I thought you would appreciate an offer uncluttered with—with—"

"Emotion?"

A look of discomfort passed over his face, and then he nodded.

"Let me see if I understand you correctly," Elizabeth said. "You want to marry me because you think we shall both profit from such a marriage. You have considerable wealth and lands to offer me, a life of leisure. Would you agree to my teaching school, as your wife?"

He shrugged. "If you find it necessary to your happiness," he said, as if she had asked for permission to paint screens or study music.

"Exactly in what way would you benefit?" She expected protestations of loneliness, the want of children, or the social demands of a person of his resources, but Richard was capable of surprising her.

"I need a wife."

"But there are other, younger women you have known longer," Elizabeth pointed out. "Why does the urge to marry take you so suddenly? Especially as you don't seem to harbor any tender feelings . . ." She paused. "For me."

The formal posture Richard had adopted on coming into the room suddenly loosened, and he sat down on the edge of a chair, with his hands on his knees.

"I like you fine, Elizabeth," he said, sounding himself for the first time.

Because she could see that this was in fact true, that he did like her a little even if he did not love her, Elizabeth felt some small softening toward him.

"Come now, Richard," she responded with a small smile. It was the first time she used his name, and it came to her with some difficulty. "You began by saying that you thought honesty was the best way to proceed."

"I thought it was best to discuss your marriage portion with your father directly," he said, a muscle fluttering in his cheek.

"Why don't you just tell me what transaction is at the bottom of your wish to marry me," Elizabeth said. "I will find out from my father if you don't tell me, you realize."

Richard jumped up again and went over to a curio cabinet, where he began to fiddle with a china shepherdess followed by lambs of decreasing size.

"Your father is years in arrears on his taxes," Richard said with his back to Elizabeth.

Elizabeth drew in an audible breath. She had not anticipated this particular complication. That her father was so much in debt, that he could not pay his land tax. She had been controlling her temper, but now the first flush of anger spread through her. She watched Richard nudging the lambs into a line while the meaning of this raced through her head.

"If I don't wish to marry," said Elizabeth finally, "I am sure my father will find another way to manage to pay his debt. There is always the possibility of mortgage."

Richard's look had something of pity in it, and that made Elizabeth draw up.

"I don't think there's much chance of a mortgage," he said. "Not with the taxes in arrears."

"But he could sell land, if need be." Elizabeth met Richard's gaze directly. "I believe you—and others—have made offers to him."

"He could have done that many times over, but he chose not to. You know that your father wants to keep the land in the family."

"And so you wish to become his son-in-law," Elizabeth said. "To circumvent his familial scruples. The land stays in the family if you marry me and resolve his debts."

He was not a coward; he did not look away. "That is the short of it," he said. "But there is material advantage for you in it as well."

"Let me ask you, then," said Elizabeth. "What happens if I refuse to marry you?"

Richard shrugged. "I expect that in the end he will sell me the land anyway," he said. "He has no choice. It would be hard for him to borrow the cash he needs, given his investment difficulties."

"Hidden Wolf seems to mean a lot to you," Elizabeth said lightly.

He didn't flinch, but he turned back to the mantelpiece. "Yes," he said. "It means very much to me."

She waited, but Richard was silent. Finally, Elizabeth dared to ask.

"And what would you do with Hidden Wolf once you had it?"

The shepherdess was in his hands, her china skirt an impossible powder pink against his palm. He ran his thumb over the frills, and then looked up suddenly. "I would make it mine," he said with an empty smile. "Mine alone."

"I see." Elizabeth nodded. *If ever in your life you managed to keep your feelings in check,* she thought to herself, *then you must do so now.* Resolutely, she put aside what she knew of Richard's past. She could no more mention the way his mother had died on Hidden Wolf than she could have asked Richard if he had been the one to rob the Bonners, or shoot at Nathaniel. But she did not like the blankness in his face when he spoke of Hidden Wolf.

"As would be your right," she said quietly.

Richard drew a deep breath. *He's relieved,* thought Elizabeth. She rose from her chair.

"Well," she began. "Let me wish you good evening."

"But—" He came toward her, stopped at a distance that made her uncomfortable. But she could not draw back. "My offer?"

"Thank you most kindly for your offer," Elizabeth said. "I'm sure you'll understand that I need to think about this carefully."

He inclined his head, and then, slowly, nodded. "Of course. When might I expect an answer?"

Elizabeth was thinking of her cousin Jane, who had had seven offers of marriage before she accepted one. *I should have paid more attention,* Elizabeth thought. Then she was struck with a fortunate idea.

"I would like to write to my aunt Merriweather," she said. "I shall do that tomorrow."

"Your aunt—in England?"

"Yes, of course," said Elizabeth. "I could never make a decision on a matter of such importance without consulting her."

Richard nodded, but his look was thoughtful. "As you wish it," he said finally.

"As she wishes what?" asked Julian from the hall. "What interesting conversation have we missed?"

Elizabeth and Richard turned toward Julian to find him leaning against the doorway, gently slapping his gloves against his leg.

Behind him stood Katherine, her eyes fixed first on Richard and then on Elizabeth, her face as pale as the snow that dusted her bonnet.

XV

Although she was surrounded by new purchases and wore a new hat, Katherine slumped in her corner of the sleigh as unhappy and dejected as she had been on the way to Johnstown. Elizabeth sat observing her, torn between compassion and irritation. That Katherine believed something important to have been arranged between Richard Todd and Elizabeth was obvious, but Elizabeth was loath to bring up the subject for discussion. *What terrible messes we get ourselves into when we are silly enough to fall in love,* she thought.

The sky rolled over them in alternating patches of blue and clouds, now casting sunlight, now spitting flurries. After only an hour on the road the team was pushing too hard, eager to be home, the smell of snow in their noses. Galileo sang to them to keep their gait steady, his soft, breathy tenor whirling away in the wind. It was a strange but compelling winter landscape: the road ran along a high ridge, frozen marshes stretching out into the winter mists, broken here and there by stands of crooked black ash and white cedar, dogwood and alders dangling clusters of red catkins. Great stretches of evergreen shrubs showed gray-blue against the snowy backdrop. Where standing water had frozen into whirlpools of ice, islands of bulrushes stabbed up, their stems twisted and gold-brown, shimmering with frost. Elizabeth wished for someone who could tell her about what she was seeing: what the grasses were called, if the berries that the birds were eating from the shrubbery were consumed by people as well, what the strange puppylike animal she spied next to the track was. A look in Katherine's direction made it clear that she was not to be engaged in such a conversation. Kitty's whole attention was fixated a quarter mile ahead of the sleigh, where Richard and Julian rode along beside each other.

"Kitty," Elizabeth tried, and was rewarded with a sullen look. "Please tell me why you are angry with me."

The younger woman never turned her gaze away from the men. "But I'm not angry with you in the least," she said tonelessly.

Irritated, Elizabeth was tempted to let Katherine stew in her jealousy, but then she recalled how the scene in Mrs. Bennett's parlor must have looked to her. *I might as well try honesty,* she thought, *for it could do no more harm.*

"Kitty," she began again. "Richard made me an offer of marriage yesterday evening."

A tremor ran over the other girl's face, followed by a quick flow of color, but she didn't speak.

"I didn't accept him," Elizabeth said. As irritating as Katherine could be, the urge to offer her some comfort was strong. She knew that it would be short-lived, if her plans came to fruition, but for the moment she wanted to help, if she could.

"Oh?" Katherine examined her mitt. "But I'm sure you will, the next time he asks."

"Why do you think that?" Elizabeth said. "I haven't shown him any encouragement."

Katherine's head turned toward Elizabeth in a slow, steady arc. Her blue eyes glittered, not with tears so much as anger and vexation.

"I suppose you are going to tell me that you *want* to remain a spinster," she said with a small, bitter smile. "Your father may believe that—your brother seems to. But I don't believe it for one moment."

Elizabeth's first urge was to protest that she did intend to stay single. That she had no intention or will to marry. The arguments for spinsterhood came to her easily; she had been perfecting them for almost ten years. But she could not tell Kitty what she was thinking; she was too young and too much involved to be trusted.

"I don't believe that Richard and I would suit at all," Elizabeth said gently.

Katherine gave a very unladylike snort. "Suit? You wouldn't *suit*? What does that have to do with it?"

"I hope it has something to do with it," Elizabeth responded. "If two people are to live together." She had the distinct impression that Katherine was hurt by Richard's offer to Elizabeth, and, nonsensically, affronted by Elizabeth's rejection of him.

"I don't see that you can be so fussy, it's not like you have other suitors at your door. I would think Dr. Richard Todd would be a fine enough husband for *you*."

She meant to hurt Elizabeth's feelings, that was clear, and in fact Elizabeth was amazed and a little dismayed to find that Kitty disliked her so very much. But more than that, she was relieved. *Thank God,* she thought. *Thank God, she really has no idea about Nathaniel.*

"You and my father are of one mind on this," Elizabeth said quietly. "I wish I were so sure. Tell me," Elizabeth said, leaning toward Katherine suddenly and grasping her hand. "If you love Richard, why are you showing so much interest in my brother?"

"Because Richard is very good at getting what he wants," Katherine said miserably, turning her face away, but allowing Elizabeth to hold her hand. "And Richard wants you."

"Surely we can spare an hour and still be home before sunset," Julian was saying.

Richard glanced at the sky and back toward the sleigh, and resettled himself in the saddle. "The temperature's dropping," he pointed out.

"Well, it won't bloody well matter to us, will it? We aren't the ones chasing a ball around on the ice barefoot. I'd like a chance to win back some of what I lost the day before yesterday."

The wind rose around them, riffling the grasses over the frozen marsh, but Julian seemed oblivious to the weather.

"It's a damn exciting game, this lacrosse," Julian added. "I don't wonder the Indians call it Little Brother of War—a full-fledged battle couldn't make men move as fast, I'd warrant. I bet Lizzie would like to see it."

Richard had been letting Julian ramble on, but now he laughed. "I can't imagine that."

"You don't know her very well, do you?" Julian said dryly. "Lizzie was the most awful tomboy. Drove the aunt distracted, pulling her out of trees and off horses. She was a better jumper than I ever was, until Merriweather found out and put a stop to it. And then she'd go off for walks and be gone for the day."

"Elizabeth? Your sister?" Richard shook his head. "I can't see it."

"Oh, yes, she's a great one for sport, at least she was until she started reading. Although I don't know what she'd make of the dancing."

Richard's face stilled. "You were at the longhouse for the dancing?"

"I spent the whole day. Don't look at me like that, old boy. Who wouldn't be drawn in, with all the drums and that singing, the men leaping around with those masks—makes your skin rise. I enjoyed it, all except the prayers. They do seem to drag on, Christian or heathen. Say . . ." He turned in the saddle toward Richard. "Is it true what they say about the women?"

Richard kept his gaze focused on the horizon. "What do they say?"

Julian grimaced. "As if you didn't know. They tell me old Sir Johnson had wives in every Mohawk camp. A generous people, if you get my meaning."

"That was years ago," Richard said dismissively. "Generosity wears thin if it's taken advantage of."

"Oh," said Julian. "Damn shame." Then he glanced back at the sleigh, and waved.

"Was there somebody in particular caught your eye?"

Julian shrugged. "Well, you've got to admit that Bonner's sister-in-law is a rare one. Never seen the like. Many-Doves, they call her. At the dancing—" Julian broke off, and cleared his throat.

Richard sent Julian a sideways glance. "I thought your interests were elsewhere."

"Kitty, you mean?" Julian asked, recovering his good humor with a grin. "I doubt much will come of that."

"And why not?" Richard asked, in an affronted tone.

"Oh, well, the same reason you gave up on her, I suppose— Don't look at me like that, it's common knowledge, after all. She's a nice enough girl, but there's no money, is there? And that father of hers—a bit of a bore, too, if the truth be told."

Richard squinted into the sky, over the horizon, and found everything more worthy of his gaze than Julian. "Take a care," he said gruffly. "She's tenderhearted." Without looking Julian's way, he asked quickly: "Has she said anything to you?"

"About you?" Julian shook his head. "Not a word, but she looks at you when she thinks nobody's paying heed. I expect she's giving Lizzie an earful. She's in a foul temper this morning, after catching the two of you last night."

"Nothing happened," Richard said, scowling.

"But not for lack of trying, eh?" Julian laughed again. "I wish you good luck, at any rate. You'll need it with Lizzie." He pulled up suddenly. "There it is. Barktown."

"I see it," Richard said shortly.

Julian raised himself in the saddle to get a better look at the small group of cabins huddled around a single bark longhouse in the distance. "That's all that's left of the great Mohawk nation."

"Those aren't just Kahnyen'kehàka," said Richard, his eyes moving over the throngs of people. "Every Iroquois in this part of the state comes to Barktown for Midwinter. They've got no longhouses of their own anymore. There couldn't be more than forty Mohawk here, most of the time."

"So why are these ones still here, then?"

"Because Sky-Wound-Round was the only one of the Kahnyen'kehàka sachems who sent his boys to fight with the colonials. Which is a shame," Richard said grimly. "Because if he had stayed allied with Brant and the Tories, he would have had to move his people north, and there wouldn't be a Mohawk left in New-York."

There was a flicker of surprise on Julian's face.

"Moses Southern tells me you lived with the Mohawk for years."

"So I did. What of it?" Richard's face had grown suddenly still.

"Well, then, you must know a damn sight more about lacrosse than I do. Your advice would be helpful when I lay my wager. Hold on," he said, ignoring Richard's protest while he turned his horse. "I'm going to talk to the girls about this."

Elizabeth bounced up and down on her toes and stretched to get a better view over the heads of the crowds lining the playing field. Lacrosse, Julian had called this game. It was like nothing she had ever seen before.

Fourteen men dressed in nothing more than breechclouts, barefooted, their hair dressed with feathers and their faces painted, pounded up and down over the frozen marsh, steam rising from their sweating bodies. They ran and collided and struggled and ran again, their sticks flailing wildly. Each of them had his entire attention focused on the net that held the ball. It might as well be July, Elizabeth thought, for all the attention they paid to the weather.

All around the playing field Indians stood in groups, their heads moving in tandem as they followed the game. They did not look to be enjoying it, exactly; Elizabeth thought they might watch a battle from a safe spot with the same intensity and focus. The only playfulness she could see came from the children, who dashed up and down the embankment following the game, brandishing smaller sticks of their own, shouting to each other, evading the grasping hands of mothers and aunts.

There were whites as well, standing well apart, talking among themselves and laughing. They seemed to be mostly hunters and woodsmen, much like the men of Paradise. One of them was staring at Julian, Elizabeth noted with some discomfort. He was a great barrel of a man, a trapper by his dress. She didn't wonder that they knew him here; it was obvious that he had spent an entire day earlier in the week. What trouble he had been brewing she could only guess at.

"My father would not approve," Kitty said for perhaps the fourth time. "I should not be here."

Julian took her elbow in one hand and Elizabeth's in the other. "I'll talk to your father, Kitty," he said, pulling them along, barely able to mask his excitement. "This way," he said. "Over here, you'll be able to see better."

Elizabeth followed her brother to a knoll, but kept her eyes fixed on the game. Now they were close enough to the field to smell the sweat as the players thundered past. With a little start she recognized Otter, his stick held across his body at an angle as he ran full-out for the goalpost. Wood clashed on wood as the others dodged and struck, trying to dislodge the ball from his net. He feinted left and then with a neat twist sent the ball flying toward the other side of the river, where another player leapt to scoop it out of the air with a flick of his stick.

"How do you know who plays together?" Katherine asked. The excitement of the game was having some effect on her, although she still scowled.

"You can't," Julian said. "They don't mark themselves as Wolf or Turtle. You'd have to ask one of the Indians." He was looking over the crowds as he spoke.

"Wait here," he said suddenly. "I'll be back in just a moment."

"Julian," Elizabeth said in a low voice.

"I'm just going to look for Richard," he mumbled as he stalked off.

"Don't be long," Katherine called after him, stepping in closer to Elizabeth.

"Remember your promise!" Elizabeth added, to which Julian waved a hand over his head without turning back. She realized that Julian's vow was long broken, and prayed that he wouldn't write scrips when his cash ran out. More uneasy than ever, she let her gaze wander once again through the crowds. There was no sign of Nathaniel anywhere; she could only hope that he would see her here on the knoll. She felt slightly dizzy with the tension of it all, and wished that they hadn't stopped.

"Do you know any of them?" Katherine asked with a sideways glance.

Glad of this distraction, Elizabeth turned her attention to the game. "There—that player, the very tall one who just passed the ball, that's Runs-from-Bears, from the Turtle clan."

The players had thrown themselves into a ferocious huddle in pursuit of a ground ball. With a grunt of satisfaction, one—a smaller man, but sleek and flexible—managed to get the ball into his net and lope off with the others close on his heels.

Elizabeth tried not to stare at the players, at their naked chests or the hard-muscled thighs which flashed from under the breechclouts as they ran. Mr. Witherspoon certainly would not approve; she imagined the long and tedious sermon he might preach, and hoped that Kitty would keep this outing to herself at home. But it was a very strange situation for two single women to be in; the specter of Aunt Merriweather's outraged face rose and was quickly put away.

There was a tugging at her arm, and she looked down.

"Hannah!"

Elizabeth was so pleased to see the little girl that she leaned down and hugged her, pressing a kiss on one cold cheek. Hannah smiled broadly at this greeting, and touched her fingers shyly to Elizabeth's face.

"Come," Hannah said, taking Elizabeth's gloved hand, and nodding at Kitty. "Come." She led them through a small group of old men who stood watching the game wrapped in blankets and fur robes, talking in low tones among themselves while they nursed long clay pipes. Their attention was fixed on the far end of the playing field, where the players were headed.

"Julian said to wait," Katherine protested, even as she followed along.

"Julian is paying us no mind at all," Elizabeth pointed out.

The village itself was a little collection of log cabins set in a frozen circle of fallow cornfields. At the center of all this stood a longhouse. It was about the length of four cabins, constructed entirely of bark lashed together with rope of braided roots. Tendrils of smoke rose from vents in the roof, but there were no windows. A door faced the east and the playing field, hung with a tremendous bearskin worn hairless and almost transparent at the edges. Above it a turtle had been drawn in red paint on the bark.

On a prominent spot between the lodge and the playing

field, just before the remains of a great fire, an old man sat on a blanket. In front of him was a great pile of goods: bundles of pelts, a very old flintlock musket, a collection of knives, an axe head without a handle, a bullet mold, a waistcoat of brocade, pieces of calico in various colors, a brace of rabbit, striped blankets, a lace shawl, glass and metal beads laid out carefully, a tied bundle of tobacco, a statue of the Virgin Mary, and a copper kettle. In a semicircle around the old man and his treasures, a group of women stood watching the game. Elizabeth was relieved to see Falling-Day and Many-Doves coming toward them.

"Please," Falling-Day said, her dark eyes bright with welcome. "You honor us by coming to watch baggataway on the last day of Midwinter. Please sit." She was gesturing to another blanket.

"We can only stay another few minutes," Katherine said to her, distantly. "We have to be going very soon."

Elizabeth took Katherine's arm, squeezed it hard.

"Thank you so much for your thoughtfulness," she said. "But we would really like to watch."

They joined the women, who nodded at them impassively with hooded eyes before they turned back to watch their sons and brothers and husbands.

The old man was certainly the most ancient human being Elizabeth had ever seen, older even than Chingachgook. One of his eyes was covered with a milky gray substance, and his long hair had thinned to a baby-fine white. But he watched the game with a keen interest and awareness that made it clear that he was not feeble.

"That is my great-grandfather," Hannah whispered to Elizabeth. "He is the clan elder here, he looks after the wagers."

"What is your great-grandfather's name?"

"Gau'yata'se," Many-Doves answered for Hannah, coming up beside Elizabeth. " 'Sky-Wound-Round.' And that is my uncle." She indicated another older man, who paced the edge of the river. "He is the keeper of the faith, called Bitter-Words."

Elizabeth watched as Bitter-Words raised a turtle's-shell rattle above his head to the rising cadence of his song. His whole body moved with the rhythm, and each step was accompanied by the music of shell necklaces and strings of animal teeth hanging from his neck and wound around his waist and knees. On his head was a complex headdress in the likeness of a fox.

There was a gasp from the crowd and Elizabeth turned to see the small, lean player darting from one end of the field to the other, leaving his pursuers behind to send the ball flying; it made contact with a large boulder with a satisfying smack. There was a rustling among the observers and a great deal of more animated discussion.

"Did he score?"

"Yes, the Turtle clan have made their sixth goal," said Hannah, with a small frown. "Now the Wolf and the Turtle are both within one point of a victory."

A woman broke out of the crowd with a terrible scowl on her face and stepped out onto the ice, waving her fists in the direction of the players and upbraiding them loudly.

"My cousin," Falling-Day explained to Elizabeth. "She is clan mother here. Her son plays for the Wolf, and she don't think much of his performance today."

"She asks Tall-As-Trees why he wears eagle feathers when he runs like a three-legged rabbit," translated Hannah cheerfully. "Maybe she will take a switch to him like she did last year."

Falling-Day cast a glance at her granddaughter, and Hannah bit her lip. She ducked her head, but her grin remained.

"It is a great honor to play for the clan in the Midwinter games," Falling-Day explained more to Hannah than to Elizabeth.

Elizabeth watched as the ball made a great arc over the heads of the players to be scooped out of the air once again.

"The Wolf have the ball," observed Many-Doves. "Maybe there will be a quick end to this."

"Let's hope so," muttered Katherine. She grasped Elizabeth's arm. "There's Richard," she said.

Elizabeth followed Katherine's line of vision until she caught sight of Richard. He was walking along the playing field on its other side, his head bent low in concentration as he listened to the young Indian who kept him company. The more animated the man became, the more slowly Richard shook his head.

"Do you know that man talking to Richard Todd?" Elizabeth asked Falling-Day.

The older woman inhaled, nodding. "Half-Crow. Of the Caghnawaga Turtle clan, in Canada." In a low singsong voice, Falling-Day began to recite Half-Crow's family history and genealogy. Listening to Hannah recently, Elizabeth had come to realize that to ask any Kahnyen'kehàka about another Kahnyen'kehàka was to ask for a detailed history of his clan; she would have found this interesting, under other circumstances, but right now she was hardly able to concentrate. One of the players had caught her attention.

He was running down the marsh full-out toward the goal, his hair flying behind him, the muscles flowing on his back. His long, powerful torso twisted gracefully as he swung the stick in an arc to snatch the ball from the air, revealing a barely healed wound which showed raw red on his right shoulder. She drew in a breath as he followed the swing through and turned full circle, revealing his face. It was painted in red and black, in a slashing geometric pattern that accented the strong nose and high brow.

"Nathaniel," Elizabeth breathed.

Falling-Day broke off her narrative. At that moment, Nathaniel let the ball fly and it hit the boulder that served as a goal with a small thud. The spectators rose up with one voice, all restraint suddenly abandoned.

"You'd never know that he's white," Elizabeth said softly.

"Sometimes it's hard to tell," Falling-Day agreed. "That's why we call him Deseroken. 'Between-Two-Lives.' "

With great satisfaction, Julian collected his winnings from a blank-faced and quite pungent trapper known only as Dutch Ton. He pocketed the coins and bills with a small smile, and then turned his gaze over the crowds.

The players were being led away by the elders to a ceremonial washing at a hole chopped in the ice; later there would be prayers and long rites where the men would dance. The social dancing, when the women would get a chance, wouldn't start until the evening. Julian knew that there wasn't time to wait. His sister would want to be on her way, and he was bound to accompany her. Already Galileo was pacing a worn path around the team, eager to get on the road. Julian thought of sending the women ahead with Richard in attendance. Richard was too bloody pigheaded to be good company anyway. He hadn't wanted to watch the game, didn't want to be anywhere near the Indian village. Although he had taken one look at the game in progress and told Julian to lay his coin on the Wolf clan, and he had been right.

Julian walked along, looking for his sister and contemplating the great satisfaction of a wager well placed. With a sigh, he acknowledged the necessity of moving on; Elizabeth was suspicious already, and it wouldn't be politic to have the judge find out about the wagering, regardless of the outcome. As put out as Richard was with him, Julian knew he couldn't necessarily count on his silence, either. The sad truth was, no one had any faith in his ability to keep things within bounds.

About fifty yards from the longhouse Julian stopped on a rise, so that the whole scene was spread out in front of him. He watched as a crowd gathered around the old sachem who was distributing the spoils to the winners. The players were returning, dripping ice water and sweat, dragging a whole troop of children along behind them, hollering and dodging in and out, fighting over the honor of carrying the men's lacrosse sticks. The old man who had run most of the prayer business was chanting, shaking a rattle over his head.

There was Elizabeth, observing with that crease between her eyes that meant she would remember every detail. How his sister could manufacture enthusiasm for the most bizarre events was ever a mystery to him. He supposed she would stay for the ritual storytelling and dreamtelling and never have to suppress a yawn, in spite of the fact that she wouldn't understand a word.

Julian called across the playing field and Elizabeth turned toward the sound of his voice, and along with her, Many-Doves.

It shouldn't have come as a surprise anymore, but Julian was struck almost dumb by the sight of her. Many-Doves—a ridiculous name, but it suited her. He couldn't think of her as Abigail; Abigail was a name for a girl like his sister, proper and boring and without a clue about men. No, Many-Doves reminded him of the madonnas the Italians painted over and over again: dark and light at the same time, silent, but with eyes that looked right into a man and wouldn't let him go. As if she knew everything there was to know about him without a lot of questions and discussion. It was no wonder so many white men went native, he thought. Another luxury he couldn't afford.

Many-Doves stood focused on the approaching players and Julian watched as her expression suddenly lost its usual remoteness. He noted with some regret that her look was for the player walking toward her, the big pockmarked buck who had dominated the game. Even from fifty yards Julian could see that he was covered with gooseflesh, and still breathing hard. Many-Doves stood waiting for him like a queen for a knight who had just championed her.

She didn't step toward him or even smile, but it was there on her face, her eyes fixed on his. Many-Doves lifted her arms, sending a red-striped blanket into a billowing arc over his head to settle it on his shoulders. She stepped up close to draw it across his chest.

Once or twice Julian had had women look at him that way, the way women look at men when they imagine themselves in love. The way Elizabeth was looking at the next man.

Julian watched astounded as Nathaniel Bonner, half-naked and painted like a savage, came to a halt in front of his sister. Elizabeth stepped forward with a blanket and she raised her face up, showing herself to be more like Many-Doves than Julian would have ever imagined. His tight-hearted, self-sufficient, don't-come-near-me sister. Looking at Nathaniel Bonner with her eyes like torches in the night.

"Where the hell have you been hiding yourself?"

Startled, Julian turned to find Richard with Kitty trailing behind. "We won't be home before dark at this rate," Richard said.

"Do let's be off," Kitty said, in a less angry tone, glancing uneasily between Richard and Julian.

Julian turned the two of them away from the longhouse and toward the sleigh.

"Go on, tell Galileo we're on our way directly," he said, pushing them off. "I'll get Elizabeth and follow you."

Kitty hesitated, but Richard was walking off already with great impatient strides.

"Go on, Kitty my dear," said Julian with a smile. "We'll be right there."

XVI

When the parlor clock struck midnight, Elizabeth rose. What she was thinking was madness, and yet she imagined doing it so clearly that it felt inevitable. It would take her an hour, now that she knew the way. She could find Hidden Wolf: the skies were clear, the moon near full. It didn't matter that she had been up since sunrise, or spent ten hours on the road. She could be back before the moon set. Who would know?

With her dress half buttoned and one stocking on, Elizabeth lay down again and buried her face in the pillow. She was so vexed and irritated that she could easily cry, or shout, or throw something.

When Elizabeth had last seen Nathaniel this morning, he had been shivering with exertion and cold, his face bloodied under the paint. But he had smiled when she put the blanket around his shoulders, an ecstatic, ravenous smile, a smile that steadied her in her resolution.

I'll come to you, he had whispered while Julian stood waiting impatiently, watching. *I'll come as soon as I can.*

He might not even be back from Barktown; perhaps he wouldn't be back for days.

Elizabeth found the candle on her bedside table and went to the hearth. She crouched before the banked fire and held the wick to the pulsing scarlet embers until it caught, a single small flame. Then she sat there on the cold floor with her arms around her knees and stared as it began to consume the mixture of tallow and bayberry.

Tomorrow she would go to the cabin. She would go alone, to see to the last preparations for school. In two days she would teach her first class. All those children, in her care. She recited their names to herself, in a rush: Ian and Rudy McGarrity, Liam Kirby, Peter Dubonnet, Praise-Be Cunningham, Ephraim Hauptmann, Obadiah and Elijah Cameron. And the girls: Dolly Smythe, Marie Dubonnet, Hepzibah and Ruth Glove, Henrietta Hauptmann, and Hannah Bonner.

He would find her there; of course he would.

I must sleep now, Elizabeth thought. Tomorrow, when I'm rested, tomorrow I'll see Nathaniel. Sleep's the thing, she told herself firmly.

She put the candlestick on the mantelpiece and went to her window. The moonlight lay like a quilt of blues and pearl-grays over the woods and the hills, painting the village in stark lines. Hidden Wolf rose like a protective specter, silent but benevolent and watchful. Elizabeth followed the path with her eyes as far as she could, and then imagined it where it disappeared into the woods. Lake in the Clouds, in shadow.

Something moved on the path, just a speck at first. She blinked, thinking she had imagined it, but it was steady, as steady as a candle flame, growing larger. It disappeared into shadow and then emerged again. Elizabeth stood utterly silent, her fingers cramping on the windowsill as the speck grew into the indistinct shape of a man. Another five minutes and the moonlight lay like a cloak on his bare head and shoulders; a tall man, moving fast, silent as the woods. Nathaniel.

She held her breath as he approached the house, her heart beating loud enough to wake everyone. Loud enough to wake the dead. Nathaniel stood below her window, his face cast half in shadow, the moon picking out one cheekbone, one half of his mouth, one eye.

He raised a hand; she raised hers, held up one finger. He nodded, and disappeared into the dark.

• • •

Silently, Elizabeth closed the door of the sleeping house behind her and pulled her shawl tight. She started at the long shape of her own moon shadow, flat and stark. There was no sign of Nathaniel. She thought for a moment that she had imagined him, dreamt the whole thing.

She had almost walked past him when he reached out and caught her wrist, pulled her up against the wall of the house. They stood there, shoulder to shoulder, Elizabeth trying hard to calm her breathing, the candle flame shaking with the beating of her heart. She followed him to the barn where he stopped to look at her, his face all angles in the moonlight.

Wait, he whispered. She stood shivering, her hair breaking in waves around her shoulders like a wild sea.

He came back, gestured her forward.

The horses shifted uneasily in their stalls. Elizabeth stood opposite the oxen and felt their dull eyes on her, blinking, blinking, their great bulk radiating pungent warmth. Nathaniel's hand pressing her wrist told her to be quiet. They stood like that for minutes, until the animals grew tired of them and turned inward once again.

The candlelight jumped on the rough board walls, a small circle, as valuable as gold in this darkness. Nathaniel took the candlestick out of her hand, his fingertips touching her wrist, sliding over the beating of her pulse. Elizabeth let it go with an indrawn breath.

When he had found a secure spot for the candle on the tack shelf above their heads, he sat next to her on a narrow bench. He bore the scars of the game: a crust of blood over an eyebrow, a bruise on his cheekbone. His hair was tangled, his cheeks stained dark with a growing beard. She held on tight to her own hands, which wanted to raise themselves and touch him, make sure that he was real, that this was real.

"Talk to me."

Elizabeth told him. She told him about Richard's proposal, about the corner her father had put himself in, about Richard's plan for Hidden Wolf. She told him about her discussion with Mr. Bennett, most of it word for word. She talked and talked in a low voice, feeling his eyes on her the whole time, but unable to meet his gaze.

"And there's this." From the pocket of her dress she drew forth a folded piece of newspaper and put it in Nathaniel's lap. She watched the candlelight on his face while he read.

WANTED. Any word on the whereabouts of the old Indian Sachem Chingachgook, known also as Great-Snake or Indian John. To settle a debt.

   Jack Lingo. Leave a message at the Trading Post, Stumptown.

He rubbed the stubble on his jaw thoughtfully.

"Who's Jack Lingo, and what does he want from your grandfather?" Elizabeth asked.

"He's an old *voyageur*," said Nathaniel. "He wanders the bush causing trouble and looking for the Tory Gold." He raised one brow. "Is that what you want to talk about?"

She swallowed hard.

"No. I think we should talk about Richard."

"What about him?"

Elizabeth looked Nathaniel straight in the eye. "I wish you had told me. About Richard's mother."

He looked at her, surprised. "Would it have changed something?"

Elizabeth wound her fingers in her shawl. "No. But it makes him easier to predict. And to understand, with his mother buried on Hidden Wolf."

"My mother is buried there, too."

"I didn't mean he had a better claim. Just that it makes me see him a little more clearly."

Nathaniel's watchfulness eased a bit. "It's not just his ma that draws him to Hidden Wolf, you know. It's more complicated than that. It has to do with Sarah."

"I don't know if I want to hear this right now," Elizabeth said, dropping her gaze. Sarah was one subject she had not anticipated in this discussion, one subject she had been pushing away from herself firmly for days.

"Never underestimate the force of a blow to a man's pride," Nathaniel said. "Or what he might do to see it set right. Richard wanted Sarah, once upon a time. And now he wants you."

"Well, I'm very sorry for his early trouble and loss," Elizabeth said. "But I can't marry him to salvage his pride, and I won't marry him and watch him turn you off Hidden Wolf. And he won't buy it, either, not if I have my way."

Finally, a grin. "I'm right glad to hear that," Nathaniel said. "But what did you have in mind?"

"I could just pay my father's debts, but it would mean all of my savings," Elizabeth said. "And in a few years' time he'd most likely be living beyond his income again, or making bad investments—"

"And there'd be no more funds to bail him out," Nathaniel finished.

She nodded.

"So."

Elizabeth glanced around. The candlelight cast a meager oval; it painted Nathaniel's face in quiet tones, softening the strong lines of his face. He was looking at her with infinite patience, and something more, something she had been hoping for. She drew in a deep breath.

"I will let Richard court me," Elizabeth said slowly. "Until my father is sure enough of me to sign the deed of gift. That will have to be done in Johnstown, before Mr. Bennett, as magistrate. And then—" She swallowed hard.

"And then?"

It took every bit of courage in her, but she met his gaze. "We could marry. You and I—" She pushed on, stumbling, her voice cracking. "Immediately. At that moment all property I own becomes yours. And that would include Hidden Wolf, of course."

His face was utterly blank.

"You want to stay single," Nathaniel said evenly, his face masked. "You've told me that any number of times."

"Your memory does me no good service." Elizabeth tried to strike a lighter tone, but she was unable to control the trembling of her voice, or even to meet his gaze directly.

Nathaniel was watching her closely, something on his face she couldn't quite place. Fear? Anger?

"I don't want your charity."

"This is not charity!"

"What would you call it, then? You want me to marry you so you can give me your property. What did you intend to do about the taxes?"

Elizabeth blinked. "Pay them."

"Aye," said Nathaniel hoarsely. "You intended to pay them. There's a word for what you're asking me to be, but it ain't exactly polite."

Shocked, Elizabeth drew her hand away. "I was thinking of you—"

"Goddamn it, woman," Nathaniel hissed. "It's not your pity I want."

"No," Elizabeth said, lifting her chin to meet his gaze, her own eyes blazing. "You want justice. And you said—you said that you wanted me, too. But perhaps that was just talk."

He jumped up, towering over her; she stood to meet him, her fists balled at her side.

"And what about you? What about what *you* want?" He was full angry now, his hands on her shoulders, hard, pressing.

Elizabeth felt her heart melting like the candlewax, felt it running down to her feet. She pushed his hands away.

"If you weren't such an idiot, perhaps you'd see what I'm trying to tell you!" she spat out. "This is for me, too. Do you think I'm fool enough to throw everything away, to hand over everything I own"—she swallowed, hard—"for no reason? I *had* come to the conclusion that I'd be better off as your wife than my father's daughter—but now I wonder."

She stood breathing harshly, her chin jutting up toward him, watching him with eyes that dared him to doubt her. He stared back.

"You realize what we'd have to do? Marry on the run and disappear long enough that he can't petition to have the marriage annulled, or the deed?"

"Yes." Elizabeth nodded. "Yes, yes. I thought of that."

He drew back and looked at her hard as if she were some new creature he had never seen before. His temple was beaded with sweat in spite of the cold.

"Do you want to be my true wife," he said, "or is this a marriage on paper you're proposing, a lie?"

"Oh, Nathaniel," Elizabeth said, suddenly miserable.

"That's not what I had in mind, no. But if you don't want me you'll have to say so and perhaps there's some other way to stop Richard."

He moved toward her, and then he hesitated.

"Forgive me for my bluntness," he said hoarsely. "But I'm asking you now to tell me what it is you want, in no uncertain terms."

"I want you," whispered Elizabeth, blinking hard. "I want you. And if there's some way to set things right with you and yours in the process, then that's all the better."

Nathaniel took her hands and drew her down to the bale of straw. Elizabeth felt his whole frame trembling.

"I told you," he said softly, his mouth against her hair. "I told you once that you only had to ask. I just wasn't sure what you were asking."

"I was afraid, too. You never said what it was exactly you wanted from me. You still haven't said it."

His fingers moved on her temple. "You want the words. I guess that's fair, seeing as how I made you speak up."

"It would be a help," Elizabeth admitted. "It's hard to propose marriage without any assistance at all. At this moment I can almost feel sorry for Richard."

Nathaniel laughed softly at that, and tilted her head up so he could look her in the eye.

"It's what you want. You're sure?"

She nodded.

"Well, then." The muscles in his throat flexed as he swallowed. "I ain't got much to offer except Lake in the Clouds, maybe not even that—"

"And Hannah," Elizabeth supplied.

"And Hannah. And a life you weren't born to, and a lot of trouble to start with—"

"And your father," she interrupted again.

"And my father. Elizabeth." He took both her hands, turned the palms up to kiss them and then pressed them to his chest. She could feel his heart beating, a slow, rolling thunder.

"None of that matters, if you don't want me the way I want you. If you come to me—" He looked away for a second, into the shadows, and then back at her. "You have to know what you're getting."

"I can see what I'm getting," Elizabeth said.

"Can you? You think you can see to my soul, do you? You don't know what kind of husband I was to Sarah. You don't like it when I talk about her, I can see that. But I think you'll have to hear about it sometime."

"What kind of husband were you to Sarah?" she asked woodenly.

"Not a very good one." His mouth was a thin line, his brows drawn together. "We married for the wrong reason."

She waited, uneasily.

He looked over her head into the dark. "I been thinking about it a lot lately. I guess I married her because I wanted to be red and she married me because she wanted to be white. So neither of us got what we wanted."

"She gave you Hannah."

He nodded. "You're right," he said. "Hannah made it worth the trouble. But there was trouble, no mistake, Elizabeth. We married too young."

"I'm not so young," Elizabeth said. "And neither are you, anymore."

"Will you listen," he said. "I'm trying to tell you—"

"What a terrible man you are, how you beat women and bully children, and throw all your money away on gaming and drink—"

"I've killed some men in my time, not counting the ones in battle," Nathaniel interrupted her.

"Well, then, there must have been sufficient reason," Elizabeth said, a bit paler.

They stared at each other for a moment.

"Will you try to stop me teaching school?"

"Of course not."

"Will you tell me how to run things? Will you listen, when I have something to say, and act on it? You have so far. I think," she said, her voice trembling, "that you'd be a good husband. Better than most, when you're not being contrary."

"Maybe you just want to get away from the judge."

"Of course I do. But—" She felt a nerve in her cheek fluttering. "But I wouldn't marry Richard Todd to get away from him, or any of the men I met in New-York—"

Nathaniel put a thumb on her chin, fanning his fingers over her cheek. "I think you're saying that you're fond of me," he said with a half smile. "And that you're willing to chance the rest because of it."

She inclined her head into his palm. "In the past week, I have been thinking that perhaps there is such a thing as friendship and equal partnership between a man and a woman. Where there is respect and—affection."

Nathaniel touched his forehead to hers, but she kept her gaze cast down.

"So," Elizabeth said lightly. "Why is it you're willing to . . . go along with this?"

"Well, I thought that would be obvious enough," Nathaniel said. "But since I promised you the words, I'll tell you. I want you with me. I want you there to talk to, and to argue with, when nothing else will do. I'm sure there'll be enough of that."

Elizabeth drew in a sigh and let it go, turning her head so that her face was hidden against his neck, her mouth close to the pulse at the base of his throat.

"I want to watch you with Hannah, see what you've got to teach her. To take you into the wilderness in the spring and show you where the flag lilies grow. When it's hot, to sleep with you under the waterfall. To kiss you whenever I please. To take you to bed, and have you there with me whenever I reach out for you." His voice was soft and low against her ear. "To get you with child, and watch it change the shape of you as it grows."

Elizabeth lifted her face up to him until her mouth waited just under his.

"That's why I want you," he said. "If you'll have me."

"Yes," she whispered. Elizabeth put her arms around his neck, and turned her mind to kissing Nathaniel.

His hands were on her back, moving in circles. He kissed the corner of her mouth, took her lower lip between her teeth and worried it gently. Touched her upper lip with his tongue and then claimed her, his arms surrounding her, one hand cradling her head.

She let her eyelids flutter closed as the angle of his head deepened. At first there were many sensations: the feel of a chest as hard as oak through layers of buckskin and fur and cloth, the exquisite rough pleasure of a day's growth of beard, the taste of him, slightly salty, and still sweet. Slowly, her whole consciousness became centered there where their mouths joined: the soft but persistent pressure of his lips, the way his head dipped and coaxed hers. He had been gentle and tentative and now there was more, a direction and growing intensity in this kiss, in the way his hands held her head so that he could take her mouth in deepening and hypnotic waves.

His tongue touched hers and she started, and drew away. She looked at him with eyes slightly out of focus, and then leaned forward to put her forehead against his shoulder.

"It's late," Nathaniel said hoarsely.

"Yes," Elizabeth agreed. "It is late."

"And you're tired."

"Oh, yes. You must be, too. It was exciting, watching you on the ice."

"So," Nathaniel said, pulling her closer.

"So," Elizabeth echoed, faintly.

"I want you," he said. "I want to be with you."

Elizabeth forced herself to meet his eye, knowing how deeply she blushed, knowing somehow that it would please him to see that.

"I would like that, too," she said, her voice wobbling. "I think."

"Good. Good. But"—he looked around himself—"not now, not here."

She nodded. "All right."

"It's getting late," he said again. "And there's a lot we need to talk about. This will take some planning, if we've got to elope. It can't be before mid-April, at any rate."

Elizabeth's heart fell, to think of that: two months.

Nathaniel took her hand, rubbed the palm with his own. "Well, now, Boots," he said, his old teasing tone back. "It does me no end of good to see that you're impatient about it. But we can't be on the run in the thaw. The whole world turns to water and mud and we couldn't get anywhere, not having to go north into the bush. And that's what we'll have to do if we don't want to be caught. Anyway," he said, grinning down at her. "I want to have the schoolhouse done first. Settle my business with the judge, so to speak, before I run off with his daughter. And it gives you two months to get the school started. Which is why you came to Paradise, after all."

Elizabeth drew in a shaky breath. "I don't know if I can pretend for that long," she said. "To be interested in Richard, I mean." She looked up at Nathaniel. "What if I can't do it? What if my father—"

"Don't mistake me, Elizabeth," Nathaniel said, his eyes narrowing. "I'll marry you one way or the other, and God help any man who tries to stop me. But I want to take you home to Hidden Wolf. If there was some other way to do it, I would. But I can't see one. Can you?"

She shook her head. "I wish," she said. "I wish with all my heart that my father would see reason and right and just sell you the land. I don't like starting out like this, with artifice. It makes me afraid."

Nathaniel began to speak, but she put a finger on his mouth to still him.

"There is no other way, I know. So." Elizabeth smiled ruefully. "I will play the game and hope that I can do you—us—some good in the process. But if I can't—" She looked up at him. "I would go with you into the wilderness, you know."

"Maybe you shouldn't be so hasty," Nathaniel said. "You haven't been introduced to the blackfly yet. But between now and then I'll have to keep a wide berth of you. Can you ignore me, do you think, when we do cross paths?"

She smiled. "I'll try to think of Hamlet, and be 'cruel but not unnatural: I will speak daggers to you, but use none.'"

"You are the most quoting woman," Nathaniel said softly, raising his hand to smooth her hair out of her face. "And will you speak love or daggers to Richard Todd?"

"I am supposed to keep him waiting and hopeful," she said. "I don't think daggers would do the job."

"What about kissing? Is that part of the job?" Nathaniel was smiling, but there was something wolfish about it that made Elizabeth wriggle.

"Well, I don't relish the idea, but I suppose it might be necessary at some point."

"No," he said suddenly, pulling her close again, pressing her mouth with his own, hard. "No. Young ladies of good family don't let themselves be kissed, if I may remind you."

Elizabeth felt a completely idiotic grin overtake her; she couldn't help it. Despite the seriousness of the situation, despite everything there was to gain and to lose, she had to smile. Nathaniel wanted her, all of her.

"What a memory you have, Mr. Bonner."

"When Richard gets too close you remember that your kisses are mine, by rights." And he bent to her mouth. When he lifted his head she was breathing hard.

"Two months is a long time," Elizabeth whispered, reaching up for him again.

"You can send word to me through Many-Doves," he said, between kisses.

"Many-Doves, yes," Elizabeth murmured back to him.

"But don't say anything to Hannah yet, she might let it slip."

"No, of course not," she mumbled against his mouth.

"Elizabeth," he said firmly, holding her away. "Early April, I'll be waiting for word. I'll meet you then, before you go to Johnstown with your father, and we'll settle the details."

She sat back, wiping her hair away from her face.

"Until then, you have to hold me far from you," Nathaniel said. "For all our sakes."

XVII

Anna Hauptmann looked up from a bolt of huckaback as the door to the trading post opened, letting in a blast of late March wind and Elizabeth Middleton. The preoccupied look on Anna's face was replaced suddenly with a smile.

"Miz Elizabeth! Well, it's about time," she said. "You ain't been by since the lake opened up. I was beginning to think maybe you forgot about us down here."

Elizabeth pushed her hood back onto her shoulders and pulled her gloves off, shaking her head.

"It's been very busy," she said. "I hope you'll excuse me."

"Never you mind, we're just glad to see you. Take off your wraps. There's room there by the warm, if these men will mind their manners. I wonder where Ephraim and Henrietta have got themselves to. They should come and say hello."

"Oh, don't bother them, please," Elizabeth said. "I came in because I was wondering if you happen to have material for handkerchiefs."

Anna was turning to the high wall behind her before the sentence was completely out of Elizabeth's mouth.

"Better than that," she mumbled, pulling out a drawer and peering in. "The Kaes girls spun me twenty yard of good plain cloth in the fall and we sewed up handkerchiefs out of the rests, save you the needlework. Unless you was wanting lawn? I ain't had any nice lawn in a year or more. Now," she continued, without waiting for Elizabeth's reply. "The question is, where they got to since the last time I seen them. How many was you wanting?"

"As many as you've got," said Elizabeth. "It's one item I didn't think I'd need in the classroom, but I've come to see that I can't do without. The children seem to all have colds. The sudden change in the weather, I suppose."

"Thaw's the season for it, sure enough," said Anna, climbing up on a stool to investigate cubbyholes out of her reach.

Elizabeth left Anna to her rummaging and turned to look over the room. There was a new sign on the wall. *All grains and flowers took in trade,* it read. An unbidden picture came to Elizabeth, in which her father attempted to pay for his tobacco with an armful of daisies, and she almost laughed. But then she saw how carefully the placard had been painted, and she bit her lip.

The usual crowd of men was gathered by the hearth. Elizabeth nodded to them from a distance. Julian waved one hand over his head in her direction without bothering to get up. Anna's father was sound asleep, the fringe of his long gray beard spread over his chest like a moth-eaten blanket. Moses Southern gave her a curt nod from his perch on a barrel of pickled eggs, but Jed McGarrity jumped up and came forward to pump Elizabeth's hand with both of his own.

"I'm glad to see you, Miz Elizabeth," he said. "I keep trying to catch you after church on Sunday. Been wanting to tell you what a fine job you're doing. You keep them young'uns hopping, that's sure enough so."

Elizabeth smiled. "It is certainly good to hear that you're satisfied with the progress your boys are making."

"Satisfied! The missus and me can't hardly wait till they come home and tell us what stories you come up with. Yesterday it was that Trojan horse that got them Greeks into such a mess." He stroked his whiskers thoughtfully. "Wonder if our generals knew about that trick. Might of worked when we was trying to shift the Tories out of New-York, back in the war."

This was greeted with a sharp glance from Moses Southern, and a broad smile from Julian. "You could have done with Lizzie's help, I'm sure," he said. "She is a very handy tactician.

Don't know how that particular skill serves her in the classroom, but it's stood her in good stead elsewhere."

"Don't you go criticizin' the schoolmarm," said Anna from her perch on a stepladder. "Ain't my Ephraim reading the Good Book to me every evening? Even that great hulk Liam Kirby is tame as a kitten these days. Don't know how she done it, and for sure she ain't going about it the way most would"— Anna sent Moses a narrow stare—"but whatever she's up to, it's working."

There was an uneasy silence as Julian settled back down into his seat and Elizabeth retreated toward the counter once again. Lately she was finding it harder and harder to cope calmly with Julian's teasing. He seemed to take every opportunity to goad her. The fact that Richard Todd called regularly on her now did not seem to make any difference. Elizabeth wondered once again if Julian had somehow gotten a hint of her plans. She was thinking this through once again when she was called out of her thoughts with a jerk.

". . . Nathaniel," said Jed McGarrity.

"Pardon me?" asked Elizabeth as calmly as she could. "I'm afraid my thoughts were—elsewhere." *What a fraud I've become,* she thought.

"I said, Nathaniel is moving along quite smart on the new schoolhouse. He's got Otter helping him raise the walls, and I'd warrant they'll be done with the bulk of it in a week. You'll be in that school come mid-April, no doubt."

"Well, that is good news," Elizabeth said, trying to sound prim and pleased at the same time. "I haven't been by to see in a long time, I've just been too busy with teaching."

"You should go on along, then, have a look."

"I think not," Elizabeth said, looking down at the wares on the counter. "Nathaniel has made it quite clear that he doesn't like me interfering."

"Is that so?" Jed asked slowly, his head tilted to one side. "That don't sound much like Nathaniel."

"Oh. Well." Elizabeth wondered how she could remove herself from this discussion of Nathaniel before she said something completely incriminating. "Perhaps I misunderstood. But I am glad to know that the schoolhouse will be finished soon."

"Injuns in the classroom," muttered Moses Southern behind Elizabeth.

"I beg your pardon?" She had heard him quite clearly, but she wanted to give the man an opportunity to back down. Elizabeth had realized for weeks that this confrontation was waiting for her, and she dreaded it. The scowl on Moses Southern's face made it clear that her worries had been well founded.

She straightened her shoulders and met his gaze full on.

"Did you have a problem with the school you wanted to discuss with me?"

"Moses is of the opinion that Indians don't belong in the classroom," said Julian easily, his eyes fixed on Elizabeth's face.

"Your Jemima is doing very well in my class, Mr. Southern," Elizabeth said quietly. "I am very pleased that you decided to send her to school after all. I don't think you have to worry that her education is suffering in any way."

"Jemima ain't the problem," Moses barked, causing Anna to come out from behind her counter, a yardstick clutched in one fist.

"You watch yourself in my place," Anna said. "I won't have none of your tricks."

Moses turned on Anna. "If she wants to teach redskins, then she should do it somewhere else. She brings them two niggers into her own house to teach 'em; she could do the same with the Bonner half-breed. And what that young squaw is doing there, I want to know. That Mohawk ain't got a thing to teach a decent Christian girl."

Julian had been following this outburst with a look of mixed amusement and curiosity, but now he looked away.

Everyone was looking at Elizabeth, waiting for her to reply to Moses. Even Jed McGarrity, who had supported Elizabeth in every one of her ventures and at every turn, looked as if he needed an answer to this question. They all wanted to know what Many-Doves had to do in the classroom.

She drew in a breath and clutched her gloves tighter in her hands to control their trembling. Anger could be a very good thing, she knew, if she could just harness it and turn it to her advantage.

"Abigail is my assistant," she said slowly. "She has been a great help to me. She works with the younger students while I have lessons with the older ones."

Moses began to bluster again, but Elizabeth held up a hand to stop him, and something in the set of her face told him that she was serious.

"Now, Mr. Southern. I run my classroom the way I see fit. Thus far, I have had good success with my students, your daughter included. You will concede, sir, that I do not tell you how to set your traps, or what game you should hunt. I ask the same courtesy of you, that you allow me to judge where and when and whom I teach. And since you are so interested in the tutoring that goes on in my home, let me tell you that you are welcome to come by and join us at any time. We are reading the works of Thomas Paine at the present. You may be familiar with his philosophy on the rights of man?"

Moses' mouth opened and closed awkwardly, and then snapped shut suddenly.

"I don't like this business," he said. "And I ain't the only one. Just wait and see—"

"And I acknowledge your objections," Elizabeth countered icily. "Now, if you will excuse me—" And she turned back to the counter, where Anna stood with both fists on her hips. She had found a basket of cloth rests and Elizabeth looked through them. "These will do nicely," she said, fingering the squares. She did not flinch when Moses Southern thundered past her and out the door.

Elizabeth looked up into Anna's eyes, and she saw there a look perhaps not of complete agreement, but of grudging acceptance. She knew that she was testing the limits of the villagers' tolerance, and knew too how much she depended on the support and goodwill of those who would defend her in public.

"Thank you," she said softly.

Anna folded her mouth into a straight line, as if she were considering taking up the subject Moses had dropped. She would do it less combatively, Elizabeth knew, but the end result would be the same: she was uncomfortable with the fact that Many-Doves had a hand in the teaching. They all were. Elizabeth was suddenly very tired of the struggle. She looked down at the basket of handkerchiefs.

"What's this?" she asked, pulling out a solitary piece of fine embroidered lawn. It was edged with knitted lace and slightly yellowed with age.

"Oh, Lordy, I forgot all about that. Bought it in Albany some many years ago. Never found nobody wanted to buy it, though. Too fancy for the folks around here. Old Olga Schlesinger used to come by regular, offer me a bushel of taters for it. But I couldn't part with it at that price. Since she died ain't nobody been interested in such a fancy piece."

Anna glanced up at Elizabeth with amusement sparking suddenly on her broad face.

"Looks to me like a hankie a bride might need on her wedding day. If only we had a bride in these parts, maybe I could sell it."

Elizabeth saw too late that she had extricated herself from one difficult subject only to land in a topic area even more sensitive. Her first impulse was to deny hotly that she was anywhere near being a bride, but she could not do that. Richard had been a steady visitor to her father's home for the past weeks, and Elizabeth had encouraged him. They had walked out together. She had visited his home. All this was common knowledge. Of course, Anna was thinking about a wedding party. What was worse, Elizabeth needed to encourage her further.

Julian roused himself to come look over Elizabeth's shoulder. "Thinking about your bridal clothes already, sister? I had no idea Todd was quite so quick off the mark." His tone was light, but he watched Elizabeth very closely.

"Now, you leave Miz Elizabeth alone," Anna said, shooing Julian away, but she grinned broadly. "This here is women's business."

"That's quite all right," Elizabeth said with a prim smile. "Please do wrap up the handkerchief. I may well have a use for it one day in the not too distant future." And she sent her brother a cool stare, thinking how surprised he would be if he only knew what she really had in mind.

The door opened behind her. Elizabeth tensed, suddenly sure that Nathaniel was standing there. She hadn't seen him at all since their long talk in the barn, four weeks ago. In the past few days, she had started taking walks she thought might put her in his path, but with no success. Nathaniel was as good as his word: he avoided her completely. When the sugar-maple sap rose a week earlier than expected, Hannah had asked her to come to Hidden Wolf for their celebration, but close questioning had made it clear that this was her idea and not an invitation passed on from Nathaniel. As much as it hurt her to disappoint the child, she had found excuses enough to stay away.

Making every effort to settle her face in a neutral expression, Elizabeth turned.

"Dutch Ton!" exclaimed Jed. "What the devil are you doing in Paradise?"

Elizabeth recognized the trapper immediately as the man who had run the betting at the Barktown lacrosse game. His blue eyes squinted out at them from a network of grimy wrinkles in a face sprouting tufts of dun-colored hair. Even from where she stood across the room, Elizabeth took in the waves of odor which drifted off the man. Her students had taught her that an acute sense of smell was a luxury she couldn't afford, but even the worst of the children had nothing on Dutch Ton's aged fragrance. She pressed one of the new handkerchiefs to her nose, closed her eyes and counted to ten.

"Close the door!" Anna barked, bustling forward. "You old fool! What do you mean, standing there like a mummy! Speak up! If you came for a bath—which I must say is the one thing I would recommend for the sake of our noses—you're in the wrong place. I don't rent out tubs no more."

Elizabeth opened her eyes once again. Dutch Ton looked much as he had when she last saw him: a barrel of a man wrapped in rags and tattered pelts, every sort of weapon and implement dangling from the confusion of leather belts crisscrossing his torso and waist. He was squinting as he looked around the room. When his gaze finally reached Elizabeth, his mouth fell open to reveal a few blackish stumps of teeth.

"What do you mean, staring at Miz Elizabeth that way?

You're putting the fear of God in her, can't you see that, you ijit! Speak up, man. I heard you was in Fish House. What brings you all the way here?"

The man blinked slowly, his gaze still fixed on Elizabeth.

"I got a letter," he said finally in a strangely high and cracked voice. "I'm lookin' for the schoolmarm to read it to me. It's from my sister."

There was a pause, in which Anna turned and sought out Jed McGarrity. "Jed," she said. "Take this old fool out of here."

"But I got a letter," Dutch Ton protested, holding up something that might have been paper. "From my sister. And I cain't read."

To Elizabeth it looked like a hunk of old newspaper which had been left out in the rain, but the look on the man's face moved her.

"I could have a look at it," she said to Anna.

The trapper was quick for such a big man; he was halfway across the room to Elizabeth before Anna and Jed's protests began.

"Now, Miz Elizabeth," Jed said. "Let me tell you about that letter."

"I may as well look at it," Elizabeth murmured.

"Well, you won't be the first," Anna said, disgruntled. "He shoves that nasty thing in everybody's face, has been for the last twenty year. Nobody can read it. It ain't in English."

"Lizzie's good at languages," said Julian, who had situated himself in the corner, uncharacteristically out of the conversation. He looked a little flustered when Dutch Ton glanced his way, and then relieved when the man looked away without seeming to recognize him.

"Is it German?" asked Elizabeth, who had taken the letter from the trapper and retreated behind the counter, both for a surface where she could lay the letter out, and because her eyes were watering with the smell of him at close quarters. "Could your father read it?"

"He can't read," said Anna. "Never learned. I tried to read it to him, figured it was German. But no luck." She looked across the room to where her father slept on, oblivious.

Elizabeth was trying to extract the sheet of writing paper from its envelope without tearing either of them, but it was hard work. The outer sheet had clearly been submerged at one point and left to dry, for the only ink left on it was a dark blur. She worked the papers apart with Dutch Ton leaning over the counter toward her.

"It's from my sister," Dutch Ton said to nobody in particular.

"Well," said Elizabeth after a minute or two. "It's badly damaged, I'm afraid, and quite faint. But I don't think it's German. Did you come over from Germany?"

The look of surprise and confusion reminded Elizabeth of her younger pupils when they listened to the recitations of the older students, and heard questions asked and answered which seemed to them unfathomable.

"Came on a ship," he said, as if that should clear everything up. And then, nodding toward the letter. "Can you read it?"

There was a sudden shifting and coughing from beside the hearth, and Anna looked up.

"Däta," Anna said. "Waking up from his nap."

The old man stretched a little and then sat up, blinking. He looked at the small crowd gathered around him and he grinned, exposing three long and very canine teeth.

"What have we got here?" he asked, his voice scratchy. "What's up, then, Annie girl?"

"Dutch Ton," said Anna. "Came with his infernal letter."

"Who's this?" asked the old man, his gaze settling on Elizabeth and ignoring the trapper completely.

"The schoolmarm," said Jed McGarrity. "Ain't you met Miz Elizabeth yet?"

"She don't come in much, Jed. That ain't my fault. The judge's girl. Aha. You look like your brother."

"Pleased to make your acquaintance," Elizabeth murmured. "Mr.—"

"Call me Axel. That's my name. Axel Metzler." He peered at her. "You're a pretty one," he said, exploring in his beard until he found a spot that needed scratching.

"Elizabeth, would you read the letter or give it back to the man and let him get on his way?" interrupted Anna. "Lord knows I'll never get the stench out of my goods."

"It's from my sister," the trapper intoned yet again.

Axel sent a long look toward Dutch Ton, and then he turned to Elizabeth. "Can't read it?" he asked her.

She shook her head. "It might be one of the Scandinavian languages."

The old man stretched out his hand, and Elizabeth put the letter in it. He puzzled at it for a few minutes. Elizabeth wondered if she should point out that he was reading it upside down, but the way he grinned at her told her better.

"Twenty year he's been bringing this letter around," said Axel. "Enough is enough. Now I'll read it to him."

Anna was watching her father closely, as if she expected some magic from him. Jed McGarrity looked from Elizabeth to Julian quizzically, but got only a puzzled shrug by way of explanation.

"So," said Axel, clearing his voice. "Your sister writes she is in good health, that the crops are good, that her children are growing, that her husband is a hardworking man."

Dutch Ton stood dumbstruck, considering. "Agatha?"

"Ja, your sister Agatha. She misses you. Oh and the old cow with one horn died."

The trapper nodded absently and sat down on a stool, still staring at the mangled letter.

"And the hay shed burned down but no real trouble, they built a better one. Oh, and the neighbor—"

"Däta," said Anna.

"I'm just reading a letter." He grinned up at her. "Let me."

But Dutch Ton stood up, took the letter from Axel, who was looking a bit disappointed to have his services broken off so abruptly, and tucked the paper into a gap in his coat.

"You see?" asked Axel Metzler of Elizabeth and Anna when the door had closed behind him. "How easy it was?"

"What if he finds somebody to really read it to him someday?" asked Jed.

"Not bloody likely," said Julian with a snort.

"Däta always was a storyteller," said Anna by way of explanation. "Can't stop him once he gets started."

"Well, then," said Julian. "Let's have a story. What have you got to tell, old man?"

Axel sent Julian a narrow and appraising look that made Elizabeth shift uncomfortably, but Julian seemed unperturbed.

"Tell the one about the Bear Dancer," said Jed.

Axel waved a hand dismissively. "Not today."

Elizabeth had been sitting silently and wondering if she dare speak up. She felt the old man's gaze on her, and before she knew how she could say what she wanted to say without arousing Julian's curiosity, she spoke.

"Tell us about Jack Lingo and the Tory Gold."

There was a little silence, and Elizabeth thought he would refuse. He was chewing on the stem of his cold pipe, considering. She dared not look at her brother, or even at Anna. No one could know how interested she was in this story.

"Ja, sure," said Axel finally. "That's a good one. Jack Lingo. Taught me everthing there was to know about the beaver. Back in '57 it was when I first ran into him. Hard times, girly. Pray to God you never see the like."

With a sigh he leaned forward and put his elbows on his knees.

"The Mingo were selling scalps to the French and they weren't fussy about where they got 'em, neither. Me and the missus had a little place on the Mohawk back in them days, near Albany, until they burned us out. Oh, ja, hard times. My Gret went to stay by her sister—she was big with this one here—" He jerked his thumb toward Anna, who nodded her approval. "So I think to myself, a man has got to have some cash, and I went into the bush, looking for beaver. Down on the Mohawk they was all gone, hunted clean out. But up in the bush I was thinking I can make me some money to start fresh.

"Now I weren't no boy, you know. More than forty, I was then, but green as a stripling. I run into Jack. Good thing, too. The bush ain't kind. No, it'll do the same job to a man as a Mingo war club but not so quick, most of the time. Ever seen what a spring bear can do to a man? Or a painter, dropping out of a tree?

"A painter?" asked Elizabeth, confused but also amused by this image.

"He means a panther," interjected Anna. "Pa! Get onto the Tory Gold! That's the story we want!"

"You'll take the stories I got, missy," Axel said good-naturedly, his great splayed thumb packing down the tobacco in his pipe. "My whole life I'm telling this story, and you know better?"

Anna waved him on impatiently.

"Naja. So. The Frenchies were all over the lake in them days. Feeling good about things, like they had the whole north woods to tie up in a pretty package and send back to their king. I was up in the bush trying my hand at the beaver and making a fine mess of it when they took old William Henry and turned him inside out."

"Fort William Henry," interjected Jed.

Axel went on as if he hadn't heard him.

"The Frog Eaters and the Mingos made short work on it. Drove the Tories and the militia out and cut 'em to pieces. Now they say it was Montcalm who found the Tory Gold, hid under the floorboards. Don't know what it was doing there. Never in my life have I known a soldier to be paid in gold. I seen a gold guinea coin myself once, a long time later in Albany. I imagine that a thousand of them gold joes in a pile would look to a man a little like heaven. But that Montcalm was an officer and they say a good one. He packed all that gold up and he got together some of his men and he sent it back to Montreal, thinking to send it on to France, I reckon. But that's where he made his mistake."

Axel hunched forward, gesturing to Elizabeth with one knotty finger until she leaned toward him.

"He sent them overland, through the bush. They had the water all tied up, you see, and they could of put that gold on a boat and had it in Montreal in no time. But they set off overland, and that right there was the mistake."

Leaning back, Axel paused to draw on his pipe, looking contemplatively at the ceiling. Elizabeth smiled, recognizing the studied pause of a born storyteller.

"They all went into the bush," he repeated. "And not a man jack of 'em come out again. Nor the gold. Now, this is where the story gets peculiar, like." Axel nursed his pipe once again, staring now at Julian, who had moved up close and sat at attention.

"Jack Lingo was in the bush that day up to no good. Stole more beaver than he ever trapped hisself, they say, and I ain't gonna disagree. Lazy, you know. Said to me once he spent years paddling the fur route up from Montreal to Grand Portage and back again, and didn't see he should have to work no more. So."

There was a crackling from the fire as Axel paused to light his pipe. Elizabeth felt her brother's attention on her and she turned to him, one eyebrow raised, meeting his curiosity and suspicion full on. Julian yawned. He might want her to think him bored, but Julian could not hide his intense interest in this story.

"The mistake Jack Lingo made that day was, he stole from a man smarter than him. Chingachgook was in the bush, you see. Don't know what Lingo was thinking, trying to steal from Chingachgook, but I guess he weren't thinking much at all. So here's what you got: Jack Lingo decides that Chingachgook don't need his canoe no more, and he climbs in and paddles off. He's on his way out of the bush, when he runs into a river of blood. Them Frenchies, cut up bad. Scalps gone, other parts, too." Axel glanced at Elizabeth and cleared his throat. "But the chest was there. Why? Dunno. Maybe they was coming back for it later. Maybe they was just interested in the scalps and never bothered to look inside.

"Now Old Jack wasn't a complete fool, not him. He got a look in that chest and saw what was there, and he knew sure enough what to do." Axel turned suddenly to Elizabeth.

"What would you do, now, missy?"

The question took Elizabeth by surprise. She sat up, considered.

"Load the strongbox in the canoe and take off," supplied Julian before she could answer.

"Ja, that's just about what Jack wanted to do, but just then

Chingachgook caught up with him. Now." He tapped his pipe against his knee. "There ain't no worse crime in the bush than stealing. And there weren't no tougher man in the bush than Chingachgook."

Elizabeth thought of the old man up at Hidden Wolf, his kind smile, and she tried to imagine him in his prime.

". . . so now Jack's got Chingachgook in front of him and Chingachgook's canoe behind him, and the chest between them. What did he do?"

"He ran like the devil," muttered Jed McGarrity.

"Like the devil!" echoed Axel with a little laugh. "Ja, like the devil hisself! And it must have been the devil who looked out after him that day, because he got away. Any other day, Chingachgook would have killed him."

"So what happened to the strongbox and the gold?" asked Julian, when it was clear that the old man had told all of the story he considered worth telling.

"Well, now," said Axel, wiping his watery eyes with a dingy handkerchief. "That's the question, ain't it?"

"What do you think happened to it?" Elizabeth asked quietly.

Axel shook his head. "This is what I know," he said. "Chingachgook ain't a stupid man, and he ain't a rich one, neither. Unless he been sitting on that gold all these years, he ain't got it. Me, I think he ain't got it. Jack Lingo thinks otherwise, he been spending all this time trying to get Chingachgook to give him a share. Note now, missy, I ain't said a fair share. Lingo never much understood that particular word, in any language."

Julian had a preoccupied look. "Where is this Jack Lingo?"

"Why, I thought that would be naked as a peeled egg," said Axel. "He's in the bush. Looking for the spot where Chingachgook hid the gold. Some say it's up there on Hidden Wolf. Ain't that so, Dr. Todd?"

Elizabeth looked up with a start to find Richard standing not ten steps away. There was a look on his face she wasn't familiar with, the blue eyes narrowed and steely above the bright red-gold of his beard. In the past month Elizabeth had avoided the topic of Hidden Wolf with Richard, and the look on his face made her glad she had done so.

"That's what they say," Richard said finally, his eyes coming to settle, heavily, on Elizabeth.

"Your beau has come to see you home, sister," said Julian, reaching for his coat. "I'll come along as chaperon."

"Beau?" said Axel, sitting up straighter and grinning. "I guess I ain't the only one with a story to tell, then."

"My brother speaks out of turn," Elizabeth said with a sharp look to Julian.

Richard seemed to come suddenly awake. He gave Elizabeth a grim little smile. "Does he?"

Anna had been watching the exchange quite eagerly. "Now, you men," she interjected, handing Elizabeth a wrapped parcel of handkerchiefs. "Don't make the schoolteacher blush. A lady ain't supposed to be too clear on matters such as these." She stood back and looked Elizabeth over as if she were a daughter in need of comfort and protection rather than a woman almost thirty, just a few years younger than herself. "It was good to have you come by and I hope you'll come again soon to talk when the menfolk ain't quite so troublesome."

"Thank you," Elizabeth said. "I'd like that." And she was surprised to note that she was not just being polite, that she meant it. Anna's straightforwardness was welcome to her after so many weeks of playacting.

Suddenly Elizabeth remembered something and she turned to Richard.

"I thought you were leaving for Johnstown today."

"Hitty Cameron had her pains start," said Richard. "And by the time she was safely delivered, it was too late to set out."

"Is that so?" asked Anna eagerly. "Has she got a girl or a boy?"

"A fine, healthy son," said Richard with a nod.

"Hitty Cameron?" Elizabeth was still having trouble sorting out the villagers. "Has she married one of Archie Cunningham's sons?"

"Well, now," said Anna easily. "She ain't exactly anybody's wife just yet, but I expect that she and Noah will go to housekeeping now that they've got a boy."

"Oh," said Elizabeth, flustered. She had heard of this local habit of starting a family before marriage, but it was a difficult one to come to grips with.

"Very well for Hitty," said Julian impatiently, trying to urge Elizabeth toward the door. "But it's time for my tea now and I'm afraid I'm not willing to wait any longer. Are you two coming along or not?"

"Go on ahead," Richard said, before Elizabeth could answer. "I will see your sister home."

Julian raised an eyebrow in question at Elizabeth, and she gave him a reluctant nod. He shrugged his shoulders and took his leave from the men at the hearth. "I'll be back to hear more about that gold," he called to Axel with a flourish, and the door fell shut behind him.

"Is there anything I may bring you from Johnstown?" Richard asked when he had settled Elizabeth into his sleigh and tucked the lap robes around her.

"Is that what you wanted to talk to me about?" she asked, surprised.

"No, but it will do for a start. And do I need a reason to talk to you?" he asked, clucking to the chestnut geldings to set them on their way.

Elizabeth had quickly realized that the hardest part of her role in the current affair was not missing Nathaniel, but coping with Richard. His possessiveness was a trial she had not really anticipated. She felt his gaze on her now, a sidelong glance of paternalistic condescension which marked her his asset, his almost-wife. Sometimes it was more than she could bear.

"I suppose not," she said tightly.

"Miz Elizabeth!" called a young voice, and Elizabeth smiled and waved at Peter Dubonnet, the youngest of her schoolboys. She was surprised to see him salute her with an axe; he was a slight child, and she wouldn't have thought him strong enough to be effective at splitting kindling. But a half-filled wicker basket stood to one side and he turned back to it as the sleigh moved on. In the classroom Peter had the serious demeanor of a child with too much responsibility, and Elizabeth wondered where Claude Dubonnet kept himself while his son chopped wood.

"There might be mail waiting in Johnstown," Richard was saying, and Elizabeth turned back to the conversation at hand.

"I suppose there might be," she agreed.

"Perhaps word from your aunt Merriweather."

"Yes," said Elizabeth, now more distinctly uncomfortable. "Perhaps. Will you be disappointed if there is none?"

Immediately Elizabeth regretted this question. She dared not look at Richard, and so she looked instead at the way the softened snow puckered and fell in on itself over Henry Smythe's fallow cornfields.

"I am a patient man," Richard said finally.

"I see that you are," Elizabeth said. "If I may make an observation, you are also a stubborn one."

He shrugged a bit, as if to concede this point. Irritated, Elizabeth decided to have her way just this once with Richard, and risk the possibility of putting him off.

"When are you going to tell me about your childhood?" she said to him. "You seem to always evade the subject."

"The way you are evading the subject of my proposal?"

"We have discussed your proposal at length, on a number of occasions," retorted Elizabeth. "You have yet to tell me anything about your childhood."

"You're mighty interested in stories today," Richard said, clearly put out.

"Do you mean Jack Lingo?" Elizabeth said.

He grunted.

"It was an interesting story, but it has nothing to do with the matter at hand."

"There's nothing to tell," Richard said stiffly.

"Between strangers, perhaps not," Elizabeth said, just as stiffly. She wondered herself why she was being so insistent about this, why it seemed so important to get Richard to talk about his time with the Mohawk.

"Are we to be strangers no longer, then?" Richard asked in a voice which struck Elizabeth as toneless and, at the same time, vaguely threatening.

The sleigh track entered a narrow place where the river negotiated between a steep hillside and a wall of rock, so that the path bordered directly on the water, rushing high now with icy runoff from the mountain. Just beyond the turning, Elizabeth knew, her father's house would come into view. But right here they were not visible from the house or from the village. With considerable discomfort Elizabeth watched as Richard brought the sleigh to a halt.

This is what my curiosity reaps, she thought to herself grimly. For weeks now she had managed to avoid this kind of encounter with Richard, but there was nowhere to go, no excuse to be made.

"Elizabeth."

She met his gaze with a raised eyebrow.

"Do you believe that your aunt will give her blessing to the match between us?"

Elizabeth called up an image of aunt Merriweather. She was a kind but sometimes rash woman of strong opinions, and one of those opinions was that a woman without considerable resources of her own was better off married. Love was not a staple of aunt Merriweather's philosophy, and she would not know what to make of Nathaniel. Richard, on the other hand, would be a more familiar kind of creature to her in spite of his unconventional childhood.

"I really don't know," said Elizabeth finally.

"Will you go against her wishes if she does not support your plans to marry?"

What a fortuitous formulation, Elizabeth thought. *At least in answering this I can look him straight in the eye.* "If I feel that it is in my best interest to marry, I will do so, even if my aunt does not agree."

"And have you decided whether it is in your best interest?" He was leaning toward her now, not with a look that was passionate, but with the focused demeanor of a man who knew how to do a job, and was determined not to cut corners.

"Perhaps," Elizabeth said, willing her voice to be steady, but knowing that it creaked a bit. She put out her hand against Richard's shoulder in a clear attempt to stop him, but he caught it in his own and brought it up to his mouth. Elizabeth snatched it away with a little indrawn breath.

"I'm a patient man, Elizabeth," Richard said, his brow folded in a line which said just the opposite. "But I'm not a fool."

Elizabeth experienced a most inopportune and almost irrepressible urge to giggle. She bit the inside of her cheek hard, trying to focus her thoughts and bring herself to reason. It was imperative that she remain calm and friendly and also crucial that she find a formulation which would reach him. And quickly.

"Your advances are most inappropriate, Richard," she said in a tone she hoped was sweet, but feared was sharp. "Have you no respect for my good name?"

Relieved, Elizabeth saw him draw up at this. He was already sitting back, a surprised but not completely dissatisfied look on his face, when the rock face began to slide.

At first there was a sharp crack like the sound of a branch snapping under a load of snow, followed by a rustling. A shower of pebbles and ice fell over them, and before it was clear to Elizabeth what was happening, the horses had begun to rear. With a muttered oath, Richard reached for the reins but they slipped away from him and over the lip of the dashboard. A large spar of rock fell just then, and Elizabeth saw it bounce off the back of one horse and strike the next.

"Hold tight!" he bellowed, lunging after the reins as the sleigh lurched and then began to fly forward, rocking madly from side to side.

Numbly, Elizabeth did as she was told. She braced her feet and fixed her hands on the dashboard. The wind ripped her hood from her head and she felt a spattering of wet snow across her cheek and mouth. The air seemed suddenly very cold, and it was hard to breathe in spite of the great wind in her face. The horses careened around the corner, setting the sleigh tipping for a brief and terrifying moment on one set of runners.

Then the path straightened out and the sleigh slammed down once again with a jolt, the runners screeching. Richard was leaning out over the backs of the geldings, shouting to them, but they raced on, great gouts of ice and mush hurtling up from their hooves.

Elizabeth closed her eyes and tried to remember a prayer,

any prayer, but none came to her, and it was more terrifying to be blind to the dangers than to watch them.

When she opened her eyes, Nathaniel was running toward them. Numbly, she realized that he must have been hunting, for he came leaping downhill, racing on an angle to intercept the team.

Richard was raging at the horses. There was just a split second for Elizabeth to note to herself, quite insanely, that she was finally seeing that part of Dr. Todd which he kept so carefully hidden from her, when Nathaniel launched himself at the team, grabbing the bridle and pulling the horses to a stop with his own weight.

For a moment the only sound was the rough belling of the dogs, who settled at a single sharp word from Nathaniel. The whole episode had lasted only seconds, Elizabeth was sure, but she felt as though a century had passed.

Slowly, almost majestically, Richard rose from the sleigh and pointed a finger in Nathaniel's direction. Elizabeth saw that it trembled slightly, and she looked up, alarmed, to see that Richard fought for his breath, his chest heaving. His color was choleric, and his voice wavered.

"This was your doing!"

"Richard!" Shocked, Elizabeth reached up a hand to touch his arm. From the corner of her eye she watched Nathaniel take this in; she sensed rather than saw him stiffen.

"I believe Nathaniel deserves our thanks," she said, withdrawing her hand.

"He deserves a beating," bellowed Richard in response.

"He saved our lives!" Elizabeth shot back at him.

"He tried to kill us," Richard corrected her without taking his eyes from Nathaniel.

"If you can't get a hold of your team," Nathaniel said, "then at least get a hold of yourself, man."

Beside Elizabeth, Richard stilled suddenly in a way which was more frightening than any shouting. Elizabeth sent a beseeching look to Nathaniel.

"Please—" she began, and then faltered. *Please,* she wanted to say, *please stop this, I'm frightened. Please. Come here and let me look at you.* A glance passed between them, and Elizabeth saw Nathaniel call himself to order, the tension leaving his jaw slowly.

"I heard the shot," Richard said, his fists balled at his side.

"Shot?" asked Elizabeth, incredulous. "What shot?"

"Somebody shot at the rock face," Richard spat out without even looking at her. "*Nathaniel* shot at the rock face to make it slide," he corrected himself.

"That's a damn fool thing to say," responded Nathaniel in a strangely reasonable tone. "And once you calm down and think it over, you'll see that for yourself. Now," he continued, touching his cap in deference to Elizabeth. He let his gaze shift over her face one beat too long. "I'm glad I could be of help and I'll be on my way again." He whistled to the dogs, and without another word to them, he slipped into the woods.

With a sinking feeling, Elizabeth watched him go. She knew she should look away, that Richard was watching, but it was impossible. She could not. In the confusion of the past few minutes, she realized, he had not once used her name.

"He did that," Richard said darkly, out of the sleigh now and checking the harnesses, locating the reins. "He did that on purpose."

Elizabeth's heart had begun to slow its pace, but now it picked up again. Richard was looking at her with such a dark scowl, his brow drawn down into a sharp vee. *He knows,* she thought numbly. *He knows.* She looked into the woods where Nathaniel had disappeared and wished him back. She had not been afraid of Richard when he seemed intent on kissing her, but she was afraid now.

"I'm sure you're mistaken," she said, finally.

But Richard wasn't looking at Elizabeth; in fact, he seemed to have forgotten her. "Of course he did it, of course. He'd do anything to keep me from getting to Hidden Wolf."

Elizabeth shut her mouth and focused her gaze on her own hands, folded into a tight knot in her lap.

"You must be mistaken," she said again.

"Let me tell you this," Richard said, snapping the reins sharply, too sharply, thought Elizabeth, given the agitation which was still evident in the way the horses jerked. "He'll have to kill me to do it, because I won't let any man stand between me and Hidden Wolf."

Elizabeth's fear dissipated suddenly in a cool wave of anger. *No man will stand between you and Hidden Wolf*, she agreed silently. *But you haven't reckoned with me.*

XVIII

Elizabeth looked down at the small notebook in front of her and closed her eyes in concentration.

"Skennen'kó:wa ken," she said finally and then, unsure of herself, she looked up at Many-Doves for confirmation.

"Skennen'kó:wa," replied Many-Doves. I am well.

Many-Doves was a demanding teacher of the Kahnyen'kehàka language, and not given to premature praise of her student. In the dim early morning light Elizabeth found it hard to read approval or dissatisfaction from her face. Hannah, on the other hand, grinned at Elizabeth broadly from her post at Many-Doves' shoulder when she did well, or shook her head sadly when she erred.

"Shiá:ton!" said Many-Doves, nodding almost imperceptibly toward the notebook.

Elizabeth dipped her quill and carefully sounded out the phrase. Then she looked with some satisfaction on the growing list of words and phrases she had collected thus far in her early morning lessons. It struck her, suddenly, that there were no *p* or *b* sounds, or any *l* sounds, either, which explained, perhaps, Falling-Day's discomfort with Elizabeth's own name. When she put this question to Many-Doves, the younger woman shrugged. "It seems we have no need of them," she said. "Our stories are still worth listening to."

This was an idea that would require some contemplation, but her teacher was not quite finished with her for the day.

"What do you say when someone is at your door?" Many-Doves asked, holding up a hand to forestall Hannah's help. "Let her think."

"Tasatáweia't," suggested Elizabeth. "Come in."

Many-Doves smiled, finally, and Elizabeth bent to sound out the complicated word, wondering what symbol she should use for the little hiccup of air that Many-Doves insisted on, as if a sound were swallowed whole. She settled on an apostrophe, but wished for something better. She worried too about her *t*'s and *d*'s; Many-Doves used something that fell between the two sounds. But because there was no model for her to use, Elizabeth had to settle for depending on her own ear.

She showed Many-Doves her work. "Is this correct?"

"Kahnyen'keha tewatati," came the gentle response. We should speak Kahnyen'kehàka.

Elizabeth bit her lower lip. "Tohske' wahi?"

"Tohske' wahi." Many-Doves nodded.

When they had worked their way through three more phrases, Many-Doves rose and opened the shutters. The spring morning came in, half light and a breeze still cold, but with an undercurrent of warmth. Elizabeth put the cork in her ink bottle and closed her notebook. By the time she had secured it safely away where curious eyes would not stumble on it, Hannah had taken her place with her primer open in front of her, and Many-Doves had begun copying out the day's Bible verse on the chalkboard. Elizabeth had just time to note to herself what an innocent scene they made when the first students arrived at the door.

They came in wet and noisy, their dinner buckets clattering and their boots thumping, voices raised in arguments and stories and silliness. Elizabeth found herself in the middle of them before she knew it, surrounded by their smells: cedar smoke, evergreen, bear grease, damp wool tangy with a full winter's wear, sweat. She wiped noses and peeled off coats and hung up soggy mittens, answered questions and directed them toward their places, until she found herself in front of the room and ready to begin, with their eyes—blues and grays and greens and every kind of brown—fixed on her.

The children were seated at two tables: the younger ones in the first row and the older in a row behind them. Many-Doves sat at a small table in the corner under the window, watching quietly as the children bent to their horn tablets to begin work on their daily penmanship assignment. "Put not your trust in princes," Many-Doves had written in her careful hand.

Elizabeth sent Liam Kirby back to study with Many-Doves while she heard the littlest students read. When she looked up from her charges, Elizabeth noted how Many-Doves' and Liam's heads were bent together over the tablet. Two human beings couldn't look less alike, thought Elizabeth: slender and self-contained, Many-Doves' whole quiet energy was focused on the work before her while Liam's riotous ginger hair and his substantial size were as hard to overlook as his excesses of energy and enthusiasm. He jiggled, he thumped, he whistled between his teeth; he could not sit still, although he meant to. At thirteen, Liam was her oldest student and there he sat stumbling good-naturedly over the first primer. Many-Doves' gentle suggestions worked like a persistent rhythm to his starts and stops.

Elizabeth acknowledged to herself once again that she had not properly anticipated the challenges of teaching. Liam was nothing like his brother Billy. He had not blinked an eye on the first morning when Elizabeth had asked him to take a seat next to Many-Doves, who could give him the attention he needed. What he lacked in imagination and intelligence he made up for with jittery goodwill and a dogged determination.

A horn tablet slid under her nose, bringing Elizabeth up out of her thoughts.

"Please, miz," said a small voice. "Ain't I finished yet?"

Elizabeth directed her attention to the single line of print wandering up- and downhill. She took a deep breath and gave Jemima Southern a regretful smile.

"I'm afraid not," she said, and in a low voice so as not to disturb the other children, she began to go over the reversed letters and backward shapes on the tablet.

"Please, miz," interrupted Jemima. "I cain't work on my tablet, could I practice on the board instead, please?"

Elizabeth looked first at the child, who had her mother's mild looks but her father's sullen temperament, and then down at the tablet in her hands.

Writing on the board was one of the most coveted of classroom privileges. The children argued about it at every opportunity. Of course, they would and could argue about anything: bringing in the firewood, cleaning the boards and sweeping the floor, passing out books, who should leave the room first and come back in last. In the recess Elizabeth had heard the boys arguing about whose father could piss in a higher arc, one argument she had kept far away from. She had found that there was no subject or task too small to quibble over. But writing on the board was the most contentious issue of all.

The others watched her with a mixture of curiosity and caution, wondering how she would deal with Jemima. The child was bright, and needed direction. But she was also cunning and disagreeable. In another classroom, with a male schoolteacher, both her intelligence and her wiles would have been crushed in short order. How to cope with one without undermining the other? Elizabeth knew that Jemima had lessons to teach her, but sometimes it was hard to be philosophical when confronted with her smug little smile.

The fire crackled in the hearth while she considered, feeling the weight of all the children's attention on her. Even Hannah, who rarely looked up from her work, was watching.

"Go on now, 'Mima," called Liam from the back of the room just when Elizabeth thought that the child was not going to give in and would have to be brought to task publicly. "Set down. Cain't you see she won't be budged? She ain't gonna let you take no shortcuts."

"Thank you, Liam," Elizabeth said, trying to suppress a smile and only partially succeeding. "I think Jemima and I understand each other well enough."

A flicker of disappointment flashed over Jemima's face, but she went back to her table without further complaint. She settled herself onto the bench with tight little movements, taking care not to touch Hannah. The two children might have been in separate classrooms.

· · · ·

On Saturday Elizabeth dismissed school with a heavy heart and took more time than she needed to set the cabin in order before starting out. She stood on the little porch for a moment, looking at the way the world around her dripped from every twig, and pulled her shawl and her hood up over her head in a vain attempt to stay dry.

Within ten minutes her skirts were muddy and Elizabeth was anticipating a cup of tea and a dry pair of shoes, even while she dreaded the evening at home. Kitty Witherspoon and her father were coming to call, and Richard was expected back from Johnstown. She wasn't sure what she dreaded more, Richard's attentions or Kitty's unhappiness about Richard's attentions.

There was a crackling in the bush, and Elizabeth paused.

"Come on, then, Dolly," she said kindly. "Come along and walk with me."

As the eleven-year-old emerged from the wood, Elizabeth smiled. "You needn't be afraid," she said kindly. "I'm glad to have your company on the walk home."

This was not strictly true, but Dolly Smythe was so painfully shy that Elizabeth felt obliged to encourage her every effort to reach out. Dolly bobbed her head and attempted a half curtsy, all elbows and awkward goodwill, her gaze directed firmly downward. Elizabeth was sure this was due to the fact that the child was terribly cross-eyed. She expected her to fall into step beside her and walk the rest of the distance in silence, but Dolly surprised her.

"There's somebody watching," she said breathlessly.

Elizabeth came to a stop, sliding a little in the mud. She looked into the woods, but saw no sign of anyone at all.

"What do you mean?"

"Somebody's watching." Dolly shrugged, unwilling or unable to be more specific. "I heard 'em, just now."

Elizabeth considered for a moment, feeling the way her heart picked up a beat.

"Probably one of the boys," she said. "Wanting to scare us."

Dolly glanced up, one of her rare direct looks. Below arched brows the color of wheat, one green-gray eye darted toward Elizabeth with the other lagging behind. She dropped her gaze suddenly.

"No, ma'am," she said simply.

"Well, whoever it is, they'll catch a cold," Elizabeth said, sounding cross when she knew that she should be sounding frightened. She wanted to call out Nathaniel's name, force him to show himself, but she closed her mouth in a firm line and set out again, with Dolly slipping and sliding beside her.

There were three kinds of meat for dinner, pickled tomatoes, Curiosity's best beans stewed with fatback, drop biscuits, a trifle laced with more brandy than was seemly, and there was Kitty, staring at Elizabeth as if she had just murdered her own family before she sat down to eat. Because her father and Mr. Wither-spoon seemed content to discuss the weather for the entire meal, and because Richard had not arrived as expected, Eliza-beth was able to avoid any topic which would cause her to deal with the younger woman directly. Kitty's anger toward Eliza-beth was implacable: Richard was at the heart of it, and Eliza-beth could not make amends. Not at the moment, at any rate. She concentrated on her meal and spoke only when Mr. Witherspoon directed a question toward her, or when Julian tried to draw her into one of his stories.

The judge seemed perfectly willing to continue the discus-sion of the thaw as they settled in the parlor after dinner, but Julian had had enough and he let it be known.

"There must be something to do at this time of year besides discuss the weather," he said impatiently.

"There's nothing to do here, there never is," Kitty said dra-matically.

"Daughter," Mr. Witherspoon admonished softly, but Kitty turned her face away from him.

"Todd had the right idea, didn't he?" said Julian. "There must be something worth doing in Johnstown. Should have gone with him," he said. "I don't wonder that they've thought up a party of some kind."

Given the crushed look on Kitty's face, Elizabeth wished that her brother would stop, but he went on, oblivious, won-dering what could be keeping Richard in Johnstown, and how he, Julian, should have had his share in the fun.

"You'll have your wish soon enough," the judge said. "We start for Johnstown next week. Things to look after, you know." He was looking at Elizabeth thoughtfully.

Elizabeth did her very best to remain impassive, glad for once that her brother's manners did not give her the opportunity to speak.

"Next week? In this weather? Whatever for? Not that I should complain, it will be good to get out—won't it, Lizzie? Oh," he went on, not giving Elizabeth a chance to agree or decline. "Lizzie won't want to come away, will she, there's her school. Responsibilities to see to, and all that. She's not free to go off at a whim anymore, are you, Lizzie?"

"I think Elizabeth will come along this time," the judge said with a knowing lift of one brow. "There are business matters to attend to, after all. Taxes, and so forth."

Elizabeth's first thought was one of relief: it was already nearing the end of the first week of April, and her father had not mentioned the deed of gift or the property transfer for months. She had begun to fear he had changed his mind about this arrangement. Many nights she had lain awake wondering what she would do if this were the case, how she could get word to Nathaniel, what he would say. Now it seemed as though he was about to make an announcement, without Richard present. It was confusing, and it was worrying, and she knew these things showed on her face. She could feel Kitty Witherspoon watching her closely, her own mouth folded into a tight line of disapproval and hardly concealed envy.

"What's all this about, Father?" asked Julian, relieving Elizabeth of the necessity of an answer.

There was a forceful knock at the door, and the judge got up, smiling.

"That will be Richard," he said. "Let's ask him, why don't we?"

Elizabeth folded her hands in her lap and forced her face into calm lines. This was what she had been waiting for, preparing for. She would make it seem as though she were finally accepting Richard. Suddenly she was glad of Kitty's presence, which would explain her unwillingness to come directly to a clear answer, or to show any joy or even enthusiasm. Even the men would understand that. They would agree on a day to go to Johnstown to sign the deed before Mr. Bennett, as magistrate. Somehow she would have to get word to Hidden Wolf.

She was so wound up in these thoughts that she barely took in the way the room had fallen silent.

Elizabeth looked up expecting Richard and saw Nathaniel instead. He stood filling the doorway, his face tight with barely controlled anger. From one hand hung the carcass of a beaver, its great tail dripping water and blood; with the other hand he held a silent and terrified Liam Kirby firmly by the neck.

"Are we at home for such a purpose on a Saturday?" Julian interrupted while Nathaniel was laying out the story of finding Liam taking the beaver from his traps. "I should think this could wait until a more opportune moment."

The judge didn't even glance in his son's direction. "It cannot," he said shortly. "If a resident of Paradise seeks me out in my official capacity, then I am always at home. Now," he said in his deepest voice. "Carry on, Nathaniel. And please, Julian, let the man talk."

"There ain't much more to tell you can't see for yourself," Nathaniel said. "The boy has been stealing from my traps, pretty much the whole winter. But this is the first I caught him. I don't usually walk the trap line this time of day, you see."

Liam stood in the center of the room, his vision focused on his own boots and the puddle he was creating on the carpet. Where his ears peeked out from his hair they were a peculiar bright shade of red. He had not yet spoken, but he twisted his cap in his hands convulsively.

"What do you have to say for yourself, Liam?" asked the judge.

"I ain't done nothing," he said in a hoarse whisper.

Elizabeth stood immobile, looking between them. She saw the bruise rising on Liam's cheekbone, dark against his pallor, and the fear and anger in his eyes.

"Liam has always been a good boy," Mr. Witherspoon said in a conciliatory tone. "Isn't that so, Judge?"

Nathaniel had been angry, but controlled. Now he swung to

face the judge, and his restraint was clearly at its breaking point. "He's been stealing from my traps, I caught him red-handed. There's laws against stealing, still on the books, I'm assuming. Either you'll do your duty or you won't. Which is it?"

The judge held up a hand in a placating gesture. "This is a first-time offense, after all—"

"I tell you, this ain't the first time my traps have been tampered with. And that's not the least of it." He paused, his stare as harsh as his tone was quiet. "You know it ain't."

"Are you talking about the theft you alleged—"

Elizabeth flinched as she saw Nathaniel's color rise.

"Father," she said, cutting them both off. She stood, immobile, knowing that every eye in the room was focused on her. Liam was looking at her as his salvation; the judge and Mr. Witherspoon were mystified at her interruption; Julian and Kitty wore their suspicions openly. Even Nathaniel, whose face she knew as well as her own, was looking at her with doubt and impatience and something like anger.

"What is it?" the judge asked. "Did you want to speak for the boy?"

"No," said Elizabeth, and then, faltering, "I mean to say, I can't speak for him or against him." She took in Liam's hurt stare, and decided that she dared not look at Nathaniel. "However, it would be appropriate to give him the chance to tell his version of what happened. Liam, will you talk to me about this?"

The boy's mouth worked in a terrible grimace; Elizabeth thought he was close to tears.

"If you won't defend yourself, and the evidence is against you, then there's nothing I can do for you," she said gently. "If you have been stealing, then you must face the consequences."

"You're awful eager to have one of your students punished, Lizzie," added Julian. "I'm not convinced he's done anything."

"Pardon me!" interjected the judge with considerable irritation. "But that is for me to decide!"

"I'm not eager to have him punished," Elizabeth corrected Julian sharply, ignoring her father. "But the law must be served, must it not?"

"How do we know the charges are true?" asked Julian, casting a glance toward Nathaniel, who stood silently watching the exchange. "He comes here with fantastic stories—"

"Are you calling me a liar?" asked Nathaniel in a tone as reasonable and measured as if he were asking for a cup of tea.

"I'm asking for proof," Julian said, just as calmly.

"There's proof to be had," Nathaniel said, tossing the beaver onto the rug at Julian's feet. "If you're interested in what's been took from me and from mine. If you want to hear about traps fooled with and stores broken into and folks being shot—come up to Hidden Wolf with me now and ask Otter how he got a bullet in his leg. If you're interested in the truth."

Elizabeth was so shocked at the news of Otter that she spoke before she could stop herself. "Are you accusing Liam of this?" she asked and then realized, too late, that she sounded as if she were doubting Nathaniel's word.

Nathaniel blinked slowly. "Not all of it," he answered without turning toward her. "Not of the shooting."

"Exactly who are you accusing, then?" asked Julian.

"Right at this moment I am accusing this boy of stealing a beaver from a line I set up on the stream we call Little Muddy. I come upon him not an hour ago. Look, you'll see his hands are still bloody."

"What exactly do you want me to do with him?" asked the judge when he had examined Liam's hands. "Sentence him to gaol?"

"That would be a start," said Nathaniel, leaning now on his rifle with an air that was half amusement and half irritation.

"No!" The boy's head snapped up. "Won't you speak for me, Miz Elizabeth! Tell them I been coming to school every day and working hard. Ain't that so?"

"Surely not gaol—" Elizabeth began.

"Enough," said the judge over the boy's renewed protests. "I find Liam Kirby guilty of poaching trap lines and fine him five dollars sterling and a week in custody—"

"Fi' dollars sterling!" howled Liam. "That pelt ain't worth five dollars!"

"—but due to his age and the first-time nature of the crime, I suspend the sentence and stipulate that the fine can be worked off, or paid in trade directly to Nathaniel Bonner. I hope that will satisfy all parties."

The judge was immediately drawn into a loud discussion of the law with Liam and Julian, but Elizabeth's attention was still focused on Nathaniel. *Otter*, Elizabeth thought. *He's worried about Otter. He never would have let himself go that way otherwise.* She knew she must look away, or let everyone in this room see those things on her face that they must not yet know about her. She dropped her gaze.

"There's just one more thing," Nathaniel said, directing himself to the judge.

Liam was suddenly quiet, as if he thought Nathaniel might demand something even more horrendous than a five-dollar fine.

"I was coming down to tell Miss Middleton that her schoolhouse is finished," said Nathaniel, turning to look at her directly for the first time.

"Oh," said Elizabeth, and then as an afterthought: "What good news."

"I'm going into the bush, hunting," he interrupted her. "But you can move in now without my help. I expect the doctor can lend a hand."

"Yes, I expect so," replied Elizabeth faintly. "Thank you kindly, Nathaniel."

"You're welcome," he said, touching his cap. Retrieving the beaver, he slung it over his shoulder with a flick of his wrist and left the room without another word. They heard the door slam behind him.

"Insolent savage," muttered Julian. "Come on now, Liam old man. Stop sniveling and tell us what really happened."

Nathaniel was angry. He was angry with himself for saying more than he'd meant to, back there in the judge's parlor. Walking up Hidden Wolf at a pace which would have left many younger men gasping, he made himself stop, to clear his head and to listen. His frustration and rage turned him inward, set him apart from the world around him, just when he needed to have his senses sharp. It wouldn't do to get shot now, not now, when things were starting to happen. He couldn't afford his anger right now; he couldn't afford to be thinking of the judge, or of Julian Middleton with his knowing half smile, or of Liam Kirby, bloody handed.

With his head cocked to one side, Nathaniel listened to the sounds of the spring thaw. He heard other things, too: three or four different birds, a squirrel, rodents in the soggy mass of winter debris on the forest floor. Far off, the thud of axe on wood. He touched his weapons: the knife at his side, the hatchet tucked into his belt along his spine. He checked the powder pan on his rifle and set out once again, cutting up the worst inclines, through thickets that seemed impenetrable, walking in the middle of swollen, ice-cold streams. Whoever it was following him, they were very good. But he was better. He knew this as a fact.

Once he had circled the strawberry fields, Nathaniel let himself think again. Now, this close to Lake in the Clouds, it was safer. He called forth Elizabeth, her face, the way her hair curled at the nape of her neck, the sound of her voice. He thought of Elizabeth with Richard, and he pushed himself faster toward home.

XIX

Curiosity had been spending an increasing amount of time with Elizabeth. At first it had seemed a natural thing that she would find work to do in the sitting room while Daisy, Polly, and Almanzo had their lessons; they were her children, after all, regardless of their ages. And Manny's mind was seldom on the work at hand unless his mother was carding wool in the corner.

Over time, Elizabeth imagined that Curiosity's interest would wane, but instead it seemed to become more focused. While Polly read aloud in her low and pleasing voice, Curiosity's hands would fall to her lap and she would incline her head in concentration. Perhaps, Elizabeth thought, it was that Curiosity wanted to be part of the lessons herself. One day she asked her outright, and found to her surprise that she had amused Curiosity with this invitation: in response, the older woman picked up the first tract to hand—it happened to be a treatise on taxation written by Alexander Hamilton—and read a paragraph out loud without stopping to breathe. Her manner was most unusual: she leaned forward at the waist and read in a loud voice directly into the page, as if she were arguing with it. Elizabeth was enchanted. It turned out that Curiosity had read every book in the judge's library, and had something to say about each of them.

Gradually Elizabeth learned to carry on with the lessons

while Curiosity flitted in and out, or sat close by, openly listening.

When Elizabeth set up a corner in the kitchen and began tutoring Benjamin and George, slaves of the Glove family, Curiosity never left at all and Galileo would just as often come to join them. James Glove let the boys come for lessons in arithmetic and writing once or twice a week when they weren't needed elsewhere. This had caused some concern in the village, but thus far the Gloves hadn't given in to pressure: they owned the only mill, and they wanted the boys to be more than one kind of help to them. Elizabeth had soon found out that Benjamin had a good head for figures, but less talent for the written language, while George was just the opposite. In a roundabout way, Curiosity let Elizabeth know it would not be to anyone's advantage if she shared this information with Mr. Glove.

Curiosity greeted the young men like royalty when they came into her kitchen and praised them to their faces when they got up to head for home, pressing gingerbread or pie into their hands and smiling a smile that Elizabeth seldom saw otherwise. Soon Elizabeth realized that Curiosity always kept Polly weaving or spinning by the hearth during these lessons. Benjamin and Polly were of a similar age, and Benjamin was a likely young man. Elizabeth wondered how Curiosity would manage to see the courtship through, given the fact that Benjamin was a slave, but she was sure that there was some well-thought-through plan. That much she had learned about Curiosity and Galileo: they did nothing by chance.

Clearly, Elizabeth had won Curiosity's approval and she felt the benefits of this state every day. It went beyond attention to her personal and material needs: Curiosity began to favor Elizabeth with information. She would bring tea to her room unexpectedly, and sit with her while she drank it, speaking of nothing in particular and still managing to pass on gossip which Elizabeth found often to be useful. Beyond that, Curiosity was plain amusing, and Elizabeth had come to depend on her in the weeks when worry about Nathaniel and their plans was sometimes more than she thought she could bear alone.

Thus, on the morning after Liam Kirby had been tried and

sentenced in the parlor, Elizabeth was not at first surprised to wake to Curiosity's knock at her door. Plagued by uneasy dreams, she had not slept well and she was glad to let herself be coddled a bit.

"Dr. Todd ain't come back yet," Curiosity said directly, handing Elizabeth a cup.

"He must have had more business to deal with than he expected," Elizabeth murmured. Of all people, she was least comfortable discussing Richard with Curiosity.

"Business, huh." Curiosity shook her head, the tower of her headcloth wobbling a bit with the strength of the motion. "Business waiting for him here, too."

Elizabeth raised a brow, waited.

"Didn't you hear Nathaniel yesterday?"

Bent over her teacup, Elizabeth searched quickly for an answer which would satisfy, but Curiosity seemed not to need one.

"Otter got himself shot and the doctor gone. I was thinking I might just go up there myself, see if they need any help with looking after that wound."

"Oh, yes," Elizabeth agreed, suddenly quite awake. "That's an excellent idea. You could take up some of that poultice you made for Nathaniel's shoulder—" She stopped suddenly. Curiosity was looking at her in a way which said more than words could.

"I was thinking I might stop and look at that schoolhouse of yours first. And that maybe you might come along, keep me company." She paused. "It's a long way for an old woman like me up Hidden Wolf."

Many logical replies to this unusual request for Elizabeth's company on an outing went through her head. All of them were familiar to Curiosity. There was something going on, and Elizabeth wasn't sure what it was.

"Father wouldn't like it."

Her lips pursed, Curiosity considered Elizabeth.

"You real worried about keeping your daddy happy these days."

Elizabeth thought hard and came to the conclusion that silence was the only viable strategy. But Curiosity had decided to open this subject, and she wasn't so easily dissuaded.

"You think I ain't seen you, bitin' your lip when the judge talk. Trying to look like you agree when you don't. Settin' your face in a smile when Richard Todd come by making sweet. You got them fooled, all right. But let me tell you, that smile about as believable as teats on a bull. Now you telling me you don't want to go up to Lake in the Clouds when I can see you ready to jump out the window to get there."

Curiosity tapped her foot, once, twice, while Elizabeth squirmed.

"What if I told you a little bird come by this morning and asked me to come up to the lake, and that little bird asked me to bring you along."

Elizabeth felt herself flush. "What did he say exactly?"

"What *he*?" Curiosity said. "I never said nothing about no *he*." Unexpectedly, she grinned. "There something you wantin' to tell me?"

It was a temptation. Elizabeth thought that she could trust Curiosity; she was sure of it. But to admit that she was carefully, knowingly, willfully deceiving her father was more than she could do.

"Not yet," Elizabeth said apologetically. "Not quite yet."

Curiosity shook her head slowly, a finger against her mouth. "You know what you're doin', child?"

Suddenly Elizabeth wasn't sure at all. She felt herself very close to tears. "Yes," she said finally.

"Well," said Curiosity, without a smile now. "I believe that you do."

There was a tap at her door, and the judge's voice through it, solicitous: "Are you coming to services this morning, daughter? The Witherspoons have invited us to dine with them afterward."

Elizabeth met Curiosity's eye and her raised brow. "You gonna disappoint that bird?"

There was another tap. "Daughter?"

"Please make my excuses, Father," Elizabeth called to the judge. "I was thinking of a walk."

·   ·   ·

They found the schoolhouse just as she had imagined it. It was full of sunlight and smelled of freshly cut timber and strong soap. In the main room there were six six-paned window sashes, two on each wall. From the far side there was a stretch of clear spring sky and the glint of yellow-green on the willows that bordered the lake; from the door there were the deep shadows of the forest. Against the drab green of the hemlock, the delicate branches of a stand of red osier glowed bright in the sun.

"Falling-Day has been here with her girls," observed Curiosity approvingly. "Not a muddy footprint to be seen." Her footsteps sounded through the room. "My, look at this. A study? And a view of the lake from the window. This is prettier than many a cabin in Paradise, Elizabeth."

Elizabeth was silent, because she was afraid that if she spoke she would be overcome by emotion. She walked through the classroom again, the floorboards solid underfoot, to stand in the study. The small window above the desk gave her a view of the little marsh that stood between the clearing and the lake, where the heads of trumpet weed and cinnamon fern were beginning to unfurl themselves.

She turned around to smile at Curiosity. "We'll need curtains."

"My, yes," she agreed. "And a hook rug or two, I'd say."

"I want to go to Lake in the Clouds now," Elizabeth said and she found herself thankful once again, this time for Curiosity's silent acceptance.

He was gone off into the bush to hunt. Of course. He had told her that in her father's parlor crowded with people, but somehow she hadn't heard it, or hadn't believed him. Elizabeth tried to pay attention to what it was Hawkeye was telling her, but somehow all she could hear was a three-beat refrain that echoed in her head without pause: *how could he, how could he, how could he.*

"I expect him back in a day or two," Hawkeye repeated and then Elizabeth produced the nod he had been waiting for. She was glad that the women were otherwise occupied, gathered around the cot where Otter lay, examining his wound. Hannah was there, too, mesmerized by the contents of Curiosity's basket and asking questions about her poultice. Many-Doves reached in to adjust the dressing and Otter batted at her, scowling. Falling-Day and Curiosity were deep in conversation.

"How did it happen?" Elizabeth asked Hawkeye, hoping for a long story, one which would allow her her own thoughts while he related it. But Hawkeye was watching her closely, and she saw understanding and compassion on his face. That was very hard to bear, and she bit the inside of her cheek to stop herself from asking that question which was running through her head.

"How do you think?" Hawkeye asked. "Somebody drew a bead on him when he warn't paying enough attention."

Elizabeth glanced at him from the side. "Has it been bad?"

He shrugged. "It's getting worse." And then, after a pause: "Nathaniel ain't took off for good, you know."

"I realize that." Elizabeth was unable to meet his eye. "I just wanted to thank him. For the schoolhouse."

"Is that so?" He took her by the arm and led her outside the cabin to the porch. The rush of the waterfall was louder than she remembered. Elizabeth let herself be shown to a rocking chair. She spread her skirts and folded her hands on her lap, and waited for this visit to be over so she could go home and worry in the peace and privacy of her own room.

"Nathaniel thought it would be best if he wasn't around for the next few days," Hawkeye said, surprising her.

"I see." Her tone was sharper than she intended; she was surprised to see Hawkeye smile in response.

"He made a point of taking leave from your folks yesterday, because then if something should happen around here—if somebody should go missing, for example—then maybe they won't think of Nathaniel first."

Startled, Elizabeth looked up. "He told you?"

Hawkeye nodded.

She was relieved and embarrassed and glad and frightened all at once. "And do you—" She stopped, unable to say the word.

"It ain't for me to approve or disapprove," Hawkeye said softly. "I will say that I'm worried. I told him plain, I don't believe you realize how dangerous it is, what you're up to."

"I'm not afraid," she said clearly.

He grunted. "You should be."

"I trust Nathaniel to look after me."

His look was keen. "That ain't the point," he said. "And you know it."

They were silent together for a while. Elizabeth looked at Hawkeye, at the set of his jaw and the way his eyes narrowed when he looked away, over the glen. There was a calmness about him, but she thought she saw something else, just below the surface. A waiting. There had been an old colonel at home who came to call on aunt Merriweather, a veteran of the French and Indian wars, who had some of the same wariness. Elizabeth wondered if all old soldiers had this feeling of cautiousness about them.

"Nathaniel is very much like you." She was surprised to hear herself say this, but found that it was the right thing. His reservation slipped a bit, and he grinned.

"Aye," he said. "That he is."

"There's the story of how you stole into a fort under siege to rescue your wife and her sister."

"Well," Hawkeye drawled. "That ain't it exactly, but I suppose it'll do for a story."

"It was a dangerous thing to do," she pointed out.

Hawkeye shrugged. "Breathin' was dangerous back in them days."

"The point is," Elizabeth continued resolutely, "that you would do the same in his place."

He laughed out loud at that. "I would," he agreed reluctantly.

Elizabeth said, "My father is talking of starting for Johnstown on Wednesday. Can you get word to Nathaniel?"

Hawkeye walked to the far end of the porch, and looked off into the gorge and the falling water. Without turning back to Elizabeth, he said, "Such a pretty spring day. Maybe you should take a little wander."

The hair on her nape had begun to rise. She wasn't sure why; she knew exactly why.

"Hannah!" called Hawkeye, and then when the child appeared at the door, he spoke a few words to her in Kahnyen'kehàka. Elizabeth, confused and still on edge, didn't follow anything of what he said. But she saw that Hannah was looking at her with a shy smile.

"Come," the child said. "I'll show you where the wild iris grow. They're up early this year."

Light-headed, Elizabeth rose. "I'd like that."

"I'll see Curiosity back home myself," said Hawkeye. "In case you're delayed."

To keep herself focused on thoughts other than their mysterious destination, and because she thought it prudent, Elizabeth tried to remark their path. Following Hannah, who was unusually quiet, they crossed from the glen over the narrowed gorge into the forest, where they passed through a carpet of anemone under a plantation of sugar maple and white birch not yet in leaf. Elizabeth saw that pieces of bark had been cut in neat rectangles from most of the birch trunks, and the sugar maple bore the signs of recent tapping.

They made their way up toward the backbone of the mountain, through stands of beech and maple interspersed with more birch and an occasional hemlock. Elizabeth had spent some of the difficult eight weeks learning about the forest from her students, and now she named the trees to herself. Occasionally she would ask a question, and Hannah would answer, naming the wild cherry for her, the yew, the trout lily which spread its strange yellow flower with mottled purple leaves in such profusion. She pointed to a porcupine's den and, calmly, the tracks of a bear in the mud. Hannah answered Elizabeth's questions without any of her usual elaboration, and after a while Elizabeth stopped asking. It was very cool in the wood, but she had begun to perspire.

At the top of the ridge, Elizabeth turned to look down on the forest, and stopped in wonder. It was as if they were alone in the world; there was no sign of Lake in the Clouds, or the village, or of anything having to do with human beings. Just the mountains and their spotty canopy of evergreens filling in with the tender first green of oaks and maple and beech, thousands upon thousands of them, as far as she could see.

Hannah was moving on, and Elizabeth followed her through forests, all red and white pine now, circumventing a marshy spot where a spring came to the surface. They came out of the wood onto a rocky plateau. A hawk passed overhead with a bit of moss trailing from her beak. The wind picked up, blowing Elizabeth's skirts around her legs.

Silently, Hannah gestured with her chin. Elizabeth saw now where they were: below them was Lake in the Clouds, the gorge pointing in a crooked finger away from the mountain. With its weathered square-cut logs, the cabin looked like something grown out of stone. Under her boots, Elizabeth could feel the pulse of the water in the rock as it rushed to that point in the cliff face where it would explode in a waterfall. From here they could not see it fall, but they could hear it, muted.

There was a three-note trilled birdsong which Elizabeth would not have noticed, but Hannah raised her head and trilled back.

"Runs-from-Bears," Hannah murmured in explanation.

There was no sign of him. Elizabeth realized that this was meant to be so: he had followed them at a distance. They would not have let Hannah walk through the forest by herself otherwise. Not given the events of the past few days.

Another call, from below. In response, Hannah pointed down the cliff. The incline was fairly steep, rock and scrabble and boulders. There was no visible path.

Elizabeth looked at the path and back at Hannah. "You want me to go down there?"

The little girl nodded as if this were nothing so terribly unusual.

"Aren't you coming?"

Hannah shook her head. "Take off your boots," she said practically. "It'll be easier barefoot."

Her nerves humming, Elizabeth complied. After a moment's thought she took off her stockings, folding them neatly.

"Go on," Hannah said, smiling now. "He's waiting for you."

·   ·   ·

It was strange to feel the ground under her bare feet and she went slowly at first, testing each foothold. Twice she grabbed at a shrub growing from the rock face, so that her hands were sticky and pungent with evergreen sap. Pausing to catch her breath, Elizabeth wiped her fingers on her handkerchief. She wished for something to drink. She wished herself on level ground. She wished herself back in England, at aunt Merri-weather's whist table with a book hidden on her lap. She wished for all these things, and none of them.

She hadn't known that fear could be intoxicating.

He was waiting for her. She tried to gather her thoughts, but they slipped away in a flurry of images, all of them Nathaniel.

Elizabeth worked her way down another thirty yards in stops and starts to a little plateau like a pocket torn in the cliff face. She wondered where she should possibly go from here, and then, from the corner of her eye, she caught a flash of move-ment.

Nathaniel was standing behind her. He had materialized out of rock, it seemed, and now without a word gestured for her to follow him. He put his hand on her shoulder to guide her up; she felt its heat through the layers of her cape and clothing. Nathaniel pointed to the first foothold and then the next, and she moved as he directed her. Then he scrambled past her to pull himself up into a crack in the rock face. He turned back and reached down a hand.

He stood poised there, his face composed, his eyes flashing something she could not quite name, but which was familiar to her, and offered his hand. Elizabeth looked at Nathaniel's hand, the broad expanse of it, the long, hard curve of his fingers. She gave him her own hand and let him pull her into the side of the mountain.

She realized it was a cave even as she came through, but it confused her to see sunlight refracting on the walls. Coming from the dark into the glare, she blinked for a moment until she could make sense of the light and noise. The outermost face was not rock, but moving water: they were behind the waterfall, not a hundred yards from Lake in the Clouds. The rush of falls produced a breeze which caught the loose hair at her nape and temples and set it dancing. A fine mist swirled through the small cave. It felt good on her flushed cheeks.

Nathaniel was standing before the wall of water, sun on his hair and shoulders. From the back he was a stranger, a wild frontiersman with his loose hair and buckskin shirt and beaded leggings. There was a knife at his waist, and his rifle leaned against the wall within arm's reach. Then he turned and his strong profile came into view. Distracted, the rush of her own blood as loud in her ears as the falling water, Elizabeth saw the wolves' skulls which had been wedged into a long crack in the wall. While Nathaniel walked toward her she counted them: seven. There were seven.

He stopped before her, his eyes moving over her face. She saw that his brow was beaded with sweat although it was cool here. *He's as nervous as I am,* she thought thankfully. She was glad it was too loud to talk; it gave her an excuse to look at him, to remind herself of the things she knew but had begun to doubt: the way his jaw curved, the straight line of his eyebrows, the way he looked at her. She hadn't been imagining it: it was there, his wanting her. Nathaniel caught her hand and drew it up between them and then turned to lead her back farther into the cave, through a narrowing and then into another room.

Here the light was less but so was the sound of the water. Elizabeth moved forward tentatively, starting at the feel of something furry brushing against her bare feet. She pushed up against Nathaniel and yelped softly.

"No, no," he said calmly. "Look. It's just pelts."

This cave, bigger than the one before it, was crowded. There were baskets and barrels, a makeshift table with a betty lamp at its center. Provisions hung from pegs driven into cracks in the walls, strings of dried squash and apples and braided corn. On smaller pegs nearest Elizabeth was a selection of clothing, bullet pouches, knives in their sheaths and powder horns. And everywhere, on every surface, were pelts tied into neat bundles.

"The winter's work," said Nathaniel, following the path of her gaze.

"Hidden Wolf," she said, finally understanding.

"Hidden Wolf," he confirmed.

Everything of value, everything they needed to get them through the next year, was here. Anybody who wanted to force them out would only have to find this place. And they had brought her here without a word of discussion or warning or caution. Nathaniel had claimed her, and she had become one of them. This made Elizabeth immeasurably happy and unusually shy; she didn't know where to look. And he was so silent; why didn't he speak? She glanced up at him, and saw that he was waiting.

"I came to tell you—" she began, and then faltered.

His grip on her hand tightened. He waited.

"I wanted to say—" she began again, and then stopped once more. When she managed to meet his eye, she saw something frightened there. She watched him try to control his expression.

"Thank you so much, Nathaniel. For the schoolhouse." This came out sounding very prim and dry and it was not at all what she wanted to say. But he was being distant and reserved; thus far he had done nothing more than take her hand. Irritated with her own clumsiness and with Nathaniel's unwillingness to set her at ease, she pulled away and made a study of her bare feet.

"You've changed your mind," he said woodenly.

"No!" Elizabeth's head jerked up, surprise cutting through the awkwardness between them. "No. How could you think such a thing?"

"Maybe I was expecting more of a greeting," Nathaniel said, and now there was at least the hint of a smile. "From my bride."

All the fear and frustration of the past eight weeks had been pulsing close to the surface, and with one word Nathaniel had pricked it open. Very slowly Elizabeth leaned forward until her forehead rested on his shoulder, shuddering with pleasure and relief at the feel of him, at his smell.

His arms came up around her. Nathaniel knew that she needed comforting. He took his time, letting her get used to the feel of him again. He touched her hair lightly, her back. Little by little she relaxed against him.

"We leave on Wednesday," Elizabeth said after a while. "And I'm worried."

"About what?"

She shivered a little. "I'm worried that I'll have to make a binding oath to Richard in front of Mr. Bennett before my father will sign the deed." Nathaniel could tell by the rush in her voice that this was the very worst she could imagine. He felt more of the tension slip away from her, now that she had shared the burden.

"Todd is coming to Johnstown with you?"

She nodded. "I'm afraid so."

"Well," said Nathaniel, smoothing her hair. "We'll have to think of a way to change his mind about that."

She pulled away then, frowning. Nathaniel tensed, feeling the jealousies of the last weeks begin to simmer again. "Unless you're worried about hurting his feelings."

"Because I don't like him doesn't mean I want to see him hurt," Elizabeth said, with a look Nathaniel thought her students must be familiar with. "It just means I don't want to marry him. As you know very well."

"We ain't got much time," he said slowly. "And I don't see that we should spend it with Richard Todd between us."

"Then promise me he won't come to any harm."

Nathaniel said, very evenly, "He won't come to any harm unless he puts himself in harm's way."

"Are you always this sure of yourself?" she asked suddenly, her irritation showing in the way she suddenly met his gaze, unflinching.

"I'm sure of some things," he responded calmly. "One of them is that Richard Todd ain't to be trusted."

"I didn't say that I trusted him," Elizabeth said. "In fact, I don't trust him. But I still don't like the idea of his being hurt."

Nathaniel felt his temper rising to the surface. "You're mighty worried about the man's welfare, seeing that you don't like him much."

"You are not being rational," said Elizabeth stiffly.

"Maybe not," Nathaniel said. "But maybe rational ain't what's called for right now. It was damn hard, let me tell you, watching the man who has been doing his best to run me and mine off this mountain, seeing him lay claim to you as if you was a good horse. I told you he won't come to harm if he stays out of harm's way, and that's the best I can promise. Is that good enough for you?"

Her color had risen, and her fingers twitched as if she wanted to hit him, or touch him. She put her chin up with that same flick of the head she had shown him the first time he spoke to her, when he had called her a spinster. One part of Nathaniel wanted to remind her of this, wanted to see her ruffle and flush and become uncertain. Because on the other side of the teasing there would be peacemaking, and they could get on with what had been started in the stable back in February. Nathaniel wanted that, but he was cautious. In the next few days he knew he would need all his skill and wits to keep them together, and alive.

And there was the matter of Richard Todd, still unresolved. He could see her weighing things, her eyes narrowed.

"Elizabeth. Is that good enough for you?" he repeated.

"Yes," she said grudgingly. "It is."

"Well, then." Nathaniel nodded. "Then this is what we've got to do. We've got to keep Todd away from Johnstown—never mind how, I'll work that out later." Reluctantly, he stepped back a bit from her. "Now maybe we better talk about how we'll meet up, before I send you home."

"Oh," Elizabeth said, feeling suddenly deflated. She tried hard to hide her disappointment, tried not to look at him, his face, his mouth. And failed miserably. She bristled with the need to put her hands on him and still she didn't dare.

She said, "I've just spent eight weeks being pleasant to Richard Todd. Which I didn't enjoy, though you seem to think I did. I thought you and I would have . . . a little time together."

There, she thought, blushing and cursing herself for it. *I've as much as dared him to kiss me, and what if he won't? What if he doesn't?* There was a need in her that she couldn't name and didn't know how to tell him about, but she knew she must touch him, must have him touch her, or simply die.

He saw all this, and it made him glad and it frightened him, too. "Elizabeth," he whispered, catching her up tight against him. "By Christ, don't you think I know how long it's been? But if I start, if we start—" And then he paused to kiss her, anyway, because she was so close and there was her smell that undid him, dried flowers and ink and her woman smell, and there was nothing more in the world he could think of doing. A rough kiss that drew from Elizabeth a sigh like the wind in the trees. Nathaniel pulled her up tighter against him and went on kissing her for a long time, until he could force himself to stop.

He buried his face in her neck, inhaling her scent. "If we start this now—"

She said, "It's already started." And she was right, he knew it; it was started and it couldn't be stopped. There was nothing to do but to draw her down into the pelts, reaching behind her to snap a cord with a jerk of his wrist so that she could lie there in a jumble of fisher fur as dark and rich as her hair while he kissed her mouth, and kissed it again, and touched her, her face, her throat, letting his mouth follow, his body tense with purpose even while hers softened, drawing him in.

Her eyes glowed in the half-light as he untied her cloak and tugged it out from under her. Concentrating on her face, Nathaniel pulled free the lace kerchief tucked into her bodice, drawing it over her skin. He dropped it behind himself and then, slowly, ran his knuckles over the swell of her breasts and down her body, half fearing that she would protest. But instead there was only the way her flesh rose to him, and the sound of her indrawn breath. She touched him then. Slid her hand into the open throat of his shirt to draw him down into a kiss deep enough to put an end to his indecision.

There were buttons and ties and hooks to be dealt with between long kisses. She helped him with her own clothes until only her shift remained, and then watched with a little frown of concentration as he sat back on his heels to pull his shirt over his head. He felt her hands on him while his face was still caught inside, her tentative fingers touching the Kahnyen'kehàka tattoo that circled his chest, tracing faded scars. When he had stretched out next to her she found the one she wanted, a puckered bullet wound on his shoulder. She lifted her head to press her lips to it, the shy touch of her tongue moving him to hastiness. He drew her close.

"Is this what you want?" he asked, his cupped hands pressing her buttocks through thin muslin, seeing that she did want it in her face and the way she moved into his hands. But he needed to hear her say so.

She surprised him. "It's you I want," she said clearly. "Not Richard Todd. You." And he understood that he had underestimated her frustration and anger and pure iron will.

He pushed the shift off her shoulders, helped her turn this way and that until she was free of it, her body white against the dark fur. The luxury of her breasts, firm and round and full, struck at him like a fist.

"Holy God," he muttered, burying his face in the curve of her throat, his hands clenching on her back. He could feel all her furious determination draining away to sudden uncertainty.

"Are you—is everything—all right?" she asked hoarsely.

Nathaniel captured her bare shoulders and leaned over her, his blood leaping at the feel of her softness against his chest. That she would need to ask such a question, that she would have no idea of her own beauty or of the value of what she offered him.

"Elizabeth," he said, resting his forehead on hers. "You are the finest thing I've ever seen. But it's been a good long while, and I'm having a hard time minding my self-control."

She smiled then. "Nobody has asked you to," she whispered, and she blushed, the color seeping down her neck and over her chest.

He followed her blush, forcing himself to slow down and start the whole game anew, light kisses and then more demanding ones while he explored her. With an open palm he drew circles over her nipple until she gasped, her fingers curling hard around his arms. When he found her breast with his mouth she cried out for the first time, arching up to him while he suckled. Her flesh swelling against his tongue, Nathaniel felt his whole body shudder with the pleasure of it.

She had broken out in a fine sweat; he licked it from between her breasts and her throat, working his way up to claim her mouth in a kiss as heavy and demanding as the ridge of flesh he pressed against her hip. As he rocked against her, hip to hip and tongue to tongue, he ran a finger up her thigh to touch her heat for the first time.

He realized that she was trying to talk to him, and he came

back to himself a little. His name. She was summoning him to her. He drew it from her mouth, swallowed it whole. Gave her back her own name, fed it to her with his tongue. Between kisses he untied the thong that held his breechclout and leggings, and then he gathered her up against himself, wanting to feel her, all of her skin against his.

"Elizabeth," he whispered.

She focused on him finally, her eyes cloudy with wanting.

"Richard Todd can't have you, not ever. You have to leave your father's home and come to me. Because once this is done, you are mine to keep and protect, and I am yours. Do you understand?"

"Oh, yes," she whispered, her hands flitting over his shoulders.

"When I'm dying," he said. "When I close my eyes at the last, it'll be your face I see, right at this moment."

When she could think again, the first coherent thought that came to Elizabeth was that she had lied. To Nathaniel, and to herself. *I'm not an idiot,* she had told him back in the snowy strawberry field. *I know what it means to mate.*

But she had been an idiot, to have thought it would be a simple, mechanical act of commitment. It had seemed the logical and the right thing to do; there was no clearer pledge she could make, no better way to make him understand that his jealousy of Richard Todd was unfounded.

And, she admitted to herself, she had suspected that she would enjoy it. His kisses had made her curious. But she had underestimated herself, her wanting and its own strength. The depth of her own response was as compelling and surprising as the burning mix of pain and pleasure he had brought to her.

He had pulled pelts over them, and Elizabeth moved tentatively underneath, appreciating the strange indulgence of fur against her bare skin, and the warm, damp trace of him on her thighs. Nathaniel was lying on his side behind her in the same curve, the hard length of his leg following the line of her own in a casual embrace which seemed to Elizabeth almost more intimate than the act that went before it. His breath on her shoulder, he stroked her arm from wrist to elbow and back again.

"What are you thinking?"

She turned to him then, determined not to be timid. "I was thinking that some things don't lend themselves to rational analysis."

He grinned, his teeth flashing white. "Is that good or bad?"

"Good," she said simply, and then dropped her gaze, in spite of all her intentions. She studied the dark blue jagged line which crossed his chest and continued in a loop around his torso, to a destination somewhere on his back. She wondered where exactly it went, but she was too comfortable and too shy to follow it right now.

He raised her chin with his finger. "You're not asking, but I'll tell you anyway what I'm thinking. I'm thinking about how fine it is to have you here like this, next to me." His gaze held her steady, as if daring her to doubt him.

"Oh." Elizabeth could feel a slow warmth seeping through her bones, pooling in her breasts and lower, lower. *This is how it starts,* she thought. *With words. With his voice, so deep that it echoes down inside.*

"And I'm wondering if you're regretting this, already."

She watched him swallow, the column of muscles in his throat moving.

"Oh, no," she murmured, pushing her face into the curve of his shoulder. "Quite to the contrary."

He smoothed her hair. "Is that so?"

With a little jolt of satisfaction, Elizabeth realized that Nathaniel was asking her for reassurance. This made her flush with pleasure, and it gave her the courage to say something she might not otherwise have said.

"I wasn't sure that I would, but after a bit, I did like it. This. Being with you."

"So did I," he said solemnly, but Elizabeth could feel him smiling.

She moved closer to him, the feel of his chest against her cheek and the weight of his arm around her shoulders already familiar. The beat of his heart and the rush of the waterfall were hypnotic.

"It's nice here," she said groggily.

He took her head between his hands, forced her to meet his eye. "Elizabeth, we have to talk."

"Of course," she said. "But the questions that come to mind right now aren't . . . seemly."

He laughed then, a comfortable sound. "For instance?"

Elizabeth closed her eyes to gather her thoughts. *Did I please you?* she wanted to ask, and *May I look at you, at all of you?* and *What is it that you think of while you're holding me? Did you cry out at the end in pain, or pleasure?* And *Is your child started inside me now?* But this last thought was too much; it filled her with anticipation and joy and a bottomless terror. She pushed it away.

He was watching her closely. Elizabeth thought that perhaps he knew all these things that were in her mind, and others that she could not yet put words to. She knew too that there wasn't time for this now.

"Boots?"

"All right, if you must know." She opened her palms on his chest, ran them over his shoulders, thick with muscle. "I was just wondering how often we would do—this."

He laughed again, and cupped her face in his hand, rubbing a thumb across her lower lip before he kissed her. "I would say that we should get married first before we start negotiating that point—" There was a scuffle under the pelts as he held off the hand she raised to cuff his ear. "But out of curiosity, Boots, how often would suit you?"

Very much awake now, she beat on his shoulders until he captured both wrists and flipped her to her back, leaning over to pin her arms up and away. His hair fell forward to brush her breasts, his earring glimmering bright silver against his skin. *Look, oh, look at you,* she thought, struck by the wondrous beauty of him, the long, elegant body arched over her with muscles tensed. She closed her eyes because the sight of him blinded her.

"Constantly," he whispered against her mouth. "We will do this at every opportunity."

·   ·   ·

Nathaniel brought her a bowl of water from the falls and tore strips from an old homespun hunting shirt so that Elizabeth could wash, but there was not enough time in the world to put herself in order. She brushed with increasing dismay at her wrinkled skirts and then, in near panic, she presented herself to Nathaniel.

"You look like you've been up to mischief," he said finally. He himself looked as he always did; buckskin did not wrinkle, it seemed.

"Mischief, is it?" she muttered. "It's not amusing, Nathaniel. I can't go back home like this. You know I cannot." In a fit of irritation, she turned her back on him while she tried to tuck her lace more neatly into the line of her bodice so that it covered the red flush that still mottled her chest.

"Do you take a chill easy?" Nathaniel asked.

She pulled up, surprised. "What?"

"Are you one of those women who take a chill easy in the cold? Get sick and take to bed?"

Elizabeth raised her chin. "I haven't been ill enough to stay in bed since I was twelve and I knocked my head climbing a tree. I can't even remember the last time I had a fever." She said this with some pride, and was surprised by Nathaniel's grin in reply.

"Come." He took her by the wrist to pull her to the next cave over her protests.

"Please, Nathaniel, think a minute. What am I to do? We can't afford to have any suspicions raised—"

Just before the waterfall he stopped. "Has anyone taught you yet how to drink out of a stream?" He shouted, to be heard above the rushing water.

Mystified, Elizabeth shook her head. "Why?"

He grinned, grasping her firmly by her upper arms. "Because," he bellowed. "Folks generally fall in once or twice until they get the hang of it."

She realized too late what he was about. Before she could protest or try to extract herself he had tipped her back headfirst into the falling curtain of icy water, and pulled her back out, sputtering, every nerve in her body jumping in protest.

"Nathaniel!" But he was tipping her back again, and this time he leaned forward to kiss her as she went, claiming a mouth already open in exclamation. She clung to him, her fingers twined around forearms as unyielding as oak as she kissed him back, feeling the hard graze of his jaw like a blessing, his mouth like a hot brand in the stream of water cascading over them.

"Now," he said, when they had stumbled back from the precipice, dripping and gasping. "I expect you can go home without raising suspicions."

It was well past midday when Nathaniel announced Elizabeth's ascent up the cliff face with a three-note bird call. She came over the lip of the incline to find Hannah waiting for her. The child was sitting cross-legged on a flat rock in the sun, her braids gleaming blue-black. In her lap was a bouquet of wild iris not yet in bloom, slender purple heads nodding inside their paper-like sheaths.

"How beautiful," Elizabeth said, but she was watching Hannah's face.

"Grandmother promised to show me how to make a poultice of these for Otter," the child said, matter-of-factly.

Elizabeth saw Hannah take in her damp hair and the sorry state of her clothing. For once, Elizabeth was supremely grateful for the Kahnyen'kehàka sensibilities which forbade personal commentary or questions of a kind which would have come naturally to any of the other children. She considered the various things she might tell Hannah, and quickly discarded them all; this was not just one of her students, but a child she would raise, her responsibility. Her daughter. Elizabeth wouldn't start out by lying to her, and so she would say nothing at all.

When Elizabeth had put on her stockings and boots, they started back.

It wasn't until they had entered the birch and maple grove closest to Lake in the Clouds that Hannah stopped suddenly. Elizabeth tensed, looking around herself, but she could see no sign of trouble.

"What will I call you?" Hannah asked in her straightforward manner, but without her usual grin.

"What do you want to call me?" asked Elizabeth, who had been thinking of the same thing.

"I remember my mother," Hannah said, and for the first time there was a wariness there. Elizabeth wanted to touch the child, but thought better of it.

"That's a very good thing," she said. "My mother died when I was just a little older than you are now, and the memories I have of her are very precious to me."

Hannah nodded thoughtfully. Then, with her chin, she directed Elizabeth's attention to a steep hang deep in shadow, where Curiosity was crouched in a riot of new ferns. As Elizabeth watched, her long, thin frame unfurled and she waved in their direction.

"Hello, there," she called. It was amazing how quickly the older woman could move. Before Elizabeth could think of what to say, she was with them, and handing Elizabeth a basket full to the rim with every sort of plant and root the forest had to offer.

"It's time we got on home," she said. "Although I'd like to know where you got them flag lily this early, Missy Hannah. Never mind," she said with a halfhearted scowl in response to Hannah's grin. "I guess I ain't traipsing up to that spring on the ridge to get 'em. No, you go on now, get on back to Falling-Day so she can poultice that leg."

For the first time, Curiosity seemed to look closely at Elizabeth. "We got to get this one home. Looks like she fell in a stream. That what happened?"

"Why, yes," Elizabeth said lamely. "Exactly."

"I thought me so." But her sharp look said much more.

Hannah had already started off. Elizabeth called, and the child stopped, looking over her shoulder.

"Thank you," she said, when everything else that went through her head turned out to be insufficient, or too complex to say right there and then. "And tell them at home, too, please. Thank you and—goodbye."

Hannah nodded, and then sped on her way.

"Come on along now," Curiosity said. "Got to get you back home and in dry clothes before you take a chill."

"Curiosity," Elizabeth began, but the older woman stopped and laid one long, cool hand on her forearm.

"No," she said, not unkindly. "I expect it's better if you let me tell the stories for right now. I got one or two might interest you."

XX

"You know how many babies I delivered in my time?" Curiosity began. To Elizabeth's relief, she answered her own question. "Don't know myself, but I expect it's close to a hundred since I come to Paradise, more than thirty year ago. Ain't been called on too often since the doctor decided he know more about birthin' than I do. He will come an' fetch me, however, when he needs smaller hands. What is so very particular about that, Elizabeth, is that the very first child I put in his mama's arms was Richard Todd hisself.

"I see I surprise you, but it's true. In '61 that was, the very year your granddaddy Clarke bought me and Leo free and sent us up here to work for your mama. I hadn't started to breed yet, myself, and neither had she, but with Cora's help we managed when the time came."

"There was no doctor in Paradise then?"

Curiosity laughed. "No ma'am. No doctor, no trading post, nothing. In '61 there was only four families up here besides your folks, remember. Hawkeye and Cora had been up on Hidden Wolf for a bit by that time—Nathaniel was two that summer that Richard was born. The others were all Carlisle's tenants, including your daddy, to start with. Has the judge told you about Carlisle? The old Tory who owned all this land until after the war when it was took away from him and sold at auction. Let's see, there was Horst Hauptmann and his first wife, the one that took the yellow fever and run off with it. James and Martha Todd and their oldest boy, Samuel, and the Witherspoons too. No, there was no doctor here then—it was up to us women, always has been and I don't expect that will ever change much. Your mama had a way about her in a birthin' room. I have always been sorry that she left before I could get to know her."

Elizabeth had never spoken to Curiosity about her mother. She knew very little about those few years her mother had spent in Paradise, and the circumstances surrounding her removal to England, except that she had been carrying Elizabeth, and the pregnancy had not been easy. There had always been a slight worry in her that if she asked Curiosity for the stories of her mother, she would hear something she might have to hold against her father.

The older woman had stopped to forage in a pile of moldering oak leaves, her quick fingers uncovering a crowd of peaked mushroom caps tinged scarlet.

"Mind you never et nothing looks like that, now," she said, distracted. Then she brushed her hands on her apron and carried on. Her step was slow and measured, moving along at the same pace as her story.

"Now Mrs. Todd wanted a doctor for her laying-in, being used to things as they was done back then in Boston. She come from a family with money, you see. But her time come upon her unexpected like, and your mama and me was called on to attend, green as we was. It was Martha Todd's good luck that Cora was at hand, too. A levelheaded woman, was Cora. I learned a lot from her. Just a year ago it was that a fever took her and I miss her every day.

"Mistress Todd was a particular woman but she brought that boy into the world without much fuss. And given the size of him, I think to this day she had misreckoned her time." Curiosity hiccuped a little laugh. "A big, fat child, with a shock of red hair like a rooster's comb. And lungs. Lordy. So you see, I know Richard as long as anybody here in Paradise."

"I wonder why you're telling me this story," Elizabeth said, slowly.

."Do you?" Curiosity stopped to look at her hard. "Well,

now, Elizabeth. I'm telling you what I know about Dr. Richard Todd because I think you're underestimating him. And that's a dangerous thing to be doing."

When it was clear that Elizabeth was not going to enter into a discussion just yet, Curiosity started to talk again.

"It was in '65 that the trouble came, in the fall. Your mama was long gone to England to bring you into the world. Your daddy had just come back hisself, went over that summer to try and fetch you'all back, but come home empty-handed. Left your mama with Julian on the way, though, so I guess they got along a'right."

Curiosity sent Elizabeth a sideways glance.

"Richard was just three, but a likelier young'un you'll never see. Big for his age, and sassy, and smart. Worshiped his brother, Samuel, followed him everywhere, as little brothers will do. A few more families had settled here by then, the ones that was braver than most. This here a mighty lonely spot, you understand, and the Mohawk hung on for a long time.

"It was a Friday evening. I recall it clearly."

Her voice dropped low, and Elizabeth had to strain to hear, although some part of her didn't want to hear this at all.

"The judge and the Reverend Witherspoon had gone into Johnstown to do some trading. I remember Mrs. Todd calling after the judge not to forget to fetch her a cone of sugar. Don't know why, but that stick with me. I had spent the whole day setting soap, and when the men was gone, I went down in the root cellar to sort through some taters. It was cool down there and I was hot, and I fell asleep. This was the old house in the village, you understand. It was a good cellar, though, deep and solid, and I never heard a thing. When I come up in the evening light, the house was gone, the whole village, too. Everything still burning, and everybody—most everybody—dead or gone."

Curiosity's voice had fallen into a singsong that made Elizabeth's skin rise. She shivered in her damp clothes and pulled her cape closer around her, but Curiosity seemed not to notice.

"The only men that survived that day were your daddy and Mr. Witherspoon because they was in Johnstown, and Axel Metzler and the old Hauptmann—they was hunting up on the other side of the Wolf. And my Galileo, he was fishing up on the other end of the lake and he heard what was going on, but there weren't nothing he could do but sit and pray. The only woman come through besides me was Mrs. Witherspoon, who climbed up a spruce when she heard the Mohawk coming and hid there. We thought at first she was took with the others. She sat in that tree for two days without making a sound. It was Axel Metzler who found her and talked her down, gentle like, though she was never quite the same after what she saw from that tree.

"The Mohawk killed the livestock and the men outright, pretty much, although they took their time with Mr. Todd. And then they took the women and children and headed out. There was six of them. Martha Todd with Samuel and Richard, and Mary Clancy with her Jack and Hester. That was the last we saw of Missus Todd and Clancy. They both died on the march north, is how the story goes. Don't know what happened to Mary, but she was a delicate thing and I have to say it don't surprise me much she didn't hold out. Martha was tough, though. She would have made it if she hadn't been big with child. She couldn't keep up. When she fell down once too often they took a tomahawk to her.

"I know how harsh that sounds, and they ain't much I can do to put a good face on it except to say that the way the Mohawk look at it, a woman who can't keep up will die one way or the other in the bush, and a swift tomahawk were the best she could hope for."

"Where was Hawkeye during all this?" Elizabeth asked.

"He took Cora and Nathaniel off to the Genesee Valley that fall. It was a shame he wasn't here, that's true enough, as he has always been on good terms with the Mohawk and might have been able to steer them away from Paradise. But the Lord had other plans," Curiosity said. "And he didn't see fit to lift the yoke."

Elizabeth was trying hard not to imagine Martha Todd and the way she died, leaving her two sons in the hands of the men who had killed her husband.

"Them was hard times," Curiosity said. "Hard, indeed."

"Did they mistreat the children?" Elizabeth asked against her own better instincts.

"Lord, no." Curiosity looked at her with some surprise. "The Mohawk know the value of a child. It was the children they wanted, you see, to start with. To take the place of their own kin, lost in the wars.

"So, now, where was we? They headed north with the children, moving fast once the women was dead. Two or three days out, it was, that Jack managed to slip away in the night, which is how we learned about what happened to the women. He had a grandfather over in German Flats, and he went to be raised up by him. I hear he a cordwainer now and a good one. But the other three—the Todd boys and Hester—they was adopted into the tribe, and there they stayed. We had no word of them for some many years."

"You know," Elizabeth said. "I have asked Richard about this part of his life many times and he is unwilling to tell me anything about it."

"Well, I cain't tell you much either about what went on those years he lived with the Mohawk. A' course, it won't be much different from the way any boy is raised. They train all the young'uns hard, but it feel like play to 'em, the way it's done. So they say. And the Todd boys was both strong. Every Indian in the northwest knew who Samuel was, he made a name for hisself at lacrosse. They called him Throws-Far, I believe. And Richard—well, big as he is, he could outrun just about anybody. Still can."

Curiosity stopped and turned to look at Elizabeth. Unexpectedly, she smiled.

"Your hair look pretty like that, Elizabeth, all curled around your face. It's a shame and pity you cain't let it go free."

"Why, thank you," Elizabeth said, surprised but pleased.

"Welcome. Now, let's see. We heard some few years after the children was took that Amos Foster was trying to buy those boys back from the Mohawk."

"Who?" asked Elizabeth.

"Martha's brother, Amos Foster. He had settled in Albany and made hisself a fortune at trade, you see. But his wife died without givin' him children and he wanted to find his sister's boys to raise up as his own. So he spent a lot of time going from village to village up in Canada until he found 'em, but it didn't do him no good."

"They wouldn't take money for the boys?" Elizabeth asked.

"Don't rightly know if they would have or not. I expect not. Any more than I would sell one of mine. But it didn't matter anyway, because Samuel didn't want to be redeemed. Most didn't, you realize. Not the ones that was took young and adopted in. Now, the way I heared it happen was that Samuel wouldn't have nothing to do with the uncle when he finally found them. Wouldn't speak English to him, even. Wouldn't answer to his Christian name. Not that you could mistake him, or Richard, either, both of them big and red-haired as they come."

"And Richard? Did he want to go with his uncle?"

"Richard was different. He would have left the Mohawk, I expect, if Samuel had come along. But he wouldn't leave his brother."

"How do you know all this?" Elizabeth asked suddenly.

"That uncle of Richard's," said Curiosity matter-of-factly. "He took a slave by the name of Archimedes along with him when he traveled the villages."

"And you know this Archimedes?"

"I do. He's my Galileo's brother. When Richard's uncle come back through Paradise to see the judge, Archimedes sat in my kitchen. That was the year Manny was born, and Archimedes dandled the boy on his knee the whole time."

Curiosity's smile was different now, turned inward. But she shook herself and sighed.

"So you see, some of what I'm telling you, don't no other white folks know. Except Richard hisself."

"I don't understand," Elizabeth said slowly. "Mr. Bennett told me that Richard was eventually redeemed by his uncle."

"It's true enough that Samuel stayed and Richard left," Curiosity agreed. "But not because the uncle paid a ransom. Although I guess that's the story people tell. No, Richard run off the fall he was eleven. Slipped away from a hunting party and made his way back to Paradise."

"But that was in Canada—" Elizabeth stopped. "He made his way through the endless forest by himself?"

"He did. With no more than a knife and a bag of nocake on him, he walked the length of the bush down to Paradise. Took him the winter."

"He was eleven years old," Elizabeth repeated to herself.

"Yasm," Curiosity agreed. "He surely was. But he kept himself fed, eating mostly rabbit, I guess, and squirrel, whatever he could snare. He ran to keep warm and found his way by the stars. So I guess you could say it was the eight years he spent with the Mohawk that kept him alive. Richard Todd is as white a man as you will ever see on the outside with his velvet and brocade, but the boy inside him was raised a Mohawk. And a warrior."

Elizabeth was thinking hard.

"What made him change his mind and leave his brother behind?"

"That I cain't answer. Guess nobody could, but Richard. And Samuel, but he's dead. Died fighting with the British in the revolution."

"Do folks around here know about Richard's escape and the winter he spent in the woods?"

"A' course they do," Curiosity said. "He come back here, after all. It was Chingachgook who found him, brought him into the trading post that February. Thin as a whipsaw, telling his story in half English and half Mohawk. Hawkeye and Cora wanted to take him in, but he wouldn't go near Hidden Wolf at first. Later he couldn't stay away," she said, sighing. "But at first Reverend Witherspoon took him and kept him until the spring, when his uncle came to fetch him to Albany."

"Richard lived with the Witherspoons?"

"He did. Let's see, Kitty would have been about five. Mrs. Witherspoon had died that winter, and I guess the reverend thought it would do her good to have the boy in the house for a while. It was Kitty that taught him English again. I remember the way she tagged along behind him, hanging on to his coat-tails, chattering the whole day long." Curiosity smiled a little. "She would do it to this day, if only she could."

"So she would," Elizabeth agreed.

They were silent for a while. There was an unreal quality to the clear spring air, filled with birdsong and the rustling of the woods coming to life again. It was early afternoon, but to Elizabeth it felt as if a week had passed since Curiosity had brought her morning tea. She could smell Nathaniel on her skin. The feel of his hands on her hips came to her, and she drew in a sharp breath. There was a sudden urge in her just to turn on her heel and go back to him, to hide there under the waterfall and never come out again. She felt vulnerable without him as she had never before felt in her life.

"Nathaniel's training must have been much like Richard's," Elizabeth said after a long time.

"Uh-huh," Curiosity agreed. "Ain't many men as good as Nathaniel—in the bush or out of it. I would trust him with my life, no question. But there's a difference between Richard and Nathaniel, and it's one you don't want to forget about." She stopped, and she took Elizabeth's hand, palm up, in her own. It was a strangely personal gesture, and it moved Elizabeth.

"Some men get an idea in their head and they cain't let go. It festers, and turns into a kind of poison. Richard's got the Wolf in him, you see, Elizabeth, and if you take it away from him, there's no telling what might happen."

She said, "I don't have any choice."

"Yes you do," Curiosity said softly. "Right now you do."

"It's not right, what Richard wants to do to them," Elizabeth said.

Curiosity was looking at her with a kind of understanding that made it clear that there was nothing to hide, and Elizabeth met this look with thankfulness.

"It's not Richard I love," she said, willing her voice strong and sure, but hearing the tremor that betrayed her.

"I can see that, child," Curiosity said, and dropped Elizabeth's hand. "Just you two make sure you don't forget about Richard. Because he surely won't forget about you."

When they had walked another ten minutes or so in silence, Elizabeth cleared her throat.

"There's more to the story that you're not telling me," she said quietly.

"That so?" asked Curiosity.

"There's Sarah," Elizabeth said, the familiar name feeling strange in her mouth.

"Why, yes, now that you mention it." Curiosity seemed to be considering. "Weren't clear to me how much you was told about her. Or how much you was wanting to know."

For the first time since Curiosity began telling her story, Elizabeth laughed, but it wasn't a joyful sound. "That's a question I can't answer," she said. "Except to say that I have a feeling I need to know more than I want to know."

Curiosity nodded. "That's the way of it, many times."

It was clear that the older woman was not going to talk until Elizabeth gave her some direction. She was tempted to let the subject drop, but also loath to let the opportunity go.

"I know that Richard Todd courted Sarah." Elizabeth paused, wondering if she should cross this line. Finally, she shook her head. "I suppose the details aren't important," she finished.

Curiosity was looking troubled, her brow drawn down into a deep furrow. "I think it's best if Nathaniel tell you hisself about what passed back then. What I know ain't gonna set your mind at ease, you see, 'cause I don't know the whole story. Nobody does, except Nathaniel and Richard, now that Sarah's gone. One thing you got wrong, though, and that is that Richard never courted Sarah. Not the way you mean."

"I see," said Elizabeth thoughtfully.

Curiosity grunted. "I doubt you do," she said. "But I've said enough for one day."

The sky which had been so blue and unencumbered just an hour ago was now disappearing in a rolling bank of clouds. Against the steel-gray horizon, the yellow-green of the budding trees stood out in stark relief. They were almost home; there was no time to draw Curiosity out, even if Elizabeth had known how to do that. And she was tired to the bone, chilled through and in want of her room where she could be alone to think.

When they emerged from the wood to start up the last small rise, Curiosity stopped suddenly and laid a hand on Elizabeth's arm in a fierce grip. Elizabeth looked up, startled, to see that Curiosity's attention was focused on the house.

Richard Todd stood at the door, filling the frame. At his side, looking the worse for travel but wearing a welcoming smile, was John Bennett, magistrate.

XXI

"Sneeze," whispered Curiosity.

Puzzled, Elizabeth began to turn to her, but Curiosity's hand clamped down on her wrist and squeezed, hard.

"Sneeze!" Curiosity hissed. "And put some work into it." She let Elizabeth's wrist go and set her face in a smile. "Well!" she called out. "Look who come to call! Mr. Bennett, it is good to see you, sir! It has been some seasons since you last come to visit us here in Paradise."

Elizabeth hung back while Mr. Bennett and Curiosity exchanged pleasantries, trying to make sense of what was happening, but it seemed that her mind would not work. Richard was back from Johnstown, and he had brought John Bennett with him. These two facts danced through her head, bumping into each other, but she could not make them intersect in a meaningful way. Curiosity cast her a furious glance, and Elizabeth stumbled forward. Richard had brought Mr. Bennett to Paradise. Mr. Bennett, who belonged in Johnstown, was here.

Then her father appeared at the door, waving a letter. "Word from your aunt Merriweather!" he called cheerfully.

With a rush of understanding as cold and clear as the waterfall she had willingly stood in just an hour ago, the truth of the matter hit Elizabeth. Richard had brought Mr. Bennett to Paradise, and it would no longer be necessary to go to Johnstown to sign and notarize the deed. It could be done now, this afternoon. Her father's property would be signed over to Elizabeth this very day. Just as soon as she gave Richard her vow.

The men were near enough now for Elizabeth to see the self-satisfied smile on Richard's face. And why not? What excuse could she have now, to put him off? She saw the pieces of his plan, and they were simple and beautiful, his strategy flawless.

For the first time in her life, Elizabeth felt close to a faint; the world wavered, and reluctantly cleared. Thoughts of Nathaniel and Hannah flashed through her mind, Lake in the Clouds in snowdrifts, Otter's bloody leg, and then Nathaniel again, framed in the light from the waterfall. Hidden Wolf. Richard thought that he had won; she could see it in the set of his mouth.

Elizabeth was overcome with a white anger so pure and hot that she felt all the blood drain from her face and settle in her fingertips, just as her thoughts settled suddenly into complete clarity. *You think you've got me in a corner,* she whispered. *But think again, my laddie.*

All this had taken only a few seconds; Curiosity still stood, waiting for Elizabeth with one brow raised. The men waited, too; she had yet to say a word to any of them. The three of them were without a clue of what a woman could do when everything she held dear was threatened. She felt contempt for them, which she struggled to keep from her face.

Elizabeth looked Richard straight in the eye, and focusing all her attention on his perfectly tied cravat, she manufactured three tremendously loud, credible, and completely unladylike sneezes.

That evening, thoroughly rested, Elizabeth stretched out in the comfort of her own bed, marveling at the agility with which Curiosity had managed the whole affair. Muttering a steady litany of dire predictions which included fever, sore throat, and putrefaction, Curiosity had whisked Elizabeth away from the men and installed her in bed with hot bricks at her feet and a cup of tea at her elbow. For good measure she had gone down to the kitchen to mix up a sweet-smelling poultice of onions and mustard seed, which sat now beside Elizabeth's bed, untouched and congealed in its bowl.

At first the men had come, one by one, to scratch at the door, but Curiosity had dealt summarily with all of them, sparing a smile only for Mr. Bennett's good wishes. Richard's offer of medical services she met with a look of shocked propriety; she talked down Julian's protests of Elizabeth's solid good health; she let the judge plead for a few minutes of Elizabeth's time and pacified him with hopes of a quick recovery. Curiosity had kept them all at bay, allowing only Daisy and Polly into the room, sending them running silently back and forth with Elizabeth's wet clothes for all to see, with demands for steaming kettles and chamomile tea, more vinegar to bathe her forehead, more broth for her to sip. The men had no chance of prevailing, and after a few halfhearted attempts, they retired to the parlor. Only the occasional sound of Julian's raised voice betrayed what might be going on behind that door.

Elizabeth was safe, for the moment. But only for the moment.

She was left to nap, to sneeze on occasion, drink tea, think of Nathaniel and the events of the morning, and weigh her options. Which seemed to be very few and all very unattractive. If she ventured out of bed, they would congregate in a moment's time to get her to participate in the signing of the deed. Richard would first propose to her once again, this time in front of Mr. Bennett, and that if she were burning with fever and at death's door. Of this Elizabeth had no doubt.

Curiosity had summed up the situation in her own way. "You heard tell about that spot between the rock and the hard place?" she said, eyeing Elizabeth's healthy color with something bordering on disapproval. "Well, then, missy, welcome to it."

This was in the evening, when the men had begun to mill about in the foyer.

"As bad as crows," Curiosity sniffed. "With the smell of fresh meat in the air." The sound of steps on the stairs caused her to ruffle up and set her mouth in a thin line. "I'll deal with 'em."

"No," Elizabeth whispered, frowning. "I'll have to talk

sooner or later. Perhaps you should allow Father in." She thought quickly. "Or perhaps Richard."

"Your daddy," Curiosity agreed reluctantly. "But you forget about Richard. He know the sound of a cough. Here." She took a brick wrapped in muslin from its place by the fire. "Hold this to your face."

When Elizabeth's color had risen perceptibly, Curiosity tucked the brick under the covers, and with a conspiratorial look, she opened the door to the judge's tentative knock.

He stood at the foot of her bed considering her closely. Finally he managed a smile.

"Well, my dear," he said. "I suppose this is not the time for a lecture on the inadvisability of walking in the woods."

Elizabeth almost would have welcomed such a lecture, if it would keep the subject she feared at bay. But her father had already arrived there.

"So. You see that Mr. Bennett has come. He is ready to witness the signing of the deed, which will endow you with a valuable piece of property. May I assume that this meets with your approval?"

"If you wish to pass your property over to me, Father, then I will not object," Elizabeth said. Curiosity was watching her closely; she sneezed into her handkerchief.

"Good," her father said. "Very good. But before we take that step, Richard would like to speak with you."

Elizabeth managed to pull herself up to a good height in her bed. She set her face in what she hoped was an expression of shock.

"You aren't suggesting that I allow Richard into my room while I am undressed?"

The judge let out his breath in a hiss. "Well, I suppose—"

"Really, Father," Elizabeth interrupted, struggling to put away a persistent memory of herself naked on a bed of furs, with Nathaniel stretched over her.

"He is a doctor, after all," her father said, quite meekly now. And seeing that Elizabeth would not be convinced, he added: "Richard does have an important matter to discuss with you before the deed is signed. One you cannot be completely ignorant of," he added.

Elizabeth said, "Perhaps it is just that my head aches, but please do tell me. Is there some reason that Richard Todd cannot wait with his important matter until our business with Mr. Bennett is concluded?"

If so much didn't hang in the balance, Elizabeth might almost have enjoyed watching her father become flustered. He considered one line of argument and discarded it; visibly took up another. There was a tic in his cheek.

"Let me be plain, daughter," he said finally. "I would like to see a formal agreement between the two of you before any legal arrangements are made regarding the property."

"I suspected as much," Elizabeth murmured. As chilling as it was to have this stated so unequivocally, it gave her room to ask some questions. "And why is that the case, exactly?"

"It is the only resolution to a complex of problems which I should not trouble you with, given your condition." The judge looked quite pleased with this formulation.

Elizabeth's fingers twitched and she twisted them in the coverlet lest they give away her anger.

" 'Scuse me," drawled Curiosity in a dry voice. "This poultice needs looking after. I'll return directly, Elizabeth."

"Now," Elizabeth said when Curiosity had closed the door behind her. "Please tell me, Father, what influence it is that Richard Todd exerts on you."

But the judge only raised a brow. "No influence beyond that of a trusted friend and adviser," he said. "And one I will welcome into the family."

"Then it is very unfortunate," Elizabeth said, feeling how anger propelled her forward but unable to stop herself for the moment, "that you cannot marry him yourself, for you certainly like him more than I do."

"Elizabeth!"

"No, let me finish. I'm wondering if it wouldn't be better to sell the land to Richard outright, and leave me out of this business transaction altogether. There is not much for me in it, after all." Too late, she asked herself what would happen if he suddenly decided to do just that.

"No!" her father said, so loudly that she jumped a little. A look came into his eyes which would have frightened Elizabeth if it hadn't surprised her so much: he was desperate. She saw him struggle to compose himself.

"Think, Elizabeth," he said in a strangled tone. "With you as mistress of the holdings, you will be able to exert some influence on Richard. In how the property is managed, for example. And there is a material advantage for you in this, or I would not allow it. You must believe that."

Elizabeth was quiet for a moment. There was, after all, nothing more to say. Her father's motivations, whatever they might be, would not be made clear to her today. He gave her no choice; he would not trust her with the whole truth. His treatment was not that of a loving and concerned father, but of a panicky businessman. Threats, right now, could only raise his suspicions. Tears would do the same, as he had never seen her cry. If she went down to Mr. Bennett and flatly refused, before him, to marry Richard, what then? The deed would not be signed, and God only knew what other plan her father might be hatching. She wondered if his concern for the management of the property was sincere. Family feelings were, after all, not so very strong in her father; only twice had he come to England while she was growing up. A thought occurred to her which might at least gain her a little time.

"I would like to see the letter from my aunt Merriweather."

Unexpectedly, the judge colored. "Yes. Of course. It's in the study; I'll have it brought up to you. Please excuse me now, for the moment, daughter, I must return to my guest. We will expect you later this evening, when you are feeling more yourself." But he was already halfway out the door.

Elizabeth was close to despair when Curiosity appeared again, this time carrying more tea, which she deposited unceremoniously on the dresser.

"Get up, now, Elizabeth, and get dressed. We got to get you downstairs."

"What?"

But Curiosity had grabbed the covers and flung them back, and had moved off to select a dress from the few hung on pegs behind the dressing screen.

"I can't go down there!" Elizabeth shouted in a whisper. "Richard will corner me immediately."

"Get dressed," Curiosity said, thrusting a chemise into her arms. "Trouble down to the Gloves' place, somebody hurt bad."

"The Gloves?" Elizabeth asked. "I don't understand—"

"Child." Curiosity stood with her hands on her hips and her elbows and chin thrust out. "Wake up now. You can't always be daydreaming when the fat in the fire. Somebody hurt down to the Gloves', and they need the doctor."

"They need Richard?" asked Elizabeth. And then: "They need Richard! But how—"

Curiosity yanked Elizabeth's nightgown over her head, and grinned. "For a smart woman, Elizabeth, you thick as custard at times."

Elizabeth narrowed her eyes at Curiosity. "Tell me—" she began, but she was interrupted by the sound of a horse in full gallop approaching the house.

"Never mind," she said, suddenly full awake. She thrust her arms into the chemise and began to button it. "How long do you think this emergency will occupy Dr. Todd?"

"Oh, by the time they get him there, pretty much all night," Curiosity said, as she worked Elizabeth's buttons with quick fingers. "Enough time for you to see to business, at any rate."

When Richard had ridden off with Julian in attendance, Elizabeth decided that a fifteen-minute delay before going downstairs was absolutely necessary. While she waited, Elizabeth made a bundle, in which she packed two changes of clothing, some sewing things, an extra pair of walking boots, her hairbrushes, soap, a small hand mirror, writing materials, her mother's cameo, and the bit of jewelry she had owned, and after long deliberation, three books. This was an absorbing and even frightening task, but when she was done she saw by the clock on the mantel that only five minutes had passed.

The bundle was too large; there was no doubt of it. She discarded the boots and the nicer of the two dresses, the hand mirror, and with some regret, the books. She would leave the jewelry and the cameo at Lake in the Clouds in Hawkeye's care. Then she sat looking into the fire, and thinking of the way the day had begun.

Elizabeth touched her mouth with a cold finger, feeling rather than seeing that her lips were still puffy and a bit tender. As was the saddle of flesh between her legs. She didn't know if thoughts of Nathaniel could sustain her in the next hour, or if they would distract. In any case, he could not help her. She must do what she needed to do to secure her own future; it was one she hadn't imagined on coming to Paradise, but it was what she wanted.

Is it?

Instead of moving into her beautiful new schoolhouse tomorrow, she would be on her way south, eloping. Eloping. The enormity of it struck her, and she felt her mouth go dry and sticky. Her students would think terrible things of her; they would probably hear them from their parents. Nathaniel was well liked, in spite of his connection to the Mohawk, but they wouldn't like him helping himself to the judge's daughter, and her property.

Life would be easier if I had never met him, she whispered to herself, and was shocked at the sound of the words in the room. At the truth of them. Without Nathaniel, she could lead a good, important, rewarding life, teaching the children who came to her with a routine of books and work. Quiet, peaceful, safe.

Boring. Lonely. Mastered.

Things would be hard when they came back to Paradise, but she would build up her school, slowly. People would get over it, and then life would settle down to a routine.

Elizabeth drew a deep breath, touched her handkerchief to the perspiration on her brow, and went down to the parlor.

Suddenly and without a struggle, the judge acquiesced to fate. Richard had been called away to see to one of the Gloves' slaves who had got his leg wedged underneath a falling tree on the far side of Hidden Wolf and no one knew how long he would be gone; Mr. Bennett had obligations in Johnstown and must be away in the morning. And here was Elizabeth, out of her sick-bed to comply with her father's wishes. There was no excuse the judge could offer that would not look strange and perhaps occasion questions from Mr. Bennett that he didn't care to answer.

The original patent was produced and examined, and subsequently the judge took his quill in hand and signed the deed of gift. Elizabeth and Mr. Bennett then countersigned the document. Finally, it was witnessed by Mr. Witherspoon, who had dropped in for the evening, and, with an especially notable flourish, by Curiosity Freeman. They drank Elizabeth's health with Madeira. Without a trace of suspicion, Mr. Bennett congratulated Curiosity on her doctoring, and Elizabeth on her improved health.

A single woman newly in possession of a good fortune, Elizabeth took her leave from her father and his guests, and retired to her bed.

XXII

She fell asleep. Deeply, utterly, completely asleep. Having feared that she would jitter to pieces waiting for the house to quiet, Elizabeth courted disaster of another kind. If not for Curiosity, she might have slept until morning.

But Curiosity was there, and she came into Elizabeth's room deep in the night. She brought with her a dark cloak, some bread and meat tied into a serviette, a cup of hot tea laced with rum, and a key.

Silently, Elizabeth held up the last object and raised an eyebrow in question. By the light of the single candle, the stark, broad bones of Curiosity's face came into relief; Elizabeth was glad to see her smile and become more familiar.

"The sec'tary," she whispered. And then, with a hug and a look which admonished and encouraged all at once, she slipped away, her white nightdress trailing behind her in a long comma.

Her father's secretary. Of course. He would have locked the deed of gift up with his other papers. Elizabeth closed her hand around the cold metal to steady her shaking.

It was easier than she imagined, getting down the stairs and into the study. There wasn't any time to waste, but she didn't let herself think of that, or of anything but the key and the lock and the documents she needed. Even when it was open in front of her she didn't dare to stop and breathe easy; by the light of her candle she sorted through the papers and found the ones she wanted, thrusting the others back into the cubbyhole, barely looking at them. Then she stopped.

She pulled them out again, even as some other part of her mind screamed at her to get out, to go.

There, on cream-colored heavy paper, a handwriting she had recognized, but more than that. Her own name. The letter from her aunt Merriweather, addressed to her. And opened. The seal broken. In the flickering light the careful pen strokes danced.

The fourteenth day of March, 1793
Oakmere

My dearest niece Elizabeth,
    Never before in my life have I more wanted those magical powers which no mortal can possess. It is only by borrowing such divine gifts that I could transport this letter to you as quickly as I would wish. Such is my concern for your welfare and future.

Elizabeth crumpled the letter against her breast as if the paper could stop the erratic beating of her heart. She dared not take the time to read the rest, or even to think about what she held in her hand, and what it might mean. She stuffed the letter into her pocket along with the deed of gift and the patent.

With hands suddenly much more steady but a heart as cold and heavy as clay, she locked her father's secretary and left his house, not bothering to take a last look around her at the rooms which she had thought would be her home for the rest of her life.

It almost ended before it began.

Elizabeth headed for the wood above the house, thinking of the shorter route to Hidden Wolf by way of the north end of Half Moon Lake. This took her around the barn, and there, where she had stood with Nathaniel two months ago, she walked into Kitty Witherspoon.

They paused, both breathing hard, like statues in the moonlight. Kitty's clothing was disturbed; a white breast glinted between the edges of the bodice she clutched in one hand. Her loosened hair hung in frowsy ropes to her waist. Her complexion was gray, but her eyes glittered.

She opened her mouth; whether to speak or scream, to greet or condemn, Elizabeth never knew, because it was at that moment that Julian appeared at the open door of the barn.

"Kitty dear," he said, as if Elizabeth were not there at all, as if he were talking to a wife across the dinner table. "Come away now." .

He considered Elizabeth for a long moment, one brow cocked. "Feeling better, are we, sister?"

Then he glanced over his shoulder at Kitty, and with a shrug that conceded a battle lost, he disappeared into the dark.

PART II

Into the Wilderness

XXIII

April, 1793

The night was close and very cool, dark but not dark; they moved through a world cast in a million shades of gray. Elizabeth peered out from under her tent of oiled buckskin, her curiosity dampened but not banished by exhaustion. She balanced on the edge of sleep, rocked by the steady rhythm of the canoe as it traveled down the Sacandaga.

It was her first canoe journey, but there hadn't been any time to think about that, to worry about it or enjoy the prospect. Keeping watch had been work enough while the men retrieved the craft from its hiding place in the woods on the edge of Half Moon Lake. They had all been tense. Even Hawkeye's usual commentary had been replaced by brisk hand signals as he directed the loading. It had seemed to Elizabeth that there couldn't possibly be room for it all, furs and provisions and something that looked like a roll of bark, her own small pack, the weapons, and more. But it had all fit, and in very short order. And then without any discussion, Nathaniel and Runs-from-Bears had taken up their positions, sitting on their haunches at either end of the canoe with their paddles at the ready.

Hawkeye had helped her into her place and walked out beside them until he stood in water to his knees. For the first time since they had left Lake in the Clouds he spoke to her, a few low words about the importance of keeping her balance, and the fragility of the birchbark craft in which she sat. Then he put his hand on Nathaniel's head, spoke a few words to Bears, and after a moment's hesitation, he leaned forward to touch Elizabeth's cheek.

"I still got my better stories to tell," he said. "So keep your wits about you." And he pushed them gently off.

The canoe slid down the lake and past the village in just thirty silent strokes of the paddles. She counted, holding her breath. There was nothing to do, no other way to help. Right then, every nerve in her body alive and jumping, Elizabeth had believed that sleep would never again be possible. But an hour later, she settled enough to allow her to rest her weight against the pelts that separated her from Runs-from-Bears.

Blinking sleepily, Elizabeth watched the riverbank, the looming shapes of trees, the wide expanse of grassy marshes which stretched sometimes as far as she could see on both sides of the river in a forest of gray-silver grasses rippling in the wind. The only constants were the running river and the tightly controlled swing of Nathaniel's arms as he paddled. Behind her she could hear, if she tried hard, the slice of the paddle as Runs-from-Bears matched his rhythm to Nathaniel's lead. In the end, the sounds of the night and the river and her own exhaustion conspired to lull her away.

The river curved and turned on itself again and again, sometimes smooth, more often rushing white; she dreamt of it as a great snake beckoning into the woods, its ancient scaled back glimmering in deep greens, sapphire-blues, golds and tarnished silvers. Then she woke, still full dark, to find that they had pulled up to the bank. Nathaniel had to raise his voice over the steady trill of crickets to be heard.

He had warned her, while they were still up at Lake in the Clouds, about the portages. There were three, he had explained to her while he filled his powder horn to the brim and did the same for his bullet pouch. The first would be the easiest. She would need to help carry the provisions and gear. He didn't ask if she could or would, he simply told her what needed to be done. It was not a situation either of them had anticipated, and there was no discussion necessary.

The sky was filled with stars so bright it was hard to look at them. In this light, Nathaniel's face seemed stern, almost angry. He helped her out from her spot between the bundles, letting her go as soon as she stood on the bank.

At her feet a fat frog glistened in the moonlight. It let out a deep croak, and leapt into the river with a splash. Elizabeth felt the spongy give of sphagnum moss through the soft soles of the moccasins she had put on in such haste, along with a doeskin overdress and leggings which Many-Doves had offered. She had let the women dress her as if she were a child, so distressed had she been at the necessity of this deception. Now she was glad of it; the cured leather felt strange against her skin, but it was comfortable and warm in the night chill, and she could move in it freely. Elizabeth patted her chest to feel the crackle of the papers she had secured there.

She accepted the shoulder pack Runs-from-Bears gave her, and stood patiently while he adjusted it. It was a considerable weight, but slung as it was at that spot on her back where she could best bear it, she felt as if she could walk for as long as necessary.

"Sata'karite ken?" he asked her. Are you well, do you manage? She pivoted, surprised, to see him smiling at her in a kindly way.

She nodded. "Wakata'karite."

"Many-Doves said you are a good student," he said, and turned back to his work.

Nathaniel unloaded the canoe and strapped on a considerable shoulder pack of his own while Runs-from-Bears stacked the bundled furs in a tower as high as his ear. Elizabeth watched as he slung a line around it and then placed one broad leather loop around his chest and a narrower one against his forehead. When he stood up, the long pack of furs stretched down the full length of his back.

Then, in a movement so fast that she could barely follow it, Nathaniel simply leaned over the canoe, gripped it on either side, and flipped it up to hang suspended above his head like a long and absurd hat.

That was the beginning of the first portage. They walked through the near dark for an hour until they found the river again, and the process reversed itself. By that time Elizabeth's knees were wobbling so that she was glad just to crawl into her spot. Before the canoe was back in the pull of the river, she was asleep.

She woke gradually the next time, aware of the awkward way she slept with her head hard to one side. The sun was coming up, and it was raining, but she was too sleepy to find the oiled buckskin and pull it over herself. And the noise. She swatted feebly around her head as if to shoo it away. Then she felt Nathaniel's hand on her cheek and she started and sat up suddenly, dislodging bundles from her lap.

The falls were someplace ahead of them, not in sight. Elizabeth wondered at how loud they could be at what must be a considerable distance. It wasn't rain that caused her hair to curl, but the fact that the air was dense with mist. This was the one he had warned her about, the portage to circumvent the waterfalls and rapids the Kahnyen'kehàka called Hard-to-Get-Around. They had four miles to walk through the bush, with a full load of furs and provisions and the canoe. As tired as she was, as much as she feared what lay ahead, Elizabeth welcomed the challenge. She was determined not to disappoint him.

But then, she wondered if she had done that already; displeased him somehow. He was so quiet. Since they had been on the water he hadn't said a word to her, hadn't once smiled, hadn't touched her except when she needed his help.

They went through the routine once again and then they set off on a well-trodden path. The river quickly dropped away, and the sound of the falls lessened. Elizabeth breathed deeply, glad of the exercise and the feeling that she was doing her part. They had moved fast on the water and this was slow, but she was expending her own energy now and that felt right. Every step took her farther away from her father and Richard Todd. She thought of the unread letter next to her heart and set her jaw a little harder.

Just when the pace of the march had begun to wear on Elizabeth, they stopped. There was a little clearing surrounded by scraggly pines, hard-packed earth and a well-used fire pit testifying to its ongoing use to travelers. Elizabeth hoped, although she would not ask, that they would rest here, and in fact Nathaniel flipped the canoe gently to the ground at the edge of the clearing.

"Best look after your own needs now," he said quietly as he took the pack from her shoulders. "Don't go too far, and don't use any leaves you can't put a name to."

She nodded, avoiding his gaze, and went off into the woods. Fumbling with the ties on her unfamiliar clothing, Elizabeth lectured herself sternly on the need for flexibility and self-reliance in new and challenging situations.

When she came back to them, the men were already eating. Runs-from-Bears handed her a hunk of corncake studded with nuts and cranberries and a piece of dried venison, which she accepted thankfully. Nathaniel was staring into the wood and seemed not to notice her. She sat cross-legged on the ground with her head bowed while she chewed, willing her eyes to clear of tears. They ate in silence and Elizabeth wondered miserably if they would ever talk again. When Runs-from-Bears got up and walked into the wood, she did not watch him go.

She felt Nathaniel's hand on her shoulder.

"Come," he said softly. "Come, you must be thirsty."

A few paces into the woods there was a small spring that erupted from a tumble of boulders, pooled and then ran away in a stream back toward the river.

Nathaniel lifted her chin with one finger. "I'm sorry," he said tersely.

"What are you sorry about?" Elizabeth asked, jerking her head away. "You haven't done anything." She knew how terribly bitter she sounded, but she was too unhappy to dissemble.

"You're ill at ease and I ain't helping much," he said. When she didn't deny this, he smiled.

"Don't have much excuse for it, though. Except things was pretty tense, and I'm quiet when I'm worried."

He crouched and leaned forward to drink from the spring, and then, wiping his mouth with his hand, he gestured for Elizabeth to take her turn. But his hair was bound back in a tail and hers was not; it swung forward and caught the water, spraying her with droplets. Concentrating, Elizabeth tried again with her head at another angle.

Nathaniel watched her grow furious with herself for her clumsiness. Knowing the danger of touching her, he hesitated but then caught up her hair to hold it for her while she drank. The heavy silkiness of it filled his hand and caught his fingers, revealing the slender white back of her neck. That sight made everything in him clutch in a fist of urgency and lust and protectiveness.

She managed it with his help and gurgled a little laugh, turning to him with water flashing in her eyelashes. Then she stopped, her own face suddenly mirroring the look he knew she must see on his own, the wanting, the tension of not enough time for wanting.

He dropped her hair as if it were on fire.

"Now you know how to drink from a stream," he said hoarsely.

"Nathaniel," she said.

She put her chin up at that angle that meant he had better listen. If it weren't for the fact that the sun was rising and that back in Paradise people might already be aware that she was gone, he knew he would take her right here. The stunned look on her face said that she would have him, and gladly.

She cleared her throat.

"They can't possibly be after us yet," she said. "Curiosity won't let them near my room until nine, at the earliest." There was a little catch in her voice, something strange in the way she related this. He met her gaze steadily and she blushed.

"Your brother knows you're gone," he pointed out.

"Yes," she said. "He does. But he can't exactly tell them that, can he? Nathaniel." She paused, and then that lift of her chin again. "It wouldn't hurt you to talk to me a little, you know. It won't make them move any faster, and it would be . . . a comfort. This is hard for me, if you hadn't realized."

"I realized," he said, less gently than he intended. "And you're right, it won't make them move any faster but it might make us slow down some."

Her face clouded at this, and Nathaniel swore softly to himself even as he watched his hand lift of its own accord. It slid through the tumbled hair and his fingers found the nape of her neck, holding her there. She closed her eyes and swayed toward him. Nathaniel met her halfway, dipping with his head to tilt her face up to him. He caught her mouth briefly, and then let her go.

"Tonight," he said. "Tonight we'll talk. Once we're wed. That is," he said, with the first full smile he had been able to summon up since she had come sprinting through the night to Lake in the Clouds. "If we don't find better things to do."

They were back on the water by mid-morning. The men paddled hard, and the canoe moved through the twists and turns of the Hudson with an agility and elegance which Elizabeth soon took for granted. Even the patches of white water came and went without causing her much concern; it wasn't until later, when Mrs. Schuyler asked about this stretch of their journey, that she came to realize how much she had assumed.

But it was hard to pay attention to anything but the incredible beauty of the river and the lands which bordered it, the mountains in the grip of spring. A good four weeks early, Nathaniel pointed out. And the warm weather was their good fortune. Elizabeth thought of this journey with the added burden of a snowfall or heavy rains and she said a silent prayer of thanks.

She saw things she had never imagined; a moose with impossibly long legs walking nonchalantly into the water to browse the new shoots, swallows careening and dipping by the tens and hundreds, a doe heavy with fawn frozen at the edge of a marsh, a line of turtles on a partially submerged tree trunk, their knobby shells glowing gray-green in the sun. A bear cub on its own, gnawing at a flyblown carcass of a fox on the shore. Elizabeth pointed this out to Nathaniel.

"Wolverine," he corrected her. "Or some call them forest devils." She looked again and saw the long, bushy tail.

There were rich smells, the water itself and sun on fertile mud and acres of wildflowers in blossom. At the river's edge, willows trailed pale fronds in the water where dragonflies hovered.

And there was Nathaniel to watch, in front of her. He had taken off his shirt in the heat of the sun. At first she looked away, the vestiges of aunt Merriweather's training still strong enough to make her start at his nakedness. But of course she must watch him, this man she had held in her arms just a day ago. This man she would hold tonight. She was at complete liberty to look at him to her heart's content. A little self-consciously, knowing that this would not escape the attention of Runs-from-Bears, Elizabeth settled in to make a thorough study. The way his muscles contracted and then relaxed, the shape of each of them as they rolled and flexed in his shoulders and upper arms, the easy, knowing grip of his hands on the paddle. She had time and ease now, to study his tattoo. Like a long bolt of lightning it looped around his left side and up his spine. The rhythmic swing of his hair hid it and then revealed it again where it disappeared into his hairline at the nape of his neck.

The force of her staring finally caused him to glance over his shoulder, to catch a look on her face that she would have preferred not to share, at that moment. He grinned at her and made a comment to Runs-from-Bears. There was a low grunt, of agreement or laughter, Elizabeth couldn't tell. She decided not to ask for a translation.

Gradually she began to take in signs of habitation. A gaudily colored duck building a nest in the wreck of a canoe half-hidden in reeds. At a distance, two men fishing in a marsh. Smoke rising from a cabin peeking out of a grove of pine trees. A canoe paddling upstream, slowly, the boys in it nodding to them in passing.

It was on the last portage that they first ran into the trapper. He was alone, a small, wiry man with a battered coon cap too large for his head and grime and tobacco juice worked into every crease on his face. He nodded at them from under his canoe, his eyes sliding in a disinterested way past Elizabeth to move greedily over the furs that Runs-from-Bears carried. Elizabeth imagined she saw Nathaniel shift the weight ever so slightly. He was dressed again, his chest crisscrossed with leather thongs and a wide leather belt around his waist that supported a long knife in a beaded sheath, a bullet pouch, and a tomahawk tucked flat to the right of his spine. His rifle was slung easily across his shoulder pack, his powder horn under his right arm.

When the man was long gone, Nathaniel stopped, settling the canoe on the ground and then entering into a long conversation with Runs-from-Bears that Elizabeth had no chance of following at all.

"What's wrong?" she asked.

But Nathaniel was hefting the canoe again, and he didn't speak until he had it balanced where it belonged.

"Bad luck, to run into him," he said. "We'll have to move faster."

Elizabeth glanced back to where the path disappeared into the wood. "Who was that?"

"Dirty-Knife," said Runs-from-Bears with a disgusted shake of his head.

"To the Kahnyen'kehàka he's Dirty-Knife, but he goes by Claude Dubonnet otherwise," said Nathaniel.

"Peter Dubonnet's father? My student Peter?" Elizabeth had never seen the man before; he had been in the bush, trapping, all winter.

"Aye," said Nathaniel quietly. "And headed for Paradise, no question."

"But why didn't he speak to you?" she asked, mystified.

"Because he's Dirty-Knife," said Bears. Elizabeth saw that there was no further explanation forthcoming.

"Oh. Well." She knew she should be alarmed, but instead there was a vague sense of disconnection. Claude Dubonnet would be in Paradise this evening and tell them who and what he had seen.

"We knew they'd be coming sooner or later."

"This is too soon," Nathaniel said. "And they know we didn't head for Johnstown."

"Can we be in Albany by morning?"

"It would be better if we could get this settled today," Nathaniel said. "We'll have to stop in at Saratoga, hope that the Schuylers have come up early, given the warm weather."

"The Schuylers?" asked Elizabeth, with growing alarm. "Do you mean Major General Schuyler and his wife? Catherine?"

He nodded.

"My father speaks of Philip Schuyler quite often, Nathaniel," Elizabeth said. "He considers the general a trusted friend."

Runs-from-Bears grunted, a dismissive sound.

Nathaniel didn't seem worried, either. "I don't doubt he

tells himself that," he said. "But I have a feeling the Schuylers'll be glad to see us."

Once back on the water they moved fast on the strong spring currents of the Hudson. In just two hours of winding waterway, they came to the juncture where the river joined the Fishkill, quickly passing what looked to be a small abandoned fort on the north shore of the smaller river. Here the white water was enough to buffet them hard, but Elizabeth's anxieties were focused elsewhere. On the west side of the river she could see the rising smoke of a small settlement just beyond the trees, and then there was a cleared path up through woods to a setting that reminded her of the England she had left behind. Not the narrow and grimy streets of London, or the wild, unrestrained countryside of Scotland where she had gone walking with her cousins, but the England of her growing-up years, clipped and tended, the England of afternoon visits and whist tables and musicales. It took her breath away to see that world appear suddenly on the banks of this wild and unpredictable river.

There was a fine wooden house, Georgian in style but of modest size. Near it were neatly fenced outbuildings of many types; she saw two barns, and at some distance, the steeple of a small church. Placid, fat cows grazed lazily on the pasture which was surrounded by forest. Beyond that, a man with a span of oxen turned soil in a wide expanse of field. In a garden behind the main house, women worked with hoes. Children ran back and forth in a game involving a ball; she could hear their shouting above the river. Then the canoe was at the bank, and there was nothing left to do but to get out and go up to the manor house with Nathaniel on one side and Runs-from-Bears on the other, just as she was, in Kahnyen'kehàka overdress and leggings, carrying Many-Doves' wedding dress of finest white doeskin carefully embroidered with beads and quills in the pack on her back.

XXIV

"Nathaniel!" cried a voice before they had climbed all the way up the bank. "*Sakrament,* if it ain't Nathaniel! And Runs-from-Bears!"

In front of them had appeared, seemingly out of nowhere, a huge man dressed in rough work clothes. He clenched an old pipe in one corner of his mouth while he talked, but managed to bellow quite impressively all the same over his shoulder. "You there, Johnnie! Go on and tell 'em in the house, Nathaniel Bonner has come to call and Runs-from-Bears with him, and a young lady just to put the sugar on top!" As if to verify the importance of this errand, he lifted his wig off his head completely, revealing a pate as creamy white and bare as the moon, and set it down again with a determined tug. Then he grinned and stuck out one reddened hand in Nathaniel's direction, lurching forward at the same time to intercept him.

Elizabeth didn't know what to make of this man, but he certainly was not the prim and disapproving country gentleman she had expected. He shook hands with such enthusiasm that she found herself grinning absurdly.

"Good to see you, Anton," said Nathaniel with a broad grin of his own. "Let me make you acquainted—"

But at that moment the children, who had heard the commotion and given up their game, arrived on the scene. They were older than Elizabeth had first thought, boys of about fourteen, and a girl perhaps twelve with plaits flying free and wild, her cheeks red with exertion and her dress ripped. There was a moment of frozen silence, and then the whole band of them launched themselves at Runs-from-Bears, the boys in a unified front at his head, the girl flinging herself around his torso. In no time at all they had pulled him down to the ground and sat, looking pleased with themselves, on his chest and arms.

It was Elizabeth's strong impression that Runs-from-Bears, thoughtful and serious as was his habit, was enjoying this game. Otherwise, she reasoned, he could simply have tossed them off. He had a smile on his face which said this was an indignity he could live with. That lasted as long as the first pinch, which one of the boys inflicted with a total lack of decorum to Runs-from-Bears' nose.

"It's all right." Nathaniel laughed at Elizabeth's horrified look. "They just need to get this out of the way."

The wrestling match which followed was punctuated by a conversation which made it clear that the youngsters and Runs-from-Bears all considered this confrontation fair price to pay for stepping onto their territory. Anton was watching them with some great amusement, his hamlike fists on his hips, when he seemed suddenly to remember his company.

"Come on now, enough for the moment. Your granny will be wondering what we're up to. And where's the general? Johnnie!" He turned and started back toward the house in a thumping march, turning back toward them so suddenly that his wig threatened to part company with the shiny slope of his head.

"Boys! Mathilde! Leave Bears alone before he decides you'll do for his dinner!" And he laughed uproariously at his own wit. "Aren't you coming?" he said to Nathaniel and Elizabeth. "Let's go up to the house, see what's keeping General Schuyler and the missus."

Nathaniel took Elizabeth by the arm and with a backward glance at the wrestling match that carried on behind them, he set off.

"Who is that?" she whispered when the big man was a few steps ahead of them and bellowing once again toward the house.

"Anton Meerschaum. The overseer. Look," Nathaniel said, "here she comes. Brace yourself for Mrs. Schuyler."

It was a bit like being enveloped in a great warm fog. Mrs. Catherine Schuyler took one long look at Elizabeth, listened to Nathaniel's brief introduction, and drew her into her home and her protection without a question or word of doubt.

In a short time she saw her guests settled at her good dining table. The door to the kitchen passage began to swing busily and in minutes two young women had set and filled the board, casting shy glances not so much at Elizabeth as at Nathaniel. There was no opportunity for talk, but Elizabeth was not unhappy with that for the moment. She listened to Mrs. Schuyler ask Nathaniel and Runs-from-Bears about people and happenings in Paradise, and she realized with some surprise how familiar the woman was with the smallest circumstances of her home.

When they had eaten—Elizabeth managed only some ale, cold fowl, and a bit of bread—Mrs. Schuyler put her small hands flat on the table before her. This was a strange gesture; Elizabeth's own hands were folded tightly in her lap. But it was also, somehow, a comforting one, as it matched the kind but firm set on the woman's face.

"Tell me, Miss Middleton," she began. "How exactly it is that you come to visit us in the company of Nathaniel Bonner and Runs-from-Bears?"

In the months Elizabeth had spent in the city of New-York waiting to travel north, and the four months she had been in Paradise, she had slowly become familiar with what Yorkers called straightforwardness of purpose. But still, Mrs. Schuyler's directness took her by surprise. Elizabeth glanced at Nathaniel and saw that he was not in the least worried by the nature of the question. On the river he had been cautious and watchful and tense, but here he was relaxed. He shrugged at her, as if to push her off on her own in this conversation.

"We are—were—on our way to Albany," she began. And then, realizing how important it was to remain calm and to keep Mrs. Schuyler's gaze firmly in her own, she continued. "I have some business to attend to. And we are to marry there." And then, calmly: "Nathaniel and I."

"That much I assumed," Mrs. Schuyler replied. "Are you eloping?"

"I am twenty-nine years old," Elizabeth replied slowly. "And I have decided to marry."

Mrs. Schuyler's round face had been calm, even impassive, but now there was a little tic at the corner of her mouth.

"Your father does not approve of your choice?"

"I haven't sought his permission," she said. "For reasons that I do not wish to share." Too late, Elizabeth realized what Mrs. Schuyler would most certainly assume as the most probable reason for wanting to marry in haste. In the same moment, she also realized that this might in fact be the case. She had been calm, but now she felt herself coloring, but she kept her gaze on Mrs. Schuyler and would not look away.

"Well, Miss Middleton," Mrs. Schuyler said. "I think very little of elopements, I must tell you. Our eldest daughter eloped and it was a terrible day for me. A terrible day. But then again, these are different circumstances and you strike me as an intelligent woman."

She addressed the men without looking away from Elizabeth.

"Is she that, Nathaniel?"

"She is," he said, almost grimly.

"Does she get on with Hannah?"

He nodded. "Aye."

"And Bears, what do you think?"

"I think she has earned the name Chingachgook gave to her, Bone-in-Her-Back," said Runs-from-Bears. "But today I gave her the name Looks-Hard."

This was the longest sentence Elizabeth had ever heard from him in English, and certainly the most startling thing she had heard him say as well. She thought of the canoe, and her careful study of Nathaniel, and she bit down hard on her cheek, determined not to say a word.

"But she thinks hard, too," he finished with a rare grin.

Mrs. Schuyler seemed to come to a conclusion. "I would say she must," she said with a sudden smile that transformed her face into something almost pretty. "To see the value of Nathaniel Bonner where other Englishwomen would see only buckskin and hands that know the meaning of work." She nodded to Elizabeth. "Your father is a business associate of my husband's," she said. "And we owe him our friendship. But Cora Bonner was more than a sister to me, and my eldest son would not be alive today without Nathaniel's help in a most difficult time. He has a home with us, whenever he should wish to claim it. Now, so do you, as his wife."

"She ain't my wife yet," Nathaniel said. "But we was hoping you could lend a hand and call in the preacher."

There was a scuffle at the door, and a giggle. Mrs. Schuyler sent a disapproving look in that direction. "We hadn't planned on a wedding today," she said. "But we would be honored, Nathaniel. I believe that the preparations have already commenced." There was another stifled laugh from behind the kitchen door. She rose.

"I have some things to speak to the housekeeper about if there's to be a wedding—"

"We don't need anything too fancy," said Nathaniel. "Just a legal ceremony and your good wishes'd be appreciated."

"Is that so?" Catherine Schuyler smiled. "I think it will take a bit more than that. I need to talk to my Sally about shifting the girls around so that we can provide Miss Middleton with a room."

"We won't be staying the night," said Nathaniel. "We've got to be on the way to Albany."

Mrs. Schuyler had been moving toward the kitchen passageway door, but she stopped, and drew herself up to her full height before facing Nathaniel.

"Nonsense," she said. "You will have your wedding dinner with us, and retire here, like the civilized people you are. Whatever business you have in Albany can wait until tomorrow." Her look dared Nathaniel to challenge her.

Elizabeth knew that Nathaniel's worries were well founded. In the hurried conversations with Hawkeye before they left, it had become clear to all of them that it was not enough for Nathaniel to marry Elizabeth. It was crucial that they file the paperwork in Albany and that Nathaniel pay the taxes as her husband, so that there could be no challenge to the validity of the deed of gift, or her status as a married woman. All this had to happen before Richard Todd or her father could raise suspicions that might slow down any part of the process.

"We should be on our way," Elizabeth agreed, regretfully. "Although your kind offer is greatly appreciated." She would have liked to spend her wedding night here in the privacy of a room of her own rather than out in the open with Runs-from-Bears nearby.

"There's business needs doing in Albany, and it can't wait," Nathaniel added.

Mrs. Schuyler's bright blue eyes narrowed just slightly as she looked back and forth between them.

"What business is that?" she asked finally.

"I have some property," Elizabeth said. "The taxes need to be paid. And there are some debts of my father's I'd like to settle," she added, and then wondered why she had.

"I believe that my husband can be of some assistance to you in that matter," Mrs. Schuyler said quietly. "Unless there is some other reason you wish to be on your way so quickly."

Elizabeth saw doubt flit across Nathaniel's face, and then, with a glance at her, he shrugged. "If General Schuyler can lend a hand with sorting out the paperwork, then we'll stay and be glad of the warm," he said. "It's cold at night still on the river."

"So it is," Catherine Schuyler admitted with considerable satisfaction, and she excused herself to go speak to her housekeeper.

"Bears," she said, turning back from the door. "Perhaps you could go after Anton and General Schuyler and see what is keeping them. I would guess they are down at the sawmill. They will want to hear the news, and then," she said with a satisfied smile, "there is work enough to keep them busy."

Elizabeth, keenly aware of being alone with Nathaniel, walked to the window to look down the sloping lawns toward the Hudson. It was mid-afternoon, a beautiful and clear day. Her wedding day. She put her forehead against the pane of glass and forced herself to breathe deeply.

He came up behind her and she put out her hand to him.

Nathaniel took it silently, and tugged her so that she had to pivot to face him, stepping backward until her shoulders touched the wall. He was unshaven, and his face was worn with sleeplessness. But in his eyes there was no tension, and something else, something fine and welcome to her.

"We could both use a good night's sleep," she said softly, feeling the rough flocking on the wallpaper against her lower arms where she pressed her hands flat.

"Could we both?" Nathaniel asked with a half smile. "Aye, I suppose we could." With one arm propped on the wall above her head, he leaned in toward her, his head at an angle. From the corner of her eye Elizabeth saw the door crack open and then slap smartly closed; heard the giggle.

"People are watching," she whispered.

"Then let's make it worth their trouble," he said, and he kissed her there against Mrs. Schuyler's good wallpaper.

When she could trust her voice she said, "Is that the best you can do?"

Nathaniel grinned at that. "Well," he said slowly, his breath moving the hair at her temple. "I'm mighty tired, you understand, and I'm looking forward to a good night's sleep. But I'll give it another go."

There was a warm, newly familiar pulsing in Elizabeth's stomach as Nathaniel leaned toward her, his shoulders blocking out the rest of the room to put them in a corner of their own. First there was just the touch of his tongue at the indentation of her upper lip, and then there was his mouth, warm and curious, and the taste of him, and what it did to her, the memories it pulled to the surface. She raised her hands and put them on his chest, letting her fingers curl into the fabric of his shirt, holding him tight while she kissed him back. He slid his arm around her waist and pulled her up closer. She felt him from head to toe.

"I hear there's a wedding today," said a man's voice at the door. "And I see that it won't be one minute too soon."

The contrast that General Schuyler drew to his overseer would have been comic if it weren't for the obvious regard they had for each other. Philip Schuyler was a genteel, fastidious man of carefully chosen words, trim build, and elegant if somewhat outdated dress, but he consulted his overseer as if he were a king rather than a rough, loud barrel of a man wearing a twenty-year-old wig with a mind of its own.

"We could send MacDonald," General Schuyler suggested, and then listened with great attention while Anton Meer-schaum explained why such a thing was impossible.

"Then I'll go myself," he said quietly. "If you and Miss Middleton will trust me with your business concerns."

Nathaniel glanced at Elizabeth, and she nodded at him. It was right for him to handle this discussion with Philip Schuyler, but she was inordinately pleased that he was sensitive enough to ask her permission to do so.

They had the patent and the deed of gift on the table in front of them. General Schuyler had looked at them carefully; Elizabeth knew that the date on the deed had not escaped his attention. But no look of surprise or censure came from him. Then, with precision and an understanding of the law that was simple and exacting, he outlined the steps that needed to be taken to secure their claims.

"Will you return to Paradise, then, if this business in Albany can be seen to without your attendance?" he asked Nathaniel.

"No," Nathaniel said shortly. "It's best if we stay out of Paradise a while, until things settle a ways. If you will look after the paperwork, and keep it safe."

"That I will," said Philip Schuyler. "And I will arrange for word to be sent to the judge. Unless, Miss Middleton, you would like to write to him yourself?"

Elizabeth shook her head. "I would much appreciate your assistance, sir, if you would be so kind—"

"It is a small thing," he said. "I am delighted to oblige."

It was clear to Elizabeth by now that Nathaniel's status here was more than that of son of a dear friend. He was treated with a respect and regard that she had not anticipated, but which she found deeply gratifying. In the hour they had spent talking about the business concerns, at least seven men had come in, hats in hand, to greet Nathaniel and Runs-from-Bears, each of them with real joy and enthusiasm. Two of them had been Mr. Schuyler's sons, young men of fifteen and twenty years, eager to talk. They were sent on their way with promises of an evening party, and the discussion returned to the matter of the property and taxes.

Elizabeth's attention wandered to the rest of the household, which had been thrown into a panic of activity. Three of the Schuylers' grandchildren were in attendance, she had found out, as well as the four youngest of their own eight, as yet unmarried children. The house, while neat and well planned, was ill suited to numbers of this kind and it bulged with people running this way and that, all with jobs to do. The parlor was being scrubbed, although Elizabeth saw not a speck of dirt anywhere. There were young women with their sleeves rolled up, boys with baskets of food and greenery, candles and silverplate, and everywhere was Mrs. Schuyler's Sally, directing the preparations with a sharp eye.

Mrs. Schuyler herself appeared and gestured to Elizabeth.

"Nathaniel?" Elizabeth asked. "Do you need me here? Can I go ahead with Mrs. Schuyler?"

He touched her hand briefly and nodded. Elizabeth was reluctant to leave him, but she followed Catherine Schuyler upstairs.

"I want you to know," said Mrs. Schuyler as soon as she had closed the door behind them in the room which had been prepared for Elizabeth. "That we are very pleased and honored to be able to be of assistance to you today. That is simply true. But," she added, and she held up one hand. "This is a strange business, if you'll pardon my saying so, and I'm uneasy about it."

"Your husband sees no legal impediment to my marriage," Elizabeth said lamely.

"Come, my dear," Mrs. Schuyler said, sitting down on the edge of the bed. "My husband is a man above all things, and he sees only that piece of this puzzle which concerns him. There is something else afoot here, and I wonder what it is. No." She stopped herself. "I am not going to ask, and I don't want you to tell me. I trust Nathaniel, and he loves you—that is enough." She turned to look out the window. In the distance, a mill could be seen on the banks of a waterway, but it stood quiet now, the fields and pastures abandoned for the moment.

"You are tired, and you would like to rest and prepare yourself. The minister will be here in an hour's time. Can you be ready by half past five? Good. Then afterward we will have our dinner and a little party."

"How kind of you," Elizabeth said.

Catherine Schuyler stood. "I am near to sixty years old, and I hope that I have learned some things from the mistakes I have made in my life. Perhaps the most important is the need to let young people make their own decisions. Now." She looked about herself in a businesslike way. "I will have a bath sent up, and our Jill will look after your needs. You will ask for whatever you require." This was not a question, but a statement of fact. Elizabeth nodded her thanks.

At the door, Mrs. Schuyler hesitated. "You will have a good husband in Nathaniel Bonner," she said. "I only wish this were being seen to in a more orderly fashion. That you had some lady of your family here to advise you."

"I doubt anyone could be more helpful than you have been," Elizabeth said quite truthfully. But she touched the letter still secured against her skin, remembering it for the first time in over an hour, and dreading the moment when she would have no choice left but to read it.

When she had bathed, and washed her hair with what she knew must have been Mrs. Schuyler's finest imported soap, and dried herself, Elizabeth lay down on the bed, completely relaxed and comfortable and totally unable to sleep for even five minutes. She had sent Jill away so that she could dress in privacy, but then she lay on the bed wrapped in the robe that Mrs. Schuyler had provided. Hung up to air were three dresses: the one she had worn last night on her way up Hidden Wolf, the extra dress she had packed, and the fine doeskin overdress lent to her by Many-Doves.

Many-Doves had made the dress for her own wedding to Runs-from-Bears. There were a hundred hours in the fine bead and quill work on the bodice and skirt, and it shimmered where

Jill had hung it to air, the fringe on the hem fluttering in the breeze. Elizabeth had never imagined herself in any wedding gown at all, much less one as beautiful and rare as this. Her cousins had been married in satin and silk and brocade, in dresses that cost more than a laborer's yearly wage. But aunt Merriweather had been firm on the matters of trousseau and etiquette, and the money had been spent gladly.

Reluctantly, Elizabeth found her aunt's letter and spread it out on the bed before her.

The fourteenth day of March, 1793
Oakmere

My dearest niece Elizabeth,

Never before in my life have I more wanted those magical powers which no mortal can possess. It is only by borrowing such divine gifts that I could transport this letter to you as quickly as I would wish. Such is my concern for your welfare and future.

I am afraid that such strong words will alarm you, but my dear Elizabeth, my concern for you is real. What terrible thoughts have consumed me since your letter arrived this evening. I sit here, writing by candlelight—a privilege I oft denied you in the name of economy—after even my maid has retired, because I know that I will not be able to sleep until I have put down on paper what is in my heart.

You write to me of your father's wishes for your marriage, to Dr. Richard Todd of the town of Paradise, once of Albany, and you ask my guidance and advice as any young woman of good breeding must. You write nothing shocking of this young man, no hint of poor character or of any trait that is less than admirable. Yet you do not want to marry this Dr. Todd, and you say so clearly. What you do not write, but which is very clear to me also, is that your father exerts his influence on you, because the connection would be an advantageous one for him. If you had come to me with this even a year ago, my answer would have been quite simple. I would have urged you to marry this young man without haste. But all has changed.

Permit me to be candid with you, Elizabeth. Do not

marry where your heart is not. Do anything but marry only to please your father.

In the years we were fortunate enough to have you make your home with us, I did not often praise you. But my dear, I did admire you, although your clarity of purpose and single-mindedness sometimes bemused and perhaps even irritated. It is only since you are gone away to make a new life for yourself in the Colonies (for such they will always be to me) that some of this has become clear to me. The reasons for this are twofold; the first is your recent long letter in which you describe your school and your work with the children of Paradise; the second, the work of an authoress of whom I shall write below. On this basis, I have had occasion to examine my own behavior toward you and to find it lacking.

You have found a calling in life, something which is denied to most of our sex. To give this up for marriage, when there is no material need to wed, seems to me a sin.

Now, I anticipate that such a material need does indeed exist. Do not forget, my dear, that your beloved father is also my brother, and as much as I love and cherish him, I also know him too well to overlook his weaknesses. Your brother's recent troubles are, I fear, to lay at your father's door, for he has no head for business or for money, except a propensity for spending it. In any case, it does no good to decry your father's follies; they can no longer be undone, and we must face them and deal with them. You write not one disloyal word of your father, but I imagine that he is in debt, and that to the extent that it is necessary for him to seek this Dr. Todd as a son-in-law.

Well, I will not have it. I cannot stand by and watch your father take away from you a calling upon which any husband must certainly impinge. Is the schoolhouse you wrote of, so carefully and lovingly planned, to be abandoned so soon? Even the best-meaning, best-loved, and most rational husband in the world who claims to share his wife's dreams does not gladly share the same lady with the children of strangers.

Marry not, Elizabeth. And so that it will be possible for you to pursue your studies and your teaching, I am prepared to do what must be done. Along with this letter I enclose a contract, duly notarized, which bestows on you a monetary gift of two thousand pounds sterling, which should make it possible for you to purchase those properties of your father's and thus render him solvent. The land will thus remain in the family, in your able hands to do with as you see fit; my brother's financial difficulties will have been resolved, and you will not be obliged to marry at his whim.

You are wondering why your old aunt should take it into her head to reverse every bit of wisdom you ever heard her give over tea. There is a simple, and yet quite apt, explanation for this, my dear, and you are at the heart of it.

Shortly after you left us, when I had begun to miss your company and good conversation at my table, I finally took up that volume you so kindly gave me as a gift on the morning of your departure. You will be surprised to hear, perhaps you will even question the veracity of my claim, but it is true. I have become an admirer—a critical admirer, but an admirer no less—of Mrs. Wollstonecraft's A Vindication of the Rights of Woman. *Most especially I was struck by the truth of her observation that there are many women who are worthy of education, but who are denied the reason and support of their fathers and brothers. Such women must usually struggle through the world on their own, but in your case I hope you will accept the help and direction of an aunt who loves and admires you, and respects those noble causes to which you have dedicated your life.*

Aunt Augusta Merriweather

Postscript. Mr. Colin Garnham, a business acquaintance of your uncle Merriweather's, leaves tomorrow for New-York. I will pass this letter and its contents to his able care, and authorize him to spend what is necessary to get this letter into your hands at the earliest opportunity. He will deposit the funds entrusted to him with the bank in Albany. I make you this gift not from your uncle's resources, but from my own. Such is my faith in you, dear niece; I know you will fulfill my highest expectations.

Elizabeth felt for a moment as if all the air in the room had suddenly disappeared. She read the letter again, and again. Her aunt Merriweather, dour, dear old Merriweather, had simply handed her everything necessary to do what she wanted to do with her life. Security for her father, financial independence for herself. The freedom to teach her school, because it stood on land she owned.

She read the letter a fourth time, and put it down to pace the room. The polished floorboards were cool to her bare feet, but she barely noted that.

Her father.

Elizabeth stopped where she was, held her newly throbbing head in her hands. Her father had read this letter and known that his troubles were solved, but he had kept this information from her. Knowing what he knew, he had pushed, until he could push no longer, for Elizabeth's engagement to Richard Todd. These ideas did not fit together, and yet they must.

It wasn't the money, then. Or the land. In spite of his protestations of wanting to keep the land in the family, her father was so desperate to pass the patent over to Richard that he had lied to her. He had stolen this letter, hid it away from her.

Jill announced herself at the door, and Elizabeth flung it open, frightening the woman so that the tea things she carried swayed and clattered dangerously on their tray.

"Pardon me, please," Elizabeth said. "But I must speak to Nathaniel, immediately."

"Shall I fetch him, then?" the girl asked, flustered. "Is something wrong?"

Elizabeth took the tray from her, nodding. "Please tell him to come to me, that I need him. Straightaway. And please— don't alarm anyone else. Just send him to me."

She was sitting on the edge of a chair with the letter on her lap when he came in.

He hadn't escaped Mrs. Schuyler's attentions, that was clear. Sometime in the last hour he had bathed and shaved and he was wearing a fresh shirt, linen this time rather than homespun or buckskin, creamy white against the tanned column of his neck. There were shadows under his eyes, but he smiled at her, a relaxed smile. She tried to smile back.

"You'll have the Schuylers in an uproar, inviting me in here."

She handed him the letter. He walked to the window to read it, leaning with one shoulder against the jamb as he did so. The light moved on his face as his eyes scanned the lines, one after the next. Then he raised his head and looked at her.

"When did this come?"

"Yesterday. I found it with the deed and the patent in the secretary last night. I just read it now."

He was watching her, waiting.

"Nathaniel. What does it mean?"

There was a guarded look about him. "It means you don't have to marry me anymore, if you don't care to."

She stood up and crossed the room. "That's not what I meant," she said peevishly. "I was asking about Richard, and my father, and why—"

"I know what you meant. But there's something else we got to get settled here first. You can do what you like now."

"Of course I can," Elizabeth snapped. "But I could do that before as well. Do you imagine that I was doing this against my will?"

"In the name of a good deed," he said, shrugging. "Maybe against your better judgment."

Elizabeth drew up, feeling her face flood with a bright, burning indignation. "Then you know me not at all, Nathaniel Bonner," she said. "And perhaps you had better reconsider yourself what it is you said you wanted from me. Unless—" She hesitated, and pushed on. "Unless you've already had that and satisfied your curiosity."

Even in her discomposure, Elizabeth could see how the anger took hold of him, how his lids lowered and his jaw settled hard.

"Is that what you think of me?"

She hesitated, and he grabbed her by the upper arms, pulled her in close. "Answer me. Is that what you think of me?" His grip was punishing, but she bit her lip rather than cry out.

"Let me go," she said. "At once." Nathaniel dropped his hands and stepped back.

"No," she said finally, rubbing her arms. "It's not what I think of you."

There was an almost imperceptible shifting of his mouth.

She said, "And what do you think of me? That I am here to fulfill some good cause?"

"If you don't need to be here, and you're still here, then I want to know why," he said, his voice hoarse now, on the edge of anger but steady.

"I'm here because I love you," Elizabeth said in a voice more calm than she would have imagined. "In case you hadn't noticed."

"You never said." There was something of an accusation in his voice.

"Neither have you!"

He looked out the window, his hands clenching and unclenching at his sides.

She laughed, because otherwise she knew she would cry. Woodenly, she moved across the room to stand in front of the bed, far away from him, where he could not touch her.

There was a hesitant knock at the door; neither of them turned.

"Is everything all right?" Mrs. Schuyler asked.

"Fine," Elizabeth and Nathaniel barked in unison.

"The minister has arrived," she sang out.

"Please allow us a few more minutes of your patience, Mrs. Schuyler," Elizabeth answered, her gaze fixed on Nathaniel. "We'll be down shortly."

When her footsteps had faded reluctantly away, Elizabeth blinked.

"Won't we?"

He came across the room in three strides and bore her down on the bed before him, pinning her there with his hands and knees. His expression was absolutely ferocious; she thought that this must be the way he had looked in battle when he had an enemy squarely in his rifle sights.

"You could have what you want for yourself." His voice dropped, very low. "Live in the schoolhouse, teach. The land's yours to do with as you please. There's money enough to buy you independence, from your father and from me, too. If you don't want to sell us Hidden Wolf, we'll be good tenants."

Her eyes swam with tears; his face doubled and tripled. She could not raise her hands to touch him or to wipe her own cheeks.

"Is that what you want?"

"No," he said, a muscle in his cheek jumping. "No."

"Tell me," she said, her voice barely audible.

"Damn the land," he breathed against her face. "And damn your father and damn your aunt Merriweather and most of all goddamn to everlasting hell your know-it-all Mrs. Wollstonecraft."

"Tell me why," she said, more forcefully now, straining up toward him.

"Because I love you, damn it. Since you have to hear it. Because I love you. That's why I want you."

"Well, you have me," she whispered, no longer fighting him. "If you really want me."

He groaned then, gripping her harder, his fingers pressing into her wrists as he pulled them up and over her head. He dropped his face to the curve of her throat, nuzzling her like a loving and thankful child, his mouth open against her skin.

Then he was a child no longer. He kissed her, a bruising kiss, stealing from her even her gasp of welcome as he reached under her robe, his hands as hungry as his mouth. She moaned with the terrible pleasure of it. He yanked at his own clothing and then he was with her, sinking deep inside with a cry, whispering in her ear, shocking, entrancing words in bright colors as piercing and immediate as the thrust of his body into hers. She arched against him but another part of her waited, terrified, for the next knock on the door.

It was over quickly. When he began to shudder in her arms she held him tightly until his trembling subsided, stroking him and wiping her wet cheeks against his hair.

"I would guess this is what they call putting the cart before the horse," she said softly, when he was quiet.

He laughed then and gripped her closer to him.

"You didn't get much out of that," he said. "I'm sorry."

"I beg to disagree," she said, stretching under him a little.

His head came up in surprise. "Do you now?" One hand slid over her damp skin to capture a breast. "Well, let me show you, then."

"Oh, no." Elizabeth began to untangle herself from him, pulling back from his embrace. "Mrs. Schuyler will be outraged. We're late already."

But his hands were everywhere, touching her, his mouth moving across her bare shoulder. She tried to stop him and managed only to press his palm against her breast.

"Nathaniel!" With a great shove she removed herself from the bed and stood there with the robe half draped about her, her hair dancing wildly, her chest heaving with every breath. "Listen to me!"

He focused, with considerable effort, on her face.

"Don't look at me that way!"

"What way?" He reached out to touch her; she scrambled away.

"Like you want to—devour me whole."

"Darlin'," he said, finally producing a smile. "That's just what I had in mind."

She clutched her robe tighter, and tried to modulate her voice.

"Nathaniel. We are supposed to be in the parlor being married, right now. Do you realize that the whole household is waiting downstairs for us while we—"

A wolfish grin, flashing white.

"While we—do—this." She stamped her foot. In irritation and frustration and fierce, undeniable arousal.

"All right, then," he said, sitting up. "I suppose *this*"—that grin again, scalding her—"will have to wait. If you think you can keep your mind on the business at hand, as unsatisfied as you are."

"I am perfectly satisfied!"

He raised one brow, and his voice came hoarse. "You don't know the meaning of the word, Boots. Not yet."

Elizabeth choked back a hasty reply, realizing that she could not enter into this conversation, not without fear of repercussions which might keep them here while the whole household waited. Pressing her lips together, she whirled away from him and stood in front of the mirror, trying to bring some order to her hair with shaking hands. He pulled his clothes into shape and came up behind her. Gently, he caught her wrist and took the brush away from her.

"Let me," he said, and he did, he brushed her hair while she stood and watched him in the mirror, unable to break away from his gaze.

"Leave it free."

"But—"

"Leave it free," he repeated. "Please."

She nodded, finally.

"I'll be waiting downstairs," Nathaniel said. "Don't be too long."

She watched him go, his hand on the handle, the way it turned. His shirt, somehow, looked completely as it had when he came in. He was unruffled, with no sign about him of what he had just done. Elizabeth looked in the mirror at her own flushed face and cursed him soundly, but silently.

"Nathaniel!"

He raised a brow.

"What about the letter, and my father?"

His look of preoccupation cleared, completely and absolutely.

"I don't know what it means," he said. "But I'm guessing we'll find out soon enough."

XXV

She who had always been punctual to a fault, who had always saved her strongest censure for those who could not keep their appointments, she was late for her own wedding. It took longer than she would have thought for her color to settle, for the tremble to leave her hands, and then she put on Many-Doves' wedding dress, looked in the mirror, and had to work hard not to start weeping.

Elizabeth recognized herself not at all. She did not understand how this could be her, Elizabeth Maria Genevieve Middleton once of Oakmere. She stared at her image for long minutes. Soon Mrs. Schuyler or Nathaniel would come to her door again, and what could she say? That she must have a wedding dress that was satin and lace, in which she would feel like who she was? That she could not attend her own wedding as an imposter, wearing clothes she had no right to? In the end, because she could not do otherwise, Elizabeth took off the dress and the leggings and put on her good gray dress with its neat, round lace color, the same dress she had worn in the night to go looking for Nathaniel. It was not fashionable, certainly. But it was her own. Now, in the mirror, she saw herself.

It took another few minutes to tame her loose hair into something that might not affront sensibilities. From the hem of her shift she pulled the satin ribbon and this she wrapped around her head to hold her hair away from her face, tying it to a bow under her ear. It was too girlish, but it was better. The curls drifted around her temples and she resisted the urge to comb them back, tuck them away. This much she could do for Nathaniel, if she couldn't wear Many-Doves' beautiful dress.

They were waiting for her; she felt the hush fall on the house when she stepped onto the stair. She had never been more frightened in her life, more acutely aware of herself and her shortcomings, more self-conscious. Poised there at the head of the stair with so many strangers watching and waiting, she sought out Nathaniel and found him, as she knew she would, smiling at her. And it was then that she discovered that it was possible to be terribly frightened and extraordinarily, inconceivably happy, all in the same breath.

Later she remembered very little about the ceremony. The Reverend Lyddeker had a distracted smile, a Dutch accent, and sprinkles of tobacco on his shirtfront; Mrs. Schuyler stood nearby with her daughters Cornelia and Catherine to either side of her, with the late afternoon sunshine setting on their blond heads like halos. The room smelled of fresh-washed curtains and pipe smoke and the grove of spruce that stood outside the open windows. And there was Nathaniel, smiling down at her. When he had her hand in his and felt her tremble, he leaned over and brushed her ear with his mouth.

"Come now, Boots," he said softly while they waited for the witnesses to come to order. "If you can stand up to Moses Southern, you can stand up to this. It won't be long."

There were only two real surprises: her own calm, now that it had come this far, and the ring that Nathaniel put on her finger. She hadn't thought about a ring, because she hadn't expected one. It was a simple gold band; she had no idea where he had got it or how, but she was very glad of its cold and unfamiliar grip. It was something to concentrate on when the final words were spoken and she found herself no longer a spinster, but Nathaniel Bonner's wife, and being soundly kissed by him in a room full of approving strangers.

The long board had been set with linen and china and crystal, dominated at its oval center by four silver waiters with bril-

liantly polished domes, slightly misty with heat, these surrounded by another ring of open dishes. There were pickled
oysters, cold venison, brook trout stuffed with walnuts and
cornmeal and fried in butter, a massive ham studded with pep-
percorns, puree of squash, snowy mounds of rice, stewed corn,
green beans in a rich cream sauce. On the sideboard, jostling for
room with a legion of ale and wine bottles there was a massive
tipsy pudding, a bowl of fruit fool, plates of shortbread and of
ginger cake. Around this feast the wedding party crowded,
shoulder to shoulder, the room filled with ten different conversations in English and Dutch and Kahnyen'kehàka, the smells of
roasted meat, pipe tobacco, fragrant beeswax candles, and the
great bouquets of spring wildflowers which flanked the cold
hearth. It had taken more than an hour of introductions and
congratulations and toasts to the couple and their hosts to get
settled here, and Elizabeth was pleased to finally sit quietly. It
was a loud and familiar company, and a jovial one.

Under the table Nathaniel's hand was lying pleasurably
heavy and sedate on Elizabeth's leg. She leaned against him
comfortably, very aware of the right to do this now. She was
not in the least hungry in spite of the wealth of delicacies that
Mrs. Schuyler had seen piled on her plate. From her spot she
could look out over the lawns toward the river and the wilderness beyond it, cast now in the early evening shadow. She might
be out on the river right now, she knew, if it weren't for the
generosity and kindness of these people, their willingness to put
down their work in order to make a wedding party for her. So
deep was she in this daydream of what might have been that she
started when a hand settled on her shoulder.

"You know what you got here, I hope," said Sally Gerlach
to Elizabeth as she filled her wineglass. From underneath an
enormous mobcap the housekeeper's owlish gray eyes blinked
solemnly. "I don't know as anybody here will tell you the truth
about him, but I will. The truth is what a bride needs, you
realize. She can do without lace on her drawers, but the
truth—" She laughed, and with her the rest of the table
laughed, too, the Schuylers and their children and grandchildren, Anton Meerschaum, the minister, other men whom Eliz-

abeth had been introduced to but whose names she could not remember, and Runs-from-Bears, who sat to Elizabeth's left and ate with great delicacy from surprisingly small servings of squash and venison.

"Now," Sally said. "Who'll tell this girlie about her man and young John Bradstreet."

"It's a tale that's been told too many times already," Nathaniel protested.

"What story is this?" Elizabeth asked.

"That's a curious one you've got there," said the Reverend Lyddeker with a very unclergylike wink. "She'll keep you busy."

"That she will, Dominie," Nathaniel said, squeezing Elizabeth's knee. She shifted a little. As if he had read her thoughts, he leaned over and spoke into her ear, his warm breath stirring her hair.

"I understand you're unsettled," he said softly. "But try not to wiggle too much, Boots. We've outraged these good people enough for one day."

She pinched him then as hard as she could. Nathaniel hiccuped and caught her hand. He pressed it down against the hard plane of his thigh, laying his own hand flat over it with fingers intertwined.

"Now tell me the story," she said.

"Aha, and demanding too," noted the dominie, peering at her over his wineglass.

"John is the Schuylers' oldest son," Runs-from-Bears supplied kindly overhearing this last comment.

"And by God he would be under the ground these almost sixteen years if it weren't for your Nathaniel," piped up Anton Meerschaum. He thumped the table for emphasis so that the china clattered, and Mrs. Schuyler sent him a look that would have made him cower, if he hadn't turned his whole attention to the oysters in front of him.

"That is the simplest version of the story," agreed Mr. Schuyler. "But you should know, Elizabeth, that we are talking about the war. Perhaps that is a topic not welcome to you?"

"Because she's English doesn't mean she's a Tory, Philip,"

said Mrs. Schuyler in a slightly disapproving tone. "She may have no opinion on political matters at all."

"Bone-in-Her-Back without an opinion is a strange idea," Bears noted dryly, earning a laugh from Nathaniel and a sour look from the bride.

"Nathaniel wouldn't marry a Tory," interjected Cornelia with some force. She was eighteen, beautiful in a butter-and-cream kind of opulence that glowed, and when she looked at Nathaniel—Elizabeth had seen her looking quite often—there was a hesitancy and shyness that was not otherwise there. Elizabeth feared that the girl was opening herself to teasing of the worst kind, but Nathaniel stared down Cornelia's grinning brothers and answered her directly.

"You're right," he said. "Unless it was a reformed one." Under the table he found the soft web of flesh between Elizabeth's thumb and first finger and began to massage it lightly.

"I'm not a Tory sympathizer," Elizabeth confirmed, pulling her hand away. "And I would like to hear the story of Nathaniel at the Battle of Saratoga, if you'd like to tell me."

"I don't think you've got much choice," Nathaniel noted.

"Well, then," said Mr. Schuyler. "Catherine must start, as it begins with her, back in Albany."

Mrs. Schuyler was ready to do her part. "Nathaniel was with Sky-Wound-Round's warriors when they came to town to negotiate terms with Philip. And he brought me a letter from his mother."

"But tell what he looked like!" called one of her grandsons.

"He looked like a healthy nineteen-year-old, the son of my dear friend Cora Bonner, on his way to war."

"Oh, Ma," drawled Rensselaer. "He looked like a Mohawk out for scalps."

"In those days," said Run-from-Bears easily, "he was Kahnyen'kehàka, and he took his share of scalps."

There was a sudden silence. Elizabeth felt all the attention in the room focus on her; even Nathaniel's thumb had stopped its slow and careful revolution on the palm of her hand.

"That sounds like a different story," she said to Bears in what she hoped was a neutral tone. "I'm curious about this one right now." And she leaned a little harder against Nathaniel while she threaded her fingers through his. But her mouth was suddenly very dry, and she picked up her glass.

Mrs. Schuyler was frowning at her son. "Rensselaer, you were four years old in September of '77."

"Nevertheless, I remember well enough," he came back, more subdued now. "How could I forget a Mohawk showing up at the door with his head shaved for battle and you making him come in and have a bath. And he did it, too. I watched to see if that tattoo of his would wash away, but it didn't."

There was a welcome ripple of laughter in the room.

The younger Philip Schuyler, a shy twenty-year-old who had barely spoken a word thus far, and who couldn't meet Elizabeth's eye, now addressed Nathaniel.

"Do you remember how we watched over your weapons and your wampum for you?"

"Yes, I do," Nathaniel said. "Don't forget, it was my first time going to battle, and I was just a little younger than you are now. There ain't much I don't remember."

"I think it was seeing that white men were going to fight with the Iroquois that put the idea in John Bradstreet's head in the first place," said Mrs. Schuyler thoughtfully. "About running off, I mean."

Elizabeth glanced up at Nathaniel. "Men? Was your father with you?"

"No," answered Mrs. Schuyler for Nathaniel. "Cora wouldn't let Dan'l near a battlefield that fall, he was down with a recurring fever. She didn't much care for Nathaniel going off, either, but he was—" She broke off then, and clearly didn't know how to continue. Elizabeth had already figured out for herself that at the time all this had happened, Nathaniel must have been very recently married to Sarah and obliged to accompany her father into battle, but she didn't know how to make Mrs. Schuyler aware of her knowledge.

"The other white man was a Scot," said Nathaniel. "Married into the tribe, by the name Ian Murray."

"Is that the one who took Works-with-Her-Hands as wife?" asked Runs-from-Bears, showing the first curiosity since the story had begun, and then looking thoughtful when Nathaniel nodded.

Mrs. Schuyler leaned toward Elizabeth. "So you see, the war party came in one hundred and fifty strong, with Nathaniel and this Ian Murray in it. And our John couldn't stand being down in Albany when the war was taking place on the doorstep up here."

"So John ran away from your home in Albany to follow Nathaniel and the Hode'noshaunee up to the battlefields," Elizabeth summarized for herself.

"Indirectly, he did," confirmed Mrs. Schuyler. "It was about a week after the battle at Freeman's farm—" She paused as if to gather her thoughts, but there was a tic in her cheek that did not escape Elizabeth. At first she thought it was anger, but then she saw the set of Mrs. Schuyler's mouth and realized that there was much more to it, fear still not resolved after sixteen years.

"When there was no more news of fighting, John thought he could come up here and rescue his pony," she finally continued. "And to this day when I think of it, him taking off in the night with a sack of food and an old musket to travel some thirty miles through Burgoyne's lines—he was twelve, you must remember—" She put her hands flat on the table and her mouth compressed into a tight line.

"He'd get his ears boxed all over again if he were here," finished young Catherine with a wince. "Never mind he's twenty-eight years old."

"And rightly so," said Anton with an upraised finger. "Just look what it did to his parents, the worry."

"So how did he find you?" Elizabeth asked.

"He didn't," Nathaniel said. "And that's where the story starts, I guess."

He took his time to fill his glass and then, when the whole room had settled, he began.

"We missed the first battle by a day. At the time I was mad as hell about it—pardon me, Dominie—that's how young I was. More than a thousand dead, you couldn't walk ten paces without stepping in blood in some spots, and me disappointed to

have missed it. We stuck around, though, because Gates pulled
back before the Tories were down for good——"

Mr. Schuyler looked suddenly very put out. Elizabeth wondered what the story was behind this, but Nathaniel moved on
with a nod to his host.

"And another battle was a sure thing. So they set us to work
like the rest of the militia and the soldiers, building fortifications
and the like. It was frustrating, let me tell you, being sent up to
battle and to end up with a shovel in my hand. I was glad of it
when they called me in to put me on scout duty."

Nathaniel paused to drink, but the rest of the table was perfectly still. Even the teenagers, who had been rocking on their
chairs and itching to be let free, were suddenly fixed and attentive.

"So I got familiar with the terrain on the other side of
things——"

"Behind the British lines?" asked Elizabeth, puzzled.

There was a disapproving frown from Mrs. Schuyler and
Elizabeth realized that this story was a precious one, with its
own parameters that didn't allow stray questions. But Nathaniel
was patient, if his audience was not.

He raised a brow. "A passing familiarity with the enemy's
situation is generally what you need, Boots," he said. "So I did
some looking around. The Hode'noshaunee fighting for Burgoyne, well, they had already started heading out by that time,
and they weren't in a hurry to turn me in. Now, it must have
been about ten days after we set up camp that Varick came to
find me."

"My aide," clarified Mr. Schuyler.

"Just when I had come to the conclusion that we'd all die of
boredom or blisters before another shot was fired. And here was
this news that the boy had took off from home and they suspected he was on his way to Saratoga. So I come up here, and
sure enough, the Tories had grabbed him when he showed up
and stuck him cold and wet in a barn. He had the good sense at
least not to tell them whose son he was. And that's where I
found him, coughing and fever-rid."

He paused to smile at Mrs. Schuyler, as if to remind her that
there was a happy ending coming to this story.

"Well, short of it is—" He held up a palm to stop protests from the younger Schuylers. "I got him back down to our camp near the lake, and we found him a doctor, a woman tending the wounded."

"A doctor or a woman?"

"Both," said Nathaniel.

"A woman surgeon?" asked Elizabeth, confused.

"The White Witch," said Runs-from-Bears. "I've heard tell of her."

"And so has every soldier who set foot on that battlefield," agreed Mr. Schuyler.

"A Kahnyen'kehàka healer?" Elizabeth was curious enough to risk the displeasure of the rest of the audience with another question.

Nathaniel shook his head. "No, a white woman, and English by the sound of her. Ian fetched her, and then it turned out she was his Auntie Claire. Brought her into camp just when I was thinking we couldn't do much for the boy. And she hunkers down next to him and listens to his chest and then she forces something down his gullet, and she bundles him up. The thing to see, though, was the way he settled down when he heard her voice, talking low to him, telling him to lay his head down. Like my own ma would have done if she had been there."

"How old was this woman?" Elizabeth asked, and then ducked her head at the good-natured laughter. "Out of curiosity—" she began feebly, but Nathaniel had put his arm around her and he gave her a little squeeze.

"Well, maybe it'll put your mind to ease if I tell you that her husband was there too, came along to camp. A big red-haired Scot, wounded at Freeman's farm. I ran into him later again on the Heights, and I was glad of it, too. I've thought of them many times since that day."

He turned to Mr. Schuyler. "Without her John Bradstreet would have died, so maybe we should be drinking her health."

"And so we should," agreed Mr. Schuyler, and raised his glass. "To Nathaniel, who brought young John through the lines," he said. "And to the White Witch—"

"Claire Fraser," Nathaniel reminded him.

"To Claire Fraser, who brought him through his fever."

"What happened then?" Elizabeth asked when they had touched glasses.

"Not much. We settled him down at camp, far enough from the fortifications at Bemis Heights to be safe, and there he stayed through the next battle, until he was well enough to set up. By that time everything was said and done, Burgoyne routed and this whole place burned on retreat. Mr. Schuyler came up when the surrender was arranged, and fetched John. And that's the story."

"Nathaniel!" scolded Mrs. Schuyler. "False modesty does not become you in the least."

"That's what happened," he repeated.

"Oh, yes, of course," she said with a grim smile. "But you left out a few facts. For example, that you had to travel eight miles through enemy territory to find him."

"That stands to reason," he agreed. "Wouldn't have been much challenge, otherwise."

Mrs. Schuyler turned to Elizabeth. "Imagine," she said. "Nathaniel, himself just nineteen, walking into the hay barn— It stood right over there, you see where the cows are grazing? That's where they were holding John prisoner. And Nathaniel just picked him up and walked out as if he had been sent to fetch him. They could have shot them right there, but Nathaniel never blinked. And imagine he just keeps walking, past the troops and the officers and the artillery, with a big twelve-year-old across his shoulders, and he walks overland, through marsh and rough terrain, eight miles, until he gets to camp. For two weeks he manages to keep this boy alive—remember, in the middle of this he went off to fight in the Bemis Heights battle."

"I wasn't alone on the Heights," Nathaniel muttered. "Anton over there did his part, and so did others on this place."

"And fought so that Morgan and Arnold both came looking for him to see if he could be enticed to leave Sky-Wound-Round and join them. And through all this, he made sure our John was taken care of. Can you imagine that?"

"I can," Elizabeth said without hesitation.

Sally Gerlach had been standing very still through the whole story, but now she came alive, breaking the spell in the room with her laugh. "A bride ain't prone to disbelieve any good thing you got to say about her man," she pointed out. "Just happens in this case it's true."

Mr. Schuyler was nodding. "So perhaps you won't wonder that we were pleased to be of help to you today. And I will look after matters for you in Albany tomorrow, so that you can rest assured."

At some gesture from Mrs. Schuyler, the servants began to clear the table, and she rose herself. "It's been a long evening. Perhaps you are ready to retire?" There were grins around the table, which she extinguished like so many candles with a single severe sweep of her head.

"Yes," said Elizabeth, wishing for some degree of poise that she didn't possess. "Thank you very kindly."

"We'll say good night, then," Nathaniel agreed.

"Ma!" said Rensselaer. "What are you talking about? It's not ten of the clock yet."

"Aye, you're right," said Nathaniel as he helped Elizabeth up. "But we've had a long day, you understand, and my bride is uncommon tired. As you can plainly see."

Elizabeth put a hand on his sleeve. "If you'd like to have a drink with the gentlemen—"

He hesitated.

"Please go ahead," she said, quite sincerely wishing that he would, thinking that right now it would be very good to have a few minutes to herself.

Nathaniel wasn't grinning at her anymore; there was something else there, a kindness and an understanding that made her breathe easier. She nodded and had begun to turn away when he caught her by the wrist and pulled her up short.

"I won't be long," he said against her hair. "Don't go to sleep without me."

It was not so very dark that he needed a candle to find his way to her. There was moonlight, and in it, Elizabeth asleep. He stood there and watched her for many minutes, until he could believe what he was seeing: his own good fortune. She slept deeply, her head turned hard to one side to reveal the line of her throat rising up from the simple nightdress, her skin as white and as soft as the light itself. Nathaniel watched her sleep, and then he lay beside her and listened to the sounds of the house settling in for the night, and the way she breathed, and the beat of her heart. And he lay watching Elizabeth sleep and wondering at himself, how he had come to this place in his life, that he should have this woman beside him as his wife.

He slept, finally. Chastely and completely content.

XXVI

She woke in waves, coming up from her dreams reluctantly. It was colder; there was rain at the window, drumming softly, a persistent spring shower in the first filtered gray light. Elizabeth stretched, and turned, and there he was, Nathaniel, watching her. Lying on his side, the bare skin of his arms and shoulders covered with gooseflesh.

"You're all cold," she said, raising the blanket so that he could slip under. And he came up against her, his long body against hers, and put his forehead to her temple.

"You're all warm." His arms went around her easily and they lay quietly in the pooling of their heat and breath, until she turned her face to him, her lips just brushing the stubble on his cheek.

"I fell asleep," she said. "You should have waked me."

"Aye, well. You're awake now, and so am I." His hands were revolving in slow circles on her back, and his gaze was low and steady and not in the least sleepy.

"Nathaniel?"

"Hmmmm?"

"There was a conversation we didn't finish yesterday."

"Forgive me, Boots, but I don't want to talk about your father just now." His mouth touched the crest of her cheekbone and she shivered.

"I didn't mean that," she said, stemming her hands on his bare chest, feeling the beat of his heart against her palms.

He drew back a little, his teeth flashing. Her wicked, wolf-like husband.

"What you said about . . . satisfaction," she managed to say.

"Ah," said Nathaniel, looking quite satisfied himself. "I knew you'd be thinking about that."

"Well," she said, when it was clear that he was more interested in exploring the soft flesh below her ear than he was in talking. "Are you going to explain?"

"Explanations at this hour of the morning?" He shook his head, one hand slipping down the length of her thigh and starting its return, bringing the hem of her nightgown with it. "But a careful demonstration, that's another thing altogether."

"It's daylight," she said quite softly, and without conviction.

"So it is. But we've done this before in the daylight. In fact, we've only done this in the daylight, and it's worked out pretty fine, I'd say."

She pressed her mouth together hard, her brow furrowed.

"Must you tease me?"

"Now that you ask," he said, his hand continuing in his upward quest. "It is my understanding that as your husband it's not only my right but my duty to tease you. And it's a task I'll take to heart, in case you had any doubts." He nuzzled her neck, and she arched against him as one hand settled on her bare hip.

"Nathaniel," she said, pushing away. "I need to— There's something—"

Reluctantly, he let her go. "Aye, well. Then see to it, Boots, but my patience ain't bottomless, you do realize."

"Oh, yes," she said, grinning herself this time. "I do realize that much." She slipped out of the bed and took her dress from its peg on the wall, and pulled it over her head, nightgown and all. Then she stepped into her shoes.

"You're not going out in the rain," Nathaniel said, astonished. "Not when there's a perfectly good alternate sitting right under the bed?"

She glanced over her shoulder at him. "I am," she confirmed.

"But why?"

"Because for the next few weeks or perhaps more, I'll have to do without the Necessary, won't I. But today I can still take advantage of the privacy." She draped her shawl over her head and around her shoulders.

"I don't see that walking through the rain is an advantage," he mumbled. "Seems like a damn inconvenience to me."

"You're not a woman."

He grunted. "At least you noticed that much." He rolled on his side and held out a hand toward her. "Give me a kiss, before you go out into the wet."

But she was already at the door, fluttering her fingers at him.

Nathaniel lay back against the pillows, his hands crossed behind his head, and watched the rain misting. It was just sunup, but they would have to be on their way within the hour. Less, if they could manage it. No time for lessons in satisfaction, or anything else, for that matter. Sooner or later Todd or the judge would think to look to Saratoga.

They would have to lie low until Schuyler had a chance to deal with the authorities and the paperwork in Albany, and then to wait at least two weeks beyond that point, moving for the whole time. Todd would be after them; of that Nathaniel had no doubt. With a sigh of regret he made himself throw back the covers and get out of bed, stretching expansively. He used the pottery contrivance Elizabeth had not wanted, noting with some amusement the elaborate motif of flowers and angels which decorated it inside and out. Then, yawning, he reached for his leggings, happening to look out the window. From this part of the house he could see the kitchen garden, the new-tilled earth dark and damp and fertile in the warm spring, and beyond it, the pastures that lay between the house and the wood.

In that moment, a man appeared at the edge of the forest where it gave way to the cow pasture. He paused there, looking sharp, and started toward the house. He was wearing a cap, but his beard glinted gold-red even in the faint light. There was the spark of a knife at his belt and the barrel of a long rifle pro-truded from over his shoulder. He was dressed like a back-woodsman, but he moved like a Kahnyen'kehàka hunter.

One part of Nathaniel's mind knew what he would see be-fore his eyes had followed the trajectory: Elizabeth emerging from the outhouse, her head bowed under the shawl to keep the misting rain off her face. Richard Todd was moving fast and he would intercept her just as she reached the kitchen door. A minute was enough time, but just.

Nathaniel had his rifle in his hands and had checked the powder pan and load in twenty seconds; in another fifteen he was standing in his breechclout and bare feet with his sights trained on Mrs. Schuyler's kitchen door, at a height of precisely five feet and ten inches. Five inches taller than Elizabeth; three inches shorter than Richard Todd.

Sally Gerlach stood at the board with her hands in a vat of dough, and stared at the half-naked man before her.

"Open the door," he said calmly.

"I need to wipe my hands."

"Nathaniel!" Elizabeth screamed from outside.

"Open it now," he said again. "Or I'll shoot through it."

For her age and size she moved fast. Dipping under his sights, she grabbed the handle with one floury hand and threw the door back with a crash.

"Mother of God!" she shouted.

Elizabeth was turned from them, struggling to pull away from Richard Todd. He had hold of her upper arm, leaning over her with a look of outrage so bitter that it made Nathan-iel's nerves hum. His finger tightened ever so slightly on the trigger.

She was looking over her shoulder at him in fear and out-rage. Nathaniel sensed rather than saw this, for his attention was focused, clear and razor sharp, down the barrel of his rifle to a spot just above Richard Todd's left eyebrow.

"Dr. Todd," he said without smiling. "Early, ain't it, for a morning call? I'll ask you just once to take your hands off my wife, and I hope you'll take heed, man. It would be a shame to make a mess of Sally's floor."

Richard's expression went suddenly blank and his eyes narrowed. He hesitated for two heartbeats and then, with a disdainful jerk of his hands, he released Elizabeth.

She stumbled into the kitchen, pulling her shawl around herself. With a look divided between disgust and complete fury, she came to stand, very straight and still, behind Nathaniel.

Nathaniel slowly lowered his rifle, but kept his finger on the trigger. At that moment, Runs-from-Bears appeared in the door frame behind Richard, his tomahawk in one hand.

Elizabeth drew in a sharp breath.

"Don't worry, Boots," Nathaniel said easily. "No harm is going to come to Dr. Todd today. Unless he puts himself in harm's way. Ain't that so, Bears?"

Richard still hadn't spoken. His face, as impassive as it had been, settled even further.

"Sally," Nathaniel said easily, his eyes still fixed on Richard. "I think Mr. Schuyler would like to know he's got company."

"Yes, indeed," Richard spoke up. "Tell him we've got a matter of the law to deal with, and we'd appreciate his counsel."

The woman hesitated, touching Elizabeth's shoulder. "Perhaps you should come along with me," she said. "Mrs. Bonner?"

"Don't call her that!" Richard fairly spat.

"That is my name." Elizabeth spoke before Nathaniel could. From the corner of his eye he could see her, her chin up, her eyes flashing with a heat and trembling anger he had never before experienced from her. But she had control of herself, and Nathaniel was pleased to see that.

"And I'll thank you not to interfere in things that are none of your business," she concluded.

Nathaniel watched Richard closely, seeing the way he struggled with his temper, ready to act if he lost the battle.

"This is my business," Richard said finally. "And I have no doubt Mr. Schuyler will agree that the law's on my side here."

"Ja, and the devil, too, most likely," muttered Sally Gerlach, and she turned to leave the kitchen.

.   .   .

They assembled in the parlor, at Mr. Schuyler's insistence, at eight o'clock. This gave Elizabeth and Nathaniel time to dress, and Richard Todd time to clean up and collect himself.

Thus Elizabeth found herself in almost exactly the same spot where she had stood to be married, less than a day ago, once again with Nathaniel at her side but this time with Richard Todd's cold and angry stare to contend with. Elizabeth was calm, now that there was nothing left to do but confront him. She thought over what had come to pass, and could not find it in herself to either regret or be ashamed of what she had done. This gave her the ability to meet Richard's stare with complete equanimity.

Mr. Schuyler stood, with his arms at his side, in front of the hearth, and kept his silence while they took their places. He was stern and closemouthed, his dark eyes hooded. He had been dressing for travel when Sally had knocked in much agitation on his door, but he had handled the strange situation in his kitchen as if it were nothing out of the ordinary. Now, Elizabeth could not tell if he was angry, and if so, where his anger was focused. In any case, the friendly and deferential man who had told stories at her wedding party was gone.

"There is some business that needs to be aired, it seems," he began. He pursed his mouth, glanced at each of them in turn, and then carried on. "Perhaps Dr. Todd will tell us to what end he has intruded on the peace of my household and attacked one of my guests." This was said very quietly, but there was no doubt that Mr. Schuyler would have an answer.

Elizabeth saw a flicker of doubt on Richard's face.

"That's simple enough," he said. His voice was hoarse, as if he had been shouting. He looked directly at Elizabeth and ignored Nathaniel.

"I'm here to fetch Elizabeth Middleton back to Paradise, at her father's request."

"Am I a sack of flour, or one of your runaway slaves?" Elizabeth began, but Mr. Schuyler shook his head gently at her. At the same time she felt Nathaniel's hand at her elbow. She dropped her head to gather her thoughts.

"I am an adult, in full possession of my faculties," she said, and then she met Mr. Schuyler's gaze. "And as you know, sir, I am a married woman. Dr. Todd had no right to order me about before I married, and he has less now."

"You are not legally married," Richard countered. Elizabeth felt Nathaniel stiffen beside her, but Mr. Schuyler spoke first.

"I beg to differ," he said. "Nathaniel?"

Without taking his gaze away from Richard, Nathaniel took a piece of paper from his shirt and handed it to Philip Schuyler.

"A signed marriage contract," he affirmed. "Witnessed by myself and my lady, yesterday evening in this room. They are legally wed, Dr. Todd, and—pardon me, Elizabeth—Nathaniel, I assume the marriage was consummated? Yes. Well. So whatever your feelings on this, Dr. Todd, there is nothing you can do about it." He hesitated, and then spoke quickly. "I might also add that your behavior this morning shows an appalling lack of manners and good breeding."

"Miss Middleton had made a legally binding vow to me," Richard said softly. "And I intend to hold her to those terms."

Elizabeth uttered something between an outraged laugh and an oath.

"That's a lie," Nathaniel said. "And he knows it himself."

"I have witnesses." Richard had gone very pale.

"Another lie," Elizabeth spat.

"I see no such witnesses here, Dr. Todd." Mr. Schuyler's calm was now offset by splashes of red which appeared suddenly on his cheeks and neck. "This marriage has taken place and is legal. Whatever else you may seek to undertake in terms of action against the lady—assuming that your evidence does indeed exist—I would hope that you would be gentleman enough to accept the fact that her favor has been granted elsewhere."

"I am man enough to claim what is mine," Richard responded.

"Richard Todd," Elizabeth said, her voice trembling with a deep, unrelenting anger. "How can you stand there and utter such an outrageous lie? I never made you any promise, and I most certainly did not make a public vow."

He blinked, slowly, his head swiveling toward her in what seemed an endless arc.

"Your father is in debt to me," he said. "As you know. If

you do not honor your vow"—he continued to speak over her rising protests—"then I will simply take his property. All of it."

"How much money does my father owe you?"

"More than you possess," he said dismissively.

"You are an arrogant, overblown boor—" Elizabeth began. This engendered a look of surprise from Nathaniel, one of shock from Mr. Schuyler, and a sudden shuffling from behind the closed doors. "And as such, sir, you have not the slightest idea of what I *possess*."

Looking decidedly uncomfortable, Mr. Schuyler raised a hand. "It was a reasonable question," he agreed. "How much money are you owed, man?"

"Three thousand," said Richard. "Pounds." And he threw Elizabeth a defiant look.

Mr. Schuyler let out a gasp of surprise. Elizabeth, herself unable to grasp what Richard was claiming, took Nathaniel's arm.

"Over ten thousand dollars?" Mr. Schuyler said. "How could this be?"

"Not that I need to explain myself," said Todd. "But the judge invested in a questionable land deal down in Ohio country. Against my better advice."

Mr. Schuyler was looking at him closely. "Of course," he said dryly. "Your better advice." He shook his head. "Ten thousand dollars. That is hard to imagine."

"Well, it's true," Richard flared. "And all the judge's property together is worth perhaps three and a half. Our agreement —and you will see that it was a generous one on my part—was to take the first patent as full payment. Upon my marriage to his daughter. It was perhaps not completely equitable as far as my interests are concerned—" He paused, as if to let this insult sink in. "But it was the only way the judge would agree."

Elizabeth felt very cold suddenly, thinking of what might have happened, the situation she might have been in, had she married this man. A wave of nausea washed over her. She felt Nathaniel's firm grip on her arm, steadying her.

"This ain't about Elizabeth, it's about Hidden Wolf," Nathaniel said.

Richard swung around to look at him. "Yes," he said. "It is."

"Hidden Wolf is no longer my father's, and you cannot have it," said Elizabeth. "Even if you sue him for nonpayment."

"The court may think otherwise," Richard said. "I'm sure they would be willing to hold off the transfer of property until the matter is cleared up, at any rate. And it could take a long time."

Nathaniel was looking at Mr. Schuyler. "We have the money he's owed."

There was a strangled laugh from Richard. "You have ten thousand dollars?" he asked, incredulous. "Have you been robbing banks in addition to stealing young women from their families in the dead of night?"

Nathaniel's hand closed hard on Elizabeth's arm to keep her still.

"You and I are going to have a discussion about that mouth of yours," he said slowly. "Someday soon. And when we do I expect you'll be eager to make an apology."

"We do have the funds," Elizabeth said, directing herself to Mr. Schuyler. "From my aunt Merriweather." It occurred to her now that the money bestowed so generously, which had yesterday seemed like a fortune, was not enough.

"Your aunt has gifted you only two thousand pounds, as I understand it," Richard pointed out. "That leaves three and a half thousand dollars."

Elizabeth's head snapped up, and she felt herself drain of color. "Well, gentleman that you are, Dr. Todd, I see you do not scruple to open post addressed to another."

"That was your father's doing," he said, not discomfited in the least.

"You are a scoundrel," she said. "And a common thief."

He smiled, and before she knew what she was doing, Elizabeth felt herself moving toward him. Nathaniel's hand on her shoulder stopped her.

"We've got the rest of the funds," he said to Mr. Schuyler.

"Oh," drawled Richard. "The mythical Tory Gold?"

Nathaniel did not turn his attention away from Mr. Schuyler. "The money can be paid out today, in Albany."

"Well, Todd," said Mr. Schuyler. "It seems that there is a happy end to this tale, after all. Today you will receive the monies owed you—providing you can produce the notes, that is. Judge Middleton will retain that property which he has not deeded to his daughter, and the lands he gifted to her remain her own property, and her husband's. And our business is settled."

"No." Richard shook his head, his smile disappearing. "Hidden Wolf was promised to me as part of the marriage contract, and I intend to sue for it."

There was a pause in the room, a gathering tension that jumped from Richard to Nathaniel and back again. Elizabeth knew that she stood outside this flow of energy. They had come to the heart of the matter now.

"Give it up, man," Mr. Schuyler said roughly. "Your chances are next to none, and you'll do nothing but injure your own good name in the courts. And hers."

"Good name?" laughed Richard. "She has no good name left to protect."

Nathaniel had been holding Elizabeth back, but suddenly he was gone from her, moving forward in two powerful leaps, so quickly that she barely understood what was happening before his fist met Richard's jaw with a dull cracking sound. Richard staggered and then caught himself. Elizabeth's stomach turned over neatly and rose into her throat.

Mr. Schuyler stepped forward and pushed against Nathaniel's shoulder, hard. "You forget yourself!" he shouted. "Think where you are, man! By God, I will put you both out if you do not control your tempers!"

Nathaniel was breathing hard. He looked away, and then back at Mr. Schuyler, dropping his head in a brief nod of acknowledgment.

Richard's eyes flashed with a narrow satisfaction. His jaw was turning color quickly, and a trickle of blood stained his lip, but he grinned.

"Nathaniel Bonner, called Wolf-Running-Fast," he said, his voice tight with menace. "Listen to me. I am going to Albany to file a breach of contract against this"—he swallowed hard—

"*lady* of yours. And to that end, I insist that she accompany me there to face that charge, and to be questioned in this matter."

"Never," Nathaniel said. His voice, so low and reasonable, made Elizabeth's hair stand on end. He glanced out the window, his fists clenching and unclenching at his sides. When he looked back, his face was impassive. "You have no power over us," he said. "And I will warn you once, and only once. You will stay away from me and mine, and we will stay away from you. But if you can't do that, if you ever lay a hand on my wife again or on any member of my family, I will kill you."

Richard did not blink. "She will come and face the charges against her," he said. "Or I'll see that a bench warrant is issued."

"Dr. Todd, you go too far," Mr. Schuyler said, disgusted. He turned to Nathaniel. "Let me deal with the man," he said. "Please take your wife upstairs."

"Mr. Schuyler, I am not going to Albany with him," said Elizabeth.

"Of course you are not. Of course not. Please, go up to your room now and I will sort this out."

Elizabeth hesitated. Nathaniel took her arm, and she glanced up at him.

"Go on, now," he said, opening the door for her. "I'll be up directly."

Mrs. Schuyler and her sons were in the hall with Runs-from-Bears, who stood with his rifle cradled in his arms. He exchanged a glance with Nathaniel and then followed Elizabeth upstairs, where he stood outside her door with his back to the wall.

She paced. She paced the room, alternately reading aunt Merriweather's letter and then stopping to make calculations on a scrap of paper. In addition to the gift of seven thousand, they needed another three and a half thousand dollars, and they needed it today. She herself had about half that much in the Albany bank, her entire annual income from her mother's small bequest. She thought that Nathaniel probably had the rest, given the offer to purchase he had made to her father. But she worked the numbers again and again and came out always at the same place: not enough money to pay off Richard, and pay the outstanding taxes on her own property, and her father's. They were at least five hundred dollars short.

It was an hour before he came to her, closing the door quietly behind him. She walked up to Nathaniel and put her arms around him, her head on his shoulder, trembling in anger and frustration.

"I had no idea," she said. "That it was so very bad. Ten thousand five hundred dollars."

He stroked her hair and said nothing.

"Tell me I don't have to go to Albany."

"You don't have to go to Albany," said Nathaniel. "But I do."

She pulled away. "Then I'm coming, too."

"No." He smiled grimly. "No, you ain't. I'm going with Schuyler and Todd because things would look bad if I weren't there to represent your interests. As it is I don't know what's going to happen."

"Can he get Hidden Wolf?" she asked, barely able to control the tremble in her voice.

"I don't think so. Neither does Schuyler. But we don't know what tricks he's got left yet, and I can't ask Philip to handle this on his own."

"Yes you can," Elizabeth said, knowing that he could not, but unable to bear the idea of this.

He smiled, and stroked her hair.

"I don't want you to go," she said, feeling her chin tremble and wishing that she could stop it.

"I know that," he said. "I don't want to go, either. But this is bad business, Boots, and we've got to get it settled. Now, listen."

He leaned forward and kissed her, quickly.

"Schuyler got him to agree to let you stay behind. Which is the right thing, because we don't know who's waiting down there in Albany to speak against you. Could be your brother—" He put a finger on her mouth to quiet her. "We ain't talking about the truth here, we're talking about how he can make things look."

Nathaniel took her by the hand and led her over to the chair by the hearth, and he pushed her into it, gently, leaning down over her.

"Listen to me now. This is what he wants. He wants you to stay here, under house arrest, while we're in Albany."

"House arrest?" she asked, incredulous.

"He says he don't trust you to stay put. Says that when it comes time for you to testify, he wants to be sure you'll come forward."

She was watching Nathaniel's face, the play of his features, the way his eyes moved.

"I think that the minute we're downriver, somebody'll show up here at the door—the judge, most likely—and force you to come back to Paradise. Take you by force, if need be."

Elizabeth lifted her chin. "I know how to fire a musket," she said.

He did her the favor of not grinning. "Aye, well. That's a good thing to know, under the circumstances." He picked up both her hands and held them tight.

"You're strong, and you're brave enough for ten. All right. When we're gone, Bears is going to stay behind. And at the first opportunity, he'll give you a signal. You remember the birdcall up above the waterfall? When you hear that, you go on out for a walk. He'll meet you behind the field where the men are sowing flax, near the mill. You can see it, there. Bears will take you into the bush, Boots, and you'll have to walk hard and fast to keep up with him. But he'll keep you safe, as long as you listen to him and do what he says."

Nathaniel's hands were warm and full of energy in her own. Elizabeth held on to him tightly.

"Where are we going?" she asked.

"To Robbie," he said. "Up near the lake the Kahnyen'kehàka call Little Lost."

"Robbie?"

"Robbie MacLachlan," Nathaniel said. "Listen, Boots. I ain't got much time here. They're waiting on me. There's no-body in this world more disposed to look after you and keep you safe for me than Bears and Robbie MacLachlan."

Elizabeth leaned forward and kissed him, hard, catching his

face between her hands, feeling the bristle on his cheeks against her palms.

"Are you scairt?" he asked, his hands on her upper arms, holding tight.

"Yes."

"Good," said Nathaniel. "You need that, hold on to it."

He started to pull away, but she grabbed his shirt and held him.

"When will you come?" she asked.

"I hope it won't be more than a week," he said. "But I can't promise it won't be more."

Nathaniel pulled her up with him from the chair and kissed her soundly. "You know I'll be there as soon as I can. We got that demonstration left unfinished, after all."

She nodded, her mouth pressed into a hard line, her eyes glittering.

He brought her hand to his mouth and kissed her ring; then he smiled and was gone.

From the window, Elizabeth watched him walking down the lawn toward the river where the canoes waited. She could see the party gathered there, Mr. and Mrs. Schuyler, Anton Meerschaum, and Richard Todd. There was no sign of Bears, but she knew he would be outside her door.

Unable to watch anymore, she turned away and caught sight of the scrap of paper with her calculations. She grabbed it, along with aunt Merriweather's letter, and flew down the stairs with Runs-from-Bears right behind her. Her skirt fluttered as she ran across the lawns, her heart beating in her throat so that she feared she would not be able to speak even if she could catch them.

But they were still there, standing in front of the canoes. Nathaniel looked up to her and his face first cleared of anger and then closed in worry.

Richard Todd turned to Mrs. Schuyler. "She's to stay in the house."

Even in her distraction, Elizabeth took note of Mrs. Schuyler's expression, the combination of condescension and righteous indignation. "Mrs. Bonner is our guest," she said. "Not a prisoner. And she has the freedom of Saratoga while she is with us."

Richard cleared his throat and looked away. "As long as she's here when the court calls on her."

"If such a thing should be necessary," Mrs. Schuyler said tightly. "Which I doubt."

"Mr. Schuyler, you are an officer of the bank in Albany?" asked Elizabeth, ignoring Richard. When he nodded, she continued. "I have funds there, and I release them to my husband for withdrawal as he sees fit. This will be in order?"

"It will." His dark eyes were hooded again, but he smiled at her.

"Thank you." She turned to Nathaniel and tugged on his arm, to pull him off to where they could not be heard. Then she put the papers in his hand, aunt Merriweather's letter and her calculations. She pointed to one set of figures and then another, and looked up at him.

"There's not enough!" she whispered.

"I'll manage," he said. "Don't worry yourself, Boots." He pulled her further aside. "There's the furs, don't forget."

"Then there'll be no money for supplies," she countered.

Nathaniel looked over her shoulder to where Richard waited. Runs-from-Bears stood to one side, alert.

"There's money enough," he said. "Leave this to me, can you?"

She nodded then, and because he was so close and because she could not do otherwise, in spite of their audience, in spite of the danger, she kissed him. Put her hands on his shoulders and went up on her toes to kiss Nathaniel, to show him what she couldn't say, didn't know how to say: how much the idea of his going hurt, how proud she was of him, how much she loved him, that she would miss him. She was crying, because she didn't know how not to. Her tears wet his cheeks.

She let him go and wiped his face with her fingers. Then Elizabeth looked up over his shoulder and saw how close Richard was, how his mouth twisted with disgust. And at his elbow, Runs-from-Bears with a hand on the shaft of his tomahawk.

"You'll have enough of him sooner than you think," Richard said when she met his gaze. "Sarah did, and so will you."

Everything in Nathaniel stilled. Elizabeth felt this, the way all his focus came down, small and tight, on the sound of Richard's voice behind him.

"Think, man," he said without turning. "Think what you're doing."

"I know what I'm doing," Richard said, not taking his eyes from Elizabeth. "I'm telling your wife what she needs to know. Being so fond of children as she is."

"What is he talking about?" Elizabeth asked, frightened.

"I'm talking about the fact that he can't give you children. Has he told you that?"

Elizabeth glanced up at Nathaniel and saw that he had gone away inside himself, his face a mask.

"Nathaniel?"

"You see on his face that it's true."

"Hannah," she said. "There's Hannah."

"Hannah's mine," said Richard.

"Nathaniel?" She touched his face, and he seemed to come back to life. He took her hand, and pulled her farther away from Richard.

"Go now," he whispered. "Remember to wait for the sign from Bears."

"I don't understand—" she began.

"Elizabeth," he said. "It would take too long now. Do you trust me?"

She nodded.

"Then believe me. Hannah is my daughter. I will answer your questions when I come to you, anything you care to ask me. Will you wait for that? Can you?"

Once again, Elizabeth nodded, but slowly.

"I love you," he said against her mouth. And he walked away from her down to the river.

Elizabeth turned back to the house and after a few yards Runs-from-Bears fell into step beside her. She heard the splash on the canoe as it entered the river, but she never looked back.

XXVII

The most remarkable thing about Runs-from-Bears, Elizabeth came to believe, was not the contrast between his ferocious appearance and his dry good humor, but his willingness to talk. She had been very quiet on the first day because it seemed appropriate to be silent in the infinity of these forests, unlike anything she had ever experienced or imagined. And she had thought that Bears would have little to say to her; she was shy of him, and worried that she wouldn't be able to meet his expectations.

And when they had finally made camp, Elizabeth had not really wanted conversation, tired as she was. It was then, sitting before the little fire and turning the cleaned possum on its spit of green wood, that she had found out that Runs-from-Bears was almost as curious about her as she was about him, and that he had things to teach her.

By the second day on the trail to the northwest, Elizabeth had begun to like him very much, and to learn how much she didn't know. The business of staying alive in the bush was serious and exhausting but also absorbing. With his guidance, she had managed the rudimentaries of cleaning small game and fish. Struggling with a possum—an animal she found almost too ugly to eat—or the skinning of a rabbit, she was very thankful that there wasn't time for him to go after bigger animals.

Rabbits were the quickest game, but she soon learned that

while they were available in abundance, they were also too lean to sustain people who walked hard all day long. Bears addressed this problem with a supply of rendered bear fat, which he squeezed from a skin directly into his mouth. Elizabeth could watch him do this, but she was not so hungry that she could manage it herself. The corncake, dry now and requiring much chewing, was filled with nuts and she hoped these would meet her needs for the time being. It was certainly true that she was hungrier than she had ever been in her life.

Elizabeth learned to strip kindling with her fingers from a birch trunk, locate deadwood, and although she was terribly slow at it, to start a fire with flint and iron. Above all other things, Elizabeth was learning to see in the woods: Runs-from-Bears pointed out wolf and deer and panther scat, beaver dams and lodges, old abandoned duck nests appropriated by mice, the way that squirrels scattered refuse on the ground beneath the trees they favored, raccoon tracks like the imprint of the human hand, how to tell otter from fisher prints, and the alternating pattern of the black bear's track. They skirted a thicket of hawthorn and he stopped to show her the way a shrike had impaled a small mole on a long thorn. She thought she would be very hungry indeed before she resorted to stealing the shrike's dinner, but she didn't say this to Bears.

Sitting in the early morning with her food, Elizabeth looked at the stretches of white cedar lining the shore of the little lake where they had camped and she saw that deer had been foraging there, shearing off the underside of the foliage in straight lines that aunt Merriweather's gardeners would have been proud of. Interspersed with the cedar were ragged spruce branches hanging low. She asked Runs-from-Bears about this.

"Deer don't care much for spruce," he agreed. He said this once in Kahnyen'kehàka and then repeated it in English.

This was the fourth full day out of Saratoga, and deep in the bush. They were eating the last of the corncake and dried berries, but Bears thought they would get to Robbie MacLachlan's by midday, and he didn't seem concerned about their lack of provisions. Elizabeth watched Bears eat, more neatly and fastidiously than she could manage without fork or spoon. There wasn't a wasted movement to the process, and he seemed to take little pleasure in it. His eyes scanned the bush as he chewed. Elizabeth knew that he was seeing things that she couldn't even imagine.

She was looking forward to Robbie MacLachlan, although she barely dared admit this to herself. Only four days walking and she was tired to the bone, and gritty, and she feared that she smelled. Much of her exposed skin was itchy with welts; she had learned, finally, what Nathaniel meant with his threats of the blackfly, although Bears told her they weren't bad this year. He certainly seemed to suffer less from them than she did. Mrs. Schuyler had given her a home remedy, but thus far Elizabeth had resisted the pungent ointment.

The early morning sun shone on Bears' hair so that it cast out blue-black tones. The tattoo that stretched over his cheekbones to meet on the bridge of his nose seemed to shine in the same shades of blue, standing out in relief against his skin, deep bronze and scattered with the evidence of a hard-won battle with the pox. Looking at him now, Elizabeth realized that his tattoos were not an abstract design of fanned lines, as she had thought, but identical to the tracks he had pointed out that a black bear had left on smooth tree bark.

"Does tattooing hurt?"

"Hen'en." *Yes, of course.*

"Then why do you do it?"

Bears touched his cheekbone with one finger. "The pain is important."

Elizabeth had the idea that she was slowly coming to see the way Bears thought. She wasn't surprised, now, to hear him accept the pain as a natural and necessary thing, instead of denying it. She decided to keep this to think about on the trail, when she would have long hours to consider it carefully. Something to keep her mind off Nathaniel.

"Do you think much about Many-Doves?"

He inclined his head at her. "As much as you think of Nathaniel."

"Why do you call him Nathaniel, and not by his Kahnyen'kehàka name?"

"I call him what he is. Right now he is Nathaniel."

Elizabeth thought about that in silence for a while.

"Why do the Kahnyen'kehàka call Nathaniel Okwaho-rowakeka?"

"Wolf-Running-Fast," translated Bears.

"Hen'en, ohnahò:ten' karihóni'?" *Yes, but for what reason?*

He blinked solemnly, which, she had slowly come to understand, was an indication that he would reply to her question with a question. "What do you know of the wolf?" he asked.

Elizabeth knew very little of wolves, she realized, and she admitted this openly.

"Wolf is a hunter," said Bears. "But most of all, Wolf never hunts alone. The pack is the most important thing, and he hunts for the pack and with it."

"But Falling-Day told me he had another name—"

"Deseroken. She gave him this name, Between-Two-Lives, when he came to live in her longhouse that winter when he took her daughter to wife. But before that he was Wolf-Running-Fast. He would tell you this," Bears concluded. "If you asked him."

"But he's not here, and you are."

He nodded, satisfied with this logic.

"You make me work very hard for the answers to my questions," Elizabeth pointed out.

"You ask many questions," Bears said. "Quid pro quo."

She could not suppress a laugh, to hear Runs-from-Bears switch from Kahnyen'kehàka to Latin. He pursed his mouth at her. "You are surprised."

"Hen'en." She wiped her brow with her kerchief. "I forget sometimes that you have had European schooling as well. You do not let it show, normally." Suddenly encouraged by the turn in the conversation, Elizabeth found herself asking a question which had long bothered her.

"Why—" She sought the right wording, and then moved forward cautiously. "Why is your head not shaved?"

She had surprised him, something that did not often happen.

"We are not at war," he said. Then, seeing that she didn't understand, he raised his hands to his own head, and grasped his hair at the crown, a handful, twisting it up and away. Although he more and more often spoke Kahnyen'kehàka to her, he said this in English.

"A warrior who takes my life honorably in battle takes my scalp back to his people, as proof of his skill and bravery. I would do the same to him. I have done the same, but not often. I was very young in the last wars. Now there is no fighting here. If I were to go north to Stone-Splitter or west"—he gestured with his chin—"to join Little-Turtle, then I would shave my head again and dare my enemies to take my scalplock."

He was watching her, his eyes hooded.

"You are thinking we are savages, and in need of civilization."

"No," said Elizabeth. "I am hoping that you never have to shave your head again."

"Hmm," said Bears, and she saw that she had surprised him again. "Toka'nonwa." *Maybe.* He rose. "We have about six hours to walk, Looks-Hard, and we'd best get going."

Her legs were still quite stiff, but Bears kept a steady pace that did not tax her overmuch. And Elizabeth enjoyed the walking. Her pack contained primarily her own things and some of the dwindling provisions; for the first part of the day, at least, it did not seem heavy to her. It helped to have the freedom to move. She wore the shirt-like overdress and leggings that Many-Doves had lent her, nonsensically it seemed, with her own shift underneath them. Her hair was plaited now and tied with a strip of rawhide, and the end swung with the rhythm of her walking at the small of her back. Tucked into a wide belt was a knife in a beaded sheath which Bears had taught her how to sharpen on the first day. Thus far she had used it only for cleaning game, but it was good to have it anyway. In a little purse she carried a sharpening stone, a tinderbox, and a small store of buckshot sewn into elongated linen capsules.

She was still wearing Many-Doves' moccasins, and she was very glad of them. Elizabeth wondered how she would ever wear her own shoes again, or even her beloved boots with their elegant little heels and fine needlework. She thought much of Paradise, particularly of her students, and of Hannah, who was her daughter now. It would have been a wonderful idea, to have a daughter, if it hadn't been for Richard Todd. He had managed to steal this joy from her, and Elizabeth resented it deeply.

What was so very frightening about this was not the memory of Richard's hateful smile when he claimed Hannah as his own child, but the complete lack of emotion from Nathaniel. No mortification or surprise or anger. Things Elizabeth would have expected, even if—and this was an unwelcome thought—Richard's claim were true. She told herself, as she had already a hundred times, that it did no good to contemplate his incredible declarations until she could talk to Nathaniel about all of it. She wondered with considerable discomfort if Nathaniel might have told her more of Sarah, and of Sarah and Richard, if she had been willing to listen when he tried to talk to her about his first marriage. She could not help thinking that he should have told her, anyway.

They began climbing again, through the woods on a path that Elizabeth could barely discern, although Bears showed no hesitation at all. Above their heads a woodpecker drilled in the soft wood of a cedar above a clinging mass of orchidlike flowers with brilliant crimson stripes. There were birds all around, busy with their nests. She had found out that many of them did not have Kahnyen'kehàka names and so she had stopped asking, satisfying herself with observing their habits and making up names of her own. So engrossed was she at the sight of a porcupine perched up high and stripping buds from a maple tree that she did not notice that Bears had stopped dead in his tracks.

He swung his rifle around and up in a fluid gesture. Elizabeth had barely picked out the buck grazing upwind from them when the shot sounded and the animal leapt wildly into the air and then fell.

"Robbie will be glad of the meat," he said by way of explanation. The birdsong had stopped, replaced by the echoing of the gunshot.

They walked into Robbie's camp a few hours later, although Elizabeth did not realize that they had done so until Bears had hefted the small buck over his shoulders and dropped it to the ground.

But it was a homestead, of a sort. There was a small natural clearing, sunlit, and surrounded by stands of birch and maple. The woods as far as she could see were completely clear of underbrush; she had come to recognize the significance of this, the difference between tended forest and bush. Off to one side there was a deep fire pit, lined with rocks and well used, with a trivet on one end and a spit on the other. On two sides of this open hearth there were logs at a comfortable distance. One of them, the one that faced away from the mountain and looked down the trail, had a shiny spot in its middle. The cabin itself she had not seen at all at first glance, because it was built into the side of the mountain. It was not so much a cabin as a lean-to, stripped logs weathered into the color of granite, with a roof of evergreen boughs over bark. There was one small window, just an opening in the wall with a propped-up shutter. It was a tidy place; the walls were hung with snowshoes and traps at regular intervals.

Bears had pulled back the rough pelt that served as a door, hooking it back over a great rusty nail on the wall. He called in, a kind of whooping hello in Kahnyen'kehàka and then in English.

When it was clear they were on their own, they made themselves comfortable in the clearing. Bears set to butchering and cleaning the buck. While Elizabeth knew that she should watch this process, she was glad to forgo the lesson for the moment to fetch water from a mountain spring behind the cabin. She filled the cavernous iron kettle and began to cut the chunks of meat he passed to her into pieces, using a flat rock as her board, and shooing away flies with ever-increasing irritation.

They worked for a few hours, until there was a stew cooking over the fire pit: venison and wild onions she found growing nearby, dried beans and squash and corn from the stores in the cabin. The smell of it made her stomach growl, but this was such a common experience in the recent days that she had learned not to be embarrassed by it. The rest of the meat Bears hung on hooks inside a hollow tree stump as high as himself. It was capped by a little shingled roof, and it had a door on leather hinges. There was a pile of split oak under a tarpaulin, and he used this to start a slow fire in the bottom of the tree trunk. He showed Elizabeth how to feed the fire, which would burn for days until the meat was thoroughly smoked.

He had held back some of the raw liver, and he offered her a strip.

"Makes the blood strong," he explained.

She could put it on a stick and thrust it into the flames, or she could do as he did and chew it raw. Elizabeth saw him grin at her, and so she ate it raw to show him that she could.

Her handkerchief, now in a truly deplorable state, could not deal with her bloodied fingers and dirty hands, and so she went to wash in the spring. In that quiet corner between the cabin and the mountain, she took a few minutes to think on her own. It occurred to her that she had now spent more time with Runs-from-Bears than she had ever spent with Nathaniel. This was not a welcome thought, as much as she was coming to like him. She could hear Bears singing softly to himself. The black-fly song; he had taught it to her, and she hummed along.

The blackfly is bringing a message
He's coming to tell us how poor he is.
The truth of the matter is,
He is so old-fashioned and brings
always the same old message.

She washed out her handkerchief and then used it to clean her hands and face and neck. Even with only cold water and without soap or other conveniences, she felt better for it. Elizabeth listened to Bears while she unplaited her hair and finger-combed it, sorting out every tangle until her hair fairly stood on end, snapping and crackling with energy. There was a clean shift in her pack, an appealing idea, but then Elizabeth looked down at herself and decided that she would wait to change until she could have some sort of bath, even if it was in the cold waters of the lake they had passed on the way to the cabin, the one called Little Lost. With a sigh, she spread her wet handkerchief on a rock in the sun and walked back around the corner to the clearing. There she stopped short, for Bears was no longer alone.

· · · ·

He was without a doubt the biggest man she had ever seen. Far bigger than her uncle Merriweather, who dwarfed all the men of the neighborhood. Bigger than Bears by half a head, at least, and half again as broad. Not fat, certainly, but layered with slabs of muscle. When he turned toward her it seemed to take forever, and to go on with the thoughtfulness of a tree flexing in the wind. He was old, more than seventy: the great sweeping mustache, his eyebrows, and the hair tied to a tail at the nape of his neck were blindingly white. His eyes, slate-blue, peered out at her from a nest of wrinkles.

Two things happened when their gazes met, both of which surprised Elizabeth. He smiled shyly, revealing a set of teeth as astoundingly white as his hair, and at the same time he blushed a shade of scarlet she had never before seen on any human being, male or female. This change in color was so furious, fast, and profound, and it flared so bright in contrast to his hair and teeth, that she was immediately put in mind of aunt Merriweather's prize rose campion, rose-red blossoms with their cover of woolly white down. Her own smile faltered to see him color so, for she thought that he must be uneasy about her sudden appearance.

He had pulled the cap from his head and stood at attention, although he did not look away.

"So here she is, then," he said. His voice was soft and somewhat higher than she would have guessed, on the basis of his size. "But look at her, she's nae but a great mass o' hair and eyes sae big as moons. A bonnie thing, tae be sure, but ower young tae be oot traipsin' through the bush wi' the likes o' you, Bears." He bowed in Elizabeth's direction with tight military precision. "So there's nocht tae do but make oursel' acquaint'. Robert MacLachlan, at your service, Mistress Bonner."

"Please." Elizabeth glanced at Bears, who was clearly content to stand back and watch her handle this encounter on her own. "Please do call me Elizabeth."

"Oh, no, that wadna do." His color had faded somewhat, but then he tilted his head hopefully and it flared again.

"I would like you to," she said. "I would be honored."

"Wad ye noo? And wha' will ye call me, then?"

"Whatever you like." Elizabeth laughed.

"Aye weel. Ma mither called me Rab, and most o' ma friends call me Robbie, but Cora Bonner, bless her immortal soul, Cora called me Robin."

" 'For bonny sweet Robin is all my joy,' " quoted Elizabeth, and she thought that he might ignite, so bright did he blush. "From Shakespeare," she explained, embarrassed for herself more than for him.

"Oh, aye. *Hamlet*. Though the man borrowed Sweet Robin fra' an auld Scots song." He threw her a sideways glance. "But he put it tae guid use, wi' *Hamlet*. Will ye read aloud, then, if ye're asked nicely?"

"I have done," she said solemnly. "Though I have no books with me."

He waved a hand dismissively. "Aye, but I do. Great lot o' good it does me, though, for ma eyes canna manage the print on the page these days. Muny's the evenin' I spent at Lake in the Clouds listenin' tae Cora read, and readin' in turn." He raised one perfect eyebrow. "She was a rare woman, was Cora."

"So everyone tells me," Elizabeth said. "But I see the evidence of it, in her son."

He smiled at that. "Aye, so ye must, tae hae marrit the man. Ne'er took a wife, mysel', for the only one wha' wad hae suited me had been lang syne acquent wi' Hawkeye by the time I met her. Forbye, her faither wadna hae looked kindly on me, wi' me bein' nought but a common sodjer. Mind you, 'gin Hawkeye hadna seen her first—" His color sputtered like the flame of a poorly cleaned wick. "But wha' am I thinkin'? I'll fetch ye sumthin'—wad ye care for a wee bit o' ale? Yon venison is ripe for the eatin'. Come and set yersel', lass. No, bide a while, that log's no' a suitable place." He stood scratching his head for a moment and then walked over to the woodpile. After a moment's consideration, he went down on his knees to heft a stump which Elizabeth would not have been able to span with both arms. It was as high as her knee, and it made a considerable thud when he set it on the ground. Then he fetched a fox pelt from the cabin and spread it neatly.

"You'll set better so," he said with a shy smile.

After quite a bit of back and forth, attention to the fire, and concern for Elizabeth's comfort, they were finally settled around the pit with bowls of stew, Elizabeth on her makeshift throne and the men with their legs stretched before them. Robbie insisted that she take his only spoon, a great scooplike affair carved of wood which looked quite reasonable in his own tremendous fist but dwarfed Elizabeth's. The stew was hot enough to burn her mouth, but she ate the fresh meat with great pleasure. Runs-from-Bears showed his usual abstemiousness, eating quickly and then leaving them to go back to work on the hide, close enough to hear without taking part in the conversation. Robbie ate slowly, although Elizabeth wondered that he managed at all between his solicitous concern for her comfort and the stories he had to tell of Cora and how he had met her when she was visiting her father.

"I couldna bring masel' tae like the man—a better officer you couldna find, but he was as crabbit as an auld witch. Noo, there was a mannie wi' gey few pleasantries aboot him. Yon yin had a glower that wad frichten a magistrate."

"But you would have overlooked sour looks, I expect, for Cora," Elizabeth pointed out, smiling both at his easy pragmatism and the way it suited his language, so broad and throaty, r's rolled and t's swallowed with a distinct Scots hiccup. It would have set her own brow on high a few months ago, but she had lost many of those preconceptions that she brought with her from England.

"Aye, and muny times ower, for her sake."

When Elizabeth had had her fill she listened quietly with the empty bowl in her lap, asking questions now and then but mostly content to let Robbie's memories take her along with him.

"And she brought a fine son into the world, and he grew up into a fine man, and noo he's yer own. But here ye sit, lass, and while I'm pleased tae hae your company, I'm wonderin' where he is, that new gudeman of yours, and why he's sent ye into the bush this way. Bears just said there was trouble."

For all his blushes, there was a keen intelligence to Robbie MacLachlan and Elizabeth thought he would see through partial truths quite easily. It was clear to her that Nathaniel trusted this man implicitly, and beyond that there was something about him which set her at ease. He was looking at her now with a quiet expectation, good humor and understanding on his broad features.

"There is a dispute," she began. "About some property, and who has a right to it. It belongs to me, and now to us, but there is someone else who believes he has a prior claim. Nathaniel is in Albany, to resolve the question."

"But he was worrit for ye, otherwise he wadna hae sent ye awa' from him."

She nodded. "The other party is fairly insistent on his claim."

"A claim tae ye, or the lan'?"

"Both," she said.

He grinned. "Aye, weel. He's no' daft. There's nae truth to his claim?"

"I have legal title and I am legally wed," Elizabeth said. "But he will not accept either as truth."

Robbie shook his head. "There's nane sae blind as he wha' winna see."

Bears had looked up from his work; Elizabeth felt his attention on her and sent a look his way, but he was not ready to speak.

"This person has threatened me with a warrant to appear before the magistrate in Albany," Elizabeth concluded. "And as I did not care to be forced, here I am."

Robbie MacLachlan's anger had a color all its own, a deeper, more vibrant red that flowed down to mottle the soft flesh of his neck.

"Forced?" he said very softly. "No, I'll no' accept that. And neither wad Nathaniel."

"He didn't," Elizabeth agreed. "It was unpleasant."

"Aye, lass, that I can weel imagine. Who is the blaggart?"

Runs-from-Bears cleared his throat. "Irtakohsaks," he said.

Robbie started at this name, turning away from Elizabeth.

"Irtakohsaks? Cat-Eater?" he asked, incredulous. "Then I mun take it back, he is a bluidy daft bugger, is Cat-Eater." His color flared. "Ye'll excuse my rough tongue, lass. I've been too long wi' only masel' for company. But Cat-Eater! And it canna be other than Hidden Wolf he's wantin'."

Bears nodded.

"Cat-Eater," Elizabeth echoed. "Is that Richard's Kahnyen'kehàka name? I've never heard it before."

"And you won't use it to his face, not unless you've got a musket primed in your hand," said Bears with one of his rare grins.

"Cat-Eater. You wadna think it tae look at him, wad ye, the coof that he's become. Aweel, I'll hae the tale in peace this e'en, but I'm sorry tae say I hae work tae do." He stood with a great groan. "Ye've been four days i' the bush, as I understan' it, and I'll miss ma guess if ye wadna like some hot water and a wee bit o' time tae yersel'."

Elizabeth paused. "Hot water?"

He nodded solemnly. "Oh, aye. I see Bears kept the best for a surprise. Come this way, my dear, and see. And bring your things, ye'll have need o' them."

The cabin was built not onto the side of the mountain, Elizabeth realized as soon as she stepped in past the great pelt at the door, but into it. The room she found herself in was very small, and practically empty; a small barrel, some dried meat and other foods hanging from rafters, pelts stretched on racks, but otherwise no sign of habitation. No place to sit or sleep at all, no hearth. But there was a great wooden door of an unusual shape, carved to fit the natural opening in the wall of rock. Robbie gave it a push, and it swung silently inward. Then he ducked and disappeared inside. There was some rumbling, followed by a spark of light which grew into a steady small flame in the open doorway. Robbie's head and shoulders appeared, a small lantern of pierced tin in one hand. He gestured her forward, his color flushing bright.

Elizabeth followed him gamely through a chain of small caves crowded with his things, the tools of his trade, primarily, but also less expected items: a small bookcase, filled to bursting; an open box filled with seashells—Elizabeth looked again, unwilling to believe her eyes, but there they were; and hung on one rock wall, a small but exquisite oil painting of a horse in a peeling gilt frame. She saw these things as the small circle of light bobbed past with Robbie's step, and then they disappeared again into the dark. Ahead of them was the persistent sound of dripping water, and a heavy, mineral-laden smell. Elizabeth could not see far ahead of herself, for Robbie's great expanse of back blocked the way. There were a number of natural chambers, some empty, and some set up as living or storage space. He showed her one with a narrow cot which she could use for her own, and then moved on to the next.

"There's light here, in the day, d'ye see? The spalt in yon wall isna so verra great that the beasties could get it, but the fresh air is a fine thing. And wi'oot it I couldna cook here in the winter."

Elizabeth saw that there was in fact a cleft in the ceiling of the natural chamber before them. It crested like a moon, with a wide center tapering at both ends. On the swept rock floor there was evidence of a small fire pit.

"O' course, this isna a guid spot tae set when it's raining," Robbie conceded. He looked thoughtful. "Tell me, lass, what name does Nathaniel hae for ye? Does he call ye Lizzie?"

"My brother calls me Lizzie, but Nathaniel has got into the habit of calling me Boots."

Robbie's laughter echoed in the caves. "Boots? Aye, and it suits ye weel. Did ye ken that the newest and youngest officer in any Tory regiment is called Boots?"

"I wasn't aware," Elizabeth said with a dry smile.

He set off again through the corridor. "Boots. It's no' sae bad as Lizzie, dinna ye think?"

Elizabeth did agree. "By whatever name you care to call me, Robbie, I am finding it increasingly warm the farther back we walk. Do you sleep here in the winter?" She had begun to perspire.

"Aye, as the season moves along, so do I." He nodded. "By January I've settled doon back here."

They had come to the end of the corridor, which widened into a cave just tall enough for Robby to stand in. The walls shimmered wet in the light of the lantern and then flared bright as he set his flame to a torch set in the wall. The floor was even, but about five feet from where they stood it sloped away suddenly into a dark pool of water, fed by a trickle down the far wall. In the small space before the pool began there was evidence of Robbie's long habitation of this place. A cot, neatly made, shelves, a rough table.

"It is a fine wee bit o' water, this." He turned to Elizabeth with one brow raised. "Can ye swim?"

She shook her head, feeling her hair beginning to curl and stick to her dampening face and neck.

"Aye, I feared so. Nathaniel must teach ye, then, for it's nae good, not knowin' how tae swim in the bush."

Elizabeth's face fell. The sudden and unexpected gift of a hot bath in complete privacy was something she could not easily relinquish.

"Noo, lass. Ye'll hae your bath. Just take care that ye gae nae further than the rope." He picked up a coiled line which lay on the ground with one end knotted securely to a bolt in the wall, and gave the other to Elizabeth. "The floor drops oot, sudden, and we'll no' hae accidents wi' Nathaniel Bonner's new wife."

He looked around himself. "There's drinking water there in the jug, for the spring water isna pleasant, for a' it's a fine tonic. Be sure and drink, lass, for ye'll sweat here like ye've ne'er sweated afore. And nae more than a few minutes in the water, the first time, until ye've had a chance tae accommodate yersel' tae the heat. Will that serve?"

It did serve. When Elizabeth had the cave to herself, she undressed in the small light of the lantern, and then with some hesitancy immersed herself in the warm water. Elizabeth took her minutes and more, and then reluctantly emerged to wrap herself in the rough blanket Robbie had left for her. She had meant to take the opportunity to wash her linen, but once on the edge of the bed, tingling from the pleasure of the soaking, her muscles loose and her hair wrapped around her head, she fell into a good and restful sleep, and she stayed there for many hours.

"Do ye ken where ye are?" Robbie asked. He stepped back from Elizabeth and looked around himself, as if he were as unfamiliar with this part of the world as she was. "Do ye ken north fra' south?"

They were on their way down to the river to fish, and after

just a day in his care, it was clear to Elizabeth that Robbie was as much a teacher as Runs-from-Bears. Their progress was slow, for he found it necessary to point out to her everything edible in their path. Now, in reply to his question, Elizabeth studied the sky, what she could see of it. There was no hope of determining the position of the sun. With a bit of an apologetic smile, she shook her head at Robbie.

"That," he said, his brow furrowing, "willna do. Ye must be able tae set off richt if ye dinna want tae gang agley." He was slipping more and more into Scots as the day went on. Elizabeth sometimes had trouble understanding him, but thus far he had always been aware when she became confused, and then he repeated himself as he did now. Slowly, saying exactly the same thing.

"You know," Elizabeth decided to point out to him. "Perhaps it's a big enough challenge learning Kahnyen'kehàka right now, without adding Scots to my lesson plan. As much as it would interest me—" she added hastily, seeing his raised brow.

"Aye, and weel ye should learn Scots, ma dear," said Robbie. "For there's nae better tongue for settin' a man richt. Cora could make her men wither an' wilt wi' it when the mood was on her, though she could talk English wi' no' a trace of the Scots when she chose—which was seldom the case, sae lang I kent her. Nathaniel can be a feisty de'il betimes, and ye'll hae need o' Scots enough tae put him in his place."

"No doubt!" laughed Elizabeth. "But at the moment, don't you think it would be sufficient if I learned north from south?"

Robbie scratched his head thoughtfully. "Aye," he said finally. "Ye've the richt o' it, lass. And p'rhaps makin' a Scots woman o' thee is no' the best thing tae be doin'. Ye've done weel for yersel', so as ye stan'." He walked over to a pine and ran a large fist down its branch, coming away with a few needles. These he held out to Elizabeth.

"Take the straightest, stoutest one there. Aye, that'll do."

Elizabeth wondered what good a single pine needle might be when she was lost in the bush, given the fact that there were millions upon millions of them around her, but she thought it best to bide her time.

"Now," said Robbie. "Wha' we need is a bit o' silk."

"Oh," said Elizabeth. "I have a silk ribbon, but it's back with my things." The thought of the ribbon she had worn in her hair for her wedding made her stop suddenly.

"Nathaniel's on yer mind," said Robbie. "It stands writ on yer face. Well, lass, if it's iny comfort at a', there's nae man whose word I trust more, unless it's his faither." He cleared his throat. "And if ye'll permit me an observation, he's done weel for hisel', has Nathaniel. He deserves a guid woman, and I'm glad tae see him wi' one."

"Do you think he was lonely?" asked Elizabeth, and was surprised at herself, to have spoken this question out loud.

But Robbie did not seem surprised. "His good fortune is, he need be lonely nae longer."

Elizabeth looked down at the pine needle lying on her palm. "Did you know Sarah?" she asked, and felt her throat swell with this, with the saying of the name which preoccupied her to such a degree.

"I did." Robbie hesitated, and then began to rumble about in the pouch on his belt. At length he pulled out a handful of bullet patches, which he stirred with his thumb.

"Silk patches are the best thing when your target's far off an' less than willin' tae stan quiet," he explained. But he looked up from his palm at Elizabeth thoughtfully.

"Sarah was a comely lass," he said softly. "But she was no' the richt wife for Nathaniel."

The pale yellow silk looked very out of place between his two thick fingers.

"It's ten year or more since I put this bit of silk by, thinkin' someday I might have need o' some careful shootin'. So, my dear, listen noo, and closely. Stroke the needle gently with the silk—that's right. We want it tae bristle. Let me see yer face. Wha' e'es ye've got, lass, the color of the sky when the gloamin's fadin' fast. Noo, rub your finger on yer forehead, there, where there's a sheen. Wha' ye must do, and gently, mind, is tae stroke the oil fra' yer finger onto the needle. Can ye manage? Lovely."

They stood with their heads bent over Elizabeth's palm.

"The Kahnyen'kehàka women are an unco' strong race," said Robbie. "Stronger than will suit most men."

Elizabeth frowned. "Nathaniel certainly knew enough about the Kahnyen'kehàka. That couldn't have been a surprise to him. And he doesn't seem to be afraid of strong women."

She realized how defensive she had sounded, but Robbie's smile was understanding.

"Aye," he said. "His mither was a strong woman, and he found one agin in ye. But there's nae denyin' it, the Kahnyen'kehàka women take things in their own hands the way ye wadnae think tae do."

Elizabeth thought of Richard's claims, and she stilled suddenly.

"It runs contrary tae everythin' ye've been told aboot richt and wrong," said Robbie. "But I've no' a question that ye'd find satisfaction wi' the Mohawk way yersel', if ye had tae live it."

"I doubt that," Elizabeth muttered.

"Oh, but think," said Robbie easily. "Ne'er a man tae run yer life. The longhouse ye live in belongs tae your mither, and one day may be your own tae do wi' as ye see fit. The bairns are yours, and the gettin' o' them—" He paused and flushed.

"As a marrit woman, perhaps ye'll permit me tae say more than I should. The gettin' o' bairns is a woman's business, ye see, among the Kahnyen'kehàka. She may take a man and he may suit her weel, but if he doesna, then she can turn tae another and nae one will say her nay. Includin' her own man."

Elizabeth looked up at him, shocked.

"A man would not tolerate such behavior," she said.

"But ye're wrong there, lassie. A Kahnyen'kehàka wad thole it, an' ye'll look far and wide i' the world for a better race o' men, braw and bonnie. Noo mind, I'm no' sayin' that he wadna dislike it. Kahnyen'kehàka are prideful people. But it is their way, or it was, before they scattered and left their hamelands."

He turned his attention to the pine needle. Plucking a single white hair from his head, he made a loop of it between thumb and forefinger. This he offered to Elizabeth, and she took it.

"Slip it under the wee needle so ye can lift it, and wha ye must do, lass, is tae let the needle float on the top o' the dub in yon dail stump at your knee. The water, ye ken, poolin' there. Mind noo, if it goes under we mun start afresh."

Robbie glanced at her, for she was staring at him.

"Go on, then, see if ye can make it float."

Reluctantly, Elizabeth turned to this task. Trying to gather her concentration, she did as she was directed. When the needle landed gently on the water, she slipped the hair away. From his pocket, Robbie took his own compass and compared it to the pine needle, which turned slowly and then stopped.

"So," he said, quite visibly pleased. "Ye've made a compass."

"Yes," she said quietly.

He cleared his throat. "I see I've told ye sumthin' ye didna know about the Kahnyen'kehàka, and it doesna meet wi' your approval."

"A child not being able to name her father with certainty does not seem to me a good way of ordering things, no," Elizabeth agreed.

"Oh, but ye've misunderstood," said Robbie. "If the woman has took a guidman then her bairns are his. He will claim them, and be glad o' them, too, and provide for them a'."

"But why would she want another—man," Elizabeth said, and she heard the confusion and irritation in her own voice. "If she had the choice to start with, and if she loves him?"

Robbie inclined his head. " 'Gin she loves him, why I suppose then she wadna want another," he agreed. "Unless he couldna do for her wha' she needed done."

Elizabeth drew in a sharp breath. "Are you saying that Nathaniel wasn't enough of a husband to Sarah?"

"No," said Robbie clearly. "I didna say that. Tae be clear, lass, and nae mistake, it wasna Nathaniel alone wha' was at fault. They call him Deseroken, but it was Sarah wha' was caught betwixt the red and the white."

Nathaniel was very clear to Elizabeth suddenly. She saw him, still bloodied from the lacrosse game, his face drawn and tired. *I married her because I wanted to be red and she married me because she wanted to be white.*

She did not realize she had spoken those words out loud but Robbie was nodding.

"That's the short and the long o' it," he agreed. He sighed, and gestured with his chin. "The needle is showing you north and south from east and west."

Elizabeth blinked hard.

"Come, lass," said Robbie gently. "Ye've got a fine man an a', and lan' tae live on, and your school, and a bonnie dauchter tae raise, wi' more bairns tae come."

She glanced up at him, her eyes glittering with tears.

"You're sure of that?" she asked.

He nodded, his color rising and falling like the tide. "I am," he said. "And so must you be."

Within three days, Elizabeth felt as if she had always lived on Robbie's mountain, and that she might always live here. The old soldier was good company, with interesting stories to tell and things to teach her. Some of the lessons she perhaps did not enjoy as much as others: there was a long discourse on the best way to remove ticks, an exercise which Elizabeth found distinctly distasteful, but which she finally mastered to his satisfaction. Bears came and went, bringing the results of his hunting with him so that the lessons Elizabeth had long anticipated were no longer avoidable. She would never have to butcher such large game herself, but she put her hand to the rest of it, learning to deal with the details of drying and smoking meat and curing the hide. It was hard work, smelly and dirty, but still it was engrossing in its own way. The worst thought was that she would not have Robbie's caves available to her when she had to put her hand to this kind of work at Lake in the Clouds.

"I will miss the hot springs," she said to him on the morning of the first-week anniversary of her wedding.

"Are ye' awa', then?" he asked, looking up from his corn-cake.

She shrugged. "I'm not sure what Nathaniel has in mind. But he did say we should stay away from Paradise for a month or so."

"Weel, as much as ye wish him here, I'll be sad tae see you awa', lass."

"Why do you live up here so much by yourself?" asked Elizabeth, a question she had been wanting to ask for days.

He smiled. "Have ye no seen the truth of me yet?" Although he did not blush as strongly or as often as he had the first days of their acquaintance, Robbie's color was still a thing to behold. Right now Elizabeth noticed how mottled his neck was with it, there where the soft folds of skin disappeared into the hunting shirt.

"I was a sodjer for so lang, and I had enough o' men, and their doin's," said Robbie. "Sometimes I'm bored wi' masel' and lonely for conversation or a bonnie face, and so I take masel' awa' and find it. But mostly I'm content tae live here tigither wi' the beasties. If only I could read, but ma eyes willna have it. If I gae amang people agin, it will be because o' that, because I canna live wi'oot voices, if I canna have books."

Elizabeth had been spending the evenings reading to Robbie, and she knew what pleasure he took in it. Often he would stop her to recite in a strong voice, with great emotion and certainty.

"Perhaps we could get you some spectacles."

He turned slowly to her, nodding. "Aye," he said. "I've had that thoucht, masel'. But tae tell ye true, lass, I dinna much like the idea o' Albany. Havena been tae such a place for ten year, or more. However," he said with a sigh, "wha' canna be changed maun be tholed. So, there's work tae be done. Nathaniel will be by sometime soon tae fetch ye hame, and he'll be verra surprised tae see what's been made o' his guidwife."

"What's been made of me?" asked Elizabeth, curious.

"Why, a woodswoman, o' course," said Robbie with a smile. "Or the beginnin's o' one, at the verra least."

XXVIII

On the next afternoon Elizabeth went down the mountain to the river by herself, taking a fishing line with her and Robbie's instructions to bring back some catfish or trout for supper. The path through the woods was familiar to her now, and she moved along quickly and quietly. Too quickly, she thought later, thinking over what had happened.

With many blushes, Robbie had warned her about the dangers of surprising bears as they foraged, especially bears with young. While black bears were generally timid creatures who would rather run than confront a human being, he said, she must be careful not to disturb them, and that especially when she was in her courses. The smell of blood would make them curious at the very least, and aggressive, in the worst case.

In fact, she had just finished her courses—an event which had taken her by surprise, for she had lost all sense of time, except for the eight days since she had last seen Nathaniel. The clutching and first trickle of it had reminded her of time passing, and then presented her with a new challenge; it was one that had preoccupied her for a good day until she had found ways to cope with the materials at hand. Once this had been addressed, Elizabeth had been a little relieved: she was not ready for the idea of a child quite yet, not until she felt more of a wife. But she had been sad, too, thinking that it would have pleased Nathaniel, and proved Richard quite decisively wrong.

It seemed a long time ago, that tousled conversation in their wedding bed, but Elizabeth wondered if satisfaction, or the relative lack of it, had something to do with the fact that she hadn't got with child. She thought of what had happened in that bed often, piece by piece, of the touch of him and his ferocious need, how different that had been from the first time under the falls. How complex the whole undertaking was, and how much there was to learn about it. She admitted to herself that she missed Nathaniel's touch very much, and thought that he wouldn't be disappointed to find in her a new curiosity about him. It was this thought that was in her head when she came to the river's edge and looked up to see the bear not twenty feet in front of her. She stood tall in the sun with her coat glistening wet, her attention fixed on Elizabeth and her soft black nose twitching. Elizabeth knew it was a female, because a very small cub played at her feet.

Her mind went very still and blank, and then in a flurry she turned and lunged at the nearest tree, scrambling up it as she last had as a twelve-year-old with a vengeful cousin in full pursuit. Even as she climbed, she knew the stupidity of this gesture, for bears climbed trees, and this one could come after her if it chose to. But she climbed anyway, the sound of her breath ragged in her own ears, drowning out what else there might be to hear. She climbed until she could climb no farther, and the young beech threatened to bend and deposit her back where she had begun.

It wasn't until then that Elizabeth stopped and looked down the trunk. The bear stood there, looking up at her quizzically, her nose still twitching. They were about as far apart as they had been on level ground, but now Elizabeth had nowhere to go. She closed her eyes and forced herself to breathe deeply until her vision cleared and she could hear something besides the rush of her own blood. When she looked down again, the bear was still there, but she had turned her attention back to foraging.

It took a good ten minutes for Elizabeth's heart to come back to a normal rhythm. In another ten, she noted that she had scraped her hands quite badly, and that they were sticky with sap as well as her own blood. More blood, she thought with dismay. The creature would never go away. And it seemed the case. She was playing with her cub now, batting at it and rolling it back and forth good-naturedly, while it squawked and mewled at her, and then finally rooted and found what it wanted.

Elizabeth sat in the fork of her branch with her knees tucked under her chin and watched them. The bark against her back was smooth, and there was a natural indentation here which provided a secure seat, if not an especially comfortable one. When it seemed sure that the mother had forgotten about her, she could watch them with interest. They were beautiful creatures, with deep, glossy coats and bright expressions. The cub was droll and absurd in its attempt to gain its mother's attention, squeaking and howling in an astounding range of sound. The mother ignored it placidly to disappear through a stand of pine. Elizabeth saw her emerge on the other side and walk into the river. She stood there staring down into the shallows, and then, faster than the eye could follow, with a wing of water flying, she flipped a fish onto the bank with a great swipe of her paw.

Elizabeth had a good view from her perch: a winding stretch of the river, and the canopy of trees, filled in now completely but still tender with spring color. On the eastern horizon storm clouds were gathering.

The bears seemed to like the little clearing at the river and were in no hurry. Elizabeth wondered if this was intentional on the mother's part, if she waited purposely for Elizabeth to come back down. Just when this idea was taking on unfortunate detail in her mind, the animal rolled to her feet and swayed off into the bush with her cub running behind her. Elizabeth let out a sigh of relief, and prepared herself for the climb down, which seemed much more imposing now than it had when she had feared for her life.

There was more rustling from the underbrush; she froze, and decided that she had better stay where she was until it was clear that the bear wouldn't be coming back. Impatiently, she settled back into her hiding place and looked down at the river.

And there was Nathaniel, just pulled to shore in a small canoe loaded with provisions.

.   .   .

She dropped out of the tree in front of him, but he didn't start. Nathaniel didn't seem surprised at all to have his wife appear so suddenly from overhead with her face scratched and her hands bleeding. Elizabeth stepped up to him, and put her arms around his waist, her face on his chest, and she felt herself tremble, and then, slowly, stop trembling.

"Good day to you, too, Boots," he said softly, his mouth against her hair. The pack he was carrying slipped to the ground and his hands moved to her back.

Elizabeth pulled away then, looked at him hard.

"You've been a long time," she said. "What happened?"

He shook his head, smoothing her hair. "Time enough for that later," he said, bending down to her. But she dropped her head, as much as she wanted him to kiss her.

"But what *happened*?" she repeated. "Did Richard prevail?"

Nathaniel lifted her chin with one crooked finger and ran his thumb along her lower lip. The shock of this, the pressure of his thumb, reverberated through her and her breath caught in her throat.

"Not the way he hoped," he said. "But it ain't over yet, I'm sorry to say."

"But—"

"We could talk about this," Nathaniel interrupted her, his thumb at the corner of her mouth, pressing lightly. "Now or later. There's other things on my mind, at the moment. But if you're set on talking—"

His breath was warm on her face. She blinked at him, paralyzed.

"Aye." He smiled. "I thought so." And he pulled her up to him and kissed her, a slow, thorough kiss, all Nathaniel, his heat and his mouth and the driving intensity of him. Elizabeth opened to him and kissed him back, her fists clenching on his back.

When he pulled away from her, he wasn't smiling anymore.

"I was worried."

"What were you worried about?" he asked in a low voice, kissing the corner of her mouth. "You knew I'd come back to you, now, didn't you?"

She swallowed hard, nodded.

"Good." He grinned. They stood looking at each other, his hands holding her by the upper arms.

"We should go up and see Robbie," she said. "He'll be happy to see you, too."

"Aye," said Nathaniel. "But not so happy as I am to have you in front of me again." He looked up the beech tree.

"You thinkin' of telling me what you're doing climbing trees, Boots?"

This made Elizabeth remember. "There was a bear," she said. "With some curiosity about me."

"That much I can believe," he said, his eyelids lowering. He pulled her to him again and this time she didn't protest. There was nothing in her but his nearness and wanting him. He supported her weight, for she could not, and he kissed her until she was gasping with it.

He was trembling himself when they broke the kiss.

"Let's get these things up to Robbie," he said hoarsely. "We can do it in one trip if you help."

"I was supposed to bring fish." She glanced over her shoulder to the river. It had begun to drizzle.

"Not this afternoon," said Nathaniel. "There's other business to attend to."

Robbie was about to go out to check his trap lines, but he stayed a while to greet Nathaniel.

"It's good tae see ye, man," he said for perhaps the fourth time, clapping Nathaniel on the shoulder. "I was wonderin' if we'd end oop goin' doonriver after ye. But we managed, didn't we, lassie, we managed and then some. She's a fine wee lassie, Nathaniel, and a unco braw one, make nae mistake."

"I haven't," Nathaniel agreed, and laughed out loud to see Elizabeth blush with this, her pleasure at having him back again and teasing her. The urge to put his hands on her was almost too strong to deny. As much as he liked Robbie and wanted to talk to the man, he wished him away to his trap lines.

"Before I gae," Robbie said, as if he had read Nathaniel's mind—a thought probably not too far from the truth, he realized, for not much escaped the old soldier—"There's sumthin' ye need tae ken. Jack Lingo's been up in this part o' the bush."

Nathaniel turned quickly, raised an eyebrow. "There's nothing new about that."

"Sae you've nae fear o' the man. Well, I dinna like the awd whoreson prowlin' aboot, no' when there's a bonnie young guidwife here and in ma care."

Nathaniel thought for a moment. He could walk out with Robbie, to talk. It wouldn't take long. He looked at his wife where she knelt by the fire, tending to the contents of the cook pot. She blushed and looked away, and his blood leapt at that, at what she was thinking, for it was clear on her face. Even Robbie could see it, for he blushed brighter than she did.

"Did you speak to him?" Nathaniel asked.

"No. But there's sign o' him, and a lot o' it. And Dutch Ton wi' him."

Elizabeth looked up at the mention of this name.

"I know him," she said. "Dutch Ton."

The men looked surprised, and so she told them the story of the letter from his sister. Robbie laughed until the tears leaked down his face.

"Wha' a daft storyteller Axel is," he said finally. Then he shook his head and stood. "Dinna fash yersel', Nathaniel. I doubt they've mair on their sma' minds than usual. And ye'll be safe come nicht, in the caves."

"Is there more to tell?" Nathaniel asked, glancing over at Elizabeth.

"Naethin' that canna bide a while." He was pulling at his roundabout, checking his bullet pouch, touching the hatchet and the knife thrust into his belt in a thoughtful way. Then he picked up his traps.

"I willna be back afore mornin'. I mun walk my far traps, an' there's nae avoidin' it. But it comes tae me," he added, dropping his gaze and clearing his throat. "I doubt ye'll miss me."

"But I will," Elizabeth said quite sincerely, coming forward. She smelled of wood smoke and her own musk, and Nathaniel reached out and put his hand on her, pulled her in to him. She came willingly, and stood there tucked into his side. They took leave of Robbie, and Nathaniel was pleased to see that she was genuinely fond of the man. It was the right thing to have done, sending her here. Given the goings-on in Albany. He grimaced a little at the thought of the conversation they must have. But not now, not this afternoon, not even tonight.

"Come," she said, when Robbie was gone. "There's food. You must be hungry."

She turned back toward the fire, but he caught her wrist, drew her up and back to him.

"I'm not hungry," he said. "At least, I don't want to eat right now."

There was a glitter in her eyes, not of tears, not this time. She had wept the last time he held her, but he was determined that she would not weep today.

"It's raining," she said softly. "Perhaps we should go inside."

"Where's Runs-from-Bears?" Nathaniel asked.

"He went out this morning, hunting. Why?" she asked, and then she looked away, knowing why. "It's full light," she said.

Nathaniel caught her waist between his hands. "We've had this discussion before," he said. "But the last time we were very rudely interrupted."

"So we were," she agreed. And then, with a frank gaze which pleased him inordinately: "I wondered if you'd remember."

He laughed then, and buried his face in her neck. "I couldn't forget if I wanted to," he said against her ear. "Will you have me in the daylight, Boots?"

She nodded; it was all she could do, he could see that. And this pleased him, too. Everything about her pleased him. Outwardly, she was hardly the same woman, wearing buckskins with her hair plaited. Her eyes were all the grayer for the browning of her skin in the sun. But when he touched her, when she spoke to him, she was still there, the woman he had married. Elizabeth, with her warmth and her smile, her intelligence and curiosity and bravery. Robbie had seen those things in her, although she could not see them in herself.

With a little shrug and a smile she had left him to take the cook pot off the fire and cover it, and then scatter the coals. She would not look at him, although he kept his gaze on her.

Elizabeth went to the cabin and glanced over her shoulder at him, and Nathaniel followed her into the dark, warm caverns inside the mountain.

They were completely and utterly alone. Outside there might be winter, or a hailstorm, or a world on fire, and they would not know, here in the middle chamber, the one where Elizabeth slept. Nathaniel piled the packets and sacks from the canoe in the space already crowded with the odds and ends of Robbie's life. The torch in the corridor smoked a bit, but here the air was clear and warm and flickering with the light of beeswax, for Robbie had left a brace of candles, clearly his best and most precious supply. Elizabeth had hesitated about lighting them, but Nathaniel had not, pointing out what she knew to be true: that Robbie had wanted them to use the candles; this was his wedding gift to them. They burned bright and they smelled sweet, and Elizabeth was glad of them, here in the heart of the mountain.

"What are you thinking?" Nathaniel asked, and she realized he had been watching her face. He was crouched down, rummaging through the plunder from the canoe.

She drew in a breath. "That we are more alone here than we were . . . under the waterfalls." She looked down the corridor, and thought of something she could offer him. "Would you like to bathe?"

"Later," he said, grinning up at her. "I brought you something."

"I don't have anything for you."

"Ah," he said. "But you do." And he hooked her leg out from under her so that she sat down hard next to him, her breath bursting from her with a surprised whoosh.

"Oooh." She laughed, rubbing her backside. "You might simply have asked, Nathaniel."

He put a small packet in her lap. She opened it carefully, feeling his eyes on her. Inside the paper there was a handkerchief, a beautiful piece of the finest linen embroidered white on white, edged all around with exquisite lace. Elizabeth looked up at him, surprised.

"You never got to use the wedding hankie you bought from Anna," he said.

"Did you know about that episode with Anna?"

"Curiosity told me."

"Curiosity." She smiled. "We owe her a great deal."

"Aye," Nathaniel agreed. "We do. But she's pleased with herself and with you. She said to tell you that you did good."

It was Elizabeth's turn to laugh. "I doubt that my father agrees with her. Her part in our getting away isn't known?"

"Seems she managed that pretty well. You don't need to worry about Curiosity," Nathaniel noted. "And your father looks none the worse for wear, although I didn't talk to him."

Elizabeth didn't want to talk about her father just now. "How are things at Lake in the Clouds?"

He ran a knuckle down her arm. "You worried about Hannah?"

"You are reading my mind again. I'm not so sure that is a desirable trait in a husband," she teased. "But yes, I have been wondering how she feels about all of this."

He smiled. "She's taking full credit for the whole plan. You don't need to worry about her, Boots. You'll be a good mother to her."

Elizabeth looked down at her hand in his. She saw how rough her skin had become in such a short time. It was sunbrowned, the beginnings of calluses on the pads of her thumbs. But these were stronger hands, and she was not ashamed of them.

Nathaniel had seen her hands, too, and his face was suddenly drawn.

"You weren't born to this life," he said, all of his playfulness and teasing gone.

"Then I'm very fortunate, aren't I?" she said softly. "To have come to it the way I did."

She lifted the handkerchief to touch it to his cheek and, as she did, two pieces of jewelry fell out: a hair clasp of silver, and a pendant, a long chain slithering after it.

"Oh," she breathed, picking up the chain so that the single pearl enclosed in a clutch of silver petals and curling leaves twirled to catch the candlelight.

"It was my mother's," said Nathaniel. "And the wedding ring, too. She left them to me to keep for Hannah, but I asked her and she thinks you should have them for now."

Elizabeth picked up the hair clasp, a wide lozenge of silver etched with a pattern of winding flowers. "Was this your mother's, too?"

"No, I bought that in Albany. I kept thinking about your hair, the color of it spread out, how it put the fisher pelts to shame . . ." He paused. "And so I bought it for you. You'll be thinking me extravagant."

"I'm thinking that you are a love," Elizabeth said, blinking hard. "Shall I put it in my hair now?"

"No," he said firmly. "I don't want your hair up right now. But will you wear this?" He touched the silver chain.

Elizabeth was already turning, gathering her plait away to expose her neck. The pearl touched the hollow of her throat and slid down between her breasts while Nathaniel's fingers worked at the nape of her neck, his breath on her hair. Elizabeth felt her skin rising, every nerve awakening. His hands moved to her shoulders, and then there was his mouth, warm and open below her ear. She heard herself gasping, a strange, inarticulate sound.

"Do you like it?"

She flexed and turned in his arms, rising on her knees to come closer to him, and hugged him with all her strength. For once, she had no words and so she just held him.

"I'll take that as a yes." He grinned.

"Yes," Elizabeth said, taking his face between her hands to kiss him briefly, rubbing her cheek against his, enjoying its roughness. "Yes, I like it. Yes. Thank you."

His hands were on her waist, where they moved up and down, slowly.

"You're welcome," he said, pulling her even closer, leaning in and then away, hesitating still.

Elizabeth wondered at him, that he did not start what they both wanted to start. His hands drew slow circles under her arms, the thumbs stretching out to trace the swell of her breasts, but he was content to watch her face, it seemed. She was not content, not at all. Now that he was here with her after so long.

"Is there anything wrong?"

"Not a thing in the world," he said huskily. But still he didn't kiss her; there was just the sliding pressure of his hands, and the sweep of his thumbs.

She met his eye and held it.

"There's no hurry, Boots," he said easily, drawing her forward to kiss her, finally, just a brushing and then he was gone. "There's no one in the world to interrupt us, and nowhere to go." With his hand covering the small of her back, he brought her up against him and pressed his mouth to her temple, traced a path with his lips to her ear. The other hand slid up under her shirt to cup a breast at that moment that he found her mouth and kissed her in earnest.

"Unless you'd like to talk, just now," he said a good time later.

"You make me shiver so," she murmured.

Nathaniel laughed and buried his face in her neck. "Shivering is just the start of it."

"Of what?" she asked.

"Of this," he said, his hands moving again.

"This . . ." Elizabeth echoed. "What do you call this?"

He did not laugh this time, but she saw something else in his face, a kind of pleasure and power and satisfaction. Her lack of experience and her curiosity aroused him. She was aware of this, slowly. She could taste it in his kiss, feel it in the way his mouth moved on hers.

"I've read about it," she said. "But I'd like to know what *you* call this."

He stilled suddenly, surprised. "What have you read about?"

"This—" she said with an edge of impatience. "What goes on between men and women. My uncle's library is very extensive, and I have read all of it. In the *Summa Theologica* Thomas Aquinas most usually uses the term *carnal intercourse,* and then there's *coition,* or *vera copula,* but it is hard for me to think of—us—in those terms. I remember a medical text very clearly which used the term *venery.* I think to the effect 'The Passions of the Mind have great Influence, as also excessive Venery.' Although more commonly I think that word is used to refer to love of the hunt." Seeing the disbelieving look on Nathaniel's face, she stopped.

"Go on," he said.

"Well," she said slowly. "There were other terms. *Sexual congress* and *consummation,* and of course the biblical *fornication,* but as we are married—" Her voice trailed away.

"Vera copula?" Nathaniel echoed. Elizabeth felt herself begin to flush, not with embarrassment this time, but with irritation.

"It's a simple question, Nathaniel," she said. "I just would like to know what you call this act, as almost all of the terms I have read do not seem appropriate."

He was smiling at her, and she didn't like it. She began to pull away, but he held her tight.

"Let me go."

"Oh, no."

"Why are you laughing at me?" she demanded, her throat tight with longing and mortification.

"I'm not laughing at you," he said, dipping his head to kiss her, but she turned away and he caught the crest of her cheek instead.

"You are. It's quite clear that you're laughing at me, and I won't have it. I've been worried about you for so long and waiting and . . . wondering. And you gave me this necklace of your mother's and now you are laughing at me." She knew she made no sense, but the choices available to her at this moment were anger or tears, and she would not weep. She would not.

Nathaniel's face had cleared of all laughter, but he didn't try to kiss her again.

"I'm sorry," he said. "But I just can't imagine you sitting in your uncle's library making a study of this topic in his medical texts."

"Why not?" she asked. "I read all his books."

He shrugged. "Why not. Well, I suppose because you were so set on yourself as a spinster. I'm surprised you could bring yourself to read about something that didn't concern you."

"I hope to never have plague or gout, either, but I read about those things," she said, knowing that she sounded peevish. She was not being completely honest with him, and it irritated her to be made to explain herself when all she wanted, really, was a simple answer. And the demonstration he had promised her so many days ago on the nature of satisfaction. She glared at him, but he looked back at her without flinching.

"And I was curious," she added, reluctantly.

Nathaniel nodded. "Aye, I can believe that. But most young ladies don't have the opportunity or the nerve to take up a study of the subject, do they?"

This insight took Elizabeth by surprise, and she nodded.

"Wait a minute," Nathaniel said. He stood, unfolding his long legs and pulling her up with him. Then he settled himself on the cot, and her next to him, tucked into his side with his arm around her shoulder. Elizabeth came to him willingly, although she was a bit surprised at this change in direction and purpose.

"So tell me about the other words."

Elizabeth sat away to look at him, but his face was open and his expression guileless, and he waited for her response.

"What do you mean?"

"You said almost all the terms that didn't suit. Which ones did?"

She tried to turn away, but he kept her where she was.

"No," he said. "We've started this discussion and we'll finish it, by God, otherwise you'll never be satisfied. Tell me what you read, Boots." He still was not grinning, and Elizabeth settled in next to him, with some reluctance.

"Two phrases come to mind," she said slowly. "The first is from *Timon:* 'Lovelie Venus sported and with Mars consorted.'" And because Nathaniel was quiet, she carried on without daring to meet his eye. "The other was from a collection of letters. I can't remember anymore who the author was, but the sentence remains with me. 'They were made one flesh by bodily fellowship.'"

"Is that all?"

"Do you want to hear more?" she asked, surprised.

"If you want to tell me."

She shook him a little, in frustration. "This all started because I wanted you to tell me about *your* words, and now you've made me give you a history of my reading habits and I must say, Nathaniel, you have quite ruined my mood."

"Oh, have I?" His hand had moved up her arm to her neck, where his fingers tangled lazily in the loose hair curling there. Her skin rose at this gentle plucking, and she gave up her frown with a small sigh.

"Maybe not altogether, then."

"Perhaps not," she conceded, as his fingers continued on their quest.

"Now, about those words you're so curious about. If you ain't satisfied with the fancy terms you know, Boots, then I suppose we must find others that will suit."

She stilled then. His hands were moving over her, but it was his voice that had her whole attention. He kissed her cheek, the corner of her mouth, her ear. "I'm going to undress you now. And then I'm going to make love to you—that's the name we'll put to it for the time being—and as we go along, I'll tell you what you want to know." He blew lightly on the moisture he had left on the soft flesh under her ear and she shuddered with that. "I'll tell you what it is we're doing, in my own words. Will that serve?"

She nodded, because she could not speak.

"And I'll ask you questions now and then to see if you've been paying attention."

Elizabeth's mind was fuzzy with the heat of his mouth at her ear and the pressure of a palm against her breast. It seemed that suddenly there was not enough air to breathe. He took his time kissing her, a long, soft kiss that made every nerve in her flare and then pulse. In response to his gentle prodding, she raised her arms over her head and Nathaniel pulled the shirt up and away, his hands so warm on her naked arms, running down her sides to pull her shift out and up. Then it was gone too and her skin rose in gooseflesh; he was looking at her, his eyelids heavy and his wanting so clear on his face.

"And if you get confused, well, then we'll start again."

She looked down at herself, her plait lying over one shoulder, a dark cable against her white skin. Her breasts, and between them the flower of silver and pearl. Nathaniel leaned back and pulled her down against him so that it was caught between them, her breasts pressed flat against his chest. He kissed her mouth while his hands moved lower to cup her hips. There was a spreading sensation in her that ran like a warm tide.

As she sank further and further into the universe that Nathaniel created with his hands and mouth and body, Elizabeth's perception of their physical surroundings faded, the smells of mineral springs and beeswax giving way to Nathaniel. On some level she had an awareness of her pores opening and her own scent rising to meet him. He was murmuring to her, talking to her between kisses and tangled clothing, laughing softly against her mouth, puffy with his kisses.

As they lay on their sides face to face, Nathaniel slid a knee up her thigh until it lodged there at the juncture of her. He was watching her face while he did this, his eyes flickering with satisfaction at her gasp. The warm, hard surface of his knee rocked against her, and her flesh answered with an increasing dampening and a sparking rhythm. In the back of Elizabeth's mind a connection was made, between the pleasure of this particular kind of touch and what might be possible, what he might have meant about satisfaction. Because she could not find the words to ask this question, she hooked her knee over his hip to draw him closer, but he held back.

"Not yet," he whispered against her mouth. "Patience."

Patience took on a new meaning, then, in the next long minutes. She had often used the word with her own students as they strove toward some new skill, and she vowed to herself never to use it again.

"Nathaniel!" she said finally, her voice breaking, and he looked up from her breast.

"There's no special word for this that I'm aware of," he said, grinning at her. In response she batted at his head, hit him with the heel of her hand above the ear. He caught her hand and then the other one, coming up to take her chin in his mouth, suckling softly. She moaned then, and he stopped it with a kiss, his length against hers and his weight concentrated where their hips strained together.

"Yes, there is," she gasped finally, her fingers flexing and stretching without effect. "It's called teasing. And if you tell me to be patient—"

"But if you're patient, darlin', you'll hear those words you wanted. If you still do want them. Aye, I see that you do. Well, then, listen, listen to me." With his mouth at her ear he flexed and suddenly he was poised there at the quick of her. She gasped, her eyes wide and startled, at the silky, hard touch. "Do you know how fine you feel to me?" he murmured, his eyes flickering with this, with his pleasure.

But he drew away, his mouth trailing down between her breasts. She cried out in disappointment and frustration and then stilled, her whole being startled and frozen, as Nathaniel finally settled between her legs and set about the business of teaching her, with great deliberation, about one kind of satisfaction.

"Nathaniel?" she gasped, her fingers in his hair, her mind reeling in panic and shock and confusion. This could not be; there must be a mistake. But the rough caress of his cheek against her inner thigh was real and so were the hands that cupped her, spread-fingered. He murmured to her, soft words, as soft as the first touch of his lips and tongue, and suddenly all the questions and doubts and all the words in the world disappeared in a blaze of pleasure and Elizabeth let them go without any regret.

And when she had finally learned about satisfaction of one kind, when she lay subdued and sated, her flesh still pulsing and leaping, then he came to her and taught her about another. Arched over her, belly to belly and mouth to mouth, Nathaniel taught Elizabeth what she had wanted to know, and he took his lessons in turn.

When she slept, he covered her with a blanket and stood looking down at her. Carefully, gently, he smoothed damp curls away from her face, resisting the urge to kiss her temple because she needed her sleep, and because he wanted a few minutes to himself to think. But then, because he could not do otherwise, he sat carefully on the edge of the cot to watch her. Supporting his weight on one arm, he leaned in and lowered his face to hers, close enough to feel the heat of her on his skin. In the soft candlelight he traced the sweep of her eyebrow and the curve of lashes on her cheek.

Nathaniel wondered that she could be both women, this peaceful one and the one who had wound herself around him with such purpose, her mouth open in a circle of surprise and wonder. The close memory of her heat, her weight in his hands, her unapologetic desire, stirred him almost to the point of waking her. But he mastered himself by degrees and leaned slowly away to rise, feeling the cool air on his damp flesh. He blew out all the candles but two. One he left on its shelf on the wall, the other he took with him to the spring where he lit a torch.

With a soft grunt of appreciation he walked into the pool and submerged himself, holding his breath as long as he could in the heavy hot water, and coming up with an explosion of breath and spray, shaking his head. He floated, spread-bodied, feeling his muscles expand and loosen, his hair sweeping around him. With his eyes open or closed he could see only Elizabeth. This evening they would sit together and eat and talk; he had missed talking to her. Tonight he would sleep with her alongside him. In the night she would turn to him and he would have her again, because he wanted her already with a will that surprised even himself. He rolled in the hot water and submerged himself again and again, letting the images of her wash over him with the water.

In the morning they would emerge into the daylight and confront what waited for them. In the morning there would be no choice but to face it all, because by the day after, they would be on the run again.

XXIX

"You cannot be serious," Elizabeth said, wiping a strand of hair away from her forehead with the back of her hand.

Nathaniel looked up over the edge of his tin cup, wondering exactly how angry she could get.

"I cannot, I will not believe this," she said, stirring the porridge with such force that it jumped out of the iron cauldron to hiss and bubble on the rocks below it.

"If I understand this correctly, you are telling me that Kitty Witherspoon has forsworn herself against me in a public court of law, and along with her Martha Southern and Liam Kirby." She glanced up at him, her mouth set hard. "Liam Kirby! The ungrateful—" She stopped, but reluctantly.

Nathaniel was silent. There was nothing he could say to make this news better; in fact, there were things still to tell her that she would not like at all.

Robbie sat to the far side of the fire, cleaning his traps and getting ready to deal with the beaver he had brought in, but his attention was primarily on Elizabeth. He caught Nathaniel's eye now and shrugged sympathetically.

"What could motivate Kitty Witherspoon to do such a thing?" she muttered.

"Marriage," said Nathaniel.

"Marriage?" Elizabeth cocked one brow, her mouth pursed. "Richard has offered to marry her?"

Nathaniel nodded. "And none too soon."

She blinked, tugging at her plait and then flinging it back over her shoulder. "Kitty is with child?"

"Curiosity says she is."

With hands that were less than steady, Elizabeth turned to the kettle and began to scoop out bowls of porridge. One of these she thrust into Nathaniel's hands. The other she passed, absentmindedly, to Robbie.

"By whom?"

"Your brother, no doubt," he said. " 'Course, that ain't common knowledge. Although Curiosity suspects, it seemed to me."

She sat down heavily next to him, and stared into her bowl.

"I know that Kitty would be very glad to get Richard, but why would he want her, under those circumstances?"

Nathaniel waited, knowing that she did not really want an answer from him; she had a habit of thinking out loud when she was trying to work through something difficult, and he was learning to let her get on with it and not interrupt.

"I expect it was the price she set on her testimony," Elizabeth muttered. "The man is really beyond all reason and propriety." She shook her head, and began to eat. After two spoonfuls, she let her bowl rest in her lap, and turned to Nathaniel.

"What a terrible muddle this is," she said. "What can I do, except deny them? I never told any of them that I was engaged to Richard, but they are three and I am only one. If I thought there was any chance of speaking sense to them—" She broke off.

"Come, lass, ye mun eat," said Robbie. "Naethin' ever looks sae bad wi' a belly fu' o' parritch."

"I hope you're right," Elizabeth said softly. Robbie had carved her a spoon of her own and she worried the end between her teeth, looking at Nathaniel in a distracted way.

"Must I go back and face these charges, and Kitty Witherspoon? Or Kitty Todd, perhaps by then."

Nathaniel tipped his bowl to his mouth while he considered the best way to reply. "Eventually," he said. "But you won't go alone, Elizabeth."

She noted his rare use of her name. He was looking at her with a calm affection; there was nothing of humor or teasing or lust in him at this moment, just the wish to reassure her. This was a comfort, because since the encounter of the previous evening, Elizabeth often found herself lost in thought and suddenly blushing furiously for no clear reason. He might have teased her, but he seemed to understand how much his lessons in satisfaction had rocked her sense and understanding of herself. It would require a great deal of thought, the whole business of being together with him. This evening they would talk it through. If she could find the words, if they could keep the talking separate for a while, from the rest of it. In the meantime there was news of home.

Nathaniel tugged on her plait to get her attention. "We have to give my father some time to see what he can manage."

"Hawkeye?" she asked, confused. "Manage what?"

"Hawkeye is a skilfu' negotiator," Robbie offered. "Gi'e him time tae talk sense tae nonsensical folk, and see if aught comes o' it."

"He won't persuade Kitty Witherspoon if Richard Todd is willing to marry her on the strength of her testimony," Elizabeth pointed out. "She'd testify against God and King—or President, in this case—for that particular reward."

"You sound as though you're regretting the loss of the man." Nathaniel grinned at her.

"Not in this world, or the next." She laughed, reluctantly. But she recognized that this idea of Richard marrying Kitty irked her, although she couldn't say why, and didn't want to think about it overmuch. Not with the way Nathaniel was looking at her.

"What power would Hawkeye have with Martha Southern or Liam Kirby?" she asked. "Or better said, Moses Southern and Billy Kirby, for I doubt Martha and Liam volunteered their testimony without considerable encouragement."

Robbie was waving a great beaver tail as if it were an outlandish new fashion in fans. Elizabeth could hear that he had a story to tell by the way he cleared his throat.

"Hawkeye once persuaded a rantin' Huron war party that it wasna a guid notion to cook his Cora for their dinner, and tha' wi'oot a weapon on him," said Robbie. "And they walked awa', the twa o' them, wi' their scalps. He's a sicht tae see and hear when he's in a persuasive frame o' mind, is Hawkeye. I dinna believe that Moses can stan' fast. And young Billy—" He laughed softly. "He hasna a chance."

Nathaniel was watching Elizabeth closely, wondering how much information he could give her at one time. She had her chin in the air, her eyes flashing with anger and frustration. In spite of the bad news that would keep them on the run, in spite of the trouble that might still take Hidden Wolf from them, Nathaniel could not look at her without a very real satisfaction and joy.

"What are you thinking?" she demanded.

"Well," he said slowly. "I'm thinking that you're my wife, scowl on your face and all. No matter what comes, nothing and nobody can change that fact, Boots. And I'm glad of it."

"Oh," she said, her anger draining away to be replaced by a softer smile.

Robbie cleared his throat. "It's a fine day on the water and I for one wad be glad o' fish for my supper. Ye realize, Nathaniel, that this lassie o' yours canna swim? Little Lost is the richt place to larn the art o' it, shallow as it is wi' a guid sandy bottom."

"So it is," Nathaniel agreed.

"You'll need help with the beaver," Elizabeth pointed out to Robbie.

"Aye, weel, I hae made my livin' wi' these beasties, an' they wi' me, for muny a lang year, aye? So I'll make do. And the truth o' it is, lass, that trout wadna taste sae bad after the venison." He was skinning a beaver as he spoke, and he squinted up from this work to grin at her.

Nathaniel was glad of an excuse to have Elizabeth to himself again. There was more to talk to her about, and it would be easier if they were alone. And Robbie was right: she needed to know how to swim. When he pointed this out to her, she listened to his logic, but he could see that the idea was causing her some uneasiness. The sight of her flushing was enough to make Nathaniel's blood leap with wanting her, although it had been just a few hours since he had left her last.

"I have nothing to wear," she said in a low voice and out of Robbie's hearing. And seeing his grin, she pushed him, hard. "Will you behave?"

He caught her up against him. "Do you want me to behave?"

"In company, at least," she said firmly. With a little shake of her head, she pulled away from him and turned to Robbie, who was looking into the innards of a beaver as if something of immense interest were waiting there, his color the shade of poppies in bloom.

"If you can manage," she said, "we'll go down and see about those trout."

"Ach aye, lass, gae on wi' ye." He did not look up from his work. "I can manage if you can."

The lake was smooth and clear and shone like a sheet of beaten silver in the sunlight. The forest came down to its shores for almost three quarters of its irregular shape, giving way reluctantly to broad banks of deep green moss. A series of coves were hidden from view; Elizabeth had been here with Robbie, and he had pointed them out at good distance, warning her to keep away.

"The loons are nestin'," he had told her in hushed tones.

Elizabeth had thought it unusual that Robbie would be so concerned about the privacy of these birds, but in this as in other things she had taken his direction, and now when she came with Nathaniel to the edge of the lake they were rewarded. A pair of loons paddled past with their eyes blazing like rubies, each with a fuzzy chick nestled comfortably on a checkered black-and-white back.

"So simple in their coloring and still anything but plain," Elizabeth said quietly. "Geometric detailing to the point of gaudiness."

Nathaniel lifted his head and called across the water, "Whooo whooo whooo," until one of the pair raised its daggerlike beak and gave back the call. They watched the birds disappear around the corner.

"Come, Boots, there's a warmish patch over there that will suit."

Elizabeth hung back a little, for she was worried, in spite of the emptiness of this corner of the world and their isolation, about the public nature of swimming. Nathaniel glanced back at her and grinned.

"You can leave your shift on," he called, once again reading her mind with an accuracy which she was starting to find somewhat irritating.

"Am I so predictable?" she asked when she caught up to him. At the water's edge a series of flattish boulders cooked in the sun, extending out in a jumble into the shallows where small fish darted. A bloodred lizard with a speckled back flexed and disappeared into the cracks. Nearby, a blue heron paced long-legged on the shore, ignoring them completely.

Nathaniel had set his rifle to one side and stripped down to his breechclout in a few movements. "About some things," he conceded.

She dared not look at him as he stood there in the warm sun, his skin glowing and his hair moving in the wind, for on her face would be evidence of what the sight of him did to her.

"I like your hair plaited," he said, surprising her. When she looked up, one brow raised, he continued. "You tug at it when you're thinking."

"Do I?" she asked, amazed to find that he was right, she had her plait in one hand and had been pulling at it. With one hand she undid the silver clasp that she now wore to secure it at the top; this she wrapped in her handkerchief for safekeeping, hesitating for a moment while she traced the flowers etched into the metal.

"What are you thinking about?" he asked.

She turned away from him to undress. Peeled the moccasins off her feet, untied her breeches to step out of them and then pulled the long overdress up and over her head. There was a breeze and it felt good on her bare arms and legs, pressing her shift to her back. She curled her toes against the warmth of the rock under her feet, and then she faced him, trying to smile but unable to.

"All morning," she said. "All morning I've been feeling you —the evidence of you—on my thighs, and I have not been able to think of much else. What that means—what it might mean." She could not bear to look at him anymore, and she dropped her gaze. "I may be with child, already." He was standing very close to her, but he didn't touch her.

"Well, it wouldn't be for lack of trying," he said calmly. He paused. "Is it that you don't like the idea of a child, or you don't believe I can give you one?"

Her head jerked up at this, and she found a look she did not recognize on his face, a vulnerability that he had never shown her before.

"I like the idea very much," she said, answering only one of his questions. She watched him struggle with what he was feeling, the way the muscles in his throat worked as he swallowed.

"It would interfere with your teaching," he said finally, and he raised one finger to push a strand of hair away from her face.

"But only for a while," she said. "There is no reason, given the way we shall live, that I should have to give up teaching completely." This proposal which she put to him with such thoughtfulness was one which had woken her in the night; she had watched him sleep and worked through how best to present it. She knew that the fine perspiration on her brow and the tremble in her hands did not escape him. But she held his gaze until he nodded, slowly.

"If that's what you want."

Elizabeth sensed his hesitation, and her spirits fell. He did not want her to teach once she had children to look after; aunt Merriweather had been right.

"You would prefer not to share me," she said, and then added hastily: "With other people's children."

"Elizabeth," Nathaniel said, crouching and pulling her down to sit next to him. "I won't ask you to give up your school, no matter what comes, and I won't resent the time you put into it. There's womenfolk enough to look after affairs at Lake in the Clouds, including children that come our way. But it's no good, pretending that there's nothing else on your mind. We have to talk this through or it will fester. Ask me what you want to know."

Elizabeth looked out over the lake. A loon was diving, disappearing in a smooth arc to drop into the belly of the lake and come up and repeat the process over and over again.

"I don't know where to start."

"Hannah is my child," Nathaniel said after a long pause.

"I know that," Elizabeth said softly. "But Richard—"

"He knows nothing of me," Nathaniel said, and for the first time there was an edge of anger in his voice. "Except what he imagines and wants to be true."

"And what Sarah told him," Elizabeth added and she regretted it, for he stiffened beside her.

"And what Sarah told him," he acknowledged. "But what she told him and what he heard ain't necessarily the same things. You know that from personal experience with the man."

Elizabeth glanced at him. This had not occurred to her, but the truth of it was obvious.

"Did he make up the whole thing?" she said, remembering even as she did Curiosity's troubled face when she spoke of Sarah and Richard.

"No," said Nathaniel, the muscle in his cheek working. "I can't claim that, either. He tried to take Sarah from me, and he came close to getting her."

"Why? Why would she turn to Richard?" This question hung in the air for a very long time, until Elizabeth turned to Nathaniel and saw the stony look on his face, the unresolved anger and the hurt.

"I don't know," he said. "She didn't explain herself to me." It was the first thing he had ever said to her which was untruthful, and they both were aware of this.

She couldn't keep the disappointment from her face.

"Give me some time," Nathaniel said.

You've had time, she wanted to say. But she watched him striding out into the depths and then swimming strongly, his legs and arms cutting the water like blades.

She forced herself to look, not at him, but at the lake. At this setting, more beautiful and peaceful than anything she had ever experienced. She watched the slow glide of a turtle shell through a stand of bulrushes, hearing the gentle gurgle and hiss of the moving waters. Across the lake the heron was still stalking, joined now by an osprey which circled and then dove, and dove again. The woods were filled with birds, and the sounds of their calls. She squinted into the shadows and saw a pair of eyes reflecting back at her; a doe heavy with fawn, wondering whether it was safe to come to the lake to drink.

Nathaniel swam for what seemed like a long time and then he came back to her, streaming water. The sun reflected off him in a million colors.

"I'm sorry," she said stiffly when he came to kneel in front of her. "It's none of my business."

"It is," he said. "It is your business."

"I wouldn't let you tell me."

"I should have made you listen."

She lifted her chin; looked him straight in the eye. Elizabeth fought hard with the impulse to smooth things over, to make him feel better. "Yes," she said finally, with a nod. "You should have. Although it would not have made any difference to me, in the end."

Rivulets of water ran down his body and over the rock, fading in the sun almost as they watched. Elizabeth saw the pulse in Nathaniel's throat. His eyes were narrowed in the glare of the sun, his face impassive.

"I haven't talked to anybody about this since my mother. She said I should put it behind me for Hannah's sake."

She started to ask another question, but he held up a palm to stop her. "Listen," he said. "Listen and I'll tell you. Although I doubt you'll be glad of it."

He settled in front of her, straight-backed and cross-legged with his breechclout covering him, the long muscles in his thighs tensed. His hair hung damp over his heavily muscled shoulders. He was completely at ease in his near nakedness, and hers; Elizabeth blinked hard and looked away, concentrated on the mountains layered in shades of green and blue as far as she could see. When she had gathered her thoughts, she looked back at him. This was Nathaniel in front of her, her husband. With a story to tell her that she needed to hear, in spite of what it did to him, the pain it caused him. She fixed her eyes on his and held his gaze.

"Tell me," she said.

Nathaniel wondered what she thought she was going to hear. He was afraid to tell her the whole story; he also knew very well that she would not be satisfied with less than all of it. But she had expectations of him and he feared—he knew—that he was bound to disappoint her in some of them.

"First you should know about me and Richard, before Sarah. How things got started. You know the story of how he came back to Paradise?"

"From Curiosity," Elizabeth confirmed.

"One person who you can count on to tell it to you true," he noted, satisfied with her source. "Well, you know then that Richard's uncle came to claim him, took him off to Albany. But he was never gone for long, he was always coming back to Paradise for a week or a month at a time. He said it was to visit the Witherspoons, but there was more to it than that. It was my mother that interested him."

"Richard came to see your mother?" Elizabeth repeated. She was trying not to ask questions; she wanted to leave the storytelling to him. But it was hard for her, he could see that.

"He couldn't stay away from her," Nathaniel said. "He loved her in the same way that he came to hate me, with everything that was in him. He used to come up to Lake in the Clouds to talk to her whenever he could manage, but mostly when I was out walking the trap lines or hunting with my father. He would sit and talk to her, or help her with whatever work she had her hand to. Candles or hoeing or wash, whatever. At this time he was less than fourteen, so you have to think of that, how strange that was. She would tell us when we came home that Richard had been to call, sometimes with Kitty. She said he was a poor soul."

Nathaniel paused, struck suddenly with loneliness for his mother. Talking about her had brought her face to him suddenly, and very clearly. Elizabeth touched his hand and he took it gratefully.

"But to me he was barely civil. Less than. You could call it simple jealousy—I had my folks and he had nobody. I had Lake in the Clouds and he had no chance of ever getting close to it." He glanced at her, saw the deep furrow of concentration between her eyes. "You haven't seen the graves yet. It's mostly our folks, but Todd's mother is buried there, too. My father found her and brought her back to Lake in the Clouds to bury, what was left of her. I remember seeing Todd out there once in the middle of the night one summer by full moon."

"Did your mother fear him?"

Nathaniel had to laugh at that idea. "My mother didn't fear anybody or anything, except illness. Richard Todd had her sympathy and her pity, but he didn't scare her. Though sometimes it seems to me that he should have.

"So things between me and Richard weren't exactly friendly but there wasn't any trouble, at least not then. When I was nineteen I left home to go to Barktown, and I was gone more than two years. I lost track of Richard until just before I came back, in the middle of the war. Did you ever ask Richard about his training?"

"His medical training? No," Elizabeth said. "He mentioned something about the physicians he studied with—"

"Adams and Littlefield. Littlefield was Clinton's personal physician on campaign."

"Sir Henry Clinton? The general?" Elizabeth looked confused.

Nathaniel shook his head. "It's a common enough name, I guess. There was a General James Clinton, too, but on the Continental side. Littlefield was his physician, and Richard was training under Littlefield, this was in '79."

"Richard saw battle?"

"Richard saw slaughter," Nathaniel corrected her. "Sullivan came up from the south and Clinton moved west along the Mohawk and then down the Susquehanna to meet him. They weren't after Tories, though. They were hoping to set an end to the whole Iroquois nation."

Elizabeth put out a hand to stop him. She cleared her throat gently. "I don't understand. You fought under your father-in-law for the Continentals, did you not? And those Kahnyen'kehàka you fought with, are they not Iroquois?"

"I forget sometimes what you can't know about, " he conceded. "You realize the Hode'noshaunee is a league of six nations? Well, within the league there wasn't always agreement on who to back in the war, not even within the tribes. Some fought with the Tories and some fought against them. By '79 all Washington wanted was every Iroquois out of the northwest, and fast. So Sullivan and Clinton marched that summer. Burned more than forty towns before they finished, and burned the crops in the fields and the orchards and anything that would take to a torch. Those who didn't die fled north to Canada, or if they didn't they starved in the winter after."

Nathaniel was talking fast, as if he could spit this information out like a mouthful of bitter medicine. He saw her hands trembling, and the way she clutched them together in her lap. It was not comfort he needed right now, but her attention; she seemed to realize that, and he was grateful.

"Clinton burned Barktown," she concluded.

"It was burned, but not by Clinton hisself. There was a big militia party from Johnstown, and they decided to get a jump on things. Thought they'd show up to report for duty with some good marks to their credit."

"Where were you?" she asked, her voice hoarse and low.

"Sky-Wound-Round sent me to Albany, to talk to Schuyler about what could be done to make peace between the Iroquois and the army." Although his face was blank, his eyes flashed with a bright anger. "Sky-Wound-Round was still hopeful in those days that the Kahnyen'kehàka could have a home here."

"But he does have a home here, I met him at Barktown."

"He lives in exile in his own homelands," Nathaniel corrected her. He watched her think this through, and then accept it, reluctantly.

"You didn't know what was happening with the campaign while you were talking to Schuyler?"

"No, and he didn't tell me." Nathaniel stopped. He thought hard about what he could say to her. If he should leave her with the impressions of Schuyler that she had taken away from Saratoga on her wedding day, or if he should tell her the whole truth. Not for the first time that day, Nathaniel thought of

Hannah, of what it would be like for her as a young woman, half Kahnyen'kehàka. Hannah would need Elizabeth's help, which Elizabeth would not be able to give unless she understood the realities of what it meant to be living in a white man's country when your skin was more than white.

"Schuyler let me talk to him as if there were some room for peace. And the whole time we talked about which of the chiefs could be brought over and which tribes might be able to survive on this side of the border, Clinton was getting his men on the road with the taste for red flesh in their mouths. Now, Schuyler claims he told Clinton to leave Barktown alone, given the fact that Sky-Wound-Round had fought for him at Saratoga."

"You didn't believe General Schuyler?" Elizabeth asked evenly. If she was shocked by this idea of considerate and elegant Philip Schuyler as complicit in a plot to wipe out the Iroquois, she did not show it.

"There's no question that the campaign plans came from Schuyler," Nathaniel said quietly. "None at all. For him, most Indians are savages and worthy of extermination, and he would own that to my face if I asked him. You're thinking of Runs-from-Bears. I'm not saying that Schuyler can't see the human being in some individuals. He can be loyal where it's called for. He did what he could to spare Barktown, but you have to remember, Elizabeth, that for him a bad Indian is one who doesn't see an advantage in being white." He gave her a minute to digest this, watching her face. He could see questions forming there, doubt and hesitancy and reluctant agreement.

"So how is it that Barktown was burned?" she asked.

"The Johnstown militia decided to do that on their own authority."

"I see," Elizabeth said, matching his tone.

"No you don't, but you will soon." He cleared his throat.

"So I went home and I found the village still smoking. The men—Sarah's father and her two brothers, both less than twenty, her uncle, other men and boys who were my friends—all of them dead. Took by surprise in the night. The women had fled or were doing what women always do, trying to keep alive and pull things back together. Sky-Wound-Round himself they took hostage, thinking they'd show up at Clinton's doorstep with more than just Indian hides to show for their trouble."

"Falling-Day?" Elizabeth asked numbly. "Sarah?"

"They took them along with Sky-Wound-Round, and Otter and Many-Doves, too. Otter was five at the time, Many-Doves was just seven."

Nathaniel had been staring at his own hands, lying flat on his knees; now he looked up at her, and he let her see his face the way he knew it must look. She was frightened; perhaps of him, perhaps of what he was telling her. It was hard to say. Nathaniel was suddenly tired, and he wanted to lie here in the sun and sleep with her next to him, listening to her breathe. Just sleep, with the sounds of the lake murmuring at them. But there was more to tell, and he could not turn away from this story, not once it was begun. With as little detail as possible, he told her about how he had tracked the militia, catching up to them on the next morning and then keeping well out of sight. To them he would have been just another Mohawk, and he knew better than to show himself.

The group of mismatched and poorly trained civilians, most of them with little battle experience, could hardly be called militia. Nathaniel recognized one or two of them from the distance. In that first day of following them the biggest surprise had been the acknowledgment that these civilians, poorly outfitted and provisioned, and led by nobody in particular, had been able to take Barktown with enough stealth and skill to cut down some of the strongest and most fearless of the Kahnyen'kehàka warriors. Two things consumed him and focused all his energies: catching up with his family and solving this mystery.

Both had happened on that evening when he caught sight of them from a bluff over their campsite.

Elizabeth was leaning toward Nathaniel, concentrated completely on this story. She hadn't interrupted him or asked any questions for quite a long time, but he could see her growing impatience. "What? What is it?" he asked.

"They were well treated?"

"They didn't abuse the women, if that's what you mean,"

Nathaniel said. He could see that this had been on her mind, for she settled back a bit, and some tension left her.

"They weren't bleeding or wounded, at least that I could see from that distance. But they were well guarded, better than I thought they would be, an older man and a bunch of women and children. It didn't fit together, none of it. The massacre, or the taking of the hostages, or the sorry excuse for a militia. But then I finally got sight of the man in charge, and things fell into place."

"Was it someone you knew?"

"Never saw him before. A slight man, didn't look much like a soldier at all, wearing spectacles. Looked more like a school-teacher."

She made a sound of impatience.

"It was Joshua Littlefield," Nathaniel said. "On his way to join Clinton at Canajoharie."

"The surgeon?" Elizabeth asked, and then something flooded her face, understanding and a blank horror. "Richard." She leaned forward and took his hands. "Richard was there. Richard told them about the village, how to get to it, how to surprise them. Was it Richard?"

Nathaniel nodded. "I hadn't caught sight of him till then, or maybe I did and I didn't recognize him. I'd been living in Falling-Day's longhouse for two years at that point. But there was Richard with Littlefield, and he was doing a lot of talking. It was Littlefield who was leading the militia to Clinton's camp, but it was Richard who was making the decisions."

"He took them hostage," Elizabeth said.

"I assume it was his idea," Nathaniel agreed. "Although I didn't figure that out straightaway. Not until it was too late."

A wariness came over her face.

"I thought if I could get to Richard, I could explain to him about Sarah, that she was my wife, that those people were my family. That Sky-Wound-Round was under Schuyler's protec-tion. I wasn't thinking straight," he said, still now after so many years feeling the shame of this, that he had made such an ele-mental mistake in assessing his enemy.

"He wouldn't listen?"

"He had me arrested as a spy," Nathaniel said simply. "And

he would have seen me shot then and there if it hadn't been for Sarah."

Elizabeth felt slightly nauseated and wished very much that Nathaniel would stop this story. She dropped the hand that she had been holding and wished for a handkerchief to wipe her face. Here was a Sarah she hadn't anticipated. A young woman who had stood up to the men who held her captive. Capable of convincing them that they would have Schuyler's wrath to deal with if they shot one of his best and most valued negotiators and translators. Nathaniel could only tell her about this in a disjointed way, he explained, because he himself had not heard what Sarah had to say.

"Somebody came up behind me and put a musket butt to my head, and that's all I remember till the next morning. I don't know exactly what she said, but she scairt Littlefield enough about Schuyler to put a stop to an execution."

"What did Richard say to you?" Elizabeth asked. "How did he explain himself?"

"Explain himself? Richard Todd? He didn't have a thing to say. Stayed just behind us for the rest of the march, watching to make sure we didn't try to run, and hoping that we'd be so stupid. To this day I wonder if he really thought he could talk Clinton into shooting me. He may have thought that; he was only eighteen at the time but he had a way with men. I'm sure it was him who got the militia riled up enough to attack Barktown, told them how to do it. Who else would know how to do that, but a man raised by the Kahnyen'kehàka? And he made it look like it all came from Littlefield, that was the real genius of it. Whether or not he thought he could see me shot at Canajoharie, he surely enjoyed watching us march."

Nathaniel had a picture of himself as he must have looked: Blinded by his own blood, with his hands bound behind him, and wheeling, his head a flare of pain. It was the sight of Otter walking in front of him that had kept him focused and able to put one foot in front of the next. Otter with his back straight and his five-year-old eyes sparking hate, so determined not to shame his grandfather or his mother. Otter who had insisted on calling Richard "Irtakohsaks," *Cat-Eater,* to his face, and who had been whipped for it. He thought of the Otter Elizabeth knew, and the one she didn't, and then he told her this story. Her head snapped up in surprise when he had finished.

"It was Otter, wasn't it, who shot at the horses that day, when we bolted?"

Nathaniel nodded.

"This is more complicated than I anticipated," Elizabeth murmured. "I am presuming that Clinton believed what you had to say?"

"Aye, once we got that far there was no question of hostages or executions. Littlefield went to report to Clinton straightaway, and you could hear the man bellow across the camp. He came thundering out of his tent and found us where they had dumped us, and he spent an hour apologizing to Sky-Wound-Round and trying to set things right. Gave us provisions and horses and sent us on our way. Promised to punish the men who were responsible—something that never happened, to the best of my knowledge. And he had the gall to send his greetings to my folks. But he couldn't send us home to Barktown," Nathaniel finished. "Because there wasn't a home to go back to anymore."

"What of Richard?"

"Did Clinton punish him, do you mean? No. He hadn't done anything but put ideas in Littlefield's head, and Littlefield was the one who caught the trouble. When we left Canajoharie the last I saw was Richard standing there, scratching his chin, watching us ride away. But then at least I knew the truth about him."

"And what is that?"

He reached out to her, took her hand in his own. She looked at it, strong and brown and capable of so much, of gentleness and affection and of harder things, when it was called for.

"Richard Todd is determined to take everything I ever had or ever wanted away from me," Nathaniel said.

Sarah, thought Elizabeth. She was standing between them; Elizabeth could almost see her. Nathaniel was thinking of Sarah, who waited to play her part in this story.

"Tell me the rest," she said. "Tell me about Sarah."

To her surprise, Nathaniel dropped her hand and stood up to look out over the lake. "You're avoiding your swimming lesson."

"I want to know about Sarah," Elizabeth said, a little surprised at him. He was looking down at her with an impatience she hadn't anticipated. He didn't answer her; she could see a muscle fluttering in his cheek.

"Nathaniel?"

"What?" he asked sharply. "What do you want to know about Sarah? She was my wife, and she left my bed for Richard Todd's. Isn't that enough to know?"

Shocked, Elizabeth rose to face him. She felt herself flood with anger and embarrassment and then with more anger. She cleared her throat. "But—"

"I'm damn tired of questions," Nathaniel snapped. "Maybe we could get to the end of them one of these days."

Elizabeth's hands were trembling, and she pressed them against her sides under her arms. "You have been telling me all along that I need to know this story."

"Well, you don't," he interrupted, his face suddenly blank and unreadable. "You're a clever woman," he said. "But there's a blindness in you for some things, Elizabeth. There's no easy answers here. Nothing I can tell you about Sarah to make it all clear to you. She's dead, let's leave her lie in peace."

"But what about you, what about your peace?"

He grimaced. "Well, I suppose I've got some coming to me now, maybe. Or at least I will once Todd has been dealt with and the Wolf can't be taken away from me anymore."

"I see," Elizabeth said tightly. She was turning away, pulling on her clothing, jamming her legs into her leggings and yanking at the ties. "As long as you've got Hidden Wolf."

"Where are you going?"

"For a walk."

"You can't run off."

"I'm not running off," she said hoarsely. "I am going for a walk. You seem to need some time to yourself, and so do I."

Suddenly his anger left him visibly, flowed away from him like a breaking fever. They stood there almost nose to nose, each breathing heavily. Sweat ran down Nathaniel's face, although they stood in shadow.

He said, "I had one wife who ran away, and I wasn't counting on another one."

Elizabeth blinked in surprise at this. He was afraid, Nathaniel was afraid of telling her what she wanted to know. It made her curious and angry and sad, all at once.

"Nathaniel Bonner," she said quietly. "It is you who don't want to talk to me."

He was mute, his jaw working in a tight circle as he stared at her. Nathaniel leaned in toward her then, his face a mask. "Maybe you're sorry you took me, then," he said. "Maybe you're wondering if you should have listened harder to Todd."

Elizabeth drew herself up. "I didn't want Richard Todd, I never did. And I'm not taking his side here, or Sarah's. Do you understand that clearly? For as long as you have known Richard he has been trying to gain advantage over you. Unfairly, and in ways which are insupportable." She took a deep breath. "I do not need to know the details of what went on between him and Sarah. But I am very distressed by the fact that you don't trust me enough to tell me the whole story and let me decide for myself—"

"Decide for yourself? Decide what? If I was at fault, if I drove her off?"

She shook her head slowly, and then began to turn away, but Nathaniel took her by the arm, held her there where she did not want to be.

"Goddamn it, I listened to you and now you listen to me. I can tell you another truth, Elizabeth, and it's the one that should concern you most. I wanted you from the first and I want you now, and that has nothing to do with Sarah or with Todd or with anybody in this world but with you, and me."

"I want some time on my own," she said, not meeting his eye.

"It ain't safe."

"I managed well enough while you were gone," she said sharply, pulling away. "I can manage now."

He hesitated. She could feel him thinking, and then suddenly he stepped back.

"I'll wait for you here," he said at last, his voice sounding as strange and hoarse as her own. "Don't go out of shouting distance."

She nodded without looking at him, and set off into the woods.

XXX

Once she was lost, there was nothing to do but admit it to herself. Elizabeth had been walking uphill for what must have been an hour when she stepped out of the woods and found herself on the edge of a meadow; it wasn't until then that she realized that she had bypassed the turning which would have led her back to Robbie.

There would be a price to pay for her preoccupation, but she could not contemplate that at the moment, not when she saw what she had in front of her. The world lay revealed, in a way it hadn't been since she had gone into the bush with Runs-from-Bears. There was an expanse of mountain meadow in tender greens and patches of unfurling bracken, spotted with blossoming goatsbeard in gaudy yellow. The edge of the meadow was framed by a low wall of sedge grass, and beyond that the rolling hills gave way to the mountains.

And on it all, light and shadow moved in a complex dance, the clouds throwing down great ragged fists of deep indigo to be swept suddenly away by slanting shafts of sunlight. Every touch of moisture on every evergreen needle seemed to spark. The world was layers of glowing color and light and a soft, warm breeze like a caress against her face. Elizabeth sat down, simply, and with her knees tucked under her chin and her arms wound round her legs, she let herself take it in.

It belonged to no one, and never could; the mountains and

the scattering of lakes in greens and azures and the endless, ageless forests. The thought came to her that it was a great vanity and self-delusion to believe that such a world could be claimed, could be owned, by simply putting a name on it. She felt humbled, and childish. And still, her anger was there and she did not know how to resolve it. With her chin on her knees she looked down the mountain to where Nathaniel sat by the lake.

He was her husband, and he loved her. And it struck Elizabeth, very clearly, that all along she had both depended on and resented him for his extreme common sense. His clearheadedness had sometimes been irritating. But today there had been another Nathaniel there, vulnerable and uneasy and defensive. Things she had never seen in him before, things she didn't know how to cope with. She wanted something from him that he didn't want to give, and she had pushed him until he wouldn't be pushed anymore. Elizabeth realized how insensitive she had been, and her cheeks colored with embarrassment. The urge to get up and go back to Nathaniel was almost more than she could withstand. But she pressed her forehead against her knees and counted to ten, and then to a hundred, forcing herself to count slowly.

She did want to know about Sarah. The young woman who had saved Nathaniel's life, and the lives of her family. Who had turned to the man who had been responsible for the deaths of her father and brothers, the massacre of her village, the desecration of her home. Sarah, who had been dead for five years but who had left a daughter behind, a bright, beautiful daughter. Elizabeth knew that she must have the story in its entirety; she needed it for herself, and she owed it to Hannah.

He doesn't trust you with her, not yet. That acknowledgment had hurt her pride, and she struggled now to come to a quiet place with the truth of the matter. Nathaniel did not trust her completely, and she would have to wait until he did.

From the edge of the wood came the strident *killy killy killy* of a kestrel irritated by intruders too close to its nest. She turned to see the vibrantly colored bird swooping and fluttering. But there was no fox or squirrel. Instead there was a stranger stand-

ing there with a coonskin cap in his hands. A man with a
beautiful smile and gold-brown eyes.

She rose slowly to her feet and stood her ground, realizing
even as she did that she had purposely and foolishly disregarded
Nathaniel's directions to stay within shouting distance. She was
without weapons and out of earshot. It did not occur to her to
ask him his name as he approached her. For months she had
been hearing stories of him; she would know Jack Lingo anywhere.

He walked with the rolling limp that was his hallmark, one
leg shorter than the other. The fringe on his hunting shirt
shimmied with it. The grin never left his face, clean shaven and
quite handsome. Fans of wrinkles at the corners of his eyes gave
him a kindly air. He was not very tall, but was elegantly built.
Even to her untrained eye he looked strong, the shoulders filling out his shirt and straining at the upper arms.

A few feet short of her, he came to a stop and bowed so that
she saw that his hair, luxuriant curls, was shot with white.

"Madame Bonner," he murmured in a deep, gravelly voice.
There were green flecks in his golden eyes. He bowed from the
waist, all politeness and condescension. "Finally I make your
acquaintance."

Nathaniel slept in the sun, as he had wanted to do. Forced
himself to lie there, to still his breathing. To put thoughts of
Sarah and of Elizabeth out of his head, and to sleep. He woke
instantaneously and reached for her, but his hand found the
more familiar shape of his rifle. He judged the time by the slant
of the light, and by the grumbling in his stomach. She would be
back at Robbie's, waiting for him with things to say. He did not
relish the conversation, but he could not go longer without
seeing her.

Downwind from Robbie's camp, Nathaniel heard the *thunk*
of an axe and the occasional pause. This part of the bush was as
familiar to him as the country around Paradise, and so were
Robbie's habits. Nathaniel had hunted here with his father every season while he was growing up, staying behind for long
weeks to learn trapping from Robbie. Hawkeye had been will-

ing to leave Nathaniel because Robbie knew the value of the business; Cora had let him go for other reasons. She had been worried about Nathaniel's restlessness, and hoped that the time with Robbie would be enough to satisfy his need for adventure. A hope that had not been realized.

Robbie was known up and down the bush for his understanding of the beaver and their ways, for his generosity and gentleness, and for his fair dealings with the Hode'noshaunee. For thirty years he had traded with them, his furs for their squash and beans and corn, for moccasins and hunting shirts big enough to fit him, and for thirty years he had been knowingly and willingly underpaid. His furs were the best to be had, and worth a fortune season by season. But Robbie had not a greedy bone in him and he was content with the arrangement, because it released him of the need to go among men. Twice or three times a year he had come to Paradise, to spend a few evenings at Cora's hearth. Since she had died he had not even gone that far.

The thought of Lake in the Clouds brought Nathaniel back to Elizabeth and Sarah. He had lost his composure today about Sarah, something he hadn't done in many years. Elizabeth had taken offense. He shook his head, knowing that he had given her cause.

She was so strong and so sensible that he forgot at times what it must be like for her, how strange it all was. Looking back at those first days she had spent in Paradise, he remembered admiring her for coping so well. That was when it had started. With the tilt of her chin and the flash of her eyes and the curve of her mouth, with the starch in her and her feistiness. The question was, could she stand to see him for what he was? She demanded the whole truth, but he worried that she would turn away from him, once she had heard it all.

He asked himself something she had not asked, and that was whether it was her or the land he had wanted more, wanted first. It was something he wondered about from time to time, but he couldn't remember anymore what had come first. Whatever had been in his head back then, the truth now was that he wanted her more than he needed her. The having of her would keep him alive.

Nathaniel came around a bend and heard a shout of laughter.

Robbie, in the best of moods. And Runs-from-Bears, laughing, too. They were sitting there at the fire, cleaning a small deer, and deep in conversation. There was no sign of Elizabeth.

"Where is she?" he asked, without stopping to greet them.

"She's a wee thing, that lass of yours, but surely ye havna lost her betwixt the lake and here, have ye, man?" Robbie was grinning, but he saw the look on Nathaniel's face and his face went blank.

"Kát-ke?" Bears asked—When?—even as he stood and reached for his rifle.

"Two hours," answered Nathaniel. "She headed up-mountain."

They split up to look for signs. Of Elizabeth, or of Jack Lingo, or of the two of them together. There was no time or need to discuss the matter. All three men knew Jack Lingo and what he was capable of; Robbie had cleaned up after him on more than one occasion. Nathaniel and Bears had heard stories from Hawkeye, told in a low voice out of the women's hearing.

The fist in his gut, low and tense, reminded Nathaniel of the morning of his first battle, at Bemis Heights. When the fog still lay over the land and all was still, thousands of men quiet, waiting for the killing to start. He pushed away the thought of his own foolishness. He could not afford that now, not until this was resolved. He would not think of the worst, because it would unman him.

He ran upmountain, his rifle cocked and loaded and primed, ready in his hands. He could reload at a dead run, but he knew that if he needed to use it and failed, she would be dead already, and his life over. Jack Lingo was a formidable enemy.

Nathaniel ran hard, light-footed and focused, stopping now and then to listen and then run again. He wanted to be the one to pick up the trail. Unbidden, the feel of her came to him, her skin pressed to his, and her smell; he frowned and sought a prayer instead, any prayer. But Christian or Kahnyen'kehàka, nothing came to him except the memory of her, how she felt to him.

Ahead he saw the forest give way to the upper meadow and he stopped. Looked harder around himself, and found her. Her heel print. Seeing it, its orientation, he knew the way she had come here, how she had traveled bearing east when she should have kept on north. Not that it mattered anymore; the outline of her foot was flanked by another print. A man's foot, with a drag to it.

Nathaniel stopped to listen, and hearing nothing, walked to the edge of the meadow where he saw the small huddled form of his wife.

It was uncomfortable sitting with her back to the beech tree. Not so much because of the bindings; she could not free herself, but they were not excessively tight, either. But she itched, and she could not scratch. Soon, she thought, she would have to shout. She had waited for as long as she could bear for Nathaniel to come and find her, but it seemed a very long time indeed. Perhaps Robbie would hear her, if Nathaniel didn't. Perhaps she could convince him to keep this to himself. She was mortified at her own foolishness.

She looked up and saw Nathaniel at the edge of the wood. A great flood of relief and gratitude filled her, but before she could call out to him he had faded back into the shadows and disappeared.

For a while, she was patient. He must believe that she was in danger, that she was being watched. He couldn't know how innocent the whole thing had been, how politely Jack Lingo had spoken to her. Nathaniel was worried for her well-being, when all he need do was come and cut her loose so she could pass along Lingo's message and they could get on with things. Her stomach rumbled and her face itched abominably and the kestrel which had warned her—or tried to warn her—of Jack Lingo's approach had rewarded her stupidity by perching above her to void in a bright orange streak down the front of her overdress. She had borne many indignities for her thoughtless behavior, and she was ready to own up to her mistakes and to carry on. But still Nathaniel didn't come. Her irritation increased with the itching of her nose.

He startled her in the end, speaking to her from behind even as he cut her bonds.

"Swimming would have been a far sight more pleasant," he said.

"No doubt," she agreed, rubbing her wrists. When she could turn she saw his frown, and she answered him with one of her own, although she would have preferred touching him.

"I began to think you wouldn't come back at all."

"The thought crossed my mind."

"Oh, very amusing." She pursed her mouth. "He did me no real harm, if you're worried about that."

He cocked one eyebrow. "I don't expect you'd be so feisty if he had."

"He was very gentlemanly," she said.

"Then you're the first to think so," Nathaniel said, frowning. "Most women who have made his acquaintance ain't seen that side of him." He turned away. "Let's go back," he said, and started off without looking at her. He was definitely in a bad humor.

"I was the one accosted," Elizabeth said lightly. "You needn't be so short with me."

Too late, she saw the error of this. He swung around on her, his face all thunder. "By God," he whispered. "You can be a stupid woman, Elizabeth. Do you have no idea what he might have done to you?"

"He did nothing except bind me to that tree," she countered. "And tell me a number of quite fantastical stories. I don't like to be called stupid. I may have been foolish to have walked so far—"

"Foolish, aye. And stubborn and thickheaded and plain ignorant, for good measure." The muscles in his throat were working hard. "And if you ever decide that you must defy common sense again then you won't have to worry about being called stupid, because you'll be dead or hurt so bad you won't give a damn." And he reached out his left arm and pulled her in to him, buried his face in her hair.

"Promise me," he said. "Promise me you won't do that again."

Chastised finally and thoroughly, Elizabeth nodded.

They stood like that for a moment, listening to each other breathe.

"Don't you want to know what he had to say?" she asked. "He gave me a message."

"Not now, not here," Nathaniel said, letting her go. "He may still be around."

There was a fallen tree, its dark, crumbling trunk sprouting great layers of pale mushrooms like a scaly beard. On it, Runs-from-Bears perched nonchalantly. Elizabeth was glad to see him, but he spoke directly to Nathaniel. It appeared that Jack Lingo's trail had been picked up and he was off the mountain, headed north.

"Robbie's on his tail, make sure he don't swing back," Bears concluded in English. Clearly for Elizabeth's benefit, although he still didn't look at her.

They were silent for the rest of the walk back to the clearing. Elizabeth noted that neither of them put their rifles out of hand, and she wondered if Runs-from-Bears had told the whole truth. Something occurred to her.

"What of Dutch Ton?" she asked. He glanced over his shoulder at her.

"No sign of him."

Now that the first flush of agitation and fear was abated, Elizabeth began to shake. She pressed her palms hard together, spoke sternly to herself. Once at Robbie's, she went immediately into the caves and to her cot, and she sat there while she was slowly consumed by trembling. Nathaniel came to her.

"My face swells when I cry," she said. "It isn't a pretty sight."

"Pigheaded and vain, too," he noted dryly. But he sat down next to her and put an arm around her shoulders. She hiccuped a little and buried her face in his shirt.

"He might have killed me?"

He nodded.

"But he was so polite."

Nathaniel waited, saying nothing while her trembling slowly subsided.

"I will grant you that the things he had to say were . . .

strange. But I never thought I was in real danger. He was so very apologetic about binding me."

"It was my fault for letting you go off on your own," he said grimly. "I should have warned you about him. Now." He wiped her cheeks with his hand. "Tell me what he had to say."

She drew in a wavering sigh. "He wants the Tory Gold," she said. "And he's convinced you've got it, hidden away. You and Hawkeye and Chingachgook. He described to me how he came upon it, although he cast himself in rather a different role in the story than Axel did in his telling of it."

Nathaniel grunted. "Aye, and so he would."

"He wears one of the coins around his neck. It is most unusual, I have never seen anything like it. A five-guinea gold piece, with George the Second in profile—"

"Got a good look at it, did you?" He looked vaguely intrigued. Elizabeth described it to him in detail, down to the hole Lingo had punched through the sovereign's temple in order to string the coin on a piece of rawhide.

"A thousand of them would be an overwhelming sight," she finished.

"And a conspicuous one," Nathaniel agreed. He was studying her hand, turning it this way and that in his own. "He had a message for me?"

"He said, 'Tell your worthy husband and his father and grandfather that the next time I will take what pleases me until payment is forthcoming.'" But he said it in French. A rather different French than I was taught, but that was his meaning." She grimaced in her attempt to smile. "At the time I didn't think it through, but I suppose that was a threat against my person?"

"Or Hannah."

"Hannah," Elizabeth breathed. "Oh, no."

"It ain't a pleasing idea, that's true." He leaned back. "He's getting impatient. Wonder what's pushing him."

"He said he wants to go to France," Elizabeth volunteered.

Nathaniel pulled up short and saw that she was not joking. "He has never been out of the north country," he said. "What would he want in France?"

"To join the revolution, he said."

"Ha! The man never fought for anything or anyone but himself."

She said, "I told him you didn't have the gold. That if you had had such amounts of money you would have bought the mountain long ago."

He rewarded her with a grin and a hasty kiss. "And what did he think of that?"

"It made him angry," she admitted. "He didn't believe me. He wanted to know how it was that you had managed to pay Richard off if you didn't have any money. Monsieur Lingo is very well informed."

"And what explanation did you have for him?"

She found the strength to meet his eye and she drew in a big breath. "I told him that you had the very good sense to fall in love with a well-to-do spinster and marry well."

"Is that what I did?" he asked, smiling broadly.

Elizabeth nodded, her own smile more tentative. "Yes. I think so."

He pulled her close. There was a great deal of satisfaction and relief in his face. "And so I did. Very well, in fact. You see how well. No, don't stop me." He was tugging at her clothes impatiently, spreading his hands wide against her warm skin.

"Did I say the right things to him?" she asked breathlessly.

"Aye," Nathaniel said, taking her hands above her head to lay her back against the cot. "You did, indeed. I'm well satisfied with you, Boots. Maybe it's time I showed you that again, don't you think? Would you be interested in another lesson in satisfaction?"

In reply, she pulled him down to her, and buried her face in the curve of his neck. Speechless, for once, in the face of what he had to say to her.

Later, his high spirits left him. While she slept out her adventure and what they had done together, he sat quietly and thought it all through, and his conclusions were not easy ones. Todd was too much on his mind, and had distracted him from other problems. The idea of Jack Lingo in a frenzy because he smelled money in the air was more than just mildly irritating.

He had put his hands on Elizabeth, and had made threats, and thus intruded himself on a set of circumstances which were complicated enough already.

They were expected in Albany, where Elizabeth would be asked to depose in a civil action being brought against her by Dr. Richard Todd for breach of promise. He was demanding satisfaction in the form of option to purchase lands included in her dower. Knowing he was out of his depth, Nathaniel had sought legal advice and found, to his immense relief, that she was not bound by law to appear. Mr. Bennett had been quite clear on this: she had not been formally served with summons papers, had she? When Nathaniel assured him that she had not, Bennett had shown his own relief and noted that it would be a very good thing indeed if the serving of such papers, on Elizabeth or on Nathaniel as her husband, proved impossible.

Nathaniel had paid Bennett's retainer and got out of Johnstown before Richard or his lawyers could find him. On the way north he had stopped briefly in Paradise to see his daughter and father, and to lay plans. Before leaving he had made sure to visit Anna Hauptmann, and to tell her in plain hearing of half the village that he was off to fetch his bride to Albany so she could testify on her own behalf and clear up these misunderstandings. The idea was to put Richard's mind at ease, although it meant lying to Anna, which he didn't like doing. She had always dealt fair with the folks from Lake in the Clouds.

Tomorrow, Bennett would show up in court without his clients, and if all went well, Richard would be angry enough to set out into the bush to find Elizabeth and serve the summons himself. They would lead him on a chase for a week or so, enough time for Hawkeye to try to talk Richard's witnesses out of perjuring themselves. It was not the best of plans, and there was all kinds of room for trouble, but it was all they could come up with on short notice.

In the morning he and Elizabeth would go north, and Runs-from-Bears would go back to Paradise, where Hawkeye would be glad of his help in case Jack Lingo made good on his threat and wandered in that direction. Not to mention Many-Doves, who had been directly displeased to see Nathaniel come home alone.

When Elizabeth stirred and woke, Nathaniel would have to make all of this known to her. He hoped there was enough to satisfy her curiosity for the moment. With any luck, she wouldn't ask those questions he wasn't yet ready to answer.

Late in the night, Elizabeth lay awake watching the guttering of a single candle near its end. She knew that she must give herself over to sleep soon, as reluctant as she was. Her body had adjusted well to these demanding circumstances, Nathaniel's attentions, her own hungers, the increased work and physical activity, but she would need all her strength for what was ahead of them. Still she could not sleep, not yet. It would be hard to walk away from Robbie tomorrow, but the idea of going off into the bush with Nathaniel was very welcome to her. The rift that had opened between them today had not yet been healed.

"Do you realize I've never spent a full day alone with you?" she asked.

"It won't be easy," he said. "The terrain's more than tough in places."

"I don't mind," she said. It was more than that, but she was shy to tell him. She was proud of how much she had learned and how far she had come, and she wanted to show him those things. And if it kept Richard Todd at bay and gave them a chance to settle this business, she would be content. The solitude would give them time to learn to know each other. This thought made her aware of other things, of the heaviness in her limbs, and the fact that her lips were tender. She pulled hard on her plait, taken aback and made uneasy by how easy it was to become aroused, how easy to lose her train of thought when Nathaniel was near.

"There will be time to talk," she said out loud. There were so many things she didn't understand and needed to know about. Questions slid into her consciousness and then out again, lazily.

"You still don't know how to swim," he murmured.

She stretched a bit and turned in his arms. Felt the weight of them around her, the solid strength of him an endless comfort.

"Never mind," he said, sifting through her hair, strand by strand, but in a distracted way. "There'll be time for that, too." There was an awareness about him when he was thinking hard, an underlying hum that she could feel in the rush of his blood. Elizabeth did not like having his thoughts elsewhere, not at this moment. She moved closer to him, bedded her head on his chest, and looked hard inside herself for words that would not come.

His arms flexed and then relaxed again. He smoothed the hair away from her face and cleared his throat. "You're thinking about Sarah," he said. "But you're afraid to ask."

She didn't respond.

"It wasn't right of me, the way I flew at you today when you brought up her name."

"No," Elizabeth agreed. "It wasn't right."

"I ain't exactly proud of what it is I've got to tell you."

"Tell me anyway," Elizabeth said. "Or we'll never get past this."

When he didn't answer, she lifted her head to look into his face. "Nathaniel. I promise I'll do my best not to judge you unfairly," she said.

"That's what I'm afraid of," he said. Then he cleared his throat, and began.

"When Barktown burned, Sky-Wound-Round and Falling-Day took the younger children and they went north to Canada to winter with Falling-Day's people, because there was no food. I wanted to go along with them, but Sarah didn't. She had been trying to talk me into taking her home to live at Lake in the Clouds ever since we married, and it looked like the right time to go. I couldn't argue with her anymore. Didn't want to, really, not with the village wiped out the way it was."

Nathaniel turned a little so that he was lying on his side curled around Elizabeth's length. In the flickering candlelight his features seemed more animated than they really were. She lay with one hand at rest on her abdomen, and he covered it with his own.

"So we went home, and they took us in. Glad to have us, too. My ma especially had always wanted a daughter and she was pleased with Sarah. That's what you have to understand about Sarah, she had the gift of making folks love her. There was a childlike quality to her when she was pleased that went to the heart, and I guess that would be the simplest truth: she had a girl's way of looking at the world and she never learned to settle for less than that." He paused. "Or to cope with more.

"Don't misunderstand me, now. She was a good worker and never shirked, but she could play harder than anybody I ever saw. Learned every song my mother knew in three months' time, and my mother had an ear for a song. My mother, now, you'd have to understand that she was hard on her own kind, she demanded a lot. But Sarah won her over, and it was the music that built the bond between them."

"That's how she learned Scots," Elizabeth noted.

"Aye. They sang together in the evenings." His voice trailed off, and Elizabeth felt a deep sadness for him.

"I remember my mother's voice very clearly," Elizabeth said. "And it's still with me after all these years."

He had been staring toward the ceiling, but he looked down to Elizabeth. "You haven't told me much about your mother."

"Another time," she said quietly. "Go on, please."

"Well, let's see. Sarah settled in at Lake in the Clouds real fast. Some in the village weren't glad to see her and didn't make her welcome, at first. But when she put her mind to it she could win over anybody. Sometimes I had the feeling that she felt obligated to prove to the world that she could be a Kahnyen'kehàka and a human being, too. The trouble started then, because I like the Kahnyen'kehàka way of life, and she didn't. We were both young, you see. Young enough to think we could just decide what we wanted to be, that it didn't take any more than that, the wanting.

"It went on for a long time before I took real note of what was happening. She wanted to be called Sarah, and if I forgot and called her by her Kahnyen'kehàka name she would get pretty mad. I remember my mother asking once how the Mohawk keep raccoon out of the corn and Sarah just looked at her with a blank face, and then claimed she didn't remember. And then one day she wouldn't answer me if I spoke to her in Kahnyen'kehàka, and I suppose that's when I couldn't pretend anymore.

"It was about that time, maybe three years since we had settled down at Lake in the Clouds, that Sky-Wound-Round took his people back to Barktown to rebuild it. Just after the

war had quieted down, it was. Schuyler gave them safe passage
—the Wolf and the Turtle and a few Bear clan, they went back
to the Big Vly in the spring. It was the first Sarah had seen of
her mother or her people in all that time. She was glad to see
them, no question, but in the end she didn't want to be there,
in the longhouse."

"But you did?" Elizabeth asked.

He said, "I did, at that time. You're wondering why I
wanted to give up my own place and take on her people when I
had folks of my own, but I don't know if I can explain it to you.
I guess the only thing I can say is that the life suited me. And I
was at that age where I didn't want to be living under my
father's rule. Now, you might be thinking that we get along
fine, and that's true enough. But I was a son then and now I'm
a father myself, and things look different to me." He shook his
head.

"Sarah got what she wanted, in the end. Not so much because her will was stronger than mine—"

Elizabeth made a small sound, and he grinned, reluctantly.

"But because it wasn't clear we would have been welcome,
anyway. Or that I would have been."

"Wouldn't have been welcome?" Elizabeth asked, surprised
and more than a little insulted for him. "After all the time you
had lived with them?"

"That's it, you see. Falling-Day had come back expecting to
find her oldest daughter with a child at the breast and she hadn't
ever even shown the signs of starting one. The Kahnyen'kehàka
take the business of getting children serious."

"What did Sarah think of this?" Elizabeth asked, because it
seemed the safest thing to ask and also because she was truly
wondering.

"I don't think she much minded, to tell you the truth,"
Nathaniel said. "She never held it up to me, never made any
complaints. She wanted me, or she wanted Lake in the Clouds.
Whichever it was that was more important to her, the result was
we didn't go back to the longhouse."

Nathaniel had been talking calmly, this story with all of its
threads unraveling evenly. But there was a pause now, and Elizabeth thought that if she relieved him of the responsibility, he

would just stop and turn inward. He glanced at her from the corner of his eye and sighed.

"Well, I was angry. Although I wouldn't admit it to anybody, even myself. I didn't like the way things were going, and I didn't like Sarah much for keeping me there, and I suppose I blamed her for not getting with child, unfair as that was. So I started spending more time in the bush. Went farther afield every time I went out, and stayed away as long as I could. Spent the season up here trapping with Robbie the winter of '82, didn't get home until the spring. With a fine lot of furs to show for my trouble but with a hatful of guilt, too, for leaving Sarah alone for so long. Robbie had done some talking to me."

Elizabeth had an image that was very real to her, of a younger Nathaniel, moodier and ill at ease with himself, spending long evenings in Robbie's company. She could well imagine that Robbie had talked to him, sparing him little truth, but doing it gently.

"He sent you home to Sarah," she concluded for herself.

There was a grim look to Nathaniel's smile. "That he did, with as much good advice as he could stuff into my head."

"But it didn't work?"

"It might have," Nathaniel said. "I was willing to make some compromises at that point. But no, it didn't work."

"Because?" Elizabeth prompted, gently.

"Because while I was gone Richard Todd had settled in to Paradise and built a fine house, started doctoring and making a place for himself in the village."

He was silent for a time, with no sign of what he was thinking with the exception of the fluttering of a muscle in his cheek. Elizabeth had come to recognize this sign, and knew that she had best leave him some room. When he looked at her again, the old anger was back, uncompromised by all the years that had passed since this hurt.

"I saw right away what had happened, that she had fallen in love with the man. She could never hide what she was feeling, not from me."

"But why?" Elizabeth said. "Why, given what she knew of him, what she had seen him do?"

"I don't know. Yes, I do. At least some of it. Because he

never chided her about leaving behind the Kahnyen'kehàka in her," Nathaniel said. "Because he was a challenge." There was a long pause, filled with tension. "Because he paid attention to her."

"Your mother," Elizabeth countered. "She must have known, she must have tried—"

"Oh, she tried," he said easily. "And so did my father. But there wasn't much to be done about it. They weren't obvious, you see. They didn't flaunt anything. To this day, I don't think anybody in Paradise has any idea of what went on."

"Curiosity does," Elizabeth said quietly.

"Because Curiosity was there for the first birthing," Nathaniel said. "Before that point she knew as little as anybody else."

"Then Hannah is in fact Richard's child?"

"No," Nathaniel said curtly. "She is mine. She was conceived the night I got home from the bush, and nine months later Sarah brought her into the world. Along with a son, who died in my hands." He sat up, his hair falling forward, and he looked Elizabeth directly in the eye, but he didn't touch her. "Hannah is my child, and I'll ask you kindly to take that as fact and never question it. Can you do that for me?"

He was looking at her impassively, but there was a wariness about him.

Elizabeth nodded.

"Now, you know about Sarah," he said, lying down again, next to her but somehow not next to her any longer. "And it's time we got to sleep."

But of course she didn't know about Sarah; she knew less of her than she had known to start with. Still, it wasn't Sarah who mattered right now. Nathaniel needed things from her that she could give him, at least for this moment, at least for now: her silence and her acceptance. Although he did not invite it, Elizabeth put her arms around Nathaniel and held him until she felt him begin to relax. In time she fell asleep herself, wondering about these wounds of his, and if it might be in her power to heal them.

XXXI

"I wish that man would set still," Curiosity grumbled out loud as she bent to pull on her shoes. "I'm too old to be running around this village ever time Dr. Richard Todd take it into his little head to go hightailing it into the bush."

Galileo stretched and yawned his acknowledgment, snapping his suspenders into place. "I'll have the team ready in ten minutes," he said as he closed the door behind him.

"You'd think I was the only woman in this part of the world to have ever borned a child," she called after him.

Then she looked up, eyes narrowed, at Moses Southern.

"How long she been at it?"

He fingered his beard, and refused to meet her eye. "Since early this evening."

"Hmmph." Curiosity stood and stamped her feet one after the other to make her shoes sit right. "Could go on all night."

"Did the last time," Moses agreed. "How much you charge for a birthing?"

"How much a healthy child and your woman worth to you?" She didn't like the man, and she wasn't about to make this easy on him, although she wouldn't have turned down his request for help. Not that she expected to be paid. Moses Southern would offer the judge something for her services, as if she were still a slave. Without waiting for an answer, she lifted her chin toward the basket on the table. "That belongs in the wagon," she said. "I have to tell the judge I'm going."

Once in the hall she relaxed a bit, and allowed herself a grin. She liked being called on, and she liked especially the business of helping other women bring their children into the world. This particular woman was one who needed some talking to. It was exactly the opportunity she had been hoping for. Childbed was just the place for some home truths.

The judge answered the knock at his door immediately. When he saw she was dressed to go out, he raised an eyebrow in question. Since his daughter's elopement and, more recently, the realization that Elizabeth was not going to appear in court as she had been requested to do, he had been keeping to himself. There was the smell of brandy about him. Curiosity's nostrils flared, and he drew back a step.

"Mistress Southern's time has come," Curiosity informed him.

"Richard isn't here to attend her."

"No, sir, he ain't." *Out in the bush running after another man's woman,* Curiosity thought. *And shame on you for letting him go after that daughter of yours.*

"Who will cook our breakfast?" He looked down at her blurry eyed. Curiosity could see that he would sleep through the morning and never miss his breakfast; he had been drinking for days. She wondered if she should take the time to talk some sense to this man, and then put the thought aside. Wouldn't do any good anyhow.

"My Daisy will see to it that you and Julian are looked after."

He nodded, and turned away from her. Then he turned back, suddenly.

"Did you know?" he asked. "Did you know about her attachment to Bonner?" It was the first time he had asked her outright.

"She never said his name to me," Curiosity said, looking him straight in the eye.

·   ·   ·

In the wagon, she laid a hand on her husband's arm. "Stop by the Witherspoon place."

"What for?" asked Galileo. "What're you plotting, woman?"

She grinned. "Why, a birthing is a long business. I need some help. Thought mayhap Miss Witherspoon would like to lend a hand."

He grunted. "I see through you."

"But she won't," Curiosity said. "Not until it's too late."

"Why not let these people sort things out for theyselves?"

" 'Cause," she sniffed. "I cain't. Wait and see, Leo, if it ain't worth our trouble to do what we can for Elizabeth when she ain't here to look after her own interests."

"You think she willing to buy them Glove boys free, you might be disappointed."

"Mayhap I will be," Curiosity said. "But I doubt it. That girl has got a good soul."

Moses Southern was waiting for them when they pulled up. He looked surprised to see Kitty Witherspoon with them, but just as he was about to comment there was a wavering cry from the dimly lit room behind him and he half turned, looking over his shoulder. His dogs whimpered and pressed close to his legs, and he pushed them off with a curse.

"Are the children here?" Curiosity asked.

He shook his head and gestured with his chin down the track to the neighbor.

"You go on now," she said to him. "Go on over to Axel and set in front of the fire, Mr. Southern. We'll send word over when the child come along."

Moses Southern was surely the sourest human being the Lord had ever seen fit to blow his breath into, Curiosity was thinking. He was looking up at her with his lips sucked right into his mouth, his mean little eyes narrowed down tight. He turned his attention to Kitty Witherspoon, who stood just behind Curiosity with her arms folded and her chin tucked down to her chest.

"Miz Witherspoon, don't you let her go talking no nonsense

to my wife, now," he said as he reached behind him for his cap, which he pulled down hard onto his forehead.

There was a look on Kitty's face, just one step removed from disgust. It couldn't have been clearer if the girl had spat on the ground in front of Moses Southern and cursed in his face. But he was looking elsewhere. Curiosity put a long, cool hand on the girl's arm to keep her still.

"Mr. Southern, don't you worry none. When the urge to talk comes upon me, I'll call on the Lord instead."

With a grunt, he turned and stamped away, splattering mud with each kick of his heavy boots.

"That man has got the temperament of a wasp-stung mule," Curiosity muttered as she took her basket from Galileo.

Inside, the small cabin was poorly lit by a sluggish fire that cast shadows in jagged shapes. There were two rooms, separated from each other by a faded calico curtain washed almost to transparency. Near the hearth laundry had been hung to dry: a little girl's dress, some mismatched stockings, a pair of longjohns, more patch than anything else. From the rafters hung a few ragged bunches of wildflowers dried to gray and dust along with the meat and the corn. There was the reek of salt pork and cabbage and vinegar, tallow candles and swaddling clothes left too long without tending. From the door Curiosity could see Martha Southern in bed in the second room, the great mountain of her belly rearing up and dwarfing the round face, streaked with sweat and blotched red and white.

Kitty was wrinkling her nose. Curiosity took one look at her and led her out of sight.

"Kitty Witherspoon," she whispered. "I can surely use your help here. But only if you don't let that woman think she's worse than dirt. You don' like the way she live her life, but she do the best she can. Now, are you here to help, or should I send you back home to your daddy like the child you are?"

At first she thought that she had been too harsh, for the girl went pale and then flushed. But the distance in her eyes went away and she blinked at Curiosity.

"I'll open the windows."

"Good idea," said Curiosity with a smile. "And we'll need water. But first come say how-do. She won't bite, you know.

Not at this stage, at any rate." She paused, and cast a knowing look at Kitty's middle. "Seems to me your turn ain't too far down the line. That true?"

Wordlessly, Kitty nodded, spreading her ringless hands over her waist.

"I thought me so," Curiosity said with a nod. "You'll be glad of women around you when your time come along."

"My husband will attend me—" Kitty's voice faltered.

Curiosity said, "Will he now?" And watched the young woman blush.

"He will be my husband."

Will he now? But she could be kind when it was called for, and so she didn't say it. She had watched this girl grow, and it saddened Curiosity to see her juggled from man to man. Always settling for a piece of what she thought she wanted. Julian's child in her, and telling herself that Richard Todd would not know the difference.

"So be it," she said quietly. "But one way or the other, you'll be glad of your own kind."

There was a moan, cut off suddenly.   •

"Miz Southern. How is that child coming on?" Curiosity moved into the next room with sharp little taps of her shoes.

"Slow," Martha Southern whispered. "Miss Witherspoon, I am surprised to see you here. Thank you kindly for your help."

Kitty cleared her throat and nodded.

"She's a mite scared," Curiosity pointed out. "But it's a chore we women have got to share, ain't that so?"

With eyes darting everywhere but Martha's belly, Kitty managed a nod. "I'm not sure how much help I can be."

"Well, settle in," Curiosity said, tying her apron into a tighter wrap around her slender self. "And we'll find out the answer to that question. Now," she said. "This is going to take a good while. Get over there, Kitty, and help me get this woman out of bed. Ain't no way a child'll get down to business while it's got such a easy life. What we got to talk about until the next pains come on?"

Kitty calmed after a while, putting her hands to whatever task Curiosity set her and doing it well. When a pain came down hard on Martha, Kitty would sometimes pause and blanch. But then she would carry on. Silent and watchful and grim, she pressed her lips hard together and worked without complaint.

But Curiosity could not move the girl to a talking frame of mind. It was an unusual experience, for she had always had the knack for getting women to open up, but Kitty was closed to the subject of what had gone on at the Albany courthouse. Martha would have been an easier nut to crack if it hadn't been for Kitty. The minute Curiosity raised the topic, she saw them glance at each other and then away, united in their discomfort as they were in nothing else. As if she had produced a rude noise or a bad smell and they were agreed that it would be rude to draw her attention to it.

The child got down to business just past midnight. Martha asked to be allowed to set, but Curiosity pushed her a little further, encouraging her to walk between them from one end of the small cabin to the other. With increasing regularity and for longer periods, Martha would falter and sag between them. What had been a thoughtful look on her plain round face turned more to pain, and then moved beyond that, too.

"Don' you hold your breath," said Curiosity. "Come on and talk to me, now. Tell me, Kitty. Did I see you come back from Albany with a new bonnet?"

It was straw, she was told. With a velvet ribbon. And then Kitty was silent again.

Martha tensed suddenly and let out a low moan.

"She's gone a gusher," Curiosity said, stepping around the puddle on the floor. "Don't look so took back, Kitty. It's just her waters. The child getting impatient now."

"Waters?" asked Kitty.

"I guess your daddy never told you much, did he? And why should he, probably forgot the little he once knew about a woman's insides."

Martha laughed out loud at that, and even Kitty grinned.

"Glad to see you ain't lost your sense of humor," Curiosity said as they settled Martha into bed. "It will stand you in good stead in the next hour or two."

"Another hour or two." Kitty looked suddenly panicked.

"Took me three to push the last one out," Martha said. "But he was oversized."

"It's one of them mysteries," Curiosity agreed. "Takes no time at all to get one planted and hours of hard work to make the trip in the opposite direction. Kitty, we'll need that basin of warm water now."

While the younger girl was in the next room ladling water at the hearth, Martha gestured Curiosity to bend down to her in the bed.

"Yes, child."

"There ain't nothing to tell you about Albany. We never was in the courthouse, never saw the judge or anybody."

"Did you hear Richard Todd talking to your man at all?"

Martha shook her head, and put her hands to her belly. "Starting again," she panted. When the contraction had let up its grip, Martha collapsed against her pillow and blew a damp tendril of hair away from her face. "I like Miss Elizabeth," she said. "I wouldn't do nothing to cause her misery."

"You wouldn't lie to the judge?"

"I can say what I saw, but I wouldn't make nothing up."

Curiosity grunted softly.

"Can I have something to drink?"

When she had finished sipping from the cup Curiosity offered her, she wiped her mouth and glanced at the older woman fitfully. "But it weren't right, her running off that way in the dead of night. I wouldn't have thought it of her." She said this softly, but she meant it. Curiosity wasn't surprised, she had heard it before in the village.

"We do what we got to do," Curiosity said quietly. "Ain't that so, Miz Kitty?"

Kitty was standing at the foot of the bed with the basin in her hands. She watched as Martha coped with the next pain, grabbing hold of the rope Curiosity had tied to the foot of the bed so that the tendons on her lower arms stood out in relief as she pulled. The bed creaked and groaned with it, and at the end Martha put back her head and howled. The water sloshed in the basin as Kitty took a step backward.

"You come over here by her side," Curiosity said. "Help her

sit up when the pains come, so she can put some muscle behind her push."

Kitty hesitated, and Curiosity shot her a sharp look.

"I got things to do down on this end," Curiosity explained. "She cain't keep her misery to herself anymore, and she will yell it out. A little noise ain't goin' to turn you blue, now is it?"

"I didn't know it hurts so much," Kitty said. "There's nothing I can do."

"You can stop whining," Curiosity shot back at her. "It's Martha here who's got the hardest work to do. Don' you go running out on her."

Kitty came forward reluctantly. Curiosity took the basin from her and set it down, and then she took the girl by the wrist, startling her. She pressed Kitty's palm against the bulk of Martha's belly.

"Feel this child trying to find its way into the world."

There was a sudden tightening and a ripple. Kitty's face rippled and changed, too. Not in horror, but in sudden understanding.

"It feels like a hand," the girl said, hoarsely.

Martha moaned softly.

"Let's hope that's a foot," she said to Kitty. "Otherwise we got our work cut out for us."

Kitty was looking between Martha and Curiosity. Her sleepiness was gone, the distant look in her eyes banished for the moment. "Will you come to me when it's my time?"

"I surely will," Curiosity said. "If you want me there. Now will you do something for me?"

"I can't tell you about Albany and the court and Elizabeth," Kitty said. "I promised Richard I wouldn't. He says it's important."

Curiosity laughed. "Men got one kind of important," she said. "Women got another." She was folding the nightclothes back, her slim, dark hands busy and knowing as Martha's flesh bulged and buckled.

"It's coming," Martha panted.

"So it is," Curiosity agreed. "Whether it's got a mind to or not." But her face was suddenly set in worry lines that she could not hide.

. . .

The public house was a dark, small place, an extension tacked onto Anna Hauptmann's trading post without attention to detail or comfort. It had once been a pigsty, until her father claimed it for his own purposes in a fit of boredom. Axel rebuilt one wall to put in a hearth, and he began to divide his day between his daughter's place of business and the distillery he set up in the barn. There he turned out a respectable ale and a clear schnapps that earned a reputation as far away as Albany. He kept the secrets of the distillery close to the vest, but Axel was soon forgiven this lack of generosity because he sold his products cheap, as he was more interested in company and discussion than he was in profits. Within a year the tavern was known up and down the territory as a place a man could go after sunset and be sure of a welcome and a strong drink. In the winter it was warm and in the summer the doors stood open, and it was a rare evening that Axel had less than three men to entertain him. As the floor was usually awash with tobacco juice, they were relatively safe from skirted visitors, a situation which was not the least of the tavern's attractions.

Julian Middleton had soon become his most reliable patron. The hunters and trappers who came out of the bush to call had adjusted to Julian without any trouble, once they had figured out that he could be ignored. He was the overdressed, underworked son of a man who couldn't hold on to his money or govern his daughter, but he had a gift for light talk and looking the other way, and so they tolerated him. Night after night Julian sat in front of Axel's fire and took up whatever subject was offered to him while he drank warm ale or warmer cider from a crusty old jug that had to be plucked out from among the cinders. Some of the farmers came in, too, but only for long enough to toss back what they weren't allowed at home, rarely contributing to the conversation. Sometimes Julian chose not to talk; nobody much seemed to mind that, either.

For his part, Julian saw the crude tavern as the only amusing spot in Paradise. The drink was cheap and the company was anything but demanding. When he had money to spend on schnapps, he applied himself to an appreciation of its rude integrity. Since Lizzie had solved all their financial problems—or the ones she knew about—there was a bit of swag in his pocket, and Julian had been making a careful study of Axel's art.

This evening there wasn't much company. Moses Southern had been turned out of his home while his wife churned out a third or fourth child—Julian couldn't remember how many he had; didn't care enough to ask. Perched on a stool in the corner, Galileo sat whittling by the light of a pine knot. On occasion he answered a question when Axel thought of something to ask him, but mostly he kept to himself. Julian was glad to see Galileo there; he could drink what he wanted and still be sure of getting home to his bed. He thought of offering the man ale, but he looked at Moses and discarded the idea; he wasn't in the mood to argue. He had had his fill of arguments for years to come—Richard Todd had seen to that. Richard, who had never been much fun as a sporting man, was turning out to be even less amusing these days, now that he fancied himself wronged. Here or there, Tory or Yank, high or low, men you owed money to were all the same, Julian noted.

Bonner had paid off the family debts in good, hard cash, but Todd wasn't satisfied, wouldn't be satisfied until he had a pound or two of flesh. There was more of the savage in him than he cared to admit. Not that he didn't have cause to be angry; Lizzie had publicly embarrassed him and he wasn't the kind to take that lightly.

There was no denying that his clever sister had saved the family from bankruptcy, but she had set the village on its ear to do it. Who would have thought it, virtuous, bookish Lizzie marrying a wild backwoodsman with a half-breed daughter and a reputation for violence. It hadn't escaped Julian that she had had an eye on Nathaniel, but he had put that down to a surprising bit of fun; he hadn't really thought she would go as far as she had, or he might have done something to stop it. The trouble was, he forgot that Lizzie was a woman, and that she was prone to womanly weakness. If she hadn't handed the land over to a bunch of Indians, he might be thankful to her for finally relieving him of the family's scrutiny: her eloping had put the minor matter of his gambling debts into perspective.

Trust a woman to fall in love and get carried away with it. The fact was, virtuous Lizzie had turned out to be nothing more than a cheat and a thief. She had stolen lands from their father, and sooner or later she would have to pay the price. She had stolen the mountain, but worse, she had left them as if she had the right to just walk away. The thought of it was enough to make his gut clench. He would remind her where she belonged, as soon as the opportunity presented itself. She would come back, and bring with her what she had taken from him.

His glass was empty. He was just contemplating how to cope with this fact when the door opened. Julian peered over his boots, half raised up on one elbow. He had been hoping for some decent company, anybody with more brain in his head than Moses Southern, but there was a slight figure outlined in the shadows at the door. A woman, breathing hard. Julian knew that sound, and he stilled, trying to make himself invisible.

Kitty Witherspoon stepped into the light, and Moses jumped to his feet.

"Curiosity sent me," she started, and then pressed her fist against her cheek, pulling her face into half a mask. "We need help. The child is turned and she can't shift it."

Moses just stared.

"I'll fetch Anna," Axel said, turning for the inner door which led to the living quarters.

"Wait," Kitty said. Then she caught sight of Julian before the hearth, and her color flared. Julian met her cold look with a nod of his own, and the quick flash of a single dimple. It didn't move her; he hadn't thought it would, but what else was there to do but try?

She turned her face away. "Curiosity said to send for Falling-Day."

"No!" said Moses, the word exploding from him in a mist of ale. He cleared his throat. "Anna will do fine."

Kitty's head snapped around, and she looked him straight in the eye. "But Curiosity said—"

"I won't have that red bitch touching my wife!" Moses thundered.

Kitty stepped back from him as if he had raised a hand to her, just as Axel stepped forward for the same reason. But it was Julian she was looking at.

"You watch your language, now," Axel said.

Kitty cast a sidelong look Julian's way, her mouth curved down. He knew that look, what she meant to say with it. He looked away.

Kitty said, "Martha is in a bad way."

"Julian ain't got nothing better to do," said Axel. "He can go along and fetch Falling-Day."

The evening was a loss anyway, and it unnerved him to have Kitty standing there, her arms crossed over her middle. He nodded, and his boots hit the floor with a thump. He hadn't had a conversation with her in— How long was it? A week? Not since Todd had told him to back off. Just as well, really. She was a sweet enough girl, but she had a way about her that reminded him of old Merriweather: she would eat him whole, if it suited her, and never blink. That was the problem with English-women, and with most American ones, as well. If Todd was willing to step in and take credit for that swelling under her apron, so much the better.

He thought of a jaunt up to Lake in the Clouds and found it didn't displease him. That buck of Many-Doves' was still out in the bush, after all. And since Nathaniel and Elizabeth had run off, all the Mohawk had been staying out of the village.

But Moses had other ideas. "Ain't no way in this world I'm letting that redskin into my cabin."

Axel combed his beard thoughtfully with the fingers of one hand while he looked Moses over, from head to foot. "Ja, what kind of fool are you, then? Curiosity knows what she's doin', after all. If she's calling for Falling-Day, she must need her. It's yer wife and child, man."

"I have to get back." Kitty looked at Moses, frowning. "Maybe you should come along with me and see what distress your wife is in. Maybe that would convince you."

Moses nodded. "I'll do that," he said, cramming his cap on his head. "But I ain't coming alone."

In the end they all went. Anna, still flushed with sleep and with her plaits draped over her shoulders, carried a basket of odds and ends. Axel had a bottle of schnapps tucked under his arm. It had its medicinal uses, he pointed out. And failing that, it was a dandy rub for sore joints. Moses herded them out of the door, sullen and wild-eyed. Julian brought up the rear, reluctantly.

"You'll go off to them Mohawk otherwise," Moses had reasoned. Julian had no intention of going anywhere, he explained. Voluntarily he would seek no exertion beyond the lifting of his glass. The man wouldn't listen.

"I ain't so sure of that," said Southern. "Your sister married in up there, didn't she? And then there's that young squaw."

"I hope you aren't holding me responsible for my sister's actions," said Julian, ignoring the second comment studiously. "For she certainly would never take any responsibility for mine."

"You talk too much," was Southern's only reply.

Well, then, Julian thought to himself. *I needn't point out the obvious to you.* With all of Moses' concern about Julian running off, he hadn't even taken note of the fact that Galileo had slipped away into the night as soon as Kitty had made the purpose of her errand known. He had been gone for a good half hour, perhaps more.

In the cool night air Julian found himself surprisingly close to sober; he almost was to the point of appreciating the ridiculous picture they made tramping along in a row, when from ahead there was a long, rippling scream that rose and faded away just as suddenly. It was then that they came into the dooryard of the Southern cabin.

Anna had been muttering the whole time to Moses, a line of argument about women's work and men's folly and Falling-Day that had affected Moses as much as the pale moonlight that lit the way. At the sound of the scream she had turned to him with something like triumph on her face. And then she lifted her skirts above her unlaced boots to reveal her legs, unexpectedly slim and girllike, and ran. She ran like a woman half her age and disappeared into the open maw of the cabin.

The men stood there, Moses included, and listened to the next scream spiral and rise and then break. When it finished, Anna appeared in the doorframe with the faint light of the cabin behind her, her face as angry and red as Moses' was suddenly set and thoughtful. She opened her mouth and then it snapped shut, suddenly, to be replaced by a concentrated frown.

"Thank the Lord!" She disappeared back into the shadows while the rest of them turned to see what she had seen.

Axel cleared his throat, and waved the torch he was carrying. "Evening, Hawkeye," he said, nodding. "Falling-Day."

If not for the white flow of his hair, Julian thought, the man could have been mistaken for his son in the near dark. They were that much alike, from the shape of the hairline to the set of the shoulders. The Bonner men were strong breeding stock. He thought of his sister and wondered if she had already found this out for herself.

Moses, on the other hand, resembled nothing so much as a great horny toad. He was inflating his lungs, sticking his chest out in front of him. If it weren't for the infernal screaming, Julian thought that it might be quite amusing, watching Moses make a fool of himself.

"You want to have a word with me while the women look after your wife, I'm here to talk," Hawkeye said easily to Moses. He sent Falling-Day a sideways look and she disappeared into the cabin without a word.

"I don't want your squaw here."

"First off, she ain't a squaw," said Hawkeye. "That's a damn impolite word, and I'll thank you not to use it. Second, she ain't mine. Now, you want Falling-Day out of there, you go in, then, haul her on out," he suggested. "See how your wife feels about that."

Moses spat, jerking his head at the last minute so that the spittle flew into the shadows. Hawkeye didn't flinch, but in the torchlight Julian saw something in his eyes, a flickering. Moses saw it, too; he stepped back, wary.

Axel laughed, and stepped between them to thrust his bottle of schnapps at Hawkeye. "Damn it, Dan'l. I'm too old to get caught up in a pissing contest in the middle of the night, and so're you. Have a swallow, and let's set."

Hawkeye kept his gaze on Moses for another three counts. It was damn impressive, the heat the man could throw with a stare. Julian wondered if he could learn to do that.

Then Hawkeye's attention traveled around to him.

"We got the making of a party, that's true enough," he said to Axel, taking the bottle. "Though not a particular happy one, by the looks of young Julian here." As if to agree, Martha's voice rose again and then ebbed. There was a lot of hurried movement inside the cabin, where the door still stood wide open. Moses had turned his attention in that direction, and stood staring.

"She's in good hands," Axel said to Moses in a kinder tone than he had used before. "Falling-Day has got a knack for the business."

"I don't care to be beholden to her," Moses snapped. "And if some harm comes to my wife or my child, she'll pay in kind."

"*Maria nah,*" sighed Axel. "What a fool you are."

"Let me just make one thing clear," Hawkeye said, in a congenial tone of voice which had no obvious connection to the cold expression in his eyes. "I'll mind my manners for a few more minutes here, out of respect for Martha. She was done a dirty turn by her daddy when he married her off to you—hold it now," he said quietly. "Hear me out. I won't have you talking like that about a woman who's in there trying to save your wife's life. Do it again and I'll feed you your teeth one by one."

"Are you threatening me?" Moses thundered.

Hawkeye blinked at him slowly. "You do catch on, eventual."

"You heard him, didn't you, Middleton? Heard the whoreson threaten me?" Moses had turned toward Julian, who leaned against the woodpile with one shoulder. Then he looked Julian up and down, his mouth curved in disgust. "What am I asking you for? Your sister is as bad as any of them, selling out to that pack of savages and thieves." His laugh was a harsh barking sound. "A few years ago we would have had a way to deal with the likes of her," he said, grinning. "A lesson or two for the teacher that she wouldn't forget. How to stick with her own kind."

Moses seemed to have forgotten about Hawkeye, forgotten about everybody but Julian, who stood listening to the ranting with one brow cocked. The man didn't even take note when Hawkeye came up behind him. He let out a surprised whoosh of air when the rifle butt tapped him on the back of the head, and collapsed in an awkward bundle at Julian's feet.

Hawkeye stood looking down at him.

"The man is a damn nuisance," he said. "I'd rather listen to Martha holler."

"He'll be hollering loud enough tomorrow, wait and see," noted Axel.

"I'm afraid I've had enough of the festivities," Julian said as he stepped over Moses. "Although it's been highly amusing."

"Tell me, Middleton," Hawkeye said, leaning on the barrel of his rifle. "What does it take to rouse you?"

Julian laughed softly. "Rousing is quite outside my sphere of experience since I've been here. Something I don't have in common with my sister, if you'll allow me an observation without taking your rifle to my skull."

"Wouldn't dream of stopping you," said Hawkeye. "Go on and talk about your sister, I'd like to hear what you've got to say."

"Oh, I'm sure you would," Julian agreed. "But you're mistaken if you're looking to me to defend her good name. It is a lost cause, I fear. And beyond that, I haven't the energy or the inclination."

"Your sister don't need your protection anymore."

"For her sake, I hope you are correct in that," Julian agreed, the usual mocking lilt gone from his tone.

Hawkeye said, "Someday, something is going to take you by surprise and wake you up."

Julian shrugged. A picture came to him: Many-Doves bent over a book in his sister's schoolhouse. The sweep of her brows, the color of the skin over her cheekbones.

"I very much doubt that," he said, turning away.

From the open cabin door there was the faint mewling cry of a newborn baby.

"Stay and drink the child's health," called Axel behind him. "His daddy can't."

But Julian waved a hand over his head lazily without bothering to turn back. He was not surprised to see Galileo was waiting in the shadows. They walked on together in silence to the wagon. Julian climbed up without a comment, resting his head on the back of the seat to watch the stars revolving over him.

Later, lying awake in his bed listening to his father's restless turning in the next room, he was amazed at himself. What had come over him, he wondered, to have passed up such a rare opportunity as a free drink?

XXXII

For all of her life she had been coddled and spoiled, Elizabeth knew; finally, the time of reckoning was at hand. She drew in a ragged breath, cursed halfheartedly, and tried in vain not to yelp.

"I'll stop whining," she muttered out loud. "I will, I will stop being such a coward."

Nathaniel was sitting cross-legged with her bare foot balanced on one of his knees. He paused in his work to look up at her. "There's not a cowardly bone in you," he said. "And you're doing fine."

Elizabeth was determined to look only at his face and no lower; certainly she had no intention of looking at the needle held so purposefully between his long fingers, but as that was almost impossible she looked away completely.

"Good thing you brought a sewing kit along," he observed, dropping another shard of wood onto the small pile beside her.

"A lady," she said through clenched teeth, "is always prepared for mishaps."

He grinned up at her briefly. "Once Bears opened up his palm with a knife, he was that crazy to get a skelf out."

"That sounds perfectly reasonable to me," she said, and then yelped again. "And what is a skelf, if I might ask?"

Nathaniel held up a small shred of wood impaled on his needle. "That's a skelf. What do you call it?"

"Misery." Elizabeth grimaced. "Otherwise I suppose I'd call it a sliver. *Skelf* must be Scots."

"Hmmm," Nathaniel agreed absently. He had a set to his jaw she didn't like, and so she looked away.

There was an eagle circling over the tops of the pine trees, raw, gliding power. She could hear the way its wings cut the air. Or she could, she was sure, if she just concentrated hard enough. Vaguely she was aware of the sound of running water from the stream just behind them, and the way her own sweat ran down her face into her eyes and stung, stung, stung. She rocked her head back and bit her lip.

"Would you relax, Boots?"

"As soon as you get the last of it out of my foot, yes, why then I will be happy to relax," she shot at him. He was frowning, one corner of his mouth turned down in concentration, and her tone seemed not to unsettle him in the least.

They were in a secluded glen between a mountain and an incredible fortress of boulders which seemed to have tumbled down directly from the heavens. Many of them were taller than Nathaniel, most of them were slick with moisture and a deep green moss. They had been crossing the rockfall when Elizabeth had misstepped and landed with all her weight on a nest of deadwood.

Moccasins had their limitations, oh, yes. Any of her boots, which had been such an extravagance and had earned her her nickname—those silly, vain, immoderate, oh so lovely boots with their leather soles—would have kept her feet protected. The muscles rolled and cramped in her lower leg.

"When my hair got plucked I got water in my eyes, often as not," Nathaniel said in a conversational tone.

Unexpectedly intrigued, Elizabeth came up on her elbows. "Your hair plucked? Your scalp, for battle?"

"Aye, and the rest of it." He grinned without looking at her. "It's not attractive to the Kahnyen'kehàka, in case you didn't know. Chest hair and the like."

"But you . . ." She paused, looking at him hard. He had shaved this morning, as he did every morning, with a straight-edged razor. More than once she had wondered why he bothered, but she liked him clean shaven, the line of his jaw and the angle of his chin, and so she had not said anything at all. Every evening, in spite of his careful attentions, his cheeks were rough with new growth, something she had learned to anticipate and also to appreciate. She looked at him now, the deep, thick growth of the hair on his head and the way it hung in waves over his shoulders. It struck her that there was little hair on him otherwise, and that this might be unusual.

"If you pull it out by the roots and you keep doing it long enough, it gives up eventually," he explained.

Elizabeth twitched as another splinter was pulled from her foot.

"You mean to say that you plucked the hair from your chest? Every day?"

"Not me," said Nathaniel. "There was an old woman in the Turtle longhouse, she did the tattooing and the hair pulling, mostly. Said I had a good face and that it would be worth the trouble to get rid of the hair, so I could find a wife. Took me on as a project. Every morning and every evening she'd just about sit down on top of me to keep me still and she'd go to work on me with her shells."

"You're making this up," Elizabeth said.

"I ain't," Nathaniel said, distracted momentarily from his story while he concentrated on her foot. Then he pulled another sliver. "She had shells tied together with a piece of rawhide, notched on two edges so she could grab with them. Or she used her fingers, for the scalp."

"I'm glad to see she didn't mind those growing back," Elizabeth said dryly. "So how long did it take?"

He shrugged. "I guess maybe three years, at least until my chest was clean enough to suit her."

"Well, I would hope that was enough," Elizabeth said. "What else could she have had in mind? Not your legs . . ." Her voice trailed away.

Nathaniel said, "She was trying to do me a service, but I drew the line below my belly. Thought any girl who couldn't see past the hair on my"—he raised an eyebrow at her—"legs wasn't worth worrying over."

"The question is why you put up with it at all," Elizabeth said, flustered.

"Maybe I was just vain, did you think of that? And besides, Ya-wa-o-da-qua told stories while she worked." He was squeezing the tender flesh of the ball of her foot between two fingers, and then he plucked suddenly and made a satisfied sound. "Not much more to go," he said. "But there's one pretty deep, so you hold tight now, Boots."

Elizabeth had been propping herself up on her elbows, but she lay back down and put an arm across her eyes. "What does her name mean?"

"Ya-wa-o-da-qua? Pincushion. Don't laugh, it's true. Hold still, Boots." There was a sharp jab of the needle; she thought she was prepared for it, but she reared up anyway, and there was Nathaniel, grinning. There was a swipe of her blood on his cheek, and a wickedly long and bloody sliver on the end of the needle. "I think that's the last of it. You did good."

"I sniveled," she corrected him, out of sorts. There was blood running down her foot; it was a most disquieting sensation.

"But nicely," he allowed. He helped her up and then to the stream, where he saw her settled on a boulder with the injured foot in the water. This stream came off the mountain and it was ice-cold even this far into the spring, but it numbed the ache in her foot and she swished it back and forth, not unhappily. Nathaniel was rummaging in the packs, his back to her.

"We'll make camp here and get you poulticed. There's a storm coming on anyway."

"So say the blackfly," Elizabeth agreed, rubbing her neck. The exposed skin from collar to her hairline was raised to washerboard consistency by a hundred tiny welts. After a few days of dampness, the blackfly moved in armies of thousands and millions, and today there had been a particularly difficult confrontation with them. Her skin felt warm to the touch and she was almost light-headed with it, but she knew that in the morning it would be gone. Until the next encounter with the little beasties. She cast an irritated look at Nathaniel; he was scratching, too, but less. He had coated his face and hands with ointment, and it had kept him relatively protected.

Elizabeth struggled hard not to let her irritation get the upper hand. There was a point, she concluded, at which the only possible tool was numbness; she could not manufacture an artificial cheerfulness when she itched and hurt and smelled. But Nathaniel didn't seem to mind her mood; in fact, the more taciturn she became, the more his own dry humor rose to the surface. It was something she hadn't anticipated, and she liked him for it tremendously. It almost made up for the infernal blackfly.

Nathaniel came up behind her with his hands cupped. Elizabeth tipped her head back to look at him upside down and dissolved in a genuine smile as he smoothed pennyroyal ointment over the mass of tiny welts. Her nose wrinkled at the smell, but the relief was undeniable. She let her head rest against the hard plank of his abdomen, her plait brushing the ground. He looked down at her, all seriousness, while he wiped her face gently with a square of muslin that had once been a part of her second shift.

"If you coated yourself with this every morning you'd be better off," he said.

Elizabeth sighed softly in response. Mrs. Schuyler had given her the concoction of pine tar, castor oil, and pennyroyal before she set off with Bears, vowing that a liberal coating on face, neck, and hands would ward off any biting insect. Thus far, though, Elizabeth had preferred the blackfly to the pungent stink and its deep brown color. But she knew that unless the insects simply disappeared, she would soon have to resort to grease or ointment, or learn to live with ravaged skin. They might spend another two weeks or more living in the bush, and it was time she faced that reality.

"Do you really know where we are?" she asked, suddenly wondering.

"I do."

"Amazing. Have you never been lost, then?"

"No, I can't say that I have. Although I was mighty disoriented once for a few days."

Elizabeth laughed out loud, and reached up with both hands to pull his head down to her, where she kissed him and rubbed a tender cheek against his.

"Don't get too friendly," he said. "There's more yet to come. We got to clean out that wound. A bit of salt would do the job, or some spirits. I've got some of Axel's schnapps along."

Elizabeth thought of the jagged hole and blanched. "Is that really necessary?" she asked.

"Aye," he said, "we best get it over with. Then we can work on making you feel better."

It was a hot, searing kind of pain that spiraled instantaneously into a great burst of color, but it didn't last long. Elizabeth bit down hard on the urge to scream; if no other lesson had been learned, Nathaniel had made it clear to her how important it was to keep their noise down to a minimum. But tears brimmed in her eyes and the world doubled and tripled. When it cleared, Nathaniel bound her wound with her third-best handkerchief dampened with Axel's schnapps, and then slipped the delinquent moccasin back on her foot. With a few deft motions he pulled her legging down and laced the moccasin over it. Elizabeth observed while he sewed the tear in the sole with the same needle he had used to fish the splinters out.

"Very handy of you," she noted, still out of sorts.

"You should be able to walk on this tomorrow."

"I intend to walk now. Can't we camp on the shore back there?" Just before her misstep, they had come past a small lake with a good protected place to settle under an outcropping of rock. At that point they had thought to walk for another three hours, but now Elizabeth was glad to have a valid excuse to go back. It had been an unusually pretty place, even for this wilderness. And since she had finally learned the basics of swimming, she took every opportunity to practice.

Nathaniel took all the packs and let her manage on her own, limping gingerly. She felt slightly silly, and looked around herself as if there might be curious neighbors watching. Instead, she caught a pair of fox cubs at play in the sun before their burrow hole, their red coats gleaming bright. They looked at her without fear, and she looked back.

Once settled, Nathaniel gathered wood for a fire. The shore was lined with a wide margin of sweet flag, and he pulled up great armfuls of the long green spikelike leaves to lay over the burning wood. The smoke that rose and filled the air would keep flying things away.

Elizabeth breathed a sigh of contentment, knowing that she should rouse herself to see to the food, but she was feeling strangely indolent. Reclining on the smooth, warm expanse of rock, she enjoyed the feel of the breeze on her inflamed face.

"I must look a sight," she said. "And you needn't bother to contradict me."

"I wouldn't dream of it, Boots."

She snorted, and liking the sound of it, snorted again. "If I had the energy I'd make you pay for that," she said, and grinned in spite of herself.

"Now you're fishing for more than compliments," he said, eyeing her with one raised brow while he shredded a long stalk of grass and tossed bits into the fire, absentmindedly.

She looked out over the lake, thought about swimming, and then lay back down lazily.

"And if I were? Isn't that my right?"

He came to sit beside her. "Aye, that it is. So what is it you want?"

She managed to look him in the eye. "A day abed with you without the need to get up and go."

Nathaniel leaned over her. "I please you, then, do I?" He wasn't smiling anymore, but there was a contented look about him.

She pushed at him a little. "You know that you do."

"Well, then, Boots, I'm glad to hear it. Because you please me mightily, too."

"I don't recall using the word *mightily*," Elizabeth said primly, and she yelped as he grabbed her, pulling her up against him to pinch her bottom.

"Mightily! Ow! Mightily!" she conceded, laughing and trying to squirm away from him.

He settled down with her half-pulled across his chest.

"Can we do that, tomorrow?" she asked. "Stay abed?" She knew the answer before he shook his head, but it was a disappointment anyway.

"Wouldn't be wise. We'll have our days abed, if you haven't got tired of the business by then."

"Oh, now who's fishing for compliments?" she asked. She sat up to look around herself. There was a small island in the middle of the lake, populated by beech trees and crowned with a few tall pine trees that reflected unevenly in the water.

"Shall we swim out there?" she asked lazily, lying down again.

"Not with your foot the way it is," he said. Instead of rising, Nathaniel stretched out and pulled her head to a more comfortable spot on his shoulder. This pleased her, but it was hard to ignore the rumbling in her stomach.

"There's trout enough for the taking," she suggested.

But Nathaniel was pointing into the sky, and she followed the line of his arm and drew in a sharp breath.

Above them the eagle still circled, but she wasn't alone.

Against the gathering clouds, the pair dodged around each other and then seemed to purposely collide in midair. With locked talons they plummeted downward in a free-fall interrupted by a series of complex somersaults. Suddenly they tore free of one another.

"They mate for life, but they go through this every season anyway," Nathaniel said. The pair was rising again, the sound of their wings clearly discernible. Talons struck and the birds fell in a swoop that ended in a long roll. Once more the performance was repeated, and this time the male covered his mate in mid-fall with a great scream of triumph, a sound almost human.

"Not exactly lovely Venus consorting with Mars," said Nathaniel. "But you might call it sporting."

Elizabeth stifled her laughter against his chest. "Very unseemly, this conversation."

"But you like it anyway."

"I like it precisely for that reason," she said, suddenly thoughtful. "It is a great luxury, the freedom to speak what is on my mind. What other person in the world—male or female —could I ask about these things?"

"Don't go imagining I'll always have an answer," Nathaniel said.

"It isn't an answer I want—"

"Aye," Nathaniel interrupted her, squeezing her hand. "It's

the freedom to talk. I know, I know. So you're in the mood for talk just now?"

Elizabeth didn't answer. She looked into the shadows of the forest, wondering about the eagles. "She didn't seem to enjoy it very much, did she? Nor did he, for that matter."

"They don't take joy in mowin', not the way folks do." He glanced at her out of the corner of his eye. "It's a good sign, anyway," he said. He had a thoughtful look about him.

She still found it strange sometimes to hear that Nathaniel took such things seriously, signs he read from the animals and the stars and his own dreams, in which he sometimes flew over the world. Her first and strongest impulse was to reject it all as wishful thinking, but slowly she was beginning to wonder not so much about the truth value of Nathaniel's beliefs, but at his powers of observation.

"Do you think we'll be like that, always struggling and then coming back together?" she asked.

He rubbed a hand across her back. "I expect we'll tussle," he said. His rubbing became slower and more purposeful, and she shifted a little and murmured against his chest.

"You're tired," he said. "And you hurt, I guess."

"It's not so bad," Elizabeth admitted. She was tired, that was true; she thought she might never move another muscle. But if she gave Nathaniel any encouragement at all, they would forget about swimming and food altogether for a while. It would take her mind off her foot; he could make her forget anything and everything when he came to her.

"Come, then," he said into her hair, tugging on the clasp to release it. "Come consort with me, darlin'. If you've the mind for a little venery, that is."

She could feel him smile, but she didn't rise to his teasing. Instead Elizabeth ran her hands over his chest, breathed in his smells. She could get dizzy sometimes, this close to him. With one finger she traced the line of his jaw, and thought about kissing him. She intended to kiss him, and very soon, but for the moment she was content with thinking about it.

"Boots, tell me, tell me what you want," he said against her ear.

She squirmed a bit and buried her face in the curve of his

neck, gasped as she felt him cup her hips and pull her up against him. She slid a hand down his belly.

But Nathaniel caught her hand and held it away from him, his head tilted hard to one side and his expression suddenly preoccupied and distant. Elizabeth froze, seeing his concentration directed outward, to the forest. He heard something. She softened her own breathing, closing her eyes to screen out distractions in an attempt to hear what he did. There was something, just above the sounds of the lake. It might have been the wind on the cliff face, but the treetops stood unruffled against the sky. It came and went and then came again. Singing. Very faint, but clearly singing.

Nathaniel was on his feet, reaching for his gun. "Stay here," he said softly.

"No." She stood up, too, and then staggered.

He pushed her back down, gently. "Scoot all the way under there, and keep yourself small. Do you have the musket? Good. I'm just going to have a look."

After a moment she did as he had directed, sitting with her knees under her chin and the musket in the valley of her lap. She watched him skirting the lake. He stopped to listen and then walked on again, disappearing into the bush with a brief look back toward her. Elizabeth stood up then, unable to stay still. Listening with all her power of concentration, she could hear nothing at all except the sounds of the lake, and the birds. The singing—if it had been singing—had stopped.

They weren't often apart in the last days, and when they were, it was a strange thing. It was true that she was more and more at ease in the forests, but Elizabeth knew that she was still very vulnerable. While Nathaniel hunted she saw after her clothes, or his, or cooking, any task to take her mind off what frightened her most: what would happen if he didn't come back. It wasn't so much being lost that worried her, although that was a real danger, one too vivid to be contemplated for long. But what worried her more was coming back to Paradise without Nathaniel. Facing Hannah, and Hawkeye. And her own life, without him. The longer he was gone, the more detailed her anxieties became.

There was a shrill whistle; she turned to see Nathaniel

emerge from the forest farther up the shoreline. He came toward her at a trot. His preoccupation was still there, but some of the tension was gone.

"Man hurt," he said.

"Who?"

"Don't know him. He's got shelter up there, but he's in bad shape." Nathaniel began to gather up their things.

"Very bad?" she asked, reaching for her pack.

"Aye," said Nathaniel. "He's dying."

XXXIII

Nathaniel set her to hauling water. In spite of her foot, and the fact that the stream was a good distance, and the awkward makeshift rawhide bucket, and the great deal of water they would need; in spite of all that, he set her to the task, and waited until she had started off for the first time before he went into the shelter. The fact was, he didn't know whether or not the man was dangerous, and he just didn't care for the idea of Elizabeth nearby. Not yet.

The singing had faded away just before he came upon the camp, where he had found the stranger in an uneasy and fevered sleep. Looking at him, it hadn't taken much for Nathaniel to figure out that he was on the run: his skin was the deep color of wild plums in August, his hair and beard like mottled fleece, his hands great overused tools. On his heavily muscled upper chest there was a brand that Nathaniel could just see through the opening in the homespun shirt. A runaway slave, of a good age, but strong. And he was dying. The deeply sunken eyes gave it away. That, and his left arm: below the shoulder it had swollen to twice its normal size, straining the hunting shirt he wore to bursting. The stink of putrefaction hung about him like a burial blanket.

Before he fetched Elizabeth, Nathaniel had spent some time looking around. Things were out of kilter here, and it worried him. A lean-to carefully built out of the materials at hand by a

man who knew his work, who had more intelligence and imagination than tools. Inside the shelter there was a makeshift cot
and a flattish boulder that served as a table. On an old blanket
spread out neatly Nathaniel saw an ancient musket, but no evidence of shot or powder, some snares, a single beaver trap, and
the remains of a meal of rabbit and fiddlehead ferns on a mat of
woven reeds. In a rough carved bowl covered by a flat rock
there was some dried meat and peas, but otherwise no provisions. Outside there was a hatchet, a short shovel, a hammer, a
knife, a whetstone, a single cook pot, all scattered to the ele-
ments and already showing the first faint glimmer of rust. This
had been the first sign that something was very wrong; Nathaniel knew instinctively that a man who could plan and build this
camp would never have treated his tools in such a way; they
stood between him and extinction.

Nathaniel reached up and poked a hole in the roof, and then
he started a small fire below it, burning the filthy grass bedding
and then the roofing material itself—bark shingles mostly,
lashed together with cord braided of roots—to drive the stench
away. Even while he worked, the man didn't wake, and Nathaniel wondered whether he would at all, or if he would slip
away without even telling them his name.

When Elizabeth returned for the third time with the filled
bucket, he sent her back down to the lake to bring him as much
sweet flag as she could carry. She went without a complaint,
trying to hide her limp.

Through all this the man slept, twitching and starting. He
cried out in pain and then mumbled, slipping back down into a
deeper sleep. In his dreams he was fighting a battle other than
the one that would kill him. Nathaniel couldn't make sense of
his fears, of the things he had done to protect himself. There
were piles of rocks, fist-sized and right for throwing; dried
grasses twisted into torches, maybe thirty of them that Nathaniel could see just inside the shelter. A pike constructed of three
long branches bound together with a sharpened stone at one
end, as if to fight something he had no wish to be near. And
then there were the pits.

They were the first thing he had pointed out to Elizabeth
when he brought her up here, one by one. Each had been

covered by bark mats, and Nathaniel had only narrowly missed a fall before he saw them, spaced irregularly around the camp. He had searched them out, yanking the covers off and throwing them onto the cold cook pit. They were all of the same good depth, but not so deep that you couldn't climb out—except a man who fell in wouldn't be in any shape for climbing: each one was studded with slender branches sharpened to a lethal point.

When the sweet flag was burning inside the shelter, Nathaniel asked Elizabeth to start the cooking fire and see to the food. It was twilight, and they were both hungry. She did as he asked, but he could see by the set of her jaw that she had gone long enough without information. He joined her at the cooking pit, hunkering down beside her while she worked. And he told her what he knew about what was to come.

"A doctor?" Elizabeth asked feebly, when he had finished.

"It's too late to take the arm off. Even if there was time to go fetch somebody."

"I see." She was cutting meat into chunks and tossing it into the pot. There was a settled quality to her face when she worked through a problem. Nathaniel watched her thinking, almost seeing the darting of the ideas behind her eyes. Looks-Hard was Runs-from-Bears' name for her, but it was a good one.

"He could take some broth, couldn't he?" she asked quietly.

"I expect he could," Nathaniel said. "He probably ain't had anything for more than a day."

"How long do you think it will be?"

He shrugged. "Hard to say. He's strong, and he's fighting. But he's been lying there for a while, and fever takes a lot out of a man. I expect he's about burned out now, so maybe a day."

She caught his eye; he knew she was thinking about Todd. It worried him, too, but they couldn't leave the man to die alone.

"How close behind us do you think Richard is?"

"Don't know, really." He cleared his throat, and then tried again. "We have done some backtracking, but he knows his way around and we leave a good trail. Two days, I'd guess, if we set still. Maybe less."

She digested this in silence, her hands moving automatically about the task in front of her.

"I don't want anyone killed," she said. "If it comes to that, then I think we should go back with him."

Nathaniel watched her work, but his real attention was turned to the forests around them. He knew what she wanted; he didn't know if he could give it to her, and so he promised her nothing at all.

Behind them, there was a shifting and a groan from the shelter. They waited, tense, and then stood when the singing started. The voice shaky at first, and then settling a little into a fine tenor.

"Why, that's Latin," said Elizabeth.

"Aye," said Nathaniel. "The Agnus Dei." And to her quizzical expression, he finished: "From the mass."

"How is it that you recognize the Catholic mass?" she asked, her brow creased in confusion.

"Lots of the Kahnyen'kehàka are Catholic," Nathaniel said. "Not to mention the Scots."

"But not you," Elizabeth said. It was a tone he had never had from her: wary, and put off.

"Oh, aye, once I was," he said softly. "A long time ago."

There was no time to explain any more, because the singing in the shelter had suddenly stopped.

"We had best introduce ourselves," Nathaniel said, brushing off his leggings. "It's the polite thing to do."

Elizabeth had expected the man to be frightened, and uncommunicative. Nathaniel had told her that he was an escaped slave, and she anticipated that such a person would be wary of strangers. Instead, he had a slow smile and he was willing to talk, even eager. His language was accented in a way which reminded her very strongly of Axel, which surprised her again. But she resisted the urge to ask him questions.

The first thing he did, after drinking two bowls of water and introducing himself as Joe, was to apologize that he had no chair to offer her.

"Been meaning to rig something," he explained. "But this sore arm of mine has been keeping me from my work."

Elizabeth glanced uneasily at Nathaniel, but he seemed to take this tremendous understatement in stride. She herself could not bear to look at the arm for long. It lay there tight and so swollen in its wrappings that she thought she could almost see it pulse.

"What happened?" Nathaniel asked. "Get your hand caught in a trap?"

He nodded. "A few days back. But I expect I'll be up and about tomorrow." His eyes turned to Elizabeth, their whites murky gray.

She tried for what she hoped was an encouraging smile. "I've got some broth cooking," she said. "You must be hungry. I hope you don't mind, we added your dried meat to ours."

"Beholden to you." There was something gracious about him that contrasted with the nervous plucking of his fingers at the blanket. "But it's near dark," he pointed out. "And you should both be inside before."

"Before what?" Nathaniel asked.

Joe's head swung toward him in surprise. "Before the Windigo come."

"Windigo?" echoed Elizabeth, turning to Nathaniel.

"The stone men," said Nathaniel softly. There was a new expression in his eyes that Elizabeth did not like at all.

Nathaniel paced up and down while she scooped the thin stew into a bowl.

"He seems so reasonable," she said in a low voice. "Does he really not know he is dying?"

Nathaniel ran a hand through his hair. "Hard to say."

Joe was singing again, his voice hoarser now.

"Does his mind wander from the fever?" she asked. "Is that why he fears—what did he call them?"

"The Windigo. No, that's not the fever. He was afeared of them before he got hurt—it took a long time for him to do all this, these pits."

A thought occurred to Elizabeth and she wiped a stray hair from her cheek as she observed Nathaniel.

"You believe him."

Nathaniel's irritation was easily read from the way the muscles in one cheek jumped. "I've never seen a Windigo," he said. "But yes, I believe him."

"Well, he is being pursued," she said. "Given what should happen if he were caught, I suppose it is not surprising that his fears have grown out of proportion." She held out a bowl to Nathaniel.

He took it slowly. "Not all things lend themselves to rational explanation," he recited. "Do you remember saying that to me?"

She blushed. "I do. But that was about something else, something I had myself experienced. And he's—his mind is wandering, from the poison in his blood. How am I to credit the idea of giants covered with hair set on human flesh?" She glanced toward the shelter.

"The Hode'noshaunee and the others to the east, my grandfather's people, all of them know of the Windigo who live in the bush."

"Has your father ever seen one, or your grandfather?" Elizabeth asked, and then looked away, embarrassed. Nathaniel was disappointed in her, and it made her unhappy to see that on his face. "It does not signify," she said. "He believes, and he is frightened. Perhaps we can put his mind to rest for the little time he has left. I will try to remain open-minded," she offered. "Although I will admit to you that it is hard, Nathaniel."

"Aye, well," he grunted, tipping up the bowl and swallowing. "Let's hope the evidence you'd need to convince you don't decide to come up and shake your hand."

"I was born on a farm on the Mohawk," Joe told her later, when he had taken as much of the broth as he could hold, and in response to her gentle questions. "German Flats, maybe you been down that way. Never learned no English till old Sir Johnson bought me to work his mill, when I was maybe twenty.

That was more than forty year ago, but the Dutch ain't washed out of my mouth yet."

"Did you stay with Johnson long?" Nathaniel asked.

Joe squinted in Nathaniel's direction. "Thirty years, near to. When he died, Molly sold me to a widow woman in Pumpkin Hollow." He had been talking easily, looking back and forth between Elizabeth and Nathaniel, but suddenly he looked away from both of them, out into the open. "Could I have more water?" he asked.

There was some vague memory stirring in Elizabeth, but she couldn't quite bring it forth. She held the bowl of water for Joe as he lifted his head.

"It's sweet, the water up here," he said when he had finished drinking. "Land of plenty," he added. His lips were cracked and discolored with fever, but he smiled weakly anyway.

"There's a pretty sunset," Elizabeth said. She could see it above the trees, all cinnamons and crimsons. The storm had sputtered and then blown away. Tomorrow would be fine and clear. She thought of telling him so, and then hesitated, thinking of what the day would bring.

When she looked down at Joe, his head had dropped back on the cot. "Night comin' on," he whispered. "Time to be indoors. They come in the dark."

She waited, and he took this as encouragement, turning his head toward her.

"Saw the first one over by that big pine, when I settled in here some weeks ago. If there was still snow on the ground you could see his tracks. Scared him off with a torch, that time." He worked the fabric of the blanket between his fingers. "Eyes red as raspberries."

"What do you suppose he wanted?" Elizabeth asked. She was very aware of Nathaniel just behind her as he fed the small fire.

Joe had begun to blink drowsily. "You think I'm a crazy old man."

"No," Elizabeth protested feebly.

He laughed softly. "Well, I'm old enough. But I saw what I saw."

Nathaniel had brought in a small sawed-off log from Joe's

woodpile and upended it, and it served as a sort of stool at the head of the cot. Elizabeth sat there now, and leaned toward Joe. "Tell me, if you like. I'm truly interested."

"Are you? You got that look about you like that young Father Mansard, wondering what trouble I got up to. And looking forward to my confession, see how to set me straight with the Lord."

She had to laugh. "I've never been compared to a priest before," she said. "But I assure you that my interest is real."

"You should be interested," Joe said in a tone that was almost fatherly. It made Elizabeth suddenly wonder about his family, if he had had one he left behind, and what worries they had for him. But his gaze turned toward the deepening dark of the sky in the doorway, and it was troubled.

"They play games with you," he said softly. "Like to scare people. Come close and throw things, run away. Like children set on mischief, throwing rotten apples at a man sweating in the field 'cause they know he cain't run after 'em." He paused, his thoughts very far away. The silence went on until she wondered if he was falling asleep. When he spoke, Elizabeth started at the new strength in his voice.

"In the night sometimes, I hear them moving around. But they don't like fire."

"How could any people survive winter in the bush without fire?" Elizabeth asked.

In the growing dark she could still clearly see the surprise on his face. "The bear do," he said. "The bobcat and the rest, anything with enough of a fur coat."

"So this creature is not a man?"

There was a faint smile on his face. "I see you, Miz Elizabeth. You more and more like that Father Mansard, that Jesuit. You want to talk logic, and I'm talking Windigo. My skin ain't the same color as yours, and you see that, and you believe it. But if I tell you there's another kind of man, with enough of a pelt to live in this bush in the winter, then you sit back and get a frown line."

"You think they sleep through the winter?" Nathaniel asked from behind Elizabeth.

"Never said that. Don't know. All I can say is that in the

night I seen them here, usually a big male, but once there was two of them. Chunking things at me, and howling. And I drove them off with fire."

"Perhaps they meant you no harm," Elizabeth said.

Joe's face contorted. "I wonder if that very same idea is going through the rabbit's head when the shadow of the owl falls over it." Another wave of deep sleepiness moved on his face, but he kept her gaze firmly in his own. "They like to play with folk, scare 'em. But don't be fooled, these ain't no fairy folk. Will you keep that in mind?"

Elizabeth wanted to assure him that she would indeed, but he had slipped away suddenly into sleep. When Nathaniel spoke behind her, she jumped.

"I'll set up in here."

She didn't protest.

By the light of the fire they dozed, and woke and then dozed again. Joe talked in his sleep, mutterings that couldn't be followed. Once Elizabeth rose to go out of the shelter and relieve herself, and when she came back, Nathaniel was sitting up with his arms slung around his knees, staring into the low flames. She stood looking at him for a moment, the strong profile lit by the fire, his eyes hooded with worry. There was grass caught in his hair, and she went to him and took it out.

He caught her wrist and pulled her down next to him.

"When she was a girl," said Elizabeth, "My cousin Amanda would come into my bed at night because she feared the Green Man. Did your mother ever tell you of him?"

When Nathaniel shook his head, she sighed. "I think that for many years I have put the story out of my head quite willfully."

"Tell me."

Elizabeth took a minute to gather her thoughts.

"Oakmere sits on the edge of a great wood. Nothing like these woods—" she said hastily. "But still, for England very large, and old. And there are tales of the Green Man that the common folk tell. I believe it was one of the upstairs maids—a young woman called Maisie—who told it to Amanda one day, although Amanda herself denied that. She claimed to know nothing of it, only that she woke sometimes at night to see a man looking in her window. A man grown out of a tree, she said, with moss for a face and hair of oak leaves and fingers like sticks which he used to scratch upon her window."

Nathaniel leaned in closer to her, and she took his hand to cradle between both of hers.

"Amanda was a flighty girl, very dramatic. But when she came to my bed at night to be comforted, I had no doubt that her fear was real."

There was a mumbling from Joe, and they both looked toward him. When he had settled again, Elizabeth continued.

"I was five years older, you see, and it had always fallen to me to be the sensible cousin to all of them, but especially to Amanda. And I suppose I was well suited to that role. It was one thing that finally gave me some . . . presence in the family. I remember how strangely my uncle Merriweather looked at me, that first night that Amanda woke the whole household screaming and would not take comfort from her mother, nor from anyone but me. He looked at me as though he had never seen me before, and I suppose in a way that was true. He was never cruel to me, I was just . . ." She paused.

"You were invisible to him," Nathaniel supplied.

She nodded, reluctantly. "And so they left it to me to convince Amanda that the Green Man was no more than a tale told at the hearth on a winter's night to entertain. But it didn't matter really what I said to her, she often ended up back shivering at my bedside in the deep of the night, when there was rain especially."

"What happened?" Nathaniel asked.

"She married at eighteen, and moved away," said Elizabeth. "When she had been married some weeks she came home to visit, and I asked her, when I had the opportunity to address her privately, how she was sleeping. I thought perhaps that she might even have forgot about the Green Man."

"But she hadn't."

Elizabeth paused. "No. I remember quite clearly the expression in her eyes, resigned and a little sad. 'He's come along, too,

Lizzie,' she told me. 'Along with the ponies and the silver. I suppose he is mine, and I must learn to live with him.' "

"What are you trying to say?"

"I'm not sure. I suppose I mean to say that we each of us have our personal demons, and that for some they are more . . . tangible than for others. And we carry them with us wherever we go, although we would much rather leave them behind."

"And what demon do you carry with you?" Nathaniel asked, very quietly.

"I am tempted to claim that I have none," she said, leaning against him and staring into the low fire. "But I fear you know me too well already to accept that."

He brought her fingers up to his mouth and kissed them. His eyes rested on her face in a caress as warm and direct as his touch. "Listen, now, because I want you to hear me."

In the night outside the shelter, there was a long, high howl, but Nathaniel's gaze held her steady.

He said, "You'll never be invisible again. Not to me, never to me."

XXXIV

A strong man crying in his sleep was a difficult thing to face with equanimity, but Elizabeth sat with Joe and watched the pain gradually pull him into a reluctant consciousness. Half awake, he seemed to be unaware of them for the moment. Elizabeth was almost glad; she didn't want him to know that Nathaniel had gone to fetch wood, thinking that it would distress him. She herself breathed a secret sigh of relief when he came back into the firelight with his arms full of the logs Joe had split and stacked. Nathaniel went out again because the water was low, this time carrying a torch and his rifle in the crook of his arm.

"You are very uncomfortable," she said to Joe. "Tell me, is there anything specific I can do for you?"

His head turned back and forth on the cot with eyes closed. Elizabeth had dampened a square of muslin from her pack and she wiped his face, noting how dry his skin was. He did not sweat anymore, and there was no fever. She knew this could not be a good sign.

"Joe," she said softly. "Do you have any message for us to take back to your people?"

He opened his eyes.

"It's a poor joke," he said, his tongue thick and his words indistinct. "To come so far and die of a scratch."

"I wish I knew what I might do to comfort you," she said. "I don't even know any prayers of the Catholic church."

Suddenly he was much more awake, and there was something like a smile on his face; she then saw that it was a grimace. "I ain't Catholic."

"But—"

"She had me baptized, and she made me learn the prayers, and every morning there was mass to sing before the work started, but I ain't Catholic. Not inside."

"Yes," Elizabeth said softly. "Of course you are right. Are there other prayers you'd like to say, or perhaps the Bible—"

"Don't need prayers," Joe said. "I need a new arm."

She thought he had drifted off again, when he spoke up softly.

"Do you know Johnstown?"

"A bit."

"I never thought I'd miss it, but I do." And then, after another long pause: "You know the new courthouse? Right across the street there's a blacksmith by the name of Weiss, Hans Weiss." His voice trailed away.

"Do you want a message delivered to this Hans Weiss?" Elizabeth prompted him.

Joe shook his head. One hand moved across the blanket and for the first time he touched Elizabeth, his fingers finding hers and wrapping around them, squeezing.

"There's a slave there, works the smithy. They call him Sam, but his name is Joshua. Big, strong man, 'bout thirty years old. I would much appreciate it if you could get word to him. Tell him I got this far, would you?"

She nodded, unable to speak.

"Tell him how sweet the water is up here, tell him that, too. And give him this." From under the blanket, Joe drew forth something not quite small enough to be hidden between his splayed thumb and finger. He pressed it into Elizabeth's palm, and closed his hand over hers.

"He'll know, when you give him that."

It was a single disk of glossy dark wood, unlike anything Elizabeth had ever seen. On the outer edges its carved geometric pattern was worn thin with handling. There was a hole drilled through the center, and in it a small stone had been wedged, perfectly round in shape but almost flat. A smaller hole near the edge was empty. In the dim light of the fire Elizabeth could make out nothing more of it, but while she tried, Joe fell back into sleep.

The morning came, and the night chill burned off quickly along with the mist on the lake. Elizabeth watched it break up and float gracefully into nothingness as she fished, crouched on the shelf of rock where they had thought to make camp. The woods seemed unusually quiet today, but she thought that it might be her imagination.

Nathaniel preferred fishing in the Mohawk way, with a spear, but she had more luck with the hook and line that Robbie had taught her to use, and which she kept wound into a ball in her pocket. Nathaniel had noted with some pleasure and perhaps a little surprise that she had a talent for this kind of fishing. With a bit of the stew meat as bait it didn't take long before Elizabeth had two fat trout on the line, thrashing angrily, the early sun rippling up and down their sides to spark the rainbow. With averted face and her mouth pressed hard, Elizabeth dispatched them one by one with a sharp blow of the head to the rock, as Robbie had shown her. With her knife she cleaned them in the lake, her chilled fingers moving fast. The clear waters clouded with the blood and then with a school of darting minnows with strangely enlarged heads, pleased to be let in on the feast. Elizabeth paused, thinking of a quick swim— the heavy smells of Joe's sickness hung about her and the lake, as icy cold as it was, would have been welcome. But she was uneasy here by herself, with thoughts of what might be happening at the camp. On the way she gathered sticks to build into a latticework over the cook fire. Her stomach rumbled in anticipation.

Joe was asleep again, deeper this time than before. He had roused only long enough to take a bit of water, Nathaniel told her. And he had asked for her. He seemed to be declining, slipping further and further away from them.

While they watched the trout sizzle, Elizabeth cooked some of the small store of oats into a thin gruel, in the hope that Joe would wake enough to take some nourishment.

"We need meat," Nathaniel said. "I'll go see what I can scare up. If you can cope."

Elizabeth was silent. Normally she would have sent him off without any qualms; she knew he would not go far and that he would be back in a few hours with a brace of rabbit or grouse, something they could manage quickly. In the meantime she would otherwise have bathed, washed out her things, or gone searching for wild onions and other greenery to supplement their meat. But this time would be different. Joe might well die while Nathaniel was away.

She felt him watching her, and was not surprised to have him read her thoughts.

"I don't like it much either, Boots, but we have to eat. And we'll be moving fast once we leave here. When he goes it will be quiet, you can be sure of that—he just won't wake up."

"He shouldn't be alone," she said more to herself than to Nathaniel, and he nodded his approval.

By late morning Joe had begun to come out of his sleep; she could tell by the twitching of his face and hands. While she sat next to him mending a rent in her leggings, he started awake, his whole body jerking, and then he reached involuntarily toward his ruined arm and cried out, a terrible sound.

"Shhh." Elizabeth stood, and sat again, and stood, one hand to her mouth, wondering what she could do. "Shhh," she repeated, and then something came to her from a school lesson long ago, learned over her books at Oakmere. She leaned in close to Joe, trying to ignore the smells rising from him, and crooned. "Schlaf, Kindlein, schlaf." *Sleep, little one, sleep.*

When he looked up at her his face was quieter; he seemed to be looking beyond her. "Nobody could mistake me for a child, Miz Elizabeth," he said clearly.

She sat down heavily, wiping her own forehead with a trembling hand.

"You thought I was out of my head."

"I thought you were disoriented."

He grunted. "Same difference. Is there water?"

"Of course," she said, flustered. When he had drunk, she sat with the bowl in her hands, not knowing what to say.

"You got that bijou I gave you?"

She produced it from around her neck; she had strung it there on the long silver chain with the silver and pearl pendant Nathaniel had given her, afraid that otherwise she might lose it.

"What is it?" she asked, curious. In the light the center stone had proved to be an opal, milky white except when the sun touched it, and then blazing in beautiful pearl tones.

"Made of wood from the fever tree," Joe explained, reaching for it. She put it in his hand. "Come all the way from Africa with my mama." He glanced at her, and then shook his head. "She hid it under her tongue all that time, thinking she would need good medicine on this side of the world where the devils roam. Trouble was, she didn't have enough medicine for all of 'em."

Suddenly he began to cough, a great raking cough that came up deep from his belly and convulsed him in pain. When it had passed, he fell back against the cot.

"In my lungs," he said. "Don't expect it'll be much longer now."

"I have some gruel," Elizabeth offered, wishing for the ability to provide some other, some real comfort. "Would you like that?"

He blinked at her slowly. "Thank you kindly," he said, already more than half asleep.

Nathaniel returned in mid-afternoon with three rabbits, two grouse, and a wild turkey, which he set to cleaning immediately in the hope that there would be time to smoke some of the meat to carry away. He moved fast and worked neatly, and when Elizabeth stopped to talk to him he was as pleasant and easy as ever, but he was worried. She could see it in the way the muscle in his cheek jumped, when he was quiet and thought her attention elsewhere. She worked with him and they talked of unimportant things, grateful for this quiet time while Joe slept. The weather was warm and Elizabeth began to sweat in the direct sun, but she didn't mind this. It seemed a long time since she had been warm through, and she said this to Nathaniel.

"This is the warmest spring I remember since I was a boy,"

he said. "That's our good fortune, although it don't seem that way to you right now."

"I didn't mean to complain," Elizabeth said quietly.

Nathaniel sighed. "You ain't complaining, and neither am I," he said. "You're mighty jumpy, Boots." He was cleaning a grouse and looked around him for a place to dispose of the entrails. "Too bad there's no dog," he said. "But I expect a fox will be by for this soon as we turn our backs."

"But there is a dog," Elizabeth said. "Joe's dog, I mean. He was out here when I got up this morning to start the fire."

Nathaniel turned to her, his face puzzled. "I never saw him."

She nodded. "A big red dog. Quite ferocious-looking, but he got up when he saw me and wandered off into the bush."

"Did you ask Joe about him? Or did he say anything, ask about the dog?"

Elizabeth shook her head. "I didn't think to. Is it important?"

Nathaniel shrugged, but he looked thoughtful. "Don't know," he said. "Just strange that he wasn't here when I first come up. Maybe he was off hunting for himself."

"Perhaps," Elizabeth agreed. It occurred to her that any dog of Joe's would have tried to come into the shelter at night, to sleep nearby. She asked Nathaniel if this was true, and he nodded. "That's what I was thinking," he agreed.

While they built up a smoky fire and set the strips of meat to slow-cook over it, Elizabeth thought it through.

"Perhaps it was a stray," she said. "Run off from somebody else."

"Could be."

"I did see a dog," she snapped then, and he raised a brow.

"Hold on, there. I never said you didn't."

"But you're thinking it. You think I imagined the whole thing. Or that it was—that I saw something . . . unreal."

"To tell you the truth, I hadn't been thinking along those lines. But you are, Boots. So tell me what's on your mind."

"No," Elizabeth said firmly. "There's nothing to tell. There was a stray dog in the camp in the morning, and now he's gone."

Nathaniel looked at her for a good time.

"Come out and say what you're thinking," Elizabeth said finally.

He shrugged. "Robbie has a blessing."

Elizabeth was struggling to be reasonable, and failing. "I'm not sure what relevance that has to the topic at hand," she said, knowing how petty she sounded.

"Then listen," Nathaniel said, and his voice went into another register, light and with a rhythm that was not his own:

> I wish ye the shelterin' o' the king o' kings
> I wish ye the shelterin' o' Jesus Christ
> To ye the shelterin' spirit o' healin',
> To keep ye fra' evil deed and quarrel,
> Fra' evil dog and red dog.

Elizabeth stood up abruptly, holding her bloodied hands away from her. "It was not an evil dog, it was a perfectly nice one, although it did smell distinctly of skunk. Could not have been more real. Now if you've had enough fun at my expense, I'm going to see how Joe is doing."

Nathaniel stood up to intercept her, catching her shoulders with the heels of his hands. "I'm sorry," he said with a half grin. "I won't tease anymore."

She hesitated. "I still must go look in on Joe."

"But you'll come back?"

"Eventually," said Elizabeth.

They had a tense afternoon, focused as they were on Joe and his needs, and the chores, and getting provisions ready. Nathaniel hummed along when Joe sang the mass, and this set Elizabeth's nerves even more on edge. She checked on Joe in the late afternoon. He roused himself enough to drink a sip of water, but he seemed barely to know her. Elizabeth sat watching him for a while, and then she went out to pace the little clearing up and down, making wide curves around the pits. Nathaniel had climbed down into one of them to pull up the stakes, which he threw on the fire one by one.

Elizabeth stopped suddenly, turning toward her husband.
"I'd like to bathe."

He inclined his head. "What about your foot?"

"I've been walking on it all day without discomfort," she
said. "And I smell. Come down to the lake with me."

Nathaniel shook his head. "I want to get two more of these
cleaned out first," he said. "If we're going to leave tomorrow—"

"Are we leaving tomorrow?" asked Elizabeth.

He met her eye, and then nodded. "I would guess we are.
And I don't think much of leaving these for somebody to fall
into."

"Nathaniel, I know we don't have a lot of time, but please
come along," she said, trying not to wheedle but not quite
succeeding. She had an urge to be away from the clearing, but
she did not like herself for it.

"You go on ahead," Nathaniel said. "I'll follow in a bit."

She turned almost before he had finished speaking, but
turned back reluctantly.

"Perhaps we shouldn't leave him."

"I think he'll be fine for an hour," said Nathaniel. "I'll
check in on him before I come down."

Elizabeth set off quickly and in just a few minutes she was
standing on the lakeshore. It was a beautiful afternoon, sunny
and clear, and there was no sign of blackfly anywhere, just the
squabbling of blackbirds and the melting, flutelike song of a
hermit thrush. With impatient fingers she undid her ties and
stripped down to her shift, wrinkling her nose at her own smell.
Once again she wished, fruitlessly, that she had not used the
soap she had brought along so quickly.

It had been a long, warm day but the water was still quite
cold. Standing in the lake to her knees, she undid her silver hair
clasp, noting that it was already quite tarnished and needed a
good polishing; another task that would have to wait until they
could return home to Paradise, along with other chores such as
mending her shift and trimming her hair. Carefully, she
wrapped the silver clasp in her handkerchief, and tucked it under a rock on the bank.

Elizabeth ran her fingers through her plait, hastily combing it until her hair snapped and crackled around her all the way to her hips, and then she inhaled and submerged herself. She pushed herself in mercilessly, feeling the gooseflesh rise bump by bump. Under the water she opened her eyes, and came almost face to face with a turtle, which started away with a whoosh. In a mood suddenly euphoric and restored, she broke the surface of the water and began to swim slowly toward the small island in the middle of the lake.

She was tired by the time she reached it, and dragged herself up on the bank with arms slightly trembling. There was a patch of sunlight and a small grove of paper birches, slender as young girls, whispering among themselves in the breeze. Elizabeth used one of them to sit against, drawing up her knees under her chin and lifting her face to the sunlight. Her hair hung veillike around her, the shorter strands around her face already lifting and drying in the breeze, curling and twisting lazily. Between her breasts Joe's disk and Nathaniel's pearl cluster felt slightly cold against her wet skin.

On the lake there was little sign of wildlife, with the exception of the usual birds fishing. Elizabeth had noted that there were no beaver, and she wondered why that was. On most lakes this size they had seen evidence of them, but there were none here at all. It occurred to her that Joe had probably chosen this lake for that reason, as it would be of less interest to the trappers. The thought of Joe made her think in turn of Nathaniel, and she glanced into the forest where she knew he would appear, but saw no sign of him.

Directly across from her was the projection of flat rock where they had been lying when they had first heard Joe singing, and Elizabeth noted how it looked like a stage from where she sat. It was just as this thought crossed her mind that the dog came out of the shadows and into the sunlight.

He was very large, even larger than she had thought him this morning. He stood in the light, his rough coat shining deep red, his tongue lolling, and looked toward her. He was not all that far away; she could see the rim of red in each of his eyes, and the glint of his teeth. Elizabeth sat very still, wondering what he would do if she should swim over to him and try to coax him back to the clearing to prove to Nathaniel that she had not imagined him. So concentrated was she on the animal that she didn't notice Nathaniel until he had already stripped and entered the water.

She stood up then, waving her arms above her head in an attempt to direct his attention to the dog.

He felt the cold of the water in his gut, but the sight of Elizabeth brought his blood up warm. She stood on the bank waving at him with her arms pulled over her head. She couldn't have any idea how she looked, how that gesture made the wet shift strain against her. Her skin, impossibly pale, and the dark circles of her nipples, and the darker triangle between her thighs, all this was brought into relief as she stood there waving at him with no hint of the turmoil she was causing. The wet fabric clung to her breasts, perfectly round. Nathaniel concentrated on moving himself through the water because the sight of her was too much to bear.

He came to his feet and walked onto the bank knowing that his arousal was plain to her; his breechclout revealed rather than hid it. He saw this in her dazed look, her eyes half closed in anticipation already, before he ever touched her. He heard her draw in breath, but then she looked away behind him to the far shore, distracted. He frowned, and pulled her to him without discussion. Her mouth was warm and she came to him willingly, pressing up against him in spite of the cold lake water that ran off him to soak her again.

"The red dog," she mumbled when he came up for air.

He would have laughed, if there hadn't been the fire in him, the need to have her now, and without delay. "Forget the godforsaken dog," he said, lowering his head to hers again, and then lowering her to the bank.

Before he got her shift off her he had broken two ties, but she didn't complain; instead she reached for the thong on his hip. But there was no time for that. He pushed her hand away, and his breechclout with it.

"Come, come to me," he whispered to her, pulling her underneath him.

Elizabeth looked up into Nathaniel's face, felt his breath on her skin. There was something of pain in his expression, in the deep lines etched on his forehead. He was frantic with it, with the need; she had never seen him like this before, and it excited her deeply. She cried out then, at the strength and persistence of him, at his urgency. There was a sudden sharp pain in her lower belly; she tensed, but it was gone before she could even gasp. But Nathaniel wasn't. Nathaniel was still with her, murmuring to her, sweet words at her ear, the flat of his tongue on her neck, holding himself over her with one arm, the other hand beneath her, pulling her up to him again and again, harder and then harder still. When she began to shudder he raised his head and watched her, a look of fierce satisfaction on his face.

"Have mercy," she gasped.

He shook his head, spattering her with lake water and sweat. "I'm nowhere near finished with you yet."

Nathaniel knew he was pushing her, maybe too hard. He moved in her without any concern for her comfort, focused only on the gathering tension that boiled up from the center of him in response to her heat.

She pulled his face to hers and kissed him, then, and he felt the first trickling break in the dam inside her. He thrust himself deeper into her, met her tongue with his own, and then it happened; she let go, every muscle in her first relaxing and then flexing around him. It was the kiss, the depth and intensity of it, that sent her over the edge. He wondered if she heard, from a place deep inside herself, the sounds of her own surrender, but he couldn't stop to ask her, or even to comfort her.

Nathaniel found himself up on his knees, holding her tightly in his arms, her legs wrapped around his waist. He had no memory of lifting her, or how they came to this position, but her bottom was cushioned against his tensed thighs and her arms were wound around his neck. He pulled her waist in with one arm and thrust one last time, searching with his mouth for her ear in the wild confusion of her hair.

"Open to me," he whispered. "Open to me now." His release came then with hers. It left him in long, slow ribbons, spooling endlessly into her. She reared back with her head to look into his eyes, and he saw it there, her awareness of each pulsing, and the power of her response.

· · ·

She was near sleep almost as soon as he lowered her to the bank, a stunned look on her face and the deep flush that ran from her breasts to her hairline already beginning to mottle.

Nathaniel curled himself against her on one side, brushed her hair away from her face.

"Did I hurt you?"

She shook her head, and then with a visible effort, turned on her side to fit herself to him. "Never," she said. And then, sleepily: "What got into you?"

Nathaniel said, "Joe died, just before I came down. In his sleep."

She tensed for a moment. He expected tears, but she simply put her face against his and trembled a little.

"That blessing of Robbie's," she said. "What was there in it about healing?"

" 'To you the sheltering spirit of healing,' " he recited.

Elizabeth turned her face up to the sky.

"Amen," she said. "Godspeed."

XXXV

The morning was wet and cold and inhospitable, but there was no time to waste. Nathaniel dug the grave, the shovel rasping hard in the unwilling earth while Elizabeth packed their gear, tucking the newly dried and bundled meat in every available space. She worked in the wet because it did not seem right to be in the shelter where Joe lay, where they had sat with him through the night, sleeping fitfully.

She paused to warm her damp hands over the sputtering fire. Nathaniel was working hard, and she watched him for a moment, secretly. It seemed inappropriate, somehow, the joy she took in the sight of him—given the task at hand. But it was difficult to look away. There was such concentration in him, such focus. He would do what must be done and do it simply and well. It made her own dread and unease seem immature and silly; but still, it was almost inconceivable, the idea that they would lay Joe to rest in that simple hole with nothing to shelter him but the earth itself. There was no time to make him a box to lie in, even if there had been the tools to make such a thing as a coffin.

Nathaniel paused to wipe the misting rain from his face with the sleeve of his shirt. He smiled at her, a grim smile but an encouraging one.

"I've got everything ready," she said. "Shall I—" She looked over her shoulder toward the shelter, and paused.

"I ain't quite that far yet," Nathaniel said. "If you feel like washing go on down to the lake, we can take care of him when you get back."

She nodded, unable to talk.

He hefted the shovel again. "Take your time," he said. "There's the pits to finish."

They were both anxious to be gone, but she couldn't help him with much of what he needed to do first. And so she left him there, nervously, but glad to be away from the clearing.

The forest sagged with the rain, each leaf dripping, rivulets running into streams, streams running down to the lake. She followed them, and was surprised to find, when she came out from under the canopy of trees, that the rain had stopped. Later in the day the sun might manage to burn off the haze, but right now Elizabeth stood on the lakefront and felt as if she had stumbled on some fairyland: mists floated over the surface of the water so that the island disappeared and reappeared, in what seemed to be an almost willful manner. The sounds of the forest and the birds echoed and swelled and faded only to come again, and Elizabeth was reminded of early mornings at home in her girlhood bed, when she rose and fell on the tide of sleep, content to coast between the muted colors and sounds of her dreams and the day that coaxed her awake.

Cupping her face to her hands, she drank and then sat, strangely without energy. She thought of stripping down to wash. It seemed a foolhardy thing to do; she could not imagine simply walking into the lake and swimming, blinded in the mists with no sense of direction. But she was sticky with perspiration and meat drippings and she knew that they would be moving fast for two or perhaps three days, stopping only when it was no longer light, with little hope of time or opportunity to bathe. And so she settled down on the bank and washed herself systematically and as well as she could without stripping down. The sleeves and neckline of her shirt would dry soon enough.

As she watched, the mist cleared suddenly, revealing the curved end of the lake and the table of rock with its overhang. For the first time since the previous afternoon, Elizabeth thought of the red dog. It had been sitting just there, not twenty feet away from her, and it had remained there while Nathaniel swam toward her, walking off into the bush while they had been occupied with each other. On a sudden whim she wiped her wet hands on her leggings and stood, tossing her plait over her shoulder.

Elizabeth scrambled over the boulders, bumping her knee as she climbed onto the platform of rock. Then she stood, looking down at the smooth gray slab. There was evidence of their short stay in the ashes of their fire and a scattering of sweet flag, but nothing else that she could discern. Still, Elizabeth persisted, walking slowly with her gaze turned downward. If the dog would not show himself, a single print would be enough to point out to Nathaniel. She did not take the time to ask herself why it was so important to prove to him what she knew to be true.

The sheltered rock face was dry and clean, but at its edge where it turned downward and disappeared into the dirt, rain dripped from the overhang and pooled. There the earth had turned to an expanse of mud, crisscrossed with the delicate prints of small birds. She jumped off the slab and felt the claylike mud give slightly under her weight. It felt tacky underfoot, and she looked behind herself and saw her own prints, already filling with water at the outer edges of the heel. Intent now, she walked a little farther.

At first she didn't really believe what she saw. She had wanted this, yes, but it was hard to credit anyway: not one paw print, but a whole line headed into the underbrush. Not a cougar, or a deer or any of the others that Nathaniel had taught her to recognize, but a dog, and a large one. For a minute she stood staring into the shadows under the overhang, thinking about going back. Nathaniel would need help with Joe.

Later, she could not even say why she had gone on, what had been in her mind except the vague feeling that she had missed something important. Something that Nathaniel would not have missed.

There were puddles of water, here and there, among the dog's prints. Strangely shaped. Four of them, at an even interval. Elizabeth looked at them, and felt her pulse double even as her thoughts slowed down to a preternatural slowness; then she recognized them for what they were. Footprints. Human foot-prints.

They were much bigger and deeper than the dog's prints; perhaps that was why she hadn't seen them immediately. Eliza-beth crouched down and she stared, harder than she had ever stared at anything in her life. And two thoughts came to her: they were fresh; and they could not be Nathaniel's. He had not come down to the lake since the rain began.

There was a tightness in her throat which exploded in a rush of blood and snapping nerves. In an instant she was running, her thoughts flashing as quickly as her feet as they flew over the rock face.

She knew that Richard must be ahead of her. He would want to deal with Nathaniel first if he intended to take her back to Paradise against her will. Elizabeth caught a painful breath, half sob, half curse, and launched herself into the bush, catching her foot on a root and falling hard, pulling herself up with a wrench to move on. She felt like a lumbering cow without speed or grace, stumbling once and then again, scrambling inef-fectively in wet leaves, pulling herself forward, soaked already to the skin with the dripping of the trees. With the sound of her own breathing blocking out all else, she made a halfhearted attempt to turn her toes inward and run on a narrow track as Nathaniel had taught her to do.

It could not have taken more than two minutes for her to reach the clearing, but she got there winded and unable to do anything else but clutch her arms to her heaving ribs and strug-gle for breath. Elizabeth paused in the damp shadows of a stand of white pine and tried to hear past the pounding of her heart in her ears. It began to rain again, in earnest now.

Something was different, but it took a few seconds for her to realize what it was: the empty grave had been filled in a high arc of fresh earth. Nathaniel had buried Joe without her.

She wiped the rain from her face and tried to gather her thoughts. From where she stood, there was no immediate sign of him. To walk into the clearing went against everything he had taught her, but he could be lying there out of sight, his head laid open to the rain, while Richard stood over him and waited for her to stumble in.

At that moment Nathaniel appeared in the doorway empty-handed—she had time to wonder where his rifle was—and Richard came out of the bush at the far edge of the clearing with his own gun to his shoulder and his sights on her husband.

Nathaniel was turned in her direction and saw her first. Surprise and sudden awareness flashed across his face; he tensed and disappeared back into the shadows as Richard called out.

"Bonner!" he bellowed. "Show yourself!"

"Richard Todd," Nathaniel called back in an easy tone. "Still showing up where you're not wanted, I see." Elizabeth could make out Nathaniel quite easily. He was gesturing with his chin in a hard motion for her to move away into the bush.

"I'll have to tie you up," Richard said. "Or shoot you. Take your choice. Either way you're going back to Paradise."

Nathaniel was gesturing to her more forcefully, but Elizabeth only clasped her arms closer around herself and shook her head.

"That's a fancy trick you got in mind," Nathaniel called back, frowning at Elizabeth.

"I guess they'll hang you for killing her," Richard called. "I won't mind watching."

For a moment Nathaniel's face froze and then something like real amusement passed over it. He laughed out loud, but Elizabeth was overcome with indignation.

"Cain't say that I'm sorry to disappoint," Nathaniel said. "She's alive as you and me."

"That grave says different," Richard called.

It was then that Elizabeth saw the rifle leaning up under the lip of the roof, on the corner farthest from Richard and out of his line of vision. Nathaniel needed his rifle now; that thought went through her head very clearly, and without taking the time to think any further, Elizabeth lowered her head, and ran.

She dodged the pit between herself and the shelter, not hearing, not daring to listen to the voice raised in surprise behind her. With one hand she grabbed the rifle and then dove, head-first, into the open doorway, casting the gun away from her as she did, hoping that it wasn't primed. She was vaguely aware of Nathaniel catching it as she hit the ground with her shoulder.

There was a scream from outside the shelter followed by a

muffled gunshot. Elizabeth rolled and was up on her feet instantaneously, looking around herself for Nathaniel, but finding instead only the empty room and the stripped cot.

The second scream was louder, and drew her out of the shelter with a jerk. Elizabeth stood just beyond the open doorway, looking into a scene that made no sense.

Nathaniel stood with his rifle sights trained downward. His hair hung in wet ropes down his back, and rain poured over his face, but his concentration was complete. With a terrible rush of awareness Elizabeth realized why he was aiming into the ground.

"For God's sake, man," bellowed Richard, his voice cracking high and hard. "Get me out of here!"

Elizabeth began to move past Nathaniel, but he grabbed her arm and pulled her up short. "Wait," he said. And then, to Richard: "Where's your rifle?"

From the pit where he sprawled, half in, half out, Richard's voice came loud. "It went off, you heard it. Even if I could reach it I couldn't reload. It's at the bottom."

Elizabeth pulled away from Nathaniel and walked forward, slowly. The rain was cold but she was flushed from head to foot. Then she reached the edge of the pit, and stopped. "God above," she whispered, turning to Nathaniel with a hand pressed hard to her chest. "We have to help him."

Richard had been running when he went into the pit; he had gone down with one leg outstretched and the other bent, and the first stake had taken him through the fleshy part of the lower leg. The bloody broken end of it thrust up through the fabric of his legging. He craned his head to look up at them, his eyes wild with pain and fear. Elizabeth saw that he had tried to catch himself by flinging out an arm; the second pike had pierced his right hand.

She felt her stomach slowly clench and then turn in on itself, pushing up. With a hiccup, she turned away and was sick. Nathaniel supported her while she retched. Miserable, Elizabeth turned to him, drawing the back of her hand across her mouth. The focused set of his face calmed her.

"This is going to be messy," he said. "But I can't get him out of there without your help."

"Elizabeth!" She looked down at Richard, reluctantly. There was blood, but not so much as she had feared. She watched in amazement as he reached with his free hand inside his shirt. Then he was holding something up toward her, a rumpled piece of paper, sticky with blood and pockmarked with rain, the ink running.

"Take this," he gasped.

"Don't," said Nathaniel behind her.

But it was too late; she had leaned forward and taken it from him. "What is it?"

Richard threw his head back and his eyes fluttered in the rain, his face transformed by a sickly smile. "Your summons," he whispered, and fell away into a faint.

It was a damn shame they couldn't leave him where he lay, Nathaniel thought, but then he kept this sentiment to himself. Elizabeth was distraught enough; he would need her usual calm good sense to deal with what was to come, and he couldn't afford to upset her further. She had helped without complaint through the worst of it, pale and thin-mouthed but determined, not wavering until they had deposited Richard, bleeding profusely, onto the stripped cot where Joe had lain.

"What in the name of God are you doing?" Richard asked when he had roused himself. He was watching Nathaniel pour schnapps onto a piece of muslin.

"For your hand," he said tersely. "To clean it out."

"Mohawk foolery," Richard said, yanking his hand away. "Bind it and be done with it."

Elizabeth was standing to one side with her arms wrapped around her, one foot jiggling hard. She hadn't spoken to Richard since he regained consciousness, but to Nathaniel her growing anger was almost palpable.

"Do it," she said to Nathaniel. "It might fester otherwise."

"You have a degree in medicine now in addition to your other new skills?" Richard interrupted himself with a howl as Nathaniel grabbed his arm and slapped the wet dressing against the gaping wound in his hand. "Goddamn it to hell!" he screamed.

"Nathaniel just buried a man who had a wound on his hand fester," Elizabeth said. "Perhaps we could do the same for you."

"That would suit you very well, would it not?" Todd shot back at her. "Then you could tear up that summons and forget your obligations."

"I've already torn it up," Elizabeth said. "And burned the scraps. And I am not obliged to you in any way at all. Although it seems we must tend your wounds out of common courtesy. Not that such a concept would mean anything to you."

Nathaniel followed this exchange with some surprise. For the first time since he'd known her, he saw Elizabeth out of her head with anger. Too mad to make sense or see what needed to be done. He tried to catch her eye but she was staring at Todd.

"We'll talk about business matters later," Nathaniel said. "Right now that spike has to come out of your leg."

He saw the grudging acceptance of this on Todd's face. To Elizabeth, Nathaniel said: "I don't much like the idea of bending down there when he's got that look on his face. Will you hold my rifle on him?"

Elizabeth's color flared. "Gladly," she said, putting out one hand to accept the gun with a small, tight smile.

"It's primed, now, so mind you don't shoot him. Unless you have to."

"She can't manage that piece," Todd said, his voice hoarse.

"I can," Elizabeth said, pulling the rifle up with a jerk, and taking many steps backward to accommodate its length. She went down on one knee to brace it on the boulder that served as Joe's table, but it was longer than she was, and Nathaniel could see that it was almost more than she could handle. Not that she would ever admit that in front of Todd. They could stop and sort out the musket, or get this over with.

"Elizabeth," Nathaniel said. "Keep it aimed on his shoulder, just there."

"She wouldn't shoot me," Richard said dismissively.

"She just might if you keep talking at her that way," Nathaniel noted.

Elizabeth gave Todd a very grim smile. "I suggest you do not test your hypothesis, Dr. Todd. The results might surprise you."

With quick motions of his knife Nathaniel cut the leggings

away around the wound. The spike had passed through the muscles of his lower leg and pushed up and out much like an arrow.

"This is going to hurt like the devil," he said cheerfully. "Tear up your leg something awful. But we can't leave it in there."

Todd's stare was direct. In the midst of his thick red-gold beard, still wet and caked now with dirt, his mouth was set straight and thin. "So do it," he said.

"Hold her steady there," Nathaniel said quietly to Elizabeth. "He's going to holler."

"I am perfectly steady," Elizabeth said. "Let him make all the noise he likes."

Nathaniel turned back to Todd and knelt to pin down his foot with a knee. With his left hand he grasped Todd's thigh to immobilize it. With his right hand he took firm hold of the broken spike.

Sweat ran into Elizabeth's eyes. She blinked, and blinked again, looking down the softly gleaming barrel of the long rifle to fix her sights on Richard's shoulder, as she had been directed. But the muscles in her hands and lower arms and shoulders began to cramp almost immediately, and in spite of all her efforts the rifle sight wavered disconcertingly between Richard's shoulder and his belly. She thought longingly of the short-barreled musket in her pack, which she had shot a number of times.

But she mustn't distract Nathaniel.

His back was to her. He moved suddenly, and with that movement Richard's face contorted horribly, his mouth and eyes flying open and his head falling back and then bolting forward. As Nathaniel pulled, Richard's upper body came up off the cot, his left arm and fist following in an arc aimed squarely at Nathaniel's temple.

It happened very slowly, Elizabeth thought later, because she could remember individual moments. Nathaniel's profile fixed in utter concentration, his fist curled white-knuckled around the bloody shaft. The spurt of blood and its smell, hot in the damp air. The roaring wild anger in Richard's voice as he threw his weight forward, the blur of his fist as Nathaniel's head snapped away to the side.

The recoil slammed into her shoulder and sent her spinning, the rifle dropping out of her hands. In the small space of the shelter the sound of the shot was deafening, echoing on and on. But it was not loud enough to drown Nathaniel's grunt of surprise as he pitched forward across Richard's legs. Elizabeth landed on her rear, and inhaling sharply she drew in some of the cloud of blue gunpowder, the acrid taste filling her mouth immediately with saliva.

By the time she regained her feet, Nathaniel was already lifting himself off Richard, who scrambled back and away. He pushed with his hands to right himself, shaking his head as if to clear it. Elizabeth stood immobile, unable to talk or even to reach out to him as he turned toward her. There was surprise on his face, and shock, and confusion. Nathaniel looked down at himself and she looked, too, and saw the bullet wound, a round ragged hole on the right side of his chest. *That's where it came out,* she thought quite clearly as the bile rose into her throat. *I shot Nathaniel in the back, and that's where the bullet came out.*

He was touching his shirt with one finger, as if he could not believe what he saw. His breath came in great gasps, and when he looked up at her, it was with a face suddenly bluish-white in color, and sagging with pain.

He sat down heavily on the edge of the cot.

"Jesus Christ Almighty, Elizabeth," he whispered. He coughed, and there was a trickle of blood from the corner of his mouth.

She fell to her knees in front of him with her arms wrapped around herself, and rocked toward him, not touching, not daring to touch him.

"Forgive me," she said, her eyes fixed on his face. "Forgive me, forgive me."

She had forgotten completely about Richard Todd, who had pulled himself into the farthest corner at the head of the cot, his hands pressed against the gaping wounds in his lower leg. The sound of his voice startled her as much as the rifle shot had.

"You married the wrong man," he said with a grimace. "But you sure as hell shot the right one."

It was enough to bring her up out of her trance. Elizabeth leaned toward Nathaniel, still afraid to touch him. "I forbid you to die," she said. "I won't let you."

There was no answer, just the desperate sound of his breathing. But his eyes held hers and he blinked, slowly.

"I need something to bind this leg."

"Nathaniel," Elizabeth said, ignoring Richard. "I will not let you die, do you hear me? But you have to tell me what to do for you."

But he could not. She stood and paced the small room, almost tripping over the rifle where it had fallen. She kicked it, and then turned back to Nathaniel. On her knees in front of him, she scrambled madly for a clear thought. *His shirt,* she thought. *Get his shirt off.*

Her hands were trembling so that she could barely manage the ties. When she found that he could not lift his arms, she took his knife and she slit the sleeves and sides, until he sat barechested before her with his head and upper shoulders against the wall, his hair dripping down over his chest.

It was a simple hole, an angry red hole that could be covered with two fingertips. She looked at it, a handbreadth below his right nipple, and Elizabeth was overcome with panic and terror. Then she pinched the web of flesh between her thumb and finger as hard as she could, willing her vision to clear.

"It's not so bad," Nathaniel whispered when she opened her eyes again. "Missed the ribs, I think." He coughed again, and a bubble of blood appeared on the wound, bright red.

"What shall I do?" she asked, trying to modulate her voice. "Can you tell me what to do?" In response, his eyes rolled back in his head and he slumped against the wall. Elizabeth put her head to his chest and felt his heartbeat, too fast. Too fast. His breathing, shallow. His skin clammy and cold to the touch.

She stood to yank the blanket out from under Richard and tucked it around Nathaniel, tight around his shoulders but tented over the bullet hole. She thought of leaning him forward to look at his back, and her stomach rose. Not yet; she couldn't, not yet.

Richard was pale, his forehead beaded with sweat.

"You must tell me what to do," she said to him. "You must."

Blood welled from between the fingers pressed over Richard's wound. "Give me something to dress this leg of mine first. The muscle is badly torn."

"Your leg can wait," she said. "Tell me what to do for him."

Nathaniel gasped, his eyelids fluttering. Elizabeth looked at the blood bubbling from his chest with every breath, at his face, tinged blue with the effort to breathe, and then into Richard Todd's eyes, filmed with a different kind of pain, long hoarded and treasured. She leaned toward him and brought her eyes within inches of his.

"Listen to me," she hissed softly. "You will tell me how to bind this wound. You will do that, and do it clearly and without delay. Because if he dies, then I will gladly sit here and watch you bleed to death. Do you hear me?"

There was a flicker of something in his eyes. Surprise. Perhaps respect. Richard Todd hesitated while the sound of Nathaniel's labored breathing punctuated the silence. At length, he nodded.

Elizabeth had never been so tired in her life, and yet she knew that she dared not sleep. She could not afford to sleep. On either side of the shelter, with the makeshift fire between them, Richard and Nathaniel were alternately dozing or in need of her attentions. It was just hours since the events of the morning, but it felt to her like years.

She went outside, desperate for fresh air, and sat down for the first time in what seemed to be days. But there was no escaping it; if she closed her eyes it all played itself out in her head again. The feel of the rifle in her hands, the way it had jerked to life as Richard reared up. The sound of Nathaniel's laborious breathing, louder than any gunshot. It would be with her for the rest of her life. Elizabeth put her head on her knees, willing herself to cry, wanting to scream, to be done with this terrible anger. With a sudden heave, she brought up everything in her stomach, her whole body coated in a cold and sticky

sweat. When the retching finally stopped, she raised her head
and found the red dog sitting across from her.

"You," she said flatly.

It thumped its tail twice and then went down to the ground.
The dog observed her calmly. There was still the smell of skunk
about it, and Elizabeth could see burrs caught in the tangled
deep red coat.

"I'll have to go for help, you know." Saying it out loud
made it real, and she was overcome with fear at the idea. But
there was no other way. They could not stay here; she could not
nurse them and hunt for them and keep them and herself alive.
She needed to get them out, and neither of them could walk. It
would be weeks, she thought, in Nathaniel's case. If ever.

She jumped up, wiping her mouth on her sleeve, and the
dog rose, too.

"I have to find my way back to Robbie's, and there's no
time to waste," she said. The dog thumped its tail in agreement.

Nathaniel was propped against the wall of the shelter on a bed
of blankets and balsam branches. She had tried stretching him
out, but his breathing was least labored when he sat upright.
Now he opened his eyes and looked at her steadily. His color
was very bad, but she smiled at him, and brushed his hair away
from his face.

"I suppose I will never live this down," she whispered.

He caught her hand and squeezed it tight. On the other side
of the fire, Richard was awake and listening, but there was
nothing she could do about that.

"Listen, Nathaniel," she said, leaning toward him. "I've
filled the big kettle and the bucket with water, you can reach
them, right here. Are you listening?" When she had his attention, she pointed it all out. The dried meat and beans, the
ammunition and his rifle and knife. Richard's weapons as well,
all within Nathaniel's reach and out of Richard's, at least until
he was well enough to move. There were enough provisions to
hold them both for three days; four, perhaps.

She dared not look at him, and so she glanced up at the roof
and the hole he had torn in it on that evening they first came

across Joe. Could it have been less than two days? "I've brought in Joe's woodpile, all of it. Richard will have to manage the fire, but I expect he'll be able to. You must stay warm."

Nathaniel squeezed her hand again. "Elizabeth."

She turned her face to him.

"It was an accident," he said. "Don't tear yourself up so."

She shook her head, hard. "There's perhaps five hours or so of light today to walk by. I could be to Robbie's by the day after tomorrow, in the morning."

"Take the compass," he said, and began to cough. He crossed his arms over his chest and the pain shook him. Elizabeth waited until it had passed.

"I've got the compass, and food enough," she said. "And I remember the way, I'm sure I do."

The muscles in his throat worked as he swallowed. "It's faster," he said, "if you skirt the swamp."

Elizabeth hesitated, and then set her face in what she hoped were calm lines.

"Yes, all right. The swamp at the outflow of Little Bear?" Between them, they worked through the route until she could recite it to his satisfaction.

Nathaniel squeezed her hand. "The musket," he said. "Load it with shot. Keep it primed."

Elizabeth shuddered at the thought of ever firing another gun, but she nodded.

"Watch—" He coughed, his face contorting. "Overhead."
For panthers in the trees, she thought. The skin across her shoulders rose in goose bumps.

On the other side of the fire, there was a shifting. Elizabeth did her best to ignore Richard, but she could see Nathaniel's attention focusing on him. She put her hand on his cheek and turned his face back to her own.

"Richard says the bullet seems to have done minimal damage," she told him. "If you stay still, and warm, and fed, the wound will close itself and you will heal. If you don't—"

His half grin closed like a fist around her heart. "Boots. I'm not that easy to get rid of."

She leaned toward him. There was the taste of blood on his

mouth, bright and coppery. "As if I'd let you get away," she said, her voice trembling.

Elizabeth sat with him while he drifted off, holding his hand. For the first time since she'd known him, his fingers were colder than her own. She studied him, the joint of the thumb, the scars, the hard places on his palm, the short, blunt nails that he was constantly cleaning with his knife. Elizabeth wet the corner of her kerchief in the water kettle and wiped Nathaniel's hands clean of the dirt of Joe's grave, and of his own blood. Then she stood, and walked over to Richard. He looked up at her, his face impassive.

"I'm going for help," she said quietly. "But I want you to know something before I go."

Elizabeth crouched down to bring her face closer to Richard's. She could see that he was in considerable pain, but that he was never going to admit it. For a moment she wondered at him, what a complex man he was. Then she thought of Nathaniel alone with him, and at his mercy. She said: "I've shot one man I didn't mean to. It won't be hard to shoot the next one, if I've got good cause."

"Promise me you'll answer the summons to appear before the court, and I promise you I won't lift a hand to hurt him."

"Or to help him, either." She almost laughed. "Your word is less than worthless, Dr. Todd. I will make you a promise. If you hurt him, then a court of law would be the best you could hope for. I doubt Hawkeye would be so kind. I know that I would not."

He was watching her closely. "You're not as tough as you think."

"For your own sake, you had best hope that you are wrong." She began to turn away.

"Wait."

Richard shifted on his pallet, grimacing. The wrappings on his hand were bloody. "I swear on my mother's grave that I'll do what I can to keep him alive until you get back. If you promise to meet me in a court of law and answer the charges against you."

"I am starting to wonder if you are completely sane," Elizabeth said quietly. His face was haggard, every crease caked with dirt. There was no sign of the elegant Dr. Todd who had proposed to her in such formal terms in the Bennetts' parlor, the man who painted landscapes and wore velvet waistcoats. And yet, somehow she had the sense that while much of the paint and glitter had been scraped away, the real Richard Todd was still not completely in evidence.

"Do we have an agreement?"

Nathaniel coughed in his uneasy sleep.

"On your mother's grave?"

He nodded, and Elizabeth inhaled. "Then I agree. But only if my husband survives, is that clear? If I find him in good condition on my return, then I will answer your charges in court."

Richard's smile was a frightening thing.

Elizabeth turned away and made herself ready. With the musket and knife tucked into her belt and the powder horn slung over her shoulder, she lifted the pack of provisions to her back, and glanced at Nathaniel. Without another look at Richard Todd, she set off, the red dog trotting beside her.

XXXVI

The red dog woke her at sunrise by pushing its cold nose into her neck. Elizabeth gasped and rolled over and then, suddenly remembering where she was and why, she sat up. There was a muffled woof and a single, appreciative thump of a tail.

"Wretched beast," she muttered, rubbing the heel of her hand on its bony skull. The fire had gone out, insufficiently banked. It was the animal's warmth that had kept her from waking in a shiver. She wondered if fleas would be worth the comfort. "I don't suppose you can fetch wood, can you? Never mind. No time anyway."

How long had she slept? She had made a hasty camp at twilight and fallen immediately to sleep. Eight hours, perhaps; it felt like less. Elizabeth ate a breakfast of raw oats and dried meat, staring into the bush as she chewed. A long day of walking ahead of her. She forced herself to swallow and took another mouthful. The dog watched her, one brow cocked. Then she snuffled and rolled onto her back, waving her bent paws slightly and casting Elizabeth a hopeful look.

"You don't really think I'm going to stick my hand into that mess, do you?" Elizabeth asked, even as she leaned forward to scratch the dog's freckled belly. She was surprised to see that the teats were elongated; a bitch, with a few litters in her past. Elizabeth thought of uncle Merriweather, how much boyish enthusiasm he had shown when one of his retrievers had whelped. It was the only time he had ever gone into the kitchen, to visit the litter in its nest of wood shavings by the hearth. And how cook had hated having him there, disrupting her routine and staff.

"Treenie," Elizabeth said, thinking for the first time in many months of the cook at Oakmere, a wiry twist of a Scotswoman with a face like an overripe tomato, a carving knife for a tongue, and fists like raw joints of beef.

The dog rolled to her feet and stood wagging her tail.

"It's as good a name as any," Elizabeth said. "I must call you something if you're going to come along."

They walked. For hours, they walked and Elizabeth talked to the red dog; it was the only way to keep her mind focused on the journey and off the cause of her errand. She was pushing hard, stopping only to drink at the river and relieve herself. Both of them ate on the go. Treenie disappeared on occasion, foraging ahead and loping back, almost puppylike, with the remnants of a rabbit or groundhog on her muzzle. Red squirrels chattered and scolded above them, and there was the persistent drone of a woodpecker no matter how far they went.

The river meandered, but Elizabeth resisted the urge to make even the most obvious of shortcuts. With considerable luck, she might survive being lost in these endless woods, but Nathaniel would not. She walked harder, chewing tough chunks of dried rabbit and tossing Treenie the gristle. They were following a moose trail, fairly well marked; Elizabeth pulled up short in surprise to find a series of nests in the gentle hollows. Apparently turkeys had found the spot to their liking in spite of the traffic: each nest of twigs and dead leaves contained a large clutch of pale yellow eggs speckled brown. The hens were just out of sight in the underbrush, fussing furiously. Not hungry enough to rob nests, Elizabeth walked on without pausing. Treenie, not quite so fastidious in her appetites, hung back; a sharp word brought her to attention, and she slouched reluctantly past the easy meal.

By midday the air was growing heavier and hotter. Sweat trickled down her back and sides and glued her hair to her temples. When a swarm of blackfly rose like a malignant cloud,

Elizabeth thought with longing of the pennyroyal ointment and the bear grease, but she had left them behind for Nathaniel, as she had left almost all the provisions. She tied her kerchief around her nose and mouth and wiped the tiny black creatures from the corners of her eyes every few steps. Treenie's eyes and nose were circled with a trembling black mask; again and again she resorted to plunging into the river to find relief.

Eventually the river fed into a small, misshapen lake. Most of these lakes had no name, and in fact Elizabeth thought this one deserved none; it was too unpleasant a place. To her right was a vast tangle of dreary tamarack and cedar interspersed with deadwood, bracken, and thorny shrubs. To her left, the lake itself was ringed by dead trees, their stumpy bare branches looped with garlands of lichen. On the far side of the lake the river spread into the deep shadows of the swamp, where the only real color came from the birds—yellow warblers flitting like wayward sunbeams, a red crossbill sitting low in a black ash—and from the luxurious carpet of deep green moss and ferns that covered everything. The air shimmered with heat and flies.

"Here it is, Treenie," Elizabeth said, wiping the blackfly from the corners of her eyes. "The worst of it."

She forced herself to sit on the edge of the river. While she recited to herself what Nathaniel had told her of the route, she ate, because she was hungry. Ravenously hungry, so that the last of the oats, all of the dried meat, the handful of beans disappeared in little time. This evening she would have to take the time to fish, or to snare. But first there was the swamp to be got around.

Keep your wits about you, Hawkeye had said to her so many weeks ago. *I've still got my best stories to tell.*

"I'll have a few of my own," Elizabeth muttered. She wished for Hawkeye, for Robbie, for Runs-from-Bears, even for her brother. Any way at all to be led.

"I'm frightened," she said aloud.

The dog looked up at her, panting, and then snapped irritably at the insects hovering about her head. With an impatient snuffle, she started off. Elizabeth followed.

· · ·

Nathaniel woke with a start and reached for her, remembering even then that she was gone, off to fetch Robbie. Who would either dig his grave or cart him out of the bush; what it would be was not quite clear. Breathing was a necessary misery. Beyond that, he itched, and he was thirsty, and his bowels gripped.

"Breathe deep," Richard Todd said from the other side of the fire. "You have to force the bad lung open."

Nathaniel blinked and attempted to focus on the man. The sweat had drawn crevices in the grime on Richard's face, and his hair clung to his temples.

"You've got a fever," he observed, his own voice sounding hollow and hoarse in his ears.

"Leg's full of muck," Richard said. "Need to clean it out."

"Sorry I can't be of assistance."

Richard managed a hollow laugh. "I'll wager."

Nathaniel struggled up by holding on to the wall, and then hung there, coughing. No blood this time; that was good. When his vision cleared again he made his way out of the shelter and around the corner, where he squatted while the world around him faded in and out of focus. What he wanted to do was to get down to the lake and lie in the water, where it would be cool and he could listen to the loons. He could wait for her there on the island where they had last come together . . . yesterday? He shook his head, rubbing his eyes. The day before yesterday, in the evening.

He forced himself to take three deep breaths, and then hauled himself to his feet where he stood, swaying. The wind was up and there was the smell of a storm in the air.

She would be halfway through the swamp now, if she hadn't lost her way. If the storm didn't overtake her, she would be out by sunset. If the storm didn't overtake her.

Treenie moved along with a certainty and steady enthusiasm that buoyed Elizabeth's spirits. She followed the dog closely over hummocks of fern-covered moss and around deep pools of water. Where she waded, Elizabeth jumped; her moccasins were already wet through, but she could not quite make herself stomp knowingly through murky waters. Her affection and appreciation for the dog grew with every damp mile.

By the late afternoon two things were clear: she should have saved the last of the dried meat, and there was a storm on the way. The constant drone and cackle of woodpeckers was replaced by the creaking of deadwood in the buffeting winds. In those rare spots where the sky showed itself it was as dark and unwelcoming as the swamp, churning with threatening clouds. She had thought to be out by the time it was full dark, but light was dwindling with the first trembling thunder. Treenie's ears twitched and she let out a low whine.

"Yes, and I know how you are feeling," Elizabeth muttered. "But at least we are free of the blackfly."

The dog woofed at her dejectedly as the thunder rumbled again. With every new flash of approaching light they moved faster. Elizabeth stumbled for the first time with the distinct crack of a tree being hit: catching her leggings on an upthrusted snarl of cedar roots, she stepped into a pool and sank immediately to the waist, her moccasins settling into the ooze at the bottom. While she disentangled herself she tried to remember what she knew about appropriate behavior in a thunderstorm. To be waist-deep in water, she feared, was almost as sensible as to stand under the lone tree on a grassy meadow.

The rain started just as she pulled herself to her feet. It crested and fell back in sudden jerking waves, cold against her heated cheeks. Treenie stood regarding her with a very clear brand of canine panic on her face while she tried to scrape the worst of the mud from her feet.

"You are a terrible coward," Elizabeth said loudly. Whether she meant this for Treenie or herself, she was not sure.

The thick ground covering of moss absorbed the rain like a strange sea sponge, giving it up again with a loud hiss under each footfall. Elizabeth watched her feet closely, determined to avoid another tumble, and so she walked into Treenie before she realized that the dog had stopped. With a startled hiccup she looked up to see a huge beech tree directly in their path, wider around than Elizabeth could reach. This occurred to her because she was tempted to put her arms around it; it was the first beech she had seen since they entered the swamp.

On one side of the beech was the river, which had inexplicably regained a semblance of banks, and on the other a great jumble of boulders, slimy with streaming lichen and clusters of red-yellow mushrooms. They had begun to scramble over when Elizabeth paused. In a flicker of lightning she had caught something on the trunk, what she had taken at first to be the claw marks of bears. She pulled herself up and stopped, to Treenie's great annoyance, to read.

CRESCENT ILLAE, CRESCETIS AMORES

The names had been obscured by real claw marks, but the sentiment remained: "as these letters grow, so will our love." Elizabeth reached up to trace the carving, wondering if she were developing a habit for hallucinations.

Treenie had Elizabeth's overdress between her teeth, and she tugged, hard.

"We're nearly out," Elizabeth said, thumping her on the back. "And thank God." In response the air lit with a triple pulse of blue-white light, followed almost immediately by the deep bass of thunder. Too close. She slithered down the boulders to the other side, and came up against a dead tamarack, already leaning precipitously.

Treenie backed up against her knees, so that Elizabeth nearly lost her balance. She looked at the shivering dog, and then looked again. In the startling blue-white light which seemed to pulse on and on, every hair in her coat stood on end. And then the thunder sucked all sound from the world: the howling of the red dog, Elizabeth's own scream, and the crack of a tree splitting open as easily as a ripe peach pit, just a few feet behind them.

Elizabeth ducked under the tamarack and ran.

"She's likely sitting under a tree right now."

Todd's voice, hoarse and weaker than it had been, came out of the shadows.

A thump, and the fire flared up around the new log. Then it

settled back down to hissing and sizzling under the persistent drip from the vent hole.

"Or maybe wading down the middle of the stream." Todd wheezed, and produced a wet cough.

Nathaniel's backside was sore, but there was no hope of breathing easily if he were to lie down. Swearing to himself, he shifted the thorny spine of a balsam branch out from under him, getting his hands tacky with the pungent sap.

There was a flash of light, and in the distance, the answering rumble.

"Have you ever seen a man killed by lightning?" Todd went on.

"No," said Nathaniel, wiggling his shoulders for easier purchase against the log wall. "But then the storm is young, and I may have the pleasure yet."

"If she dies, the court will take the Wolf away from you."

"Just yesterday you thought I killed her in cold blood."

"Well, she does have an irritating way about her," Todd pointed out. "I've seen wounded cougars with more pleasant personalities."

Nathaniel dipped his tin cup into the water kettle. "Listen to you. All your shine is rubbing off, Todd."

"Tell me you wanted her for more than the land and I'll call you a liar."

"I ain't got the strength to get mad," Nathaniel said wearily. "But I could work myself up, if you want to push things a little further."

There was a streak of white past the open door, and a high-pitched squeal as an owl swooped down and off with a struggling prize. Nathaniel started, feeling the sweat pearl on his forehead.

"You couldn't throttle a rabbit," Todd observed. There was a pause, and the sound of chewing. Nathaniel had almost fallen asleep when the voice came again.

"Besides, if you ever were going to kill me, it would have been back then. When Sarah died."

Nathaniel felt his pulse beat pick up; he was suddenly not sleepy at all.

"You think it was my fault, I know you do. Everybody does."

It took a lot, but Nathaniel kept his peace.

"Well, it wasn't. Nobody could stop the bleeding. Curiosity couldn't, either, nor your mother, nobody. I did my best."

The storm swelled again, and the fire sputtered.

"Goddamn it man, I know you're awake. Say something."

"You're sicker than I thought," said Nathaniel. "To be running off at the mouth the way you are."

Richard grunted. "Fever," he said. "Does the talking."

"You got nothing to say worth listening to." Nathaniel tossed his cup and it clanged against the kettle.

"Not like you can walk away from me, is it, if I want to talk to you. But if you don't want to listen, then let me ask you a question."

"For Christ's sake, Todd. Save your breath."

"Why'd you marry her?"

He let the question hang there, not knowing which woman it was Todd was asking about. The one who lay all these years in her grave, a child in her arms whose father couldn't be named with certainty. Or the one out there on his account, who might not make it through the night.

Nathaniel said, "If you could have one of them, right now, which would it be?"

"Why, Sarah," said Todd softly, but without hesitation. "It was always Sarah. She was mine first."

Nathaniel looked hard across the fire, but he could see nothing of the man except one arm, bent up at an angle across his face. He wondered if the poison had got into his blood already, to have him talk so crazy.

"She never told you, I know it. But she would have run with me, that winter I ran away from Kahen'tiyo. If she could have."

"Sarah would've been ten years old," Nathaniel pointed out, trying to keep the irritation and anger from his voice, and not succeeding. That Falling-Day and her family had spent the winter that year in the Kahnyen'kehàka village to the north, he knew to be fact.

"I was only eleven. And she wanted to come with me," Todd said. "She knew even back then that she didn't belong."

"Sarah was Kahnyen'kehàka," Nathaniel said weakly.

"I taught her to think otherwise," said Todd. "Although she took some reminding, when we finally ran into each other again."

"Reason enough to kill you, right there." Nathaniel's fingers groped and curled and found no purchase. He forced himself to think of Elizabeth, and then he drew in three deep, pain-wrenching breaths, and then three more. "But I won't," he said finally. "At least, not right now." He closed his eyes, but it wasn't any good. Some things wouldn't go away in the dark.

"How come you're telling me about this now?" he asked. "All this time you kept quiet."

"I'm sicker than you are."

"Well, I don't care to hear your confession," Nathaniel snapped.

"That's not the point," Richard said. "You never have got the point."

"Then spit it out, man. What do you want of us?"

There was a long pause. "The leg's infected," Richard said. "If she doesn't get back here quick I won't have much chance."

Nathaniel said, "You can't have the Wolf, living or dead."

"But you could bury me there," he said softly. "If I don't make it, you could bury me next to Sarah."

"And if you live?"

"Then I'll do my best to get the mountain," Richard said.

Elizabeth fell for the second time climbing over a huge hummock. The carpet of moss gave way and she sank in to the ankle, coming to a full stop while the world revolved around her in a fury of wind, never-ending lightning, and thunder more predictable than the beat of her own heart. With a gasp, she sat back awkwardly on one haunch.

She was so wet, she could not remember what it was like to be dry. The buckskin clung to her heavily, and she thought lazily about simply taking all the wet things off and just making her way without. "Eve on the way back into the garden," she said aloud.

Treenie crowded in close, her teeth chattering visibly. Elizabeth slung one arm around the animal's neck to steady herself and slowly pulled her ankle out. A deep scratch, but no other injury. She had begun to pull up, when she felt the dog tense.

Just on the other side of the stream, the ragged frame of a dead balsam was thrown into relief by a huge flash of light. The bolt struck at the tip and rent it to the root with a noise so absolute that Elizabeth felt rather than heard the whoosh of the explosion: the balsam burst into a single flame, and fell in a slow and graceful arc like a torch flung into the stream. Unable to turn away or close her streaming eyes, Elizabeth watched as the burning tree discharged a volley of small missiles which flew through the air, streaming fire. Some landed heavily in the water, but one fell at her feet with a thud. She squinted, and looked harder, trying to make sense of it: a jay, its claws turned down on themselves in death. One half of its feathers strangely disheveled and standing on end; the other half charred raw and slightly steaming.

Elizabeth pulled herself to her feet, wiped the rain from her face, and set off again.

The familiar night sounds provided some comfort: the odd barking cry of the fox, the echoing owls, the wolves, forever calling, the shouting of the tree frogs and crickets singing without pause. Drifting in and out of sleep, taking note of the state of the fire and the storm, paying attention to Richard's small sounds, Nathaniel dozed and slept and thought of Elizabeth. Willed her forward, through the swamp and then due south, to Robbie. He willed her dry and whole and healthy, he willed her good spirits and easy thoughts and a clear trail. He willed her back beside him.

Richard sat up suddenly, startling Nathaniel out of his thoughts and fully awake. His hair stood out in a mane, his beard caked with grime. In the firelight his blue eyes blazed with fever and the madness of wanting and a clear, focused fear.

"What?" Nathaniel asked, even as he heard it himself. But he asked again, "What?" hoarsely. He reached for his rifle, the cold metal of the barrel as familiar to him as any part of his own body. His hands shook as he cocked the trigger. The sound was lost in the crackling of the fire.

Fear was commonplace in the bush. Once, deep in concentration as he aimed at a running buck, he had lost his footing and begun to slide over the edge of a cliff. As a young man, he had seen a panther drop out of a tree onto a boy's back and reach around to lay his throat open with a casual swipe of a paw. More than once, he had capsized in icy white water. But this fear was colder, because he could put no face to it, beyond the ones that Joe had described. No face that he wanted to see.

With his bad hand cradled against his chest, Richard was holding up his left palm toward Nathaniel. *Wait,* he mouthed. *Wait.*

Against the first gauzy light of dawn the huge form materialized in the door all at once. Nathaniel's nostrils flared: sweat and tobacco and beaver musk and bear grease, and all the other smells together that made the Kahnyen'kehàka smell. Fear gave way to relief so suddenly that Nathaniel broke into a running sweat. He lowered his rifle sights to wipe his face with one sleeve.

The man in the doorway came forward. The firelight picked out his rough-cast features: an old tomahawk scar ran from his scalp down the left side of his face; one ear was mangled. Nathaniel didn't recognize him, but that didn't matter. He would be related somehow, through Sarah. And a Kahnyen'kehàka out hunting or traveling wouldn't be alone.

It took three heartbeats for Nathaniel to realize that something was wrong with Richard, who crouched motionless on the other side of the fire. All the wariness and anger in his face had disappeared. Above the beard, his face had taken on the look of a child, blank with fear.

The man's eyes were narrowed and fixed on Richard. Suddenly, unexpectedly, they widened in surprise. The large mouth broadened into a smile, splitting the tattoos on his cheeks with deep dimples, turning him from a warrior into a boy.

"Irtakohsaks," said the man to Richard Todd. "Et-shitewa'kenha, karìwehs tsi sahtentyonh."

Cat-Eater, Little Brother. You have been gone a very long time.

XXXVII

Such a warm and excessively sunny morning seemed improbable after the night of storms, but Elizabeth woke to just that. She might be wet through, every muscle might protest at the need for action, but the early morning sunlight was welcome on her face.

And there was a rabbit, fresh killed, bleeding into the grass at her feet, and evidence on Treenie's muzzle that she had indulged herself first.

"Very generous of you," Elizabeth praised her. "But how am I going to start a fire?" She hauled herself into a sitting position and stretched arms overhead, wincing slightly. She was not quite hungry enough to eat the flesh raw. But eat she must.

Eventually, she found a cranny between some boulders where the accumulation of autumn leaves was thick and deep enough to provide some dry tinder. This she fed carefully until there was enough of a flame to cook the rabbit on an improvised spit of green wood. In the end she burned both her fingers and her mouth and ate it near to raw anyway, while Treenie made short work of the odds and ends.

She wished desperately for the time to sit quietly and dry out, even as she sorted through her things and made ready to set off. In the bottom of her pack she found a forgotten store of nuts, which she cracked between her teeth while she surveyed the damage. The gunpowder was damp, but she was only a morning's walk from Robbie, if she didn't lose her way. For that long she could do without the musket. The knife was easily dried and oiled. Finally, Elizabeth changed into the spare hunting shirt, which was not quite so damp as the overdress on her back, loosed her hair so that it could dry in the breeze and the sun, pinned her hair brooch to the inside of her shirt to keep it safe, checked the compass, and set off with her moccasins cold and wet on her feet.

She found herself humming after a bit, and stopped, surprised and a little shocked at a disquieting truth: she was no longer panicked. The thought of Nathaniel made her walk faster, but somewhere during the storm she had lost the kind of breathless fear which had threatened to overwhelm her since the shooting. Under clear skies washed into brilliance, panic was replaced by a calmness of purpose.

The forest thinned by mid-morning into something approximating a meadow, or as close to a meadow as she had ever experienced in the great northern woods. About an acre in diameter, it was predominantly knee-high grasses and blueberry thickets. Recognizing the place as the one Nathaniel had described to her, Elizabeth stopped and took her bearings again. She was to leave the river and turn due south, here, and make her way over the hill before her. There would be a deer trail, Nathaniel had said, that crossed a brook with an abandoned beaver dam.

With a start Elizabeth found herself nearly tripping over a fawn hidden in the grass, a tiny thing with huge round eyes that looked up at her without fear or interest. Treenie pushed forward eagerly.

"Mind your manners," Elizabeth said to her sharply. Dejected, the dog loped ahead in search of an uncensored meal. Elizabeth was hungry, too, but on the other side of this hill she would come to the lake called Little Lost, at the foot of Robbie's mountain. The thought of delay was unbearable.

She tucked the compass into her belt and went down on one knee to retie a moccasin, feeling her hair, dry now, falling in a veil past her cheek and shoulder to touch the ground. It was a strange feeling to wear her hair loose, almost as disconcerting as it would be to walk naked through the meadow. Feeling suddenly vulnerable, Elizabeth stood.

"Not so long ago, the Indians would have fought over those long curls of yours," said a voice behind her. "Killed each other for the privilege of scalping you. But of course, your hair is magnificent, Madame Bonner."

Elizabeth drew one very slow and deep breath. She turned, her thoughts churning as fast as the racing of her heart.

Jack Lingo. He was directly before her; she could see the individual hairs in the eyebrow which he raised in a quizzical arch.

"I see I have surprised you."

His gaze flickered away, over her shoulder. Behind them Treenie was growling, a sound which would have made Elizabeth's hair stand on end in other circumstances. The trapper pursed his lips.

"Your animal?" he asked, bringing up the barrel of his rifle.

"Yes," Elizabeth said hoarsely. The clack of the hammer striking the lock seemed very loud. With the hiss of the primer powder, she simply reached out and pushed the barrel hard to one side and held it there in her fist. She felt it jerk in her hand with the blast of sound and smoke. Above her own coughing, the other sounds came all together: Lingo's curse, and the dog's scream. She turned in time to see the flash of one red haunch disappearing into the trees.

Elizabeth turned on her heel to go after her, but Lingo had her by the wrist with a grip that did not yet hurt, but soon would.

"Let me go," Elizabeth said.

"It was just a graze, thanks to your foolish intervention. You needn't worry about the animal."

Elizabeth stilled suddenly.

The eyebrow peaked again. "You don't believe me, and why should you? But in this case I am telling the truth. She has gone off to tend her wound. She may live."

He jerked with his head toward a log on the ground, letting go of her wrist.

"Sit."

She stood, and watched his face cloud with something she

could not name. Not anger. Anticipation. Her stomach rose and turned in on itself.

"Mr. Lingo," she said, and faltered.

"Sit," he repeated. "We may have a long wait ahead of us. And please, you must call me Jacques."

"Jacques," she said. "Please let me go."

At that he gave her a broad smile. His teeth were very white and even, overlarge in his face. "Do you beg me already? You disappointed me last time, madame. This time I will wait for your good husband to come and confront him myself. Perhaps with your assistance we can finally resolve this misunderstanding between us."

Elizabeth could not gather her thoughts. He intended to keep her here with him; she could not be delayed. Perspiration trickled down her face.

He was looking at her sharply. "Unless you are already widowed?"

She jumped. "No."

Lingo reached over and took the useless musket out of her belt. He tapped the muzzle against one tooth, thoughtfully. "So soon tired of married life? No, I thought not. He has a way with the women, does Nathaniel. There was a little wench up in Good Pasture, she would have followed him anywhere once he had her. But he was not interested in a wife at that time. Or shall we say, not in a poor wife. But I bore you."

"Mr. Lingo," began Elizabeth. "Come along with me if you must, but I have an errand that cannot wait."

"Cannot wait?"

Elizabeth shifted uncomfortably, using all her concentration to set her face in neutral lines. To tell this man that Nathaniel lay wounded and defenseless a day and a half's walk away did not appeal to her at all. On the other hand, if she did not tell him he might keep her here all day, which would be disastrous. She had no doubt that he could outrun her, even with his limp. Remembering the look on Nathaniel's face when he had found her after her last conversation with Lingo, she knew that she was in very serious trouble.

"I have to fetch Robbie," she said finally. "There was an

accident. Richard Todd was hurt. Nathaniel can't carry him out, alone."

The blue eyes narrowed. "I have no patience with lying women," he said. "I have relieved more than one of that breed of their tongues."

Elizabeth drew herself up, and called forth every bit of dignity she possessed. "Richard Todd is injured, and I am on my way to Robbie. I'd like my musket back, please."

She regretted that *please*. It had sparked an unpleasant smile.

"Mais non, you cannot leave so soon. And it would not do you any good. Robbie is away."

"Away?" She cleared her throat. "If he is walking his trap lines, he will be back soon enough. Now." She nodded and took a step backward. "Excuse me—"

"But I most certainly do not," said Jack Lingo. "Look, here comes an old friend of yours. Perhaps you will find his conversation more to your liking."

Even in total darkness, the smell would have been enough to put a name to the man who came up behind her.

"Dutch Ton," said Lingo. "The beautiful Madame Bonner, of whom you speak so often. I think we will make camp right here, don't you?"

In the late afternoon she made her first attempt at escape, and failed. The men had been drinking for hours, quarreling and singing in turns; sometimes they seemed to forget her, and other times they discussed her openly, as if she were not capable of understanding their comments.

Elizabeth watched the sun track through the sky, feeling the skin on her nose and across her cheekbones burning and stretching with the heat. Lingo would not allow her to change her position; he walked with her to the edge of the forest when she relieved herself, turning away slowly after a disquieting moment when he seemed to be set on watching her.

She guessed the hour to be three in the afternoon when they fell asleep. Lingo sat against a sapling with his rifle cradled across his lap, his ankles crossed and his chin on his chest. Dutch Ton, twice his width, lay spread-eagle in the meadow grass with his mouth open to the sky, the ginger stubble on his face glistening with saliva. Elizabeth watched them breathing for a long time, and then she simply stood up and began to walk away.

When she had reached the edge of the wood, a rifle shot clipped a tree branch just above her head. Lingo had caught up to her before she could even think of running. Without a word, he wound one fist in her hair and yanked her back to camp. She would not yell, though she could not stop the tears that welled up at the pain.

This time he did not banter politely as he bound her. The rope was old and sticky with some substance Elizabeth could not—did not want to—identify. He pulled a loop tight around her left wrist, and tied the other end to his belt. Then he fell with a grunt back down to the ground, scratching the crotch of his breeches intently. He laughed out loud when she looked away.

"What do you think, has he grown tired of her?" he asked Dutch Ton. "It is hard to imagine, looking at her. But then again perhaps she is unresponsive."

"She can read," Ton pointed out. "A teacher."

Lingo spat into the fire.

"We might shave her head," he said thoughtfully, leaning over to touch a curl where it lay on Elizabeth's shoulder. "No scars, after all. But a clear message."

She jerked away. Some time ago she had decided that it would not serve her in any way to involve herself in a discussion with either of these men, and so she bit her tongue and fought hard to keep her face calm. With each passing hour that became more difficult.

Lingo had uncorked the bottle and drank again, deeply.

I am not thirsty, Elizabeth chanted to herself. *I am not thirsty*.

He leaned toward her on one elbow, held out the bottle. She pressed her mouth into a hard line and blinked, slowly.

Lingo lowered the bottle, but stayed stretched out before her, staring up at her face. There was graying stubble on his face now, and a network of wrinkles at his eyes and the corners of his mouth. The skin on his neck was loose and soft.

"You are older than you first appear," Elizabeth said out

loud, surprised at the creakiness of her own voice, unused now
for hours.

His expression hardened, and he snorted softly. Then with
his mouth pursed and his elegant brows drawn together in a
tight vee, he lifted one hand with a slow and deliberate motion
and encircled her ankle with it. She could feel the heat of his
palm through the soft leather of her moccasin, the length of his
thumb, the firm pressure of four fingertips.

When Elizabeth was suffused with color, he smiled, and let
her ankle go.

At nightfall the men made a small fire and cooked a hen turkey
Ton had snared. Lingo threw Elizabeth a piece of charred meat.

"So, how long do you think it will take for Todd to die
without medical attention?" he asked in a jovial tone. "Perhaps
he is dead already and your troubles about the mountain are
over. You would owe me a debt, then."

Dutch Ton had been sucking on a bone, and the face he held
up in the firelight glistened with fat. He looked between Elizabeth and Lingo with his usual perplexed gaze. She caught his
eye, and held it until he blinked and looked away. He had
brought her water earlier in the evening, enduring Lingo's ridi-
cule. Elizabeth had hopes of him.

"It is very rude of you to deny me conversation," Lingo said,
sighing. "Ton here has such a limited view of the world."

"Have you had any more letters from your sister?" Elizabeth
asked Ton.

Lingo raised his voice. "Of course, maybe Todd and Bonner
are both dead. In which case you will need consolation in your
grief. You would prefer Ton's . . . assistance to mine?"

"If you still have that letter," Elizabeth persisted, "I would
very much like to look at it again."

"She is trying to seduce you, Ton. Tell her she needn't work
so hard at it."

Elizabeth was glad of the twilight, hoping that it masked her
heightened color. Dutch Ton was staring at her and she managed a prim smile. "The letter?" she repeated.

"Don't have it no more," he said. "Didn't need it, once it was read to me."

"Oh, what a pity," Elizabeth said lamely. "Then perhaps you could tell me something about yourself."

Lingo laughed softly. "*Oui, Ton.* Tell her about the day down at the schoolhouse, and how close you came to killing her husband."

Elizabeth started. Ton had dropped his gaze and was poking at the fire with a stick.

"Five good beaver pelts," said Lingo. "That's all it took to have him shoot your precious husband. But of course, he failed to kill him and never collected."

In her cold fury Elizabeth said, "I didn't realize that you were quite that lazy. To have a simpleminded man fight your battles for you."

Before she realized what he was about, Lingo had reached across the fire. He used the back of his hand rather than his fist, but still Elizabeth's head rocked back and she tasted blood in her mouth. The blow echoed in her head.

"Let me show you what Ton will do for a beaver pelt," said Lingo. "I think you will find it most instructive. If the smell of him doesn't choke you first. And then I will take my turn and demonstrate to you that I am very capable of settling my own scores."

"Nathaniel and Hawkeye will track you down," Elizabeth said, her voice faltering.

"The north woods are very large," said Lingo. "And we know them as well as your men. Better."

"But think," Elizabeth said softly. "Am I worth the last chance you have at your gold?"

His smile startled her. In the firelight, his pale eyes seemed totally without color. "Perhaps," he said. "Just perhaps you are. I have the idea that you are a screamer, madame. A weakness of mine, you see, that I indulge on occasion." He was tossing more wood on the fire as he said this, and there was a swoosh as it caught, and the crackle of resin. An explosion of sparks flew up and into the darkening sky; Elizabeth watched them scattering like malevolent spirits.

He lifted his hand as if to salute her. The rope that bound

them together jumped to life. It had been lying coiled to one side of the fire, but now she watched him loop it around his wrist, once, twice, until it stretched high across the fire between them. The first tug Elizabeth was able to resist without moving. She held his eye, and lifted her chin.

He jerked harder, and she rose awkwardly. Another yank, and she fell forward onto her knees, directly before the fire. She scrambled to her feet.

Lingo stood and gathered the rope in both hands. Realizing that he intended to pull her into the flames, Elizabeth began to struggle in earnest, leaning back with all her weight.

"Stop," said Dutch Ton quietly.

Lingo laughed breathlessly. "It won't kill her," he said, jerking again so that she stumbled half into the fire. "Just a scar or two in payment for that mouth of hers."

The skin on Elizabeth's wrist had peeled away, but she was too concentrated on the fire to take note of that, or of the blood. She struggled for her footing, sliding forward two inches for every inch she regained. The toes of her moccasins were singed. Tossing her head back in an effort to keep her hair from the flames, she saw Dutch Ton towering over her. His large, placid face was creased in concentration.

Coming up next to her, Ton closed his fist over the rope in front of her own two straining hands. For a single strange moment Elizabeth was reminded of childhood games with her cousins. Then Ton grunted, and pulled. With a shout of rage Jack Lingo was hauled through the fire, scattering burning wood and embers everywhere.

They had stumbled backward together, and Elizabeth stood heaving for breath, watching while Lingo bellowed and hopped, slapping at himself. There were burnt spots on his hunting shirt and breeches, and a livid red welt on his hand.

And then he looked at her, and she knew that the unholy tales Nathaniel had kept from her about Jack Lingo were all true, and more, and worse. He grinned, and she moaned.

He pulled the rope up again, and producing a knife from its sheath at his belt, he cut it with a single movement. Then he launched himself at Dutch Ton.

Elizabeth backed away. The men circled each other slowly,

Lingo lithe and winding; Dutch Ton much like a bear, all hulk-
ing muscle. She could hear the sound of Ton's breathing, even
above the steady stream of curses in French and English. With a
scream, Lingo rushed the bigger man and threw his weight at
him.

Without stopping to think about the outcome of this fight,
Elizabeth circled the fire to the jumble of provisions, keeping
her eyes on the men while she searched with shaking hands.
Her knife, her pack, her musket, these she grabbed up and
turned away, and then turned back. There was no time to look
for her wedding ring or the silver hair clasp that he had taken
from her, and no time for regret, either. After a split second's
hesitation, she took up Lingo's rifle, too, and she ran into the
woods.

In the meadow there had been enough of a moon to cast a
weak shadow, but once the woods closed around her she was in
total darkness. Elizabeth stopped, closed her eyes, and forced
herself to breathe deeply.

There was a fluttering above her in the trees, and she looked
up in time to see the faint glimmer of a wide white breast.
Then the owl called, and her pulse slowed.

He would be after her, if he survived the fight. And Elizabeth feared that he would survive. Dutch Ton had drawn
Lingo's anger on himself and given her this opportunity; he
would most probably pay dearly. She could not find it in herself
to be thankful for this, not right now. All she could think of
now was getting away, of finding Robbie.

Her vision was adjusting slowly to reveal the faintest outlines
of trees.

Blue-eyed people are at an advantage in the night woods,
Nathaniel had told her once while they made camp on a moon-
less night. He had winked one hazel eye at her and drawn her
into the darkness of the balsam-branch shanty where there had
been only Nathaniel and no thought of anybody but him until
the sunrise. She had not feared the dark then. She had never
feared it before. But Jack Lingo had looked at her over the fire,

his pale blue eyes promising things she did not want to contemplate.

Elizabeth stifled a small hiccup of fear and began to sort through the weapons. As she tucked the musket into her belt she realized that she had neglected to pick up the powder horn.

Instead, she had Lingo's rifle. In the afternoon she had watched him clean it, polishing the walnut stock lovingly. A Kentucky rifle, he had told her with some considerable pride in his voice, in spite of her studied lack of interest. She ran her hands over it in the dark, familiarizing herself with its dimensions, touching the trigger lightly. It was primed, but to shoot it accurately and hit a moving target would be a miracle.

Miracles are a luxury you cannot afford, she told herself sternly. *You have only yourself to depend on.*

Elizabeth looped the strap over her head, swung the gun across her back, and set off cautiously. She thought of Treenie now, hot regret welling up in her eyes.

She had feared hunger and exhaustion, and found instead that she was suffused with energy, uplifted with it, rendered almost weightless. By the time the night sounds had begun to recede and she was able to make out irregular patches of sky, Elizabeth had begun to hope that she had evaded Jack Lingo. She would soon reach the crest of the hill, and there would be enough light to check her compass. In the early light, walking steadily, she could make Robbie's camp in two hours from that point.

There was a spring and a trickle of water; she drank at length, glad of the icy cold. She filled her palms and splashed her sunburned cheeks with it. When she looked up, she realized that it was light enough to see the ferns and grasses that circled the spring. She took a handful of wild mint, tucked half of it into her shirt and the other into her cheek, and drank again.

Able to move more quickly, Elizabeth picked up her pace, pausing now and then to listen. Near the crest of the hill, she paused for a longer time, and felt her pulse take up an extra beat. Six weeks in the bush under the tutelage of Runs-from-Bears and Robbie and Nathaniel had made her aware of certain things. She could not always put a name to what she heard, but she could say if it was out of place. The faint crackling might be a moose, or it might be a man. She headed uphill again, hoping for a clearing at the top. What advantage this would bring her she was not sure, but it was a goal and she moved toward it.

And then stopped, finding herself at the edge of a small clearing. Afraid to step out, she hesitated.

She started at the sound of his voice, yelping one high, clear tone.

"Don't run," he said easily. "It is such a waste of energy. In the end I will catch you anyway."

But she ran, without looking back. She felt his knife thump against the rifle on her back; heard him curse and stop to retrieve it. She ran faster, into the woods again, downhill now, she ran hard and clean, her toes turned safely inward, leaping over a small stream and dodging a deadfall. Branches tore at her hair like grasping hands. Elizabeth heard Lingo behind her, and she ran harder.

The scream was like a woman's, high and shrill. It pulled her up short as nothing else save Nathaniel's voice could have done. Elizabeth tripped and righted herself and turned back to see the panther dropping out of a tree to take Jack Lingo to the ground. She had passed under that tree just seconds before.

Elizabeth stood taking in great burning gulps of air while she watched. Unable to turn away, unable to run as she knew she should, she must. She watched first in horror as they struggled, and then in disbelief and amazement and unwilling admiration as Lingo extricated himself from the dying animal.

He stood looking at her, blood dripping from the scratches on his upper body, his bloody knife at his side. She turned to run again, and again she tripped.

In seconds he was on her, one foot on the small of her back as he reached down to cut the rifle strap. He was careless with the knife; the cut burned. Then he was up again, kicking her until she rolled over to face him. Lingo leaned down, his breath rancid on her face, his eyes glittering. His sweat dripped onto her, and his blood. She heard a hoarse whimpering, and knew it was her own.

"This will take a very long time," he said, not bothering to grin now.

She tried to roll away and he slapped her, and slapped her again, until she lay still looking up at his face and the canopy of trees with her ears ringing. Behind him was a wild cherry tree in full bloom, framing his scratched face in delicate white blossoms. It was a strange sight. Elizabeth smiled.

Lingo started at her smile, and then his face darkened. His eyes traveled down over her breasts. With a small flick of his knife he cut the first tie, nearest her throat.

"There's no hurry," he said, his eyes darting wildly. "Let me tell you first what I've got in mind." He was speaking French now, his voice low and easy, talked on and on while he played with the knife, laying the flat of the blade on her cheek, touching the tip to the corner of her eye. She learned that steel had a smell, bright and hard.

Elizabeth wished for the ability to close her ears as she could her eyes. She turned away inwardly, tried to gather her thoughts. She could not reach for her knife. The musket was useless.

"I see I have lost your interest," he said after a while. The knife jerked again, cutting her skin this time with the tie. He grinned, and the bile rose in her throat.

"Ah," he said, lifting up the silver chain with the bloody tip of the knife. "You have been hiding treasures from me."

"Take it," Elizabeth said.

"Oh, I shall. When we are . . . finished."

If she struggled, perhaps he would kill her outright. For one moment, she could not decide if that was something to be wished for, or not.

She tried to fix on Nathaniel's face in her mind, but he would not come to her, as if he could not bear the sight of her pinned underneath Jack Lingo.

Elizabeth sobbed. Lingo slapped her, and her lip split against her teeth. He rubbed one finger in her blood and drew it down between her exposed breasts. She began to retch.

Lingo jerked back, his face creased with disgust. Elizabeth rolled onto her stomach and hauled herself to her hands and knees, vomiting into the soft mass of moldering leaves. Her whole body shook with it.

She heard him moving away. She hung her head and

brought up the last her stomach had to offer, blood and bile, mint and bitterness. Gagging, praying, she lifted her head and heard an unexpected sound.

He stood three feet away, his back turned to her, leaning with one shoulder against the cherry tree. It struck her almost as comical, that he would think to turn away while he pissed. She choked back something that might have been a laugh.

At her side was his rifle. The gleaming barrel, more than three feet in length, the long, polished cherry wood stock with its inset patchbox and hinged brass lid. Something etched in the brass plate in ornate script. Her vision doubled but then cleared:

VOUS ET NUL AUTRE

You and no other. Elizabeth's fingers curled around the cold metal.

Wake up now! she heard Curiosity's voice say clearly. *You can't always be daydreaming when the fat's in the fire.*

As he began to turn back toward her, Elizabeth lurched to her feet with the rifle barrel in both hands like a cricket bat. Her scream seemed to paralyze him, tearing up from the gut, every ounce of her strength and rage in it. His expression was almost resigned: one brow frozen high in reluctant admiration as his eyes traced the arc of the swing.

The edge of the stock met his head over the left ear. The cracking bone resounded like nothing Elizabeth had ever heard before and she felt his skull pop like the shell of a beetle underfoot. The force of the blow traveled up her arms with a jolt that forced her backward, the gun dropping out of her hands just as Jack Lingo hit the ground, folding in on himself.

She stood looking down at him, her hands tingling at her sides.

Petals were falling. They made intricate and lovely patterns on the spreading crimson lake; they spangled the wild tangle of his matted hair. His eyes were open, and his expression quizzical.

A woman who had always taken pleasure in a task well done, Elizabeth turned her face upward and sent a howl of satisfaction spiraling into the sky.

.   .   .

She left him as he was, and went on without weapons, without provisions. A half mile away, she stopped to listen, and hearing no sound of him, she sat down on the forest floor. After a good while, Elizabeth rose to her feet, wiped her swollen face with her own hair and checked the compass. She was off course, but not badly. She began to walk.

At Little Lost she stopped, and stumbled, and walked into the water, submerging herself for as long as she could bear it. The cold was a mercy on her cuts and bruises. She drank until she could drink no more, and finally came up on the shore where she lay with her throbbing cheek against the firm, cool sand. A loon swam by, its ruby eyes turned blindly toward her. She wondered how loon might taste.

The path to Robbie's camp was immediately familiar. It would be safe to run, if only she had the energy. Her feet hurt, and her face was a misery. She wondered if Robbie would recognize her.

The clearing, then. Finally. The worn log benches and stone-lined cook pit, the neat rows of traps hung under the roof, the woodpile. No fire burning, no sign of Robbie. She called, and got nothing but a crow's raucous cry in return. Elizabeth looked into a stand of pine and saw the bird balanced delicately on a sycamore branch, its dusty black breast spotted with yolk and eggshell. Around it, the robin darted and shrieked while the crow reached into her nest again.

Elizabeth wondered if it was possible simply to die of despair.

XXXVIII

She dreamed of Runs-from-Bears, but in her dream he had grown young, his face smooth and unscarred. As always, though, he smelled quite distinctly of bear grease and hard walking. She huddled in on herself, seeking a deeper sleep in which dreams did not rely on scent to send their message.

But her stomach was growling, and under her hip a spray of pine needles had worked themselves into a most uncomfortable spot. And the smell of bear grease was still there, now accompanied by a voice, one she recognized. Elizabeth bolted upright and knocked heads with Otter.

"My God," he whispered. "It is you."

"Otter," she said, and drawing in one deep breath to steady herself, Elizabeth reached out and grasped both of his forearms with her hands.

"Do you have any food?"

His look of surprise and shock was quite suddenly replaced by a sense of purpose. He disappeared for a moment but was back before she could rise to follow him, putting a piece of dried venison in one hand, and a great hunk of nocake in the other. Her mouth filled instantly with saliva.

Otter watched her eat. She saw his eyes moving over her face tentatively, as if he could not quite believe what he saw.

"Is it so very bad?" she asked finally, between mouthfuls.

He blinked in affirmation.

Suddenly exhausted again, Elizabeth slumped. She looked at the sky and was surprised to see that it was still very early, long before noon. She could not have been sleeping for more than an hour.

"Nathaniel?" Otter asked, warily.

"He's alive," she said. She did not often weep; she had always prided herself on that, the ability to control excesses of pain or anxiety until they could be digested in private. But now, even as she found the necessary words and told the story in a fairly calm and quite comprehensible way, tears ran down her face and drenched the remains of her shirt. She finished as quickly as she could, leaving out only what she could not bear to relate: how Nathaniel had received his wound, and what had delayed her. Otter was young, but there was a reserve about him that reminded her of Bears. She was infinitely grateful not to be asked to explain her battered face.

"We have to go after Nathaniel, and Todd." His eyes flashed at this last name, and Elizabeth remembered that there was unsettled business between Richard and Otter. She tried to remember what Nathaniel had told her of the march to Canajoharie, but her head was muddled, and the world seemed bent on a lopsided spin.

"But Robbie," Elizabeth repeated, thinking of his strength and his experience and his love of Nathaniel. If anyone could save them from disaster, it must be Robbie. "Do you know where Robbie's gone?"

"There's no time to waste, waiting for him," Otter pointed out.

Elizabeth could not hide her disappointment, although she had no wish to insult Otter. But he was looking at her, for the moment, with a narrowed gaze and for the first time Elizabeth saw Falling-Day in him, her quiet determination.

"We got to get you cleaned up before we set out," said Otter, and he disappeared in the direction of the caves.

Questions were running together in her head, all of which she wanted immediate answers for. What Otter was doing here in the bush on his own, whether Hannah and Hawkeye and the others were whole and safe, how soon they could leave, how long it would take. If he believed Nathaniel could still be alive.

She dared not let herself think about it, about the time lost, about what she had left behind under the wild cherry tree, about Nathaniel. She had not yet given up on him, and she would not, until she had seen him laid in the ground or had gone to her own grave.

Otter came back at a trot, his hands full of what he needed to tend her wounds.

Elizabeth got to her feet, and he helped her.

Back on the trail with her wounds cleaned and bound, and Otter's solid back always in sight, Elizabeth felt herself floating. She knew that she was near to collapsing, and that she must soon ask him to make camp. But they had only been under way for an hour, and she felt the press of time as surely as she felt the throbbing of the bruises that ranged up and down her ribs.

And also, there was the matter of the cherry tree. In less than an hour's walk they would come upon it, and there would be no choice but to explain. Elizabeth wanted that behind her, and so she took a mouthful of nocake to chew slowly, and she focused her energies on putting one foot in front of the other.

She had been worried about Otter's youth, about his impulsive behavior: walking behind him, she thought at great length about the gunshot which had bolted the sleigh team, and what might have come of that. But he had been trained by men she trusted and loved, and he walked with their gait and posture and keen, sweeping gaze, his rifle forward and primed. For the moment she was content to follow him. This passivity would not last as long as her collection of bruises; this well she knew herself. But for the moment, she was thankful for Otter, who set a good pace and didn't coddle her.

Elizabeth convinced herself that she was capable of walking past that spot under the cherry tree. She had nothing to hide; could hide nothing, in fact. She would not let Jack Lingo reach out from the grave to make one last attempt to keep her from Nathaniel. Not that he had a grave, or ever would.

In the end when she recognized the turn of the trail, she could not go on. Otter went those few steps without noticing that she hung back, and she heard a soft exclamation. A long silence followed.

There was a dead oak which had fallen into a small pond. She had not noticed it on first passing. Out of the thick layer of pungent green scum that blanketed the water, a rack of branches bleached the color and glossiness of old bone pointed at the sky. On each sat a single grackle, dark feathers iridescent in the late sunlight. Elizabeth counted fourteen of them, motionless, their eyes turned to her. She could not remember ever seeing grackles in these forests before. Blinking hard, she wondered if she were imagining them, or if perhaps they were part of that other forest which seemed to always be there, right below the surface: the forest of red dogs and stone men, birds shimmering in rainbows and lovers who wandered the swamp murmuring their vows in Latin. Her ability to reason these things away had been worn thin, as thin as the wooden disk that lay still between her breasts. She touched a finger to Joe's bijou and watched as the birds flew away, one by one.

She started to find Otter standing in front of her. Elizabeth lifted her chin and met his gaze. His eyes were so dark, but they were like her own in at least one way: in them she could read what he was feeling. And what she saw she could not at first credit.

"Awiyo, aktsi'a," he said hoarsely. *Well done, my sister.*

Otter opened his palms. On the left, a large gold coin shimmered against the deep bronze of his skin; His Royal Highness King George II seemed to be winking at her, as if he approved of this change in his circumstances. In the other palm—Elizabeth blanched to see it—there was a tooth. Long and yellow and wickedly curved. It was still bloody.

Otter steadied her, his fingers and the coin pressing into her shoulder.

"The panther," he said softly. Then he held up the tooth to his own necklace of teeth and claws, as if to demonstrate.

"Yes, please, you have it." Elizabeth felt nauseated and suddenly a little dizzy.

"No," said Otter forcefully. "You must wear it, it is your right." He touched his own necklace, and then hers: the bijou and the silver flower that had belonged to Nathaniel's mother.

She said: "I didn't kill the panther." Her voice had gone suddenly hoarse, and she began to shake.

"But he did, and you killed him." He paused. "It's Lingo, ain't it? I've heard tell, but I never saw the man before."

Otter was more than ten years her junior, but Elizabeth felt like a child under his gaze: vulnerable and uncertain and very afraid. It seemed that everything came back very simply to this truth, which could not be avoided. The evidence was around this turn in the path. She had killed a man. And why? Otter had not asked, but he was watching her patiently, and waiting.

For Nathaniel's sake. Jack Lingo had kept her from her errand, and by that act he may have caused Nathaniel's death. But she knew in her heart that this was not the truth. Perhaps not even a part of the truth.

Lingo had put his hands on her, and it was that, that sin which had fueled her journey, instantaneous, from the woman she had been to the woman she was now. She had raised the rifle and swung it for herself alone, for Nathaniel had not existed at all: in that instant she had been alone in the world with Jack Lingo.

She nodded. "Yes," she said. "It is—it was, Jack Lingo." She sought Otter's gaze. Those final words would not come, and so she let them float between them.

Something flickered in Otter's eyes; he was looking at her, looking hard. Seeing the cuts and the bruises on all of her exposed skin, even to the backs of her hands in a spread of color from yellow-green to indigo. "Tkayeri," he said softly. *It is proper so.*

Elizabeth took the coin and the panther's tooth from him, held them together in one hand. The tooth was very sharp, and mottled with dried blood. "I should wear these?"

"Why not? It is your right," Otter repeated.

"Why not," Elizabeth echoed. "Yes, why not."

They camped on the crest of the hill. Otter built a quick lean-to of balsam branches, beginning with a sapling which he rough-stripped and propped against the trunk of an older tree. Elizabeth ate while he worked, forcing herself to swallow corn bread spread liberally with bear fat. It was slick and the taste was overpowering, but with each mouthful she felt her body stir and waken, as if she were a growing thing supplied with water after a long drought.

She felt suddenly very anxious, and wondered if they should have continued walking. When she asked Otter about this, he shrugged diplomatically. Elizabeth sighed and sought a more comfortable position against the beech. There was a bird calling, a plaintive three-note song, and Otter singing softly under his breath while he worked.

Elizabeth fell asleep with the Tory Gold resting between her breasts, warmed by her skin.

They walked hard the next day. Elizabeth scanned the swamp halfheartedly for Treenie, but saw no trace of her. The swamp itself no longer frightened her; she saw it only as another obstacle between herself and Nathaniel. When they stopped to rest and eat, she could barely sit still, and found herself being addressed like a wayward child by Otter. She snapped at him, and he blinked his disapproval. A trick he had learned from Nathaniel. She sat, finally, and ate.

"If we push hard we could be there just after sunset," she proposed. Knowing even as she said this that she was incapable of such a thing. Walking as hard as she was able, without injuries, she had needed a full day for the stretch before them, and it was midday now. Elizabeth took another mouthful of dried beef, as salty as tears.

Otter did her the courtesy of not replying.

"You will make a good husband someday," she observed grudgingly.

"My mother does not think so." He grinned.

They made camp late, past dark and only three good hours from Nathaniel. Elizabeth could not sleep at first, as tired as she was. Every muscle trembled, and the tips of her fingers were numb. She lay with her leggings rolled to a pillow underneath her head and stared at the sky, the great sweep of stars too bright to ignore.

"You haven't asked about Hannah," Otter pointed out to

her, and just that suddenly all of Elizabeth's tension collapsed in on itself. There were other people who missed Nathaniel and worried for him; one of them was his daughter. Her daughter.

"She sent along a message for you. Said, tell her I been keeping the new schoolhouse in order, swept up and dusted."

Her throat suddenly swollen with tears, Elizabeth tried to find Otter's face in the dark. "Tell me about home," she said.

In the morning Otter had to wake her, her sleep was so deep and absolute. She sat up, disoriented, and accepted the water skin from him. They ate and drank in near darkness. Elizabeth could hardly strap on her pack, her hands shook so.

Otter was as silent and preoccupied as she was. Yesterday he had talked easily and at length about any number of topics that came to him, but now as the sun rose on a day that promised to be hot and clear, his look was dark and uninviting. He insisted on taking the time to clean his gun again, boiling water in a tin cup to purge the barrel, measuring powder carefully, and loading it with what seemed to Elizabeth enough lead to bring down a bear.

It wasn't until they were under way that she was able to breathe again. Her mind kept composing pictures for her: Nathaniel weak but clear-eyed, Nathaniel consumed in fever, Nathaniel lost to her, too deep inside himself to hear her calling. When she thought of Richard, it was reluctantly, unwilling to expend any of her goodwill on him at all. *Perhaps he is dead,* she thought with no regret, and then colored with shame and defiance, simultaneously. It would be easier, and to deny that would be the worst kind of hypocrisy.

Her thoughts went back to Nathaniel, what he would need. Food, and water, and his wounds tended. He would still be coughing, but hopefully not bleeding anymore. Perhaps Otter would know more about herbs than she did, what she should look for, what teas might help. He could hunt and provide for them, and she would look after Nathaniel, until he was well enough to walk.

He would be sleeping when they came in; she imagined this. His face thin with pain and disguised by many days' growth of beard, but when she woke him he would grin at her, and call her Boots, and hold out his hands. She hesitated to think how he might react to her bruises, but she was determined to tell him nothing of Jack Lingo, not at first. Not until necessary. A bad fall would have given her the same injuries, and he had seen her fall before. She thought that this was a reasonable story, and one she would be able to make him believe. If only Otter would cooperate. If only she could keep her voice from giving her away.

When he was fed and his wounds tended to, then he would sleep. And she would sleep beside him, and he would heal. Then they would go home to Paradise and start their life.

The unnamed lake with the island at its center where they had last been together was suddenly there before them, and the platform of rock, where they had watched the eagles mate. Elizabeth broke into a run, with Otter right behind her. It was only two minutes, but how could that be? It must be ten times that, or more. Otter was talking to her, but she could make no sense of what he was saying; could not even tell if it was English or Mohawk.

At the edge of the clearing she pulled up, hard, and saw the smoke curling at a cook fire. One of them was well enough to get outside to tend it. A great rush of hope burst through her, and she knew how afraid she had been. She paused to catch her breath, and in that moment what she had taken as a great pile of red pelts on Joe's grave rolled suddenly to one side and gave a low woof. Elizabeth watched in disbelief as Treenie came loping toward her, grinning idiotically, her whole body moving with the rhythm of her tail. There was a wound on her back, crusted with blood. Elizabeth steadied herself by threading her fingers into the dog's coat, speaking softly to her. Then she cleared her throat and started forward, calling out.

Robbie MacLachlan's familiar form materialized in the doorframe. Elizabeth's voice died in her throat, and then she increased her pace, running the last few paces into Robbie's comforting embrace.

"Weel, then, lassie," he said while he patted at her back.

"It's nae sae bad, nae sae bad a'all. Dinna greet so, ye'll break ma heart."

His great bulk blocked out the rest of the world. Wiping her face with her hands, Elizabeth looked up into his eyes, and saw no end to her troubles.

"Is he alive?" she asked hoarsely. "Tell me he's alive, Robbie, please."

"Who, then? Joe? Do ye ken Joe? If it's him ye mean, I canna hold oot much hope, for there's a new grave—"

Elizabeth pulled away from him, shook her head. "That is Joe's grave. He died five days ago." Without waiting for Robbie's reaction, she walked stiffly past him and into the shelter. On either side of the cold fire there was nothing but a scattering of straw on the earth floor. The food, the weapons, and the tools; everything was gone. She heard herself moan, pressed the back of her hand to her mouth until her lip, barely healed, began to bleed again.

"I dinna understand," Robbie was saying behind her. "Where's Nathaniel, lass? And how come ye here lookin' sae blue an' battered?"

"He was here," she said numbly. "I left him here, to fetch you. They were both injured, and couldn't walk."

"Baith injured? Who baith?" The frustration in Robbie's voice was making it break and crackle. "I dinna understand."

"Cat-Eater," said Otter.

There was a soft woosh of surprise from Robbie, and then he came forward to take her by the arm. "I came this way this morning tae look in on Joe, for he was a friend o' mine. Now ye tell me that Joe is dead, and Nathaniel and Todd were here? They fought?"

She nodded, hesitating only slightly.

"Someone came," she said, more to herself than Robbie. "Someone came and took them away."

Robbie's hand moved to Elizabeth's shoulder, and it gripped her firmly. "I've been in this part o' the bush for a guid week, lass, and there's ample sign o' Indian aboot. No' three days syne I came across an abandoned camp. They were headed this way."

Elizabeth looked up at Robbie, saw the hope in his face and

felt the stirrings of it in her own heart. "Do you think they were Kahnyen'kehàka?"

"Aye, fra' the sign I wad say they were. And they are in the habit o' passin' through this way." He cast a glance at Otter which Elizabeth could not quite interpret, but the younger man had a question which was more relevant.

"How many were they?" he asked.

"At least a dozen. Enough tae get both men oot, if need be. And they'll have had canoes, forbye."

"But where?" she whispered, and then turning to Otter, she raised her voice. "Where *is* he?"

Otter's eyes had been scanning the shelter while she spoke to Robbie, and now he went down on one knee there where Nathaniel had been propped when she last saw him. A knife had been used to scrape the bark away, leaving a small patch of white raw wood. There a single word had been written in ash by a fingertip. It was smeared now and barely legible. On her knees next to Otter, Elizabeth read it aloud.

"Kahen'tiyo.

"I don't understand," she whispered.

Robbie translated: "Good Pasture."

"Where my mother's people live," supplied Otter, and there was some excitement there, some satisfaction in his voice. She turned back to Robbie, and spread out one hand, palm up.

Robbie glanced at Otter, and then he cleared his throat. "Canada," he said. "Aboot four days' hard walk fra here."

Elizabeth had felt completely drained just five minutes ago, but a new flush of energy flowed through her. "Let's go, then," she said, standing up and dusting her hands on her leggings. "It's a good day to walk." And then she stilled, seeing their faces.

She could not stand it, the way they looked at her. Her whole life she had seen this look in the eyes of men: when she had asked for a Latin tutor, and then for one who could teach her philosophy. When she had wanted to climb Ben Nevis with her cousin Merriweather and his friends. When she had offered to write extracts of her uncle's library books. The day she had expressed her wish to leave England, and first spoke of teaching school. Now all of those things seemed so trivial compared to the task she had before her, and these men, who were stronger and braver and more honest than any she had ever known, they were looking at her with that same doubt she had borne for all of her life. Elizabeth looked Robbie in the eye, and she lifted her chin.

"Let us go," she said again.

"Elizabeth, lass," he said softly. "Ye can barely stand for weariness. Ye're covered wi' bruises that wad lay the toughest sodjer low. Ever' bone in your face shines through, and I'd wager it wad be no job worth mentionin' tae count your ribs, forbye. I hae no doot ye mean what ye say, for ye've the bluidy heart of a lion—"

She began to interrupt him, but he squeezed her shoulder again and lowered his voice another tone.

"Whate'er it is ye've got behind ye these few days on the trail, lass, it has left scars for all tae see, and others festerin' deep inside—ye needna contradict me. I may be an auld man, but I'm no' yet blinn. Pay me mind, lass. Ye mun hae a day's rest, or there willna be a wife for Nathaniel tae come hame tae."

All the reasons they must move on, now, immediately, were clear and ordered in Elizabeth's mind, but when she opened her mouth, something else entirely came out.

"I cannot let him die alone and without me," she said, looking between them. "I will not. Don't you understand, both of you? I am responsible."

"Elizabeth," Robbie said hoarsely. The tears in his eyes took her by surprise. Suddenly she was overcome by the urge to bury her face in his coat and weep until she was emptied of it all, all the weakness and doubt and softness inside of her. So she could get on with what she must do. She loved Robbie for his tears, but she could not indulge him, or herself.

Otter had been leaning against the wall, and he righted himself. "We'll walk till noon," he proposed. "And then make camp, if you'll agree to rest then, until tomorrow morning."

She could see it on their faces: this was the best she could hope for. And without them, she could not find her way to Canada. "You think he is being cared for?" she asked finally.

Otter nodded without hesitation. "Hen'en." *Yes.*

"Better by far wi' the Kahnyen'kehàka than wi' a Boston surgeon," Robbie confirmed.

"Until midday, then," she agreed. And Elizabeth walked out of the shelter and the camp without a backward glance, glad to have Treenie beside her again, and these good men at her back.

XXXIX

Men, Elizabeth concluded, could be counted on to be childish and unreasonable at the most awkward times. They had been on the trail for almost a week, and now, less than two hours from the village where they hoped to find Nathaniel alive and well, they had decided to make camp where they stood. Without her approval and simply ignoring every argument she could muster. Her attempts at rational discussion were dismissed: Otter was tense and Robbie strangely uncommunicative. Elizabeth sat in front of the fire and brooded, cleaning her musket with a rough quickness that made Robbie wince openly.

"I could go on alone," she said when she could be still no longer. "I managed on my own in the bush for days, I'm sure I could manage two hours in terrain such as this."

There was no response. Surprised, Elizabeth looked up and saw Otter and Robbie approaching a man at the edge of their camp.

He was Kahnyen'kehàka, and from the look of him, a scout. Of middle age, he was not overly tall but built as wide and strong as an oak. The man was dressed much as Otter was dressed, but he had more weapons on his person, and there was something else that made Elizabeth's irritation and preoccupation wither away immediately: his scalp was shaved clean with the exception of a long shank of hair knotted at his crown, gleaming blue-black in the twilight, and trailing an ornament of

turkey feathers. From the belt around his waist there was another set of feathers, these strangely matted and dull in color:
dark and lighter browns, one shot with dirty silver streaks, another much paler, with a definite curl to the ends. Seeing them
clearly, Elizabeth felt her mouth go dry with fear. In her lap,
the musket felt awkward and heavy and completely useless.

But he was Kahnyen'kehàka, she reminded herself. A cousin
of some kind to Otter, without a doubt. And neither Robbie
nor Otter appeared frightened. She could hear only snatches of
their conversation, on her side of the fire, but the tone was
calm. She had no wish to come closer, and the scout apparently
did not find her of interest in the least: with a glance that took
in every detail of the camp and rested only very briefly on her
face, the man turned and left them without another sound.

It took Elizabeth another minute to realize that this quiet
and imposing stranger had accomplished something which had
eluded her.

"What are you doing?" she asked Otter, although she could
see for herself that he was breaking camp.

"The sachem sends word that they want us in the village
now," he answered.

She stood, and watched them working for another few
heartbeats. "They have been watching us?"

Otter grinned at her, and she saw now that his tension had
been replaced by relief and anticipation. "All day," he confirmed.

Later, Elizabeth promised herself, she would apologize to
these men for her irritability and lack of observation. But at the
moment she could not find the words. A thought occurred to
her, but she had to clear her throat several times before she
could make herself produce the question.

"He is there?"

"Aye, lassie," said Robbie. "He is. Alive, and on the mend."

In the dark she had little sense of the village. First there were
the fields with neat rows of young plants, and then a small
corral, where a young boy stood sentry. Around him a number
of dogs lifted themselves from the ground as if suspended by

wires, propelled by a low growling. Treenie froze beside Elizabeth and met them with her own rumbling, the fur on her hackles rising. The boy spoke a short word and the village dogs collapsed again, their eyes keen and at odds with their obedience.

They turned toward the center of the village, where the night was split open by a great fire, and a singing such as Elizabeth had never heard.

"Stay close," Robbie said softly.

She nodded. The rush of her blood made her fingers jerk and tingle, the knot in her belly pulling tighter with every pulse and echo of the drums. Close against her thigh, the red dog's trembling was like her own, rumbling up from the marrow, as if every bone had been hollowed out and filled with glassy shards of panic and agitation. *He's here, he's here, he's here.* Almost, almost she could hear the voices singing what rang so persistently in her head: Nathaniel is here; Nathaniel is alive.

There was sudden silence when they walked into the open area where the fire burned. Hands stilled on drums, and the dust settled slowly around the dancers' feet. Elizabeth blinked hard as her eyes adjusted to it: the great leaping light that cast everyday browns and tans into a spectrum of golds, set off here and there with a splash of crimson or green. Around them perhaps two hundred pairs of dark eyes, waiting. Only the fire spoke now, with a crackle and low roar.

A single figure came forward. He was wrapped in a blanket, and wore an elaborate headdress on his shaved scalp.

"The sachem," Robbie said quietly to Elizabeth. "Stone-Splitter, by name."

Of all the men, the sachem was the only one to wear a headdress which included the antlers of a deer. But even to Elizabeth it was clear that his authority did not come from his ornaments or by virtue of his age—there were older men—but from a singular intensity that brought him everyone's attention. Now he was looking at Otter with obvious pleasure and satisfaction.

"We welcome our brother Tawine, who has been long absent from our fire, and we welcome our friend Yotsìtsyonta, who finally honors us with his company after so many years."

He spoke Kahnyen'kehàka, but in a slow, measured way that Elizabeth could follow, for the most part. The sachem paused, and Elizabeth felt his gaze on her, quizzical but reserved.

"You are the wife of Nathaniel, whom we call Okwaho-rowakeka?"

"Yes," Elizabeth said, and then more loudly: "Hen'en."

"He is a good man, and our brother," said the sachem, and there was a murmuring around the fire. "He has told us to expect you."

Elizabeth's throat closed tight with this, the certain knowledge that he was alive. She nodded.

Stone-Splitter said, "Tell us why you ran away and left your husband to die alone in the Endless Mountains."

Elizabeth looked to Otter, unsure if she had understood correctly. She saw by his face that she had.

"I did not leave my husband to die," she said, finding a voice that was stronger and louder than she expected. "I went only to fetch Robbie—Yotsìtsyonta." She repeated his name in Kahnyen'kehàka. "I left to get help, so that Nathaniel would not die."

An old woman came forward, her tangled mass of bone, bead, and shell necklaces and ornaments rattling with each step. In spite of the great age which drained her face of flesh, she had eyes as bright and cutting as chips of obsidian against sand. She came close enough for Elizabeth to catch the smell of her, the sharp tang of sweat and dried herbs and tallow, bear grease and buckskin. And she saw distrust in her narrowed eyes, and dislike. Why this should be, Elizabeth did not know, but she drew in a breath to steady herself.

The old woman was examining Elizabeth's face openly.

"You have been beaten," she said. "Did you shoot a husband who raised a hand to you when you were disobedient, and then run, leaving him to the hungry ghosts who walk the forest?"

"No!" Elizabeth felt Otter stirring beside her, and she turned to him. "I cannot say this in Kahnyen'kehàka," she whispered. "Please translate for me. Tell them that Nathaniel never raised a hand to me in anger, and I did not run from him. I could not manage on my own," she finished, cursing the way her voice trembled. "Tell them, please."

Her mind moved with preternatural slowness, one thought repeating itself again and again: that unless she answered these people to their satisfaction, Nathaniel would stay hidden from her. To admit she had shot him, even in error, was a chance she could not take. While Otter translated, she watched the faces around her, searching the crowd once again for a familiar or friendly face, and found none.

"Irtakohsaks tells us a different story," said the sachem.

Irtakohsaks. Cat-Eater. Elizabeth started at this name. She had completely forgotten about Richard, and what he might say and do to gain his own ends. Beside her, Otter had come to life; she could feel him crackling with energy.

When she met his eye, she saw how angry he was. "Ask them if my husband holds me responsible for his wounds."

Otter did this, but before he had finished the old woman's voice rose shrilly.

The sachem held up a hand to delay her. "He does not," he answered, looking at Elizabeth rather than Otter. "It is Irtakohsaks who spoke to us of this."

Otter's indignation burst out of him. "Irtakohsaks speaks lies," he said. "Irtakohsaks was once a child of this fire, but he turned his back on the Kahnyen'kehàka long ago. He led the O'seronni soldiers to us and they murdered us in our beds. He bound Sky-Wound-Round like an animal and forced him to march. Would you take his word above the word of Wolf-Running-Fast, our brother, who accuses this woman of nothing? Irtakohsaks does not know this woman. He is not worthy to take this woman's name in his mouth."

Amazed, Elizabeth listened as Robbie translated at a whisper beside her. She had not imagined Otter to be capable of such a speech, or thought of herself in such terms. Her impulse was to drop her head in embarrassment, but there was a stronger urge, too, one of self-preservation, and she kept her gaze firmly on the sachem, who gave Otter his whole attention.

"My grandmother," Otter continued. "My grandfather, my family. May I speak for this woman, who is my sister? I ask for this privilege because her husband, my brother, cannot speak for her."

"I can speak for myself," Elizabeth muttered, but Robbie's hand tightened on her shoulder, and she bit her lip.

Otter glanced at Elizabeth. "Grandmother is right, Bone-in-Her-Back has been beaten. But not by our brother. She tells the truth: she was on her way to find help for her husband when she was attacked."

With the realization that Otter was about to tell the story that Elizabeth knew no words for, she felt her skin rise up in fear. "Please," she said softly, but Otter ignored her.

"To keep her from her errand, he beat her until she bled," Otter said, his voice certain and strong. "And she killed him, with her own hands she killed him, in order to return to her husband."

"Did you see this?" asked the sachem. "Did you see her kill this man?"

"No," said Otter. "But I saw the man, and I saw what he did to her."

"Please," said Elizabeth, no longer able to hold back. "Please, may I see him?" Robbie pulled her closer to him, hushed her softly. "Courage, lass," he whispered. "Let the boy talk, for he does ye naucht but good."

"Onhka?" asked the old woman, her face creased with doubt. *Who?*

"Lingo," said Otter and with that single word, his agitation left him, flowed out and transferred itself to the entire crowd. The men pressed closer. One of them, wearing a headdress fashioned from the entire pelt and skull of a wolf, pushed to the front. His face was painted in great vertical stripes of red and white and in his eyes Elizabeth read doubt.

"The man called Lingo is no man," he said. "He is a ghost. He walks with the Windigo," he concluded, and there was a sigh that rose up from the assembly like the sparks of the fire, disappearing into the night.

"Sachem," said Otter to Stone-Splitter. "He walks no longer. I have seen his blood on the ground."

The old woman raised her voice. "If our warriors have never been able to kill the ghost called Lingo," she said, "then this white woman cannot have done such a thing. Unless she is *Wataenneras.*"

Elizabeth did not know this word, but Robbie's indrawn breath told her it was not good to be called such a thing.

"She is no *Wataenneras,*" Otter said. "Her medicine is good."

Elizabeth said, "Otter. Tell this woman, your grandmother, something that she knows already. Tell her that a woman's righteous anger has its own magic."

Otter hesitated, and then did as she asked.

In the old woman's eyes there was a flickering.

"Do you have proof of this?" Stone-Splitter asked.

Without turning toward her, Otter said, "Show them."

Elizabeth stepped back, shaking her head. With one hand she clutched the front of her shirt.

Robbie leaned toward her. "Ye mun show them proof o' wha' ye claim, lass, 'gin ye wish tae see Nathaniel. Ye've no' convinced the woman, and withoot her word ye'll get nae further."

But still, she hesitated. Somewhere in the shadowy longhouses Nathaniel lay, waiting for her. Within touching distance. Within calling distance. Could he hear this, what they said of her, what Otter had told? It did not matter, for by tomorrow he would hear it, if not from her, then from others. To claim her husband she must first claim Jack Lingo. For all eternity, he would belong to her as surely as Nathaniel did. They wanted to see evidence not only of Lingo's death, but of her pride in this deed; they wanted Lingo's scalp. She felt the point of his knife at her eye, and for a moment she truly wished she had it to show them.

Elizabeth pulled the chain from her shirt and held up the coin between two fingers so that it flashed in the firelight. When she could take her eyes away from that sight, she saw something on the old woman's face which surprised her. A new and grudging respect, and something else, something in the way she drew back, and held herself. Perhaps it was envy, or perhaps fear.

"She killed Lingo with his own rifle," said Otter, holding this up, too, now that Elizabeth had made her claim. The barrel gleamed red-brown in the firelight. This is why Otter had insisted on taking it, as proof. *Vous et nul autre*. She could look at it, now, without her gorge rising.

Otter said: "Bone-in-Her-Back has walked many days to find her husband. Will you take her to him now?"

The old woman turned away from the fire. At a nod from the sachem, Elizabeth followed her, alone.

There were three longhouses set at angles to each other. The great expanse of their curved and ribbed sides reminded Elizabeth of the skeleton of a whale she had seen on the shore off the New-York harbor, blazing white against a blue-green sea. Almost a year ago, that had been. She wondered at this, that it could be true.

The old woman was hesitating before a bearskin door, watching Elizabeth.

"I am Ohstyen'tohskon," she said. "This is the longhouse of the Wolf, and I am Kanistenha here." *Clan mother.*

"I thank you for your help and your hospitality," Elizabeth said, seeking the Kahnyen'kehàka words slowly. "I thank you for my husband's health."

The old woman blinked at her. Elizabeth saw that she had not gained her trust, or her respect. But then none of that mattered, not at this moment.

The singing and drums had begun again, so that inside the longhouse there was an underlying rhythm to the sounds of the night like a muted heartbeat. It was a warm evening, and only a few fires were lit in the long central aisle, casting enough light to see the raised platforms at the rear of each living area. Each of them was piled with bear pelts and furs of various kinds and on many of these there were sleeping children, their naked skin glowing softly. In the deep shadows, Elizabeth saw a young woman with a newborn child at her breast, its tiny fists curling into the soft flesh. The woman watched her with hooded eyes, as if she were nothing more than a dream.

Then the old woman came to a stop, and gestured with her chin. Elizabeth was almost afraid to look. She thought that her fear would be obvious, but Ohstyen'tohskon stood impassively, with her eyes averted. As Elizabeth turned, she disappeared into the shadows.

He was asleep, as she had sometimes imagined him to be. And thin, his face so terribly thin. They had shaved his face. Behind his head and shoulders was a rolled bearskin, lifting him very slightly. His face was turned toward her, his arms crossed on his belly. The wound was hidden in shadow, and Elizabeth was glad of it.

Carefully, quietly, she went down on both knees beside the sleeping platform. Putting her face next to his, she inhaled his smells, all healthy: clean sweat tinged with something herbal, something she almost recognized. Elizabeth leaned closer to feel his heat, and kept herself suspended just so, her face within inches of his. Every muscle in her ached with it, but she stayed, breathing in the breath that he exhaled, until the trembling of her arms threatened to wake him. She sat back on her heels.

He opened his eyes then. A smile flitted across his face, and he closed them again.

"Boots," he said softly. "I see you."

His voice, and the pleasure of it.

"Sleep," she said, touching one fingertip to the corner of his mouth. His hand came up and caught her wrist, and she inhaled sharply.

"Come," he said, and drew her up onto the platform beside him.

She hesitated. "Your wound," she whispered.

But he hushed her, pulling gently until she had slid over him and he could tuck her between himself and the wall. He had broken out in a sweat, but then so had she. She put her face into the curve of his throat.

"I thought I would never see you again." Her fingers curled around his arm, pressing with new strength, pressing hard. Hard enough to make him flinch; hard enough to mark him with five small angry-blue moons.

"I never doubted you," he whispered, holding her as tightly as he dared. "Never for a moment."

XL

He did not sleep well. Coasting on the tide of his dreams, sometimes frantic, sometimes resigned, Nathaniel rose and fell and rose again to assure himself that she was there. Whole, and healthy, if not unmarked. She slept with her mouth slightly open, and her brow creased in concentration, as if this were another task set before her to prove her worth.

The sun rose and found its way through the smoke vents into the high, arched ceiling of the longhouse, and with it he could see more of her. Old bruises, faded to the yellow-green of a cyclone sky. Overlapping, they arched across her cheekbones in the shape of a hand. Nathaniel counted the livid center of each bruise, and was overcome with a numbing anger, more disabling and deeper than any he had ever known. This she had endured for him. This and more, for he could see the healing cuts high on her chest.

There were not many men in the bush, and he knew them all. It was not unknown for a man to go out of his head with loneliness, or vicious with greed. But the man who had put his hands on Elizabeth had not been lonely; he had just liked his work. There was only one person who could be responsible, and Nathaniel groaned inwardly to think that he had sent her off on her own, worried about every danger except the one that she had met, and somehow, escaped. There was a story here, and one that would be hard for her to tell. And harder to listen to. *Give me a tenth of her strength,* he thought.

At his back, the sounds of the longhouse rose gradually. Women's voices, coaxing, impatient, amused. Hungry children, men murmuring in half-sleep. The scraping of the mortar as the daylong task of grinding corn began. Nathaniel liked the longhouse in the early mornings, the routine and comfort of it, but right now he wished for the most rudimentary shelter in the bush, where he would have his wife to himself, and he could talk to her free of curious ears and eyes. Where he could really look at her, and learn what he feared: the full extent of what she had suffered.

He heard a shuffling behind him, and saw from the corner of his eye that He-Who-Dreams stood there, watching them. The weight of the faith keeper's gaze was not so heavy that Nathaniel had to turn, and after a while he went away. Nathaniel felt a twinge of regret, for he liked the old man and owed him many favors, but now there was Elizabeth. Elizabeth with her bruised face and the shuddering that shook her even in her sleep. The faith keeper's curiosity would have to wait.

There was a harsh clearing of a throat behind him: the clan mother, with her bitter tea, and her hard black eyes that were beginning to fail her. Now he did turn, for there was no denying her. This was Falling-Day's mother and his own daughter's great-grandmother, and in her face he saw what his first wife might have become with old age. She cleared her throat again, and he sat up, knowing that he could not escape her vigilance, or her tongue.

He took the bowl from her hands and drank it in two hasty swallows, grimacing. Beside him, Elizabeth stirred, and he saw the old woman squinting at her. Then she met his gaze, and her mouth hardened.

"You are not yet healed," she said, not bothering to lower her voice.

"But with your help I will heal, Grandmother," he said, hoping to work a small opening in her resistance. Elizabeth's arrival did not please her; he had anticipated that. But then, nothing much did please her.

She grunted, and narrowed her eyes at him. Poked a hard finger in the direction of his wound, so that he twitched.

"Breathe deep!" she hissed at him. "Or your lung will rot like a bad plum, and you will drown in your own fluids."

Nathaniel did as he was told. She watched him for three breaths, and then smiled sourly as he coughed, shaking her head.

"I will send your food," she said, turning away. And then, over her shoulder: "And clothes for her."

"Her name is Elizabeth," Nathaniel called after her.

She turned back. "Erisavet." The old woman's mouth twisted around the unfamiliar sounds, and she shook her head. "You gave her the name Bone-in-Her-Back?"

"Chingachgook gave it to her."

"Ah. Well, the biggest bone that one has is in her head. Stubborn as the sun in the summer sky." And she went off.

He turned back to Elizabeth, and found her eyes fixed on him.

"Bone in my head?" she asked sleepily. "Bone-Head. Yes, it feels appropriate right now." For a moment the look on her face was much the same as the one the old woman had given him. Then she sat up and with quick hands she touched his forehead, his cheek, his shoulder, ran her fingers down his arms and then gently touched his chest. Her gaze fixed there, at the wound.

He leaned back on his hands so she could see and watched the emotions moving over her face, pressing her lips hard together. He was taken up by the strong urge to gather her to him and rock her until she could smile at him again.

"Richard told them I shot you and ran away," she said, her voice hoarse with anger.

"I told them otherwise."

"But they believed him." She glanced up at him, and away. He caught her chin between his thumb and forefinger and brought her gaze back to his own.

"They did not believe him," he corrected her. "They were testing you."

"She doesn't trust me," Elizabeth said. "The old woman— Ohstyen'tohskon."

"Made-of-Bones," Nathaniel translated. "And she doesn't trust anybody. She nursed me well," he added. "So she couldn't dislike me too much."

"Nathaniel . . . ," Elizabeth began, and then her voice trailed away.

He put a finger to her mouth, shaking his head very slightly. "Not here," he said. "Not now. First we eat—you can't afford to miss a meal, Boots, from what I can see. And then we'll go down to the river—is Robbie here?"

Elizabeth nodded. "And Otter. And—" She almost smiled. The relief of this, her almost smile, took away a little of the surprise at Otter's presence.

"And the red dog," she said. "I call her Treenie." He watched her thoughts moving across her face, and the small promise of a smile fade away.

Nathaniel leaned toward her, brushed her mouth with his own, felt her start and then come to him. "The world will be right again," he said. "Together we will make it right."

It was a busy time in the village, Nathaniel told her as she discarded the ragged clothes she wore and dressed in the buckskin overdress and leggings a young woman had brought her. The moccasins were very fine, decorated with beadwork and porcupine quills; Elizabeth took it as a sign that the clan mother was not completely set against her.

Elizabeth found herself wondering about her pack, and provisions, and the weather and the trails, and then she remembered, with something between relief and disappointment, that they would not be on the trail today. She had completed her task, she had found him, and for the moment they were not going anywhere.

She walked with Nathaniel, and looked at the things he pointed out. The new crops in the fields demanded a great deal of attention, and it seemed that every woman was there with a hoe, many of them working stripped to the waist. Elizabeth wondered if the ability to be shocked had been taken from her for all time, or if it simply required more energy than she could spare.

Nathaniel walked very slowly, and his breathing was labored at times so that he would stop, as if taken by some unexpected thought. She stopped then, too, and watched him. Content that he was in fact mending, Elizabeth felt herself beginning to relax.

"Richard?" she asked, although she meant not to. The thought of him, and what he had said to these people about her, would make her go pale with anger, if she let it.

Nathaniel shrugged. "He is still pretty bad off, I think. I don't see him. They keep him over there—" He jerked with his chin toward the last of the longhouses, where boys played with small baggataway sticks in a noisy game.

"They saved his life."

"Not yet, they haven't. I don't think he's cooperating much, but then he never thought to come back here. That much I know."

Elizabeth stopped. "Here? This is where he was brought as a child?"

"I thought you realized," Nathaniel said. "I thought Otter would have told you. He was adopted into the Bear clan. They mourned him when he ran away."

"No," Elizabeth said thoughtfully. "Otter said nothing of this. He mentioned Richard very little."

Nathaniel looked concerned. "The boy bears watching," he said finally. "Stone-Splitter wouldn't be pleased if he took vengeance on Todd, not here and now."

"I made Richard a promise," she said, more to herself than to Nathaniel.

He grunted, as if to save himself the trouble of disagreeing.

Pausing while he caught his breath, Elizabeth had time to look around her. The village was as large and ordered a community as any farming village in England, with every adult she could see at work. A trio of young girls about Hannah's age were clustered together under a young birch tree, stripping dried corn from cobs, each of them working with what looked to be the jawbone of a deer, teeth intact. They had been chattering with great abandon, but when Elizabeth and Nathaniel came into hearing distance they giggled, and fell still.

"Nathaniel!" Otter materialized out of a crowd of young

men examining a gun—Elizabeth saw with some discomfort that it was Lingo's rifle—and came at them at a trot. Robbie was just behind him, his great rosy face beaming and Treenie at his side. The dog greeted Elizabeth with great joy, took unenthusiastic note of Nathaniel, and then calmly positioned herself on Elizabeth's free side.

"You see?" she asked him. "The red dog."

He grinned at her. "Aye, Boots. I see plain enough."

"By God, man," Robbie said, clapping him on a shoulder. "Ye canna be left alone wi'oot callin' a' the trouble i' the world doon on your thick heid."

For the moment Elizabeth was content to stand and listen as Otter spoke of home, and how he had left them. She saw Nathaniel's concentration and his slowly growing alarm as he listened to Otter's story of how he came to be in the bush at all, but Elizabeth was suddenly very sleepy and could not concentrate on this involved tale of an Indian called Little-Turtle who lived to the west.

She stifled an expansive yawn.

"Did ye need mair sleep, lass?" Robbie asked, and then produced one of his blushes. It occurred to Elizabeth that his Kahnyen'kehàka name had something to do with the blossoming of flowers, and she felt a great wave of affection for the man, which she showed by brushing some of the accumulated muck from his sleeve.

"Nathaniel and I thought to go down to the river."

"Ach, weel," said Robbie, slapping Otter on the back. "We mun be on our way. Tae see aboot a canoe. Or wad ye rather walk back tae Paradise, experienced woodswoman that ye are?" He winked at Elizabeth and turned away without waiting for a response, whistling for Treenie to follow. The dog trotted off with an apologetic glance at Elizabeth.

Otter hesitated. "I won't be going back with you."

Nathaniel grimaced. "That's a discussion for another time," he said. "Right now Elizabeth and I have business."

Elizabeth looked down to find a very young boy tugging on the long fringe which bordered her overdress. He gulped hard and giggled a high, sweet tone. Then, seeing that Elizabeth was not in a frame of mind to eat him whole or otherwise bewitch him, he rattled off what seemed to be a question in a torrent punctuated by the soft whistle of his breath.

"I don't understand." Elizabeth shrugged her shoulders at him regretfully.

Nathaniel shooed the child off with a few words and then he took Elizabeth's hand. The rope burns on her wrist were scabbed over, and Nathaniel looked hard at them.

"He wanted to see the ghost coin," he said evenly. Elizabeth could see in his eyes that he knew most of what she would tell him. When she tried to look away, he pulled her closer, and leaned down to speak into her ear. "Come on, then," he said softly. "Let's get it done with. It won't go away on its own." He lifted her hand higher, turned it this way and that.

"Your wedding ring."

"He took it." Her tone was hollow, but there was a flash in her eyes: anger, and desperation. "Lingo took it, and I couldn't find it—after."

"We'll get another one," Nathaniel said.

"No." She shook her head. "I don't want another one. I want that one."

And she walked off toward the river with her husband close behind, to tell him what he needed to know.

Otter and Robbie spent their morning negotiating with Awer-yahsa about the cost of the fine birch bark canoe he had just begun to build, and having come to an understanding, Otter went to fetch Nathaniel and Elizabeth to get their approval.

"You can come see it. If you've got the inclination," Otter added, politely looking away. He had found them stretched out in the sun on the riverbank, Elizabeth asleep with her head in Nathaniel's lap and her face blotchy and streaked with tears.

Nathaniel looked up at him, this young man he had known all of his life. He had had a hand in the raising of him, and at this moment, he was especially proud to be able to claim that.

"We'll be up directly," he said quietly.

Otter nodded, and turned to go.

"Wait." Nathaniel looked out over the flowing river, seeking the words he needed there.

"What you did for her I can't ever repay," he said. "Although I will surely do my best."

"I didn't do anything for her you wouldn't have done yourself," Otter pointed out. "Nothing I wouldn't have done for my sister."

Nathaniel was silent. He watched Elizabeth breathing for a long minute.

"She would have made it on her own," he said. "She's that tough. But she wouldn't have had a chance to heal, and now she does."

Otter looked thoughtful. "She is not proud of what she did," he said, and Nathaniel knew this was more of a question than a statement. Often he was called on to explain the way that white people thought and acted, when their ways mystified the Kahnyen'kehàka. Otter was watching him, wanting to understand how this woman could take anything but pride in killing a stronger enemy. But Nathaniel could not explain this to him in any way that he would understand, and after a while the younger man went away, as thoughtful and quiet as Nathaniel had ever seen him.

After he watched her sleep for a few more minutes, counting her breaths and measuring them against his own, Nathaniel woke Elizabeth. She was disoriented and flushed, but the silence between them was an easy one. When he told her about the canoe, she managed a smile.

"We can go home," she said. "When?"

"The canoe will need a good week," he said, brushing his knuckles across her cheek. "And I'll be stronger then, too."

"A week," she echoed, looking uncertain.

"Sitting still for a week goes against the grain, I know," he said. "If it can be managed in less, we'll do that."

"I suppose I shall cope," Elizabeth said.

"Aye." Nathaniel nodded. "I know that you will."

She sighed, and started up the riverbank. "Let us go look at this wondrous canoe, then."

Nathaniel caught her by the arm, and turned her to him.

"Elizabeth."

The gray of her eyes seemed lighter now that her skin had darkened in the sun. He traced the outline of her face, touched the dimple in her chin. Cupped her cheek, and then the back of her neck. "None of it would have mattered if you hadn't come back to me," he said, hearing the catch in his voice. And saw by some miracle that he had found the words to comfort her.

On a small stream a short walk away from the longhouses, they found the canoemaker and his apprentices hard at work, their naked upper bodies and legs streaked with grime and sweat. One of the boys alternately fed the fires and stirred a great kettle of what looked like a coiled mass of stringy rope.

"Spruce root for lacing," Nathaniel explained. Elizabeth, who as a child had willingly spent hours with the cook, the blacksmith, and the carpenter, stepped in closer to watch.

The second boy was holding two long ribs of wood at an angle in another kettle while the older man poured boiling water over them. While they watched, he dropped his ladle and took the ribs in both hands, stepping backward without looking to sit on a tree stump, where he began to work the wood back and forth over his knee. His whole concentration was on a single point in the wood, as if he could will it to bend. Suddenly his mouth turned down at one corner and then blossomed into a full-blown frown. With a sigh he took up a crooked knife, and began scraping at the wet wood.

"Not thin enough to give the right bend," Nathaniel explained.

The canoemaker looked up at him and asked a question, which Nathaniel answered at length.

"That is not Mohawk," Elizabeth said, her tone slightly vexed.

"No," Nathaniel agreed. "Sturdy-Heart is Atirontaks. He came to live with the Kahnyen'kehàka many years ago." He glanced at her from the corner of his eye. "He wants to see the gold."

"I suppose it would be impolite to refuse," Elizabeth said. With a little shake of her head she pulled the chain from inside her neckline and held it out. The boys came up close, so that Nathaniel spoke a soft word to them. Then the canoemaker came, too, and looked down at her face, rather than at the coin in her fingers. Elizabeth did not mind his close inspection, for there was an honest curiosity in him that disarmed irritation. He said something to her directly and then stood waiting for Nathaniel to translate it.

"He says he will build you a very good canoe."

"Ah, well," said Elizabeth with a half smile. "Then I suppose it was all worth the effort."

She slept again, and ate, and slept, and in between she talked to Nathaniel at great length. Sometimes she talked to him in her sleep, and woke to find him listening to her with an intent look on his face. They passed three days like this, seeing Robbie and Otter now and again but otherwise keeping to themselves. In the evening when the great fire was lit and the singing began, they retired with the youngest children and the oldest grandmothers. In a few days' time the village would celebrate the Strawberry Festival, which they would be obliged to join, Nathaniel told her. She agreed to this, but for the moment she sought to avoid both Todd and a conversation with the old woman.

Made-of-Bones came twice a day to feed Nathaniel infusions and to tend his wound, bringing along a steady dialogue which required no reply, and in fact would tolerate none. Elizabeth watched carefully and even asked a question on occasion, which seemed not to please the old woman, or to displease her, either.

With every passing day Elizabeth felt stronger and more sure of herself in the village, understanding a little more of the rhythms of the place, and a surprising amount of the language. She ate with huge and unapologetic appetite. Some of the Kahnyen'kehàka food was unusual and she knew that in the past she would have surely turned away from it; in fact, her affronted stomach could not always keep it down. At night she sometimes woke with hunger pangs, but with Nathaniel's heartbeat in her ear and the smells and sounds of the Kahnyen'kehàka all around her, she would asleep again, at ease.

On the tenth morning there was a heavy rain falling. The others seemed not to mind the weather, going on about the business of preparing for the Strawberry Festival, which was planned for the next day, but bringing in some work that was normally done out of doors. Elizabeth had had enough of rain, and was content to stay under the roof.

Made-of-Bones had assigned one of her granddaughters, a serious young woman by the name of Splitting-Moon, to look after their needs. She brought them food, offering the bowls with downturned eyes and few words. Other young women had soon begun to find excuses to come by and talk to Elizabeth, in short and sometimes awkward conversations, but Splitting-Moon had nothing to say to her. Sometimes, when she looked up, Elizabeth found the younger woman watching her.

This morning she accepted a bowl of beans and cornmeal bread from Splitting-Moon, who barely acknowledged Elizabeth's thanks and did not meet Nathaniel's eye at all.

"Nathaniel?" Elizabeth asked thoughtfully when she had gone. "Splitting-Moon doesn't go out to the fields with the other women?"

He glanced up from his food and shrugged his shoulders. "Made-of-Bones is training her as Ononkwa," he said. *Medicine woman.* "She spends her time gathering herbs and roots and whatever else she and He-Who-Dreams need for medicines."

"I am afraid we are a burden to her. Should I offer to help with her work?" Elizabeth had been grinding corn for the last days, an unskilled task she could do while talking to Nathaniel.

"I don't think it will set her more at ease, if that's your intention."

"Her silence does unsettle me a bit. Is it me she minds serving, do you think?"

Nathaniel had an uneasy look about him. "It's got nothing to do with you, Boots. Or at least not directly. It's me she's uncomfortable with. There's some history between us," he finished.

Elizabeth had a sudden unwelcome memory of Jack Lingo, and his claims about Nathaniel. She put her bowl down. "What do you mean by 'history,' exactly?"

She had the surprised satisfaction—for there was no other word—of watching Nathaniel become flustered. "It don't mean a thing, anymore. But a few years back I brought Falling-Day and Many-Doves up here to visit, and I spent some time with Splitting-Moon. She wasn't happy when I left."

Nathaniel lowered his voice, and his eyes. "I was lonely, you see. It had been a few years since Sarah, and I suppose I let my guard down." He cleared his throat and looked up at her. "To be truthful, I ain't especially proud of the whole thing. She did me a good turn, but she wanted things from me I couldn't give her."

Elizabeth considered this information, and found herself strangely detached from it, with only the vaguest stirring of jealousy. The serious young woman with her straight back and beautiful, glowing skin had shared Nathaniel's bed, and had at one time thought to claim him. But he had left her, and gone back to Paradise to live without the company of a woman.

"And you? Were you happy to leave?"

He was watching her face closely. "I like it here, but I was ready to move on home."

"And I'm glad that you did," she said simply. He smiled at her, and then his face clouded again.

"It ain't kind of Made-of-Bones to make her spend so much time near us," he said. He seemed to be on the verge of telling her more, but voices rose suddenly at the far end of the long-house, and three young boys appeared. They ran, dodging fires and tools and children at play, to come to a breathless halt in front of the clan mother's fire. The old woman and Splitting-Moon had been sorting through baskets of dried plants, but Made-of-Bones looked up at the boys with a kind of irritable affection, and allowed them to speak.

Their story was told in three voices, simultaneously. Elizabeth had caught only isolated words when a translation became unnecessary, for a group of men had appeared at the bearskin door. The tallest and foremost of them was a frightening sight, with hooded eyes and a ragged scar which ran from his scalp down the left side of his face. His head was shaved for war, and like the scout, scalps hung on his belt. He was every horror tale that had ever been told about Indians, and then he grinned and produced two dimples which belied the impression entirely.

Nathaniel was rising, with a smile of his own. "Spotted-Fox," he said. "And his trading party, back from Albany. They brought us out of the bush." He glanced at Elizabeth apologetically. "I have to—"

"Go on," she said. "I understand." But Nathaniel was already gone.

The village erupted into a new kind of activity. The men had come back from trading the winter's furs, their canoes loaded with provisions of all kinds. There was a profusion of materials to sort out and store according to the instructions of the three clan mothers, as well as the Strawberry Festival on the next day. Young people had been assigned the gathering of the fruit, and it seemed impossible to step anywhere without danger of putting a foot into a basket of strawberries. They were being crushed for juice, and the heavy, sweet scent hung in the air.

Nathaniel came to find Elizabeth as soon as he could remove himself from the storytelling of the traders. He found her grinding corn, with Robbie at her side and the red dog at her feet. She looked up at him with her eyes softly shining, and Nathaniel felt a familiar stirring. They had not come together since the day Joe died, three weeks ago now. It seemed like much longer. In the night the smell of her had often pulled him aroused and eager from his sleep, but thus far he had resisted his growing need. She was still very fragile and easily startled, and content with kisses. Although he thought that soon she would want more.

"And how did they get on, the laddies?" Robbie asked. "No trouble wi' the exciseman?"

Elizabeth laughed out loud in surprise. "In this of all places I cannot imagine that they would have such a problem."

Nathaniel and Robbie exchanged glances. "We're a half day's ride from Montreal," Nathaniel pointed out. "And the English ain't thrilled with the Kahnyen'kehàka running fur into New-York."

He watched her working through this information. "They trap in Canada and smuggle furs to Albany for a better price," she concluded.

Robbie grinned at her. "Ye've got the richt of it, lassie. And a unco' lucrative business it is, too, but bluidy dangerous for a' that."

"They shave their heads," she noted. "As if they were at war."

Nathaniel said, "Stone-Splitter has managed to keep his village intact and well provisioned because he is always at war, Boots. He has always gone his own way and his people have survived for it. You see this place is much better off than Barktown."

"Hmmm." Elizabeth had to agree with that observation, but still she was uneasy. "I wouldn't want to be here if the English raid," she said, working the pestle more forcefully into the curve of the bowl.

"On that account ye needna worra, lassie." Robbie stretched and stood. "The English are no' aboot tae come doon here an' pester Stone-Splitter. They dinna like the tradin' he does, but they do depend on his braves in the event o' war."

"Another war? Between England and America? Unlikely," Elizabeth noted.

Robbie looked thoughtful. "Aye, weel. Ye've mair faith in yer countrymen than do I. But in the meantime there's celebratin' tae do. Strawberries, ye ken. The wee seeds do stick in ma pegs, but I canna resist, for a' that. I can weel resist anythin', except temptation." He winked at her. "And then o' course, there's the dancin'."

Elizabeth smiled. "Will you be dancing, Sergeant MacLachlan?"

He laughed, his strong white teeth flashing. "Wait an' see, ma lassie, and these auld bones may just surprise you." Robbie paused on the way out, and turned back to Elizabeth.

"Wad ye mind owermuch if I tak the wee dog wi' me? She and I get on richt well," he said, somewhat apologetically. Treenie cast her a sheepish look of her own and Elizabeth waved her on, amused.

When they had gone, Nathaniel sat down next to Elizabeth and slipped an arm around her waist. She paused for a moment in her work, and then tipped more corn kernels into the bowl.

"And what about you?" he asked, breathing on the soft pink lobe of her ear. "Will you be dancing, Mrs. Bonner?"

She snorted and pushed him away. "Not very likely," she said, laughing.

"And not even for your husband?"

"Don't you mean, *with* your husband?" she asked, keeping her eyes on her task.

"No," he said. "The women's dance is just that. For the women to dance and the men to watch." He turned her face to him and kissed her lightly, taking considerable enjoyment in the way she grew flustered.

"It's daylight, Nathaniel," she whispered. "And there are people about."

"But it won't be daylight forever, Boots."

"Your injury," she said, faltering.

He ran a hand up her side, his fingers gently probing. "Let that be my concern," he said. "Unless you're saying you don't want me?"

"No!" She glanced around them, her color high. "I didn't say that."

"Then you do want me."

She pursed her mouth at him, in exasperation and something else, perhaps relief, or pleasure. Then she nodded. "When we have some . . . privacy."

Nathaniel rose to his feet. "The rain's stopped, and I'm off to have a talk with Stone-Splitter," he said. "Will you come along?"

Elizabeth looked down into her bowl, and back up at him.

"Please come." He amended his question, and she took his hand and let herself be drawn up.

The sachem was sitting on a blanket in the sun, surrounded by piles of silver and copper coins. With him were Spotted-Fox and the faith keeper, He-Who-Dreams, who drew on a long pipe as he watched Stone-Splitter count. Elizabeth recognized other men, some of them by name now. They were talking quietly among themselves. They neither stared at her nor ignored her, and after a while she was able to simply listen to Nathaniel as he talked.

The sachem threw a pinch of tobacco onto the fire, a ceremonial gesture that Elizabeth recognized as an honor to Nathaniel, who then thanked Stone-Splitter for his help and hospitality, and finally announced their plans to leave the village on the day after the Strawberry Festival.

When Nathaniel had finished, the sachem spoke, glancing now and then at Elizabeth.

"He wants to talk to you directly," Nathaniel said. "He will try to do it in English."

Elizabeth was sitting across from He-Who-Dreams, who nodded to her without taking the pipe from his mouth. She glanced also at Spotted-Fox, trying not to stare openly at his scars, the mangled ear and the deep puckered valley that dragged his eye down at the outer corner.

The sachem regarded her for some time, and then he spoke to her in an English undercut with French. "Tell me of your school, and your students."

Taken by surprise, Elizabeth took a moment to gather her thoughts. "It is a small school," she began. "All children in the village are welcome to come and learn. It is my belief that each of them; white or Kahnyen'kehàka or black, is entitled to an education. I would welcome any child of this village to my classroom."

Stone-Splitter turned to Nathaniel and asked for an explanation in his own language, which took a long time. Then he turned back to Elizabeth.

"And you are the teacher?" he asked.

She nodded.

Stone-Splitter looked thoughtful for a moment.

"Bone-in-Her-Back," he began. "We see you. You are a good woman. You have brought Wolf-Running-Fast the land he needs to keep his people safe. You have shown great courage in the bush. You killed the O'seronni who walked with the Windigo, a ghost-man who has caused the Kahnyen'kehàka much sorrow, and you show us respect and a willingness to learn our ways. We see no fault in you but your pride."

Elizabeth blinked at him, confused. "Pride?"

He-Who-Dreams spoke up, his voice raspy with age but his tone not unkind. He spoke slowly, switching back and forth between his own language and a melodious French. "You call yourself teacher, and summon children to you. White children, and black, and Kahnyen'kehàka. But we ask, what do you have to offer our children? You cannot make a moccasin or skin a deer. You cannot cure hides. You know nothing of the crops, how to plant or tend them. You cannot turn your hand to hunting, or show them how to track. You do not know the names of the moons or the seasons, or of the spirits who direct them. Of medicines you know nothing. And yet you call Kahnyen'kehàka children to your school. You will teach them to read and write your language. You will teach them of your wars and your gods. You can teach them only to be white."

Blushing hot with confusion and anger, Elizabeth struggled hard to hold on to her composure. Nathaniel had taken her hand and she felt his tension, too, but she was being tested and he could not help her.

The sachem finished: "Bone-in-Her-Back, I wish you well, but we cannot send our children to you. Instead, I say that you should send your sons to us, and we will make men of them."

The men were watching her, their eyes hooded and expectant. Elizabeth searched inside herself for an answer to this man, for some way to make him understand. She meant well; she had only the best intentions for those children who came to her. Reading and writing were good and necessary skills, ones that would open up worlds for them.

Other worlds.

She cleared her throat.

"Sachem," she began. "We are ignorant of your stories, that is true. Most of my people are dismissive of your way of life. But it is also true that the Europeans are here and will not be sent away." There was a surprised murmuring, but Elizabeth continued, searching for the right words. "All I can offer your children is a command of our language, and a knowledge of our stories. It is through those stories that you can gain some understanding of how we think."

"You give us weapons to use against your own people," Spotted-Fox pointed out to her in a very good English.

"I would give your children a tool," Elizabeth said quietly. "What they do with it once they leave my classroom I cannot determine."

The sachem was looking hard at her, his face impassive but his eyes wide and flashing with the speed of his thoughts. "If you stay with us for the summer, we will teach you our stories, and you can teach us your own."

"I thank you for this honor," she said. "But we have family at home who wait for us. I will learn the Kahnyen'kehàka stories from Falling-Day and Many-Doves and Runs-from-Bears. And from Otter, who has already taught me important lessons," she added, seeing the young man suddenly at the back of the crowd of men.

"Otter goes to fight with Little-Turtle against the treaty breakers in the west," said Stone-Splitter.

Elizabeth glanced at Nathaniel, and he nodded. When she looked into the crowd again, Otter had disappeared.

"Is this your decision, then?" Stone-Splitter asked, his eyes moving between Elizabeth and Nathaniel. "Do you leave us?"

"As soon as we are ready to travel after the Strawberry Festival."

"And what of Cat-Eater?" asked the sachem. "Will he travel with you?"

"No," said Elizabeth before Nathaniel could speak. "He does not."

"He wishes to speak to you."

"We will resolve our business with Cat-Eater before we leave," said Nathaniel.

Astonished, Elizabeth turned to him. He shook his head almost imperceptibly. She swallowed hard and settled back on her heels.

"First it looks as though you have business to settle between yourselves," noted He-Who-Dreams.

Elizabeth went back to the Wolf longhouse on her own, because Nathaniel had more business to discuss with the men. She was preoccupied and unsettled by the conversation, and unsure of the answers she had given. Suddenly all the things she had taken for granted about herself and her purpose in coming to this new place were suspect. Torn by indignation and doubt simultaneously, she walked along lost her in thoughts, so that at first she did not hear the voice that called to her, and then she did not recognize it. And when she did, she suppressed both a groan and the strong urge to walk on as if she were deaf to her own name. But her training, even now, was too deeply ingrained for such behavior. Slightly light-headed, Elizabeth turned and found Richard sitting in the sun on a blanket before the Bear longhouse.

If she had been thinking of some short and less-than-friendly greeting, it died at the sight of him: this was a man with Richard Todd's voice, but he looked like no one she had ever known.

If she had thought Nathaniel thin, Richard was skeletal. Minus the great mass of his red-gold beard his face was an unhealthy white. His strong nose stood out like the spine of a supine bird, his cheekbones like arched wings. His cheeks were sunken, and his lips cracked and scabbed.

Although she had not intended to, Elizabeth approached him, noting that he smelled of sweat and herbs but not of decay.

"My wounds heal, slowly," he said, reading her mind, as well as the look in her eyes as they traveled over him. His voice was softer than she remembered. Perhaps the fever had broken his anger as it had broken him physically.

"Are they treating you well?" she asked.

"You and I have business to discuss," he answered.

Elizabeth flushed suddenly with a particular memory. "Yes. Let us begin with the lie you told in yet another attempt to keep me from my husband."

Richard waved a hand dismissively, and made a mulish mouth. "You are here, are you not? You promised to answer my charges in a court of law," he said quietly.

She had begun to turn away, and now she turned back. "I did," she said. "And I will. Before the sachem and his council, I will answer your charges."

Richard's pale cheeks flared suddenly. "I meant the court of the state of New-York."

"But you did not specify that," Elizabeth pointed out.

To her surprise, Richard smiled.

"As you wish it. We will lay this matter before Made-of-Bones and Two-Suns and She-Remembers."

"Those are the clan mothers," Elizabeth said, caught off

guard and feeling somehow that she had been outmaneuvered, but not quite seeing how.

He spread out his hand, palm upward, to reveal a horrible wound, only half healed. Elizabeth looked at it because she could not make herself look away.

"Of course," said Richard. "This is not a matter of war, but of the clans. It is for the clan mothers to decide. We will only go to the sachem if they cannot reach a conclusion."

"Do you think they will tell me I picked the wrong husband?" Elizabeth asked, almost able to muster a smile at this idea. It was clear in what high regard the village held Nathaniel, and how well disposed they all were—men and women— toward him.

Richard leaned his head to one side, looking suddenly tired. "I know this. I know She-Remembers: for seven years I called her Elder Sister, and slept at her hearth. I know that Made-of-Bones is Sarah's grandmother and held her very dear. I know that she told Sarah to put her husband aside, because he could not give her great-grandchildren to bring to the council fire."

"And I know that Sarah refused this," Elizabeth said, wishing that she could stop the shaking in her voice, but failing. "And that she did bear Nathaniel children, in the end."

He raised one reddish eyebrow. "Then you know more than Nathaniel does himself. More than Sarah knew. The question is, who will they believe? You, the O'seronni woman, or Irtakohsaks. Who has returned home to them."

"Against your will," Elizabeth pointed out.

"I beg to differ," he said slowly. "They have heard no such thoughts from me."

"You are bluffing," said Elizabeth.

"Let us wait and see," Richard said, suddenly much paler. He swayed slightly as he rose, and grabbed onto the wall of the longhouse. Elizabeth watched without extending a hand as he limped toward the door.

She was still standing there when he had disappeared into the shadows.

XLI

More tired than she could remember being since that day on the trail when Otter had found her at Robbie's, Elizabeth wanted only the sleeping platform she shared with Nathaniel. And Nathaniel. But he was still with Spotted-Fox and the others, and so she made her way back to the longhouse and crawled alone into the pile of bearskins, falling asleep even before she could consider removing her moccasins. She slept deeply, and woke staring at the endless rows of dried corn hung in the rafters, ravenously hungry.

She sat up, and found Splitting-Moon directly before her. They were alone in the longhouse with the exception of a very young child playing naked in the ashes of a cold fire, singing tunelessly to herself. Outside there was a game going on that seemed to involve the whole village. All except Splitting-Moon.

"Do they play baggataway?" Elizabeth asked, her mouth sticky with dryness.

Splitting-Moon nodded and handed her a bowl of water, which Elizabeth accepted gratefully. The younger woman began to turn away.

"Splitting-Moon." Elizabeth used the woman's Kahnyen'kehàka name. Just her name, but it was enough to make her pause. "Why do you watch me?"

For a moment Elizabeth feared the woman would not answer at all, thus closing the door between them for good. But a tremor moved her mouth, and a look of uncertainty came over her face.

"Because you have a magic that is new to me," she said finally. "I would like to understand it."

Elizabeth smiled, relieved. "I have no magic."

"But you have bound Wolf-Running-Fast to you," said Splitting-Moon.

"I married him," Elizabeth said. "There is no magic in that, just—" She paused, lacking the right Kahnyen'kehàka word. "Bonne chance."

The younger woman blinked at her, and then reaching out one finger, she touched Elizabeth's face. With some effort, Elizabeth held herself very still while Splitting-Moon traced an invisible mask lightly around her eyes.

"You have bound him to you with his child," said Splitting-Moon. "Your spirit is stronger than mine, stronger than Yewennahnotha's was. Neither of us could hold on to his children."

Elizabeth jerked with surprise; she felt her heartbeat leap and then settle again. Yewennahnotha'. *Sarah.* She heard herself laugh, a startled sound.

"Where do you get such an idea?" she asked, and then in response to Splitting-Moon's blank look, she realized she had said this in English. In her agitation, the Mohawk would not come to her and so she repeated herself in French.

Splitting-Moon's puzzlement cleared. She walked the small distance to her grandmother's hearth to look through a large basket, and returned with a broken shard of mirror, only as big as Elizabeth's palm. "You wear the mask," she said, holding it up to her.

"I am not with child," Elizabeth whispered, but even as she said this, her mind raced. She was seeing herself for the first time in weeks, her face unfamiliar with its sharper angles. Her skin was simply brown from long days out of doors, she told herself, even as she saw the faintly darker glimmering circling her eyes.

She shook her head, closed her eyes, and willed herself to recall the last time she had bled. She realized that she did not know the day of the week, or even what month it was. The days and weeks slipped away from her as she tried to count them. Five weeks? Six?

"I do not think I am with child," Elizabeth corrected herself, and with the realization that this thing might be so, she knew it to be true. She sat back on her heels, and wrapped her arms around herself, bent forward in an arch. Her whole body flushed with terror and joy, and an overwhelming sense of power and simple wonder: that she should be capable of this thing that made her, once and for all time, Nathaniel's wife.

"You did not know," Splitting-Moon said.

"No," said Elizabeth, bringing up her head to meet Splitting-Moon's gaze. "I did not realize." In the younger woman's eyes she found sympathy and joy, and for those gifts she knew she would always be thankful.

"He will be pleased."

There was a shout from the crowd outside, voices raised in a wild cheer. "Yes," Elizabeth said, drawing a shaky breath. "He will be very pleased."

Splitting-Moon nodded at her, and turned away.

With nowhere to be alone, Elizabeth lay down with her face to the wall, and put one palm flat on her lower belly. How could she have not noticed, how could she have overlooked what her own body tried to tell her? It was not the Kahnyen'kehàka food to blame for her upset stomach. She blushed at her own dull wits. Splitting-Moon, who had never borne a child, had seen what she should have known for herself.

What she had to make known to Nathaniel.

Nathaniel had looked in on Elizabeth, and finding her asleep, he had gone to watch the game. He stood on a rise not too close to the field, where he could keep one eye on the longhouse, waiting for her to appear. His injury did not hurt him especially, except for the fact that it kept him out of the game. He liked the challenge of baggataway, the way it pushed him to his limits.

He drew a deep breath into his lungs. The tissues expanded creakily, but with less reluctance than had been the case even yesterday.

On the far side of the village the river ran south to join the great lake the French called Champlain. On its bank, a flash of movement caught Nathaniel's eye. A single canoe pulling up. Visitors were not surprising: Kahnyen'kehàka would come from far away for the Strawberry Festival and there would be many more canoes before the afternoon was out. But Stone-Splitter was a cautious leader, and the sentry was already on his way to intercept the new arrivals.

Two men. By his size and shape, Nathaniel recognized one of them as Stands-Crooked, the scout who had first brought the news of Elizabeth's approach. He had been gone from the village ever since, Nathaniel realized.

The other man was Kahnyen'kehàka from his dress, and bearing, and walk. Kahnyen'kehàka in the way he looked around himself, and the way he wore the musket slung on his back. Kahnyen'kehàka in everything except that he stood a head taller than any of them, and the scalp lock on his tattooed skull was not black, but red-gold.

Elizabeth at his elbow. Nathaniel turned to her.

"What is it?" she asked, seeing the look on his face. "Trouble?"

"Maybe," he said. "I'm not sure." He jerked his head in the direction of the river.

Her eyes were good, and her powers of observation better.

"He looks like Richard," she said, her voice faltering.

The two men were approaching the playing field at a quick pace. There was a cry of welcome, and then another. Nathaniel heard the name being called out: Inon-Yahoti'.

"Who is that, Nathaniel?"

"Throws-Far," he said. "I doubt he answers to Samuel Todd anymore."

"Richard's brother?" Elizabeth's hand on his forearm, pressing hard. "His brother? I thought— Mr. Bennett said—"

"That he was dead? Died in battle? Well, that's what they think down on the Mohawk."

"You knew."

"Of course I knew he was alive. The Kahnyen'kehàka keep track of each other, you see. He fought for the British during the war, and moved up farther north when things went bad."

"My God," said Elizabeth. "Richard's brother. Does he know?"

"I'd be surprised if he didn't know his brother was alive. But on the other hand, I doubt he's expecting him to show up." He thought for a moment. "Wait here," he said, thinking of finding He-Who-Dreams, the best source of information among the men.

Her chin lifted. "I will not," she said firmly. The furrow had appeared suddenly between her brows, and Nathaniel almost laughed out loud to see it.

"Then come along." He sighed, taking up her hand.

"Wait." Elizabeth glanced toward the crowds of people, and then back toward the longhouse. She swallowed nervously, unable to meet his eye.

"What is it?" he asked.

"I saw Richard," she said in a rush.

"Ah." Nathaniel put an arm around her shoulders, and bent his head to hers. "And how was that?"

"I told him that I would answer his charges here."

"You look nervous enough about it," he noted, smoothing a hand over her hair and tugging lightly on her plait. "You've got nothing to fear, Boots. We'll deal with Todd, and the day after tomorrow we'll be on our way home."

Elizabeth looked up at him. "Do you believe that?"

"Aye," he said. "I do."

"But Nathaniel—" She paused, a muscle in her cheek twitching. "What does it mean, his brother coming here like this?"

"The sachem sent for him," Nathaniel said. "Probably He-Who-Dreams put the idea in his head."

"He-Who-Dreams takes a great deal of interest in Richard's welfare," Elizabeth noted. "I suppose he must have known him as a boy when he lived here."

"That ain't it exactly," Nathaniel said with a sidelong glance. "It was He-Who-Dreams who led the raiding party that brought Richard and his brother to the village."

This last piece of information seemed to have robbed Elizabeth of the powers of speech, a state Nathaniel knew would last only until she had chewed on it long enough to get the next issue fixed in her mind. He couldn't predict what it would be, but he did know it would give him something to consider. *Loving this woman is a far sight easier than keeping up with her,* he thought. *God grant me the energy.*

He let a hand rest on the small of her back. "You realize, Boots," he said, stopping to get her attention. "That I have never known anybody who makes me think so hard as you do."

She closed one eye, considering. "Is that good or bad?"

"Oh, good," he said, his hand sliding down the curve of her hip.

Her smile was a rare and especially beautiful thing these days. She put her hand over his where it rested on her hip. "That's lovely to hear, Nathaniel. But right now—" She looked through the crowds around the baggataway game, which was just coming to an end. "Where has Richard's brother gone?"

The sound of a single drum began, accompanied by one high, summoning voice.

"The Stick Beating Dance," he said. "That's it, then. It's a curative rite, but I'll wager Richard wouldn't ask for it for himself. That's why they sent for Throws-Far, because he can request it for his brother. How did his wounds look, when you saw him?"

"Festering, the one on his hand that I could see," she said.

"So that makes sense, then."

"I should be very curious to see Richard right now," Elizabeth said.

"Well, for once Todd ain't in an obstinate frame of mind," Nathaniel noted. "There he comes now."

The whole village seemed eager to be a part of the dance, and so Elizabeth, who was tall for her sex but not so tall as the group of men who milled around the fire, could not fix Richard in her view. Eventually they worked their way to one side, where two singers had situated themselves on a bench. One of them was the canoemaker, who blinked at her solemnly as he beat on his water drum. The other singer had a rattle constructed out of a length of horn, stopped up at one end and fixed with a wooden handle at the other.

Two groups were forming on either side of the fire, of both men and women.

"I should join them," Nathaniel said. "Will you—"

"Oh, no." Elizabeth would have laughed out of nervousness, but the mood of the crowd was subdued and focused, and so she sent him on his way with a little wave of her hand.

When Nathaniel had disappeared into the dancers, she found herself trembling with relief. Elizabeth was thankful for this extra time to think about how to say to him what there was to say. The idea was still fresh and unfamiliar enough to make her jerk with surprise, and flush with a combination of pride and reserve. What did a lady say, beyond the terribly awkward phrases of the drawing room?

"Nothing," Elizabeth muttered out loud to herself. A lady said nothing, had no real words for this condition, because it was one never discussed publicly. Announcements were made in a neutral voice over tea: *Young Winslow and his lady are in hopeful expectation,* her uncle might say.

The singing rose another notch, a wonderful, throaty chanting that was almost hypnotic in its rhythms. Nathaniel moved past in the line, his torso bent over as he danced, all his concentration there, on moving himself in those small, concise steps that sent He-Who-Dreams' prayers off toward the heavens.

A bubble of nausea rose unexpectedly in Elizabeth's throat and she swallowed it back down, taken by surprise. It was the crowd, she supposed, and the heat of the fire, and the excitement—still no clear view of Richard. But then aunt Merriweather would ask what she might be thinking, standing out in the evening breeze, in her delicate condition. Elizabeth had a sudden longing for her aunt, who would take her by the hands and look into her eyes and see what was there. *I have had good news of you,* she might say with a smile. Aunt Merriweather loved children excessively, but Elizabeth thought of her cousin Marianne at an assembly ball, her mouth in a small moue of disdain as she whispered behind her fan: "Imagine Jane Bingley dancing, and so obviously *enceinte.*"

What a terribly awkward thing it is to be English, Elizabeth thought, watching a young Kahnyen'kehàka woman heavy with child advancing with the shuffling step of the dance. All at once she realized how many others there were with a child on the way or one straddling a hip and another at the breast. She could manage this. She would have a child, Nathaniel's child, and a life with him, and her work—Stone-Splitter's voice drifted through her head and she answered it firmly. She *would* have her work, even if it was not what she had imagined it to be. She could be happy.

I am happy. It was true, in spite of all that had happened. She was content, and suddenly she was not so worried about how to tell Nathaniel. The words would come, when the time and setting were appropriate. Perhaps tonight when they retired, or perhaps tomorrow. When she had grown used to the idea herself and made herself acquainted with the child, who appeared in her thoughts already as an infant; she could almost feel the weight of it in her arms. She tried again to count days, and failed. As best she understood these things, this child would come early in the new year. If all went well.

She was jerked out of her daydream by Robbie, who materialized behind her.

"Have ye need of a translator?" he asked quietly. "I thoucht ye might like tae ken what He-Who-Dreams has tae say."

Elizabeth nodded, glancing up and behind at Robbie. "Did you see—" she whispered, and he nodded.

"I did."

He-Who-Dreams raised his voice, putting an end to their discussion.

The lines of dancers kept time with the drum, a hundred feet in soft moccasins moving back and forth. There was the swoosh of long fringe and the clinking of beads and shells and silver ornaments. Many of the men wore knee bands sewn over and over with rattles made from deer hooves, and these set a steady pace.

The sun had fallen to the horizon and hesitated there, the curve of its great belly resting on the edge of the world, bedded in a sky that melded from deep indigo to a pale lavender.

"Welcome, Throws-Far," He-Who-Dreams called, raising the ceremonial stick in his hand. "We welcome our brother who comes to us from the Caughnawaga—" He gestured. "He asks us in his brother's name to offer up our songs so that Cat-Eater might heal and walk among us again."

The crowd parted and Throws-Far appeared, carrying a basket. A huge man, broad and layered with muscle, he bore more than the usual share of battle scars. Elizabeth was close enough to see the details of the tattooing on his face and head. He had painted his face in yellow and blue, four stripes to a cheek. But no manner of dress and no amount of ornament could hide his coloring, the pale skin that resisted tanning, the coppery hair and vivid blue eyes. Those eyes met hers and she saw his attention narrow to a hard focus. Elizabeth stepped involuntarily backward and closer to Robbie.

The dancers were moving again. Spotted-Fox, Splitting-Moon, Otter, and then Nathaniel. As he passed, Elizabeth saw his attention was someplace far away.

The singing grew louder and then stopped abruptly. She watched as He-Who-Dreams reached into the basket of gifts Throws-Far had brought, finding a highly decorated pouch, closed by a drawstring. He opened it and poured what was inside into his palm.

"Great Spirit who gave us the night," he chanted, as the last rays of the sun trembled and then were lost. On the other side of the sky, the moon rose, the color of an overripe peach.

"Great Spirit who gave us the darkness in which to rest. In that darkness we send our words to you."

The tobacco crackled when he scattered it on the fire, smoke rising with a great whirl of sparks in a sweet, pungent eddy to the sky. The musicians' song swelled, and receded, swelled again, hovered above the fire like a living thing, and fell silent.

He-Who-Dreams thumped the ground with his stick.

"Cat-Eater!" he summoned. And again, "Cat-Eater!"

There was a rustling, a soft murmuring. Throws-Far watched, the firelight lending his face an animation which was not his own.

Elizabeth swayed with a new wave of nausea, catching Robbie's arm for support. Sweat broke out on her brow and trickled down her face. Her mouth filled with sour saliva.

"Wha' is it, lass?" Robbie whispered. "Are ye ill?"

Richard came. He stood across the fire from his brother.

Pale, so pale, slightly bent with one arm held at an awkward angle, supporting his weight on a stick. Behind him was She-Remembers, the clan mother of the Bear longhouse and the woman who had been nursing his injuries.

The two men stood across from each other looking through the flames, like images in a distorted mirror.

There was a fist high in her gut, forcing itself up into her gullet. Elizabeth turned away from the fire, stumbled out of the crowd, through the milling children, with both Robbie and Treenie behind her, making anxious noises. Past the place where Made-of-Bones' great-granddaughters liked to grind corn in the mornings, past a skin stretched out on a frame, half scraped. The stink of the urine in which it had been cured struck her physically, and Elizabeth stumbled into the shadows beside the longhouse, where she paused, and let it happen. And happen again. And again. She braced herself with one arm against the longhouse wall and hung there, as miserable as she could ever remember being. Robbie had disappeared, but Treenie sat patiently, as if she had seen such behavior before, and expected to see it again. When Elizabeth looked at her, she thumped her tail sympathetically and offered a doglike shrug.

"Here, lass," Robbie said when he returned, holding out a water gourd. She filled her mouth and spat. Did that again, and then finally drank in small sips.

"What hae ye been eatin'?" Robbie asked, shaking his head. "I should verra much like tae ken, so that I may stay far awa' from it."

She gave him a weak grin, and drank again.

"Lie ye doon," Robbie suggested.

Elizabeth straightened her shoulders, and glanced back toward the fire where the whole village stood, listening to a single voice. It was one she didn't recognize, but which was very familiar, all the same. Richard, and his brother, and their Kahnyen'kehàka family around them. Now, standing outside of the light of the fire, it all seemed so very strange. She had come looking for a life different from the one she had in England, but this—

Robbie's hand was a gentle weight on her shoulder.

" 'Tis a verra curious thing tae stan' betwixt worlds wi' a foot in both," he said.

"I don't belong there among them," she said. "I feel as though I'm intruding on a family matter."

"But it's his place, too, lass."

She didn't have to ask for his meaning. Nathaniel was here, because some part of him belonged here. " 'Thy people shall be my people,' " she said softly.

"Ooch, it's guid tae hear ye quotin'," said Robbie easily. "I see that ye are feelin' mair yersel'."

Elizabeth laughed a little. "I'm feeling much better," she agreed, and realized that it was true; the nausea had ebbed away.

"Dinna ye think that a rest—" he began, but he drew up short. Curious, Elizabeth turned and found Splitting-Moon standing just a few paces off.

"My grandmother asks that you come to her," the young woman said.

"Weel, then, lass, ye had best be goin'. Made-of-Bones doesna look kindly on disobedience."

"I've noticed," Elizabeth muttered, starting off behind Splitting-Moon.

The Bear and Wolf longhouses were identical in most details, a fact which set Elizabeth a little more at ease. Here, though, the clan mother's hearth was shared with a husband, the sachem, who was still at the Stick Beating Dance. The lingering scent of his tobacco made a contrast to the herbs that were so prominent at Made-of-Bones' hearth. She-Remembers seemed to be more involved in the making of the ornaments that so many wore, and the fine needlework that decorated the clothing. Bits of work in progress were piled everywhere, as were baskets of porcupine quills, shells, threads, and other things that Elizabeth could not identify. There was time to see all this, because she and Splitting-Moon arrived first.

While the younger woman fed the fire, bringing it up to a good blaze, Elizabeth examined a long row of feathered head-dresses, picking up a half-finished one to look at it closely. The headpiece itself was an elongated cap of supple wooden splints interwoven and covered with the softest doeskin. This one did not yet have feathers, but it sat beside baskets full of them: eagle and turkey, which she recognized without too much trouble, some long ones which might have been feathers of the great blue cranes they saw so often on the waterways, crow and hawk.

Splitting-Moon made a sound of welcome and Elizabeth looked up to see the bear pelt at the door pushed aside.

She laid the headdress carefully down and stood, her hands folded in front of her. The three clan mothers came in first, followed by Richard, leaning heavily on his stick, and finally, thankfully, Nathaniel. He came to her immediately.

"Are you unwell?" he asked, hooking one of her fingers with one of his own.

She squeezed tight, and managed a small smile. "I am well enough," she said. "We can talk about that later." Elizabeth was vaguely aware of Splitting-Moon slipping through the doorway and away into the night.

She-Remembers was a woman of perhaps fifty years, straight of back and very tall for her sex. Her left eye seemed to be blind, for there was an opaque cast to it and the lid hung slack. This was her hearth, and she spoke first, welcoming them all. She looked down the length of the corridor as if there were some message to be read in the shadows, and then she turned to Elizabeth.

"Cat-Eater tells us that you first seemed ready to take him as your husband, but then left in the night with Wolf-Running-Fast. He says that you promised to bring the mountain we call Hidden Wolf to him when you married, and that he has been cheated of this land, which is rightfully his. He has made a suggestion to us, and asked us to consider it, but first we would hear your side of this matter."

Nathaniel had translated some of this for her, staring at Richard, who stood almost in the shadows. His face was haggard but his attention as clear and focused as a hungry bird of prey.

She cleared her throat.

"You will forgive me if I use French when Kahnyen'kehàka fails me—" Elizabeth looked each of the women in the eye. Two-Suns seemed to be quite young to be clan mother to the

Turtle longhouse, but she had a serene air. She-Remembers had a more hesitant way about her, but there was nothing obviously hostile or unfriendly in her bearing or tone.

But Made-of-Bones. The old woman stood watching her with drawn brow. She rubbed the fringe on her sleeve between her thumb and forefinger and squinted at Elizabeth, her head cocked hard to one side.

Elizabeth said, "It is true that for some weeks I let Richard talk to me of marriage. But it is not true that I promised him anything, because I never intended to marry him. I told him so at least twice. But I followed my heart—and my conscience— and I took Nathaniel as my husband." She paused, and met Richard's eye. "I am well satisfied with him."

Made-of-Bones pushed the air out through her nose. Nathaniel squeezed Elizabeth's hand, and she returned the pressure.

"It is true that Hidden Wolf is now Nathaniel's property, but that is only true because the laws of my people do not allow women to own property when they marry. I would not hand over what is mine simply because I am a woman, if not for the law."

Made-of-Bones snorted again, whether out of displeasure or agreement, it was not clear. Two-Suns spoke up in a surpringly hoarse voice.

"The O'seronni call us backward," she said. "They do not see themselves."

"It is not the Kahnyen'kehàka way," agreed She-Remembers.

"The O'seronni are a nation of fools," pronounced Made-of-Bones with a dismissive chop of her hand. "Do you need to be reminded?" She considered Elizabeth for a moment, one corner of her mouth turned down. "Did you take anything from Cat-Eater which is his?"

"No," said Elizabeth slowly. "I have taken nothing of Richard's."

His voice came, not unexpectedly. "Except my good name," he said. He was feverish with agitation, sweat pearling on his brow.

"You have your name," she answered calmly. "And it is as good as ever it was."

"Enough," said She-Remembers. She took a moment to gather her thoughts. "By our law Cat-Eater has no claim to you or what is yours. My sisters will agree with me?" Two-Suns nodded quickly; Made-of-Bones responded with a jerk of her shoulders.

"But we also cannot make any judgments based on your own laws, which are mysterious to us. We can only advise you."

Elizabeth felt Nathaniel relaxing beside her, but she could not do the same: the expectant look on Made-of-Bones' face made her shift uneasily from one foot to the other.

She-Remembers said, "Cat-Eater tells us if he cannot have the mountain, then he would claim the child of Sings-from-Books as his daughter."

Elizabeth grabbed onto Nathaniel's arm. Her face inches from his, she watched all the color drain from him, felt the coil of his muscles. Her own knuckles were white where her hands gripped his forearm. "Nathaniel," she hissed, shaking him. "Nathaniel!" He glanced down at her, his face ragged with anger. Seeing her distress, the wild look in his eyes eased just a bit.

"She is not yours to claim," he managed finally, in a voice that was almost his own.

"I say she is," said Richard.

Elizabeth's heart thundered so that her vision seemed to throb with it. Hannah. Only once had she ever heard Richard mention her name, on her first night in Paradise at her father's Christmas party. He had looked at the little girl as if she were a stranger, and an uninteresting one at that: nothing more than a half-breed female child, and no good to the world.

"You have no interest in Hannah's welfare," she said to Richard in English.

Nathaniel said, "It is not about Hannah." And looking at the clan mothers one by one, he said: "Cat-Eater is consumed by envy and will take from me whatever he can get."

Richard put his fist against his chest, so that the livid gash of his half-healed wound flared. "I take what is mine."

"Wait," Elizabeth said, holding out both hands in a pleading motion. "Kahnyen'kehàka children belong to their mothers, is that not so? Then what claim could Richard possibly have?"

"I would bring her here to her great-grandmother," Richard said, looking at Made-of-Bones. "But she would be brought up in the knowledge that I am her father."

"You are *not* her father." Nathaniel's voice filled the longhouse. "Sings-from-Books was my wife when she bore the child."

"Sings-from-Books put you aside and took another," said Made-of-Bones.

"Did he tell you that?" Nathaniel asked. "You believed him?"

"My daughter Falling-Day told me that," said Made-of-Bones. "I believed her."

Richard shot Nathaniel a triumphant look.

A wave of nausea washed over Elizabeth, and she swallowed it back down, ruthlessly.

"You cannot take the child from the home she knows and loves," she said. "Away from her family."

"We are her family," said Made-of-Bones. "Her grandmother and her uncle and aunt can come with her, and live here at the hearth where they belong."

Nathaniel's eyes narrowed in Richard's direction. When he spoke again, it was in English. "I see it now. You'll give the old woman back her daughter and her daughter's daughters, and then you've got the Kahnyen'kehàka out of Paradise. Do they know that's what you want? To get the last of their people out of your sight? You claim her as your daughter." Nathaniel's mouth twisted in disgust. "If you could you would gladly kill every one of these people in their beds."

"That is not true," Richard said, hoarsely.

"You watched that happen before, at Barktown."

"What happened at Barktown was not my doing. If they believed that it was, I would be long dead." There was no sign of emotion on Richard's face, no movement at all, but every line in his body vibrated with tension. The clan mothers were watching him, but he seemed to have forgotten them. Elizabeth was suddenly struck with a memory of her brother, interrupted at cards when he had his last shilling on a wager, consumed by the game and his own desperation.

Nathaniel said in Kahnyen'kehàka: "I don't know what Falling-Day advised my wife, but I do know that Sings-from-Books never left my mother's home or my hearth. I claim her child as my own in the Kahnyen'kehàka way, and according to the laws of the O'seronni. And I dare anyone here to prove otherwise."

"Wait," said Made-of-Bones. She turned her attention to Elizabeth, poked at her with one broad finger. "Cat-Eater cannot take the child," she said grudgingly, "but you could send her to us. You have told us of the ways of the O'seronni, who have taken your land from you and given it to a man because you chose him to lie with. You see our ways are not so simple-minded. Would you not have the child raised here, where she can learn to be a woman?"

Elizabeth flushed with a new anger, looking into the old woman's dark eyes. "I am a woman," she said clearly. "And I have things to teach her."

"You cannot teach her to be Kahnyen'kehàka!" said Made-of-Bones.

"That is for her grandmother and aunt to do," Elizabeth agreed. "They are with her, too." She drew in a sharp breath, and let it out. "It's about that, isn't it? Not so much about Hannah, but about getting your daughter back."

Made-of-Bones said, "I had a good man, and I bred him five sons and three daughters. Healthy, strong children. All of my sons died as warriors, in O'seronni wars. Two of my daughters are gone. One at the hands of Redcoats, while she was big with child. The other, the mother of Splitting-Moon, of the O'seronni spotted sickness. There were once many women at my hearth, but now there is only myself left in my line, and my granddaughter, Splitting-Moon. Can you not understand what it is to want my child and her children here, where they belong?" She looked at Elizabeth, and then at Nathaniel. Suddenly her face hardened, the corner of her mouth turned down. "Perhaps not," she said, her voice dropping. "Perhaps you cannot imagine this. The loss of a child is a pain you will never know."

Elizabeth caught up Nathaniel's hand, and jerked it, hard.

"Let me answer," she said hoarsely. "Please." She stood like that with him until she felt his reluctance break.

The words were there, she could say them: *But he can father children; I carry his child.* It would break the back of the only argument Richard had which meant anything to these women; it would resolve the issue of Nathaniel's manhood. She felt color flooding her breast, moving up to her hairline. Nathaniel was looking at her, they were all looking at her. She dropped her gaze to the ground, cleared her throat, and tried to summon the words.

When she looked up, Throws-Far was with them. He had stepped out of the deepest shadows into the firelight, appearing like an apparition. With a nod to each of the clan mothers, he addressed She-Remembers.

"May I speak?" Into the terrible tension around the hearth, he brought a quiet voice, without anger or threat.

She-Remembers murmured her agreement, while the other two simply nodded. Made-of-Bones threw a nervous look in Nathaniel's direction.

Richard stood motionless, all the anger in his eyes suddenly masked. There was a stillness in him, the same stillness she had seen on the shore of the Hudson while he watched her say goodbye to Nathaniel so many weeks ago. He could bide his time, when it served his purposes. His intent and resolve were as clear and marked as the streaks of paint on Throws-Far's face.

"I came today because He-Who-Dreams summoned me to help. He sees more than one kind of sickness in this man, who is both my brother and a stranger to me. And so I speak, although I see that he does not want my help."

There was no tone of complaint in Throws-Far's manner or words, just simple statements put forth with great deliberation.

"This man has never lived among the Kahnyen'kehàka," said Throws-Far. "Even when his body was here, his heart was back with the O'seronni. He could not be one of us. He could not forgive me for putting the white ways behind me."

Richard was not looking at his brother, but his face trembled and the line of his jaw hardened. A drop of sweat fell onto his shirt and was followed by another.

Throws-Far directed his comments to the clan mothers, as if

they were alone. "Even now he will not see me. There is a hardness in his heart that makes him blind. But he can hear me. I can tell him that I have four fine sons and two daughters who make me proud. He is their uncle. He knows this now, and can never put this knowledge from him."

The wind rose and shook the bark roof of the longhouse. The night was all sound: the drum and rattle, crickets and the faraway echo of the wolf, and above it all the prayers of the faith keeper, drifting into the night sky for the sake of a man who stood here, his face glimmering with sweat and his eyes blank with resignation.

Throws-Far listened to the faint voice of He-Who-Dreams for a time, and then his face cleared of this preoccupation and he turned back to the clan mothers.

"A warrior can have a father's heart. So I ask Cat-Eater, would you do to this child what was done to you? Would you destroy a child to avenge our mother?"

Richard's head snapped up, and for the first time Elizabeth saw him focus on the man who stood opposite him. His face flushed a vivid red, his mouth twisted in indignation and an undisguised pain.

Throws-Far met Richard's stare calmly. "Do not let the bitterness in your heart rule your mind. Put Hidden Wolf behind you."

"Who are you to tell me what to do and how to live?" Richard asked woodenly.

Throws-Far blinked. He opened his mouth to speak again, but his words were uncertain, and even his voice was different, higher and younger: "I am your brother," he said in English. "I was once called Samuel."

Just above their sleeping platform, there was a break in the roof of the Wolf longhouse that would displease Made-of-Bones greatly. Had she known of it, she would have sent one of her grandsons immediately to climb to the roof and repair it. But she didn't know, and Nathaniel was glad of the view of the heavens, on their last night with the Kahnyen'kehàka.

He lay on his back watching the stars in the sky. They had a knowing glitter, like the eyes of the great cats when they lie in wait in the bush. Cold and hot all at once, something too bright to comprehend.

Elizabeth shifted her head to a more comfortable position on Nathaniel's shoulder. She was nowhere near sleep, which surprised him given the long events of the evening. There was a hollow feeling under his ribs when he thought about it, what Todd had tried to do. What he was still trying to do and would die trying to do, if he persisted.

"It's over now," she said softly, reading his thoughts, or the tension in his shoulders.

He let a finger trail over her temple and down the side of her face. "You don't think the man has changed because his brother tried to speak some sense to him?" He didn't like the bitterness in his voice, but it was there all the same.

"People change," she said. "I have changed."

Nathaniel grunted. "Tomorrow morning when we take this business before the sachem, then we will see how changed Richard Todd is."

She rubbed her cheek on his chest, put her mouth softly against his neck. His skin flared in an arc from the touch of her lips to his groin, and he turned, carrying her with him. Richard Todd was banished: in the faint light of the moon and the embers of the hearth fire there was only the outline of her face, her sweet, strong face in the shape of a heart. In the shape of his own heart.

He kissed her cheek and found it wet. "Why do you weep?" he asked, astounded.

"I want to go home."

"We start tomorrow."

She nodded, but she was not with him in her mind.

"Tell me," he said against her mouth. "What is it?"

"Nathaniel. It *is* over. You needn't fear Richard's claims about you—they are not true. And there is proof, now." She took his hand and carried it down to press it flat on her lower belly. "There," she whispered, her forehead against his. "We have made a child, you and I."

At first the words were as meaningless as birdsong. He heard himself draw in breath and let it out again. Under the curve of his palm her warm skin rose and fell on the tide of her breath. It was her face that told him clearly, the joy in it and the fear in equal measure.

"Are you certain?"

"It has been six weeks since I bled—" she whispered. He put a thumb against her lips, and his forehead against hers.

In that instant Nathaniel knew the depths of his self-doubt. Exposed suddenly to light and air, the fear that he had lived with for ten years simply withered away to be replaced by an elation that clenched his heart, and would never let go.

He said something he had never admitted to himself before: "I didn't believe it was possible."

She was pushing closer, winding her arms and legs around him to make a cradle of herself. With her voice and with the body which sheltered his child, Elizabeth rocked the breath of hope back into him.

"I never doubted you," she said softly. "Never for a moment."

XLII

The Strawberry Festival ceremonies required a great deal of preparation from the Kahnyen'kehàka of the Wolf longhouse, so that well before dawn hearth fires were stirred and torches lit. Half asleep, Elizabeth lay quietly listening to a muted argument between Crow-Flying, Spotted-Fox and their son, Little-Kettle, who would be taking part for the first time in the Feather Dance. He had particular notions about his face paint, it seemed, which did not suit. He was threatened with a consultation with the clan mother and the conversation took an abrupt end, just as Made-of-Bones appeared beside their sleeping platform with her usual bowl for Nathaniel.

Her mouth was set in a harder line than usual, and she did not meet Elizabeth's eye. The outcome of the discussions in the Bear longhouse clearly did not please her in the least, for while she was always short and sometimes rude, she had never before failed to respond to a greeting.

"Splitting-Moon will prepare enough medicine for your journey," she said to Nathaniel as he sat up to take the bowl. "Bone-in-Her-Back can make an infusion?"

"I can," Elizabeth answered for herself.

Nathaniel drank, and then handed the bowl back to the old woman. For a moment they both held it fast, his strong brown fingers and hers, a few shades darker and twisted with age, the nails ridged. "There is no way to repay you for the gift of my good health," Nathaniel said. Elizabeth watched Made-of-Bones take in this message: *I am thankful, but I will not deliver my daughter to you.*

She made a flicking gesture with her fingers, as if to brush away his words. "When are you leaving?"

"You know that we have unfinished business with Cat-Eater after the Feather Dance."

"This morning Throws-Far left us," she said. "His brother went with him."

Nathaniel's sleepiness was suddenly gone. "Where is Otter?"

Made-of-Bones spread out one hand and closed it in a sweeping curl of her fingers. "Gone, with the warriors. And his Windigo rifle." Her mouth turned up at one corner. *"Vous et nul autre."*

Elizabeth felt her skin rise and flush all along her back. Nathaniel put a hand on her arm; it was only that, its warmth and weight, that kept her from shaking. He was staring at the old woman; she looked back at him, one white brow raised, and then she left them.

"Nathaniel," Elizabeth said hoarsely. "What does it mean?"

Outside, the faith keeper's song began, calling the Kahnyen'kehàka to the festivities.

Nathaniel swung his legs down so that he was sitting on the edge of the sleeping platform, all tension and concentration where just a few minutes ago he had been sleeping with his body curled around hers, his hand on her belly.

"Otter hasn't gone after Richard," she said out loud, wanting it to be so.

Nathaniel shrugged. "Maybe not."

Elizabeth thought of Otter at the Stick Beating Dance, his gaze always fixed on Richard.

"But perhaps," she conceded reluctantly. "Otherwise he would have taken his leave of us."

Nathaniel grunted, running a hand through his hair. "He don't know what he's getting himself into."

Elizabeth was torn between worry and irritation, and with something smaller and meaner: she did not want to chase a

nineteen-year-old bent on revenge into another wilderness, for
the sake of a man whose greed had nearly cost her everything
she held dear in life. Or even, God forgive her, for his own
sake.

She leaned forward to put her chin on Nathaniel's shoulder.
"I owe him a great deal," she said. "But it is time to go home."

"We'll go home," he agreed, touching her cheek. "The boy
has the right to fight his own ghosts."

They took leave of Stone-Splitter and He-Who-Dreams formally, presenting their small store of tobacco as a gift. Then
they visited each of the clan mothers, and accepted well wishes.
She-Remembers gave Elizabeth a carry bag decorated with
elaborate quillwork and beads. Two-Suns had a pair of fine
doeskin leggings. It occurred to her, as it had every day that she
had spent with these people, that everything she wore and everything she ate came from them, but that this was taken for
granted: their generosity was fundamental to their character.
She wished she had some way to repay them for their kindness,
and said this to Robbie, who was busy with his gear.

"I've no' a doot the day will come when they will need your
friendship," he said quietly. "Or that ye'll remember the kindness shewn ye."

Made-of-Bones came down to the river at the last minute,
Splitting-Moon behind her. They had provided baskets of herbs
and other gifts for the Kahnyen'kehàka at Hidden Wolf, and
Elizabeth saw the old woman's eyes moving over the way these
things had been packed in the canoe. Then she repeated the
messages she had already given Nathaniel for her daughter, until
she was satisfied that he had each of them word for word.

She seemed to hesitate and then she turned to Elizabeth.
"The O'seronni medicine to keep the *brûlot* away, the one that
turns your skin brown—do you have any of it?"

Elizabeth glanced at Nathaniel, who looked as puzzled as she
felt. "I do not," she said. "Nathaniel?"

"There's a half bottle, in my pack."

The old woman produced a small satisfied grunt. "Stay away
from it," she said to Elizabeth. "And suffer the bites." And she
left them without another word of farewell.

"What was that all about?" Elizabeth asked Splitting-Moon. "I know she is upset with me, but to wish me bitten . . . ?"

"*Le pouliot*," said Splitting-Moon, glancing over her shoulder. "It is poisonous."

"I assumed that pennyroyal is poisonous to the blackfly. But not to us—I used it, we all used it," Elizabeth protested, her nose flaring as she remembered the strong tang of the sticky liquid.

"It is poison to the child," Splitting-Moon said, her gaze firmly excluding Nathaniel and Robbie from the discussion.

"In any form?" Elizabeth asked faintly.

"No. Only if you drink tea made of it. If you put on your skin, it would not cause harm."

Elizabeth frowned. "Then I don't take her meaning."

"My grandmother would counsel against any O'seronni medicine for a breeding woman. But it always puts her in a bad mood to have her family leave her." Splitting-Moon offered a rare half smile. "I am afraid that she does indeed wish you bitten."

Paddling downriver, Elizabeth looked back to see Made-of-Bones standing on a rise above them. The force of her personality subdued by distance, Elizabeth saw her for the old woman she was, in the curve of her spine and the sparse white hair lifting in the wind. A woman who had lost most of the people she loved, and feared to lose more. Suddenly Elizabeth wished she had made more of an effort with her.

Treenie whimpered a little and put her head on Elizabeth's knee, and when she looked up again, they had turned a corner and Made-of-Bones was gone.

She leaned toward Nathaniel and whistled softly so that he turned his head toward her. Behind her Robbie had already begun singing.

"She knew. Made-of-Bones knew about the child," said Elizabeth.

Nathaniel nodded.

"Do you think she told Richard?"

"She must have," he said. "Otherwise why would he take off the way he did?" Nathaniel asked, the sweep of his paddle as steady as his breathing.

There is the question, she thought. Of the answer, Elizabeth was not quite so sure as Nathaniel seemed to be.

PART III

Will Ye Go, Lassie, Go?

XLIII

Late June, 1793

By their fifth day on the vast lake called Champlain by the
French who had claimed it, and Regioghne by the
Hode'noshaunee, who knew it was the province not of men,
but the warrior spirit who commanded the wind and waves,
Elizabeth had learned that Robbie could not paddle without
singing. He sang songs of the fur traders, the marching songs
that he had learned in twenty years as a soldier, and a great
number of Kahnyen'kehàka songs, one of which the canoemaker had composed and delivered with the craft:

> *The canoe is very fast.*
> *It is mine.*
> *All day long I splash away.*
> *I paddle along, I paddle along.*

When he found that his music had a willing audience, Robbie opened up his treasure chest: the ballads and songs of his
boyhood in the Scottish border counties. He had a deep, clear
voice and an ear for a tune, and his music hung over the water
like the shimmering dragonflies that followed them everywhere.
Just now he was humming a melody that had been haunting
him for days, a simple song that Elizabeth had begun to hear
even in her dreams.

While a canoe was not always the most comfortable form of travel, Elizabeth found that with Robbie behind her and Nathaniel in front, she was content. Shifting her weight to ease the ache in her knees, she fumbled her paddle and accidentally sprayed Treenie, so that she produced a startled but sleepy woof in response. Nathaniel glanced back over his shoulder at the dog and then grinned at Elizabeth.

It took a moment to get her paddle back in the water in the right rhythm. The men did not need her help, but she wanted the challenge of the task. She needed something to distract her from the constant preoccupation with her own inner workings, for sometime in the past few days a small kernel of nausea had taken up permanent residence. When she woke in the morning it was lodged high in her belly and almost possible to ignore. By midday it had grown like a spider's web, working its way up to her chest, and by the late afternoon she could no longer take note of anything but the creeping fingers, pressing in the softest flesh at the back of her throat.

I have learned to cope with many indignities in the past weeks, she thought to herself. *But never will I become accustomed to being indisposed in public view.*

This day was hot and sunny, but the sweat on her brow was more a signal that she was approaching a crisis. Then she noticed that the sound of the water was shifting—she could hear white water now before she saw any sign of it, even before Nathaniel signaled to head to the shore of the little cove ahead of them. Elizabeth's spirits lifted in the hope that she would be able to keep her distress to herself for once.

"No rest for the wicked," noted Robbie cheerfully, heaving his great frame out of the cramped space as they pulled to the shore. Elizabeth was up and away before the men could secure their paddles, returning very shortly to rinse her mouth with lake water.

"But perhaps a wee snooze," he continued as if there hadn't been any interruption in his thoughts. "It's no' tae early tae make camp, dinna ye think, Nathaniel?"

Elizabeth cast him a sour glance. "Robbie. There are hours of light left, and this is not a long carry."

"Och, weel, lass," he said, stroking his mustache thought-fully. "Auld bones, ye ken."

"Oh, I ken, I certainly do." She hefted her pack with an annoyed tug. "Do you think I haven't noticed that we stop earlier every day? Nathaniel, you need not coddle me. I am perfectly fine."

"Maybe it's not you we're stopping for," Nathaniel answered easily. "I'm still healing, in case you forgot. And there's no hurry now, is there?"

Elizabeth looked at her husband. He had stripped to the waist, and he stood before her in nothing more than his breech-clout, sun-browned and glistening with sweat, the muscles in his arms and shoulders tensed as he lifted his half of the canoe. His wounds were still bright red patches on his chest and back, but she hadn't heard him catch his breath or cough in days. In fact, he was looking very much like a healthy male of the species, with a grin on his face that told her he was feeling anything but tired.

She gave in after they had walked the mile of the carry. Above the sandy beach where they would push off again there was a low bluff covered with scrub grass, bracketed on one side by a great wall of wild roses in full bloom. Just beyond, a stand of young birch and maple cast a blanket of cool shadow. Seeing all this, Elizabeth acknowledged that a longer rest would be welcome, and the men set about making camp.

She went down to the lake, stripping off her moccasins to wiggle her toes in the warm sand. When she had walked out to the point where the water almost reached the hem of her over-dress, she washed as best she could, glad to be rid of the penny-royal ointment even if the blackfly had not yet settled for the evening. She thought briefly of Made-of-Bones and Splitting-Moon, and for a moment she wished herself back in the long-house. In the company of any knowledgeable woman who would be able to tell her that what she was experiencing was normal, because Elizabeth's greatest fear was that she would fail somehow in this, the most basic of womanly functions.

Treenie came capering into the water, plowing right past until she was nothing but a slick of floating red fur and a but-tonlike black nose. Elizabeth considered joining her, calculated the length of time it would take to dry out the doeskin dress and leggings, and turned back to the shore where she waded, gathering as many of the fresh-water mussels as she could carry in her tented skirt. They were huge, bigger than her hand and pockmarked with shimmering limpets.

It was cool and pleasant on the beach. The dog made a halfhearted charge at a group of gulls who squawked and lumbered off like cranky old men. Since she had been traveling with them the red dog had become less of a hunter, and she seemed only slightly mystified at her lack of success. With a philosophical *woof!* to the gulls, Treenie galloped off down the shoreline after Robbie, who was gathering driftwood for a cook fire.

"Oh, the summertime is comin'," he sang softly as he went about his work. "And the trees are softly bloomin'." His voice faded as he disappeared around the curve of the little cove. Out on the water, Nathaniel sat in the canoe with his gaze fixed below the surface and a fishing spear balanced lightly in one hand.

Treenie came back along the beach, her wet coat clogged with sand, and lay down. Elizabeth joined her, content to sit for a while looking out at the lake to watch Nathaniel fish. The setting was beautiful, but she was so sleepy. Sometimes it seemed that she would never again be fully awake. With a little sigh of irritation, she roused herself finally and climbed the bluff to camp, where she left the mussels by the cook pot for Robbie to deal with. Then she took her rolled blanket from her pack and joined Treenie in the flickering silver shadows of the birch and hickory trees, where she made a quick tent and collapsed into jagged half dreams.

It was a cool and clear evening that provided a sunset over the mountains in a thousand layers of color, the kind of sunset that never failed to lift her spirits. The evenings were Elizabeth's best time, and the nap had done her much good, although her appetite was not quite restored. There was bass grilling over a lattice-work of black willow splints, and a stew of mussels, dried beans, and wild onions, which she ate with forced enthusiasm. She had a secret longing for Curiosity's best Sunday biscuits of wheaten flour, even as she crumbled the good Kahnyen'kehàka corncake into her bowl.

They were sitting on an upcropping of rock. Nathaniel was next to her, his empty bowl balanced on the long, flat plane of his thigh. From the corner of his eye, he was watching her eat while he threw bits of fish to Treenie. Robbie was on his third bowl of stew, and showed no signs of slowing down.

"Splitting-Moon told me that it was natural, you not being hungry," Nathaniel offered. "The child takes what it needs, one way or the other, so you might as well give in, gracious like. Ain't like you got much choice, either way."

"Despotic leanings already." Elizabeth smiled. "An ominous beginning."

There was something he wanted to say; she could see it on his face, along with the reluctance. She raised an eyebrow in encouragement.

"Sarah never was sick, with either of her times," he said. "It worried my mother. She said that a child setting properly will make itself known. If that makes it any easier."

Elizabeth glanced up at him. In her misery it had never occurred to her that the nausea might be a good sign. And she hadn't thought about—hadn't wanted to think about—the fact that Nathaniel had been through this before, and was better acquainted with the process than she was. He knew enough to be worried about her, and to comfort her, too. She felt selfish, suddenly, and very self-centered.

He almost laughed. "You should see your face," he said. "Only you would manage to feel guilty because you don't like being sick." He hugged her one-armed, while he tossed more wood on the fire. "It'll pass, Boots, and you'll be able to get back to teaching. That's something to look forward to, at least."

"There is quite a lot to look forward to at Hidden Wolf," Elizabeth agreed. There were things to worry about, too. How it would be to share a small cabin with four other adults was something that kept her awake at night, knowing that there was nothing to be done about it and also that the lack of privacy would be the biggest challenge she would face. As she didn't know how to raise this question with Nathaniel without sounding demanding and dissatisfied, she quickly sent her thoughts in another direction.

"It would be nice to know that I'll have any students to teach. And there is always the possibility that my father has reclaimed the schoolhouse to use as a pigsty."

Robbie looked up from his stew, the white crescents of his brows knitted together in surprise. "But Nathaniel's bought the lan' and the schoolhoose, too, fra' yer faither, so ye needna fash yersel' . . ." His voice trailed off as he saw the exasperated look Nathaniel sent his way, and he threw up one shoulder as if to ward off a blow.

"Laddie, ye'll hae tae forgi' me. I disremembered that she didna ken."

"Pardon me?" Elizabeth asked, looking between the two of them. "You bought the schoolhouse?"

"Yes, and the land," Nathaniel said. "From your father's agent while I was in Albany. I meant it for a surprise, on home-coming."

"Yes, I see that," she murmured.

Robbie looked warily between them and then suddenly stood. "I've a mind tae take a wee walk doon the shore. It's time I had a wash, for I fear I stink sae bad as a new recruit's shirttail after his first battle. Will ye join me, Treenie?"

The dog was immediately at his side, her tail generating a significant breeze.

Nathaniel began to rise, but Elizabeth put a hand on his forearm.

"Oh, no," she said. "I think not. You and I have things to discuss. Treenie is good company, and she's more Robbie's dog than mine now, anyway."

The old soldier glanced at her, his head cocked to one side. "Do ye mean it? She is verra fond o' ye, lass."

"I will miss her," Elizabeth said. "But yes, I mean it."

"Weel, then, come along wi' ye," Robbie said softly to the red dog. "If ye are tae bide wi' me, it's time I taucht ye some manners."

"That was kind of you," Nathaniel said when Robbie had disappeared toward the lake. "He seems lonely, these days."

"Nathaniel Bonner," Elizabeth said, turning to her husband

and fixing him firmly with her most concentrated schoolmistress gaze. "If you think you can distract me from the topic at hand with a few weak compliments, you are sorely mistaken."

"For a woman in misery you're sounding mighty sure of yourself," he said dryly, trying to produce a scowl but not quite succeeding.

"Oh, very clever," Elizabeth noted, matching his tone. "But making light of my discomfort—for which you are responsible, I might point out—is a tactic which will not divert me, Nathaniel."

A hand passed over her back; he smiled and bent toward her mouth. "I was hoping you wouldn't notice."

"And if insulting my powers of observation does not serve," she said, tilting her head so that his mouth caught the crest of her cheek instead of its real target, "then you will try seduction."

He laughed out loud, his eyes flashing irritation and pleasure in equal parts. "It's good to see you feeling better," he said. "Even if you are set on sharpening that tongue of yours on my hide."

"I am not easily diverted, that is true. Would you have me more malleable?" It was a challenge, edged with worry.

He shook his head. "I wouldn't change you, Boots, if I could. Aggravating as you are at times."

"More flattery," she said. "Do stop, or I shall swoon."

Nathaniel sighed, apparently resigned to his fate. "So ask if you're set on it, and I'll answer if I can."

Elizabeth thought for a moment, and then she put it to him as carefully as she could: "How is it that you went off to Albany with not quite enough money to pay both Richard and the taxes, and managed not only to do that, but also to buy a plot of land with a new building on it? If there is a price on your head for robbery, I should like to know about it."

There was an edge of irritation in the way he ran his hand through his hair. "Maybe I'm just good at dealing."

"Perhaps," Elizabeth conceded, trying to keep her tone even. "But even so, money cannot be created out of thin air. How did you make aunt Merriweather's note stretch so far?"

"It was easy," he said. His face had gone very watchful and

still. "I didn't use your aunt's money at all. That's all safe in the bank."

It was not often that Elizabeth found herself speechless, but she could not think of a thing to say to her husband, whose eyes never moved from her face. Nathaniel reached into the neck of her dress to pull out the long silver chain. Along with it came his mother's pearl cluster, Joe's bijou, the panther tooth, and finally the gold coin, warmed by her skin. This he tapped softly.

"The Tory Gold?" Elizabeth asked, numbly. "You have the Tory Gold?"

"Not all of it," Nathaniel said, sitting back, suddenly tense and very wary.

She stood abruptly and pointed at him, her finger trembling slightly. "*You* didn't have a dollar to wager at the turkey shoot!"

Nathaniel peered up at her, one eye narrowed. "Couldn't exactly toss a five-quid gold piece at Billy Kirby and ask for change. Not without giving the game away."

"The *game*?" Her voice wobbled. "The game? What game is it that you mean? The one when you convinced me that marriage was the only way to secure Hidden Wolf away from Richard? That game?"

Nathaniel stood, and put his hands on her shoulders. "I never said that," he said softly. "If you'll think back."

She pulled away. "Did or did you not have a chest full of gold at your disposal at the very time you were telling me that you could not match Richard Todd's bid on Hidden Wolf?"

"Chingachgook gave us leave to spend as much of the gold as we needed, back in December, but we couldn't," Nathaniel said. "Not without drawing the government of the state of New-York and the British army down on our heads. Not to mention—"

"Jack Lingo," Elizabeth supplied.

Nathaniel grimaced. "Aye. Jack Lingo."

"This whole journey was for naught," she said dully.

"No!" He reached out toward her but she stepped away. "Elizabeth. Even if we could have handed the gold over for the land without half the world coming down on us, it wouldn't have done any good. You know that. Your father was set against selling it to us from the start, because it was the only way he had of keeping Richard Todd in line—by marrying you off to him, for the mountain."

"Yes," she hissed. "But none of that would have come as a surprise. You might have told me the truth. You might have trusted me."

"Elizabeth. I trust you with my life. I would have told you before we got back to Paradise." Nathaniel paused, his face clouding. "I didn't tell you back to start with, because—"

"Yes?" She waited in a kind of void, terrified of what he might say, but needing the truth anyway.

"Because I was afraid of losing you, if there was another way to get the mountain. I couldn't see a way out, but I figured you might."

The words hung there between them, over the shimmering heat of the fire. Elizabeth watched them floating for three beats of her heart. There was a ticking sound in her throat.

"It was the pretense of my aunt's money that allowed you to use your own?" She wondered at how calm she sounded.

He nodded.

"But why did you not simply use my aunt's funds?" she asked. "It was there for the specific purpose of buying me out of my father's troubles. Why not leave your own resources for another time?"

The muscles in his throat were working, and the look in his eyes made her heart ache. He had not used aunt Merriweather's money because the drive to own the mountain was stronger than anything else. He had got her, and the mountain and the schoolhouse, on his own terms.

Elizabeth looked away to try to sort out her thoughts, struggling desperately for some balance, but finding none.

"So in fact, you did buy Hidden Wolf without my help." She heard the tone of her voice rising, but she could not stop it. "And so I deceived my father out of his land to offer it to you—of my own free will—but you preferred to take it away from me instead. To suit your pride and to spite Richard."

They stood almost nose to nose, each of them breathing audibly.

"That's unfair," he said, the muscle in his cheek trembling

dangerously. "We are legally married, Elizabeth, so it didn't seem to matter where the money came from—"

"Oh, really," she interrupted, her eyes flaring. "Completely insignificant, was it?"

His brow furrowed, he said: "I thought you'd be pleased to have the schoolhouse, and your own money, too."

"No, Nathaniel. *You* have the schoolhouse. You bought it and the land it stands on with *your* money."

"To give to you!" he roared.

"You are impossibly dense!" she shouted, pushing at him with the heel of one hand so that he stepped backward. His expression shifting from surprise to anger, he stumbled and righted himself awkwardly, but she advanced on him again.

"Had you thought, had it not occurred to you, that perhaps I wanted to own something of my own? That for once it would be welcome not to be *given* something, but to claim it for myself?"

He had that tic in his cheek, the one she had last seen when he held a bloodied and helpless Richard Todd in his sights.

"So you wouldn't mind accepting the schoolhouse as a gift from your aunt, but you won't have it from me?" He laughed hoarsely. "More wisdom from Mrs. Wollstonecraft?"

Elizabeth raised her face to the darkening sky and let out a half scream of frustration. "You vain, self-centered, thoughtless, bloody man!"

"For Christ's sake, woman, I was trying to give you something you said you wanted!"

"But you had to take it away from me first, did you not? You are no better than Richard Todd!"

Nathaniel's head rocked back as if she had slapped him.

Horrified at her own words and still angry beyond her experience, Elizabeth looked around herself wildly, as if seeking help in the deepening shadows.

In two long strides Nathaniel reached the pyramid of supplies and weapons on the far side of the fire, and sweeping up his rifle in one hand, he jerked it up toward her, stock first. His jaw was set like granite. "Looking for this?" he asked sharply.

She drew in a shuddering breath.

"Go on," he said, dead calm. "Finish the job you started, if that's what you think of me."

Elizabeth stood very still, her fury suddenly spent: she could feel it running down her body, dripping from her fingertips with each shallow beat of her heart.

Every muscle in Nathaniel's arm stood out in relief, his fist strained white around the barrel of the gun. His mouth was set in a line just as unyielding. Sudden tears pricked behind her eyes and in her throat, a pain past bearing.

She turned away and walked into the woods.

Robbie was sitting near the fire whittling a new penny whistle when she returned, and he met her with a look of such compassion and sorrow that she nearly lost her resolve. She shook her head at him briefly. Nathaniel was stretched out on the far side of the fire, a long shape under his blanket turned away on one side. She knew he was not asleep; she could hear it in his breathing and see it in the tension in his shoulders.

Elizabeth stood at the edge of the small camp and hesitated. Robbie was watching her; Nathaniel had not moved. She approached him and stood looking down.

"How much did you pay my father's land agent for the land and the schoolhouse?"

"Three hundred dollars," he answered, without looking up at her.

"That's very dear," she said, surprised. "For such a small plot of land."

He was silent.

"I will buy it from you," she said. "With my own money."

Nathaniel sat up and slung his arms around his knees. The firelight played on his face, bringing his cheekbones into high relief and drawing deep shadows on the hollows beneath. There was not the hint of a smile about him. "Make me an offer."

"I'll give you the three hundred you paid for it."

He grunted. "What profit is there in that?"

Elizabeth thought for a moment. "Three hundred twenty-five."

"Four hundred."

She bristled. "Three hundred fifty dollars."

"Four hundred," said Nathaniel, sticking a long blade of grass between his teeth.

"That is a thirty-three percent profit," she sputtered. "For an investment of—"

"About eleven weeks," he supplied.

Elizabeth folded her arms across her chest. "Three hundred seventy-five dollars."

"Cash?"

"You know I have no cash!" she fairly exploded. She lowered her voice with considerable effort. "I will write you a note on the bank."

Nathaniel looked thoughtful. "There's no paper or ink in camp."

Elizabeth turned to Robbie, who held up both palms in a gesture to ward off any part of the discussion.

"I suppose we could write it out on buckskin," she said through clenched teeth. "With my blood, if that's all that will settle this."

"No need," Nathaniel said at last, one brow cocked. "Your word is good, until we can draw it up legal, like. Three hundred seventy-five dollars plus ten percent interest per week until you pay the balance in cash."

"That is usury! It could be weeks until I can get to the bank." She knew she was sputtering but could not stop herself. "You can't ask over a hundred dollars a month in interest—"

"I can," said Nathaniel. "But it's high, you're right. So I'll offer you a straight cost of four hundred dollars, no interest."

He raised a brow at her, mocking. Her wolf of a husband, flashing his teeth as if he would eat her whole.

"Done," she said, in strangled tones.

Nathaniel was up on his feet instantly, holding out his hand. Elizabeth took it reluctantly, as if it were an ill-used handkerchief. But he held on to her, looking down into her scowling face.

"Pleasure doing business with you," he said dryly. "Now come to bed, because I have things to say to you." His fingers trailing over her palm.

Behind them Robbie rustled, and spoke softly to Treenie.

"No," Elizabeth said. "Not tonight." She looked off into the darkening woods, and would not meet his eye.

"Then I'll say it now, like this. I shouldn't have said that, about what happened. I ain't holding a grudge."

She nodded.

"I apologize."

"Thank you." She hesitated. "You are nothing like Richard Todd."

"Thank God," he said, with a grin. He still held her hand. "Will you come to bed now?"

"No," she said, shaking her head.

Nathaniel took her chin between his fingers and turned her face up to his. She met his gaze reluctantly. He was frowning, the straight brows drawn together. Then he let her go.

"Please yourself, then."

Without a backward glance, she walked to the other corner of camp, and rolling herself in her blanket, she lay down.

Above Elizabeth's head, the clouds closed in over the stars. There was the soft sound of the water on the shore and the ticking of the fire. Inside her there was a ticking, too; she wanted her husband. She wanted to draw him down to her and make him sweat, bring him into a fever of trying to please, because he had hurt her. The look on his face when he held out the rifle to her—it was not something she could bear to think about for long. She wanted him to come to her and wipe it away, but there was Robbie, and more than Robbie, there was her pride. Elizabeth put the corner of the blanket in her mouth and bit down hard.

She rolled onto her side and covered her ears, but she could not block out the melody or the words of Robbie's fine, deep baritone:

Oh the summertime is comin'
and the trees are sweetly bloomin'
and the wild mountain thyme
grows around the bloomin' heather.
Will ye go, lassie, go?

She was heavy-eyed with wanting the refuge of sleep, and yet she could not quite go where she wanted to be. Long after Robbie's song had faded away, the words echoed in her head. *Will ye go, lassie, go?*

On the other side of the camp, Nathaniel lay as awake as she was. She could see him, the way he sought her out, the whites of his eyes flashing toward her like a beacon calling her home. With a small grunt of effort, she turned on her side so as not to have to look at him. Between herself and the fire, Treenie lay like a great hissing log, wheezing in her sleep.

The bullet graze on her haunch was healed now.

I ain't holding a grudge.

Hot tears welled up in her eyes and she squeezed them shut hard to banish them. Pushing against a wall of hurt and indignation, she forced herself downward toward sleep.

A shuffling. She opened her eyes to see Treenie sitting up, her ears pricked forward and her head cocked at an angle. Elizabeth watched silently, as the dog trotted toward the shadowy curtain of the forest and froze, a low hum issuing from her throat. She moved forward in liquid steps, the growl escalating slowly.

Elizabeth felt the hair on her nape begin to rise. She glanced at the great mass of Robbie, snoring softly in his tattered bearskin blanket, and then, without moving her head, at Nathaniel. There was no indication that he heard anything; he lay with one arm bent under his head as he often slept, his face in shadows.

Treenie still advanced, her whole form compacted now into one tightly wound muscle. Elizabeth felt herself go slightly dizzy with fear, staring into the darkened forest.

She cleared her throat, a small sound that woke no one.

It might be wolves, although they had not seen any signs of them while they were canoeing down the lakeshore. None of the large cats would attack them like this, in a group around a fire, and bears disliked wood smoke.

Treenie could not manage a pack of wolves on her own.

Elizabeth called to Nathaniel, softly, and then finally, on her hands and knees, she moved toward him as Treenie moved toward the wood.

• • •

He was awake at the dog's first shifting, but he lay as he was, listening. As he had been taught to do, as he had done for all of his life, he threw his senses forward into the dark, feeling the shapes there by their sounds. No need yet to reach for his rifle.

When she started toward him, he almost raised a hand to stop her, but then hesitated. Behind Elizabeth's back, the dog had come to a halt and waited, her head cocked. In the flickering light of the fire, Nathaniel could see her shape change as she relaxed.

Elizabeth did not see the red dog turn back, nor did she see Robbie rise, and taking his gun, slip into the shadows. Her face was a study in concentration.

"You're awake," she whispered. "Didn't you hear—"

She glanced over her shoulder, and started at the sight of the red dog at rest by the fire, head on her paws. Elizabeth sat up, supporting her weight on one arm.

"Traitor," she whispered.

The dog's tail thumped.

Nathaniel held up the corner of his blanket. "Now that you're here."

He saw her thinking it through.

"Please."

The small scowl still firmly in place, she joined him. She lay on her side with her back to him, her body tensed.

"What do you think it is?"

Nathaniel shrugged. "Don't know," he said. "Robbie will deal with it."

"What if it's your Windigo?"

He paused. "Not in this part of the bush," he said, brushing stray hair away from her neck. Her smells were strongest here, at the hairline and the crown of her head. He resisted the urge to bury his face in the soft skin between shoulder and ear.

Robbie came back into camp and made no comment about the change in the sleeping arrangements. "Naucht bu' wolves," he said, seeking out Nathaniel's gaze for a long moment. "They've found easier prey in yon beaver pond, and willna bother us this night." But he spent some time building up the fire before he returned to his blankets.

Elizabeth lay awake, the sound of her breathing slightly labored, as if she had run a long distance. He moved closer, and she tensed slightly without moving away. Nathaniel breathed softly on her ear; she let out a small sigh.

"Thank God for wolves," he whispered. Her skin rose in response to the movement of his lips, but she did not turn to him. He pulled her back against him, and felt her resistance growing. "Don't," he whispered. "Don't, please."

She struggled, then, openly, and in one violent motion, Elizabeth turned to him to take his face between her palms. In the dark her eyes seemed overlarge, glistening, the fringe of dark lashes damp.

"I cannot ask you not to be angry at me for what I did to you," she whispered. He tried to speak, but she hushed him with a sound.

"Do not deny it, even to yourself. But I want you to promise me that you will never hold it up to me again like that."

In his arms she was all tension and terrible hurt; he could feel it writhing inside of her. Nathaniel flushed with remorse for what he had said so thoughtlessly in his anger.

"We've got tempers, the both of us."

"Do you not understand, Nathaniel? It's much more than that." Her eyes moved over his face. "You and I, we have a power over each other, it is like no other force in this world. Between us, words can do worse injury than—"

"Any rifle," he finished for her. "Yes." There was a churning in his chest that closed his throat and made each word painful.

"I'll try," he said hoarsely.

She let out a sigh. Her smells struck him forcibly, her anger and her arousal enveloping him, winding around him as he wound himself around her. Vaguely, he was aware of Robbie leaving his bed and disappearing once again into the night.

She reached for him with strong hands, demanding her due. Her roughness was new to him, her greed as arousing as her heat. At some point Nathaniel remembered the child and tried to pull away, to temper himself. But she would not have it, could not have it, and clung to him still riding the wave of her fury. He gave in, caring for her the best way he knew how. In the end she rewarded him with a shudder and a smile and deep, healing sleep.

XLIV

There was a two-day portage waiting for them when they finally reached the end of the long water the Kahnyen'kehàka called Tail-of-the-Lake, known to the whites as Lake George. The walk westward to the Hudson drained Elizabeth of the last of her energy and her patience. She wanted to be home. She wanted a hot bath and Curiosity's special soap to rid herself of the accumulated vermin of the journey. She wanted to sleep in a bed; the last time she had had the pleasure of one was on her wedding night, so many weeks ago. She wanted to see Hannah, and get on with the business of being a mother to her. Elizabeth was struggling very hard to be rational and patient and reasonable, and her inconsistent success at these basic requirements of herself did not suit in the least.

Once they had come to the juncture of the Hudson and the Sacandaga, Nathaniel insisted on a full day's rest. Elizabeth thought she would die of wanting to get on with it: they were only days out of Paradise, after all. But Nathaniel was firm, and met her objections with calm reasoning she could not counter. To his credit, he bore her ill humor with equanimity which was neither condescending nor overbearing, and in the end she had to admit that the rest did her much good. She slept for the most part, dreaming strange, brightly colored dreams of Hawkeye and Falling-Day, Runs-from-Bears and Many-Doves and Hannah, Curiosity and Anna Hauptmann.

On the last day, drenched in sweat from paddling hard upstream, they stopped a few hours out of Paradise. By this time, Elizabeth's joyful anticipation had given way to a light but persistent anxiety, buzzing quietly beneath the surface like a sore tooth as she framed the things she might say to her father, to Julian and Kitty, to Moses Southern and to her schoolchildren. Half-imagined conversations left her on edge, wanting both to rush ahead and run away. She saw herself standing before them, their minds and hearts closed to her reasoning, their indignation and disapproval weapons she could not best. *It doesn't matter, it won't matter,* she told herself again and again. She remembered Nathaniel's face when she had found him finally, the strength of his arms and of his resolve. *The world will be right again,* he had said to her. *Together we will make it right.*

Resting before the final push so that she could recover from her daily bout of nausea, Elizabeth had taken the opportunity to comb out her hair and plait it again. She had washed the grime from her face and neck and arms, steadfastly refusing to look at her reflection in the water, knowing that gallons of buttermilk could do nothing to repair her skin to its former state of ladylike pallor. For the first time in many weeks she found herself thinking of the loss of her own clothes, for as comfortable as she had become in Kahnyen'kehàka dress, she did not relish the idea of meeting her father and brother as she was.

By the time the first homesteads came into view set back from the shores of the river, Elizabeth could not remember why she had been in such a hurry to get here, and if they should not have waited until full dark. As if he had read her thoughts, Nathaniel glanced at her over his shoulder, his teeth flashing white in his face. "You sorry you took me on, Boots?"

Her anxiety left her in a great rush. Instantly ashamed of her petty worries, Elizabeth drew a deep breath and tossed her plait over her shoulder.

"Never," she said.

Rain began to fall as they pulled to shore. Treenie bounded into the shallows and waited there while the men dragged the canoe into the bushes. Elizabeth pulled on her pack, looking over the familiar setting of the lake, the far shore lost in a twilight fog. Not a person in sight, no curious boys to gawk, ask

questions, and carry news. Tomorrow would be soon enough
for a reckoning.

On the way up the mountain, a path as familiar to him as the
landscape of his own face, Nathaniel had to remind himself to
limit his stride. He was eager to be at home and anxious about
what news waited for them, but he was worried about Elizabeth
and the child, too. If he turned now and looked at her she
would lift up her chin, and urge him on. She would push herself past reason, if he let her. She wore her determination like
war paint.

The rain stopped and the cloud cover broke so that the forest
was plunged in and out of the last light of day, now near dark,
now reflecting raindrops on every leaf. The sun dropped below
the horizon with the suddenness of a finger snap, and in response the breeze rose and the great pines all around them
rustled and sighed.

They passed the old schoolhouse and he saw with some relief
that it had not been vandalized.

"I came tae ca' on yer faither here, muny years syne," Robbie was saying to Elizabeth. "Afore he wed yer mither, that was.
The judge was e'er glad o' company. A mannie wha kent the
worth o' a wee sup o' whisky on a cauld winter's eve."

"Rab MacLachlan," she answered, her tone gently teasing.
"For a man who professes to love nothing so well as his solitude
it seems to me that you are happiest in the company of others."

"You've got him there, Boots," Nathaniel laughed.

"That she doesna," Robbie protested with a grin. "I deny
that wi' baith hands and wi' a' my teeth."

The path grew steeper and the bantering slowed and then
stopped. In single file they made their way through the darkened strawberry fields, the heavy smell of overripe fruit following them back into the forest. He heard Elizabeth draw in a
small hiccup, the sound she made when she was struggling not
to be sick. Strong smells roused her stomach, these days, and the
sickly sweet stink of an acre of fermenting strawberries was
enough to set his own stomach on edge. He increased his pace

to put the place behind them, and when he paused to look back he could see that the crisis had passed.

At the place where the path left the woods and came out near the cliff face, Nathaniel stopped to listen. Cupping a hand at his mouth, he sent out the poor-will's rolling call: *purple-rib! purple-rib!* He waited, and then repeated it.

The call came back, and he relaxed. Behind him, he heard Robbie let out his breath, too.

Elizabeth was at his elbow.

"Look." She made a sweep with her arm as if to lay out the whole world for him. When he could make himself look away from her face he saw what she did: the moon was rising, rolling up the long spine of the mountain just opposite them, the one the Kahnyen'kehàka called Wolf Walking.

"He carries the moon on his back," Nathaniel told her. "Trying to take it home to his young."

"How many times have you come home to Lake in the Clouds?" she asked, her gaze still fixed dreamily on the mottled silver disk of the moon.

"A thousand, and a thousand more," Nathaniel answered, tracing the line of her cheek with one finger. "But never so willingly."

She rewarded him with a smile. "Do you think Hannah will be surprised to see us?"

"You can ask her yourself," Nathaniel said. "I hear her coming now."

Treenie was standing to attention, and she let out a soft woof. "Aye, loupin' like a deer wi' the hunter fast behind," Robbie noted.

There was a rustling and then the forest broke, and she was there. Nathaniel opened his arms and gathered up his daughter to him, her smile as bright and broad as the rising moon.

Julian Middleton sat down on the bench just inside the door to Axel Metzler's tavern as if his energy had extended just so far and not a step further.

The place was almost empty. Axel sat on a stool dipping each of his small collection of dented pewter tankards in a barrel of rainwater and handing them to Ephraim, who dried them on a ragged piece of toweling.

"Come set you by the hearth," Axel called.

"Cooler here," Julian protested.

Axel shrugged his shoulders. "Ja, sure. But it's a long walk to the cider jug."

"A man needs a little exercise now and then," Julian replied, stifling a yawn. In the end Axel wiped his hands on his apron and poured a cup of ale, sending it over with the boy, who peered at Julian hopefully from behind a curtain of sleek brown hair.

"Such industry deserves a reward." He reached with two fingers into his vest pocket. Ephraim snatched the ha'penny out of the air with a grin and a nod.

Julian had just settled in comfortably with his legs extended and his ankles crossed when Liam Kirby came flying through the door, tripped on the highly polished toe of Julian's right boot, and went sprawling headfirst toward the hearth. He came to a stop with his chin on the brickwork, but he was up in a snap.

"Good God," Julian said, examining his footgear for scratches. "So much energy after so hot a day really is in very bad form, Kirby."

Normally an excellent foil, Liam seemed not even to hear Julian's comment. Even his freckles stood out in alarm. "They're back," he said, gasping for air. "The teacher's back. I saw 'em headed up Hidden Wolf."

Axel took his pipe from his mouth and thrust it in Julian's direction. "Do you hear that, Middleton? Your sister and her husband are back."

"Yes, I heard." Julian took the last swallow of his ale and held out the cup to Ephraim again, who came forward to take it quite eagerly.

"And Robbie MacLachlan with them," Liam yelped. "In a new canoe."

"Old Rab!" Axel slapped his leg in appreciation. "Now there'll be some fun, you'll see. Rab hasn't been down this way in a long time."

"Any sign of Todd?" Julian asked the boy.

Liam accepted a cup of ale from Axel and drank thirstily, the pale liquid dribbling down his chin to stain his shirt. Wiping his mouth with the back of his hand, he shook his head. "Didn't see any."

"Ja, well," said Axel, stumping to the door to look out into the night. "He won't be far behind, the doctor. Or let's hope so, or Miz Kitty will make life miserable for all of us."

Julian buried his face in his cup, relieving himself of the necessary reply. He wouldn't particularly care whether he ever saw Richard Todd again, if it weren't for Kitty Witherspoon. If Todd didn't marry her, and soon, it was clear to him where she would turn to resolve the problem that was growing underneath her skirt. And not without cause; Julian had not been an eager student, but he could count backward from nine on his fingers as well as any old crone. If pressed, he couldn't deny that he was the responsible party; but then, no one was pressing. And there was no need to step in, not if Todd was willing to take over.

"I'm going to find my brother and Moses Southern," Liam announced. "They'll want to know."

Julian raised one eyebrow. "No doubt," he agreed. "But perhaps you'd be so good as to hold off on that until tomorrow."

The boy pulled up short. "But they'll want to go up there right away, see if they can talk some sense into them."

Axel snorted a laugh. "Ja, now that is something I'd like to see, myself. Moses Southern talking sense to the schoolteacher."

"Somebody needs to do it," Liam said, defensively.

"Nonsense," Axel muttered, returning to his chore. "Have you forgot Nathaniel and Hawkeye? Ja, you're fools, all of you, if you think you can scare them off that mountain. I want no part of any of it."

Liam stood red-faced, twisting his cap in his hands, and threw a questioning look to Julian. "If there's a mine, it's yours, by rights."

Axel said, "And you're going to march up there right now and tell Hawkeye that, are you? You so eager to have another talk with the man, after Albany?"

The boy's high color drained suddenly. "I ain't lied about

Miz Elizabeth. I never said a word about her, since then, and I won't, either."

"Amazing, how convincing Hawkeye can be with a hickory stick in his hand." Axel laughed.

Julian clucked his tongue. "You scare the boy, Axel, but you know that he has a point. But you are right, too, of course, at least in part." He paused to take a deep swallow. "It won't do any good to go up the mountain and fling accusations. I know my sister. She'll close ranks with the Bonners and you'll get nothing from her but a lecture. Axel," he finished, "I find ale is not enough to wet my gullet if I am compelled to make such long speeches. Break out the schnapps, will you?"

Liam said, "But we can't just give up the mountain. And there's the wood, and the hunting—"

"Indeed." Julian got up finally in pursuit of his schnapps.

"What do you think we should do, then? Will you come along and talk to my brother?"

"Oh, do be serious. I have no intention of running off into the night to put heads together with Billy Kirby or Moses Southern. No, I will have a conversation with my father tomorrow and see what might be done in a more civilized manner. In the meantime, if any of those men want my advice, I'll be here," Julian said, lifting his glass. "In serious contemplation."

Elizabeth wondered, at first, if she were dreaming. In the light of the moon she saw before her not just the familiar shape of the cabin at Lake in the Clouds, but a second one, similar in shape, set back and to one side. She had come to a complete halt on the path, unable to credit what her senses told her.

"I was keeping it for a surprise," Nathaniel said beside her. "Didn't know if they'd be able to finish before we got back, anyway."

Hannah was jumping up and down in excitement, yanking on Elizabeth's arm. "Do you like it? Do you like it? There's curtains and real glass, and bookshelves and a desk and a bedstead—"

The tears stinging in her eyes were happy ones, but Elizabeth blinked hard anyway, determined to banish them. She nodded at the little girl and smiled.

"She likes it fine," Nathaniel said, his hand on the crown of Hannah's head.

"I like it very much," Elizabeth confirmed. "Is it for the three of us, then?"

"That it is, Boots," Nathaniel said. "And room for more to come. It ain't exactly Oakmere, but I'm hoping it'll serve, just the same."

"It will serve all the better for not being Oakmere."

"What's Oakmere?" Hannah asked.

"The house where I was raised," Elizabeth said. "I'll tell you all about it."

The door to the closer cabin stood open now. Nathaniel squeezed Elizabeth's shoulder and then headed off toward his father. Behind Hawkeye, the rest of them stood at the door, their faces lost in shadow: Falling-Day, Many-Doves, and Chin-gachgook, on Runs-from-Bears' arm.

"Come on," Hannah said, tugging at her sleeve, and then skipping ahead.

"You look as surprised as I am," Elizabeth said to Robbie as they followed. "You didn't know?"

"Weel, lassie, *surprise* wouldna be a word I'd use, masel'. It's awfu' mild, if ye ken what I mean. It cowpit me on my doup."

Elizabeth stifled a laugh. "Pardon me?"

"Pardon my exuberance, lass. I said, it threw me doon on my behind. Ye dinna mind, then, that he had ye a cabin built wi'oot askin' ye first?"

She squeezed his arm. "I do not mind one little bit," she said. "In fact, I could not be more pleased."

Robbie shook his head, reaching down to pat Treenie distractedly. "I dinna understand why yon wee cabin should please ye when the schoolhoose broucht doon yer wrath, but then I've larned tae leave sleepin' dogs be. Run along, lass. Canna ye see that they're waitin' for ye?"

Elizabeth hesitated, looking up into Robbie's kind eyes. "You come, too."

He shook his head. "I willna dawdle, lass. But it's the new guidwife that they want. Gae on wi' ye, then."

She went up on tiptoe to kiss the soft cheek. "You've been a good friend to me in these past months, Robin MacLachlan, and I will not forget it."

Before he had time to blush again, Elizabeth had set off.

XLV

After a morning of unpacking and messages and stories back and forth—in which only the minimum had been told, and the rest promised—Elizabeth stood in front of an open chest in the bedroom of the new cabin with only Hannah in attendance. There was not a lot of furniture: a bedstead, a tick mattress, pillows and a quilt, a straight chair, and this chest. Full of things that had belonged to Nathaniel's mother and his first wife.

"I remember this one," said Hannah, gently touching a homespun skirt dyed a deep indigo.

Elizabeth hesitated. She did not relish wearing Sarah's clothes. She did not even know if they would fit her. But if she were to call on her father, she could not realistically go in Kahnyen'kehàka dress.

Nathaniel came in, and Elizabeth saw how the child's whole posture changed. He touched her lightly in greeting, his fingers barely brushing her shoulder and then her cheek.

"Your grandmother is looking for you," he said to her. "There's corn that needs grinding."

She sighed audibly.

"Come back when you are finished," Elizabeth said. "I would like to swim later, if there's time."

"Can you swim?" Hannah asked, looking at her father rather than at Elizabeth.

"I taught her, the same as I taught you," Nathaniel said. "Go on, now."

There were windows on two walls: one looked over the waterfall and gorge, and the other looked down the glen to the other cabin. They watched Hannah's long legs flashing as she ran, and Elizabeth laughed. "I don't think I've ever seen her walk at a normal pace."

But Nathaniel was looking down into the trunk and seemed not to have heard this. Something passed over his face: regret, perhaps.

"You're about the same size as Many-Doves," he said. "She could lend you a dress until we fetch your things." His arm stole around her waist, and Elizabeth leaned into him thankfully.

"When should we go do that?"

"There's no reason to waste time about it, Boots," he said dryly. "In the evening, then, if that will suit." He paused, as if wondering how much he should say.

"I believe that I can handle my father," Elizabeth said, anticipating his worries. "We have done nothing illegal, after all. And we are certainly not the first ever to marry without a father's permission."

He let out a small laugh. "But it's more than that, and you know it, Elizabeth. The whole village is involved."

While she had been exploring the new cabin and talking to Falling-Day and Many-Doves, Nathaniel had been talking with the men. The sweet smell of Chingachgook's pipe still clung to him.

"Tell me."

She could feel his thoughts moving away from her as he stared out of the window. The mid-afternoon light played on the waterfall, throwing reflections over the walls.

"Some of them don't want us here."

"We knew that long ago, Nathaniel."

"Yes, but there's more to it now. Billy Kirby and the others have been spreading rumors. Some folks are pretty riled."

She waited, and when he saw she would wait until he had told her all of it, he sighed.

"They've been saying that Sky-Wound-Round will be mov-

ing all of Barktown up here. That when he does, there won't be
any game left for the whites and no woman will be safe in her
bed. That there's a mine hidden on the mountain that we didn't
tell the judge about."

"A mine?" Elizabeth asked, incredulous. "Surely, Nathaniel,
once they see that this is all nonsense, they will leave us in
peace."

He grunted. "But in the meantime," he said. And didn't
finish his sentence.

"Tell me the rest."

Nathaniel rubbed his eyes. "There was more trouble with
trap lines, tampering and out-and-out thievery before the season ended. Somebody took a shot at Bears while he was hunting. Falling-Day set a quarter acre of corn and beans down next
to the new schoolhouse and last week it was put to the torch.
For a start." The muscle in his cheek fluttered with frustration
and anger.

Elizabeth stared at him, feeling suddenly ill. Nathaniel took
her by the shoulders. "Promise me you won't wander off on
your own without one of the men nearby. And don't let Hannah go off, either."

She nodded.

"Are you scared?"

"Mostly I am angry," she said. "But yes, a little. Nathaniel,
we can't hide. We have to live our lives."

"So we do. And we will." His fingers plucked at the tendrils
of hair on her neck. She put her forehead against him and
breathed in his smell.

"I don't care about the village," she said. "I don't care about
anything but being here with you. I can't tell you what this
means to me, Nathaniel. This place of our own."

"A bed of our own, too," he said, and she could feel his
smile. "And a door of our own, that closes," he continued,
reaching behind himself to do just that and then coming back to
her, his hands moving up to seek out the bare skin of her neck.
He bracketed her face with his fingers. "Once I promised you
time to lie abed all day, do you remember?"

She did. But between kisses, she asked where the other men
were.

"Busy," Nathaniel muttered.

"This is insane," she said against his mouth.

"What?"

"This constant need to be with you. It is not rational."

"Maybe not," said Nathaniel, his mouth at her ear making her skin rise. "But it's the right kind of insanity."

" 'Love is the noblest frailty of the mind,' " Elizabeth whispered, and Nathaniel pulled back from her with a laugh.

"You trying to quote me out of my intentions?"

"Oh, no," she said, pulling him back to her. "Nothing so rash as that."

She let herself be taken down to the bed, to their bed; she let him please himself, because it pleased her to do so. And Elizabeth discovered once again what it was like to be so caught up in this man that she thought she could easily die of love, and not regret her last breath.

Nathaniel, half asleep, lifted his head. The constant rush of the waterfall dampened other noise, even with the window sash closed, but she knew by the look on his face that he was hearing something. He had been stroking her back, and his hands stilled.

Elizabeth stilled, too, and then she heard it, very faint:

"Hellooo the house!"

"That's Curiosity!"

"Aye." He yawned. "She'll have a message from your father."

Elizabeth groaned, grabbing for her clothes. "How did he know?"

"Somebody saw us on the way in, of course." He stretched, reaching out to touch her, but she was already gone.

After some frantic rearrangement of her clothing and hair, Elizabeth rushed out onto the porch and down the stairs, pulling on her moccasins as she went. There, Galileo greeted her with a sweep of his hat and a bow and then did the same for Nathaniel, who had appeared on the porch behind her.

Curiosity came forward with her skirts snapping around her

ankles, both hands outstretched and her face creased in a broad smile.

"The judge sent us up here with your things," she said, jerking with her chin toward the packhorses so that her head wrap was set to swaying. "And a word or two. But I want a look at you, first."

"I'm afraid I can anticipate the message," Elizabeth said, standing still while she was examined from front and back, and hoping the evidence of her afternoon's activity wouldn't be so very obvious.

"Yasm, he ain't pleased with you. But there ain't no need to hurry hard words, is there, Nathaniel?"

He was untying a basket of books from a packsaddle. "They tend to improve with waiting," he agreed.

Elizabeth caught his sideways grin and responded with one of her own.

"Where you want these trunks, Miz Bonner?" Galileo asked.

"Just in the main room, please, until I have time to sort through things."

When the men had disappeared with the first load, Curiosity stepped back. "The bush was a sore trial, I see."

Elizabeth nodded, hoping that she would not have to tell all of it right now. "We survived."

"So you did." Curiosity climbed the three steps to the porch. "These chairs for admirin' or for settin' down?"

Once comfortably settled in the rockers while the men moved back and forth, the older woman leaned forward and put a hand over Elizabeth's where they were folded on her lap.

"You got news of your own?"

Elizabeth met the mild amber eyes steadily. "It seems I could not keep it a secret even if I wished to do so."

Curiosity let out a little rush of air that might have been a laugh. "Don't take much sense to figure that a newly married woman in her prime is liable to turn up in the family way. And you ain't the only one. Maybe you didn't notice that Many-Doves is already working on her first."

"Is she?" Elizabeth laughed, delighted.

"And then there's Kitty."

"Oh, yes." This mention of Kitty's condition brought Elizabeth round to thoughts of her brother. "I need to talk to you about that."

"We got time for trouble later," said Curiosity. "I ain't done looking at you yet. Your mama was one of those women who wear her condition on her face, and you take after her. How long since your courses?"

"A good nine weeks," Elizabeth said. "If I remember correctly."

"That's *good*." Curiosity squeezed her hand hard, and then sat back. "Ain't no need to color up and look away. The judge may settle right down when he hear a grandchild on the way, no matter what your brother got to say."

Elizabeth grimaced. "I expect Julian has quite a lot to say. But perhaps I should hear my father's message."

Curiosity smoothed out the material of her apron. "Pretty much what you think. You ain't welcome at his door, until you see the error of your headstrong ways and do what's called for."

"And what is that?"

"I expect he won't be satisfied unless you put your husband aside—not likely, is that, seein' what you got to show for your time in the bush. Todd will have to live without this mountain. Where is he anyway? Did y'all meet up with him?"

"Oh, yes," Elizabeth said. "We did. It's a long story."

"He headed back this way?"

"I assume so. Curiosity." Elizabeth leaned toward her. "My father's debts have been paid, and his taxes as well. All his financial problems should be resolved. Richard Todd might try to take *me* before a court of law for breach of promise but there is no claim he can make against my father, so please explain to me what this is all about. I simply do not understand."

"It's about his pride, child. You embarrassed the judge in front of the whole territory."

Elizabeth flushed. "Only because he left me no choice."

Curiosity had not lost the knack of a sharp look. "Am I criticizing you?"

"No." Elizabeth sat back. "I'm sorry, of course not. But I am nervous about . . . everything."

"Naturally," Curiosity raised a brow. "But you done good, child, and not just for yourself."

"I'm afraid that the villagers won't agree with you."

Curiosity laughed out loud, and then shook her head. "You still got some friends down there. But mostly you got folks worried. They want to know what plans your menfolk have got for this mountain, and some of them are mighty uneasy."

"Uneasy enough to burn crops?" Elizabeth asked.

Curiosity shrugged. "You scare one stupid man, he'll most likely run off. But a crowd of stupid men—there ain't nothing more dangerous, or meaner." One corner of her generous mouth turned downward. "It's our bad luck, you see, that Paradise got more than its fair share of men couldn't find their hindquarters with both hands."

Elizabeth stifled an uneasy laugh, but Curiosity was not smiling. She leaned toward Elizabeth. "I ain't telling you nothing your people don't know already, but you watch yourself, and that child, too. Stay clear of Kirby, and Dubonnet and Southern, most of all." She straightened, and the frown line between her brows was replaced with a genuine smile. "Now, there's Falling-Day."

On the porch of the other cabin Falling-Day's small, straight form had appeared with her daughter and granddaughter behind her, and Curiosity raised a hand in greeting.

"Let's us women have a look-see round this new home of yours," she said, rising. "And a little talk 'bout happier things."

There were three rooms, a great luxury in a village where most cabins had only one. The long main room had a hearth of flagstone at one end and a loft at the other where Hannah slept. Like the older cabin, there was a work and storage room as well as a bedroom. There were few pieces of furniture, some of it with the same sharp tang of newly cut wood as the cabin itself, while other things—the table and benches, the rifle rack above the door, the bookcase, the bedstead—showed signs of careful mending.

Curiosity examined everything in great detail, keeping up a running conversation with Falling-Day while they discussed spinning wheels and scraping frames, cooking kettles and lamps. Elizabeth and Many-Doves spent this time unpacking the baskets of books, while Hannah flitted back and forth, alternately picking up volumes to look through them and then trying on Elizabeth's hats and making silly faces at herself in her hand mirror.

"Ooooh," she called out, opening a small trunk filled with Elizabeth's boots. She immediately began to tug at her moccasins, engaging a sharp comment from Falling-Day.

"Oh, let her." Elizabeth laughed. "I doubt I'll have much use for them anymore." She reached over and picked up a boot of fine deep-blue morocco leather, its neatly turned toe edged in brass. "They were never very comfortable," she admitted.

The sight of all her worldly belongings spread out around her on the plank floor of the cabin made the finality of her new situation clear as nothing else had, not even waking this morning in her own home with her husband next to her. She would never return to her father's home, or to her aunt's.

"The judge will be waitin' on his supper," Curiosity announced as if she had read Elizabeth's thoughts. "I had best be on my way. I expect we will see you at church in the morning?" This was addressed to Elizabeth.

"Is it Saturday? I hadn't thought about church," she admitted, wiping her brow. "Do you think—"

"Yasm, I think. It ain't the worst idea, showin' up at services. Get folks used to the sight of you. It's why we brung up your trunks this afternoon."

"What is your opinion?" Elizabeth asked Falling-Day, who was very quiet.

The older woman thought for a moment, her broad face giving away nothing of her feelings. "The judge is unlikely to be there, isn't that so, Curiosity? So I think that it would be best for you to go, otherwise they will say that you hide from them."

Curiosity laughed out loud. "This one never did learn how to walk away from an argument, but I guess they'll figure that out soon enough." She wiped her hands on her apron, and headed for the door. "Where have those men got to?"

Hannah jumped up to join her, so that Elizabeth's sun hat slipped forward over her face. Extricating herself, she offered to take Curiosity to the sheds where Galileo and Nathaniel were talking, and the two set out together.

"There's some of my soap in one of those baskets," Curiosity called over her shoulder on her way out the door. "And some other odds and ends. Now I expect to see you and that husband of yours tomorrow, you hear?"

"Come back soon," Elizabeth said, her throat suddenly tight with tears.

"Good friends are a great treasure," Falling-Day said just behind her.

"Yes, she is a good friend to me. To us." Elizabeth turned back into the cabin. "I wanted to thank you," she said. "For whatever part you had in all this—"

"It is good that you are here," Falling-Day said. "For all of us. And since my daughter has taken a husband, we needed more room."

"I am sorry to have missed your wedding ceremony," Elizabeth said to Many-Doves. "And I am sorry all of you could not be at mine. Was this to be your cabin?"

Many-Doves shook her head. "I belong at my mother's hearth," she said. "But you need one of your own. And I think that there will be much back and forth between the two, anyway." A smile twitched at the corner of her mouth. "Especially at mealtimes."

"I'm afraid that Nathaniel would starve before I learn how to cook properly." Elizabeth gestured over the piles of books. "Philosophers and playwrights are well and good, but I should have sent for a cookery book or two, as well."

Falling-Day smiled, setting Elizabeth more at ease. She was just wondering how to broach the complex topic of laundry when from the open door she saw Galileo and Curiosity appear from the sheds leading the packhorses, with Nathaniel close behind. He made a sign to indicate that he was going to see them a part of their way, and the women waved until the small party disappeared on the path.

Many-Doves left them, picking up a hoe on her way to the small cornfield that lay in the sunshine at the widest part of the glen, at the edge of the cliffs.

"There's a meal to cook before the men get back," Falling-

Day announced in Hannah's direction. The little girl had been running around the cabin, dragging a frayed rope for Treenie to chase. In response to her grandmother's voice, she dropped her rope and the red dog collapsed in a tangled heap at her heels. She looked up at Elizabeth and then at her grandmother with pleading on her face.

"If you can spare her," Elizabeth said, "I would be glad of her help getting the cabin in order."

Falling-Day blinked, slowly, and then nodded. "If you want the child with you, yes."

Hannah let out a hoot of satisfaction and set out once more with the dog in pursuit.

Of all the Kahnyen'kehàka she had come to know, Elizabeth found Falling-Day to be the most inscrutable. While she had shown nothing but kindness and generosity, there was a reserve about her that made it very difficult to speak up in the older woman's presence. Falling-Day's silences, while never edged with the same kind of disdain that women sometimes used to make their displeasure known, were absolute and impenetrable. Elizabeth wondered, as she had many times on the long journey home, about this woman who had left her mother's longhouse against custom and expectation to take her children to be raised in her husband's village, and then to a cabin in the wilderness, in isolation from other Kahnyen'kehàka. She had seen her husband and sons killed, and carried on to raise Sarah, who had spent her life trying to be something she was not, and Otter and Many-Doves, who were unapologetically Kahnyen'kehàka. This was the woman who had, by some accounts, rejected Nathaniel as a son-in-law, but had come to live with him to raise his child upon his mother's death.

"I should like very much to have Hannah spend some time with me," Elizabeth confirmed, struggling with the urge to look away from Falling-Day's steady gaze. "She has her first home with you, but I hope that eventually she will be equally comfortable in both cabins. Your mother was very worried about her upbringing in the Kahnyen'kehàka way. I wanted you to know that I will not interfere."

There was a subtle shifting in Falling-Day's expression. "The only way to bring Squirrel up truly as a Kahnyen'kehàka woman would be to send her to my mother's hearth.''

"Oh, no." Elizabeth tensed in her surprise. "You don't want to send her away—''

"I did not say that," the older woman interrupted gently. "She is Nathaniel's child, and she must learn to live between two worlds as he does. It would be wrong to send her away from him, just as it would be wrong to let her forget my daughter, her mother. Do you agree?''

Elizabeth nodded. "Yes, I do."

"And when you hold your own child in your arms? Will Squirrel still be welcome at your hearth?''

Elizabeth felt her face flooding with indignation, but the older woman held up a hand to keep her from speaking.

"I offend you. But I speak the truth: it would be better for her to stay with us if she cannot be sure of her welcome once this new child arrives.''

After a long silence in which she knew herself never to have been so closely observed, Elizabeth said: "Nathaniel has given me many gifts, but none is so precious to me as his daughter. My own child could not be more loved.''

"Bone-in-Her-Back," Falling-Day said in the Kahnyen'-kehàka language. "You are a strong woman. You have shown yourself to be braver than most, and a true friend. And you bear Wolf-Running-Fast children who will bring great joy to this family." She hesitated, her brown eyes probing deeper. "I will trust you with the care of my granddaughter, but I will watch you.''

"I wouldn't have it any other way," Elizabeth answered. "And I will need your help.''

There was a flash of satisfaction on the older woman's face, and Elizabeth was struck suddenly by her resemblance to Made-of-Bones. She pointed this out.

Falling-Day blinked. "All women are alike when they fear for their children," she said. "Kahnyen'kehàka or O'seronni, when a mother rises to defend her own she is like sister bear.''

There was the sound of Hannah's high, lilting laughter.

There's nothing more dangerous or meaner than a crowd of stupid men.

Elizabeth thought of Jack Lingo, and there was a familiar tingling, the sparking of nerves all the way to her fingers. At the time, standing over his bloodied body, she had thought that she would never again be able to raise a hand in anger, but now she knew that she was capable of more, and perhaps worse.

"Yes," she agreed. "That is a lesson I have already begun to learn."

XLVI

When they had been home almost a week, Elizabeth left the cabin in the early morning to fetch water and found Robbie and Chingachgook sharing a pipe on the porch. Robbie was dressed for travel.

"Oh," she said. The prickling in her throat wouldn't allow any more of a greeting.

"Aye, lassie, it's time that I was awa'. Dinna fash yersel', Boots. Ye've no' seen the last o' Robbie MacLachlan."

Robbie was the only person besides Nathaniel to call her Boots, and the simple affection in his voice brought her dangerously close to tears. It had been just three months since she had come to know the old Scot, but she could hardly imagine being without him.

"Grandfather," she said to Chingachgook. "Is there nothing we can do to convince Robbie to stay in Paradise?"

Chingachgook's smile moved his face into a mass of wrinkles in which his dark eyes almost disappeared. "I have known this man for many years," he said. "It is not an accident that my people gave him the name Wind-Walker."

Nathaniel came out onto the porch and Elizabeth caught up his hand, squeezed it hard.

"Robbie is leaving."

He nodded. "I thought he might, soon."

"What about the old schoolhouse?" she asked. "Couldn't he have it for his own? It's in good repair."

Before Nathaniel could reply, Robbie spoke up.

"Ach, weel." He sighed, and shifted his rifle sling to a more comfortable spot on his back. "I canna deny but it's a temptation. I will make ye a promise, lass. Should this winter be as unco' hard an' lonely as was the last, then I will come tae bide in yon wee cabin, 'gin ye still care tae see the likes o' me on Hidden Wolf."

"You're always welcome," Nathaniel said.

"We'll look for you in the spring," Elizabeth added, smiling now.

Robbie took leave of Nathaniel and then Chingachgook, grasping the old man by the hand and the lower arm.

"Great-Snake," he said, with a sad smile. "Will I see ye again, auld friend, 'gin I come in the spring?"

Chingachgook gave him a thoughtful look. "The Maker of Life is good," he said, putting one huge, rough hand on Elizabeth's arm in the gentlest of touches. "I hope to see my great-grandson before he calls me to the Council Fire. But don't wait too long, my brother, I think he grows impatient and will not be put off very long."

"I willna tarry, come spring," said Robbie. "I remember Nathaniel's naming ceremony, muny years syne, and I wadna miss his son's, no' for a' the deer in the wood."

Elizabeth touched Chingachgook's hand. "Perhaps this child is not a son," she said, and was surprised to see him almost laugh at her.

"When I fly at night, I have seen my great-grandson in your arms," he said, as if this were proof positive. Which, Elizabeth realized, it was, for him.

Robbie whistled to Treenie, who came out of her sleeping place under the porch with her tail in a great sweep. "Come, lass, we're awa' hame."

At last he turned to Elizabeth. "Walk wi' me a while."

"Go along," Nathaniel said, taking the water bucket from her. "But not too far, mind."

"I'll send her back straightawa'," Robbie promised.

When they had walked a few minutes in silence, he cleared his throat.

"Weel, lassie." The soft wattles of flesh on his neck were flushed bright with color. Elizabeth rubbed the heel of her hand over Treenie's bony skull and waited, wondering what he had on his mind that he could not say in front of the men.

"Ye ken I've spent some time in the village wi' Axel," he began. "For he's a guid man and one I trust. A wee bit free wi' the ale betimes, but he's no' got a crookit bone in his body, and a mind sae sharp as yer own. And there's nane sae guid as his dauchter. Anna is a fine woman."

"Yes," Elizabeth said slowly. "I think quite a lot of Axel and of Anna, as well." When they had gone to the village for church services, Anna was the only one—besides Curiosity, and some of the children—to show Elizabeth a really warm welcome.

"They are mair than guid friends, ye ken. They are the kind ye can count on when others are bluidy-minded."

They had come to the small stand of white birch which marked the turning of the path down toward the strawberry fields, and Robbie paused.

"Wha' I mean tae say is this: if there's trouble, then get ye tae Axel, for it's gey certain he willna desert ye in yer time o' need."

"Robbie, you frighten me," said Elizabeth. "With Nathaniel and Hawkeye and Runs-from-Bears, even Chingachgook, as old as he is—why would I have need of Axel's help?"

"I hae no' a doot that yer menfolk can stan' for ye; dinna mistake me. But there's rough talk in the toon, lass, and I fear it will come tae a bad end. Truth be told, 'gin I could help it, I wadna leave at a'. But I made a promise tae an auld friend that I mun keep."

Elizabeth considered at length. "You know more than you are telling me," she concluded.

He nodded reluctantly, watching her from the corner of his eye. "Yestere'en I paid a ca' on yer faither."

She shot him a surprised look. There was a hollow feeling in the pit of her stomach, unease born of distrust.

On her second day home, Elizabeth had gone with Nathaniel to call on her father and brother, but a very grim-faced Curiosity had told her that the judge and Julian had just left for Albany, on business they would not name. She had never seen Curiosity so unsure of herself. Just yesterday afternoon, Runs-from-Bears had come in from his scouting to report that the two had returned home.

"Why did you not tell me you were going, Robbie?"

"Aye, weel. I thoucht it wad be better tae talk tae the judge man tae man, ye ken. And I didna tell ye straight after, for the twa o' them put me sair oot o' sorts."

"My father is not resigned," she said, an acknowledgment rather than a question.

"Tae say the verra least," Robbie agreed. "Lass, let me speak plain. I wadna fear yer faither's anger 'gin it werena for yer brother. Taegither they will stop at naethin' tae see their will done."

"I must go see him."

"Aye, that is a start. P'rhaps the idea o' ye wi' bairn will do some guid."

Self-consciously, Elizabeth put a hand to her waist. She doubted her father would see her condition without being told; it was a thought she did not enjoy.

"Robbie," she said slowly. "Why tell me this and not Nathaniel?"

He hesitated for a moment. "Lass, 'gin I had a son, I couldna love him mair than Nathaniel, do ye ken the truth o' that?"

Elizabeth nodded slowly.

"He's a rare mannie, is Nathaniel. Gey braw, and canty. But he's got a bad habit o' underestimatin' men wha' are weaker than he is. He hasna larned that weak men are tae be feared."

She said, "You think he should fear my father?"

Robbie stroked his mustache thoughtfully. "Nathaniel thinks the judge a foolish auld man, no' worth much troublin' ower. But worse, he's disremembered yer brother, and yer brother is nae man's fool."

A quick memory came to Elizabeth of Julian as a four-year-old, during one of the judge's rare visits to England. She could almost feel the short fingers, sticky with marmalade, wound stubbornly in her skirts; he had torn the fabric before he could be dragged away to greet the stranger who was his father. That evening Julian had disappeared, and stayed away for two whole days, secluded in the depths of the kitchen cabinet where he could hear the news of the house and still be warm and have enough to eat when all had gone to their beds. Only the cook's need of a rarely used jelly mold had uncovered him. When asked what he had been about, he had looked surprised that the adults could not see the sense of his plan. "I wished to make you unhappy," he had said. "Not myself."

"Julian is not stupid," she agreed. "And he is incredibly stubborn." She sighed. "Robbie, tell me truly what you think."

"I think that with yer brother's direction, a man like Judge Middleton is mair dangerous than Moses Southern. Southern may fool with yer traps and burn yer crops, but yer faither's weapon is the kind that Nathaniel canna stan' up tae."

"The law," said Elizabeth.

"Aye," agreed Robbie. "The law."

Hawkeye and Nathaniel both insisted on coming along, and so they set out immediately, in spite of a light rain. Elizabeth realized that her dislike of bad weather had been worn away as cleanly as her regard for many of aunt Merriweather's social niceties. But still, she did not want to appear before the judge with straggling hair and so she wore her summer cape with the hood pulled down low, and gave up her moccasins for her old nankeen walking boots, solid and thick and suddenly much heavier than she remembered.

"The man won't thank you for gettin' him out of his bed," Hawkeye observed, squinting up at the storm clouds.

"No, but at least we can be sure to find him in."

Nathaniel grimaced slightly. "I'm not of a mind to go running after the man, Boots. When he wants to talk to us, he knows where we are."

With Robbie's concerns so vividly in her memory, Elizabeth said nothing. She hoped that Robbie was wrong about her father and his intentions. But more than that, she hoped that he had been wrong about Nathaniel's unwillingness to see the dangers her father represented.

When they reached the river and passed over the small bridge, Hawkeye paused to look out over the water. "Ducks coming along," he said with a small frown. "Another week or so, the fledglings will be 'bout ready to fly."

"And should they not?" Elizabeth asked, made curious by his dire tone.

"Billy Kirby will be out here, egging on half the village," replied Nathaniel.

At any other time, Elizabeth would have been intrigued enough by this strange answer to ask more questions, but as they approached her schoolhouse she found herself jumpy and at odds. On her first visit here in the last week the sight of the cornfield in rubble and ashes had made very clear the animosity they faced.

As they approached the building she relaxed. The new wood, hardly weathered in the few months, shone butter-yellow in the misting rain. Curiosity's muslin curtains hung at all the windows, and there was no sign of mischief since she had been here two days ago with Hannah to bring more books and sweep. Automatically she felt for the reassuring shape of the key, which she kept always in her pocket. On Monday she would hold school again, although she knew she could count with assurance on only five students: Hannah, Anna Haupt-mann's two, and the McGarritys' boys.

Jed and Nancy McGarrity had come up to Lake in the Clouds to tell her so, carrying a bushel of plums between them which they put down on the porch. Jed took off his battered cap and squinted sideways at her, his long, homely face set in a frown. There were flecks of red on his cheeks above his beard. "My Nancy's pa didn't take to me, either, when we got married," he said. "And we done well enough, never caused no-body harm." He nudged his wife, who had not looked up from her own dusty bare feet.

"We'd be pleased if you'd take the plums in payment for the summer's schooling for our boys," she said so softly that Elizabeth had trouble hearing.

"Ian and Rudy are welcome in my classroom," Elizabeth had answered with all the dignity she could muster. She knew that these two, in their best dress and scrubbed to a shiny pink to pay this visit, would not understand her urge to hug them both in gratitude. "And thank you kindly for the plums. I am sure we will be glad of them in the winter."

Now Elizabeth anticipated the first day of school with less trepidation, knowing she would have students, even if they were few.

They came around the corner and she felt Nathaniel jerk in surprise, pulling her out of her daydreaming. Over his shoulder she saw that some papers had been nailed to the door. Protected as they were under the eaves they had remained almost dry, but they flapped weakly in the wind.

Nathaniel put a hand on her arm, but she shook him off with a frown, and went up the three steps to the door. She tore the newsprint down with a jerk, leaving the nail behind. Turning slowly to Hawkeye and Nathaniel, she finally raised her head.

"Well?" said Hawkeye finally.

She cleared her throat twice. "From an Albany paper, dated yesterday." And she read out loud:

REWARD

Today Secretary of the State Treasury Morris opens an inquiry into the matter of funds stolen more than Thirty years ago. In the aftermath of the siege of Fort William Henry and the subsequent Savage Massacre of the retreating British and Militia troops by French forces and their Godless Indian allies, a cask of gold coins was stolen from the Fort for transport to Montreal, but never reached its destination.

The Government of this State has claimed the fortune of some Five Thousand Guineas as payment and restitution for expenses and losses suffered by the Citizens of New-York in fighting France for George II.

Long believed Irretrievably Lost in the heart of the Wilderness, a reliable Source has reported a sighting of the unusual five-guinea gold pieces in recent circulation. Any report of these coins should be brought immediately to

Secretary Morris at his offices in Albany. A Reward will be made to Persons contributing to the safe return of the monies to the State Treasury.

"Well, goddamn the judge for an old fox." There was something of admiration in Hawkeye's voice.

"What's the other one?" Nathaniel asked.

Elizabeth read again, this time her voice wavering in anger:

MISSING PERSON

Sought: Any reliable word on the whereabouts and condition of Dr. Richard Todd of Albany and Paradise. He was last seen going into the bush some eight weeks ago near Fish House. Information should be directed to Judge Middleton of Paradise, concerned friend of Dr. Todd, and representative of his affianced, Miss Katherine Witherspoon. Foul play is feared.

Elizabeth crumpled the newspaper in her fist. "It's time to speak up."

Nathaniel raised a brow in surprise. "I thought we were on our way to do that."

"It's time to speak up in public view," Elizabeth said. "Or they will charge one or both of us with murder. Hawkeye, can you fetch my father to the trading post?"

Hawkeye grinned. "Trussed like a Christmas turkey, if need be."

For a moment, Elizabeth thought. These men before her were so much alike not just in their appearance and posture, but also in their simple willingness to listen to her, and what she had to say. It was a great blessing, and she blinked a brief prayer of thanksgiving.

"Julian should be there, too," said Nathaniel. "Your father didn't come up with this plan on his own."

She shot him a startled look; he knew her brother better than she had thought. "Yes, of course you are right."

Hawkeye shrugged, wiping the rain from his face. "Shouldn't be too much trouble."

"Then I'll go fetch Kitty," Nathaniel said.

"Yes, we need Kitty," agreed Elizabeth. "Affianced of Dr. Richard Todd."

"By God." Hawkeye laughed out loud, slapping his leg. "And I was starting to fear that you two had lost your spunk out there in the bush."

Nathaniel came up the steps, crooked a finger under Elizabeth's chin, and turned her face up to his. "You feeling up to this?"

"Oh, please." She grabbed his wrist and held it away from her. "Nathaniel, it would be dangerous to let this foolishness grow out of all proportion."

There was a satisfied flashing in his eyes. Her plait was gone, subjugated into a neat roll on the back of her head, so Nathaniel settled for tugging on her earlobe.

"Just as you say, Boots. So let's get a move on."

"Wait," Elizabeth said. "I'm confused about something first."

Nathaniel glanced at his father, who shrugged.

"If you paid my father's agent for this schoolhouse with the five-guinea pieces, then he must be the 'reliable source' referred to here." She held up the crumpled newspaper. "But if so, my father would have to turn those coins over to this Mr. Morris. I cannot imagine him so set on punishing me that he would willingly hand his money over to the Treasury."

Hawkeye squinted up at her. "You've got a keen eye for detail, woman, and you know your father pretty well. I don't doubt you're right; he wouldn't want to hand over the gold, if he had it."

"But of course he has at least some of it." She was overcome with a sudden sense of dread. "Nathaniel. You did pay my father for this land with the gold?"

Nathaniel said, "Let's go inside."

The schoolhouse smelled of raw wood and beeswax and the great bunch of wild lilies Hannah had arranged in a vase. An errant moth bumped sleepily against the closed window, which provided a view of the marsh and the lake, pretty even in the rain. The sun struggled to break through, touching the forest here and there tentatively. But Elizabeth's whole concentration was on Nathaniel. She pushed back her hood, and looked him straight in the eye.

"You did pay my father for this land with the Tory Gold?" she repeated.

"Not exactly, Boots," said Nathaniel. "Couldn't risk putting those coins into circulation. Once Chingachgook made up his mind to spend the gold, he gave us leave to spend what we needed to get the mountain—"

"But not to hand over the coin, because that would have brought the treasury down our necks," continued Hawkeye. "But then it turned out there wasn't time to melt the gold down before you two took off for Albany—"

"Because we left three days earlier than expected." She finished his thought for him, remembering quite clearly the hurried, hushed conversations between the men when she had come to Lake in the Clouds in the middle of the night. Another thought occurred to her.

"You knew about my father's debts to Richard Todd, or you wouldn't have been planning on taking the gold with us when we left."

Hawkeye said, "We had a pretty good idea. Your father don't exactly keep his troubles close to the vest."

The tic in Nathaniel's cheek was fluttering hard. "Are you angry?"

"I'm too confused to be angry yet." Elizabeth walked to the other side of the room, and then back again, deep in thought. The men watched her, while they dripped rainwater onto the polished floor.

"There is a very obvious question. If you did not use my aunt's gift, or Chingachgook's gold, what bought this place, then, and paid off Richard Todd?" Her voice strained high and then broke. "The mythical gold mine on Hidden Wolf?"

Nathaniel ran a hand through his hair in the way he had when he was trying to puzzle through a problem, and the dim light caught his earring with a spark. Spinning silver in a heavy elongated drop. Similar in design to the one Hawkeye wore, similar to the mass of silver and copper necklaces and bangles and kneebands all the Kahnyen'kehàka wore.

"There is a mine," she said, sitting down heavily.

"Well, not a gold mine, at any rate." Hawkeye's tone bordered on the apologetic.

"Copper? Silver? Diamonds?" She was close to hysterical laughter.

"Silver," said Nathaniel. "The Kahnyen'kehàka knew about it before the Europeans came."

She drew in a deep breath. "Aha. Since you could not risk the gold guineas, you took the silver when we left for Albany, and traded it for cash. Which in turn paid the debts. How long have you been mining the silver exactly?"

Nathaniel blinked. "Ten years, maybe."

"And you take it out . . . ?"

"Bears takes it out one canoe trip at a time."

His tone was calm, but his eyes were hooded with worry.

"Let me see if I understand," she said, quite softly. "My aunt Merriweather's gift, those two thousand pounds, that has not been touched?"

"It's earning interest."

"And there is the output from the mine, which is . . ."

He shrugged. "I'd say there's maybe twenty thousand dollars by now."

"Nineteen five," corrected Hawkeye. "But it ain't ours, not really. Bears looks after it, sees to it that it gets distributed among the Kahnyen'kehàka. What we borrowed from the silver money in the spring we'll pay back—when you two go to Albany you can take care of that, too."

"I see. With the gold, I presume. There are one thousand five-guinea gold pieces?"

"Closer to fifteen hundred," said Hawkeye, grinning now.

With an incoherent sound of surrender, Elizabeth put her face in her hands. After a long minute, she looked up.

"I married for money."

Nathaniel glanced at his father, and then at her. "It looks that way, Boots. Do you mind very much?"

She laughed. "I'm not sure. I will have to become accustomed to the idea before I can say." She found her handkerchief and wiped her brow with it. "If my father or brother should find out about the mine—"

Hawkeye grunted. "It would get loud around here," he said. "And it might complicate things in Albany, down the line."

"Of course we must go to Albany, soon, to settle our agreement on this place . . ." Elizabeth paused to look around herself. "But how is that relevant?"

Nathaniel said, "There's still that bench warrant issued for you. The mine would make things look suspicious."

Elizabeth came to stand in front of him, so that she had to raise her head to look into his eyes. She was close enough to feel the heat of him. "Did you marry me to get this mine, Nathaniel Bonner?"

"I did not." He met her gaze without flinching.

"Is there anything else you have not told me about? Land-holdings in Albany? A peerage in Scotland?"

He shook his head.

"So." She looked between them. "You two did manage to deceive my father in this, that much cannot be denied. He could legally claim the profit from the mine before title was transferred—"

"But only legally," said Hawkeye. "The way I look at it, the money that's come out of that mine is part of what should have been paid to the Kahnyen'kehàka for the land."

Elizabeth looked at them, dressed simply in worn buckskin, with work-hardened hands. They did not live easy lives; they had not profited personally from the mine. There was nothing of greed in what they had done, but there was something of pride.

"Yes, I see your point," she said finally, and there was a soft flicker in Nathaniel's face: relief, and gratitude.

"And given the fact that my father found it within his heart to publicly accuse me of murder . . ." Elizabeth held up the newspaper. "I cannot find it in mine to be outraged for him."

Nathaniel held out his hand to her. "Then let's go and settle this business."

"One thing more," she said, holding back.

The men froze.

"With the gold and the silver, there will be quite a lot of cash available to us. I will have a say in how it is spent."

Hawkeye glanced at his son, and then nodded. "That's fair enough."

"Then let us go," said Elizabeth, pulling up her hood. "It promises to be an eventful day."

XLVII

Elizabeth found Anna's trading post just as she had left it: crowded with men, and overwhelmed with the smells of human sweat, tobacco and wood smoke, wet wool and bear grease, pickled onions and drying venison. The walls were still covered with signs and advertisements, and Anna was in her usual place behind the counter, rummaging head and shoulders deep in a cubbyhole. Poised at the open door, Elizabeth saw the assembly turn their attention to her and fall silent, one by one. With her cape wrapped around her and water dripping from the brim of her hood, she made sure to meet every eye she could catch. There were only ten men, half of whom she could name. But no sign of Axel, or of Jed McGarrity, the two she would have most liked to have seen.

Leaning on the back wall, his arms crossed on his chest, was Moses Southern. He was half-turned toward the much smaller Claude Dubonnet, who for Elizabeth would always first be Dirty-Knife, although she could not call him that. He had straightened up to stare at her from the newspaper he had spread out over the pickle barrel. Elizabeth thought briefly of offering to read it out loud to them, for she had no doubt what it was that had captured their interest. More of Julian's work, she was sure.

Nearby, Archie Cunningham was trimming his fingernails with a hunting knife, flicking the parings alternately into the

fire and at young Liam Kirby's ears. Curled almost double over
the draughts board, Liam took no notice. His brother Billy sat
opposite with his back to Elizabeth, talking to a trapper Elizabeth did not recognize while he waited for Liam to make his
move.

Liam stuck out a grubby finger to move his game piece,
looked up, and jumped at the sight of her. His left hand flew up
toward his cap, catching the corner of the board and upending
it with a smack. Red and black game pieces went skittering
over the floor.

"You goddamn puppy," said Billy in a conversational tone.
At that moment he caught sight of Elizabeth, and his mouth
snapped shut.

Moses Southern hawked, a long, dragging sound, and then
without looking away from her, sent a stream of tobacco into
the bucket that served as a spittoon.

"I'll warn you once more, Southern," Anna said, bringing
her head out of the cubbyhole. "A drop of that mess on my
clean floor and you'll mop it up yourself."

"Hello, Anna," Elizabeth said.

"Well, Elizabeth! About time you showed your face." Anna
leaned over the counter to give Charlie LeBlanc a good-natured
slap on the crown of his head.

"Take your eyes off my candy jar and say how-do, Charlie.
That's Mrs. Bonner come in, the one you made moon eyes at
all winter. If you ever thought to come to church you would
have had the chance to welcome her home last Sunday."

The young man flushed a deep red and flashed a reluctant
grin in Elizabeth's direction, so that the newest gap in his teeth
became evident. "Miz Elizabeth." He bobbed his head.

"It's good to see you, Charlie."

As if they had been woken from a trance, many of the other
men tipped their caps in Elizabeth's direction and mumbled
greetings.

"You come down the mountain all alone?" called Moses
Southern, his raspy voice carrying through the room.

"And why would I not?" Elizabeth asked him with a small
smile.

Moses shrugged. "Just last week Asa Pierce got killed by a

bear up on Hidden Wolf. Lots of trouble out there in the bush for folks who don't pay attention."

"Lots of trouble," echoed Claude Dubonnet, rubbing a finger alongside his nose.

If you only knew how much trouble, Elizabeth thought, touching a finger to the chain that disappeared into her bodice.

"Oh, be quiet, you old gasbag." Axel appeared at the rear door, scratching at his beard. "Asa Pierce didn't have the common sense God gave a goat, although he was a good enough blacksmith. Hello there, Miz Elizabeth."

"Are you well, Mr. Metzler?"

"Ja, sure. Fine, fine. My joints are hollerin' loud enough to be waking the dead on rainy days like this one, but you know what they say. Live long and drink deep, and sooner or later you'll get your share of the dregs. Anna, you got time to be helping this woman, or you want me to come behind your counter and see to it?" Axel settled with a deep sigh of satisfaction into the chair nearest the hearth, a position which put him just between Moses Southern and Billy Kirby, both of whom glowered at Axel openly.

"I'll manage fine, I always have," Anna said. "Now, what can I help you with, Elizabeth? I expect you've got a long list. Takes more than four legs in a bed to start a marriage out right, after all."

The purpose of this trip had not been shopping, but as Elizabeth had no idea how long it would be before Hawkeye and Nathaniel would appear with their charges in tow, she set her mind to the many things large and small missing from the new cabin. In short order a small hill of dry goods had been piled on the counter, with a new kettle and a large sack of goose feathers at the center. By the time the women had begun to discuss fabric for aprons and sheets, they had long lost the attention of the room. Slowly the noise level returned to normal, and Elizabeth began to enjoy the process of purchasing things for her new home, although she was always aware of Moses Southern behind her.

Anna had just pulled out a tin washtub for Elizabeth's inspection when the door opened. With a rush of cool air the skin rose on the nape of her neck, and she raised her eyes slowly.

The judge was there, with Julian hovering at his right elbow.

Elizabeth had never before spent much time away from her brother, and to her surprise she found that she had missed him, even as he stood before her with his derisive half grin. Hawkeye had obviously dragged him out of his bed, for his eyes were reddened and he was unshaven; neither had he taken the time to comb his hair, and his hair fell over his right eye. Elizabeth was reminded of him at thirteen, when he had not yet learned to hide his anger or his intelligence behind a mask of equal parts lethargy and mockery.

"Hello, Father, Julian." She pulled her cloak closer around herself, glad of its protection.

"Lizzie," said her brother.

Before her, she saw her father's expectant face, and close behind him, Hawkeye watchful and waiting. Her father hung back as he always did, hoping that someone else would fix this problem he had created. Hawkeye was silent because he knew the trick of waiting until he was needed. But it was Julian who concerned her now, Julian who thought that he could some-how talk her out of her marriage, her new home, her freedoms, to come back to them. She wondered if he missed her, too, or if the lost mountain was all that interested him.

He said, "To have lowered yourself to such tricks, are you not ashamed?"

Elizabeth pulled the rumpled newspaper from inside her cloak, and held it out to him.

"This is a strange coincidence," she said. "I was about to ask you the very same question, little brother."

Nathaniel had never thought much of the Reverend Mr. Witherspoon, but he found reason this morning to revise his opinion. Kitty had flatly refused to accompany him to the trad-ing post; only her father's intercession had worked to change her mind. Word of Richard's whereabouts and health—which she demanded immediately, but which Nathaniel would not supply—were only to be had if she came along with him. Mr.

Witherspoon helped her wrap herself in a light cloak that could not conceal a six- or seven-month pregnancy, and the three of them made their way to the village in the rain.

Kitty was silent, after she found that Nathaniel would not answer questions. This left Mr. Witherspoon to inquire after Elizabeth in a manner which managed to be both polite and severe.

"She has broken her father's heart."

"She has settled all of her father's considerable debts," amended Nathaniel.

"I hope she does not already regret her hasty actions."

"You can ask her yourself," Nathaniel pointed out. "She's waiting for us." From the corner of his eye he saw Kitty start. Her face took on a set look, as if this news were unexpected, but quite welcome.

"If she would only apologize for the injury she has inflicted, I am sure the judge would forgive her and take her back into his home. The man is all kindness, when he is well treated."

Nathaniel almost laughed out loud. He looked at the clergyman at some length, the smudged spectacles sitting crooked on the long, reddened nose, the hollow cheeks and pale mouth. Watery blue eyes met his own, and in them he saw that it was hopeless: the man wore blinders and would never even know it.

"My wife has a home," he said simply. "She don't need the judge's charity."

"Father," said Kitty sharply. "Can't you see that your arguments are wasted on him? Sue a beggar and you will profit nothing but fleas, after all."

Now Nathaniel did laugh, as he was sorely tempted to ask her what kind of fleas she had profited from Julian Middleton. His laughter hit her hard; he saw her color up, her eyes flashing anger and tears.

He had grown up with Kitty Witherspoon and it was not the first time he had made her cry, in the normal rough way older boys had with little girls. But Kitty in tears made Nathaniel feel thirteen again, which in turn made him think of his mother.

Cora had taken Kitty on when Mrs. Witherspoon died. Her father had not known what to do with a little girl, and so it was Cora who had taught Kitty how to sew and cook, and who had listened patiently to her stories, answered her questions. Nathaniel could hardly remember a time in those years when she had not spent all or part of every day on Hidden Wolf.

Then Richard had come back to Paradise. It was Kitty who had brought him up to Lake in the Clouds the first time, understanding that Cora would make room for him. *Stray cats find their way to the kindest heart in the village,* his father had commented on coming home from a long hunt to find three children at his table instead of one. But he hadn't minded, not if it pleased Cora to have them around her. *My mother could have taught you something about charity,* Nathaniel thought, as Witherspoon carried on about the duties of children.

Nathaniel should have been angry with Kitty; she had caused trouble and was willing to cause more. But he had his mother at his elbow now, and he saw Kitty as she would have: still a girl at heart and mind, her slender back bent with the weight of a child who brought her no joy, fathered by a man who would never claim it, or her. Suddenly Kitty was once again the almost-sister she had been, and Nathaniel was overwhelmed with anger at Julian Middleton, and at Richard Todd as well, who had offered her a home and his name as he would make any business deal. She deserved better and he was tempted to tell her so. But he also knew that her own anger was as deep and unfathomable as her sorrow, and that words—his words— would not help right now. Having learned not only charity but the value of a well-timed silence from his mother, Nathaniel kept his thoughts to himself.

Alfred Middleton, onetime trapper and hunter, adventurer, land speculators and property holder, presently judge in the township of Paradise in the state of New-York, understood above all things how to play to an audience. This particular audience was well disposed toward his plight and would come completely over to his side with very little work at all, if only his son would hold his tongue. If only it weren't for Hawkeye, who stood watching with that infernal smirk; always knowing too much and guessing the rest. Standing there like an angel of God, ready to do battle for Elizabeth.

He hadn't seen his daughter for three good months, and hadn't expected to see her, either. Julian's plan, again. She would be easier to persuade that way, or so his reasoning went. But Elizabeth stood before him now with her eyes flashing and her cheeks flushed with color, and he realized with some surprise that she was pretty, if you could overlook the impudent way she had of meeting a man's eye. There were other men in the room who appreciated what they saw, too: the younger ones showed it plainly, the older ones with swift, guarded glances. The judge wondered for the first time if Bonner might have married her for something other than the mountain. The fact that Nathaniel wasn't here hadn't escaped the judge. All at once he didn't feel quite so comfortable with the door at his back, and he moved slightly forward.

The truth was, if it weren't for the land, he would almost be glad to see her wed to Nathaniel Bonner. She was as strong willed as her mother, but smarter: a bad combination in any woman, but impossible in a daughter. Maybe Nathaniel could handle her. God knew Todd hadn't been up to the job.

She was looking at him now, holding the newspaper out toward him. He would have blushed, if he had been capable of it. The newspaper had been Julian's idea. Together they had gone to Albany, and set it all in motion. Although he didn't like it, not at all. If the Bonners had the Tory Gold, then that fortune was in the family, in a manner of speaking—and he had no intention of handing it over to the state. In that case, Elizabeth had made a decent match: a man with some money who would look after the land. Not that he could say so out loud: the men in this room had a fear of the Mohawk that would outweigh any loyalty they felt toward him. And there was Julian, who resented everything Elizabeth had, but the mountain most of all.

His children's voices moved back and forth: the delicate, deadly thrusts of foils rather than the more blunt no-nonsense of the war club. The judge had been too long in this country to remember the rules of engagement, but his children had learned them well in his sister's household. Oh, yes. The men in the room, most of whom had fought more than one bloody war, watched in horror and amazement at what damage could be

done without knives or firearms. He listened to the cloaked
parry and thrust, and his head ached. The judge wished to be
home again where Curiosity would fix him a hot toddy and he
could contemplate his folly in privacy. He had been foolish, in
his anger and hurt pride. He had let Julian set this plan in
motion, even though Curiosity had given him that look, the
one that said that he was moving too fast and would regret it.
*You set on stirrin' up a wasps' nest, best know you got some safe place
to run, first.* The judge looked at the faces in the room and he
knew he should have listened to her. Generally, life would be
much simpler if he would just let Curiosity make his decisions.
It was Curiosity who told him to keep out of Todd's investment
schemes to start with. She had said straight-out that Richard
Todd would be more trouble than he was worth.

The door opened and Kitty Witherspoon came in with Nathaniel right behind, proving Curiosity right once again.

There was a transformation in Kitty; Nathaniel watched it happen as she stepped over the threshold. Her narrow back straightened and her head held high, she walked right up to Elizabeth.

"I want to know what you've done to Richard."

The room was close and full of people, and the mood generated more heat. Both women's faces were pearled with sweat.

"Who told you we've done anything at all to Richard
Todd?" Elizabeth asked calmly. Nathaniel sought out her eye,
but she was focused on Kitty.

"Richard went into the bush to serve you with a bench
warrant more than three months ago," she said. "He expected
to be back in a month. He promised me that he would be."

Elizabeth put her hand on the younger girl's arm. "Because
he could not keep one promise does not mean he will not keep
others."

Kitty's faced drained of the little color she had had, and she
shook off Elizabeth's hand with a small strangled gasp. Stepping
back, she came up against the counter.

"What is keeping him, then?"

For the first time, Elizabeth looked toward Nathaniel. He
raised his head, and immediately the attention of the room was

on him. He had few friends here, but his father was at his back, and Axel stood on the other side of the room with his rifle within reach. He flexed his hands at his sides, felt the rush of fear and anger thrumming softly in his fingertips.

"There's lots of distractions in the bush," Nathaniel said.

Julian said, "Was your rifle one of them?"

Elizabeth turned to her brother. "Julian. How good of you to come to the point, as usual. Since this issue interests everyone here, let me say this clearly. The last we saw of Richard was in Canada—"

There was a shifting in the room, a sudden increase of sound.

"He was injured, but he was recovering."

"Where?" Kitty's voice was hoarse.

Nathaniel spoke up for the first time. "Kahen'tiyo."

Kitty shook her head sharply. "Richard would never go to Kahen'tiyo of his own accord. He must have been taken by force."

"He was carried, but not by force," Nathaniel said. "The Kahnyen'kehàka saved his life."

"I don't believe you." Her voice wavered and threatened to break. "He ran away from the Mohawk and said he would never go back."

"He didn't have much choice about it, with his injuries."

The judge stepped forward, clearing his throat in an ominous way. "How did he get these injuries?" he asked, glancing between Elizabeth and Nathaniel.

"I didn't shoot him, if that's what you want to know," said Nathaniel. "Didn't knife him either, or chuck a rock at him, or push him off a cliff. I would have, you understand, because he came bearing arms against us. But he met with an accident before we could get down to business."

"Do you have any proof of this?" Julian asked.

Elizabeth said, "Robbie could have told you, but he has left for home. The people at Kahen'tiyo could tell you what we have told you."

Moses Southern called out, "Who's going to take the word of those Mohawk? Do you have any white people to speak up for you on this?"

"Robbie told me the story," said Axel. "Just like they're telling it here."

Moses waved Axel's evidence away with one thick hand. "But you didn't see him yourself, Metzler. MacLachlan could've been wrong."

"Richard will find his way home soon enough," Nathaniel said. "I guess you'll have to settle for his word on it, if he's white enough for you, Moses."

"By God," called a male voice from the back of the room. "You'd better be right."

Kitty held up her hand. "Wait!" she cried. "Wait! I want to know where Richard is now. I want to know why he didn't come back with you."

Elizabeth answered her. "Katherine. All we can tell you is that Richard was healing slowly from his wounds when we last saw him, and that he left the village just before we did, heading north. He did not tell us why he was going, or where."

"If he was injured, he couldn't have traveled on his own," Kitty pointed out.

Elizabeth flashed a look in Nathaniel's direction. He shook his head slightly, suddenly fearing what detail she might give Kitty. But it was too late; he saw that immediately. Elizabeth had taken pity on the young woman, and she would do what she could to calm her fears.

"He left the village with his brother."

"By God," said Moses Southern, pushing suddenly toward the counter. "By *God*! You dare to lie in our faces and think you can get away with it—"

Nathaniel had begun to move forward as soon as Moses had, but Anna came between the old trapper and Elizabeth first, her solid form acting as both a wall and a battering ram. She put out one muscled arm and gave him a shove.

"Get out of here if you can't behave no better than that," she shouted. "If you want to talk civilized, then you step back there and use a suitable tone, or I'll pick you up and toss you out the door myself, Southern. Do you doubt I can do it?"

Heaving with anger, Moses looked in turn at Nathaniel and Elizabeth, and then his eyes skittered quickly through the room, clearly counting allies: Liam Kirby had slipped out through the back door, but Billy stood watching, his hands on his belt. Archie Cunningham and Claude Dubonnet stood ready to reach for weapons. The others, men not clearly on either side of this battle, but none of them well disposed toward the Mohawk, stood aside waiting to see what would happen. Nathaniel placed himself slightly in front of Elizabeth, and saw Hawkeye coming up on her other side.

"Samuel Todd died fighting for the Mohawk fifteen years ago," said Moses Southern. "Everybody knows that."

"Well, then," said Hawkeye in an easy tone that set Nathaniel's nerves humming, for he knew well it meant that his father was on the edge of losing his temper. "They forgot to tell Samuel to go bury hisself, because he's alive as you and me."

Southern let out a grunt. "Samuel Todd is long dead. And if you're lying about that, then you're probably lying about the rest of it. Todd is rotting out there in the bush."

Kitty made a strangled noise. Furious, Elizabeth turned toward Moses Southern.

"If you insist on calling me a liar again, Mr. Southern, I am afraid you might be in real danger. You see that my husband and my father-in-law do not take well to such insults. Now." She looked around the room, her eyes pausing briefly on Julian, who was leaning against the counter, clearly enjoying the entire proceeding. Then she found her father near the door, and her eyes narrowed. "I would like to have your attention. Samuel Todd is alive, I saw him myself. As is his brother Richard. Both these facts are verifiable, if you care to make the trip. If you do not, I would ask you to desist in these ridiculous claims. Father?"

The judge stepped forward reluctantly.

"I believe you know something about this advertisement in the newspaper?"

"For Miss Katherine's sake——"

"How very gallant of you," Elizabeth said dryly. "To go to such length and expense. Julian, I expect this was your idea?"

"I don't like to take all the credit," her brother said, looking uncomfortable for the first time since he had come in. "Kitty was in a bad state of mind," he added, and then he had the good grace to flush, his neck and the tips of his ears mottling red. "Not that it was our fault, but we thought we might as well be of help."

Elizabeth turned a glare on Julian; Nathaniel felt her anger rising like the screech of a hawk before it swooped down on its prey. But it was Kitty who spoke up.

Her eyes were fixed on Julian as if she had never seen such a creature before. "Julian Middleton," she said very softly. "I fear for your immortal soul."

She held his gaze until he looked away.

Elizabeth turned to the judge. "Father, are you going to charge us with some crime against Richard Todd? Because if you are, do it now, please."

There was an uncomfortable silence.

"Father?"

"No," he said then, pursing his lips. "I have nothing to charge you with."

"Do not sound so very disappointed, Father," Elizabeth said dryly.

The judge drew himself up to his full height. "Your sarcasm is uncalled for, Elizabeth. It does you no good credit."

"You see that marriage has done little to improve me, then."

Nathaniel saw the tension in her face and in the slight tremble of her hands, and he knew even if her father did not that she was upset and hurt. He put a hand on her shoulder.

Kitty Witherspoon suddenly came to life, pulling her cloak around herself in spite of the heat. "I have heard enough. Father, please." And she pushed her way through the crowd with the Reverend Witherspoon close behind her. Elizabeth was still staring at the judge.

"Elizabeth," Nathaniel said. "We're done here."

"No you ain't," said Moses Southern. "I still got a question to ask."

Hawkeye's rifle stock hit the floor with a thump, and the group of men around Moses jumped like rabbits. Moses himself stayed steady, his fist curled white around the barrel of his own rifle.

But Hawkeye talked to all of them, drew each man in the room in with his eyes. "You're wanting to ask about Hidden Wolf, and by God it's time to get it out in the open. The mountain belongs to my daughter-in-law and my son, by law. They got the paperwork, anybody wants to doubt my word." He pointed to an old hand-drawn map on the wall. "I can draw the boundaries, if that's necessary. But I think you all know where they lie."

"You planning to keep us from hunting on the Wolf?" asked Dubonnet, his thin voice spiraling up in a harsh arc.

"I don't make the gaming laws," Hawkeye said coldly. "If you hunt out of season, it's the judge you'll answer to—ain't that so, Alfred?"

The judge nodded, reluctantly. "The gaming laws and restrictions will be enforced on private and public lands."

Hawkeye grunted. "So this is what we got to say. You can track your game onto the Wolf, same as always. Berrying, that kind of thing, that we've got no problem with. But there'll be no more timber taken from our land—" Billy Kirby made a protesting noise, and Hawkeye nodded at him. "I see you, Billy. Not another tree from our land, do you hear, and we don't care what terms you got to offer. There's plenty of timber out there otherwise. No trapping, either."

"How about looking at the Wolf, Hawkeye, that still allowed?" Moses' tone was all spit and poison.

"Well, now, I dunno," Hawkeye said slowly. "I suppose so, long as you don't get too close, Moses. As for the rest of you, stay off the Wolf past the strawberry fields. Any man found farther up than that, my son here will take you before the judge for trespassing. Now, me personally, maybe I'll shoot first, depends on what I catch you at."

Billy Kirby spoke for the first time. "Ain't like you ever caught anybody up till now."

There was a new silence in the room as Hawkeye looked at Billy. As he held the gaze past the point of no return, the younger man blanched, but he did not look away.

"You don't want to be the first, Billy," Hawkeye said, so softly that the skin rose on Nathaniel's nape. "Not now that you've had fair warning. You all leave us to our own business, keep your hounds and your hands off what don't belong to you, and there won't be any trouble."

"What about them Mohawk? How many more of them you

got headed this way?" Archie Cunningham directed this at Hawkeye, but Nathaniel stepped forward.

"My family is my own business," he said. "Anybody interferes with them, I'll deal with it myself. And the law will back me up on that, won't it, Judge?"

Nathaniel had never seen Middleton look so miserable. He cast a glance at his son, whose jaw was strung tight enough to hear his teeth grinding, and then nodded.

"That's all we wanted to set straight," Hawkeye said. "You'll find us good neighbors, if you'll leave us in peace."

Elizabeth was silent most of the way up the mountain, busy sorting through the conversations in the trading post. Snatches of sentences came to her, so that her temper flared and flared again. She saw Julian's pale face, the way he had avoided looking at Kitty at all. He had gambled on the knowledge that Elizabeth could not expose him without exposing Kitty at the same time; he had won. She could not cause more pain where there was already so much.

In front of her Nathaniel walked with his head up, watching the woods. She knew that Hawkeye did the same behind her. The men carried their rifles at the ready, and their tension hummed almost loud enough to be heard. Elizabeth fought with a wave of fear and anger. She would not be forced from her new home; she would not be Miss Middleton again, to please her father and console her brother. But she remembered Robbie's words, and she knew he was right: this would take no good end. Hawkeye had offered a truce in a conciliatory tone, he had sought out every eye in the room. But few had met him in return; she had watched carefully. It had been a rational offer; the only possible way to live together with these people who had been at war so long that they could not face the idea of its alternative. *You'll find us good neighbors, if you'll leave us in peace.*

Axel, bless him, had stepped forward. "Ja, Dan'l. We've never been anything else," he had said. "Ain't no need to expect less now. You're welcome here anytime, and you'll find most of us will be glad of the company of any of the Hidden Wolf folk."

It had been a relief, to be reminded of this. That there were other people, reasonable people, in the village. Jed McGarrity, and his family. Curiosity and Galileo and their children. The Gloves, who had greeted her kindly. And other families, enough of them to make Paradise home.

Elizabeth had accepted Nathaniel's arm to leave the trading post, and then stopped to speak to Anna about the pile of dry goods on the counter. Hurrying to catch up to him at the door, a foot on the tail of her skirt had held her up.

We'll find that mine, came a soft voice. *And then we'll find you dead in your beds.* It might have been Moses, but perhaps not. She had not turned around.

XLVIII

Elizabeth held her breath well into the second week of the school session, and then, cautiously, she allowed herself to exhale. There had been no trouble from the village, no disruptions of any kind to herself or her students. Every morning thus far, she and Hannah had walked down Hidden Wolf with no escort save for the company of Hector and Blue, Hawkeye's dogs. The hunters were sorely vexed by the unprecedented and apparently endless ban on deer tracking, and were willing to take on escort duties, even if they did not take them very seriously; they were easily seduced away by the promise of a squirrel, and would turn tail and head for home as soon as Elizabeth put the key in the schoolhouse door. Nathaniel was less than enthusiastic about this arrangement, but Elizabeth had argued for it and persuaded him in the end that it would not serve anyone to have her appear frightened to her students.

She had eight of them, each more well behaved, attentive, and hardworking than the last. Each with some talent, small or large, that she could clearly see and lovingly encourage. Each with problems small enough to address carefully after long contemplation. And five of the eight were girls, two of whom—Dolly Smythe with her painfully crossed eyes, and her own Hannah—showed real curiosity and intelligence. This final blessing she kept to herself, for she did not wish to discourage the other children by showing favoritism.

Now they worked with heads bent over precious paper, quills held tightly in curled fingers. Once a day they put aside their hornbooks to practice penmanship, and they copied today's sentence from the board exactly as she had put it there:

No man is an island, entire of itself.
—JOHN DONNE

Elizabeth watched Ruth Glove chewing her lower lip almost ragged in concentration as she carefully dipped the quill in the inkpot she shared with her sister. Behind Ruth and Hepzibah, Ephraim Hauptmann had put down his quill. No doubt he had rushed through the sentence and produced something barely legible.

"If you are satisfied with your work, Ephraim, then sit quietly until we are finished," Elizabeth said to him. "However, if you think you could do better, you might try again."

He picked up his quill with a resigned sigh. Ephraim was a good boy, but his mind did tend to wander from the task at hand. Not so Ian McGarrity, who would fill the whole paper if she let him. Elizabeth watched Ian squint at the board even from the spot closest to it, and wondered once again when she should speak to his parents about his eyesight. The McGarritys had no money for spectacles, but Elizabeth could and in fact intended to buy some for the boy when she was next in Johnstown or Albany. First there would need to be some arrangement; she would have to accept half of a pig, or a keg of maple syrup, or something that the McGarritys could spare as payment, to suit their sense of equity.

The only sounds in the room were Henrietta Hauptmann's labored breathing, the scratching of quills, and the ticking of Elizabeth's little clock on the desk in front of her. Absentmindedly, she paged through the Bible, searching with only half her concentration for tomorrow's penmanship verse. This half hour was one of the few times she had for her own thoughts in an otherwise busy school morning, for all the children were needed at home in the afternoons and she was determined to fit not only reading, writing, and arithmetic into each day, but also some rudimentary history and geography. Many-Doves could no longer spare the time to help, and thus Elizabeth could not conduct extra lessons with the older and more advanced students: Dolly, Hannah, and Rudy McGarrity needed more complex arithmetic and they were ready to start French. Perhaps in the fall. Elizabeth closed the Bible and looked out the window.

The haze on the lake had not yet burned off: it would be a hot day. She suppressed the urge to pull at her bodice, which was uncomfortably tight these days, and especially uncomfortable in the heat. As she did many times every day, she wished herself back in Kahnyen'kehàka dress. Her students wore loose-fitting overshirts of airy muslin and light, high-waisted summer frocks. Her own summer clothing was made for the damp, cool mornings of Oakmere. She would have to have some dresses made, and soon.

Elizabeth sighed again, and tried to focus on a suitable verse for the next day's lesson. For some time she had been considering "Thou shalt love thy neighbor as thyself," but each time she came across the sentence Moses Southern's scowl rose in her mind's eye and she felt incapable of adequately defending this choice. And when she thought of Moses, she must also think of his daughter. She could not deny it was a relief not to have Jemima in her classroom, but neither could she deny that this was a guilty pleasure. The little girl needed the experience of school, even if Elizabeth did not especially enjoy the challenge she presented. Once again she thanked God for her sweet-natured and biddable students.

"Miss?"

The small voice startled her out of her daydream. Ephraim Hauptmann stood before her desk, his hands folded in front of himself. His usually pale seven-year-old face was flushed the color of ripe strawberries, and under the luxuriant fringe of hay-colored hair his eyes darted this way and that, unwilling to meet hers. The classroom went suddenly even more still than it had been.

"Yes, Ephraim, what is it?"

"Please, miss," he said in a whisper that was heard in every corner of the room. "My winkle's got stuck."

Elizabeth blinked. The little boy blinked back at her, his eyes as round as pennies, his color deepening to plum. She looked more carefully at his grubby hands, crossed so primly in front of himself, and saw the glint of dark glass between his fingers. His inkpot.

Biting her lip, she looked down at her own hands, at a fading scar on her thumb. Elizabeth looked at anything and everything that might keep her from laughing out loud. From the corner of her eye, she stole a look at the class. Each child sat there completely engaged, waiting for her to solve this problem, as if it were an everyday occurrence for little boys to try inkpots on for size. Which, Elizabeth mused to herself, might be the case. She wondered what other mischief she had overlooked.

"I said, I've got my—"

"I heard you, Ephraim," Elizabeth interrupted him. "I'm thinking."

The first hushed giggles came from Ephraim's sister Henrietta, with Hannah fast behind. Elizabeth sent them what was meant to be a firm look, but which she thought probably came closer to a grimace.

"Well—" she began slowly.

Thump! Elizabeth sprang up from her chair, nearly overturning it in her alarm. The children were up, too, and looking around. There was an outraged cry from outside, and another thump which set the open window behind her desk to rattling. As she turned in that direction, she had a brief glimpse of Ephraim's shocked face, his ink-stained fingers pressed to his mouth and the small glass bottle dangling incongruously from his unbuttoned breeches.

"Oooowwww!" came another screech. Elizabeth stuck her head out of the window to see Nathaniel pinning Liam Kirby to the wall.

"Leeeemeegoo!" howled Liam, arms and legs flailing.

The children had raced out of the door as soon as she had turned her back, and they appeared in a crowd at the corner of the building.

"Look here, Boots," Nathaniel said. "You've got a Peeping Tom."

"His name ain't Tom," offered Ruth Glove cheerfully. "That's Liam Kirby."

"He knows that," Dolly hissed. "A Peeping Tom's some-body who looks in at windows where he don't belong."

Liam was squirming but Nathaniel held him fast, leaning with all his weight on the fistful of hair pulled up hard and taut against the wall. Pinned like a bug, Liam sputtered and squeaked and sent Elizabeth pleading glances.

Elizabeth turned her attention to her students. "I don't recall giving permission for you to leave your seats. Please return to them at once."

Sheepishly, with lingering last looks toward Liam, they retreated the way they had come. Elizabeth waited until she heard the door close and heard them talking inside the classroom behind her.

"What are you doing here, Liam?"

"Nothing," he spat, earning a smart cuff above the ear from Nathaniel.

"Oooww! What was that for?"

"For your sweet manners and courteous ways," Nathaniel said. "Remember it." Then he looked at Elizabeth. "It ain't the first time. I was watching today because I saw his tracks here."

Elizabeth considered the red-faced boy, trying to assess the source of his discomfort: anger, or embarrassment.

"Do let him go, Nathaniel, before you snatch him bald-headed."

With a shrug, Nathaniel stepped away and then made some considerable show of wiping his hand on his leggings.

"Liam, I wonder if you'd like to come back to school."

This earned her a raised brow from Nathaniel, and a scowl from the boy.

"Don't know why I should want to come back here," he mumbled sullenly, rubbing his sore scalp.

"I don't know why either, exactly," Elizabeth said. "But it seems as if you do. Why would you spend your valuable time listening at the window, if you did not?"

Nathaniel's sour grin told her that he approved of her tactics, if not of her purpose.

Elizabeth said, "There's an empty desk if you'd like it. Now if you'll please pardon me, we have lessons—" She stopped, remembering Ephraim's dilemma. A quick glance over her shoulder showed her all of the children gathered in a tight circle, heads bent in utter fascination.

"Give 'er a yank, Rudy," came a decisive female voice. "You're the strongest."

"Holy God!" cried Elizabeth, bumping her head on the window frame in her hurry to get into the room. "Children! Wait!" As she pushed through the circle around Ephraim, Nathaniel and Liam came in the door and joined her.

Nathaniel's mouth twitched at one corner and then the other. He looked at Elizabeth and then quickly away.

"It's all swoll up," Ephraim announced piteously. "Won't budge."

Elizabeth coughed, and covered her mouth to cough again. She turned away to bury her fit of coughing in her handkerchief. When she turned back, Nathaniel was down on one knee in front of Ephraim, surveying the situation.

"Don't suppose there's any lard to hand," he said. "Wonder who can run the fastest and fetch me some."

In a second, the room had emptied of all the children except for Hannah, who retired reluctantly to the front step at Elizabeth's suggestion.

At thirteen Liam was more than twice Ephraim's size; he had to squat down on his haunches to get a better look. He rubbed the ginger-colored down on his upper lip while he considered the dangling inkpot.

"Lordy, you don't need no lard for that job." He squinted up at Nathaniel. "What you need is a hammer."

Ephraim's head jerked up, and at that moment there was a soft *pop!* and the bottle fell to the floor with a clank. It rolled away under a desk, trailing a long comma of ink.

"What'd I say?" Liam looked from Nathaniel to Elizabeth and then at the small blue-stained appendage curled so innocently in Ephraim's lap. "How'd that happen?"

"You scared the piss out of him." Nathaniel laughed, slapping Liam on the shoulder.

"I did not piss!" Ephraim protested, blushing this time to the tips of his ears. He crossed his hands over his lap.

"Yes, well." Elizabeth took on a soothing tone. "It looks as though school is out for today. Why don't you go home and—"

"Wash up," supplied Nathaniel, the corners of his mouth curling uncontrollably upward.

"In the future—" Elizabeth continued slowly, trying to ignore Nathaniel and find the appropriate tone.

"Keep your breeches buttoned." This from Liam.

Elizabeth scowled at him, and he dropped his gaze in reply. She sighed. "I suppose that does sum it up. Best get along, Ephraim. And tell the others that school is out for the day."

The look of confusion and utter embarrassment on the boy's face was replaced instantaneously with one of unmitigated joy, which gave Elizabeth momentary pause. "I do trust we will not have any repetitions of this unfortunate event, Ephraim Hauptmann. No matter how beautiful the weather."

His face went very still. "No, miss. 'Course not." He paused, and shrugged philosophically. "Didn't feel very good, anyway."

They managed to control themselves until he was safely out the door, and then they laughed until Elizabeth's ribs ached with it.

Hannah appeared at the door. She sniffed, and raised a brow in unspoken criticism.

"Are you coming back to school?" she asked Liam when he had managed to stifle himself.

He ducked his head in sudden seriousness. "I suppose so," he said. "Until my brother finds out and takes a switch to me."

"Good," said Hannah. "We need another boy for games at recess. And you need to learn to read." And she disappeared into the sunshine.

"Miz Bonner?" Liam paused at the door on his way out.

"Yes?"

"I ain't got any money to pay tuition," he said. "But I can chop wood."

She was careful not to smile. "That would be a very acceptable arrangement, Liam."

Staring at his own bare feet, the boy spoke up again.

"It weren't my idea, you know. About Albany, and the court. I wanted to tell you I was sorry about that."

Nathaniel squinted at her, his skepticism written in the downward curve of his mouth. But Elizabeth remembered Liam as a willing and eager student, good-natured and hardworking, if not especially talented. She was willing to give him the benefit of the doubt.

"Thank you," she said. "I am much relieved to hear you say so."

The boy nodded, kneading his cap as if he hoped to wring the right words from it. "If you've got a taste for duck, well, then come down to Half Moon late this afternoon. Most everybody will be there." He cast a sidelong look toward them. "Could always use another canoe."

Nathaniel hesitated so long that Elizabeth grew uncomfortable.

"Thank you kindly for the invitation," she said. "We'll try to come."

"I don't see why we should not go, Nathaniel. If they are making an effort to include us—"

"You're sure that's what's on their minds?" he said, gruffly.

Elizabeth stopped to pick a handful of pink milfoil. She crushed one of the gray-green leaves and inhaled the spicy smell while she weighed her response.

"Do you think it's some kind of trap?"

He looked around for Hannah, who had hung back on the trail to examine a dead firebird. She was folding and unfolding the wing, studying the way the joints worked. With one part of her mind, Elizabeth wondered if Nathaniel noticed his daughter's preoccupation with the workings of living creatures: if it was unusual, or the normal way of Kahnyen'kehàka children. But his thoughts were elsewhere.

"They ain't quite that dumb, or desperate. Not yet. But then we ain't turned anybody off the Wolf, yet."

"Then why should we not?" She heard the impatience in her voice, and then tried to modulate her tone. "Please tell me why we should not go to the village for the duck hunt, Nathaniel."

"You tell me first why we should." His own tone bordered on the edgy.

"Because my students will be there, with their families. Because it would be good to see the Hauptmanns, and I need to talk to the McGarritys—"

"You need more society." He came to a halt in the path, for they had lost sight of Hannah.

Elizabeth laughed. "Society? Now you are being silly, Nathaniel. But it does seem to me that we need to show our faces in the village, once in a while. We must live among these people, after all."

"Your father will likely be there, and Julian."

"Father, at least," Elizabeth agreed. "I will not hide from my father, and I'm surprised that you would want me to."

Nathaniel let out a great rush of air, a sound of surrender that Elizabeth had learned to recognize. He was not convinced, but he would no longer oppose.

"I don't want you to hide from anybody, Boots." He brushed his knuckles along her cheekbone. "But I'm afraid you're in for more than you bargained for."

She caught his hand and kissed it. "I won't be there alone, will I?"

He smiled, finally. "Never for a moment."

XLIX

They came down to the village at dusk, stopping just above the lake to survey the shore. Nathaniel remembered fishing the lake as a boy. At dawn or dusk, wading in the shallows or out in the canoe he had felt like an intruder in a world crowded with fish and birds and wild of all kinds. That was before the village took hold and started to grow like a new kind of animal, jealous of its space and food.

Where now a crowd of children fed deadwood into a growing bonfire, he had once watched a hawk and an eagle wage a screaming battle over a mallard. Asleep on the shore, he had come suddenly full awake to see a bobcat drinking not twenty yards from him, all gold and sliding muscle. But now the shore was crowded with canoes and dugouts and anything that could be paddled, even a makeshift raft. Men paced back and forth, their movements jittery with excitement. Their voices rose like a buzzing on the wind.

"Like warrior ants, on the move," said Chingachgook beside him, and Nathaniel grunted in agreement.

"I don't see any guns," commented Elizabeth.

"Don't need any, for fledglings," Hawkeye said. "The wood ducks can't fly now, not the hens or the young."

He pointed out the long, marshy stretch on the opposite side of the lake, just above the village. There, reeds and cattails, cranberry bushes and drowned trees wove themselves into a watery fortress of a good half mile in length.

Elizabeth squinted into the sky. "Those are drakes, are they not? They seem quite irritated."

Mergansers sporting white ruffs like cocked hats circled above the lake, rousted from feeding by the commotion on the shore. Nathaniel felt their agitation whirling and swirling like a rising storm. He put a hand on Elizabeth's shoulder.

"It ain't pretty, this kind of hunting."

"Is any hunting?" she asked, surprised.

"By God, yes," said Hawkeye decisively. "There's a beauty to be found in tracking a deer and taking her down clean. She might outsmart you or outrun you. There's a challenge to it, and a skill."

"Perhaps I can go out with you sometime, and see for myself." Elizabeth had long been curious about Hawkeye's hunting absences.

"You make me an apple pie, I'll take you out tracking," he promised.

"Ah." Elizabeth smiled. "I knew there would be some condition."

"I will take you into the forest," Chingachgook said quietly, so that the whole party stopped short. Nathaniel looked back to see his father and grandfather shoulder to shoulder. They were so alike and so different: both of them white-haired, and straight-backed, tough old men who had outlived most of the people they had loved, but still they stood there looking at Elizabeth with real affection and admiration.

The dappled light moved on his grandfather's face and it seemed to Nathaniel almost as if the bone glimmered softly through Chingachgook's skin. He stepped toward the old man, as if he had cried out in pain. Then he realized that no one else had seen anything alarming. A waking dream, then. Not to be ignored, but not carrying the same urgency as a sleeping dream. He would talk to the women about it when they got home; they could tell him what it meant.

Chingachgook was telling Elizabeth about tracking, and what would be expected of her. "If you want to learn to listen to the deer, then I will take you. You must listen to them if you want to track them. I will teach you how to sing to them." His expression was somber, and her smile faded.

"I would like that." She sent a glance in Hawkeye's direction. "And I will learn how to make you an apple pie, anyway."

The path had been winding in and out of the wood to deposit them suddenly on a secluded corner of the lake. The men dragged a canoe out of its protected spot under a stand of redbud saplings.

"You'll have time enough to practice on that pie," Hawkeye said gruffly. "Couldn't go out after a deer now anyway, not until the rut starts; you'd end up in Anna's pantry."

"Anna's pantry?" Elizabeth laughed out loud.

"It's what we call the gaol," said Nathaniel.

"There's a gaol in Paradise? Is it ever used?"

"Oh, aye." Hawkeye nodded. "When old Dubonnet—Dirty-Knife's father—lost his temper over cards and took his tomahawk to Axel, for example. Don't look so surprised! It weren't much of a cut—Dubonnet was drunk, and Axel was fast. He's still drawing breath, after all. But they needed someplace to put Claude until they could decide what to do with him. Anna had an old pantry she didn't use much, so they put a lock on the door and that's been the gaol ever since."

Nathaniel caught a speculative glance from Elizabeth, quickly stifled when she saw herself observed.

"Just one night, Boots."

"Pardon me?" Her tone was slightly affronted. She didn't like being so easily read, but Nathaniel could no more pass up the opportunity to tease her than he could walk by her without touching her.

"I spent a night in Anna's pantry when I was fifteen. I could see you wondering."

"That sounds like a story for another day. I thought we were going to join the party?"

He gestured her into the canoe with a sweep of his arm.

Once on the lake his good humor fled quickly. In spite of the way the dusk colored the mountains and the lake reflected it all back, it looked like bad news to Nathaniel. On the far shore the men had divided themselves into the canoes, two to a craft, and paddled out in complete silence to form a fan that took in about the first third of the marsh. They hovered there, waiting for a signal from Billy Kirby.

Chingachgook had started singing, a low chant to the spirit of the lake. Above his voice Nathaniel could just hear Hawkeye explaining to Elizabeth what was about to happen. The words were indistinct, but he saw her back suddenly straighten and tense. She asked a question, but Hawkeye's answer was interrupted by a shout from the other side of the lake.

"Go to it, boys!"

The far end of the fan moved in first, penetrating the marsh as quickly as the dense growth would allow. There was a great swaying of the reeds, and then the shadows crystallized into distinct shapes: a whole army of wood duck hens with their fledgling young were being forced into the open water by the tightening wedge of canoes.

Chingachgook's melody rose and wavered over the lake as if to meet the frantic danger calls of the hens. The fledglings were paddling furiously, some of them trying to lift themselves into the air without success. Nathaniel scanned the marsh and the lake and estimated forty molting hens with broods of six or eight young, no more than a pound each in weight.

A mottled brown hen made a headlong dash for the narrowing space between two canoes just as there was another shout from Billy Kirby, and the men moved in from the other end.

They had it down to a science, all right. The man in the rear kept paddling while the one in front harvested. It was amazing to watch Billy Kirby at work: he could grab two fledglings in one fist and twist their necks so fast that all you saw was the heap of feathers as he tossed them over his shoulder into the empty middle of the canoe. All around him other men were hard at work, too, and the air filled with tender new feathers.

Some of the hens, better and faster swimmers, had made it out of the circle. Now, seeing their young attacked they rushed back, fairly lifting themselves out of the water in their fury. As they came within reach they were grabbed up, too, and dispatched without pause. In a matter of five minutes the canoes were filled with great fluttering mounds.

"At least it was over quickly," Elizabeth said on a hoarse, in-drawn breath.

But it wasn't, not yet. The first full boat had made it to the shore to be met by the women and children. As soon as it had been tipped up and emptied of its cargo, there was a high yodel of excitement, and the Cameron brothers jumped back in to paddle out again at full speed, ready for the next flushing.

"But they must have more than two hundred ducks," Elizabeth said, indignantly. "Isn't that enough?"

"They don't know the meaning of the word," Hawkeye murmured. And with a disgusted shake of his head and a nod to Nathaniel, they paddled for shore.

It was very hard to maintain a composed expression. Elizabeth forced herself to breathe in and out evenly; to answer in a normal tone of voice when she was spoken to. They found a spot to stand as far away from the bonfire and the growing mountain of dead birds as could be managed, and there she stayed, greeting her students and talking to their parents.

Against her will, her attention was drawn again and again to the spot on the shore where the women had begun the work of cleaning the birds. With the help of the oldest children, each carcass was headed, briefly bled, and then slit open without even a rudimentary plucking. The fledglings weren't good for anything except the breast meat, Anna explained to her.

Then why not let them grow into maturity? Elizabeth wanted to ask, but the sight of Anna's strong thumbs digging to separate the meat from the bone was more than she could take; she nodded and turned away as quickly as she could without giving offense.

Boats came and went, and the hill of inert bodies seemed to get larger in spite of the furious pace being set by the workers on the shore. Nathaniel and Hawkeye were talking quietly just behind her; Chingachgook had walked down the beach and stood watching silently, his blanket wrapped around him and his eyes fixed on some point on the water.

"Miz Elizabeth?"

Martha Southern stood off a few feet, her head lowered. She

had her new baby strapped to her chest with a shawl, and the little button of a face peered out at Elizabeth with perfectly round eyes. Elizabeth had not seen Martha since her return.

"Moses is out on the water," she said, as if reading Elizabeth's thoughts.

"Is that your new son?" Elizabeth asked, glad of the distraction. She had heard the story of the child's birth from Falling-Day.

"Yas'm, this is our Jeremiah. Three months old."

"Congratulations, Martha. He looks a fine, healthy boy."

"Yas'm, that he is."

She paused, and then held out a chipped wooden bowl which had been hidden in the folds of her skirt.

"Would you like some meat? It's just off the fire."

Four tiny breasts; hardly enough for a single serving. Elizabeth felt a wave of nausea rising in her throat as surely as the tide. She looked around herself in desperation, but Nathaniel and Hawkeye had moved off to join Chingachgook and Axel. With a start, she realized that her father stood just a few feet away on the rise that looked over the lake, and that his attention was on her, all frowning concentration, his disappointment and disapproval radiating in warm waves. She swallowed hard, and wiped her brow.

"Are you all right, Miz Elizabeth? Don't you care for duck?"

She shook her head, and then sat abruptly on the sand. Martha came closer, her gentle, plain face creased in concern.

"Martha," Elizabeth said softly. "Thank you very much for your kind offer, but I'll have to ask you to take that away, now. The smell—" She swallowed hard again, and met the younger woman's gaze.

"I'm in a family way, you see."

The anxiety on her face was replaced suddenly by an understanding and empathy so sweet and welcome that Elizabeth's nausea ebbed a few steps in response.

"Oh, I see. That's good news, now ain't it? Just a minute, let me put this down—" And she hurried off, only to return in just seconds with a chunk of plain bread.

"Bread always did help my stomach to settle," she explained, handing it over. Elizabeth murmured her thanks and took a small bite.

They were alone; the children were busy on the far side of the bonfire burning fingers and mouths as they plucked at the roasting meat, eating without thought or pause. The women were elbow-deep in blood and feathers. Anna made a comment and loud laughter rose over the lake in response. In the canoes the men were still at work, far up the shore. No sign of Moses Southern.

"Could I hold your baby? Just for a moment?"

Without a word, Martha reached into the cradle made of her shawl and handed him over to Elizabeth. Then she settled down on the sand next to her with her arms slung around her knees.

Elizabeth took the swaddled child into the crook of her arm and looked down at the face, rumpled now in a thoughtful way.

"He looks very serious," she said, testing the solid weight of him, warm and slightly damp and definitely thrumming with life.

"I'm afraid he takes after his pa," Martha said, and then bit her lip, nervously. She cleared her throat. "You never held one before?"

"Not one this small," Elizabeth said. "He's very . . . compact."

"Unwind him and he'll start working those arms and legs, like one of them crawlies with a hundred feet. When he starts to walking, I'm the one who'll need all that get-up-and-go."

The child opened his mouth to burble at Elizabeth. She made a similar sound back at him, and she was rewarded with a toothless smile.

"There!" said Martha. "He don't do that for everybody. Jemima is the only one he'll smile for regular, like."

When the baby's smile was replaced with a rumbling frown, Elizabeth handed him back to Martha, who looked out over the water again, scanning it warily. Then she settled the child back in the sling and opened her bodice to his seeking mouth.

"How is Jemima?" Elizabeth asked, watching closely.

"Fractious as ever," Martha said easily, casting her a sideways look.

The baby made mewling sounds, gulping noisily and waving a suddenly freed fist in the air.

"I wished I could've sent her to school again," Martha said softly. "You did her good, although I guess it didn't feel that way at the time."

"Maybe in the fall," Elizabeth said.

Martha sighed, patting the curve of the child's hip. "You don't care for this party much, do you?"

In the twilight Elizabeth looked over the beach. Everywhere there were bloody piles of half-dismembered fledglings, feathers ruffling in the breeze. Down the shore, another good-sized hill of carcasses had been abandoned, untouched.

"I don't understand, I suppose—why is it necessary to take them all?" Elizabeth immediately regretted this question, fearing that she would not be understood, or that if she were, that she would give offense.

But Martha was looking over the lake with a thoughtful expression. "I grew up in Fish Creek, did you know that? There were fourteen of us, and I was the second youngest, the only girl." She glanced at Elizabeth to see if this story was welcome, and then she murmured a soft word of encouragement to the child. "There was never enough on the table. We didn't starve, you understand, but you could never be sure of the next meal, either. You learned to be quick and to take what you could before anybody else caught you at it. Now, Moses is a harsh man at times, but there's always plenty on our table, and I know as long as he's alive I won't have to worry about how to feed my children. But Miz Elizabeth, you know, I still have this urge sometimes—when I take the corn bread out of the oven, hungry or not, I could eat the half pan standing there, and hide the rest under my pillow."

"Martha," Elizabeth said. "You could, but you do not. You have learned not to. When I look at this—" She lifted her chin toward the littered shoreline. "It seems so wasteful. Next year there will be no more wood ducks, and how sad that is."

"But of course there'll be wood ducks next year," Martha said, surprised. "There's always wood ducks. They come up in the spring, they always have and they always will. If that weren't

the case, the judge would make a law and put an end to the
ducking, ain't that so?"

There was a harsh sound just behind them. "What in hellfire
do you think you are doing, woman?" Moses Southern bellowed.

Martha launched herself to her feet. Elizabeth caught sight of
one white breast dripping milk and the outraged face of little
Jeremiah, suddenly deprived of his meal. Before she could rise,
Moses had pushed past her, advancing on Martha.

"You got no more brains than a mudpuppy! Get on home,
now, and wait for me. I'll deal with you later."

Nathaniel had appeared at Elizabeth's side. He helped her to
her feet just as Southern whirled around. With his eyes narrowed and his great nose red and swollen in irritation, he
looked almost comical. If it weren't for the fact that he would
take out his anger on Martha, Elizabeth would have laughed at
him.

"You leave my wife alone!" he shouted.

"Lower your voice, man," Nathaniel barked. "You're making a fool of yourself."

Elizabeth was aware of Hawkeye coming up behind her.

"I know what she's up to, and I won't have it!"

"We were just talking, Mr. Southern," Elizabeth said calmly.
"Nothing more."

"Tell her, Bonner. Tell her to stay away."

"I hear you myself, Mr. Southern. I think everyone in a ten-
mile radius hears you." In fact every man, woman, and child on
the lake had put aside their work to watch. At the very edge of
the crowd Elizabeth caught a glimpse of Martha, pulling her
two reluctant children away.

There was a soft clearing of a throat, and Elizabeth realized
that her father had come closer. Moses turned to him, his expression suddenly gleeful at the unexpected appearance of an
ally. But the judge only looked at him with a small frown.

"Moses," he said finally. "I suggest you go now, before you
get yourself into more trouble than you can handle."

New outrage spread over the trapper's already florid face.
"So you're taking her side, are you? She run off, stole you
blind—"

"Goddamn it, Judge. Tell him to hold his tongue." Nathaniel's face hardened into the mask she knew so well, the one that meant he was just barely keeping control of his temper.

"I am taking no one's side." The judge raised his voice slightly. "But I can see where this is headed, and I see no reason to ruin the evening for the whole village."

This drew Moses up short. He glanced around himself for the first time and saw the audience he had drawn. With a mumbled curse, he turned away and stamped off in the direction of a group of men gathered on the far side of the fire.

At the same time, Liam Kirby started toward them, convulsively twisting his cap in his hands. He stopped in front of Elizabeth.

"I'm sorry," he said, his gaze fixed firmly on his own feet.

"It's not your fault, Liam." Elizabeth tried for an encouraging smile.

"No, I'm sorry I can't come to school." He would not meet her eye, but even so she could see the bruise that covered a good part of his left cheek.

"I see," she said softly.

"Will you tell Hannah I'm sorry to miss the games?" His voice was so low that Elizabeth thought at first she had misheard him. His blush told her that she had not.

"I will tell her."

The boy nodded jerkily and then turned away, walking back to the group of men where his brother waited for him.

"Won't you come eat?" Anna called from the fire, gesturing to them. "More than enough to go around."

Her students, their faces turned toward her hopefully, fingers and mouths shiny with grease; the Camerons, the Smythes, the McGarritys, all of them willing to welcome her. John Glove came forward, speaking sensible words in a kind tone.

"Don't be chased off, now, if you'd care to stay and eat with us. He won't bother you anymore." He was a wealthy man, the owner of the mill, the owner of slaves; his children sat in her classroom.

Chingachgook stood on the shore, his expression unreadable. Behind her Nathaniel and Hawkeye were silent, waiting for her to make this decision. Elizabeth felt suddenly very weary, and unbearably sad.

"That's very kind of you, Mr. Glove," she said. "But I think we should be away home, don't you, Nathaniel?" She turned, seeking out Hawkeye's eye. He nodded at her silently.

There was not one bird or duck on the water, not as far as she could see: a new kind of wilderness. As the canoe moved into the new darkness of the evening, Chingachgook's song rose again, strong enough to be heard all around. On shore there was sudden silence. She thought, she hoped, that they were hearing the song of appeasing words to the spirit of the lake. Other words ran through her head: *In the day shalt thou make thy plant to grow, and in the morning shalt thou make thy seed to flourish: but the harvest shall be a heap in the day of grief and of desperate sorrow.* These words Elizabeth kept to herself, for the song said the same thing to anyone who would listen.

There was a screech of high laughter from the shore, and a splash as the boys tossed one of their unfortunate own into the water. The judge stood apart from the crowd, watching with his hands crossed on his back and his chin on his chest.

The breeze rose cool. Elizabeth turned her face to the sky, and out of the darkness a single mottled brown feather came twirling to brush against her cheek. She caught it in her fingers and examined it for a long minute. With hands slightly trembling, Elizabeth tucked it carefully into her bodice.

"A keepsake?" Nathaniel asked behind her.

"A reminder."

"Wasn't the most pleasant evening of your life, I'll wager."

"No," she agreed. "But perhaps it was one of the most instructive."

"Don't judge them too harsh," Nathaniel said softly. "Or yourself, either. It's going to take some time."

Chingachgook's song trailed away into the night sky, as light and soft as a feather on the cold night breeze.

Nathaniel lit a torch and they went down to the waterfall. The slick stone steps were familiar to him even in the dark, but she moved cautiously, digging with her toes into the deep green moss. Wedged between rocks to extend over the water, the torch threw a bright, rippling flower onto its dark surface.

In the sticky heat of the July night, she waited for him to go first. He submerged himself and welcomed the cold. When he surfaced she had unplaited her hair so that it swept around her hips. Her skin glowed in the faint light, whiter than the reluctant moon. Below her ribs there was the hint of a newly sloping curve to her belly, there where the child grew; between the rounded weight of her breasts a glistening of sweat.

He held out his arms and she came to him. She drew in her breath at the cold, her nipples hardening against his chest.

They swam to the falls and then dived under the rushing water to the cool darkness behind. On the other side of the flowing curtain the torch wavered and blinked like a benevolent spirit, the only light in the world. He showed her the footholds, guiding her hand to them one after the other. Then he climbed first and, reaching down, lifted her over the edge into the cave where they had first come together.

He lit another torch and made a new nest of furs against the cool damp. Wound together they shivered, and then they stopped shivering. Near sleep, she suddenly stiffened in his arms, all her focus and attention turned inward. She took his hand and put it on her belly, hushed him when he tried to speak. He felt it then: the soft tumbling that was the child announcing itself, a swimmer in a quiet sea.

She fell asleep with her hair drying into curls around her face. Nathaniel listened to the rhythm of her breathing, but he lay awake himself for a long time, thinking about her. Her pleasure in the children she taught; her endless patience with them. Her disappointment and impatience with the parents of those children. She had the knack of righteous indignation without bitterness, but for how long? Nathaniel wrapped a strand of her hair around his finger to tie her to him and wondered how long she could tolerate living in Paradise.

L

"Good God. They are talking of trying the queen of France as an enemy of the state."

Nathaniel produced a questioning sound around his spoonful of porridge.

Elizabeth never looked up from Mr. Schuyler's copy of the *Gentlemen's Periodical*. "The Jacobins. They will end up putting her to the guillotine as they did the king. Is there no end to this insanity?" She pushed her bowl away to make more room for the newspaper, her eyes flying greedily over the small print.

The housekeeper hovered, clucking nervously.

"Boots, eat your food," Nathaniel said. "Mrs. Vanderhyden here will fuss herself into an apoplexy if she thinks she's sent you off without a decent meal. Imagine how she'd explain herself to Mrs. Schuyler."

Elizabeth cast a distracted but apologetic look toward the housekeeper, and then reluctantly put down the paper to pick up her spoon.

"You said you were looking forward to the news," Nathaniel reminded her. "Guess you didn't think so much would be afoot."

She swallowed hastily. "Well, yes. The yellow fever epidemic in Philadelphia is truly horrifying, Nathaniel. So many have died. And then there is this Monsieur Genet from the revolutionary government—if half of this is true, he is a revolution unto himself. He is determined to pull this country into the European war, and on France's side." Elizabeth looked out the window to Catherine Schuyler's manicured garden. It seemed so peaceful here, but she was beginning to believe that peace could never be anything more than a deceptive lull in an ongoing storm. "The revolution seemed such a hopeful thing in the beginning. I can hardly imagine what it's turned into."

"I can," Nathaniel said. "Listen, Boots. I don't want to say it ain't important, what's going on in the world. But we've got a few things here to work through today." With his chin he gestured to the unopened letter on the table.

When they had come to the Schuylers' Albany estate the evening before, they had found two letters. Elizabeth had read the one from Mrs. Schuyler straightaway: it was all apologies for the family's absence, instructions on how to best enjoy herself in Albany, and a three-times-repeated invitation for them to stop at Saratoga on their way home. The second letter was from her aunt Merriweather; it was still unopened.

"I will read it later today, when our business is concluded," she said. "It will be easier then."

Nathaniel touched her knee under the table.

"We'll manage this, Boots. We've managed worse."

Elizabeth shook her head while she drank the last of her tea. "I will believe that when we have put the breach-of-promise suit behind us."

They left the neat grounds of the Schuyler estate and walked through fields that bordered the Hudson, thick with growing wheat and rye, corn and beans, separated by rows of gnarled apple trees standing sentry. Behind it all, boats moved along the Hudson so that their sails seemed to skim the sea of grain. The sky was wider here without the mountains and in it the clouds skittered along as if to keep up with the sailboats.

Albany in the late summer was almost as unpleasant a place as London, Elizabeth thought as they made their way along Ferrington Street into the center of the city. They had come on business that could not wait, and she would be happy to leave as soon as they possibly could. The roads were crowded with housemaids swinging baskets on red-chapped arms; peddlers hawking sticky peaches, sugar-sweet melons, wilted kale; young women in watered silks with feathered parasols tilted against the sun; River Indians dressed in fringed buckskin and top hats; slaves hauling bales of rags and herding goats. It was not so dirty and crowded as New-York had been, that was true. There was a pleasing tidiness to the brick houses with their steeply tiled roofs and bright curtains, but still the humid air reeked of sewage, burning refuse, pig slurry, and horse dung. Elizabeth swallowed hard and put her handkerchief to her nose and mouth, wondering to herself that she had forgotten what cities were like in such a short time. Three months in the wilderness had changed her, stolen her patience for the realities of a crowded life.

To her further surprise, Nathaniel seemed at ease. Men leaned over half doors to call out a welcome, dropped their tools to come into the street and talk to him, wiping dirty hands on leather aprons. Nathaniel touched the small of her back as he introduced her. "My bride," he said so many times she lost count. "My bride, Elizabeth." It caused her both a great deal of pleasure and acute embarrassment. She had never minded being called a spinster: there was something solid and rational about the word, and she had made it her own. But never had she imagined herself as a bride; she still could not, although it pleased her endlessly that Nathaniel saw her thus.

She rediscovered what she had first learned from the Schuylers at Saratoga: Nathaniel's reputation spread far over the territory and was larger than she could comprehend. Before they reached the main market square they had had four invitations to come and stay and countless invitations to dinner. Elizabeth collected shy looks from bachelor farmers, appreciative appraisals from merchants and calculating glances from their wives and daughters, some of them directed openly to her waist. What she carried there was not visible to the world at large, not when she was fully dressed—but they saw what they wanted to, and nodded to each other knowingly.

Total strangers seemed to know things about her.

"Don't look so surprised, Boots," Nathaniel had said after

an old trapper by the name of Johanson had inquired after her time in the bush. "This always was a town with an appetite for gossip, and we gave them enough to talk about in the spring."

"Richard gave them enough to talk about," Elizabeth amended. "I shudder to think what they must have heard of me."

"Well, now." He frowned. "I expect that your running off to marry me is only part of your reputation. They'll be thinking of Lingo, too."

She pulled up short. "What does anyone here know about that?"

Nathaniel put a hand out to take her elbow and came in closer.

"Elizabeth," he said calmly. "News like that has legs. It'll get up and walk itself across the territory in no time at all. I know, I know you don't like the idea, but if it's any comfort to you, nobody thinks badly of you. You found a real good way to make these men take you seriously—haven't you noticed?"

"I was hoping for respect," she said. "Not fear."

"They go together, around here."

"What the women must be saying—"

He pulled up, and turned her to him. "Did you look at Jane Morgan when I introduced her just now? Did you see her kerchief under a hat, in this heat?"

"I don't understand your point."

"This looks like a city to you, Boots, but this place has been in the middle of one war after another since the first Dutchman put up a hut and called it home. You see that fort over there on the island? That's there for a reason. Jane survived a scalping. I don't doubt she killed a man or two herself. I know my mother did. Women living in these parts learned how to handle weapons and they used them, or they didn't last long."

In the middle of the crowded street he put an arm around her and his cheek to her hair. "This ain't London, although it may stink as bad at times. Now will you stop fretting?"

"I'll try," she said against his shoulder.

"That'll do, Boots. I couldn't ask for any more than that."

.   .   .   .

Judge van der Poole had a goiter that rested on his bony neck like a perky second head, a fact which might have been easier to overlook if he did not have the habit of stroking it thoughtfully as he read the papers before him. His small red mouth pursed in thought, he petted and prodded the growth until Elizabeth had to look away to retain her composure.

He had received them in his home, most probably at Mr. Bennett's urging, Elizabeth thought. It was certainly more pleasant than the courthouse would have been. The thick walls and batten-shuttered windows made the house cool and dim; it smelled of smoked ham and beeswax and freshly pressed linen. The hearth was surrounded by ceramic tiles in a white and blue pattern that matched exactly the colors of the rugs on the brightly polished wood plank floors. It was a comfortable house without pretensions, in spite of the elevated position of the householder. Elizabeth found herself relaxing while Judge van der Poole read through the pile of papers before him at leisure.

When he finally spoke, it came as a surprise. "Mr. Bennett, I'm going to talk to Mrs. Bonner directly, if she will allow me."

"I think you'll find her very capable of dealing with your questions directly," Mr. Bennett murmured before Elizabeth could voice this sentiment herself.

Judge van der Poole paused to pat his goiter thoughtfully. "If we understand correctly, Mrs. Bonner," he began, peering at her from over the rims of his spectacles. "You are asking the court to dismiss the breach-of-promise suit brought against you by Dr. Richard Todd."

She allowed that this was true, and in response he went back to the paperwork, tilting his head to one side with his mouth tightly pursed.

"Most unusual, you realize. A very delicate business, this. First the defendant was not to be found, and now the plaintiff has gone missing. You have the support of some very prominent citizens, I note, but still, Dr. Todd has his rights. I think I must ask Mrs. Bonner to tell us her story from the beginning," he said. "Without her husband in the room. If he doesn't object." It was not a question.

Elizabeth felt Nathaniel's hand on her shoulder, the strong

fingers pressing briefly. He spoke a few low words with Mr. Bennett, and then he left their fate to her.

There was a little boy in the next garden, building a fort out of bits of cast-off wood mortared together with mud and straw. Nathaniel sat down in the shade of an oak where he could watch him work. The shuttered windows of the van der Poole parlor were at his back; when the wind was right he could hear only the rise and fall of voices. She was doing most of the talking, in an easy tone.

It could go wrong; they knew that. The judge could order them to sell the mountain to Richard, or he could void both the deed of gift and the land transfer. No one would be able to lift a finger, not even Philip Schuyler. Richard would come back to Paradise to find that they had done his work for him: Hidden Wolf back in Middleton's hands; Richard determined to have it. Nathaniel would be back where he started, except he wouldn't. He would still have Elizabeth for his wife and nothing could change that.

Sometimes he tired of it, the whole long battle for one small corner of the forest when so much had been lost already by the Kahnyen'kehàka.

The little boy's curls twirled around his head in the breeze. He glanced up at Nathaniel with eyes as green as the flickering leaves, tugged on a curl that fell over his forehead, and then frowned at his handiwork. With a sigh he got up and disappeared around a corner to come back with his fists full of kindling.

Nathaniel loosened the neck of his shirt another notch and made himself more comfortable against the broad back of the oak, glad of the breeze and the shade. A rider passed and hooves struck the cobblestones in a hollow rhythm. In the next garden the little boy began to hum over his work, tunelessly. Elizabeth's voice rose and fell in counterpoint, as familiar to him now as the sound of his own heartbeat. At odd moments there was the sound of the Hudson, not a quarter of a mile off, rushing south to the sea.

He dreamed of Chingachgook on the river, paddling by

torchlight. Suspended over the world as he coasted on the wind, Nathaniel watched the old man sing his hunting song, calling the deer to him. A buck appeared on the shore as if he had been waiting for this summons all of his life and swam toward the canoe, his eyes reflecting red and gold in the torchlight. Chingachgook raised his gun and his voice broke, a different rhythm now: his own death song. The river twisted and turned, and Chingachgook disappeared. In his place, Elizabeth floated on the waters of the Great River, her arms beating like wings and her hair spread around her in a halo. Her white body was swollen great with child. The river turned her like a log, darkening her skin to the color of tarnished copper as she rolled, changing her shape, uncoiling her hair. Sarah, now. Sarah's face, and in her lifeless arms, a baby, a too-still baby neither white nor red but mottled gold and chestnut and a deep earth color, a neck ringed in bruised greens and blues. Dark hair ruffled like down in the breeze.

Nathaniel woke with a start, his heart beating in his throat. She was there, kneeling next to him.

"You were dreaming." Her face was furrowed with concern. "I've never seen you sleep in the day like this."

He put his hands on her, wordlessly.

"What is it?" She caught his hands, held them still. "What is the matter?"

"Nothing," he muttered. "Just a dream." *Just a dream.* He rubbed a hand over his face. "What happened with van der Poole?"

Elizabeth cast a glance over her shoulder toward Bennett. He studied his shoe buckles, his hands crossed at the small of his back.

"There is good news," she began. "He seems to believe that Richard is alive and that we are not responsible for his absence. But neither will he dismiss the lawsuit."

"Damn."

She closed her eyes briefly. "All is not lost. He has set a court date in September. If Richard does not appear for that, then his claim will be automatically dismissed."

"It is a formality, I think," said Bennett. "He is well disposed toward you or he would not have asked us to join him for dinner. It is a good sign."

"Elizabeth doesn't seem to think so, not by the look on her face." Nathaniel rose, and helped her to her feet.

"I am not sure one way or the other," she said. "I suppose it will depend on the dinner conversation."

"Your condition is enough cause for us to stay away, if you don't care to go," Nathaniel said.

Mr. Bennett looked between them. "What is this? Good tidings?" He cleared his throat. "Well, then, Mrs. Bonner. You should certainly stay away if it will distress you, given your hopeful expectations."

She managed a thin smile. "Do you think that we can really risk the judge's goodwill?"

When Mr. Bennett did not immediately respond, she nodded. "Your silence speaks quite loudly. Well, I will cope. But first I need to go to the shops."

"You require a dress for this evening," Mr. Bennett guessed.

"I require spectacles," said Elizabeth. "And a supply of new quills."

Because they did not have any other molds, Run-from-Bears had melted down about twenty pounds of the Tory Gold in a makeshift forge and cast a fortune in bullets. These Nathaniel had been carrying in double-sewn leather pouches next to his skin since they left Paradise, ten pounds on each side. In Johnstown this unusual currency would have caused a stir, but Albany was a town built on some two hundred years of high intrigue and trading shenanigans. Comfortable Dutch and British merchants had made large fortunes running illegal furs from Canada, reselling silver spoons stolen in Indian raids on New England families much like their own, and bartering second-grade wampum and watered rum for all the ginseng root the native women could dig up, which they then traded to the Orient at an outrageous profit. A sack of golden bullets would raise nothing more in an Albany merchant than his blood pressure.

Gold went for seventeen dollars an ounce on the open market; Nathaniel stipulated sixteen and the doors to the city's warehouses opened to him on well-oiled hinges. If the merchants of Albany had ever heard rumors of Tory Gold, or been told of the state's keen interest in recovering that treasure, they were struck with a sudden and thorough epidemic of forgetfulness which would last until they estimated that Nathaniel had exhausted his resources.

Elizabeth had followed the trading quietly, but she had not missed a step of what went on; Nathaniel was sure of it. She watched with narrowed eyes as he negotiated the exchange of one bag of gold for a note signed by Leendert Beekman, not the biggest or most successful merchant in Albany, but one of the few Nathaniel trusted. While his clerks took care of Nathaniel's requests, from gunpowder, flints, and pig iron to hair ribbons and a bag of peppermint drops for Hannah, Beekman took Elizabeth's list and waited on her personally, measuring flour and sprigged lawn, sewing needles and China tea. He produced a display case of spectacles, spread out spools of thread and brass buttons for her examination, and debated with her the relative qualities of various kinds of ink. When she had chosen three dozen new quills, he produced a sheet of paper and showed Elizabeth his latest acquisition: an artificial quill. A mahogany stem was inset with carved ivory, and tapered down to a nib of copper and silver. A magical contrivance that would hold more ink than a quill, and never need to be sharpened.

She held it as another woman might hold a jewel she believed to be too extravagant to even contemplate owning. With a small smile, Elizabeth returned the pen to Beekman and thanked him for his trouble.

With their purchases wrapped for delivery and Beekman's note firmly in hand, they went to the bank, where a bored clerk with a mulish mouth and tobacco-stained fingers counted out the money in a combination of Spanish, British, Dutch, and New-York currencies, muttering exchange rates under his breath and scribbling out an accounting as he went along. Nathaniel arranged for a good amount of this money to be paid into the account of a Mr. James Scott. To his surprise, Elizabeth excused herself during the process and went to speak to the bank manager without him. Walking back to the Schuyler estate with five hundred dollars in notes and silver and his hand resting lightly on his rifle, he managed to curb his curiosity.

"Why James Scott?" Elizabeth asked. "Could not Runs-from-Bears use his own name?"

He cast a surprised glance in her direction. "Bears never goes into the bank. They wouldn't let an Indian do business there, Boots."

She drew up, flushed with surprise and indignation. "But why not, if he has money to deposit? The funds from the silver—" She glanced around herself and dropped her voice. "They are kept in that bank? I assume you were repaying the funds you borrowed from the silver mine in the spring?"

"Yes."

"Then who is James Scott?"

"I am. I do the banking for Runs-from-Bears. It's just a name, Boots."

Elizabeth shook her head. "I fear I will never understand this business."

"You could understand it well enough, Boots. You might never like it much. You realize the treasury could show up at our door tomorrow," he warned her once again. "Sooner or later somebody's going to start talking about this gold we're spending so freely, and they'll come looking for the five-guinea pieces."

"I am not worried," Elizabeth said, straightening her shoulders. "I will just tell them you married me for my money."

"That'll do the trick, all right," Nathaniel said sourly.

In their room, Elizabeth put a small purse in Nathaniel's hands, along with a sheet of paper covered closely with her strong, upright handwriting.

"Four hundred dollars, as agreed. In notes. I hope that is satisfactory. And a bill of sale for the schoolhouse, for your signature."

He knew better than to show surprise. Nathaniel read the offered document carefully; he read it again in order to gather his thoughts.

"Mr. Schuyler arranged for the withdrawal. And Mr. Bennett reviewed the bill of sale and made a suggestion or two. They were both most helpful."

"So I see. Did you withdraw all of your aunt Merriweather's funds?"

She raised an eyebrow.

"Never mind, Boots. Idle curiosity killed the cat, I'm told. Give me something to write with, and we'll see this done."

"Wait," she said suddenly, and she turned on her heel and left the room. Nathaniel was just thinking of following her when she reappeared ushering before her a mystified Mrs. Vanderhyden and Mr. MacIntyre, who ran the estate for the Schuylers while they spent their summer at Saratoga.

"We need witnesses."

When all parties had signed the document and they were alone again, she sat down on the edge of the broad bed and let out a sigh of relief, and then lay back with an arm across her face.

"Thank you."

"Don't mention it. Now I'll have to figure out what to spend this money on. Don't think I've ever had so much cash and nothing to do with it."

She peeked at him over the edge of her arm. "If you'd like to make an investment, I have something to suggest."

He grinned at her. "I was thinking of a new rifle, but I expect you'll have a better idea. What is it?"

Elizabeth shook her head. "I'm not ready to tell you yet. Hopefully tomorrow, before we leave for home."

Nathaniel lay down next to her and pulled her face up to his, traced her eyebrow with his finger. "I'll let you lead me astray tomorrow." His hand slid down her arm and up her side, probing softly with his thumb for the curve of her breast. "If you'll let me do the same for you today."

"I wasn't made for fancy clothes," he said, picking at his shirt-front. The coat, borrowed from John Bradstreet's wardrobe, was cut in severe lines, tight-sleeved and swallow-tailed, and slightly too narrow across the shoulders. Nathaniel flexed his arms in protest.

"I beg to disagree," Elizabeth said, her head tilted to one side. Under the softly gathered, high-waisted skirt—borrowed again from the selection Mrs. Vanderhyden had provided—one toe tapped softly. She brushed a hand across his shoulder.

The color suited him: deep black against the fine Holland linen, with a modestly folded jabot at the neck. The fawn-colored breeches fit him better than the coat, and they were far less discreet than his usual buckskin leggings: every muscle was visible when he moved. His hair was brushed back smooth away from his brow and gathered into a neat tail. The combination of his deeply tanned face above the startling white linen and the twirling silver earring leant him a dangerous air, which he supplemented with a scowl.

"I can't deny that you look pretty, Boots. But I like you better in doeskin with your legs bare and your hair plaited. I hardly know how to put my hands on you."

"As you've had your hands on me quite a lot today, I find it hard to sympathize." She tugged on the lace shawl tucked into the deeply cut bodice in a vain attempt to cover more of her bosom. "Rest assured, I do not enjoy this any more than you do. If I had my way I would spend the evening in bed. Reading," she added in response to his grin. "But it seems we have entered into the world of high finance and intrigue, and I suppose we must play out the game."

"I never realized you were so ambitious."

"It comes from marrying into money."

He grunted, and picked up his rifle to hook the sling over his shoulder. "Let's go on then and put it behind us."

"You are going armed to an evening party?"

"I'm going nowhere without Deerkiller, Boots. You'll have to put up with both of us barbarians at the table." One brow went up in a sharply defiant angle, and Elizabeth realized suddenly that Nathaniel truly dreaded what was before them.

Among the odds and ends on the dresser, she caught sight of the eagle feather which he normally wore in his hair. Elizabeth reached up on tiptoe and quickly knotted it into the simple black band that bound the long queue at the nape of his neck.

Nathaniel looked at himself in the mirror and rewarded her with a wolfish grin.

Elizabeth was relieved to find that the party of jurists and merchants she had anticipated was not to materialize. Instead she found herself in the company of a small group of French immigrants, aristocrats fleeing the fury of the mob that had taken over in France. Simon Desjardins and Pierre Pharoux were on their way to found a settlement on the western frontier. Her first impulse was to sit down with these Frenchmen and hear directly about the revolution in their homeland, but an introduction to Judge van der Poole's last guest put this out of her mind completely.

Mr. Samuel Hench was presented to her as a Baltimore printer on business in Albany. He had delivered a number of volumes to the judge, and been asked to stay to dinner. By the quality of his dress Elizabeth saw that he was very wealthy, and by its plainness, that he was Quaker. He was a large man, broad in the shoulder, with sharp features at odds with the mild expression of his blue eyes. Above a high forehead his hair was iron-gray.

"Mrs. Bonner," he murmured. "Mr. Bonner. Fate has brought us together this evening, for otherwise I would have come to look for thee. Or I should say, I would have been looking for a Miss Middleton, formerly of Oakmere."

Elizabeth could see the watchful tension in Nathaniel's face, and so she spoke for them both. "And why is that, Mr. Hench?"

"Because it would be remiss of me to be in this part of the world and not pay my respects to Caroline Middleton's daughter."

"You knew my mother?" Elizabeth smiled with relief.

He bowed briefly. "I knew her as Caroline Clarke, before her marriage to thy father. Her mother—your grandmother—was my aunt Mathilde, my mother's sister."

Nathaniel found himself between the Frenchmen. They had so many stories about their adventures to date, and so many questions about the western frontier that van der Poole's good food grew cold on his plate. Listening to the plans they laid out for him in detail, plans which were both daring and wildly under-

informed to the point of recklessness, Nathaniel grew both
alarmed and annoyed. But they were sincere and they saw the
things around them for what they were rather than for the price
they might fetch. He would have liked them, under other circumstances, so Nathaniel fought the impulse to give them the
whole truth in one lump and watch them choke on it. In another setting, with other company, he would have told them
the worst of what they would face, from impassable rivers to the
Seneca, who would not stand idly by and watch their hunting
grounds divided up among yet more O'seronni.

Far down the table on its other side, Elizabeth was deep in
conversation with Samuel Hench. She had that concentrated
look about her, the one that came over her when she was
reading, or listening to Hannah. Nathaniel took another forkful
of bass and onion pie, trying at the same time to turn his attention to the story he was being told of the Frenchmen's cold
reception in Philadelphia.

"Your secretary of state did not even offer us seats when we
came to call on him. He was openly hostile to our plans to
bring our families and colleagues here from France."

Mr. Bennett had been following the conversation without
taking part, but now he put down his glass with a small thump.

"Pardon me, gentlemen, but I do find that hard to credit.
Mr. Jefferson has spent a great deal of time in France, after all. If
his patience is short right now with you or your countrymen, it
will have to do with the fact that your Minister Genet has been
outfitting privateers to attack the British Navy in our waters.
But Mr. Jefferson's love of things French is legendary."

Pharoux was not going to back down. "I had great hopes of
him for exactly that reason," he said. "You see, I am an archi-
tect and an engineer, monsieur. I hoped that he and I would
have some common ground on which to build an understanding. But it seems we are not the right sort of Frenchmen. We
are on the wrong side of the revolution, and do not deserve to
keep our heads."

His voice had not risen, but his emotion caught Elizabeth's
attention.

"I for one am glad that you have kept your heads," she said.
"And I see no reason that you should not make a home here for

yourselves. But I am an immigrant myself, of course. It is easy to be generous with that which one does not possess." She hesitated, and Nathaniel knew she was wondering who might now be living on those lands these men had so easily claimed for their own.

Desjardins raised a hand in a conciliatory gesture. "Madame, I beg you to excuse my colleague's temper. It has been a difficult process, trying to make our way in this country. Last week we rented a carriage from a livery not so very far from here, at the cost of one dollar per day—"

"That is a reasonable price," interjected van der Poole, his hands folded across his ample belly and his head resting comfortably on his goiter.

"Yes, indeed. But not until we returned the rig were we told that we owed another dollar each day for the use of the horse. A miserable animal I might add, prone to crow-hop."

Nathaniel cleared his throat. "Let me guess. That would have been Morgan Blake's livery on Black Creek."

The Frenchmen glanced at each other. "You see, Mr. Bonner. We require the assistance of a good guide, an informed man with experience, if we are to make a home for ourselves and our families."

"You do," Nathaniel agreed. "But I ain't the right man for that job."

"Can we not tempt you and your good lady with land? We have two hundred thousand acres of prime forest and pastureland, on the shores of Lake Ontario—" Pharoux's enthusiasm rose as quickly as his temper.

"The survey is not complete," interrupted Desjardins. "But we have every reason to believe that the property is as it has been described to us. We call our settlement Castorland, for we are told that there is a great abundance of beaver. Would you not be interested in joining us to expand your holdings?"

Nathaniel felt van der Poole's attention focusing on him, waiting to see how he would react to this offer of yet more land, when he had just married into a thousand acres.

"We are well settled where we are," Nathaniel said. "I'm sure the judge can recommend a good man who's interested in going west."

The servant approached with a platter of beef, and Desjardins took a generous portion. "We are on our way tomorrow to visit Mr. Schuyler at Saratoga. He has a guide in mind, I am told."

Elizabeth's eyes darted between the men; Nathaniel could almost see her thoughts, the questions rising like bubbles to the surface, but her cousin stepped in with a question before she could find a way to get started.

"Speaking of travel, when wilt thou return to Paradise?" Hench asked. "Perhaps I could travel with thee. I have a few days, and I would like to visit with the rest of the family there."

Nathaniel made it clear to Samuel Hench that he was more than welcome to accompany them to Paradise, if he had his own horse and cared to leave tomorrow.

"So soon?" asked the judge, sitting forward. "You've only been in Albany two days."

"We need to be at home," Nathaniel said. He shifted uncomfortably. Having called the afternoon's dream to mind, he could not easily put it away again.

"We have heard nothing yet of your travels through the bush, Mrs. Bonner."

Pharoux's fork clattered onto his plate. "You have traveled through the bush, madame?"

"Mrs. Bonner has been all the way to Canada and back again," the judge offered.

"But this is wonderful!" cried Desjardins. "My wife planned to stay behind because we heard that the journey was too arduous for women. But perhaps if you would speak to her, Mrs. Bonner—"

"I would tell her to stay with her children in Albany." Elizabeth's fingers strained white on the stem of her wineglass. "I would tell her to wait until you and your colleagues have made a suitable home for her."

Desjardins' face fell.

"It was difficult for thee then, cousin?" Samuel Hench's question was fueled by concern rather than bald curiosity, and in response the line of Elizabeth's jaw softened, and she lowered her chin.

"It was the most difficult and the most important experience of my life," she said. "I will never be the same again."

"I see thy mother in thy nature," Hench said with a distant smile. "In thee is the same combination of fire and ice that ruled her, and in the end caused her to leave the Life to join Alfred Middleton in the wilderness."

The room fell quiet at this, and he seemed to realize what he had said. He bowed his head.

"Pardon me, cousin. I am too familiar."

"No, not at all." Elizabeth's voice was hoarse. "My mother may have left the Friends to marry my father, but she stayed a Quaker in her heart. Enough so that I value the truth, and would not have you apologize for speaking it."

Judge van der Poole said, "Since we are speaking so plainly to one another, and have come to such an understanding, then perhaps Mrs. Bonner will satisfy my curiosity. I know I have not been very clever in disguising it. Jack Lingo has long been a problem to us all, and I would like to know if I can thank you for removing that particular thorn from my side. Will you tell us what happened to you?"

Nathaniel watched her over the edge of his wineglass. She might simply silence the judge with a withering look, but some part of him hoped that she would not. It would do her good, to tell this story in this small group of men who were ready and even eager to find favor with her. Maybe then she could be done with this business, finally. She sought out his gaze.

"Boots," he said, as if they were alone. "It's your story to tell."

And so she told it, slowly at first with hesitations that had all of the men in the room leaning forward, their eyes reflecting candlelight and curiosity. She searched out her words carefully, looking down into her lap at times with a small frown. At the worst of it, she crossed her arms across her belly and met Nathaniel's eye. When she was finished, there was a small silence. Even the servants seemed to be paralyzed, until the judge gestured for more wine.

"Mrs. Bonner," began Desjardins in a subdued voice. "You are an amazing woman, if I may say so. But there is one thing you have not told us, and if I do not ask I will always be curious."

She raised a brow, not directly in encouragement, but neither did she turn away.

"What happened to Dutch Ton, as you call him? Did you find his body in the clearing when you returned there with your young Mohawk friend?"

"No," she said. "We did not. Otter found his trail, but there was no time to follow it. Dutch Ton is either dead in the bush, or he will make himself known one day."

"Does this frighten you?" asked Samuel Hench.

She shook her head. "He saved my life, once. I don't have any reason to believe that he would come after me in anger."

But Nathaniel had seen her tilt her chin like that before, and he knew how to read her anxiety. Maybe better than she did herself.

Samuel Hench accompanied them back to the Schuyler estate under a velvet dark sky. Van der Poole had lent them a lantern, and it swung back and forth on its handle with a steady squeak. Walking in a bobbing pool of light with the men on either side of her, Elizabeth enjoyed the fresh night air after the long hours in close company, as tired as she was. Samuel Hench was a surprise, but a pleasant one, and she wished for more time to spend with him.

"Didst thou not wish to talk to me of a business matter, cousin?"

She felt Nathaniel's surprise even though his face gave none of it away.

Elizabeth began slowly. "You are still in the Life?"

"I am."

"I would like to engage your help in a fairly delicate matter." She paused. "To be blunt, I would like you to act as my agent where I need to remain anonymous. The first step is to provide you with the necessary funds, and the second step is that you stop in Johnstown and visit a blacksmithy in the vicinity of the courthouse. Then there is more business of the same kind for you in Paradise with a slaveholder by the name of Glove, if you will see this through to the end."

She laid out her plan. Even in the simplest terms, it sounded fantastic and, she feared, self-interested. But for many weeks, even for months, she had been wondering how best to do what she felt she must do, and now that there was no lack of funds, and a means to her end, she could not be still. If Nathaniel objected to the large amount of money she proposed to spend, there was no sign of it. She thought that if she dared look at him she might even find him smiling.

Her cousin was another matter. It was a large plan, and perhaps too ambitious. Unfortunately, his face stayed in shadow and she could not judge his reaction.

"Thou realizes that each of the men will bring a price of somewhere around three hundred dollars? Is the blacksmith well trained?"

"I expect that he is, I have no direct knowledge of him." Elizabeth stopped and put something in Samuel Hench's hand. "When you speak to him alone, please call him Joshua, and give him this." The pale stone in the center of Joe's bijou flashed once in the lantern light. "If he would like to come see us in Paradise, we will tell him what we know of the death of the man who gave us this for him."

Samuel Hench nodded thoughtfully. "I will invite him to accompany me to Paradise, if he so chooses. I understand that the two young slaves at the Glove mill can read and write, and keep books. And they are skilled managers?"

"That is perhaps a bit too much to claim, but they are both capable and hard workers, and with considerable talents."

Nathaniel's silence was becoming more noticeable. She tried to gauge his mood with a sideways glance, and saw him lost in thought. Samuel Hench was concerned with the details of the task she set before him, and seemed not to notice.

"Just two more issues, cousin. First, there are no further directions for me on the matter of the others, just that three young women be given their freedom. Have I understood thee correctly?"

She nodded. "I will leave the matter of who, and under what circumstances, to your discretion. I do not wish to know any names, unless this becomes necessary for some other reason. But it is quite important to me that for each of the young men who are given their freedom, one young woman is given the same opportunity."

There was another long and comfortable silence. Finally Samuel Hench stopped, and turned to them.

"Nathaniel, how dost thou feel about this plan of thy wife's? It will cost something close to two thousand dollars before it is done."

"We can afford it," Nathaniel said easily. "At the moment, at any rate."

She squeezed his arm thankfully and said nothing.

"Well, then. It is a worthwhile undertaking and I will make it my Cause, under one condition. The young women will need support after they are released. Help setting up a home, and provisions, and some kind of meaningful work. Husbands, eventually. I will take on responsibility for their settling well, after thy funds have bought their freedom."

Elizabeth nodded without hesitation. "That would be a relief to me. I do not mind so much how it is done, cousin, as long as it is done. And as long as it is done without knowledge of my—or our—participation. I do not wish these people to feel any obligation to us and I do not want to further complicate our position in Paradise. We have enough to deal with as it is."

Samuel Hench smiled, finally. "If thy purpose were not wholly laudable, cousin, I might be tempted to call thee devious."

Elizabeth felt Nathaniel's arm tense under her hand. She thought he would laugh out loud at this, and was preparing to pinch him when she realized that his attention was suddenly focused elsewhere. At first Elizabeth heard nothing but the river and the night wind in the corn, but the hair on her arms and the nape of her neck rose and she felt the danger there in the pit of her belly, as keenly as she felt the child rise and kick weakly in protest at her sudden silence.

Hench wore no weapons, but Nathaniel's rifle made a solid enough sound as he swung it into his hands.

"Who goes there?" His voice traveled in the dark like an arrow.

"It's me, Nathaniel," came a female voice from the darkness behind the Schuylers' gate. Many-Doves appeared in the circle of lantern light. "Put that down, for God's sake. I've been waiting for hours. That old Dutch woman wouldn't tell me where you were."

"My God," Elizabeth said. "What has happened?"

Many-Doves said, "There's trouble. Bears was afraid to leave the other women alone, and so I came on horseback."

Nathaniel reached her in one stride. "Tell me."

"Billy Kirby arrested your father for taking a buck out of season."

"Billy Kirby?" In amazement and outrage, Elizabeth found her voice.

Many-Doves nodded. "He was voted sheriff the day you left the village."

Elizabeth made a noise of protest, but Nathaniel was focused, as he always was, on the more important issue. The anger would come later. "He's locked up?"

"Since last night." Many-Doves sent a significant glance to Samuel Hench.

"My cousin," Elizabeth said, distracted.

"This is not the time for introductions," Samuel said with a small bow, and retreated into the shadows on the other side of the road. When he was out of earshot, Many-Doves continued, speaking directly to Nathaniel.

"Chingachgook may have walked the path by now; he was injured or they would have taken him, too." And then in a rush: "The judge fined them each a hundred dollars or a week in Anna's pantry, but we didn't have it, Nathaniel. Your grandfather wouldn't let us use the gold—" Again an uncomfortable look toward Samuel Hench, but his back remained firmly turned. "And Bears said it was too dangerous to use the silver. He thinks that's what they were hoping for, with this trick. So I came after you. Do you have that much cash?"

"There's enough cash," Nathaniel said. "But maybe not enough time. I'll have to ride hard. I'll wake MacIntyre and borrow a horse."

Elizabeth said, "If we can borrow one horse we can borrow two."

"Boots." His fingers pressed so hard into her upper arms that she winced, but he held her gaze. "You can't ride hard, you know that. Not astride, I won't let you risk it."

Flooded with frustration and disappointment, Elizabeth bowed her head. He was right; she could not risk a full day's ride at the pace he would set.

"You and Many-Doves come with the wagon, and don't dawdle. I'll need you there."

It was hard to swallow; it was hard even to breathe. Just weeks ago she had sworn she would not be separated from him again; it seemed that this place still had lessons to teach her. She could not put aside the image of Chingachgook, wounded and perhaps dying while his son sat in a makeshift gaol. She pressed Nathaniel's hands, and nodded.

LI

Samuel Hench accompanied them as far as Fort Hunter, where they would cross the Mohawk. Standing at the bank of the river while they waited for the ferry, he offered to put off his business in Johnstown in order to see them home to Paradise.

"Thank you kindly, but we will manage very well," Elizabeth said, too distracted and worried to go to much trouble reassuring him. To her relief, he did not take offense or argue with her; he simply went down the embankment to negotiate the crossing.

"The river is running fast," Many-Doves observed. She had been very quiet since they set out at first light, talking only when Samuel Hench was out of earshot or when Elizabeth asked her a direct question. Whether this was worry for what was happening in Paradise, or a simple distrust of a man she did not know, Elizabeth could not tell. But she was right: the river was running fast. Elizabeth watched the ferryman, a Kahnyen'kehàka called Tall-Man, shake his head vigorously in response to Samuel Hench's request. Elizabeth felt her stomach go hollow at the idea of a delay.

"If we can't cross today—" she began. But Many-Doves handed her the reins and jumped off the wagon before she could finish her thought. Her plaits bumped on her back as she ran light-footed down to the ferry. Elizabeth could not hear what she said to Tall-Man, but she saw him listen to Doves and finally nod his head, reluctantly.

"I do not like it," Samuel Hench said when Elizabeth had joined them there. "It is too dangerous. I promised thy husband that I would see ye safely across this river. He was worried about the crossing, and told me so."

"There is no time," Many-Doves replied curtly. She did not wait to hear his response, but went to help Tall-Man with the horses and wagon.

In a softer tone, Elizabeth said: "I thank you for your concern, but we must be on our way. My husband's grandfather may be dying, and there is more trouble—"

The horses were letting out soft, high nickering. Usually biddable and good-natured, they had to be coaxed onto the ferry with hooves clattering hollowly. Samuel Hench left her to help. Elizabeth stood watching the river, ill at ease and unsure of herself.

But the winds stilled, suddenly, and the heaving of the ferry with them. Tall-Man let his sons ply their poles and work the drag line while he stood with a stern eye fixed on the river, as if this would make the waters behave. One hand he kept on the neck of Samuel Hench's mare. The other rested lightly on the wampum belt crossed on his chest. Safely on the other side, he raised a hand to the sky as if to thank the winds.

"I believe you were very worried," Elizabeth said to her cousin when they had the earth under their feet again.

"Thy husband told me of a dream having to do with a river," he replied. And then: "Why dost thou look surprised?"

"I am not surprised that Nathaniel should have a dream," Elizabeth said. "Only that you should take his dream as literally as he does."

Samuel Hench's open, honest face went suddenly very still and grim. "Cousin," he said. "If thou wilt survive in the wilderness, thou must take heavenly direction in whatever form it comes to thee."

"But there is the river, behind us, and we are all whole and ready to move on," Elizabeth pointed out, only somewhat discomfited at being taken to task.

Behind her, Many-Doves said: "There is always another river."

The younger woman was looking at Samuel Hench with an expression which had lost much of its wariness and reserve. In return he inclined his head.

Elizabeth climbed up onto the wagon, and once seated, held out her hand to her cousin. "I will remember that, or I will try to. Thank you very kindly for your company, Cousin Samuel. I wish you good luck in your business endeavors in Johnstown . . ." She paused, and smiled.

His grip was firm and dry. "I will come to visit thee in Paradise, as promised." The calm gaze held hers without wavering. For one moment she had a strong sense of her mother, and she released his hand only reluctantly.

Many-Doves spoke to the horses and they began to move away. Samuel Hench sat straight-backed and watched them go, the broad rim of his Quaker hat casting a shadow across his face so that she could not read his expression.

The weather threatened disaster: a strong rain would turn the roads to mud and add an extra day onto their journey. The wind sent the beech trees into a flutter of green and silver leaves. Overhead a hawk rose and fell on fitful breezes.

"If we push hard we can be there late tomorrow," Many-Doves said after a long silence. "If you feel up to it."

They had been eating from the provisions packed by Mrs. Vanderhyden, and there was a scattering of crumbs on her shoulder. Elizabeth brushed them away for her.

"Now you sound like Nathaniel," she chided softly. "Will not even you trust me to rest when I need it?"

Many-Doves smiled. "You are not known for your kindness to yourself."

"And neither is Nathaniel. And neither are you, for that matter. You do not faint away at what needs to be done simply because you carry a child."

Many-Doves looked thoughtful for a moment. "I was not raised to faint."

Elizabeth bristled. "I have never fainted in my life," she said tightly. "I will not start now."

"I would be surprised if you did," Doves conceded.

"Then why must you coddle me so?"

As if Many-Doves were explaining the most obvious thing in the world to a small child, she said, "Because you carry Nathaniel's son, and Hawkeye's grandson, and Chingachgook's great-grandson."

She might have laughed at the absurdity of it, if it were not for the earnest concern so clear in the dark eyes that met her own. Elizabeth said, "Why is everyone so sure that this child is a boy? I would be just as glad of a daughter."

"Of course," said Many-Doves. "So would I. But I carry a son as well."

"More dreams?" asked Elizabeth, torn between amazement and frustration.

"Of course."

"Well, I surrender," Elizabeth said, throwing up her hands. "I will continue to wonder, but please go ahead and think what you like."

On the road that would take them through the Big Vly and on to the Sacandaga they passed isolated homesteads, sometimes in twos or threes. Twice they were stopped and asked for news, which Elizabeth provided to the best of her ability. Many-Doves always sat silent during these exchanges, in spite of curious looks that came her way.

In the dooryard of a small farm on the edge of a marsh, a woman was hoeing a garden patch, her shoulders bowed under a straggling mass of gray-blond hair. From inside the cabin came the weak cry of a very young child; another leaned against the open door, dressed in a ragged shirt almost as grubby as the small face, too wan and thin to bear the weight of a smile. Even the corn in the field slumped its way around the house.

"You and I are very fortunate."

Many-Doves nodded. There was nothing to add to this simple truth.

In a rush, Elizabeth said: "Since Samuel left us I've been waiting for you to tell me what happened at home. I wonder why you're being so quiet about it. My imagination is quite running away with me."

Many-Doves grimaced. "I did not see all of it, and can only piece it together for you."

"Any information would be better than none at all."

"You might not think so, when I'm done." She paused to collect her thoughts. "I guess the simplest way to tell it is that Hawkeye and Chingachgook were fishing by torchlight on the lake the night you left for Albany. Hector and Blue got wind of a buck, chased him into the lake—and that's how it came to pass."

"Why were Hector and Blue left free to roam?"

"They weren't. Somebody cut them free."

"Somebody? Just tell me, tell me the worst and get it over with."

Many-Doves shrugged with one shoulder, as if to dislodge something sitting there with claws dug in. "Hannah caught sight of Liam Kirby disappearing into the woods. The dogs already had the scent by that time and there was no calling them back."

Dread was heavier than fear, and duller than anger. Elizabeth felt it settle into her stomach with searching fingers as she listened to the story. Two things became clear to her: it had not been a random chain of events that led to Hawkeye's arrest, but a carefully laid plan; and it would not be easily undone or set right. Billy Kirby and Moses Southern and their cohort had somehow managed to lure Hawkeye into a trap that led straight to the mine: either they would have to produce silver to pay their way out of jail, or they would sit in Anna's pantry, leaving the mountain open to exploration and the mine to discovery. Runs-from-Bears could not both protect Lake in the Clouds and keep an eye on the mountain. It was a worthy plan, and far beyond the powers of men like Kirby. Julian was behind it; of that there was no doubt. And if the judge had not taken an active part in besting Hawkeye, neither had he put a stop to its execution.

There was so much to be angry about that her thoughts collapsed in upon themselves and would not be called to order.

"Billy Kirby came up to the house later with a whole crowd

of men to arrest them both. Hawkeye went out on the porch to meet them. Looked Billy straight in the eye and said it was a good thing the new sheriff had come to call, because some thief had snuck in and cut his dogs' leads, and what was the law going to do about it?"

Elizabeth had to suppress a smile in spite of it all. Hawkeye would spit in the devil's eye.

"That's when the real trouble started." Vertical lines appeared on either side of Many-Doves' mouth, set in a downward curve. "Kirby asked Chingachgook if was he the one who shot the buck out of season, and of course he didn't deny it." She paused, and glanced at the darkening sky. "Chingachgook told Billy that it would have been disrespectful not to take an animal sent by the Great Spirit, one who came so peacefully. And he said he wouldn't be locked up in an O'seronni gaol for taking a gift. Then he just turned his back on those men and walked away."

Before Elizabeth could ask, Many-Doves shook her head. "They didn't shoot him. Moses Southern took his rifle butt to the back of Chingachgook's head and then, when he was down, he pulled his knife."

"I assume Hawkeye was tied up by this time, or Moses would be dead now."

"Moses is dead," said Many-Doves calmly. "Your father shot him."

They stopped to water the horses and let them graze. Elizabeth sat on the bank and put her bare feet in the cold running water; leaned down to scoop it into her cupped palms to drench her face and neck again and again.

"I think the judge just intended to slow Moses down," Many-Doves said. "But he's never been much of a shot, and that smoothbore of his—well, you've seen it before. A ball took Moses just over the ear. He died straightaway. Another ball hit Chingachgook in the side, passed right through." And after a longer pause in which Elizabeth said nothing: "Nobody blames the judge, not even Martha. He was there to make sure things didn't get out of hand. I guess Moses took him by surprise, and it got away from him."

"You needn't make excuses for my father."

Many-Doves was not unnerved by Elizabeth's anger. "If your father had not stopped Southern, Chingachgook would have died right there under his knife."

"If my father had stopped the whole undertaking before it started, Chingachgook would be whole and safe."

Many-Doves blinked in surprise. "Do you think that Great-Snake would rather die in front of a fire like an old woman?"

"I don't know what he would want," Elizabeth said bitterly, wiping her face dry with her skirt. "But I do know who has taken that decision out of his hands. My brother's greed has exacted too high a price this time, and he shall have to account for it."

"Your brother was not with the men who came to Lake in the Clouds."

"But he was, he was there. You could not see him, but his spirit was there. He put the smell of silver in their noses, and cut them loose. And he did not care who got run down in the hunt."

Many-Doves chirruped softly to the horses and they raised their heads from grazing. They needed a longer rest, but the women were anxious now to get back to Paradise and see this thing to its end. With the wagon juddering over the well-worn trail, Many-Doves finally spoke. "It is not greed that rules Julian."

Elizabeth had never before heard Many-Doves use her brother's name; it was an act of intimacy and ownership that surprised her almost as much as what was to come.

"A man with no center will try to fill the void that rules him. You call this greed—"

"You surely are not excusing Julian's behavior!"

As if Elizabeth had not interrupted, Many-Doves said: "He is dangerous because he does not know how to help himself, except to take from others what can never do him any good." Many-Doves sent Elizabeth a sliding glance. "Did you know what name my mother gave him?"

"I did not know that you and Falling-Day spoke of my brother at all."

"She calls him Ratkahthos-ahsonthènne'."

Struck silent, Elizabeth let the rhythm of the jostling wagon sway her from side to side. *He-Seeks-in-the-Dark.*

They rode in silence for the rest of the day, Elizabeth pushing with her feet against the splashboard until her knees ached. They came to Barktown when the sky had turned to bruised purples over the cranberry marshes. From the stores in the wagon they made presents to Sky-Wound-Round, tobacco and dried meat. At his council fire they told the story of Chingachgook, and the path that stood before him. But sleeping that night on a platform under the arched roof of the Kah-nyen'kehàka longhouse, it was not the old man Elizabeth dreamed of, but her brother as a young boy, singing himself to sleep in the dark.

The first person she saw at Lake in the Clouds was one person she did not wish to see, did not care to see ever again: her father. The judge stood on the porch of Hawkeye's cabin in the twilight, staring into the waterfall. He did not seem to hear them coming, although the exhausted horses lifted their heads to whinny with excitement at the idea of fresh hay and rest. He simply stood there. Her father, usually so meticulous about his person, was unshaven. His clothes, rumpled and splashed with mud. When he finally turned his head toward her, she saw that his eyes were sunken and red-rimmed.

"Daughter." The muscles in his neck moved beneath the soft folds of flesh. His voice was hoarse with disuse, or liquor. Or perhaps both, she thought.

"Father." Elizabeth climbed the porch and reached for the door.

"Wait."

She obeyed; and chided herself for it.

"It was an accident," he said. "I admire Chingachgook above all men, I was trying to save his life. You must believe me." And then, in response to her silence, as deep as the dusk: "I wouldn't have thought you so cruel."

She drew in a ragged breath, all anger and frustration. "If you need forgiveness, then it is not from me. Where is Hawk-eye?"

The judge turned his face from her. "He has three days left on his sentence."

"But Nathaniel—he paid the fine, did he not? Was not your sentence a hundred dollars or seven days?"

"The sentence was a hundred dollars *and* seven days. As set out by law."

"Well, then, if you truly want to be forgiven, you must commute his sentence."

The judge's face contorted. "I would, daughter. If I could."

"No, Father. You could, if you would. But you will not risk the anger of the villagers. Is that right?"

"I am bound by the law," he said, two patches of red rising on his cheeks.

"How convenient. Now if you will excuse me."

Many-Doves came around the corner from the barn just as the door opened. Runs-from-Bears held out one hand toward her and she ran up the porch steps and into his arms. Elizabeth slipped past them with her head averted, but she could not help but hear his soft murmuring.

Curiosity stood on the far side of the main room, working a pestle and mortar. Falling-Day was at the hearth with a ladle in her hand. In the middle of the room was a cot, on which Chingachgook lay, his hands folded on his stomach. His face was turned from her, but his chest rose and fell fitfully.

On the edge of his cot, Hannah perched with a book in her hands. Her voice broke off in mid-sentence when she looked up.

She was just tall enough to rest her head in the hollow spot between Elizabeth's breasts. She smelled of wood smoke and growing things, and she trembled slightly, in fear or relief, Elizabeth could not tell. She only knew that her throat was tight with joy at this greeting, in spite of the news written clearly on Curiosity's face.

Falling-Day murmured words of welcome to Elizabeth and to her daughter, who had come farther into the room to kneel next to the cot. Hannah pulled away, gently, and joined Many-

Doves, picking up her book to find her place. *Poor Richard's Almanac,* Elizabeth saw now.

Curiosity laid a hand on Elizabeth's arm.

"How much longer?"

She lifted a shoulder, inclined her head. "Tonight, I'd say."

"Where is Nathaniel?"

"He went to fetch Hawkeye."

"But I thought—"

"Maybe you can stop him," said Curiosity, "if you hurry."

Headed down the path from Lake in the Clouds at a fast clip and lost in her worries, Elizabeth was taken by surprise at the arm that shot out of the dark behind the church and caught her up. Even knowing it was Nathaniel, a small cry of alarm escaped her, to be stifled immediately against his shirt.

He set her firmly on her feet and then pinned her up against the wall of the church. She was breathing hard; he kissed her, harder.

"Nathaniel!" she hissed, breaking away.

"I'm glad to see you home safe, Boots. Although I have to say your timing ain't optimal." He touched the corner of her mouth with his thumb and she caught his hand, held it there.

"Nathaniel, tell me you're not here to break Hawkeye out of Anna's pantry."

He hushed her, pulling her farther away from the path. There were voices, coming closer. Men on their way to Axel's tavern, where the noise indicated some party well under way. Elizabeth waited until the pressure of his fingers on her arm relaxed. Then she took his face between her hands and made him look at her.

"It will do us no good if they lock you up, too," she said, keeping her eyes fixed on his. "Come back home with me. Your grandfather will be asking for you."

Nathaniel caught her hands and pushed them down, firmly. "He'll be asking for my father, too, and I aim to make sure he's there."

"Please, be reasonable. There is no window big enough for him to climb through. Anna sleeps in the next room, and the tavern is right there—it's impossible. They must have posted a guard."

"Aye," Nathaniel agreed with a grim smile. "Liam Kirby, asleep on a stool with his hat pulled over his eyes."

Elizabeth tried to calm her voice, seeking frantically for that logic which would reach him. "Nathaniel, it sounds as though every man in the village is in the tavern."

Bursts of singing came to them on the warm evening breeze, interrupted by raised voices and an occasional shouted laugh.

"They buried Southern today," Nathaniel offered in explanation. "It's an Irish wake they've got going on."

"Oh, lovely, then they are in a rare mood. Think, please. Even if you manage it somehow, they will come looking for him—and for you—immediately."

Nathaniel stared down at her sternly, his eyes narrowed.

Elizabeth knew that she was saying things he didn't want to hear, but that he couldn't deny. She recognized the expression on his face, although she had never seen him wearing it before. It was a look she knew too well: all her life, she had seen it on the faces of men when she asked yet another question, or made that final observation, the one that dug too deep and hit a nerve. Slowly, reluctantly, Elizabeth had begun to trust the fact that he liked her the way she was, that he could cope with a woman with a mind of her own without losing his sense of himself as a man. And now, here it was. That look.

She watched him struggle with it. He would either talk to her, and they would resolve this, or he would try to send her home.

The muscles in his throat began to work convulsively. His face, his beloved face, all angles and planes. The scar at the corner of his eye; the straight line of his brow. It all dissolved as she watched, anger and stubbornness giving way to something she had never imagined: desperation. The kind of bone-deep desperation that made other men—not Nathaniel, never Nathaniel—into little boys.

"Elizabeth." His voice came harsh with the effort of it, of showing her this. "It'll kill my father. It will kill him, not being there when Chingachgook walks the path. I know my father, Elizabeth. And I cannot leave him sitting in that gaol, and live with myself. Not tonight, not for another day. Don't ask me to walk away from this, because I can't."

Elizabeth pressed a hand to her mouth. Then she said: "I will go talk to the judge. He cannot be so cruel as to keep Hawkeye from his father's deathbed."

He groaned in frustration. "Don't you see? Kirby would raise an army to stop him."

She searched his face for the truth. "Are things so far gone here, then? Do they hate us so much?"

He had no words for her; for once, Nathaniel had no comfort to offer. Elizabeth stood up straighter, and glanced toward the tavern.

"I will go in there and speak to Kirby. Perhaps I can appeal to his better instincts."

"I can't let you waltz into a room of drunken men with bloodshed on their minds. And it wouldn't do any good anyway, Boots. You know that yourself."

Elizabeth let her head drop back against the wall of the church. Above her, the dark shapes of the fir trees flexed against the night sky. For no reason she could understand, Elizabeth thought of Kitty's mother hiding up in the branches of one of those trees for two days after the Kahnyen'kehàka war party had come to call, afraid to climb down and face the rest of her life after what she had learned about the cruelty of men, and how deep it could run. *Some folks sit tight and let life happen to them,* Curiosity had said to her once. *No matter what the cost.*

"But I do not," Elizabeth murmured. "And never will I."

The worry that etched Nathaniel's face in deep lines gave way to sudden curiosity.

"Have you got a plan?"

Amazed to realize that she did indeed have a plan, Elizabeth nodded. "Can you raise enough of a fuss to empty the tavern? Get all of them out here for a quarter hour or so?"

One brow shot up, incredulous. "And what good will that do us?"

Elizabeth smoothed her hand over his shoulder. "Quite simple. While you are out here amusing all of them, I will be inside."

The other brow went up, and with it, a flicker of a grin.

"Elizabeth Middleton Bonner," said her husband slowly. "Are you proposing to break a man out of gaol?"

"If you'll explain to me how to force the lock, well, then. Yes. I suppose that is exactly what I am proposing."

Nathaniel reached into his bullet pouch and pressed a knobby iron key into her hand.

"Where did you get this?"

He shrugged. "We've got some friends left in Paradise."

"Axel." She nodded. "And I know we can count on Anna to look the other way, if it comes to that."

"It's going to take more than a little luck to pull this off, Boots."

"Pah." She made a small flickering motion with her fingers. "Luck is for the unprepared and the mediocre. What we need is a plan. And careful timing. And quite possibly, a large gourd from Anna's garden."

Elizabeth thought that if she let herself contemplate the enormity of the task she had just taken on, she would begin to shake with fear, and so she spoke to him of the details. Nathaniel was already more himself: she could feel it in the way he ran his hands over her arms, see it in the distracted look on his face as they discussed timing, and decoys, and meeting places.

"We should wait another hour or so," he said, when they had sketched it out between them. "Until they're good and drunk."

"You won't burn anything down, will you?" She plucked at his sleeve anxiously.

"Nothing so dramatic as that, Boots. No, I thought I'd give Billy Kirby what he really wants, which is just a chance to beat me bloody in front of his friends. If we wait, he'll be drunk enough to think that maybe he can do it. So we've got some time on our hands here. Any ideas?"

She had an idea, oh, yes. Pinned against this wall with Nathaniel leaning over her, his warm breath stirring her hair and his fingers plucking gently, she had notions in her head that a year ago were beyond her imagining. The warm summer night and the smells of him, and the anxiety and excitement of what lay before them, all came together to hum in her veins. She lifted her face to him, knowing that he could read what was written there better than any words on a page.

With a small laugh, Nathaniel came in closer. He dropped his head so that his mouth hovered just over hers.

"You're full of mischief tonight, ain't you, Boots?"

Before she could protest, he had closed the gap between them. She spread her hands on his back and tangled her fingers in his hair and kissed him back, pressing herself to him. Two days without Nathaniel had reminded her what it was like to be alone. His shoulders flexed under her hands; she pressed her teeth to the skin of his neck, tasting his salt and sweat and wanting more, wanting all of him. But the combination of his hands on her breasts and the wall at her back struck a chord she could not ignore.

"This is the *church*," she gasped when his mouth left hers to move to her ear. "Nathaniel! Perhaps—"

His hand slid inside her bodice, just as his lips closed over her earlobe.

"Nathaniel," she whispered, pushing him away.

His thumb stopped its slow rotation on her nipple, and he lifted his head. "Boots?"

She pulled his head to her, kissed him hard. "There's something sacrilegious about this."

"Well, then," he said thoughtfully. His hand continued on its quest beneath her skirt while he kissed the corner of her mouth, his tongue flickering. "Quote me something from the Bible, if that will help. Because I want you."

She gave in with a laugh. Because she wanted to, because she wanted him. She let him bare her breasts to the night breeze. She took his kisses and gave them back, put her hands on him, greedy for the evidence of his desire. With his arms beneath her knees he lifted her against the wall, finding his way through the tangle of her skirt, his fingers pressing into her rounded flesh, seeking. He tilted her up and fit himself to her with a groan muffled against her arched neck.

So closely joined together that she dreaded ever having to let go, Elizabeth drank in the words he murmured at her ear, sounding for all the world like a prayer.

LII

They found a pumpkin in Anna's garden that was just about big enough to serve as a stand-in for Hawkeye's head, but they also found Jed McGarrity, who was using it as a pillow. Sound asleep with his fiddle cradled in his arms, he was snoring lightly and seemed not in the least uncomfortable.

"Maybe we should help him home," Elizabeth suggested.

"No time," Nathaniel reminded her. "And Nancy wouldn't let him in, anyway. He smells like he climbed right into the schnapps bottle."

"Is Jed difficult when he is inebriated?" she asked thoughtfully.

"There ain't a mean bone in the man's body."

"Good, then maybe we won't have to make do with the gourd." When there was no reply to this suggestion, Elizabeth glanced up at Nathaniel. But his attention was elsewhere, on what was going on inside the tavern.

She put a hand on his arm. "Be careful."

He grinned down at her, cupped her cheek in his hand. "You, too." And then he disappeared around the corner to enter the tavern by its front door. Elizabeth wound her hands in her skirt to keep them from trembling, and she glanced at Jed McGarrity's long face, half lit in moonlight. She crouched down next to him, shook him slightly.

"Hmmm?" He opened one eye and then closed it again. "Miz Elizabeth. Kind of you to come and call."

She stifled a smile. "Jed, wouldn't you be more comfortable in a bed?"

"Yas'm, but there ain't one handy," he mumbled.

"You stay put and I'll find one for you. If you're not fussy about where, exactly."

He fumbled at his head for a moment, as if he had a hat to tip. "I ain't a fussy man, miss. Thank you kindly."

His snoring resumed just as the first shouting erupted from the tavern.

Liam had left a betty lamp alight on a pickle barrel when he went out to watch the fight, and Elizabeth was very glad of it as she threaded her way through the trading post, around washtubs, boxes of Daffy's Elixir of Life, stacks of folded huckaback and dried tobacco leaves. The trading post was unnaturally quiet in the deep of the night, in contrast to the noise outside. It seemed that the men of Paradise enjoyed a fistfight. She just hoped they didn't take it into their heads to join in. Elizabeth put that idea firmly away, and felt once again for the key in her pocket.

There was a window cut in the pantry door, a dark square as big as her hand. Elizabeth went up on tiptoe, but she could see nothing. With the sound of her own heartbeat so loud that she could barely concentrate, she fit the key to the lock, wincing at the small scraping noise.

"Nathaniel?" came a whisper.

"No, it's Elizabeth." She swung the door open and found Hawkeye standing there, fully dressed. He put out a hand to grab her shoulder, and leaning over, touched his forehead to her hair.

"By God," he whispered. "I knew you two would come through."

Overcome with a rush of affection, Elizabeth grasped his free hand, and pulled him into the room. His face was rough with beard stubble; his hair clung damply to his temples. Blinking and squinting in the light, he looked at first like a confused old man. Then he shook his head and his gaze, razor sharp, focused on Elizabeth.

"Is that Nathaniel out there fighting Kirby? Aye, I thought so. He's been looking for an excuse for a while, but I guess he didn't think it would come like this." He paused, and ran a hand over his chin so that the bristles crackled. "My father?"

"He's alive, but the women think he's very close, Hawkeye. I'm sorry."

He nodded, as if he had been expecting to hear worse. "Not too late, at least."

She put out a hand. "We need a dummy of some sort for your cot, so they don't realize right away—"

"No time, lass." He shook his head. "I'm away up the mountain."

Elizabeth knew he was right, but having come so far so quickly, she was suddenly almost paralyzed with worry. She forced herself to say it, anyway. "Go on, then, I'll cope here."

At the door, Hawkeye paused. "You're a fine woman, Elizabeth. I'm proud to call you daughter."

She pushed at him, her anxiety almost at the breaking point. "Go," she said. "We'll come after. Just go."

He didn't need more urging. Elizabeth watched him running across the garden, as elegant and quick as a deer in flight, his hair fluttering silver in the moonlight. He disappeared into the woods without a sound.

Drenched in sweat, she set off into the garden, listening as she went to the sounds of the fight out front.

If he had ever seen a sure thing, a fight worthy of a wager, this was it, thought Julian. Nathaniel Bonner in a white fury, and sober, against Billy Kirby with a half bottle of schnapps in him. Billy might weigh a few stone more, but it would do him little good tonight. More bad luck, to have put all his money into drink and cards before Bonner showed up. Up to that point, it had been a boring affair, this Irish wake. The memorial toasts for a man few had liked and fewer still would miss were only vaguely amusing; the singing had set more than one dog to howling. It was almost enough to make Julian appreciate the

empty house he had waiting for him. He had been on the point
of going when things got interesting.

Of course, Billy had brought the fight on himself. He could
no more keep from bragging about tossing Hawkeye in the gaol
than he could stop breathing. Bonner, cold bastard that he was,
hadn't blinked. He just listened to Billy rant on and on, and
then asked in a conversational tone if the sheriff had the balls to
stand up with somebody his own size and age, or if it was only
old men he felt safe taking on, and that at the end of a rifle.
That stare of his was like a poke in the chest; drunk or sober, a
man couldn't walk away from it and call himself a man.

They had all trooped out after Billy, bellowing encouragement and calling out wagers. Drinking men would put coin on
any absurdity in the name of friendship; sober men—or men
who could handle their schnapps—could profit. If only a man
had the necessary funds. But since the accident that had sent
Moses to his comeuppance, with the old Indian to follow soon
after, the judge had not handed over a copper penny. Hadn't
even shown his face at home. Julian still hadn't figured out how
to get past Galileo and into the money chest and he was feeling
the pinch. But still, he couldn't quite stay away from the fight.
He thought Bonner would put Kirby down clean and neat;
there might be a free round, afterward.

Fifteen minutes into it, it was clear that neatness wasn't on
Bonner's mind. He had a long reach and hands like iron hooks,
and he knew how to hurt a man without taking too much out
of him. Standing aside from the crowd safe from the dust and
the occasional spattering of blood, Julian might have enjoyed
the show if he'd had anything to invest in it.

"Sweet Mary, Nathaniel ain't even broke a sweat yet," muttered Henry Smythe. In the flicker of the torches the crowd
waved like flags, the ginger fuzz that covered Kirby's back and
chest streamed with sweat.

"Better Billy than you or me, eh?" Smythe edged closer to
Julian. He smelled of boiled cabbage and wet wool.

"You're in my way, old man."

Axel stood a few yards away with all the weapons around
him, a condition he had placed on this fight; he was a man who

knew his clientele, after all. Julian moved in his direction, keeping his eyes on Bonner and Kirby.

They were circling, Kirby working his bloody fists in front of him as if he had no idea what they were for, although there was no lack of advice from the audience. Bonner didn't have too many friends in this crowd, but he didn't seem much to mind, one way or another. Shouts of support and jeers slid off him as slickly as Billy's haphazard jabs.

A shout of reluctant approval followed a left hook that took Billy in the chest, but left him rocking. Like a stunted oak in a high wind, he groaned but he would not quite topple.

"Nathaniel Bonner!" cried Anna Hauptmann. "Are you fighting with the man, or dancing? Will you knock some sense into his bloody head once and for all?" She was the only woman in the crowd, standing there in a dressing gown and bouncing up and down on her bare feet like a girl of twelve. Not a pleasing sight.

"Aw, Anna. I got a dollar on Billy there, give him a chance."

She grunted, and flung her long plaits back over her shoulders. "You want to throw your good money away, Ambrose, you go right ahead. But I guess when your Marianne gets done with you, you won't look much better than Billy there."

Nathaniel reached out with a left cross and Billy's lip split open with a pop. The crowd bellowed in response. From his one open eye, Billy threw them a baleful glare. His nose had been slightly reoriented on his broad, lopsided face, and he stood there heaving and foaming like an overworked horse in the sun.

"Christ on a pony, Kirby, fall down and stop embarrassing your sainted mother!" shouted Anna, disgusted. "Would you see to business, Nathaniel?"

Bonner just circled, as if he had nothing better to do than watch Billy Kirby bleed into the dust. If he was getting any pleasure out of it, it couldn't be seen on his face.

A blow to Billy's shoulder sent him staggering backward.

"Come on, Kirby," called one of the Camerons in a long whine. "You can do better than that."

"Me Grannie Meg could do better than that, and her dead these ten years!" Archie Cunningham shouted.

Axel let out a great bray of laughter, and the rest of the crowd joined him, tentatively at first and then with abandon. In response, Kirby roused himself, leading with his right in a long, sloppy roundhouse that gave Bonner more than enough time to step out of the way. Stumbling like a baby, Billy barely caught himself before plowing into the horse trough.

Bonner wasn't even breathing hard. He had taken only one real punch, and a graze on his cheekbone glistened raw in the torchlight.

"Ja, you look ready to call it quits, Kirby. Had enough?" Axel called.

Billy shook his head, slinging ropes of blood and spit. He started toward Bonner growling, only to be dealt a vicious uppercut to the gut. Kirby crossed his arms over himself and collapsed forward onto his knees, his head hanging down to the ground. Blood and vomit dripped into the dirt.

"That's it, then!" Axel held up one arm.

Liam Kirby, his face a study in misery and shame, crouched down next to his brother, who now sat on the ground. With a push and a roar, Billy sent the boy sprawling into the dirt. Then he hauled himself to his feet and stood glaring at Bonner, swaying crookedly. Bonner stared back, one brow cocked like the leg of the bigger dog.

Claude Dubonnet came and whispered something into Kirby's ear. Billy finally nodded, and followed him off in the direction of his cabin.

Men were heading back into the tavern, more sober now than they wanted to be, and not looking forward to paying off hasty bets. The pockets of Anna's morning coat were sagging with her profit.

"I see you slinking away, Isaac Cameron," she called out. "Never mind. If I don't get my coin from you I'll just drop by your place in the morning, see if it's any easier to part with it when your head's fit to burst."

Isaac came trudging back into the torchlight, fishing deep in his money pouch and muttering loudly. "You trained that daughter of yours poorly, Axel. What's she doing out here in the middle of the night, sticking her nose in men's business?"

"Collectin' your money, looks like." Axel laughed. "Don't

go blaming her for the liquor in your belly." He grinned at Julian as he handed over his musket.

"Ain't that so, Middleton?"

Wiping the barrel with his handkerchief, Julian merely smiled.

Bonner still stood where the fight had stopped, his face set and impassive as ever. He was flexing his right hand, opening and closing the fist like the mouth of a trap, slowly rolling his shoulders and testing his elbows. No damage to speak of, beyond a split knuckle or two. Anna was talking to him, gesturing broadly. One or two of the men stopped to congratulate him.

Watching a fight was thirsty work. Julian wondered if his brother-in-law might be persuaded to buy him a drink, in celebration of the triumph of good over evil. Then he remembered that Hawkeye was sitting over in the trading post behind a locked door, and he thought of a better plan. Just earlier in the day he had seen a stray bottle of schnapps on the counter over there.

Axel had come up to talk to Nathaniel; Julian took that opportunity to slip away.

Drenched with sweat, her heart beating hard in her throat, Elizabeth closed the rear door of the trading post behind her and took a moment to lean against the wall in order to catch her breath. She shut her eyes, willing the shaking in her hands and legs to cease. It was a mean trick she had played on poor Jed; he would be hard-pressed to explain himself tomorrow morning. He had offered to play her a tune, even as he fell onto the cot and instantly to sleep, never noticing the sound of the door locking behind him. Elizabeth hoped he would forgive her, in time. If it bought Hawkeye the chance to be with his father before it was too late, she would take on Jed McGarrity's anger, and gladly.

The noise of the fight had stopped, and the tavern was filling up again. Nathaniel would be looking for her down by the schoolhouse; she needed to be on her way.

She opened her eyes, and her brother was standing in front of her.

"Mrs. Bonner," he said, sweeping his arm in front of himself in an expansive gesture that had nothing to do with the leering grin on his face. "Whatever in the world are you doing here? Or is that a question you cannot answer?"

"I am waiting for my husband," Elizabeth said. Behind her back, she still held the key to Anna's pantry. She gripped it harder. "And what is your business here?"

He shook his head. "Not nearly as interesting as yours, I'll wager. Been in to pay your father-in-law a midnight visit, have you? Find him well?"

Elizabeth fixed him with her sternest gaze. "I hope you are not so very short of cash that you're resorting to petty thievery again."

"I see that marriage hasn't mellowed you!" He laughed softly. "If you are so concerned for my financial well-being, my wealthy sister, why then perhaps you would be so good—"

"Nothing changes, Julian, does it? You are still trying to get others to pay your way for you."

"And you will still try to change me. These games of yours are very tiresome, Lizzie. Why don't you just come back home, and put an end to this silliness?"

Her anxiety abruptly replaced by anger, Elizabeth felt the knot in her stomach tighten and break. She stepped toward her brother, and he stepped back in surprise.

"This is not a game, Julian. This is my life. I have a husband, I have a home. I am never coming back."

His temper was buried deep, but she still knew how to put a hook in it and drag it to the surface. She watched him battle to maintain his smirk, and fail. "You will," he whispered, with a new edge to his tone. "I will see to it. You cannot run off with a third of the property and think you'll get away with it."

Shaking now with exhaustion and irritation, Elizabeth pulled herself up to her full height. "I have only what was rightfully mine. And listen to me now, carefully: I will keep what is mine."

On Julian's face a flickering of anger. His mouth, narrowed down to a spiteful line. "You don't believe that Nathaniel Bonner really wants you, do you?" His eyes traveled slowly over her face, and his lip curled in disgust. "Now that he's got your father's land, what makes you think you can keep him, you with your books and your lectures. You can't breed him any children —did Richard ever tell you that, that your husband's sterile? Didn't bother to mention that, did he? But then I doubt the thought has even occurred to him—why would it, after all, when there's a woman like Many-Doves in the next bed."

The bile that rose in her throat would choke her, if she let it. It tasted of the things she saw in him now: the consuming selfishness, the bitter loneliness that had turned this man into a creature that she did not recognize, and wanted no part of.

She said: "It is very strange that you should mention Many-Doves, Julian. Just earlier today she was talking to me about you."

If she had slapped him, he could not have looked more stunned. It gave her pause enough only to catch her breath.

"Many-Doves said, 'A man with no center will try to fill the void that rules him.' She calls you He-Seeks-in-the-Dark."

He let out a rush of air that was half gasp, half awkward laugh. "Mohawk nonsense," he said hoarsely, his eyes flickering away from her. "What is that supposed to mean?"

"It means that you have no soul. You know that to be true, which is your second curse. And the harder one to live with."

Nathaniel appeared suddenly out of the darkness; she felt his presence like the shadow of the mountain itself. He put a hand on her arm, and she touched him with a finger, asking for his silence for one more moment.

Julian blinked at her, as if he could not quite focus his eyes. Then he turned his back to both of them, and disappeared into the night.

They walked home in silence, but they were not alone on the path to Lake in the Clouds. Three young River Indians overtook them in the strawberry field, alive with waves of fireflies under the horned moon. Another, larger group of Kahnyen'kehàka came out of the forest a mile farther on. Many-Doves had started the word moving in Barktown, and from all over the territory men would come to be near when Chingachgook walked the path. Nathaniel's pace quickened, and Elizabeth pushed herself to keep up.

The cabin was crowded with strangers. Onandaga from upriver. More Kahnyen'kehàka, standing quietly. A couple of white trappers were cleaning their guns by the hearth. Her father sat talking to John Glove and Galileo. She felt his gaze on her as they passed.

Hawkeye was crouched next to the cot where his father slipped further into his death dream. The only things alive about him were his eyes, fixed on Chingachgook's face, and his voice, hoarse and vaguely crackling. He was singing under his breath in Mahican; Elizabeth did not understand the words, and she did not need an interpreter.

She picked up Chingachgook's hand off the blanket, fever hot. Cradled in her own two hands, it was like a piece of driftwood, deceptively light for all its strong, polished form. She had the sense of his bones, leached hollow and pale, as if they had lain for all of his many years in the direct light of the sun. The same sun that had given his people their own particular rainbow: copper and bronze, amber and sienna.

There was a subtle shifting in the deeply fissured face. His eyes opened, a flicker of awareness, and then closed again. The snake that coiled over his cheekbones shimmered in the lamplight and disappeared into the sparse white hair at his temple.

The door opened and there was the distinctive rattle of bone and silver. Elizabeth had last seen Bitter-Words this morning at Barktown, and now here he was, standing over the cot to look at Chingachgook with his eyes as black and expressive as the night. Hawkeye rose to talk to the faith keeper, and Elizabeth took the opportunity to slip away and look for Hannah.

Outside, a huge fire was burning, and around it, more people, mostly men. Maybe a hundred of them, talking among themselves while they made camp. They were roasting deer; she counted three, and a small bear, the bones of which had been tossed to the dogs. These men would hunt to feed themselves, as they must. Billy Kirby could hardly drag all of them off to gaol.

But he could, he would, come looking for Hawkeye, and soon. And he would find half the Hode'noshaunee nation here, as they had feared would one day be the case. She put the thought away from her—what they had done tonight, and what it would mean tomorrow—because now she was tired, she was tired to the bone and she would think of her child first. Nathaniel came out on the porch behind her.

"Go sleep," he said, his arms coming up from behind to encircle her, his chin resting on the crown of her head. "I'll come fetch you when it's time. You did good, Boots. Thank you."

She nodded, leaning back against him.

"Your father—"

"Tomorrow," he said, his mouth at her ear. "Sleep first."

Elizabeth left him to this family of his that was still a mystery to her, a connection woven not of blood and muscle but common purpose. On her own porch, facing away from the gathering, she found children sleeping wrapped in blankets. She stood for a moment listening to their breathing, and watching the flicker of fireflies. A Kahnyen'kehàka woman she did not recognize sat in one of the rocking chairs, nursing an infant.

Inside, Curiosity was stirring the cook pot. Elizabeth took soup and corn bread from her. She could not remember when she had last eaten, but she still felt strangely full, a fist in her belly and her throat closed tight. She took the soup out onto the porch and then the women collected the sleeping children and took them up to the loft, and Curiosity went back to the other cabin.

Elizabeth found Many-Doves and Hannah asleep in her bed. Hannah was fully dressed, her unplaited hair scattered across the pillow. She lay down with them to wait.

From the open window, there was the sound of singing and a water drum and a slow, shuffling step toward the dawn.

LIII

"Mr. Middleton, Billy Kirby here and Claude Dubonnet with him."

Julian squinted up at Curiosity's oldest daughter. "I don't want to see anyone, Daisy."

"Yes, sir, so you said. But I don't think they'll go away on my word."

Daisy blinked at him, her mouth folded in a tight line. Another woman who couldn't tell the difference between a drunken man and one who was working on achieving that state, but had not yet succeeded. Julian reached for his coffee cup, and eyed the brandy bottle on the sideboard.

"Then get your mother to deal with them." He took another swallow and then stabbed halfheartedly at a sausage. "I'm not in the mood for their games this morning."

She stood there still, her face impassive. "My folks are up at Lake in the Clouds," she said patiently. "Chingachgook died at dawn, so I don't expect they'll be down anytime soon."

At the door, Billy Kirby said: "The whole Indian nation is up there, too, to bury the old bastard."

"Billy," said Julian with a sigh. "By God, man, can't you leave me alone? My head hurts as bad as your face looks. Go home and sleep, why don't you, and let them bury their dead."

Dubonnet, face like a pickled egg, cleared his throat. "You were eager enough to send us up there not so very long ago."

"Yes, well. I didn't anticipate you'd make a complete muddle of it when I made the suggestion. My error, I suppose."

"We didn't shoot anybody," Kirby said.

Julian lifted up his hands in a gesture of dismissal. "I have no intention of climbing that mountain to watch Nathaniel Bonner thrash you again, Kirby. Even if he does have a more appreciative audience this time—"

"Hawkeye was broke out of the gaol last night. I got an idea that it was your sister who done it."

Julian pulled up short, and then let out a hoarse laugh. "She was always too clever by half. I should have known." He took a harder look at the two men before him. The worse for wear, but dressed and armed as if they were going to war. "Tell me you are going up there to arrest Hawkeye in front of every Mohawk in New-York State."

Billy's jaw worked like a saw. "And your sister, too. Soon as I got enough men together, I'm going up there to do just that."

"By God, you are either the bravest or the stupidest pair I've ever seen. There's not enough men on the continent to pull that off," Julian said. "How long do you think you'll keep the support of the men in the village if you try to arrest my sister? And you've got no proof that it was her, do you?"

Billy jerked the battered tricorn from his head and began to knead it compulsively. "Not exactly. There's Jed McGarrity, but he ain't too talkative this morning."

Julian snorted. "The judge will need more than your suspicions before he'll put a woman in gaol."

Billy's head jerked up, his eyes flaring. "Well, what about you, then? Your word would do the job."

With a quick motion, Julian emptied his coffee cup, and then put it down softly on the table. "Don't count on it."

"Does that mean you ain't coming with us?"

Julian ran a hand through his hair. "I most certainly am not. I don't know why I should worry about the two of you, you are more trouble than you are worth. But let me point out that not only is discretion the better part of valor, it is also a more promising strategy in this little war of yours."

Billy scowled at him. "Talk plain, Middleton."

With a groan, Julian heaved himself out of his chair. "All

right, yes. How is this: if you can put a harness on your impatience now and sit on your hurt pride, you will have at least a prayer of getting what you want."

Dubonnet looked thoughtful. "And if we don't?"

· Julian shrugged. "If you go up there now, Bonner will gut you and leave you for the crows. Sheriff or not."

In a great tidal wave of grief that took the summer day and heaved it into a new shape, Nathaniel struggled from task to task until his grandfather was in the ground. Working with his father and Runs-from-Bears, they dug the grave. The faith keeper's songs and prayers provided a rhythm to work by.

It was just over a year since they had buried his mother. Behind him, Nathaniel could sense the shape of her grave. He imagined her as he always did, with her arms held out in welcome. The others were waiting for Chingachgook, too. Those who had gone before: his first son, who had died in battle, the wife who had borne him. Sarah, with the child in her arms. They would welcome Chingachgook, who would walk tall and strong among them. He had gone to this homecoming gladly.

Standing at the grave in which they had put him to rest, Nathaniel wondered where his grief had hidden itself. He envied his father, and Falling-Day, and the very rattles that Bitter-Words raised over his head, for their ability to send a voice into the heavens. He could not; his words had been taken from him. He could not even find them for Elizabeth, who stood beside him quietly, her gray eyes like bruises in her pale face.

One by one, men came forth to speak over Chingachgook. White and red, they had fought and hunted beside him; they wore their years as openly and proudly as their battle scars. In Mahican and Kahnyen'kehàka and Onandaga and English, they offered their memories. The old warriors wished Chingachgook a good journey, and counted his days in words as clear and hard as wampum beads. Axel spoke, too, and the judge, a roaring mumble of regret and self-pity that made the faith keeper stare and the Kahnyen'kehàka look away in shame for him.

Elizabeth swayed, and Nathaniel put an arm around her. She

would ever surprise him, this wife of his. Her eyes moved over him, searching his face as her hands had explored his wounds, lightly, knowingly. He had wondered if she could bear these many hours of leave-taking; he had forgotten the depths of her strength. One day it would be his turn to walk this path, and then she would stand here with their children beside her, and she would find the words to tell the story of his days. She would outlive them all to tell the tale. He would see to it.

By sunset it was over, and the Kahnyen'kehàka started to slip away in small groups over the ridge of the mountain. Once, Many-Doves told Elizabeth, there would have been days of storytelling and prayers, but no more. The Hode'noshaunee who survived in this part of the world had learned to live in the shadows. The villagers went, too, the judge last of all, lingering until Curiosity took him aside and spoke plain words. Elizabeth watched him go from her window, debating and rejecting definitions of charity and duty in her head, her arms wound tightly around herself.

It was good to be alone again. Elizabeth took her place at the long table in Hawkeye's cabin with real relief. Hannah was to her left and Nathaniel to her right; Falling-Day sat across from her, with Many-Doves and Runs-from-Bears. Hawkeye was at one end of the table; at the other end, Chingachgook's place was empty.

They ate of fresh venison and beans and squash, and Elizabeth remembered suddenly the first meal she had had at this table, in the dead of winter. They had feasted on the turkey Hawkeye had won from Billy Kirby, and Nathaniel had shown her his plans for the schoolhouse. She had wondered then if she could ever be a part of such a family, if there might be room for her here. Now she could not imagine living without these people.

She put her hand on Nathaniel's leg, lightly, and he covered it with his own.

At the head of the table, Hawkeye was watching them, his face drawn.

"Nathaniel," he said, pushing his plate aside. "You and Bears and me need to have a talk and then I'll be on my way."

Beside Elizabeth, Hannah tensed suddenly.

"Where are you going, Grandfather?" She spoke Kahnyen'kehàka, a sign of her distraction.

"Over the hills and far away," he said with a kindly smile. "I'll bring you back a treasure or two."

The women sat silently, with eyes fixed on Hawkeye. *They knew it would come to this,* Elizabeth thought. *From the beginning, they knew. All day they have been preparing for more than one leave-taking.*

But she could not be silent, not for Hannah's sake, not for her own.

"Is this really necessary?"

"Aye, lass, I fear so." Hawkeye looked down at his hands where they rested on either side of his plate. "Otherwise they'll be by, looking for me. And I won't spend another night in their gaol."

"But they have what they want, if they drive you away." Beside her, Nathaniel shifted, but he did not try to quiet her.

"Not quite. You're still here, all of you. You'll just have to carry on without me." He glanced at Hannah's stricken face. "For the time being."

Abruptly the child rose and walked over to her grandmother. "Make him stay with us," she said in a whisper.

Falling-Day put a hand on Hannah's shoulder, and closed her eyes briefly. "Your grandfather goes to look for your uncle Otter," she said, in an even tone. "When he finds him, we will all be together again. You must wish him a successful journey."

Hannah looked hard into her grandmother's eyes, and then toward Many-Doves. Many-Doves nodded firmly, and in response the child's shoulders slumped.

Elizabeth turned to Nathaniel, and saw two things: that this new loss was inevitable, and that the weight of it was almost more than he could bear.

She put Hannah to bed and read to her by the lamp; a luxury for both of them. In the pool of light, the little girl's skin seemed as smoothly polished and glowing as amber. Pausing between pages, Elizabeth found it hard to look away from her face. Such a pretty child, with a willful beauty that mesmerized and frightened all at once. Elizabeth forced her attention back to the story. Tonight, though, Hannah could not be distracted with tales of the *Arabian Nights*.

"Will you and my father go away, too?" she interrupted.

Elizabeth closed the book. *We are not going anywhere,* she wanted to say. But she knew that to sacrifice the truth in the name of comfort would be a mistake with this child. She said, "There are some things I can't be sure of, but I do know that we could not be a family without you. If we must go in the end, then we will all go together."

From the small window under the eaves, she saw that the sky was crowded with stars. Somewhere in the night Hawkeye was moving north on foot by their light alone.

"The winter is coming," Hannah said. "He will be cold, and lonely."

Elizabeth wondered if she would ever grow used to having her thoughts read so easily. "I expect that your grandfather will spend some time trapping with Robbie," she said, although she only could hope that this was true.

"If I were a boy, I could go with him to look for Otter."

She thought she had shed her share of tears for the day, and now Elizabeth found that she was wrong. And how senseless it was to cry for little girls just because they could not go to the places that little boys went so freely.

She said, "When I was eight, I stole some of my cousin Merriweather's clothes. I thought I could dress as a boy, and run away to do as I pleased."

"Did it work?"

Elizabeth shook her head. "They did not fit. You know," she said thoughtfully. "I have never told anyone else about that little adventure of mine."

Hannah smiled. It was a small gift, but perhaps enough to sleep on. Elizabeth kissed her cheek and then she picked up the lantern to make her way down from the sleeping loft.

Nathaniel and Runs-from-Bears were waiting in the shadows of the cold hearth, slumped in chairs. Bears was deeply asleep, his head turned hard to one side, but Nathaniel's eyes followed her as she moved toward him.

"You're as tired as he is."

"True," Nathaniel agreed, squinting up at her with one eye closed. "But I ain't quite so drunk."

He had not slept for two days; the slightly slurred quality to his words might have been nothing more than exhaustion. But the smell on him said something else. Elizabeth stepped back.

"You've been drinking?" she asked, incredulous.

"Aye," Nathaniel said. "That I have." Bears stirred slightly, as if he might have something to add.

Torn between unease and compassion, Elizabeth pushed out her breath audibly. "We'll have to get Bears home somehow."

"They wouldn't let him in. Or if they did, he'd regret it. Falling-Day won't tolerate any man when he's been drinking."

It was true that Elizabeth had never seen any liquor at Lake in the Clouds, but neither had she seen wheaten bread, or sugar, or coffee. It had not occurred to her that the absence of hard drink was significant.

"Never mind, Boots. We'll sleep in the barn," Nathaniel said, rising awkwardly.

"You'll sleep in your bed," Elizabeth said shortly. "But I fear Bears must stay where he is. He'll have a sore neck in the morning."

"That will be the least of it." He paused. "You ain't mad at me?"

She turned away from him to spread the hearth blanket over Bears. With her back to him, she said: "It is a strange way to remember your grandfather or to say goodbye to your father, and I do not see the sense of it, Nathaniel. But I also see no sense in adding insult to injury. Go to bed."

He put a hand on her shoulder. "Come with me."

"I will sleep with Hannah tonight."

With a jerk, he turned her toward him. "No." And seeing her face, he dropped his hand and his head, but not before she saw how his eyes glistened in the lamplight.

"No," he said, just as firmly. "Don't leave me alone."

Silently, Elizabeth nodded. She picked up the lantern and went ahead of him to their room.

.   .   .

He slept uneasily, tossing and muttering in Kahnyen'kehàka. Skimming on the surface of sleep, Elizabeth started awake more than once. There was enough light from the night sky to show her his face, deeply shadowed and outlined with worry. She wanted to touch him, to smooth the lines from his face, but she feared waking him. With a sigh, she turned away to curl on her side.

Behind her Nathaniel stilled suddenly, and she knew he was awake. He pressed his length against her back, his breath warm and harsh at her ear. He smelled of whisky and the council fire. His hands were on her hips, and then he was with her, in a smooth gliding motion. Even as she arched back against him with a soft sound of surprise, he stilled and his grip loosened, and he fell away into a true sleep.

She lay in his arms, half dreaming of Oakmere, of aunt Merriweather at the tea table with her married daughters around her. There had been much talk of husbands at these teas when the men were absent: inexcusable habits, vagaries and moods, strange affinities, male needs—unspecified, incomprehensible needs—that must be seen to. Beyond these necessities, the hearts of men had never seemed to interest her aunt, as if satisfying their stomachs and other bodily demands were sufficient evil unto the day. As if men had no hearts to speak of.

Elizabeth felt Nathaniel's heart beating against her back; her hair was wet with his tears.

Aunt Merriweather. With a care not to wake him again, Elizabeth unwound herself from Nathaniel's embrace. She found a candle and slipped into the main room to light it from the banked embers in the hearth. Bears was gone, the blanket folded haphazardly over the arm of the chair. She hoped he had found a more comfortable bed.

She stood considering the pile of goods, still unpacked, that had come with them from Albany. After a moment's rumbling, she found it wedged between the packet of new quills and the bill of sale for the schoolhouse: her aunt Merriweather's letter, the green wax seal still intact. Elizabeth sat down in the chair and smoothed her hands over the gentle curve of her stomach, considering the square of paper on her knees. Beyond the muffled rush of the waterfall, the world was silent, and the seal cracked open like a shot.

Elizabeth unfolded the closely written sheets and leaned into the candlelight until the elegant black script steadied enough to let itself be read. Thus Elizabeth learned that while she had been moving north through the bush in the hope of finding Nathaniel alive, aunt Merriweather had been nursing her husband through a sudden and final illness; that she had buried him on a rainy summer morning on the very day Elizabeth's letter had arrived with the shocking news of her marriage to a backwoodsman; and that Augusta Merriweather, widowed mother of four grown children, had nothing more pressing to do with her time than to travel to the Colonies and see what could be salvaged of her beloved niece's future and prospects. She had booked passage with a Captain Wentworth and expected to arrive in mid-September.

Traveling with her would be two servants, her eldest daughter, Amanda, and Amanda's husband, Sir William Spencer, Viscount Durbeyfield.

They were too busy the next day, all of them, to take note of Elizabeth's new preoccupation. The harvest was close at hand, and the trapping season, and there were now two men where a few months before there had been four to do the work. Elizabeth was glad to have Nathaniel so occupied, because she was not yet ready to share her latest news.

The other women spent the day in the cornfield, but Elizabeth kept Hannah by her. She was pleased to have the child's help and her easy company. They sorted through the purchases from Albany, setting aside the schoolroom supplies and gifts from provisions which needed to be divided between the two cabins. Hannah was delighted with each discovery, and her low spirits gradually rose while she dashed between cabins with her arms full of good things.

In the meantime, Elizabeth spent some time putting together a basket of supplies, from cloth and buttons to a cone of sugar and a small sack of wheaten flour.

"Who is that for?" Hannah wanted to know.

"Martha Southern and her children."

"Oh." She had found a pair of spectacles and she put them on, where they promptly slid to the tip of her nose. "And these? Ian McGarrity?"

"Yes. If his parents will allow it." Elizabeth did not want to think of Jed McGarrity right now, and so she sorted through the small store of ribbons she had brought with her from Albany. She pulled out a dark blue and a green, and wound them into a neat package, which she added to the basket.

"Do you think Martha will take those things from us?"

Elizabeth stood with a sigh. "I'm not sure," she said. "But I must try."

It was Jemima who came to the cabin door. Her homespun dress had been dyed a hasty and uneven black, and it matched the frown on her face.

"Good afternoon, Jemima," Elizabeth said softly. "May I see your mother?"

"Of course, Miz Elizabeth. Please do come in." Martha pulled the door out of her daughter's hand, ignoring the look the little girl sent her way. "And Hannah. It's so kind of you to call. Please do come in."

Hannah headed immediately for the baby in his cradle near the hearth, but Jemima intercepted her, placing her small, solid body between the other girl and her goal.

"Daughter," Martha chided softly. "Go fetch Adam out of the garden. Go on now."

Jemima hung back, staring at her feet. "What are they doing here?"

"We've come to pay our respects," Elizabeth answered, although the question had not been directed at her.

Jemima left, banging the door behind her. The child wore her anger and misery so clearly and unapologetically that some of Elizabeth's dislike gave way without a struggle.

"She's taken her pa's passing real hard," Martha explained.

"Yes, of course she has. I am very sorry for your loss. Especially sorry," Elizabeth added.

Martha nodded. Her fingers rubbed the thin fabric of her skirt, and for a moment she could not meet Elizabeth's eye.

"We put our faith in the Lord. He had strong feelings, my Moses, and they moved him too far at times."

Elizabeth made a small noise of encouragement, for she did not know how to respond to this.

Martha looked up. "You've had a loss of your own," she said. "And I'm sorry for Moses' part in it. I hope you all are taking comfort from each other."

"Thank you," Elizabeth said. "We are." Then she leaned forward. "Martha, I have come to see if I can be of any help. If it is not too early to speak to you of this."

The basket sat between them on the floor; Martha's gaze moved over it, and there was a flicker there: relief, and pleasure, too.

"Those things are for you, and I hope they will be of use. But I had something else in mind, as well." Elizabeth met Martha's surprised look, and with simple words, laid out her thoughts. By the time she had finished, Martha was looking doubtful rather than surprised.

"I don't like charity," she said. "Moses wouldn't want me to accept charity."

Hannah had scooped the baby onto her lap as soon as Jemima was out of the cabin, but now he began to fuss. Distracted, Martha took him from Hannah and began to jostle him on her knee.

"It is skilled work," Elizabeth said softly. "I cannot sew, and I have need of many things for myself, and for Hannah—and for the new child, as well. I would not call that charity."

"Can I work here?" Martha asked. "I wouldn't want to be taking these children up the mountain every day."

"Of course," Elizabeth said. "I will bring you what you need."

The frown line between Martha's eyes slowly disappeared. "I can only sew half days, until the corn is in. Two dollars for a day's work is all I'll take."

"But I inquired in Albany," Elizabeth pointed out. "Experienced seamstresses ask for two and a half, and that seems fair."

Martha jostled the boy on her lap, and produced her first

smile of the day. "Paradise ain't Albany, and you'll get plainer work from me," she said. "But we can make the difference up in trade, if you'd be so kind. I'd still like my girl to come to your school."

The door opened and Jemima appeared, dragging her younger brother behind her. Elizabeth stifled a deep sigh of resignation, and extended her hand toward Martha Southern.

At dinner, Nathaniel almost laughed out loud to hear it told: Jemima Southern back in Elizabeth's classroom, for good this time. It was only her sharpest look that stopped him; that, and perhaps the fact that his head still pained him. At the moment she could not sympathize one bit.

They were eating on their own this evening. Elizabeth had managed a stew, with Hannah's assistance, and corn bread, which she now crumbled into her bowl with some irritation.

"I know I should be glad of the challenge," she said. "But she is such a trying child."

Hannah hummed her agreement. "If we could at least have Liam, too," she said. "Jemima never acts up so much when Liam's got an eye on her."

"I guess Jemima'll settle down to schoolwork soon enough," Nathaniel offered; his attempt at an apology. He added: "At any rate, Boots, it's a good thing that Jed and Nancy ain't set on pulling their boys out of the classroom. Jed is a forgiving man, I have to say."

Elizabeth threw Nathaniel a pleading look over Hannah's head, and he nodded. For the moment Hannah knew nothing of Jed's unplanned and undeserved stay in Anna's pantry, or the role Elizabeth had had in Hawkeye's return home; nor did Elizabeth want her to know for as long as possible. The whole episode seemed unreal, still. She expected Hawkeye to come through the door any moment, and she thought that Nathaniel did, too.

"Ian looks mighty strange in those spectacles," Hannah noted.

"If you insist on reading by starlight you'll need spectacles yourself, and quite quickly," Elizabeth pointed out, ladling more stew into Hannah's bowl. She moved too quickly and gravy splashed on the table. With a small cry of dismay, Elizabeth began to mop at it with her apron.

Nathaniel appeared at her side, pulling her gently away. "Boots!" he said softly, his mouth turned down in worry. "It's just a spill. What is the matter with you? You're so jumpy."

"Maybe it's Great-grandfather," Hannah said.

"No." Elizabeth pulled away from him. "Yes. Of course it's Chingachgook, in part—but, well." She drew in a big breath, and let it out. "I thought it would be better to wait, with all that has happened in the last few days. It's so silly of me. Here." She drew aunt Merriweather's letter from her pocket, and held it out toward Nathaniel.

He raised a brow, and slowly reached out to take it. Then he turned it over in his hands. "We just forgot about this, didn't we? In the hurry to get back here. From your aunt."

"She's on her way here for a visit," Elizabeth said in a rush.

"Well, that's not so bad," Hannah said with a bigger smile. "Is it space you're worried about? She can sleep with me in the loft."

The thought of aunt Merriweather climbing the ladder to the sleeping loft might have been amusing, in other circumstances. But Elizabeth could barely listen to the child's plans for the visitors; she watched Nathaniel scan the letter line by line. He looked up in surprise. "Your cousin and her husband, too?"

Elizabeth cleared her throat. "And servants."

"Well, never mind, Boots," he said, pulling her close to wipe a smear of gravy from her cheek. "I expect we can deal with them well enough. You and me have dealt with worse in our time, have we not?"

She let out a short hiccup of a laugh, which Nathaniel took as agreement.

In bed that night, Nathaniel surprised her.

"Where did you want to run away to, when you stole your cousin's clothes?" he asked sleepily.

"You heard that?"

"I was drunk, Boots. It don't render a man deaf."

She moved her head to a more comfortable position on his shoulder. "I thought I could sign on as a sailor, and get far away somewhere where women were allowed to ride horses astride, and learn to shoot."

"And read what they pleased?"

"That was before I found out about books," Elizabeth said. "When I did find out about them, it seemed for a long time that they would be enough to make up for the rest of it."

He turned on his side, shifting her down so that he could look into her face.

"What is it about William Spencer that you want to tell me?"

"There is nothing to tell you about William Spencer," she said without a moment's hesitation. "Not a single thing."

But Elizabeth lay awake for a long time, contemplating the irony of a truth as unsettling as any lie.

LIV

With the approaching harvest, Elizabeth's students began to disappear from her classroom. Boys and girls alike would be gone one day or two in an awkwardly revolving pattern, to reappear with an apologetic nod of the head and agricultural details Elizabeth had actually begun to grasp. By the end of the first week after Chingachgook's funeral, with her own work at home increasing and the visit at hand pressing on her mind, she recognized the necessity of a natural recess in the rhythm of the school year. She proposed a small celebration to end a successful summer session, with recitations.

"And food?" Ephraim wanted to know.

"Of course," Elizabeth agreed. "We would want to offer our guests something."

"What's a recitation?" asked Ruth Glove.

"Singing and poems and such," proposed Dolly Smythe.

For the first time since she had come back to the classroom, Jemima Southern sat up to show some interest.

"Each of you would perform some small piece. Ian, you might recite a bit from *Robinson Crusoe* if you like, you have a very nice way with it. And Jemima, would you like to sing?"

The look of eager surprise on Jemima's face gave Elizabeth great satisfaction. Finally, she had found a suggestion which seemed to wake the little girl up.

The date was set for the following Saturday evening.

"Our ma makes doughnuts on Saturdays," Ephraim pointed out. "And folks smell better, too." No one seemed surprised by this connection, and so Elizabeth bit down hard on her own smile. After more discussion, she set them to the task of writing invitations to their families.

Leaning over Ian Kirby's slate while he puzzled out how to do such a thing, Elizabeth felt Hannah's hand touch her arm, tentatively.

"Can I recite, too?"

Surprised, Elizabeth pulled up to look at her closely. "Of course you may, Hannah Bonner. You are a student in this class, are you not? Perhaps you could recite some Robert Burns."

Hannah nodded thoughtfully, and turned back to her work.

When Elizabeth let the children go for the day, Curiosity was waiting on the step with a broad smile and a basket filled with bread and cake and other lovely things Elizabeth very much missed, although she would not admit this weakness. Before she could say a word in greeting, Curiosity had grasped Elizabeth by both arms and pulled her back into the empty classroom. Then she stood there, tapping one bare toe and smiling so broadly that Elizabeth found herself almost laughing in return.

"What is it?" she asked. "Good news?"

"Well, let me tell you," Curiosity said. "There's company at your pa's, arrived late yesterday. Asking for you."

Elizabeth's face fell.

"Not that Merriweather woman! A Quaker gentleman."

"Cousin Samuel," Elizabeth said, brightening. "I was wondering."

"Yas'm. Samuel Hench, and he brought a man called Joshua with him, a blacksmith."

"Did he? I am glad he was able to come and call, he wasn't sure he would find the time."

Curiosity's sharp gaze fixed on Elizabeth's face. "That cousin of yours has been holed up with John Glove all morning. Spending money."

Elizabeth turned away. "I suppose then he will want his dinner."

"You a terrible fraud, Elizabeth. Look me in the face and say you don't know nothing about the man's business here."

"Curiosity," she said, turning back to spread her hands out in front of her in a gesture of surrender. "I suppose it was silly of me to think I could hide it from you. But let's keep this between us, shall we?"

With a hoarse laugh, the older woman took Elizabeth firmly by the arms again and, leaning forward, planted a dry kiss on her forehead.

"I knew it!" she said, shaking her slightly. "I knew I weren't mistaken about you."

"But we can keep this between us?" Elizabeth prompted, again.

Curiosity nodded so that her turban wavered precariously. "We can, if we must. But some things happening now, and you've got a hand in them."

"What things?"

"Why, my Polly will be getting married, now that Benjamin has his papers. I wondered if this day would ever come. And right now Galileo is having a talk with Mr. Glove. We were thinking that maybe he would hire on our Manny, have him learn the mill business."

"But what about Benjamin?"

"He'd come work for your pa, take Manny's place and set up housekeeping with Polly."

"I believe you could run a revolution single-handed, Curiosity."

"So could most women," she said with a dismissive flutter of her fingers. "A revolution ain't nothing but a good spring cleaning long overdue, after all." She thrust her basket in Elizabeth's hands and picked up her skirts to go.

"You come down to the house this evening, all of you. We've got some celebrating to do."

"Oh, Curiosity," Elizabeth said slowly, stepping back. "I'm not sure."

"None of that foolishness. He's your pa, after all. And my Polly would be disappointed if you was to stay away." She pulled up. "You told the man yet that you with child?"

Elizabeth shook her head. "There never was an opportunity. I'm surprised—" And she broke off, with a grin.

"You think I'm going to spill those particular beans, missy, you don't know me overwell. That's for you and your man to do. Tonight seem like a good time."

"I just don't know, Curiosity. With all that has happened—"

"Chingachgook was a good man, and now he's gone. The Mohawk know the difference between the quick and the dead, and they don't make young folk stop livin' when the old move on ahead. If Falling-Day don't want to come down the mountain 'cause she don't feel comfortable, that's something else again. But you could come."

Elizabeth hesitated, and then she nodded. "I will talk to Nathaniel."

"You do that. And come along, then. You don't smile enough these days, Elizabeth, and you got plenty to smile about, ain't you?" Her eyes traveled over the line of Elizabeth's skirt.

"You have a way of looking at things, Curiosity. It is very disarming."

"I'll take that as a compliment. Now, I'll see you tonight, I hope." And with a rustle of skirts she disappeared over the step.

Hannah appeared suddenly out of the other room with a whoop and a holler.

"Oh, can we go? Please?"

"You must learn not to startle me that way," Elizabeth said, leaning back against her desk for support. "What were you doing in there?"

"Reading." Hannah held up a tract that Mrs. Schuyler had sent for Elizabeth's sake: *A Present to be given to Teeming Women by their Husbands or Friends, Containing Directions for Women with Child. How to Prepare for the Hour of Travail. Written for the Private Use of a Gentlewoman of Quality: and now published for the Common Good.*

"Oh, dear," said Elizabeth uneasily. "I suppose you've read most of it already?"

Hannah nodded happily. "I don't think my grandmother would agree with much of it. But it's interesting anyway."

"No doubt," Elizabeth muttered.

She had set up the second schoolroom as her study and a library, of sorts. Nathaniel had made her a desk, and a comfortable chair; the light was good and the view over the lake wonderful. But when she could, Elizabeth preferred to work at home, to be near him. Hannah made more use of the study than Elizabeth did. It was not hard to understand, for Elizabeth remembered very well what a rare and valuable commodity privacy had been when she was young.

She began to sort through the books on her desk.

"I'm not sure if we shall go. I need to talk to your father about it."

"If you want to go, he won't say no," Hannah said. "He can't refuse you anything."

"Is that so?" Elizabeth laughed. "Let's get home, then, and see if you are right."

Hannah cast a longing look toward the study. "Could I stay just a while longer?"

Elizabeth wanted very much to give Hannah the half hour she desired, but it was not a sensible thing to do. There was work waiting at home: the small fields of corn, beans, and squash that lay on the outer, sunny apron of the gorge demanded all the women's energy now, and Hannah's time outside of school was highly prized. Beyond that, Nathaniel and Runs-from-Bears were even more on guard these days than they had been. Billy Kirby had not yet made a move to avenge his hurt pride, but he would not wait forever.

"You can take the tract home with you until tomorrow."

The child's face darkened: disappointment, and a tinge of defiance. This lasted only for a moment, and then she turned and went back into the workroom, to reappear again emptyhanded.

"It is not fair," she said. "Being tethered all the time. I like it as little as Grandfather did, but you set him free." And she threw Elizabeth a significant glance.

"Ah," she said. "I wondered when you'd find out about that. Did the boys tell you?"

Hannah nodded. "It is easy for you to talk about staying close to home and being safe," she said. "You've had your excitement, the summer in the bush and then breaking Grand-father out of Anna's pantry."

Elizabeth pressed the ridge of her nose between two fingers and a thumb. "Those were not pleasant experiences, Hannah," she said. "I did not go looking for them, and I wish that neither had been necessary."

The little girl shrugged one shoulder, unconvinced. "Everyone else in this family gets to have adventures. When will it be my turn?"

"Soon enough, I fear," Elizabeth said. And hoped it was a lie.

There was another social call to pay, one that Elizabeth dreaded very much. But she thought that she might as well get it behind her, on the way to Polly's engagement party. Kitty would not welcome her gladly, but she could not put aside the strong feeling that the younger woman did need help, and would accept it, if only Elizabeth could find the right words.

Nathaniel was not happy about the visit, but he seemed much easier when they found out that Mr. Witherspoon had gone to pay a call on Martha Southern. Hannah too did not mind the delay; she took a chair in the Witherspoons' parlor and looked about herself with great curiosity and undisguised interest, jumping up to examine the books on the shelves with her hands crossed on her back, as if she could barely withstand the urge to touch the few well-read volumes. Elizabeth joined her and found what she had expected: Tillotson's and Butler's *Sermons*, much thumbed; *Pilgrim's Progress, Paradise Lost, Robinson Crusoe,* with bindings carefully repaired; Walton's *Life of Dr. John Donne,* Law's *A Serious Call to a Devout and Holy Life,* and Clarke's *A Demonstration of the Being and Attributes of God,* these less worn and dustier than the rest. There were also some volumes on medicine, which immediately caught Hannah's attention. She sent Kitty a pleading look, and receiving a small nod in return, Hannah settled herself happily in the corner with *The Anatomy of Humane Bodies with Figures Drawn After Life* with an air of real industry.

Kitty's still and disinterested expression was focused on Nathaniel, who was carrying most of the burden in trying to create a conversation; none of what came into Elizabeth's head would serve at all, as most of it had to do with the neat, round expanse of Kitty's middle. Until today Elizabeth had resisted the urge to calculate Kitty's condition out in months, but found now that she could not deny what she saw before her. With some shock she reckoned that Kitty was perhaps seven months gone; Elizabeth wondered at herself, that she had been so preoccupied indeed in January, to have not noticed the game Julian had been playing with this girl. With this girl who would soon be a mother, without a husband's support. She wished very much for some degree of intimacy with Kitty, so that she could discuss her situation with her openly, but the expression on the younger woman's face made it clear that this was an impossibility.

Kitty had turned her attention to Elizabeth, her pale eyes hooded.

"There was no word of Richard in Albany." It was a statement rather than a question.

"I am afraid not."

A lip curled down in gentle disbelief. "Really? You are disappointed not to have met him there?"

Elizabeth produced something that was meant to be a smile, determined not to lose her composure or temper. "I have brought you a few things from Albany." She gestured to the basket Nathaniel had put down near the door. "I hope they will be of use."

There was a notable silence.

"I will be in Albany to testify, when the time comes," Kitty said. "When Richard is back. He will buy me what I require then."

Because she did not know whether she should be affronted at such bad manners, or rightfully rebuked for having presumed that Kitty would accept any token from her, Elizabeth glanced away. On Nathaniel's face there was wariness: he did not want Kitty—or anyone here—to know about the new court date, and the repercussions if Richard were not to appear. With some misgivings, Elizabeth swallowed down what she most wanted to say.

He saw what was on her mind, and rose to end the visit. "I am sure he will, Kitty. In the meantime, we got you some odds and ends to tide you over. Boots, they'll be waiting for us."

Hannah dropped a small curtsy before Kitty. "Did you know that Polly and Benjamin are getting married?" she asked. "We're going to the party. Do you want to come?"

Kitty turned away to look out the window, her narrow back straight and her shoulders held so stiffly that Elizabeth thought a single touch might cause her to shatter.

Walking away from the house, Elizabeth had the sense of the empty windows at her back, as vacant as blind eyes.

It was Samuel Hench who gave Nathaniel and Elizabeth the news that Judge Middleton and his son had left for Albany just that afternoon. For once, Curiosity seemed not to know about the judge's movements, and seeing the joyous faces in the parlor, Elizabeth understood her distraction.

"I thought perhaps that ye would not know," Samuel said, his face troubled. "It did seem strange to me that they should go off so suddenly."

"Never mind, man." Nathaniel clapped him on the shoulder. "Let's not ruin the party for the others."

The reasoning was sound, but Elizabeth could hardly put the idea of her father and brother on their way to Albany out of her head. Most certainly her cousin had mentioned their meeting at Judge van der Poole's; Julian had reasoned out the rest for himself. She sighed, and turning, walked straight into Curiosity's arms.

"I knew you'd be here," Curiosity said with a smile. "Come say hello."

The night air was distinctly cold and much of the party was gathered around the hearth: Polly and Benjamin, looking dazed but happy, Daisy with some sewing in her lap, and a tall, sturdy man introduced to Elizabeth as Joshua.

"We met a friend of yours in the bush," Nathaniel said by way of greeting.

Joshua seemed to be perhaps thirty, although the hair on his closely shorn skull was tinged with gray. He had mellow brown eyes and a steady gaze. "Yes, sir, so I've been told. I would appreciate the opportunity to talk to you about that, after the party."

Elizabeth followed his glance toward the young people by the hearth. Polly and Benjamin were talking to Hannah, but Daisy's attention was fixed solidly on her sewing. This struck Elizabeth as strange; then Daisy glanced up and Elizabeth saw the brightness of her eye, and the look in it when she turned her gaze to Joshua.

"Yes, this is not the time," Elizabeth agreed.

Joshua sat down again across from Daisy, who dropped her head over her work. Elizabeth elbowed Nathaniel neatly to cut off any comment that might be forthcoming, and she sought out Curiosity, who winked at her meaningfully.

"He ain't going anyplace," Galileo announced. "The judge's going to set him up. We been without a smith since Asa Pierce came out on the wrong side of a disagreement with that bear, and Joshua is looking for work."

"What very good news!" Elizabeth caught her cousin's eye and smiled broadly.

"Good things come to them who wait, ain't that so, Elizabeth?" Curiosity called. She was putting a bowl of butter beans on the table and she straightened up to survey the collection of platters and servers. "Hannah child, you must be hungry. George, Manny, put down them dominoes now, and come eat. Even happy stomachs need food," she said in the direction of the hearth. "Mr. Hench, will you do us the honor of starting?"

They learned that the wedding party was set for the next Saturday afternoon, to which Hannah promptly called out: "Oh, no!"

"Saturday next doesn't suit you, Missy Hannah?" Galileo asked solemnly. "Why is that?"

Hannah ducked her head and apologized for her outburst.

"We have the school recitation planned for Saturday evening," Elizabeth explained. "But of course we shall find another time for that."

"No need," Polly said, tugging on Hannah's plait. "A wedding don't take very long, after all. Don't you like the idea of two parties in one day?"

"Our Hannah likes her parties spread out, generous like," Nathaniel said. "She doesn't like to tire herself out with her admirers."

"I don't see any problem with both things on the Saturday, if you don't, Miz Elizabeth." Benjamin raised his voice to be heard over the good-natured laughter.

"It is entirely up to you," Elizabeth said. "If you don't mind—"

Hannah clapped her hands with pleasure, and turned to Samuel Hench. "I've never been to a wedding so I don't know what will happen there, but will you come to the school party? Jed will play his fiddle, and there's doughnuts, and singing, and poems."

"I would very much like to hear thee sing," he replied solemnly. "But I'm afraid my business will take me away tomorrow."

"Why, that's not any visit at all," Hannah said. "You haven't even come to Lake in the Clouds."

Elizabeth squeezed Hannah's hand under the table and leaned in closer. "I'm sure that Cousin Samuel would stay longer if he could."

"I would, indeed," Samuel agreed.

"Cousin," she said quietly. "I hope you haven't taken offense at my father's sudden departure."

But his answer was interrupted by a knock at the door; the kind of knock that did not mean friends come to call. The laughter in the room fell away into an awkward silence and Galileo rose with a puzzled expression and went into the hall. Beside Elizabeth, Nathaniel tensed.

The man who appeared in the doorway was not especially large, but he had a great expanse of gray beard, a halo of bright white hair, and a forcefulness of purpose in his stance.

"The name's O'Brien," he announced. "Treasury agent. Here on business. The Indians on the mountain said I might find Nathaniel Bonner at Judge Middleton's." His eyes, ice-blue, hesitated at Samuel Hench and then moved on to Nathaniel. "I guess that's you. I'll have a word, now."

Elizabeth was on her feet, her hands clenched at her sides. "You are unwelcome here, Mr. O'Brien. This is a family party. If you care to call again in the morning—"

"A family party?" He smiled, exposing a scattering of sharp teeth in raw gums. "Strange family, I'd say. Where is the judge, anyhow?" This last question was shot at Galileo, who provided a brief explanation.

"If you would be so kind, Mr. O'Brien—" Elizabeth tried again.

"It's not my business to be kind when I'm on a job. Who're you?"

Nathaniel's hand on Elizabeth's wrist pulled her up short. In a long and easy movement, he stood. "She's my wife. She happens to be the judge's daughter, as well, but you can call her Mrs. Bonner. I'll come out and talk to you, if you'll leave these people in peace."

He leaned over to talk quietly into her ear. "The treasury was bound to show up sooner or later. Sit tight, Boots." Then he winked at Hannah, spoke a quiet word to Galileo, and disappeared into the hall.

The crackling of the fire in the hearth was all the sound in the room for a long moment, and then Curiosity let out a great sigh. "Come on, now, there's food here too good for the pigs. Manny, hand your plate down here, sugar, and let me give you some of this beef. You won't get this good once you start working down to the mill, let me promise you that."

Slowly, the conversation turned back to the wedding and the upcoming school recital. Elizabeth gave her cousin a grim smile.

"I see that thy life in Paradise is not dull," he said. "Perhaps I should not be surprised that thy brother does not wish to leave."

Once again Elizabeth put down her fork. "Julian? Leave? Why should he?"

Samuel shrugged. "I thought that perhaps I could convince thy brother to come home with me, for I could use an assistant. But I'm afraid the life of a merchant does not entice Julian."

"I am surprised to hear of your offer," she said. "But more, I am disappointed that he did not consent to join you. I think it would have done him much good to get away from here."

Samuel nodded thoughtfully, and then gestured toward Joshua and Daisy, who were picking at their plates while they talked. "Dost thou know the proverb about the two things that cannot be hid?"

Elizabeth smiled. "Love, and a cough. I see the first here in evidence, but what has that to do with my brother?"

"The proverb was once longer, I believe: 'Foure things cannot be kept close, love, the cough, fyre and sorrow.' I would say that thy brother burns not with love, but with jealousy. Perhaps given hard work, and a purpose, he could be saved."

"You are a missionary at heart," Elizabeth said ruefully. "I only wish there were some hope of success in this case."

"There is always hope," Cousin Samuel said.

When she finally went in search of Nathaniel, Elizabeth found him leaning against the wall of the house staring at the night sky. She followed the line of his gaze, leaning against his hard shoulder.

His arm came up around her and she moved in closer, for it was truly cold.

"The maples are turning," Nathaniel said.

She let out a small laugh of surprise. "Can you see that, in the dark? Or do you hear it?"

In response he took her hand and pulled her down to the trees that stood on the far side of the barn. In the dark, he reached up and pulled a leaf, which he stroked across her cheek and then pressed into her hand. "Go have a look," he said. "If you don't believe me."

"Oh, I believe you," she said, pulling her shawl more tightly around her. Even in the moonlight, she could see the set of his jaw, and the lines around his mouth.

"Are you worried about the winter?"

He sighed, chafing her arms with his hands. "There's enough sign that it will be a hard one, but no, I ain't especially worried about the winter."

Elizabeth rubbed her cheek on his shoulder, drawing in his smell.

"Are you going to tell me about our visitor?"

"O'Brien? He's after the Tory Gold."

"That much I surmised," Elizabeth said. "I gather you satisfied his curiosity. I heard him ride off."

Nathaniel produced a small snort of laughter. "I doubt that man has ever been satisfied with anything. But I've quieted him down for the moment."

"Do you think my father sent him this way?"

"No. The judge and your brother won't be in Albany until sometime tomorrow, Boots. Unless they ran into O'Brien on the road, which ain't likely." He lifted her hand to his mouth and kissed her knuckles. "No, it was the gold we spread around in Albany. The state wants it, but thus far they don't have any clear claim to it."

"So then we don't have to worry about him anymore."

"I don't know about that," Nathaniel said grimly. He took her hand and they started back toward the house. "I think O'Brien will stick around for a while, at any rate. He took a room at the Pierces', and he's likely to try to question you, so be prepared."

"I am not afraid of him," Elizabeth said.

Nathaniel pulled up short, and leaning down, kissed her briefly. "I know you're not, Boots, and that's what scares me. A little healthy fear is a good thing sometimes, in a man or a woman." His hand swept down over the curve of her belly, and up her back to pull her in closer. "There's been enough leave-takings for a while."

Pressed against him, Elizabeth felt a tremble in his arms. "I am not going anywhere, Nathaniel," she said firmly, determined to keep surprise out of her voice.

"That's good," he said. "Because I wouldn't know how to go on anymore, without you."

The sound of the front door closing separated them. In the shadows, she made out Joshua's solid form. He had his hat in his hands, and his expression was guarded.

"Don't care to interrupt," he said. "I'll come find you another time."

"Oh, no," Elizabeth said, stepping toward the porch. "Please don't go. We wanted to talk to you about Joe."

In the faint light, Joshua's expression was unreadable. "Can you tell me how he died?"

"You know he's dead?"

Joshua reached into the pocket of his coat with two fingers and drew out the bijou Elizabeth had worn on a chain around her neck for so many weeks. The pale stone in the center flashed like an eye in the moonlight. "If he sent me this, he's dead. It was all he had to leave behind." There was a long pause, in which Joshua looked thoughtfully at the small ornament in his palm.

"Do you know, did he take a family name?"

Nathaniel glanced at Elizabeth. "He introduced himself to me as Joe, no last name. Did he tell you, Boots?"

When Elizabeth confirmed that he had not, Joshua shrugged. "I was hoping he might have left me that, too, now that I need one. He was my father, but I guess you figured that out."

Elizabeth walked up the porch steps and stood in front of Joshua. "It seems to me a very great responsibility, to find a name for yourself. Perhaps your father meant you to take on that task when the day came."

"I'll have to think on it some," Joshua said.

Nathaniel said, "Maybe we could go set in the kitchen and have a talk. You'll want to hear what we have to tell you in privacy."

"If you don't mind bein' kept away from the party—"

There was a loud burst of laughter from the parlor, punctuated by Curiosity's voice in a rambling scold.

"I think they're managing without us well enough," Elizabeth said dryly.

"Would you mind if I asked Mr. Hench to join us? I would like him to hear this story, too."

"That's your decision," Nathaniel said.

Joshua looked down to the cap he held in his hands. "Maybe you don't understand this," he said, searching carefully for words. "Don't know why you might, after all. But it's a strange thing, having decisions to make all of a sudden. God knows I'm thankful, but it'll take some getting used to."

Settled around the hearth in the kitchen, Elizabeth and Nathaniel told the story they had to tell of Joe, how they had come across him and how he had met his death. Elizabeth cradled a cup of warm cider in her hands, and watched the firelight flicker in the deep amber fluid as she listened to Nathaniel tell the last of it.

"I didn't know him very well, you understand," Joshua said quietly, when Nathaniel had finished. "Me and Mama was sold away when I was little. But I saw him now and then in the town, and twice a year on Sunday he had a free afternoon. He walked a long way to come talk to me then, wasn't ever more than an hour, 'cause he had to be back before sunset. Strange, how much you can miss a body you never did see very much to start with. But I do miss him. The idea of him."

Cousin Samuel had been quiet through much of the story, but now he leaned forward, his hands spread out in front of himself. While they were well acquainted to honest work, they had little resemblance to Joshua's hands, heavily muscled, blunt, and the dark skin seamed with scars.

"There is an old saying that might serve well," he said. "'Grief will not recall thy father to thee, but by thy conduct thou canst revive him to the world.'"

Elizabeth felt Nathaniel's sorrow, usually held so tightly in hand, blossom suddenly up. He flushed, perhaps with embarrassment, perhaps with new purpose. For a moment Elizabeth was overcome, too, but with feelings of guilt: she had not understood, not really, what it had cost him to have said goodbye to his grandfather and father on the same day. To know one of them gone forever; and not to know if the other would ever return. Under her folded hands, a sudden faint kicking, as if to scold. She wondered if this child would read her thoughts as easily as its father did.

"Sometimes, truth be told, I am angry at my father," Joshua said in a voice so soft that Elizabeth barely heard him.

"That he ran away?"

He turned his head toward her slowly, and blinked.

"No," he said. "That he didn't go long ago, and take me with him."

They were quiet then. There were no other sounds in the kitchen but that of the wood hissing in the hearth, and the creak of the wind in the rafters, but it was not an awkward silence. After a while it gave way to talk, the sort of easy talk between men after a long day of hard work and a shared meal. They were that comfortable together, talking of matters of the world, far away: plague in Philadelphia, and civil unrest in France; of things closer to home: the weather, and the harvest, and signs of a hard winter to come soon after.

She might have had a share in the conversation. She knew that they would listen to her; they would answer her questions and ask her opinion. And because she knew this to be true, Elizabeth was content to sit and to watch their faces, and listen.

LV

An impatient fall nipped hard on those September nights, and the village pushed toward an early harvest. Deprived unexpectedly of her students, Elizabeth tucked up her skirts to help pick apples and pears from the trees between the barn and the corn. Finding a great deal of satisfaction in the filled baskets, she took it upon herself to join Many-Doves and Hannah as they waded in the shallow waters of the marsh, where they harvested wild rice and cranberries as red as rubies. On a clear fall afternoon while Falling-Day tied standing corn together with strips of rawhide to bring about the first drying of the cobs, Elizabeth picked the beans that wound up the cornstalks, pausing now and then to look over the golds and oranges and reds scattered in the forest canopy like candles against the coming night. With Hannah she went deep into the woods to gather beechnuts while squirrels chirred and barked overhead, leaping from branch to branch in shivering outrage. As she had been in the spring, Hannah became her teacher once again, pointing out the flocks of robins and chickadees gorging in preparation for their flight south, half-built muskrat shelters woven with cattails and bulrushes, a red-bellied snake working its way into an abandoned anthill where it would sleep through the cold.

She saw little of Nathaniel during the day: the season had begun, and the men went out very early with the dogs. One of them was never far from Lake in the Clouds; both of them were uneasy about leaving the women alone. Elizabeth began to understand what a great hardship it was to have Otter and Hawkeye away. For the first time she heard Falling-Day wonder out loud when her son would come home, a question which much occupied Elizabeth, along with thoughts of Richard Todd. The judge and Julian had returned from Albany with nothing to say about their trip, its purpose or success; nor had there been any sign or word of aunt Merriweather. O'Brien, who turned out to have the improbable first name of Baldwin—promptly shortened to Baldy by Axel and his regular patrons—demonstrated more interest in schnapps than he did in finding the Tory Gold, and showed no inclination to leave Paradise. And the date of the final hearing on the breach-of-promise suit approached. In an attempt to curb her anxiety, Elizabeth spent her evenings preparing for the school recital, visiting her students in their homes where she often joined in shelling beans while she listened to recitations.

Over a solitary supper—Hannah was still busy with Falling-Day—Elizabeth brought up the subject again. "Where do you think Richard could be?"

It was not a new question, and Nathaniel shrugged, as he always did.

"Your guess is as good as mine, Boots."

" 'Excessive worry will not resolve anything,' " Elizabeth recited.

"Right again."

"But I can't help wondering."

He sighed, and put down his fork. "O'Brien has been nosing around on the mountain."

"Oh, now that is one way to distract me. Something new to worry about. Did you catch him at it?"

"Bears ran across him on the north face."

Elizabeth looked up sharply. "Near the mine?"

He nodded. "Don't worry, he hasn't found it."

"How do you know?"

"Because he hasn't showed up here with your father and brother and Billy Kirby behind him," Nathaniel said.

"Of course, Billy is behind this, and my brother behind

Billy. Lord God," Elizabeth muttered. "Does he have the right to trespass, as a treasury agent?"

"I ain't exactly sure," Nathaniel admitted. "But he got off quick enough when he ran into Bears. I'm on my way to see the judge tonight, to find out for certain."

Elizabeth busied herself clearing the table. He caught her wrist, drew her across to sit on his lap with a thump.

"I don't want you worrying overmuch, Boots. It's just another week to the hearing, and we'll be clear then. I'll stick closer to home in the meantime." He blinked at her, and then tried for a grin. "I promised you life wouldn't be boring, didn't I?"

She touched her forehead to his. "Right at this moment, I would not mind boring. Do you want me to come with you?"

"No. You can't hold your temper around your father—don't frown at me that way, Boots, you know it's true. I'll wait till Julian is down at Axel's, to catch the judge on his own."

"Suddenly an evening shucking corn sounds quite pleasant." Elizabeth began to climb off Nathaniel's lap, but found that he was not ready to let her go.

"You don't need to work so hard, Boots," he said softly. "I worry about you."

"Pah," she said, tweaking his ear. She took his hand and spread it across the slowly increasing curve of her stomach. "I'm as healthy as an ox."

"And just about as heavy." He grinned, wiggling underneath her.

Elizabeth yanked harder on his ear this time. "I shall remember that, Nathaniel Bonner, the next time you want me to sit on your—lap." And with a little push she was up and away.

For the recital Anna Hauptmann promised five dozen doughnuts and a wheel of her good cheese; the Gloves, cider and ale enough for all; the other families, blessed with fewer material goods, pledged apple and pumpkin pies, corn fritters and baked beans. Curiosity announced that if she was making one cake, she might as well make two. The schoolchildren came to Lake in the Clouds by special invitation on the night before the recital to practice their singing, and to make popcorn balls, sampling extensively as they went.

There was much discussion of what to sing, in what order, and whether or not audience participation should be encouraged, or tolerated.

"Just try to keep our ma from singing," said Hepzibah, licking her fingers.

"Not during 'Barbry Allen'!" warned Jemima. " 'Barbry Allen' is mine!"

"We'll make sure your mother has a full plate," Elizabeth suggested to the Glove girls. "So she won't feel compelled to sing along."

This made sense to Jemima, who went back to squeezing popcorn into tortured shapes.

"Is the judge coming?" asked Hannah.

"He is," confirmed Nathaniel from the corner where he was casting bullets. "Told me so himself." He raised a brow in Elizabeth's direction, seeing her frown. "I think you'll be surprised at the audience you get. It's the talk of the village, your recital. Do you think you'll have your mouth unglued by that time, Ephraim?"

Ephraim mumbled an answer through a great mass of molasses and popcorn.

"He don't know his poem yet," Henrietta announced primly. "I heard him trying to say it to Ma today, and he couldn't get past the third line. Maybe Dolly will have to say it for him."

Ephraim took a threatening step toward his sister, and Elizabeth caught him up neatly. "Well, then, you'll have to come to the schoolhouse in the afternoon and practice. If your mother can spare you. Could we possibly try 'The Lass of Richmond Hill' now? All of us?"

Rudy McGarrity, blessed with his father's musical ear, provided the tone and the children were off at a great gallop, with cheerful enthusiasm if a notable lack of synchronization. They followed this with "Robin Adair" and concluded with a thunderous rendition of "Yankee Doodle." Outside, Hector and Blue raised their voices to sing along.

Elizabeth made a mental note to herself to make sure the

dogs were securely tied up far away from the schoolhouse for the duration of the recital.

Paradise was a hardworking, no-nonsense kind of place for most of the year, not much given to taffy pulling or picnics. At first worried that folks would just ignore the school recital—something he did not know how to warn Elizabeth about—Nathaniel began to imagine what might come of excesses of hard cider, high spirits, and old grudges scraped newly raw. The combination of Polly's wedding and the school recital on the heels of a rushed but successful harvest was a powerful one, and he watched its approach as he would watch a dead tree in a windstorm, to see in what direction it might decide to fall.

The day arrived, and Paradise surprised him by turning out in its best. Jack MacGregor, a man known to spit at his own shadow when it got too close, showed up for the wedding in a regimental kilt so moth-eaten and dusty that it set half the village to sneezing; Charlie LeBlanc had invested in a top hat two sizes too small, and it perched on his pinkish skull like a hen at roost. Most of the men owned nothing more than two sets of buckskins, and had had to dig to the bottom of their trunks.

"Ain't seen the back of so many uniforms since we run the Tories out of Saratoga," announced Axel, drawing sharp glances from his daughter and a giggle from his grandchildren. "*Schau,* Anna." He poked her with a long finger. "Ain't that the jacket Dubonnet wore to his own wedding? Must be ten year ago."

Even Billy Kirby had made an effort: his buckskin and his hair both approached something a man might call clean. There was no sign of Liam, or O'Brien. Nathaniel was glad of Bears, back up on the mountain to keep an eye on things.

The Bonners were barely settled in the pew behind the Hauptmanns when the service began. Yankees might be the kind to spend their free time in a church but Yorkers had other ideas, and Witherspoon knew his congregation and their worldly leanings: over the years he had learned to carve his services down to the bone.

Under the pitched roof the crowd generated a lot of heat. Elizabeth's color was high, and there was a sheen of sweat on her brow, but she smiled when Nathaniel caught her eye. Between them, Hannah hopped with excitement, until Many-Doves leaned over to give the child a pointed look. Many-Doves was getting a few looks herself: she didn't often come to the village, and people took note. He was not much given to prayer, but Nathaniel wondered if they could all get through this day without some help from Above.

In a new dress of deep green, cut generously so that she could move and breathe, Elizabeth listened to the ceremony, craning her neck to catch a glimpse of the bride. Even above the rustling and coughing of an impatient congregation, she heard Polly's calm voice as she recited her vows; she wondered if she had sounded so composed, but at the moment she could remember nothing of her own wedding except a series of disjointed images, and the feel of her hands in Nathaniel's. This put her in mind of Mrs. Schuyler, which in turn raised the idea of aunt Merriweather; Hannah tugged on her skirt, rescuing her from her worries. The congregation was on its feet and singing. Polly and Benjamin were making their way down the aisle with Curiosity and Galileo just behind.

"I thought it would take longer," Hannah said.

"Oh, it will," said Many-Doves. "Another thirty or forty years, most likely."

Elizabeth bit back her smile, but Nathaniel laughed out loud.

The wedding party had been set up on tables behind the church on the small green that ran down to the brook. Under a stand of maples flaming in oranges and reds, children already gathered around plates of sweets. Dolly Smythe called to Hannah, who disappeared into the crowd of children without a backward glance.

The men were opening a keg of rum.

"Can't have a wedding in Paradise without rum," Nathaniel said, taking in the look of surprise on Elizabeth's face. "Don't worry, Boots. I'm not about to partake."

"A toast to honor the bridal couple would not be unreasonable, Nathaniel."

He shook his head, his eyes traveling over the crowd. "Not today." And then: "I wish my father were here."

With a frown, Many-Doves dealt Nathaniel a pinch hard

enough to make him jump. "This is a wedding party," she reminded him. "Not a war council."

"Yes, please," Elizabeth added. "Today of all days. The children are so looking forward to the recital. And look at Curiosity, I have never seen her so happy."

Nathaniel moved away from Doves, rubbing his arm. "I'm no match for the two of you, Boots. I'll give it a try."

He took Elizabeth's hand and the three of them made their way toward the bridal couple. What a strange but wonderful thing it was, Elizabeth thought, to hold a man's hand in a crowd. It made her feel very young and silly and at the same time very pleased. It was just five months since she had been a bride herself, after all, and for Many-Doves it was even more recent. Elizabeth caught sight of Molly Kaes teasing one of the Cameron brothers, and she shook her head slightly to herself.

"It's the business of the day, Boots," Nathaniel said, reading her thoughts. "Harvesttime and courting go together."

"And a rush of babies in the spring," added Many-Doves, patting her own belly.

Polly and Benjamin accepted their good wishes with pleasure. Elizabeth let Galileo press a glass of punch into her hands, and she spoke a few words with Manny and Daisy. Curiosity, for once at a loss for words, simply hugged her and smiled. As the brother of the groom, George had decided to take charge of entertainment, and together with Joshua he had begun a game of boules. Many of the men were wandering in that direction.

Elizabeth finally turned away to find herself face to face with the judge, and Julian.

She looked over the crowd, hoping for some distraction which would reasonably take her away, but her father's tone, tentative and friendly, stopped her. Not for the first time Elizabeth wondered if it was her father's role in Chingachgook's death which had caused this sudden change in his attitude, or if there was some other, less visible or pleasant motivation. He had even been willing to speak to the treasury agent on their behalf; or so he had claimed to Nathaniel. Now he was trying to meet her eye, like a schoolchild looking for praise.

"You are looking very well, daughter."

His face was drawn thin, but his hands were steady and he

had lost some of the vacant look in his eyes. He held a cup of punch rather than rum, she saw with some relief. But Elizabeth could not think of one topic to discuss with him that would not soon bring them to an argument, and so simply thanked him.

"Has your harvest gone well?" he asked, directing the question to both Nathaniel and Many-Doves.

"Very well," Many-Doves said. "We are pleased."

"You are gaining weight, Elizabeth."

Her head snapping up in surprise, Elizabeth saw that her father was sincere: he did not know about her condition, or he never would have made such a remark. She had never had the opportunity to talk to him alone and pass on this information, but she thought by now someone would have pointed out to him what would soon be obvious to all.

At the same time, there was a new look on Julian's face. He had not known, but he did now.

"I did not mean to offend," the judge said, looking uncertainly between Elizabeth and Nathaniel. "It suits you, after all."

Nathaniel cleared his throat. "Well, that's good to hear," he said, his hand moving to the small of Elizabeth's back as if to keep her from running away. "Because she'll gain a sight more before she's done. There's a child on the way, I guess you didn't realize."

The deep flush on her father's face might have been embarrassment, or dismay, or joy; Julian's reaction was less ambivalent. With one piercing look at Nathaniel, he turned and walked away.

An hour before the recital was set to begin, Dolly, Hannah, and the Glove sisters were arranging food while Elizabeth hung garlands of the last of the summer asters. Excitement and silliness were running very high, and she was beginning to worry about the boys, who had been sent to fetch more cups and should have long been back from this errand.

Anna arrived with doughnuts and the distressing news that the wedding party had broken up and was drifting resolutely in the direction of the schoolhouse.

"Folks been waiting months to see the inside of this place," she said, taking the garland out of Elizabeth's hands and climbing up on a chair in a businesslike fashion. "Couldn't wait anymore. Anyway, you want the men with another hour's worth of rum in their bellies? Let me do this, you got other things to attend to, I fear. I just saw that son of mine running away from the Necessary with the McGarrity boys."

It turned out to be good advice: Elizabeth found Jemima Southern in the outhouse with a board wedged up under the handle. To her surprise, the child was perfectly calm when she finally emerged.

"I knew you'd find me," she said. And then with a forward thrust of her chin: "They don't like my singing, but I'm going to sing anyway."

"The boys are just overexcited, Jemima. You have a beautiful voice, whether or not they will admit it." Elizabeth could meet her eye calmly, because this was the truth.

The child's sharp gaze swept across Elizabeth's face. "You would let me sing, even if I croaked like a toad."

A small laugh escaped Elizabeth. "If it were important to you, perhaps I would. But more likely I would try to convince you to recite some poetry."

"My pa liked me to sing to him," Jemima said. " 'Barbry Allen' was his favorite of all." With an air of desperation, the child said: "You didn't like my pa, and he didn't like you."

There was a lot of noise from inside the schoolhouse, laughter and a little girl's voice raised in protest, but Elizabeth tried to focus on the small pale face in front of her. "Jemima. Whatever the lack of understanding between your father and me, I am very glad to have you in my classroom—don't scowl, it doesn't suit you. I will admit that you and I sometimes do not see eye to eye, but I am glad to have you here. And I am glad that you are going to sing. You will do the school great credit. Now, shall we get ready for our guests?"

Ruth Glove's small, sleek head appeared at a window, her eyes round with delight and delicious anxiety, her mouth rimmed with crumbs. "Jemima!" she cried. "Come see our doughnut tower!"

With a grumble that did not quite hide how pleased she was to be a part of the high spirits, Jemima ran up the steps and into the classroom. Elizabeth hung back for a moment, content to let Anna cope while she took this last chance to gather her thoughts.

The late afternoon was clear, the air as cool and crisp as apples. A flock of geese passed over the lake, silent as the clouds above forests of flame and deep green. She wondered if they regretted leaving the world below them behind as they hurried south, to places less colorful but warmer.

Nathaniel was on the path now; she caught sight of him once, twice, and then he came out of the woods just above the schoolhouse. He was leading the bay gelding, loaded with the things she had sent him for: more candles, in case the recital ran past dark; the corn bread and apple crumble that Falling-Day had made for the party; and the packages Elizabeth had so carefully wrapped late last night, her gifts to her students for their work over the summer.

Elizabeth was struck forcefully by the sight of him, coming toward her. It still seemed improbable, that she should have arrived at such a place in her life. She wondered what the world would be like without him in it, and found she did not want to know.

Nathaniel had just begun to believe that maybe they would get through the whole recital without trouble when the first rumbles made themselves heard.

The crowd's attention was fixed on Ian McGarrity as he fought his way through "John Barleycorn." Elizabeth stood off to one side with her arms folded, ready to prompt him, but the crowd had done her out of the job, and with good spirits. There was not one man or woman in the crowded room who hadn't learned the poem as a child, and didn't mind the chance to prove the fact by helping out Ian.

Elizabeth looked as happy as he had ever seen her; perhaps it was some of that, and her quiet energy, that was wearing off on the crowd. Even those who had kept their children away from the school in the summer after she had run off with him were scooting farther forward with every new piece, as if they would like to be up in front of the room and reciting.

But there was noise outside, and it was more than raccoons after the corn. Nathaniel didn't have to take a roll call to figure out who was responsible. Most of Paradise had managed to squeeze in, even the troublemakers: Liam Kirby right up front, his face still shadowed with fading bruises. Dubonnet, with his son sitting on his lap, directing the musical proceedings with a well-gnawed popcorn ball. The Camerons, drunk enough to sing along on "Yankee Doodle." The judge sat well to the back with Witherspoon, both of them slightly blurry-eyed but attentive. It would be all they could do to keep Witherspoon from reciting the bit of Greek poetry he called his own; the judge was sure to offer a story or two of his own adventures.

Missing were Julian and Billy Kirby, and some of the trappers who had been hanging around the tavern lately. But they weren't far off.

Ian finished with a grin and a flourish:

John Barleycorn was a hero bold
Of noble enterprise
and if you but once taste his blood
It will make your courage rise!

Elizabeth was the last person in the world to look for courage in a bottle of whiskey, or to promote such an idea, but she had allowed Ian this poem. It was a surprising but wise thing to do, and Nathaniel found himself admiring her tactical skills, once again. Latin or French poetry would have shown off her students' skills, but earned her no marks with the men of the village; "John Barleycorn," on the other hand, they could much appreciate. But it had also sent many of them back to the ale barrel, which was certainly not what she had in mind.

From his spot near a window, Nathaniel caught a flash of blue disappearing around the corner. Reflexively, he touched his rifle. He should go out there, put a stop to whatever trouble was brewing before it got out of hand. But it was Hannah's turn, and the sight of her so grown-up and pretty was hard to turn away from.

She took her place in front of the room and curtsied, completely at ease. Nathaniel didn't recognize the dress she was wearing, pale yellow with ribbons in her hair to match. It made the copper of her skin shine, her plaits stand out glossy black. She looked more like her mother with every passing year. On his deathbed, Chingachgook had called Hannah "Little-Bird," the name Sarah had gone by as a child. But there was a solidness in Hannah that Sarah had never had, something she had more in common with her mother's sister, and her grandmother.

Many-Doves and Falling-Day were sitting in the second row, off to one side. Their whole attention was fixed on Hannah.

A hooting laughter from outside, closer this time. Jed McGarrity caught Nathaniel's eye and raised a brow.

There was no help for it. Nathaniel cast a regretful look at his daughter, and slipped out the door with Jed and Axel right behind him.

The schoolhouse windows stood wide open in spite of the cool evening air, so that the building seemed to bulge and pulse with all the life inside it. As they walked away Nathaniel was aware of Hannah's voice, clear and strong. There was a hint of Falling-Day's rhythms in her tone now: a gift she had inherited from his own mother, the ability to take on voices that were not her own. She had insisted on a Kahnyen'kehàka story, and Elizabeth had not tried to dissuade her. Nathaniel followed along with one part of his mind as he made his way past the outhouse to a stand of evergreen just behind it.

"Brother Fox saw a woman with a cart filled with fish, and as he was always both hungry and lazy, he thought up a good trick. Pretending to be dead, Fox lay down on the path so that the woman would pass him. The woman saw the fox and thought that she should have his good pelt, and so she picked him up and put him in her cart with her fish. Behind the woman's back, Fox emptied the cart of the fish and crept away himself.

"Later, Brother Fox met with Wolf, and told him of this very good trick."

There was laughter from the shadows, and a wolflike howl.

"Get a good hold on your temper, Nathaniel," Axel said softly. " 'Cause they'll do their best to get it away from you."

In the schoolhouse, the barest hint of a pause and then Hannah's voice carried on:

> *But the woman was not so dumb, and having figured out what foolery had been played on her, she understood the Wolf's game as soon as she saw him lying in her path. For his trouble, Brother Wolf received a good beating instead of a fish dinner.*

"Look, Middleton, we got company." Billy Kirby straightened up out of the shadows. He had been drunker before, but not by much. With him a trapper, the nameless kind who came into the village to drink and bother women who would never have any interest in him. The stench of liquor and sweat hung around him like a cloud of blackfly.

Behind Nathaniel, Jed drew a disgusted sigh and let it go with a rush.

"Middleton!" brawled Billy, half turning. "He was there a minute ago," he said, his face creased in confusion.

"You could use a place to lie down, Billy." Axel scratched his beard thoughtfully. "Why don't you head on home?"

"You ordering him off this place?" asked the trapper, peering up from his spot on the ground owlishly. "He's the sheriff, you can't order him around like that."

"That's true enough, Gordon," said Axel with a soft laugh. "I can't order a man off land that don't belong to me. That would be up to Nathaniel here. Me, now I could tell you to stay out of my tavern—if I was riled enough."

The trapper held up a hand in surrender, and then pulled himself to his feet to shamble off into the woods in the direction of the village.

Billy wiped his mouth with his sleeve, and considered them from under half-raised lids.

"Came to fetch my brother home," he said. "He don't belong in there with that woman and her brats." Billy glanced uncertainly around himself, and then jerked with his chin toward the schoolhouse and the sound of Hannah's voice. "I don't want him hearing none of that Mohawk nonsense."

Axel moved forward another step, and Jed came up on the outer flank.

"We'll send him home for you," Axel said easily. "You go on ahead now, while you're still healthy."

Billy's face clouded with doubt, and then cleared suddenly. "Maybe I'll just come on in and join the party. Tell a few Mohawk stories of my own."

"There's children in there," Jed said. "They ain't doing you any harm, Kirby. Let them get on with their party in peace, why don't you?"

Billy flushed, the color moving up from his collar to mottle on his neck and jowls. "There won't be any peace in Paradise until things is settled," he said. His gaze flickered toward Nathaniel and away again. "Until we run you squatters out and get the mountain back. You got the gold, don't you? Think you can buy your way clear. Well, you can't. O'Brien will find it and take it away from you, and then we'll get the mountain back."

There was a scab high on Billy's cheekbone, a relic of the last beating Nathaniel had given him. Nathaniel fixed on that, and tested the weight of the rifle in his hands. Hannah's voice came into the silence:

> *"Next Brother Fox met Bear, who also wanted fish. Fox told him: 'Down at the river there is an air hole in the ice. Put your tail down into it as I did and you can pull up as many fish as you can eat.'*
>
> *"Bear, always hungrier than he was bright, did as he was told. And instead of a fine fish dinner he froze his tail off in the icy water."*

Billy had a keen look about him, eager now. "Don't want to break up your woman's little party, do you? Worried about making her mad?"

"You are surely the stupidest creature God ever put on this earth," said Jed, his voice low and hoarse. "Are you forgetting the beating you took from this man the last time you was drunk?"

"He won't fight, not now," Billy said. "Look at him, he's scared. Not of me, no. But she's got him tied up in a knot."

Nathaniel turned back toward the sound of his daughter's voice; because it was the right thing to do. For her, and for himself, and for Elizabeth. Behind him, Billy Kirby laughed.

"I guess I'd toe the line, too, for a woman who'd brain a man with his own rifle. What I'm wondering is, what old Jack got up to before she laid him low. Maybe Lingo ain't gone, really. Maybe he left a little something of himself behind, growing—"

As he swung around Nathaniel caught a glance at Axel's expression, drawn down hard and resigned.

At the last moment, some part of his reasoning self stopped him and Nathaniel lowered his aim from that point high on the bridge of the nose where the bone could be shoved into the brain, and the rifle butt took Kirby square in the mouth. His head jerked back with the sharp crack of breaking teeth, and he collapsed backward, coughing and spitting blood, his hands pressed to his ruined mouth. Nathaniel put his foot on Billy's throat and leaned in.

"Nathaniel," Jed said at the count of three, when Billy's bucking and kicking had started to ease up.

Axel knocked him away. "You don't want to hang for Billy Kirby," he said. "He ain't worth it."

His face set hard, Nathaniel reached down and pulled Billy up by the shirt, and held him at a distance while he bled and retched and tried to catch his breath. When it was clear he wouldn't die straight off, Nathaniel dragged him down to the lake, tinged red with the sunset. Kirby hit the water with a splash and Nathaniel waded in after him to pull him out, shook him as easily as he would shake a wet dog.

"Can you hear me, Billy?"

The ruined mouth stretched, broken teeth and bloody pulp. Nathaniel shook him again, and he nodded.

"I want you to hear me clear. My wife is carrying my child, and I'll kill the next man to suggest otherwise. You got that?"

Nathaniel looked up on the shore. Axel and Jed were still

there, Axel leaning on his rifle, pulling on his beard. Behind them was Julian.

"Middleton? You hear me?"

"Oh, yes, quite definitely," Julian said softly.

From the schoolhouse, the sound of singing. A young girl's voice, sweet and clear.

"Now, one more thing. You leave off beating that brother of yours, or I'll come after you and make you regret it."

Nathaniel let Billy Kirby go with a jerk and a splash. He leaned over to wipe his hands on his shirt and then he walked up the shore. Julian stood there, watching impassively as Billy vomited.

"You got something to say, Middleton, then say it."

His eyes narrowed, Julian looked away. "I believe Billy touched on all the salient points."

"When are you going to stop hiding behind other men and settle your own business?"

None of his usual grin, now. "When the return is higher than the required investment."

"You will never get the land," Nathaniel said. "Or your sister."

Julian said: "And I shall never stop trying."

"I lost my temper," Nathaniel said shortly. "It's that simple."

Elizabeth was sitting on their bed with a handkerchief in her hands which she folded small, spread open on her lap, and folded small again. In the corner was an embroidered lily of shaky proportions, bracketed by her own initials. The Glove girls had given her this gift; Elizabeth blinked at it and the flower swam briefly in what threatened to be tears.

"I was trying to save your recital, damn it."

"Yes. I know." She looked up at him finally, and taking a very deep breath, she managed a smile.

Nathaniel drew back, frowning. "Tears? It went well, Boots, didn't it?"

"It did go very well," she agreed. "Better than I had hoped."

"What is it, then? You're not crying for Billy Kirby?"

Lifting her head, she met his gaze. "You do know, don't you, that Jack Lingo did not—"

He interrupted her by pulling her into his arms. His own expression was tense with regret. "I know," he said. "I know, Boots, I *know* that. Oh, Christ, I shouldn't have told you what he said."

She put her face to his shoulder. "You do believe me?"

"Yes," he said, and he kissed her. "Yes, I believe you. It was just Billy Kirby's half mind at work."

"No," Elizabeth corrected him. "It was my brother." And the tears came then.

He held her while she wept, rocking her gently with his face against her hair. He could not correct her, and so he said nothing at all.

"It's late," he said finally. "You need your rest."

She shook her head and held on harder to him, rubbed her cheek against his. Ran her hands under his shirt and around his waist. He moaned, softly, against her hair.

There was a timid knock at the door, and they moved apart. Hannah appeared, looking woeful but determined.

"What are you doing up?" Nathaniel asked, surprised. "I thought you were asleep."

"Grandmother has my book," Hannah said. "I had other things to carry, and she said she'd bring it up."

Elizabeth had given each of the students a book, suited to their interests. Hannah had been so overwhelmed by her copy of Cowper's *Anatomy* that she had been struck speechless.

"You can get it from Falling-Day in the morning," Elizabeth said, glancing out the window into the darkness. "It's too late to read, now."

"Oh, please," Hannah said. "Please let me go get it. Grandmother won't mind."

Nathaniel glanced at Elizabeth, and raised a brow. She nodded, reluctantly, and Hannah turned and was gone. They listened to the sound of her bare feet on the floorboards and then the front door closed behind her.

"Where were we?" Nathaniel asked, pulling her back to him across the bed.

"You were about to kiss me."

He laughed. Against her lips he said, "Nothing gets by you, does it?" She kissed him back, warm and playful: she tasted of molasses and cider. Moving down the long column of her neck, he nipped and teased her until she captured his face between her hands and brought his mouth back to her own to draw him down into a long kiss that left her gasping slightly, and straining upward into his hands.

Nathaniel reached for the candle, but she caught his wrist. "I want to see you," she said. "Let me see you."

Her eyes were soft and slightly glazed with the look she had sometimes when they were alone, and sure of the time they had together. He undressed her, and her skin rose to his touch and the cool night air. When he had stripped down Nathaniel drew the covers over them: a different kind of cave, rich with their smells and echoing with the small sounds she made.

Elizabeth put her hands on him to pull him closer, wound a leg around his hip, and ran her mouth up his neck to find his ear. But he resisted her, holding back when a simple forward movement would have joined them.

"Boots," he said. "Slow down. There's no hurry."

She shook her head: whether in contradiction or dismissal, he could not tell. Twisting in his arms, she pulled away and then pushed him down. In a single movement she had straddled his belly and bent over to kiss him, all soft and warm, her breasts against his chest. There was a furious tide running in her, and he could not resist its pull, did not want to.

"Holy God," he muttered, his hands on her thighs, his thumbs seeking. "You're as slippery as the road to hell." And he lifted her. Helped her move, put her where they both wanted her to be, and arched up to meet her. Her hair fell around them in waves, pooling on his legs and belly. His fingers tangled in it where his hands gripped her hips.

He let her have her way, finding her own rhythm. In the flickering candlelight, he watched her face contort, the tip of her tongue caught between her teeth. And then her eyes flew open and her face dropped forward and she came with a shudder and a small, wordless cry.

She was content to let him lead, then. To be turned onto her back, her arms spread wide with his fingers intertwined in hers while he held her down and found his way into her again. Between them, the swelling of her belly where their child rested; Nathaniel was overcome with the need to cover them like a shield, to hide them from the world, to keep them safe at any cost, to keep them to himself alone, forever.

As was her habit, Elizabeth fell asleep straightaway, but Nathaniel lay awake in a cocoon of melancholy and worry. It happened sometimes, when they had been together; he bore it alone, knowing that it would be gone in the morning. The wind was high in the trees. There would be a strong frost.

He was thirty-five years old, but he had never spent a winter alone on this mountain without his father's guidance and support. At this moment, he could not deny that the thought frightened him.

Nathaniel curled himself around Elizabeth, listening to the sound of her heart, and let himself be lulled to sleep by its rhythm.

Suddenly and completely awake, Nathaniel sat up in the dark. Something was wrong. He shook his head to clear it. On his bare skin the air was frost-cold.

He blinked in the darkness, listening.

Two heartbeats, where there should have been three; he could not explain how it was he knew this, but he did. He reached for his breechclout in the dark.

"What is it?" Elizabeth said sleepily.

"Hannah."

He was pulling his shirt over his head.

Elizabeth sat up. "She'll have gone to sleep in the other cabin."

Outside, a faint sound: the rolling beat of hooves. Elizabeth was awake now, reaching for her own clothes, tripping after him into the other room.

The sleeping loft was empty. He dropped back down the ladder, his bare feet slapping hard on the floorboards.

"Nathaniel," Elizabeth said, trying for calm. She was struggling with the flint box and the candle. In the small new light, he grabbed his rifle from its rack over the door with one hand, his powder horn and bullet pouch with the other.

"Nathaniel, she'll be asleep with Falling-Day."

The sound of a single rider, closer now.

"Nathaniel Bonner!" A boy's voice, cracking with panic.

"That's Liam Kirby," Elizabeth said, dread flooding through her, cold and harsh.

They went out on the porch. Liam sawed at the reins, cursing. He whipped his head toward them as the horse danced away.

"The schoolhouse! Fire!"

And he wheeled, and was gone again into the woods. Nathaniel broke into a dead run for the barn as Runs-from-Bears appeared out of the darkness, racing in the same direction.

"Oh, God, my God," Elizabeth said. She bolted for the other cabin, toward the flame of a single candle, mumbling a prayer: *Let her be there, let her be there safe.* Her skirt caught on a root and ripped; she ran on, screaming Hannah's name. The women came flying off the porch to meet her as the horses thundered past, the men riding bareback.

"Hannah?" she asked, grasping at Falling-Day's arms.

Falling-Day, her face like a mask: "But I sent her back home to you, hours ago."

Elizabeth gasped. "Her book?"

In the pale light of the moon, Many-Doves' face alive with fear.

"It was left behind in the schoolhouse."

LVI

There is nothing to fear in the dark, Hannah's great-grandfather had always told her. *Only O'seronni fear what is not there.* She had spent all her life on this mountain; her Kahnyen'kehàka half was not afraid. Her other half, the white half, could be silenced for the moment. This errand would not take long, and she would be back in her own bed with the book under her pillow.

Hannah felt again for the key in her pocket. She had taken it from its nail near the door, and without asking. Tomorrow she would have to answer for that. Grandmother would be very angry with her; she didn't dare think about what her father would have to say.

Elizabeth might be angry, too, but she would understand, in the end. It was the first book Hannah had ever owned, her very own. And they had not seen what she had seen: Jemima Southern's eyes round with envy, and wanting. Jemima didn't care about bones of the arm or the flow of blood, but she wanted anything Hannah had, and the Southern farmstead was closest to the school. Hannah wanted to get her *Anatomy* before it could disappear.

In the moonlight, the schoolhouse echoed with remembered voices, dark and quiet as a fallow field. Her hands trembled as she lit a candle.

She found it in the study, on the desk. Someone—Jemima?—had opened it to an illustration of a chest in which the bone had been cut away and the muscles and ribs peeled back neatly to show the heart. Hannah had seen more than her share of blood: both of her grandmothers were healers, and neither of them had ever had the habit of sending curious little girls away. But these pictures had nothing in common with broken bones and gashes and trap wounds. Hannah had planned to grab the book up, lock the door, and speed away home to her bed, but she paused to run her finger over the drawing.

It was lovely and quiet here. The little room with its neat rows of books was hers, for the moment. Hers, and nobody else's.

Hannah pulled the door firmly closed. A shawl was draped over the chair; it was thick and warm, and it had Elizabeth's scent. She pulled it around her shoulders against the chill. The desk was too high for her to sit over the book comfortably, so Hannah sat cross-legged on the rag rug with her feet tucked under. Bent over the book in her lap, she lost herself in the secrets of the human heart.

In time she turned the page, and then, after a while, the next. The candle burned steadily while she read, but she had no sense of time passing. When the print began to swim, she rubbed her eyes and forced them to focus.

Hannah fell asleep with her cheek against a drawing of the arteries of the neck. She did not wake when the candle sputtered and went out; she never heard the sound of the door opening in the other room.

Liam cantered through the village, filling the air with his cawing: *"Fire! Fire! Fire at the schoolhouse!"* Men began pouring out of Axel's tavern before he had even started away up Hidden Wolf.

Billy Kirby, thought Julian as the village erupted into action. With his shattered mouth and pride to match, there was no doubt about who had taken the torch to the schoolhouse. The idiot would go to gaol for this, but worse, the village would stand behind the Bonners, now.

Julian had no intention of sharing credit with Billy Kirby for a crime he hadn't even contemplated—arson was not his style, so inelegant—so he took the bucket that was shoved into his arms and ran with the others for the schoolhouse. There was nothing like a fire to sober men up.

If a man had time to stop and admire it from a safe distance, a building burning in the night was a beautiful thing. The flames were well established on the west end of the schoolhouse: they shot upward from an open window, a strange reversed lightning intent on laying the heavens open. At the front of the building, window glass glittered like hungry yellow eyes. Julian was reminded of a leopard he had seen once in a cage in a London whorehouse, pacing, pacing.

People were pouring in from every direction. Women, barefooted and in nightdresses with babies in their arms. Children shivering in the cold. Men, many of them still in the clothes they had worn to the school recital in the evening. There was no movement toward a bucket line: it was out of control, and one splash of lake water at a time would be no use at all.

The judge came galloping up, his white hair unbound and fluttering. He flung himself from the saddle and stood before Julian, heaving for breath. With one hand he held the reins of the terrified horse and with the other he grabbed his son's shoulder and dug in his fingers, hard.

"I hope to the Almighty God that you had nothing to do with this, Julian."

A sudden bellowing saved him a long and tedious explanation. O'Brien, coming out of the woods, was shouting and pointing toward the fire.

"The Mohawk girl!" he roared, waving his hat. "Saw her go in a couple of hours ago, don't know if she came out."

"Lord Almighty," the judge groaned. "Are you sure?"

"There was candlelight on the east end, an hour ago."

"Which Mohawk girl?" Julian asked. And getting no answer, he grabbed O'Brien by the collar and swung him around forcibly. "Which Mohawk girl?"

The old man squinted up at him. There was ash in his white hair.

"Does it matter?" he asked, jerking away. "Wake up, man. She's cooked, whoever she is."

Wake up. Julian stared at his father, and his father stared back.

Julian shook his head, trying, for once, to do what was being asked of him, although what he wanted was to sleep. To go to sleep and push the image out of his head: Many-Doves beating on the door, her hair dancing in the flames. Because, Julian realized with cold horror, because the door had a lock, and the key was in it. He could see it. Billy Kirby, damn his soul to a hell like the one he had created, Billy Kirby had set the fire and locked the door.

In the frantic light of the fire, Martha Southern was holding her girl while she screamed, endlessly. A horse screamed in counterpoint, and went crashing off toward the lake. On the far end of the schoolhouse, a window shattered and a swirl of cinders went into the night sky like a flock of tropical birds in unlikely colors.

Wake up.

Just unlock the door. Just turn the key.

He walked away. His father, deep in furious debate with O'Brien, took no notice. There was a shawl on the ground and he picked it up. Ten feet from the door, the hair on his head rose to the heat. The door was hot to the touch; he used the shawl to turn the key, and felt the lock give with a sigh.

From the corner of his eye, Julian caught movement: two riders, bent for hell down the mountainside.

He kicked the door open, and ran into the schoolhouse.

He had always taken a secret pleasure in color, and so in spite of his terror—the kind of deep fear that opens up the bowels and makes the blood run thin—Julian saw how exquisite it was: the flames moved through the room with a seductive and terrifying symmetry. Crouched on the floor in the middle of its roaring, watching the fire weave and prance, Julian recognized nothing about this place, as if he had never been here before.

Because he hadn't. He had never been anywhere like this; of that much he was sure. Of that, and the fact that his skin was stretching and rising, and that the floor was burning his feet through his boots. Coughing explosively into the shawl, he could not remember why he had come into this place. He was alone in the screaming fire, and it would kill him if he didn't move. Whatever it was he had been looking for was not here.

Off to his right was a door: intact. On the other side of that door there would be air to breathe, and cool darkness.

Julian yanked the door open and in response the fire at his back rose and roared like an animal. He slammed the door shut, and almost laughed at the absurdity of it. Then he turned, and scanned the room.

Sitting on the floor in the corner was Nathaniel Bonner's daughter, her arms wrapped around a book. She was rocking, her eyes blank and blind with terror. The only light was the leaping red and gold reflected in the little window above the desk; that meant, he realized with some quieter, rational part of his mind, that above them the roof was on fire. He could open the door and take her through it, or they would die here together.

His mind had hitched down to a slow, uneasy trot. He thought of Elizabeth; and for the first time in days, he thought of Kitty. He had come in here to save another man's wife, and found Bonner's daughter instead. There was an irony there, and one he knew he would appreciate if only his mind would start working.

She looked up at him, her eyes like cold coals.

Julian picked her up. "Time to go," he wanted to say, but his throat burned and all he produced was an explosion of coughing. She buried her face against him, folding her body small and tight. Her book was wedged into his chest, its corners digging into his ribs. He realized suddenly that he had never held a child before in his life.

There was an explosion of glass, and Julian jerked as a shard lodged itself in his cheek. He turned, a long, slow process, and found Nathaniel Bonner trying to jam himself through a window that would accommodate only half of him. Blood dripped from his hands and ran down his forehead.

"Give her to me!" He held out his arms.

Julian looked down at the child.

"For the love of God, man!"

He put Hannah into her father's arms.

And they were gone, leaving behind only the window sash rimmed with shards like bloody teeth. Julian stood for a moment, looking out. There in the night, figures danced and contorted in the light of the fire. His father, screaming for him to come.

For once in his life, Julian simply obeyed. He opened the door and found that the fire had come closer: a wall of it between him and the exit, beckoning and calling for him as his father was screaming outside in the night.

Julian ran through the wall of smoke and flame and out the building that heaved and groaned behind him, trying to hold his breath and failing, taking in long, fiery breaths as he would swallow a bitter medicine put off too long. He ran into the open, and onward. From one side, he had the sense of a man's form launching at him, and then it hit him full force and he was on the ground. Rough hands slapped at his back and head.

Someone flipped him over: the pockmarked Indian, staring down at him. Over his shoulder, the last thing Julian saw was his father, and then, his sister's face, Madonna-white and stained with ash and terror.

They carried Julian to the Southerns' cabin, where Nathaniel and Hannah had already been passed into the care of the women. When Falling-Day had convinced Elizabeth that the little girl's injuries were minor, and Elizabeth had spent some time rocking Hannah while she wept, she went to the corner where Many-Doves was tending Nathaniel's cuts.

She was digging shards of window glass out of a gash on his lower arm. Other cuts on his head and arms and shoulders had been cleaned and stanched, but this was the worst.

"Let me," Elizabeth said, putting her hands on Many-Doves' shoulder.

There was a sheen of sweat on his brow, but Nathaniel shook his head. "This ain't much, Boots. Falling-Day will sew it up. Go on to your brother."

Many-Doves got up. "Fresh water," she said, taking her bowl with her. Elizabeth caught her hand in passing and squeezed it thankfully. Then she glanced into the small room where they had put Julian on the bed. In between the racking coughs, there were voices: Martha and Curiosity, her father.

"Elizabeth," Nathaniel said, holding out his free arm. She went down on her knees next to him and he pulled her in close. "He can't live long. You know that?"

She pushed her face against his neck, and nodded.

"Then go on to him," he said. He was looking at Hannah, who had fallen to sleep in Falling-Day's arms. "If he can still hear you, tell him I said thank you."

Axel passed her at the door, and stopped when she asked him where he was going.

He sent her a sideways glance, and then frowned at the hat in his hands. "He's asking for Kitty, and her father. I'll go fetch them."

"But it could not be good for Kitty, in her condition—the sight of him like this—"

The old man grimaced. "That's what Curiosity said, too, but what choice is there?"

Elizabeth drew in a deep breath, and nodded.

"If you were wondering." Axel's head came up, and he met her eye. "Runs-from-Bears and some of the men went after the Kirbys. I expect they'll bring 'em back in short order."

"But not Liam!" Elizabeth said, grasping Axel by the sleeve. "It was Liam who came to warn us."

Axel's eyes had a strange, cold glitter to them. "If the boy's innocent, he won't suffer for his brother's sins. But you'll note, Miz Elizabeth, that nobody's seen hide nor hair of him since."

Because she could not deny this, Elizabeth tried to think of some reasonable explanation, but a new volley of coughing was rolling through the room like the sound of cloth tearing. She went in to her brother.

The char and blisters that ran from the side of his head down over Julian's left shoulder and arm were hard to look at, but it was his color which struck most forcibly. His face was ash-white against the pillow slip, but his mouth was an incongruous cherry-red, as if he had made himself up for a masquerade. Curiosity was wiping away the vomit and blood, but the color remained. His garish lips stretched in a grimace over his teeth; his nostrils flared, and then he erupted into that cough, a sound that no human being should be capable of making. She did not know where to touch him, and so Elizabeth stood across the bed from her father and did Julian the favor of not looking away.

He inhaled in a long, racking wheeze and opened his eyes. "Hurts," he whispered.

"Yes, child." Curiosity leaned in next to Elizabeth and gently laid a cloth, damp and pungent-smelling, on the worst of the burns on his neck. His face contorted and then relaxed. She held up a tin cup and he made a clumsy effort to bat it away.

Finally his eyes focused on his father. "Kitty? Is she coming?"

The judge nodded.

Elizabeth leaned in closer. "Julian?"

She waited until the coughing passed, trying not to see the smears of blood and cinders that Curiosity wiped from his chin.

"Julian, we—Nathaniel and I, and Falling-Day, and Bears and Many-Doves, all of us. We wanted to thank you—"

Elizabeth wanted to say other things, but she did not know where to start. She wanted to scream and weep, but she was afraid that if she did, she would not know how to stop.

"What can I do for you?" she asked.

"New lungs," he wheezed. And miraculously, a sour grin, the one she had had from him every day of his life, he gave to her now in his last hour.

"I wish that it were in my power."

"The mountain," he said. "Give back the mountain."

She started. Glancing up at her father, she saw the shock draining what was left of his color.

"Julian—" the judge began, but the coughing started again.

On her father's face Elizabeth saw something small and old. She wondered what he saw in her own face, which felt to her as if it must be made of glass, ready to shatter at the slightest touch.

There was a sudden silence in the other room, and the

Witherspoons appeared at the door. Kitty stood there wrapped in a cape that could not hide her shape, holding the straining edges together over her belly with fingers so tense and white that it would not have surprised Elizabeth to see them snap off. Behind her Mr. Witherspoon was speaking to Nathaniel.

Kitty came forward to look into Julian's face. They stared at each other for a long moment, and then the coughing took over again. Impassive, she watched him convulse with it. Elizabeth could not bear to see it, and so she looked away.

When he could talk again, Julian's voice was less than it had been even a few minutes earlier.

"Will your father—" he began, and then again the long pause, much longer now, while he brought up more of his lungs. When he finished, his voice was so faint that Elizabeth was sure, at first, that she had misheard. Then he repeated himself:

"Will he marry us right now?"

Elizabeth met the judge's shocked gaze, and then she turned to Kitty, whose whole attention was on Julian. There were two spots of hectic red, high on her cheekbones.

She nodded. "Yes."

"Julian—" began the judge, with an uncomfortable look toward Kitty. "Are you sure?"

"My child," Julian said. "It is my child. Is that not so, Kitty?"

"It is," she hissed softly, and smiled. Elizabeth felt suddenly faint, and she reached for the headboard to steady herself.

Mr. Witherspoon cleared his throat. "But what of Richard?"

Kitty's stare, as furious and burning as the blaze that had brought them to this place, silenced him. She said: "We may never see Richard Todd again."

With shaking hands, Mr. Witherspoon opened his prayer book and began his second marriage service of the day. Curiosity took the signet ring from Julian's uninjured hand, and when it was over, Kitty wore it, clenching her fist to keep the ring from falling off.

Elizabeth kissed Kitty's cold white cheek, and then she leaned down to kiss her brother. He smelled of vomit and singed hair and blistered flesh, and her stomach rolled and heaved. She wanted to say comforting things, to tell him that he was ending his life well, and honorably, and that she was proud of him. But her own throat constricted and she fought with tears as he fought for breath.

His whisper caught her up, kept her captive with her ear near his mouth.

"Done now. Legal."

"Yes."

His eyes rolled in pain as he struggled to talk.

"Right thing to do."

"Yes," she said again, nodding fiercely.

Her brother whispered: "The rest of the land." His eyes fixed on hers. "Safe now, from you."

Elizabeth jerked back as if the heat rising up from his burns had flickered out to scald her. She pressed a hand to her mouth and forced herself to swallow those words that wanted to push out. Things that no one could say to a man on his deathbed. She cast a glance at Kitty and saw with tremendous relief that she alone had heard Julian's last confession, not of guilt and remorse, but of the need to pass on his misery and hurt.

He grimaced in pain, or satisfaction: she could not tell. A shudder ran through her. Elizabeth picked up her skirts to turn away, and Curiosity's strong hand found her elbow.

"Wait now," she said. "Wait. It's almost over."

And then it was. Julian heaved once, seeking upward, and finally settled against the pillow, his last breath hissing through clenched teeth.

Mr. Witherspoon fumbled with the pages of his prayer book. The judge, stony faced, sat down heavily and rubbed his sooty cheeks with his hands. Elizabeth wanted to go to Nathaniel; she wanted it very badly. She wanted Nathaniel to take her away from here to a place where she could scream until her throat ruptured with it. She looked down at Julian's ruined face; her vision blurred until all she could see was the little brother he had once been, a bright child, a new spirit in the world, full of promise that would never be fulfilled.

Her father sobbed, a hoarse, terrible sound. She walked around the bed and put her hand on his shoulder, at first lightly, and then with increasing pressure as she felt the tremor in him

grow and begin to twist into something larger and ungovern-
able.

Finally Curiosity reached down to close Julian's eyes, but
Kitty caught her wrist to stop her.

"Let me," she said softly. "It's my right."

From the single window in the main room, Elizabeth watched
the column of smoke and flame in the night sky. For the first
time, she thought briefly of her books, all gone, now. The
schoolhouse, gone.

In the other room, the women went on about the business of
caring for the dead. She should have a part in it; he was her
brother, after all. But she could not bear it, and so she stood and
waited while Curiosity and Martha did for Julian what needed
to be done. Galileo and Manny were there, too, getting ready
to carry him home through the night.

Falling-Day and Many-Doves had taken Hannah and
Martha's two oldest home to sleep, leading them away up the
mountain on horseback, with Jed McGarrity following close
behind because Nathaniel would not leave Elizabeth. She had
wanted so much to go with them, but her father sat on a stool
in front of the fire, talking to Axel and Mr. Witherspoon in
sentences which made sense, but rang as hollow as the look in
his eyes. Opposite him sat Kitty still in her cape, gazing
thoughtfully into the hearth. There was a small line of concentration between her brows. *A new sister,* Elizabeth thought
dully. *Kitty is my sister, now.*

There was a scuffing sound, and the men came through the
room carrying their burden on a plank of raw board. Julian had
been wrapped in a quilt, as they would have wrapped an infant
against the cold. Mr. Witherspoon and her father followed
them out of the cabin. Elizabeth caught the gleam of the judge's
hair in the moonlight as the small procession started away.

"We'll go home," Nathaniel said. Elizabeth pivoted to him,
and he held her with one arm. The other was wrapped from
wrist to elbow where Falling-Day had sewed up the gash. Putting her face to Nathaniel's chest, Elizabeth was met not with

his smells, his familiar and comforting smells, but with the stench of fire.

"Perhaps I should go with my father."

Curiosity had been standing at the door lost in her own thoughts but now she cast Elizabeth a sharp look. Without a word, she crossed the room to peer into her face. With swift, knowing touches Curiosity outlined the swell of her belly, prodding here and there. Her grim look was replaced with a softer, satisfied one.

"You need your rest," she said. "We'll see to the judge."

Kitty stood suddenly, her head cocked to one side and her expression puzzled. As if she had an important question, but lacked the language to phrase it. Curiosity turned, following the line of Elizabeth's gaze.

"It's six weeks too early," Kitty said. She pressed her hands into her belly as if to quiet the child inside. "It can't be, yet."

Curiosity let out a high, quivering sigh. "I feared as much."

Axel stood up so quickly that his stool fell over. "Should I go after Falling-Day?"

Without looking away from Kitty, Curiosity said: "She's got enough to handle with the children. I'll need my Daisy, if you'll be so kind. Martha and me can manage in the meantime. Elizabeth, you let Nathaniel take you home. There's more work here tonight, but not for you."

"No!" Kitty's puzzled expression was replaced instantly by a fearful one. "Please, Elizabeth. Please stay."

Nathaniel at her elbow, his fingers pressing. She started to agree, and the pressure increased; she turned, and was met with the anger in his face.

"Let me talk to you outside."

"But—"

"Outside," he insisted, pulling her along. Elizabeth caught Curiosity's resigned expression, and Martha's startled one. She let him direct her out the door, and then stood while he turned on her, his fury pushing him to a state she had never seen before.

"I won't let you do it!" he said. "Curiosity and Martha will look after her. I'm taking you home."

"Nathaniel—" She raised her hands, helplessly, and he came

up close enough so that she could see the blood caked in his hair.

"No."

"She needs me, Nathaniel. Look what she has just been through—"

He laughed, a harsh sound with nothing lighthearted in it. "And what have you been through? What have you lost tonight?"

"I have not lost my husband, or my daughter, or my unborn child."

"You lost your brother!"

"My brother was lost to me long before this night," she spat back, and then pressed a hand to her mouth. When she was sure of her voice again, she said: "I have my family, but she has lost the father of her child. And she may well lose the child, too."

His face contorted then, and he put his arms around her and pulled her to his chest, his hands cradling her head. His trembling told her what his words had not.

"I am perfectly fine," she said softly. "Nathaniel. I am in no danger at all. Here, feel." She took his hand and pressed it to her belly. "This child announces its health very clearly. Do you feel?"

The column of muscles in his throat rippled as he swallowed. He was calmer, but still there was a fine, humming tension in him. "You'll come away if it's too much?"

"Instantly."

"You'll let Axel or one of the men see you home if you're ready before I come to fetch you?"

"Of course. I will not go anywhere alone. Not until—" She thought of Billy Kirby, and saw by the new flash of anger in his eyes that Nathaniel's thoughts had taken him in the same direction. "Not until you tell me it is safe to do so."

Another hesitation, and he looked off to the horizon where the dawn was showing in its first pale streaks. "I can't stay, Boots."

"Go on ahead home, then," she said. "Be there when Hannah wakes."

"You don't understand."

"I understand," she corrected him. "You'd rather face an army than a woman in childbirth."

He glanced up in surprise. "Did Falling-Day say something to you?"

"No." Elizabeth smoothed a hand over his cheek. "She said nothing at all. But I know that you've been through this before, and that the outcome has never been easy or completely joyful. So I am not surprised that you don't want to be here."

"You're too smart by half," he said, wearily. "Maybe there's some flaw in your logic, Boots, but I'm too tired to see it."

"I must stay, if she wants me. Will you go now, and let me do what I must do?"

He pulled her face to his and kissed her, briefly. "All right, then. But I don't like it much."

Neither do I, Elizabeth whispered to herself as she went back into the cabin alone. *Neither do I.*

LVII

A cold rain began at dawn, beating down on Paradise without pause. While Kitty labored, the wind trembled and whispered in the eaves with a voice so human that gooseflesh rose on Elizabeth's nape; at times only the greatest feat of self-discipline kept her hands from shaking as she wiped Kitty's brow. She said very little through the long hours, content to let Curiosity's easy good humor carry the burden. When her thoughts drifted toward her brother, she reined them in sharply. There would be time for such things later, she told herself firmly, trying very hard not to let his face take Kitty's place on the pillow.

Through the morning people came and went with covered dishes, special teas, offers of help. Bleary-eyed and unshaven, Mr. Witherspoon showed up at the door to be comforted by Curiosity and sent home to his bed. At midday when it seemed that it would be a good while before the child could be coaxed into the world, Curiosity sent Elizabeth to rest. She obeyed without protest. Curling into Jemima's narrow bed next to the hearth in the other room, she fell into a sleep so bottomless that when she did wake she had no sense of where she might be, or why, or even what woke her.

Gradually her mind presented her with simple facts which were, at first, impossible to fit into a rational whole. Her brother was dead; her school was gone. There was a heaviness to these truths that was almost tangible, the weight of sorrow still to be explored. Just as Elizabeth realized that what she was hearing was not a storm, but the cry of a newborn, Daisy came through the room, buttoning her cloak.

"Going to fetch the judge and Mr. Witherspoon," she said, pulling up her hood.

Elizabeth held out both palms in a gesture which pleaded for good news.

"Kitty held up fine."

"The child?"

"Alive, right now, breathing better than Mama thought he would."

"Thank God," Elizabeth murmured.

"Amen," said Daisy, and she closed the door softly behind her.

Elizabeth went into the other room to be introduced to her nephew. Cradled in the crook of Kitty's arm, he looked like an undersized and ill-proportioned doll.

"Meet young Master Middleton," Curiosity said, wiping her neck with a linen square. "Cocky as a banty rooster, but a sight smaller."

Kitty looked up wearily. With some obvious effort, she focused on Elizabeth.

"I did it," she said. "I didn't think I could, but I did."

"Yes," Elizabeth agreed, not trusting herself to say much more. From Martha she accepted a cup of tea, but she could not take her eyes away from the child. Her brother's son.

Kitty touched the baby's cheek with one tentative finger. "Will he live?"

Curiosity drew in a deep breath. "If he's kept warm—there's precious little fat on him—and fed regular, and if God is kind, why then, yes, I'd say he's got a chance," she said slowly. "But it'll be a struggle, and not all of it is in your hands."

The child mewled, his tiny fists working into his cheeks.

A knock at the door, and both Curiosity and Elizabeth turned to see Runs-from-Bears come in and close the door behind him against the storm. He was drenched with rain and mud-streaked; over his arm was Elizabeth's cloak of boiled wool, and he carried her walking boots. With some surprise she looked down and realized that she was barefoot, and had been since she left Lake in the Clouds the night before.

He greeted Curiosity with a nod, and then turned his attention to Elizabeth.

"Nathaniel sends word." He spoke Kahnyen'kehàka. "You must come, now."

The smile on her face faded. "More trouble?"

"All of our people are whole," he said. "But come, there is no time to waste."

Elizabeth knew that no amount of questioning would get information from Bears that he was not ready to give, and so she did not try to talk to him on the way up the mountain. He had come on horseback, which made it clear how urgent this errand was; Runs-from-Bears disliked horses and would walk almost anywhere. He helped her up behind him and took off, and Elizabeth was immediately glad of his solid form in front of her, for he took the brunt of the cold, wet wind. As they crossed the strawberry fields the cloud cover broke up to reveal a quarter moon, a smudge of light in a brooding dark sky.

Nathaniel was waiting for them on the porch of his father's cabin, and she walked into his arms. He held her for a moment, but he could not hide his distraction and tension.

"Kitty? The child?"

"Both alive, but the boy is very small," she said. "Curiosity seems to think he may live. Have you got somebody in there?" Elizabeth asked, peering around him.

He rubbed his eyes. "Aye," he said. "Liam, in a sorry state."

Nathaniel caught her by the shoulders, shaking his head.

"No, Boots. He ain't dying."

"Did he—was he—" She could barely collect her thoughts.

"He says he'll only talk to you." Nathaniel's fingers pressed into her shoulders. "Elizabeth. Listen now, because we don't have much time. Bears found the boy beat up and unconscious on the north face of the mountain. He had McGarrity and O'Brien with him at the time."

The north face of the mountain. Wild and steep and dangerous; Elizabeth had only seen it from above. The north face of Hidden Wolf, where the entrance to the silver mine was.

"Half the village is up there now, looking for Billy."

She squared her shoulders. "I'll talk to him," she said. "And see what he knows. Is Hannah in there, too?"

"She was, but Falling-Day sent her off to bed. Though I doubt she's asleep."

"Just as well," Elizabeth said thoughtfully. "I may have need of her help."

The first thing she noticed was Hannah, peering down from the sleeping loft. And then Liam, on the cot where Chingachgook had died. Many-Doves looked up at her and blinked a greeting.

She had wondered, through the first long hours of Kitty's labor, why she was not angrier. Her brother had died needlessly; her stepdaughter had barely escaped with her life. The schoolhouse and all the books and materials collected over such a long time, the children's work, all of it gone. But she had not been able to find any anger in herself. When the thought of Billy Kirby had come to her, it was as though he were a stranger, someone she had seen once long ago. She could not even remember the sound of his voice, or his face.

Looking at Liam, so like his brother, Elizabeth felt a small flame of anger flicker and begin to burn in the hollow place beneath her ribs.

Falling-Day had splinted Liam's left leg below the knee, and bound his wrist. Between crisscrossed bandages his chest was bruised into a dark rainbow. But his face was the worst: a lumpy mass of spongy flesh, his lower lip mangled. Elizabeth touched his shoulder, and he jerked.

"Liam," she said softly. "Who did this to you?"

He tried to turn his face toward her, but caught himself with a strangled cry.

"Don't, please. I'm right here. Who did this to you?"

To see him weep was almost more than she could bear, but Elizabeth steeled herself. Taking her handkerchief, she touched it gently to his tender face. Nathaniel was watching from the other side of the room, his arms crossed on his chest and his chin down low.

Liam's sobbing ebbed, slowly.

"Did men from the village beat you?"

He shook his head slightly.

"Was it your brother?"

A nod, barely perceptible. When she repeated her question, he nodded again, more firmly.

"Liam, we have to find him."

The boy let out a small cry, and Elizabeth touched his shoulder.

"I promise you to do everything in my power to make sure he has a fair trial. But Liam, we have to find him before the villagers do, or there's no telling what might happen."

She wondered for a moment if he had fallen asleep. Then his voice came, stronger than she had expected.

"You won't hang him?"

Elizabeth glanced at Nathaniel. He nodded.

"None of us here would hang him. We will do what we can to see that he comes to trial."

"He's my only kin in the world," Liam said. "I got no place to go."

"You can stay with us," Hannah said from the shadows. She had come up in her bare feet, and Elizabeth had not heard her. "Can't he? He can stay with us."

Liam's right hand rose to wave uncertainly in the air. Elizabeth caught it.

"I tried to stop him," he whispered. His lower lip had begun to bleed again, and she touched her handkerchief to it, but he shook his head in irritation.

"Miz Elizabeth, I didn't know Hannah was in there."

"Of course you didn't," Elizabeth said firmly.

"But Billy didn't know, either. I'm sure he didn't know. He didn't know." And the tears began again in earnest.

Hannah was staring at her father, her chin thrust out belligerently. "Can't he stay with us?"

"Yes," Nathaniel said. "We'll make room for him. But right now we need Billy, and fast."

At the sound of Nathaniel's voice, Liam had stopped weeping. He took some long, shaky breaths and then he let Elizabeth's hand go.

"He's hiding in a cave on the north face," he said. "Above the deadfall. You know where I mean?"

"I do," Nathaniel said, reaching for his rifle. He glanced at Runs-from-Bears, who was lacing up dry moccasins.

"We'll be back as soon as we can, Boots."

From the doorway to the workroom, Falling-Day said in Kahnyen'kehàka: "Bring him back here and I will gut him myself." There was an edge in her voice that Elizabeth had never heard before. Her eyes were on Hannah.

"We'll take him someplace safe until tempers ease up a little," Nathaniel said to Elizabeth.

"There ain't no place safe left in the world," Liam said. In the candlelight his eyes were glazed, a watery blue. "Not for Billy, not anymore."

Nathaniel and Runs-from-Bears were just crossing into the forest when Elizabeth called out behind them. She was running, her shawl flapping in the wind. Nathaniel caught her up and smoothed the loose curls from around her face while she fought for her voice.

"Nathaniel," she gasped. "It's Sunday. I just realized. You were supposed to leave for Albany this morning."

He had been fixed on the idea of Billy, all his energy and anger of the past day pushing him forward, and he could not make sense of what she was trying to tell him. Nathaniel saw Elizabeth's frustration, and he forced himself to breathe in and out, and think it through.

It hit him, then. "God Almighty. The court date."

"Yes," she said. "Tomorrow."

They stared at each other for a moment.

Bears said: "Maybe nobody needs to go. If Richard don't show up, his suit against you gets dropped. That's what van der Poole said, wasn't it?"

"But what if Richard is there?" Elizabeth said. "He could be."

"Then I'll have to go," Nathaniel said. "If I leave now and ride hard I can be there in time."

"You cannot go," Elizabeth cried. "The men here will take justice into their own hands if you are not there to stop them."

There was a small silence, and she pulled herself up and looked him hard in the eye. "I promised Liam."

"Does it matter if Billy Kirby dies tonight or next week in Albany? Is it worth losing the mountain over?" Nathaniel shot back, exasperated.

"Bears can go and explain. If Richard is there, perhaps the judge will postpone again when he hears what has happened."

"They wouldn't let me in the courthouse," Bears said, presenting a simple fact.

Elizabeth threw up her hands and her voice came hoarse, with effort or suppressed tears or anger, Nathaniel could not tell. "Then I will go."

"No," Nathaniel said flatly. "You will not."

"Wait," said Bears, turning to Elizabeth. "You write a letter for the judge, I'll take it to Schuyler, and he can go in your place."

Nathaniel's stomach gave a lurch, a knot of anxiety unraveling. Elizabeth was lifting her skirts and turning toward the cabin already. "I'll write as quickly as I can," she said, and she was off, disappearing quickly in the darkness. Nathaniel watched her go, and then he turned to Bears.

"It may be a hard ride for no reason," he said. "I doubt Richard is anywhere near Albany."

Runs-from-Bears shrugged. His expression was blank, but his tone was hard-edged. "You watch out for that treasury agent," he said. "He's too curious about the north face."

Nathaniel nodded, his thoughts moving away already and up the mountain. He grasped Bears by the lower arm and then took off into the forest.

He knew the mountain as well as he knew the cabin in which he had been born and raised, as well as he knew the textures and planes of his daughter's face. It was Hannah's face Nathaniel carried with him through the dark, the look in her eyes when he pulled her through the schoolhouse window.

He had rocked her while she wept and sobbed and coughed, rocked her as he hoped her mother might have rocked her, murmuring to her wordlessly. Unable to console her, Nathaniel had wished for Elizabeth to help him with this, and looked up to see her flying toward them, with Many-Doves and Falling-Day just behind. Just then Julian had come bolting out of the schoolhouse with his hair on fire, to be knocked to the ground by Bears.

The sight of him had seemed to give Hannah a voice.

"I tried to get out," she hiccuped. "The smell of it woke me up, and so I tried. But it was locked. The door was locked."

Nathaniel had known real rage only a few times in his life. On the battlefield he had made his acquaintance with the pure, focused fury that lifted a man above fear. It had come to him again, seeing what Lingo had done to Elizabeth and knowing that the man was beyond a reckoning. As he walked toward the Southerns' cabin with Hannah in his arms, the same kind of jagged, razor-edged rage overcame him. Billy Kirby had set the schoolhouse to burning and locked the door.

He had to ask. "Did he see you? Hannah, did Billy see you?"

She trembled against him. "I don't know," she mumbled, rubbing her eyes now. She had cried herself dry. He could almost feel the tension in her flowing out and away; she seemed heavier now, looser in his arms. Falling-Day came up and he passed the child over to her, following them into the cabin to have his wounds tended. Thinking not of his own injuries, or the daughter who still needed comforting, or his wife, who went pale and straight-backed to her brother's deathbed, but of Billy Kirby, and how right it would feel to put a rifle up against the man's head and pull the trigger.

Running this mountain in the near total dark was not nearly as hard as it was going to be to keep his promise to Elizabeth.

Nathaniel pushed hard uphill, pausing only to listen. Twice he heard search parties and saw lanterns, not too far off. He kept his own counsel, not because he didn't need their help, but because he couldn't afford their company. Not where he needed to go.

On the edge of a ravine on a slope so steep that he could stand straight and chew grass if he chose, Nathaniel caught a flash of movement above him. The wolves who made this side of the mountain their own were watching him, eyes reflecting red in the moonlight. It was a good sign.

He skittered over a shoulder of scree accumulated over many years, feeling it shift beneath him. Paying attention to the mountain now, because the mountain was paying attention to him. The Wolf would toss him into the void like a bucking horse if he let his mind wander. When the moon was lost behind cloud cover he came to a halt and waited, because he had no choice. An owl called in the darkness and nearby, a nightjar seemed to answer.

Stopping often to listen, Nathaniel made his way along a narrow cliff and past the silver mine. From what he could see through the tangle of juniper that grew out of the cracks in the rock face, nothing had been disturbed; there were no obvious tracks, although daylight might tell a different story. You could walk past the spot a thousand times and never guess what was there: not just the silver mine, tended so carefully these many years, but the strongbox that Chingachgook had brought out of the bush back in '57, and the rest of the Tory Gold.

Nathaniel continued on up through the pines, switching back and forth where the incline was too much for him. There was the deadfall, a hundred years and more of wood downed by storm and wind, as dangerous as any bear trap. The cave was just above him, but before that there was a cliff face he didn't dare scale in the night. The long way around took him a good hour at a steady climb, until finally he could look down on the cave. Under an outcropping of rock he hunkered down, to wait and to think.

He had played in the cave as a boy, hid there when he wanted to be on his own. Right now Billy might be looking at the elk and deer he had drawn on the walls with a burnt stick. His father had shown the cave to him when he was ten; he would do the same for Hannah, when she was surefooted enough for the narrow ridge that led to it. If they were still here. If they could still call Hidden Wolf home. It seemed more and more likely to him these days that they might actually lose the mountain, or simply walk away from it. Once he would have sacrificed his own life to secure his daughter's birthright, but just yesterday he had learned that the cost of staying might be too high.

In the dark Nathaniel could not see the smoke rising from the mouth of the cave, but he could smell it, along with roasting possum. Kirby was in there; he was keeping himself warm and dry. With his rifle across his knees, primed and ready, Nathaniel waited for Billy to show his face, or for the dawn when he could go in after him. Whichever came first.

Just before sunrise he made his move. From one side, he tossed in a torch, swung his rifle up and went in with his finger testy on the trigger. It wasn't any struggle at all: Billy simply got up wearily, dropped his gun, and stood staring at the floor.

"You ready to go?" Nathaniel asked.

Billy raised his head and Nathaniel saw the ruined mouth and the flash of dark resistance in his eyes. It took nothing more than a tap of the rifle stock on the jaw to stop his lunge and toss him down. He clasped both hands to his face, bent himself into a bow and howled.

"Shut up," Nathaniel said. "If you don't want Axel and the rest of them on your tail."

Spit and blood ran down between Billy's fingers as he peered up at Nathaniel.

"Call 'em in," he said hoarsely, his torn mouth working in odd jerks. "Maybe I can strike a deal."

And he reached under the blanket that lay in a heap on the dirt floor and came up not with the knife Nathaniel had half expected, but fists full of gold coin.

"Call 'em in!" Billy shouted. "Where's that treasury agent? O'Brien!"

He coughed and laughed, and tossed the coins in the air. They clinked and rolled on the ground; Nathaniel kept his eyes on Billy.

"The judge will want to see that mine," Billy said, wiping his chin with the back of a hand. "Nice little piece of work it is, too."

"The judge is busy burying his son."

For a moment the certainty in Billy's face wavered, and then it cleared. "You're lying."

Nathaniel shook his head.

"But not in the fire." Billy's voice cracked and wobbled. "That wasn't the idea at all."

"What was the idea?"

Billy just stared at him.

"We'll head down to the village and ask, if you don't believe me."

"You can't afford to take me down there."

"It's you that stinks of fire and spilled blood," Nathaniel said. "Get up."

Suddenly much paler, Billy said: "You'll have to hand that gold over to the treasury."

"What gold?" Nathaniel said. "By the time they get back up here, there won't be any gold. They'll think it's a story you made up, desperate to save your hide."

Billy stood up slowly. "The judge will take the mine away from you."

"And if he did," Nathaniel said, "Elizabeth is his only heir now." He pushed the idea of Kitty and her newborn son out of his head. "We'd get it back in the end. So let's you and me go on down there and ask him what sits worse, the loss of a mine he never knew he had, or the loss of his son."

"You're lying!" Billy whispered.

"Am I? Let's go find out."

He made Billy shake out his boots and strip down to the skin, losing a few gold pieces along the way. Then Nathaniel let him dress again and he prodded him out of the cave at the end of his rifle. His face was as calm and impassive as he knew how to make it, but his mind was racing. There was no one who could come take the gold off the mountain now; Bears was gone to Albany, and none of the women were strong enough to manage the strongbox. He wasn't even sure he could handle it on his own, half empty as it was.

On the cliff edge Billy hesitated in the first rays of the rising sun. Squinting, he glanced up at the sky, and then over the gorge below. He scuffed with one toe and a cascade of pebbles disappeared.

"Gotta piss."

Nathaniel waited.

"Aren't you going to ask about your brother?"

Billy's head jerked around, surprised. "What about him?"

"You don't know if he's alive or dead," Nathaniel pointed out.

Billy shrugged, pulling his breeches back into order. "I was beat harder than that once a week when our folks was alive," he said. "Never killed me. No other way to knock sense into a thick head, Pa always said." He ran a hand over his jaw and winced. "Anyway, they can only hang me once. That is, if Julian really died in the fire."

Nathaniel blinked at him and said nothing, feeling the rage rising in his gorge.

"Stupid bastard, to go in there," Billy muttered.

"Maybe," said Nathaniel, watching closely. "Maybe there was something worth saving inside."

Billy studied his boots.

Nathaniel's rifle hummed in his hands, speaking to him. He gripped it hard and focused on what he could see of Billy's face, bruised and bloody. To the right the sun was rising in colors of fire. Ahead of him was the wilderness. Somewhere out there his father was living rough, because of Billy Kirby. And there was Liam—alone in the world, except for this man. The world narrowed down to this, everything in the balance because of a man like this.

"Why'd you lock the door?" Nathaniel asked, hearing his own voice low and even and far away.

The shaggy blond head came up slowly. A struggle on his face, the bruised mouth puckered. The expression of a man weighing bragging rights against the little bit of common sense he called his own.

"It's like Pa always said." Billy cocked his head to look out over the wilderness. "If a thing's worth doing, it's worth doing all the way."

"That's damn good advice," Nathaniel said, and his rifle stock took Billy in the gut and shoved him backward. There was an explosive grunt of air, Billy's eyes bulging with the shock of it. Nathaniel watched his arms pinwheel once, twice, and there was a furious scrabble and shuddering of loose rock as his boots skittered over the edge. He flung himself forward to grab at the rifle barrel, Nathaniel's shirt, his legs, the fringe on his moccasins. Then the cliff edge snapped off in his hands with a crack like bone breaking—*like Liam's bones breaking*—and Billy Kirby fell a hundred screaming yards to strike the cliff face headfirst, fell again, silently now, to strike again, careening down the mountainside until he was lost in a vast sea of juniper and hemlock.

Nathaniel stood for a long time, listening to the winds. He thought of Elizabeth, who trusted him to do what was right. He looked into his own heart and knew he had done just that, and no less. For his family, for himself. When the rush of his blood had calmed enough, he went into the cave and collected the gold coins. Then Nathaniel started down the mountainside to put them back where they belonged, and to collect Billy Kirby's body.

LVIII

In the next few days, Elizabeth found herself unwilling to leave home, even in the face of visits which could hardly be put off. Her father was not coping as well as she had hoped; there were Kitty and her new baby to look in on, and her schoolchildren seemed to seek her out at every opportunity as if they could not quite believe that she would still be in evidence if the schoolhouse was not. Determined to spend the day at home in spite of all of that, Elizabeth first took up some mending and spent all her time retrieving her needle, or nursing a stuck finger. Finally she resolved to make a list of those books and supplies which had survived the fire. She assembled paper and quill and ink, and found that even the quill felt awkward in her hand.

"You've been to the window five times in a half hour," Many-Doves said. She spoke Kahnyen'kehàka in front of Liam, a sign of her distraction and irritability.

Runs-from-Bears had left for Albany four days ago; Elizabeth could not imagine what was keeping him so long. If Bears did not come back today Nathaniel would go off after him, an idea which did not bear long consideration.

Elizabeth watched Hannah for a moment. The little girl was coping better than the rest of them were with the aftermath of the fire, perhaps because she had taken on Liam as her personal responsibility. When she was not reading to him, or helping him read, she pressed him into service of all kinds.

Immobilized by a broken leg, Liam had spent the morning mending a harness for Nathaniel; now he watched closely as Hannah demonstrated how to braid corn for drying. She picked up the sharpened deer antler attached to a rawhide loop that slipped over her middle finger, and slit the husk. Then she removed all but four good strands, which she plaited into the string of cobs which trailed off Liam's lap. They had already finished two longish braids, which Hannah had hung over the rafters by climbing the ladder Nathaniel had raised in the middle of the room. Liam would have climbed that ladder if she had asked him; Elizabeth had no doubt that he would climb up on the roof, at Hannah's request. He would do whatever he had to do to prove his worth to the household, and to earn his place.

There was a hollowness to the boy's cheek, and a kind of damp-eyed distraction that Elizabeth understood very well: she too was constantly finding herself caught between sorrow and anger at a brother who was suddenly and absolutely beyond redemption.

She forced her attention back to her list, a melancholy business. Most of the books she had here were not suitable for the children, and all the other materials, from quills to hornbooks, had been lost. On a fresh sheet of paper she began a letter to Mr. Beekman, the merchant who had been so helpful in Albany. At least there were funds enough to replace what had been lost. When she looked up again it was time to start to cook, and Nathaniel was coming up the porch stair, and not alone.

Many-Doves let her sewing drop to her lap, her whole body trembling. By the time Runs-from-Bears came through the door, she had already taken it up again and her expression was calm, although her eyes sparked when she looked up to greet him. Elizabeth looked away, not wanting to intrude.

Nathaniel dropped down on one knee next to her chair, and rubbed his cheek on her shoulder.

"All's well."

She raised a brow, and he nodded. "No sign of Richard in Albany, and van der Poole was as good as his word. The suit's been dropped."

Carefully, Elizabeth put down her quill, and then she turned to him and placed her hands on his shoulders. "Are you sure?"

"Bears?" Nathaniel asked, not taking his eyes away from her.

Runs-from-Bears came across the room, pulling some papers from inside his shirt.

"The judge sent this along, said you should put it in a safe place. And there's a letter from Mrs. Schuyler there, too."

"It is over, then?" Elizabeth asked, because she could not quite grasp it.

"Looks that way," Nathaniel agreed.

"Well, then," Elizabeth said, turning to Bears. "What took you so very long? We were concerned."

"Your aunt Merriweather," said Bears. "She ain't exactly a fast traveler."

"Who?" asked Liam, looking up from his work.

"Aunt Merriweather!" answered Hannah for Elizabeth, unable to hide her excitement. "From England, and cousin Amanda—"

"And the husband, too. Spencer." He had found a basket of corncake, and he paused to swallow. "But Mrs. Schuyler talked them into leaving the servants behind in Albany."

"At least there's that," Elizabeth said. Nathaniel's keen eyes were on her. There was a wondering there, questions unasked.

"Bears told them about Julian," he said. "And Kitty, and the rest of it."

Elizabeth pushed out a large sigh of relief. "Where are they?"

"At the judge's."

"Well, then, let's go!" Hannah said, in a businesslike way. "She'll want to see you right away."

"Certainly not," said Elizabeth firmly. "They've traveled all day, and she'll want her tea and her bed. Tomorrow is soon enough. Now if you'll pardon me—" Without another look at Nathaniel, she picked up her shawl and left them.

Bears found her an hour later, where she sat on a beech stump that overlooked the waterfall and the cabins. It had become a favorite place for her since she moved to Lake in the Clouds;

the rushing of the water was soothing, and everything she held dear in the world was within view. Soon there would be snow and this spot would be lost to her until spring. Falling-Day was predicting a hard winter from the way the corn husks had grown in a tight swirl, and the thickness of the muskrat shelters. Elizabeth pulled her shawl more closely around her shoulders against the chill.

She knew that she should go down and cook, too, but she also knew that no one would mind if she did not; Falling-Day would have enough red corn soup for all of them. Nathaniel was in the barn, skinning a deer. She caught sight of him, now and then, looking in her direction. They all knew where she was; they were all content to leave her this time on her own. All except Runs-from-Bears.

She watched him coming in her direction, and tried to set her face in a welcoming smile. He hunkered down, his hands draped casually over his knees, and watched with her.

"Things are simpler in the bush," Elizabeth said after a while. When he had nothing to add to this observation, she picked up a stick from the ground and began to break pieces off it, until she could put off the question no longer.

"Sennonhtonnon'?" *What are you thinking?*

Runs-from-Bears said: "You are one of the bravest women I have ever known. But you sit here shivering in fear of *akokstenha*."

Elizabeth flung the stick at him and it caught in his hair. "I hope you did not call her an old woman to her face. And you should understand," she said. "You just spent three days in her company." Then her voice caught, hoarse with tears, and she pressed her hands to her eyes. "How will I explain? How can I ever explain?"

Bears pulled the stick from his hair, and dropped it. "She does not hold you responsible for what happened to Julian. He made his own way."

Her head jerked up, and she saw his expression: firm, and without pity.

"She has a younger brother, too, and he has been a disappointment to her. Maybe she knows more of what is in your heart than you imagine."

Surprised out of her anxiety, Elizabeth examined his expression closely. "My aunt has been very frank with you. She must have wanted some information."

Bears produced a grin. "Quid pro quo."

"I cannot imagine what news she might have of interest to you, Bears."

He said, "Your aunt has had an adventure or two of her own. They came to New-York by way of Montreal. Where she made the acquaintance of Richard Todd."

Elizabeth heard what he had said; she heard him repeat it. But she still could not quite credit what he told her. Richard Todd was in Montreal; her aunt Merriweather had had opportunity to meet and talk with him. There was a hollow feeling in Elizabeth's stomach when she thought of the lies that Richard had probably told, made only slightly less by the knowledge that aunt Merriweather had spent the days after Montreal with the Schuylers; from them she would have heard something more of the truth. It was almost funny: she had first dreaded having to make her visitors acquainted with all that had happened here in Paradise in the past few weeks, and now her aunt seemed to be in possession of that information, and more. More than Elizabeth herself knew, or wanted anyone to know.

"She asks more questions than you do, Looks-Hard."

Suddenly resigned, Elizabeth wiped her eyes with her handkerchief and squared her shoulders. "Perhaps it would be best to see her this evening, after all."

Bears rose, and offered her a hand up. "Tkayeri," he said. *It is proper so.*

Elizabeth, Nathaniel, and Hannah arrived at the judge's door just after dark, to find the house in great turmoil. Instead of the normal lamplight, beeswax candles blazed in all the downstairs rooms. The hall was crowded with luggage and boxes which Manny was busily sorting away, but there was no sign of the visitors or of the judge. Polly appeared with her arms full of bedding in the doorway of the study. It seemed that they were in the process of moving Kitty and her son into the house, and the study was to be converted into a nursery. Nathaniel saw by the look on Elizabeth's face that she was not at all surprised at this. In fact, she was barely able to suppress a smile.

"It looks like aunt Merriweather's planning on moving in herself," Nathaniel noted, stepping over a tea chest inlaid with mother-of-pearl.

"Oh no," Elizabeth said. "Perhaps there is luggage here for a week, certainly not more than two. She did not bring a cat with her?" This last question was directed to Polly, who confirmed that there was no cat in the traveling party. Elizabeth nodded, satisfied. "Without Aphrodite she will not stay for more than a week or ten days."

"Should we go help?" asked Hannah, trying hard to curb her curiosity about a large trunk marked "Library."

"Absolutely not," Elizabeth said. "She'll have everyone jumping as it is. We'll sit here, and wait."

Nathaniel moved a stack of hatboxes and she made a place for herself near the hearth. Hannah managed to find the book-shelf and settled down in a corner. Nathaniel took Elizabeth's hand, icy cold, and rubbed it between his own. There was a jumpiness in her that was foreign to him, but he had observed that even a woman as unflappable as Falling-Day could be brought out of her calm when she believed her mother or an older aunt to be close by.

The wagon pulled up, and in almost no time at all, Aunt Merriweather appeared at the door. Nathaniel saw straight off that she was the kind of woman who made the wind move with her. She was tall, with a back as straight as a sword and a set to her shoulders that would have suited a general. In her arms was a bundle which Nathaniel supposed held Kitty's child. She handed it over to Curiosity without hesitation, and then crossed the room in a great crackle of skirts and capes, all in black. "Elizabeth, my dear," she said, holding out her hands. "Come and kiss me. I suppose this is your husband? I am so very pleased to make your acquaintance, Mr. Bonner. Such good reports I have had of you, I wonder if they could all possibly be true? And your Hannah. Come closer, child, and let me look at you. Your uncle Runs-from-Bears told me all about you—some-where in my things I have something which might interest you. Curiosity, would tea be too much? You must tell me if I am being too demanding—I am only a visitor, and I have no wish to disrupt your household. Sit here, Elizabeth, where I can examine you. Whatever are you wearing on your feet? Could we find paper and ink, do you imagine? I need your assistance at once, we must construct a list. I find your father—most excellent man, but a man after all—ill prepared to take on the task of raising his grandson. We must find the good even in the saddest of fates, must we not, Elizabeth? Have you seen your nephew today? I arrive to find that he has already been christened *Ethan,* imagine. The image of your poor brother, I would say. Kitty, you should not be out of bed, but I suppose you might come and sit with us for a few moments. This is your affair, after all."

Elizabeth was immediately caught up in a discussion of Kitty's change in circumstance. She threw Nathaniel a weak smile; he shrugged one shoulder and turned to the window. The judge was headed up the stairs with Mr. Witherspoon close behind. Galileo and Benjamin were unloading the wagon.

A couple was walking up the hill toward the house. The woman was small and finely built, pretty but pale in her mourning clothes. Her hands fluttered as she spoke. There was something whispery about Elizabeth's cousin Amanda, even at this distance.

There was not much more to see about William Spencer, whose attention and mind were not with whatever tale his wife had to tell. He was of medium height, with the shoulders of a man who sat over books all day. He stood looking down over the lake and the village, his expression easy and even and empty, somehow. His wife stood at his side, talking on, her hands moving in the air in front of her as if she could call his attention to her with magic. Nathaniel wondered if cousin Amanda had brought the Green Man with her all the way from England, and if he would feel at home with the stone men of the endless forests.

Elizabeth found that aunt Merriweather was best approached like an unavoidable march through a boggy field. Once in the middle and up to the ankles in muck, there was nothing to do but persevere for the other side.

When there was opportunity, she answered questions in the order they seemed to her most important. To answer them all would not be possible; Aunt would come back to those which most interested her, anyway. One such question had already surfaced in three slightly different forms. Nathaniel would have been a help in this conversation, but he had excused himself to lend Galileo a hand.

"If we do rebuild the schoolhouse, it will not be until the spring. There is too much work at this time of year to think of it, in any case."

Her aunt said: "But I am more than willing to finance the rebuilding—"

"I understand, and I am most thankful for your generosity. It is not the funds for rebuilding which are at issue, but simply the time. This winter we will make do with Father's first homestead. It served us well before, and will serve again, will it not, Hannah?"

Hannah's instincts were very good; she simply nodded, and resisted the pull into the conversation.

"Cannot you hire one of the men in the village, or several of them, to take on this job?" asked her aunt.

Kitty surprised Elizabeth by speaking up. "The hunting season is upon us, ma'am," she said. "And many of the men here go into the bush to trap."

"I see," aunt Merriweather said. Which meant, of course, that she did not; she was not resigned. Elizabeth anticipated other conversations on this topic, but for the moment she was rescued by the arrival of her cousin Amanda, who dropped down beside her in a great rush of silk and taffeta, and took both her hands in her own pale, cold ones.

"We have been a very long time in finding you," Amanda said in her breathy, sweet way. "I did wonder if perhaps we should never get here at all."

"But here you are," her mother noted. "And here is your tea. I do not like your color, Amanda. Do drink it while it is warm."

Hidden from her mother's view by Kitty, Amanda rolled her

eyes at Elizabeth, even as she took the cup that Daisy offered her.

"You are looking very well," Elizabeth said, squeezing Amanda's hand. "And I am so pleased to see you here. I only wish circumstances were happier—"

The judge had been sitting quietly nearby, listening with a smile on his face. But he stood and left the room quite suddenly, mumbling some small excuse. Mr. Witherspoon trailed out after him, casting apologies liberally as he went. Aunt watched them go with a closed expression and her mouth drawn down in worry.

"I fear we do not have much to offer in the way of diversion, given recent losses," Elizabeth concluded.

"Oh, but there is the child," Amanda said. "We must be thankful for the child."

Curiosity appeared at the door as if she had been summoned. The bundle in her arms was squirming and humming in anticipation. "Kitty, this boy of yours is empty again."

Kitty rose. "I must go and see after him," she said. "If you will excuse me."

Amanda jumped up, Elizabeth forgotten, to follow Kitty on her errand.

"My poor dear," aunt Merriweather said under her breath. "My poor lamb, so long without a child of her own. She holds up so bravely, does she not? Although we were most surprised, pleasantly surprised, by the good tidings we had of you, my dear. I must say at least your sense of decorum and timing is better than was that of your poor brother—not that such a thing as reputation seems to matter here. Ah, William."

Will Spencer was at the door. He bowed from the waist, and came forward.

It was almost two years since Elizabeth had last seen him: the hair on his temples had grown sparser, and there were the first fine lines around his eyes. But the same kindness and intelligence were there, too, and when she looked at him she did not see a man of great wealth and education, but the boy she had grown up with. She smiled at him, and at herself: all her worries, and here was just Will, who had hid with her in the apple orchard, taught her how to make a slingshot out of old garters, and told her stories of the Amazon. Whatever else she had once felt for him seemed all very dim and unimportant, compared to what she felt for the boy he had been and the place that boy held in her heart. Perhaps he could see all this on her face, as well, for his strained expression was replaced by a genuine smile, and he leaned over to take her hand and kiss her cheek. He smelled, as always, of his pipe.

"Will."

"It's good to see you, Lizzie," he said. "I've been very worried about you."

Aunt Merriweather put down her teacup. "So were we all. But look at the color in her cheeks. The wilderness agrees with her, after all. Is that not so, Mr. Bonner?"

Elizabeth was startled to find that Nathaniel had come in. His face was set in an expression she could not quite interpret.

"I'm called Nathaniel. And yes, it's true enough."

Growing up under her aunt's tutelage, Elizabeth had often seen the calculating look she was giving Nathaniel now: she had not yet determined his worthiness, and she would not be rushed in her appraisal or less than frank about the results of her examination. What Elizabeth had not often experienced was the kind of measured calm with which Nathaniel met this scrutiny. The truth was, Elizabeth realized, that Nathaniel would not be devastated or even especially put out if her aunt should take a dislike to him. It was this potential indifference which was so unusual. Augusta Merriweather had enough money and influence to gain the attention of almost anyone who crossed her path. Thus Nathaniel was a new experience for her and, Elizabeth saw with some relief, not a displeasing one.

"Well, then, Nathaniel. Come here and be introduced to Sir William Spencer, Viscount Durbeyfield. He is also my son-in-law, and your wife's first love."

Elizabeth's spoon went clattering to the floor.

"Mother!" Amanda's tone was all gentle sorrow and dismay.

"Now, Mother Merriweather," said William with a great frown.

"Do stop 'Mothering' me," the old lady said irritably, peering at her son-in-law down the elegant arch of her long nose. "Do you think you could hide anything from this man? Look at him." She pursed her mouth. "You might as well come out and tell him all of it."

Elizabeth met her husband's cool and somewhat amused gaze.

"I'm listening, Boots."

"We were together quite a lot as children," Elizabeth said, struggling very hard to keep her composure and her temper both. "It was very long ago."

"How long?" asked Hannah, who had surfaced from her corner and her book with an unerring affinity for high adventure.

"A million years," Elizabeth said firmly.

William held out a hand toward Nathaniel. "You'll permit me to present myself to you, in spite of this rather peculiar start we've made. Will Spencer, at your service. Mother does like to stir things up"—Aunt Merriweather's cluck of the tongue drew a smile from him—"so you mustn't be alarmed at her stories."

"I ain't so easily vexed," Nathaniel said, taking the hand that was offered to him. "Elizabeth can tell you that much about me."

Aunt Merriweather rose with a sudden flurry of skirts and lace. "I do hope that she will have a great deal more to tell than that. Elizabeth, love, come with me to my room. We have much to discuss, and we can leave the men to their own devices. They will sort things out as they see fit. Hannah can amuse herself? I see she has much in common with you at her age, Elizabeth—if you were not up a tree, you were lost in a book."

When the door had been firmly closed behind them, the old woman settled herself in the chair by the window. Ever vigilant, Augusta Merriweather did not like surprises or unexpected visitors, no matter how far she might be from home.

"Well, Lizzie," the older woman said, when Elizabeth had taken a seat at her knee. It was her other voice, the kinder one she reserved for moments of solitude. All the lines in her face seemed to soften at once. "This is a sad business, is it not?"

Elizabeth nodded, because she was not sure of her ability to keep her composure. She watched her aunt's profile for a moment, remembering small things which had been lost to her in the time they had been apart: the strong lines of her face, stronger now it seemed. She had grown older.

"Sometime I would like to hear the whole story of what went amiss with Julian, for your father is not capable of telling it. But I think not now. I find I am not in the right frame of mind for tears."

"You never are, Aunt."

"Have you never seen me thus?" She looked a bit surprised. "Well, I shall not start this evening, then. There are other matters more urgent, at the moment. Your new sister-in-law, first and foremost. Tell me, do you think there's any chance of our taking her and the child back to England with us? Or just the child—Amanda and Will would provide an excellent home. You know this to be true."

Elizabeth realized that her mouth had fallen open, and she closed it with a snap. But before she could gather her thoughts, her aunt was off again.

"It is very awkward, indeed. I have no sense of the girl—she seems as fragile as blown glass on the surface, but I suspect there is a strong will in there, somewhere. I certainly hope there is, at least, or Richard Todd may well find a way into your father's pockets in the end." Her blue eyes flashed as she said this.

"Aunt, I have no idea what you are talking about."

"Do you not? I think you must. Don't pretend with me, Lizzie, not with me. I know your father too well; I knew your poor brother, too, and having met Dr. Todd—in quite remarkable circumstances I'm sure you'll agree—I see how you were caught up here in men's games. You have managed to extricate yourself—and well done, too, I will admit."

"Thank you," Elizabeth said, suppressing a smile.

"But Kitty sits downstairs, a new widow with the key to your father's heart and property at her breast, and I do not doubt that Richard Todd will see that as clearly as I do."

"Whatever did he say to you to lead you to such a conclusion?"

Aunt Merriweather began to twist and turn the rings on her hands. "It was not so very much, at least it would not seem so much to anyone else. He said that a woman imprudent and impetuous enough to elope with a backwoodsman could not be a proper overseer and steward of this land—" She glanced out the window. "When I heard those words from him, I knew that he either did not know you at all—unlikely, given the small society here, and the fact that he pursued you for so long—or that he preferred to misrepresent you to the world to further his own ends. It was outrageously insolent of him, too, to make such pronouncements about his betters, and in public."

Elizabeth smoothed her skirt under her hands, and sought the right tone. "But Aunt," she said. "Richard's interest has always been very specifically in Hidden Wolf—the mountain. I do not believe that he has designs on the rest of my father's holdings. All of the trouble has been because that mountain is in that part of my father's property which he deeded to me— upon my marriage."

She wished for the power to keep from flushing, even as she felt the color rising on her neck and face. From the way her aunt's mouth curled down at one corner Elizabeth knew that none of the intrigues of how and why she had married had gone unnoticed, and also, more strangely, that her aunt's sensibilities had not been fatally insulted. Because she could not resist, Elizabeth remarked on this.

"I expected your disapprobation," she said softly.

"Because you ran off into the wilderness with Nathaniel Bonner?"

"Yes," Elizabeth said slowly. "And because of the way I secured my claim to the property. All of this—" She gestured out the window. "All of my life now, so different from what you hoped for me, I think."

Aunt Merriweather's bright blue eyes could be hard, but her expression now was not an unkind one. "Are you happy about the child you carry? About the man who is the father of your child?"

"I am, yes. I am very happy."

"Then I see no sense in criticizing you for living a life different from the one you would have had in England. This is not England, after all—so much I have learned on this journey. No, the truth is, Elizabeth, that I am a bit envious. Do not smile, you insolent girl, when I reward you with a confession. I assure you, I do not make many of them; old age has some small compensations."

The mixture of exasperation and amusement on the older woman's face faded away to be replaced by something more thoughtful as she looked out into the night. Benjamin was walking toward the house with a rushlight to show him the way, and the strange shapes thrown by the pierced tin of the lamp shade danced like fairy lights in the darkness. In the endless woods above them, a stag called out, a great rolling sound that echoed down the mountain valley.

"What a strange and wonderful place this is," Aunt Merriweather said. "Everything is bigger, and taller, and brighter—even the night sky is intemperate. I'm quite sure we do very well with many fewer stars in England."

"Why, Aunt," said Elizabeth, surprised out of her watchfulness. "I believe that you like it here."

There was a flicker on her face, regret perhaps, and sadness. Gone as quickly as it came, forced away by sixty-five years of studied pragmatism.

She said: "Had I been born a son, I should have come with your father to this new land to make a life for myself." She hesitated, examining the backs of her hands. "At your age I would have disappeared into this wilderness, too. Even now, I can still feel how it lights a fire in the blood." She turned back to the window. "Is that not so?"

"It is so," Elizabeth said. "It is exactly so."

They talked for a very long time, Elizabeth getting up from her place now and then to put more wood on the fire and trim the candlewick. Her aunt had always been a good storyteller, and she had much of interest to relate. Even so, Elizabeth was startled to see the time when Nathaniel finally came to knock on the door.

"The rest of them have all gone off to bed, and Hannah can't hardly keep her eyes open."

"Oh, I'm so sorry—what have you been doing with yourself?"

"I had a talk with Will Spencer, and then a longer one with Joshua and Daisy. Looks like another wedding soon."

"That will please Curiosity," Elizabeth said with considerable satisfaction of her own.

Nathaniel hesitated. "Do you want to stay here tonight?"

"Of course she does not," Aunt Merriweather said behind them. "Take her back to your mountain now, Nathaniel. I shall come tomorrow to see what kind of home you two have made together."

Elizabeth kissed her aunt's soft cheek, and the old woman held on to her for a moment. "He's a fine man, my girl. You did better for yourself than my Amanda did, but you know that, do you not?"

She wondered if Nathaniel would raise the subject of her relations straightaway, but he was more concerned about Richard Todd, and unable to curb his curiosity.

"I can't see your aunt dining at Beaver Hall," Nathaniel said, shaking his head as he pulled off his leggings.

"She said it was all very elegant. The lieutenant-governor of Montreal was there, and a Huron sachem, and a French comte escaped from the Terror—and Richard in the middle of all of them."

"I don't like it," Nathaniel said. And then, after a longer pause: "There was no sign of Otter?"

"I described him quite carefully. She saw other Indians, but she is fairly sure that she did not meet Otter. And Richard did not mention him. Apparently," Elizabeth continued slowly. "Apparently Richard was paying court to a young woman."

"It's a good thing that Kitty's squared away, then," Nathaniel said, but his thoughts were clearly still with Otter. Elizabeth thought of pointing out to him—as her aunt had pointed out to her—that Richard might still marry Kitty, who now had a much more attractive dowry to offer. But Nathaniel had already headed off in another direction.

"If he has any interest in Paradise, or the mountain, he'll be back here before winter settles in."

"Yes," Elizabeth said. "He mentioned to Will that he had business in Albany."

"Not anymore, he doesn't," Nathaniel said firmly.

"But he could not have known that at the time."

Nathaniel lay back on the bed and reached up to tug on Elizabeth's hair, which she was plaiting for the night. "He can't go after you anymore, in court at least."

She ran a finger over the stubble on his jaw, enjoying the rasp of it. "I had some chance of standing up to him," she said. "Kitty—well, I am not sure what will happen if he comes proposing marriage all over again."

"Maybe you could give her lessons in how to turn him down. Since you've got some experience at it."

"I think that perhaps I may have to do just that," Elizabeth said, leaning over to tousle his hair. "Thank goodness, I've got Aunt Merriweather and Amanda to help me, for I fear Kitty will be a reluctant student."

"So Amanda had more men to choose from, did she?"

She turned away to look for the rawhide string with which she tied her plait. "Not so many as her sister Jane, but yes, I believe she had three or four. But she accepted Will straight-away, once he got to the point."

Elizabeth gave in, finally, to his silence.

"Nathaniel. We were playmates, and I . . . enjoyed his company as a young girl. He was one of the few people who would talk to me of books, and did not scold me for my curiosity. He never had any interest in me, and he never knew I had any interest in him. In the end he married as his family hoped and wished, and all parties were most satisfied with the arrangement. If I felt any regret, it was for the friend I lost. And perhaps at first I was disappointed to see him marry to better his connection, rather than for love. But I soon came to see that he and Amanda suit each other."

"Do they?" Nathaniel asked. "He never even looks at her."

"I suppose when you and I have been married for six years we might seem the same way, to strangers."

At that he caught her by the plait, and pulled her down next to him. He kissed her soundly, and held her until she stopped struggling, and then he kissed her again until a small sigh escaped her and she lost track of the conversation, and everything but the taste of him, and the textures of his mouth and the feel of his shoulders under her hands. When Nathaniel raised his head they were both short of breath.

"Do you think you'll have enough of kissing me, in six years?"

She laughed. "Not in sixty. But must we judge them by our own standards? Amanda is a good wife to Will," she said with an air of finality.

"And I suppose he is a good husband."

"You do not like him. That is very sad, because I do."

Nathaniel lay back, his hands behind his head. The room was chilly, but he did not seem to mind the cold, for he lay there in only his breechclout. Then he turned on his side to talk to her.

"I don't dislike him. It's just that he reminds me of someone I knew once," he said. "It was a long time ago, when I first went to live at Trees-Standing-in-Water."

"When you were first with Sarah?"

"Aye." He gave her a grim smile, and then cupped her face in his hand. "I was spending half my time with her brothers and father—this was long before they were killed in the raid. The other half of my time I spent trying to convince Falling-Day and Sarah that I would be a good husband and that I deserved a place in their longhouse. Do you remember, I told you back in the bush that I had been Catholic once?"

"Perhaps that is one detail of your past that we need not share with aunt Merriweather."

"Do you want to hear this story?"

"I do. But please take your hand away, because it is distracting me."

She was a little sorry to have him comply so willingly, but then she was also interested in what he had to tell.

Nathaniel said: "There was a priest living there then, a Frenchman who went by the name Father Dupuis. But the Kahnyen'kehàka called him Iron-Dog."

She had to laugh, in spite of the seriousness of his tone. "What a strange name."

Nathaniel shrugged. "He had a beard which was ugly to them—they might have just called him Dog-Face, which is what they often call bearded O'seronni. But he also had their respect, because he lived and worked like a man among them.

"I got to know him pretty well, because Sarah wanted me to be baptized. It was one of the conditions she put on letting me come into the longhouse. I can see you're uneasy with that, but it didn't mean much to me, Boots. It was just some water and some words, and I didn't believe any of it. I would have done and said a lot more than that to get where I wanted to be with Sarah."

"So you did it to please her?"

"Aye, I'm afraid so. But remember, I was barely eighteen, and at that age a man lives between his legs, mostly. Though some hide that better than others, or deny it. The thing about Iron-Dog was that he lived and worked among us as a man, but he had none of a man's needs."

"Nathaniel," Elizabeth began slowly. "As a part of his training he was taught to suppress such urges—I think it was Saint Augustine who said that complete abstinence is easier than perfect moderation."

"That's just it," Nathaniel said. "I spent a long time watching the man, and I came to the conclusion that he never had any appetites to start with. It wasn't a struggle for him. He never looked twice at the women when they went bare-chested to work the fields, or worried about the way young folks would disappear into the woods—he just didn't care about those things, and that made him unusual for a priest, and for a man, too. It's part of the reason he lasted so long among the Kahnyen'kehàka."

Elizabeth turned onto her stomach and put her chin into the cup of her palm. "Are you trying to tell me that he had . . . unnatural leanings?"

Nathaniel drew up, surprised. "No, that ain't what I meant at all. It wasn't that he liked his own kind—I've known a few like that, and that wasn't it at all, with him. There was no hunger in him at all for human touch, of any kind at all."

Elizabeth was disconcerted by the comparison of such a man to Will Spencer; she sought in her mind for examples of her knowledge of him that would disprove what Nathaniel was proposing.

"You saw him greet me," she said. "Surely you could find nothing cold in him there."

"I never used the word *cold*."

"You might have," she said. "You are accusing him of a lack of interest in things worldly and mortal, as if he were some kind of . . . would-be saint. You are perfectly at your leisure to dislike Will, if you must, but perhaps it has less to do with him than it does with you."

Nathaniel's face went very still for a moment, but there was a great deal of movement behind his eyes as he thought. She could see him weighing words and rejecting them.

"I never said I didn't like him, Boots. I don't know him well enough to come down on either side of that, yet. But you've put your finger on something. Maybe there is something of the saint in your Will Spencer, the way there was in Iron-Dog. And maybe it's me that's at fault, then, because I might respect a saint, but it's damn hard to like one."

"He is not *my* Will Spencer," Elizabeth said, her irritation getting the upper hand. "He is an old friend and my cousin's husband. I can see nothing saintlike about him at all."

"Well, you don't share a bed with him." Nathaniel grinned; his mood was shifting as clearly as the moon moved down the night sky. "Maybe that's what your aunt meant when she said you did better for yourself than Amanda."

She rolled onto her back to glare at him. "Your ears are altogether too sharp. That comment was not meant for you to hear."

"Really?" he said, one brow raised. "I ain't so sure about that." He seemed on the verge of saying more, and then he stopped, and ran a finger down her neck and into the opening of her nightdress.

"I'll spend some time with Will this week, see if I'm wrong."

"Good, " Elizabeth said, somewhat mollified. And then, after a long pause while his finger traced her collarbone: "It's late, perhaps we should sleep."

"Aye, I can see you're tired." His hand continued on its quest over her shoulder. "Tell me to stop, then."

She made a small sound in the back of her throat, and closed her eyes. "It is very late," she said hoarsely.

"Tell me to stop." His breath was very warm against her ear.

"I don't want to," she said, turning to him. "You think you're the only one with strong appetites, Nathaniel Bonner. Well, I am here to prove you wrong."

He laughed then, his hands moving on her, stripping her nightdress away. Even in the gentle touch of candlelight his expression was severe with desire. And it struck her suddenly that Amanda did not know of this, might have never known what it was to see this look in her husband's face, to feel wanted in this way. Elizabeth tried to imagine that, the lack of *wanting* in Nathaniel's eyes, and she was overwhelmed with thankfulness for him, for his hands beneath her and his strong kisses, the touch of his tongue. When he was over her she spread her hands on his back and arched up to meet him to tell him so, but he took the words from her, stole them from her with his look, that look that came over him when he was inside her: intent on more, always more, intent on disappearing into her, on becoming part of her, sweat and blood and seed.

"You see?" he said, stealing her words and then feeding them back to her, stroke by stroke: "You see?"

LIX

Elizabeth's week was consumed by aunt Merriweather. On those few days that she was not expected at her father's, her aunt came to spend the day on the mountain. She sometimes brought Amanda and Will with her but more often came alone, accompanied only by Galileo, or Benjamin. She drew everyone who came across her path into conversation, curious about each small detail of life at Lake in the Clouds. Examining the pelts on their stretchers, Aunt Merriweather expressed a strong inclination to see an animal which could produce a fur of such value and utility. Between Runs-from-Bears and Hannah, she marched off to the nearest beaver pond at dusk and waited patiently, getting her boots wet but coming back to the cabin highly satisfied with her success.

She had soon won most of them over: Falling-Day's reservations seemed to give way quite quickly, and while Liam was openly jealous of the way Elizabeth's aunt could claim Hannah's attention, he himself went out of the way to present a good picture to the old lady, even asking for a comb on one occasion when she was expected. Only Many-Doves remained distant, and watchful, unmoved by the gifts that had been brought for her from Montreal, polite at all times but unwilling to be drawn in. It was Many-Doves who gave aunt Merriweather her Kahnyen'kehàka name: She-Pulls-the-Winds-Behind-Her.

Elizabeth smiled uneasily when she heard it, but she could not deny that it was appropriate.

Elizabeth left her aunt alone with Nathaniel for short periods of time, and thought perhaps that with enough exposure they might come to like each other. Of course, Elizabeth did not mention to him her aunt's proposed scheme for laying pipe to bring water into the cabin, or for improvements to the chimney. Nor did she tell him about the many suggestions for more traditional furnishings, stout shoes, flannel undergarments, the addition of pork to their diet or brood hens to their livestock.

Most of the time she was alone with her aunt, and little by little she had the stories of her first year in the New World drawn out of her. Some things Elizabeth did keep back, quickly relearning the skill of deflecting curiosity when it strayed into dangerous areas. She did not, would never, tell her the whole story of Jack Lingo, for she believed she knew the limits of her aunt's open-mindedness. They spoke of England, too, and of uncle Merriweather's death. Then, on a cold afternoon with the newly harvested pumpkins and squashes piled around them like a galaxy of small glowing suns in the coming dusk, they spoke of Julian, and Elizabeth saw tears in her aunt's eyes, and found her own, then, finally.

On the day before they planned to begin the return trip to Albany, Elizabeth took Hannah with her to spend the day at her father's, leaving a disgruntled Liam behind in Falling-Day's care. It was to be one of Aunt's traditional teas: the men were banished, and the women could sit comfortably and talk openly.

They were a small group: Aunt Merriweather, Elizabeth, Amanda, Hannah, and Kitty freshly out of childbed. There were dark smudges under her eyes, and her hands shook slightly. Elizabeth had seen that expression before, when her cousin Jane's new daughter had been two weeks old. As if the infant's constant demands had caused Jane to forget the boundaries of her own body.

Elizabeth knew that Kitty's condition did not escape her aunt, but in a very uncharacteristic way she overlooked the slightly rumpled gown and unkempt hair. Aunt Merriweather had plans for this tea, and Kitty would not be excused until she was satisfied.

Curiosity filled the sideboard with scones and cakes and tea brewed according to directions, and then disappeared into the back of the house, where Elizabeth followed her to ask for her company at the table. She had been feeling vaguely worried about Curiosity all week, ill at ease about the way she had vanished suddenly into the guise of a household servant in the shadow of aunt Merriweather's expectations.

"She don't want nobody like me at her tea table," Curiosity said firmly, fixing her attention on the churn. "You go on now, and talk to them. Tomorrow they'll be gone and things will get back to normal around here." She scooped up another slab of pale butter beaded with water, slapped it onto the mound on the board before her, and began to work it mercilessly with her paddles.

"She means well, Curiosity."

"Yas'm, the lady is just a visitor and don't wish to cause no disruption in the household. I heard tell."

Elizabeth could not suppress her smile. "I'm very thankful to you for all the trouble you've taken under challenging circumstances. But please do come, Curiosity. I believe that she's planning to bring up the subject of Richard, and your word counts for very much with Kitty."

The tension in the bony shoulders eased a little. "I don't do anything but show her the way. The same way I will do for you and for my own daughters, when the time come. With a little *charity*," she added, pointedly. She sent Elizabeth a sideways glance. "What's this about Richard Todd?"

Once Elizabeth had related aunt Merriweather's predictions about Richard's return to Paradise and a renewed interest not so much in Kitty, but in Julian's widow, Curiosity took off her apron, wrapped a fresh bandanna around her head and joined them. There was some irony in the fact that it took Richard to unite Curiosity and Augusta Merriweather in a common cause, which Elizabeth appreciated but could not mention to either of them.

"But I don't understand," Kitty said when the subject had finally been broached. She had been concentrating on the child in her lap, and her gaze shifted only reluctantly to the women seated around the table, all with their attention on her.

"Kitty," said Curiosity, rattling the spoon against her saucer to get her attention. "There's a simple question here, child. What are you going to say to the man when he shows up and starts talking marriage again?"

Elizabeth might have laughed at aunt Merriweather's expression, divided evenly between reluctant admiration and horror at such an uncloaked presentation of the facts. She might have laughed, if it were not for the puzzled and distinctly defiant crease between Kitty's brows.

"I cannot imagine that he should," Kitty said. "I am a widow, now, after all."

"Men rarely forget about money and connections," aunt Merriweather said. "It is one of their more dependable appetites."

Hannah looked wide-eyed from face to face, her cake forgotten on the plate before her. Elizabeth wished suddenly that she had left the little girl behind at Lake in the Clouds, but there was almost no way to turn back the conversation at this point, and Hannah would never leave without a struggle.

"You do not know Richard as I do," Kitty said firmly. "No one does. I grew up with him, and I can appeal to his better nature. If I should have that chance."

"That is the worst kind of folly for a woman, to think that she can change a man by marrying him," aunt Merriweather said.

"You heard tell of the tiger and those stripes he so fond of," Curiosity agreed.

Elizabeth cleared her throat. "What we are trying to say, Kitty, is that if Richard is still interested in marriage when he returns, we hope you would think very carefully about his motivations before you reconsider."

Kitty's head came up quickly, her cheeks sparked with red. As if he understood the fact that he was at the center of this controversy, the baby on her lap began to fuss. Amanda leaned over to burble at him. He settled, mouthing his fist with great sucking noises.

"I am not so sure of any of this," Kitty said finally in a strangled tone, refusing to meet anyone's eye.

"Katherine," aunt Merriweather said sternly. "Perhaps I must be blunt. You are no longer without connections. To marry is to compromise what you have gained."

With a rebellious flash in her mild blue eyes, Kitty said: "That did not stop your niece."

There was an immediate response on Elizabeth's lips, but her aunt silenced her with a severe glance. "Let me understand you clearly, then. You intend on marrying Dr. Todd should he renew his offer?"

Kitty's chin trembled, but she held it high. "I will listen to what he has to say."

"It's what menfolk *don't* say that's the problem," Curiosity muttered.

Kitty stood up abruptly. "I think it is very—cruel of you to talk to me this way, all of you. I have lost my husband so recently, and you are asking me to put aside the friendship of the one person in the world who has always stood by me—"

Curiosity reared up to face the younger girl, fists on hips. "Now I got to tell the truth and shame the devil," she interrupted, sucking in one cheek and pushing it out again. "I don't see Dr. Todd hiding around here. I didn't see him here even a week ago worried about was you going to bring that child into the world without a name, or not."

"He would have come, if he had been able," Kitty said, jiggling the baby madly against her shoulder. He let out a wail almost as indignant and sorrowful as the look on her face.

"Oh, dear." Amanda sent a pleading look to her mother, whose thunderous expression was fixed on Kitty. Elizabeth wished now that they had told her about Richard's activities in Montreal, as painful as it would have been to her.

Kitty said: "You need not pity me. Richard will come still. He promised me that he would. And if he still wants to marry me although I am a widow, then why should I not—" Her gaze moved around the table in search of a kind and understanding face, but found only dismay, irritation, and anger. "How else shall I ever get out of this village and into the world?"

"Katherine Middleton," said aunt Merriweather calmly.

"The world is yours *without* Richard Todd, if you so desire it. You and your son are welcome at Oakmere whenever you like. You can make your home with me."

"—Or with us, at Downings. We would love to have you." Amanda broke in on her mother.

"You see," aunt Merriweather said. "As the widow of my late nephew you are your own mistress. Marry again, and you are subject to your new husband's whims."

Kitty stood there swaying slightly, as if she could not quite make sense of these words.

"Either set down, or hand over that boy before you drop him," Curiosity said, holding out her arms for the baby.

The blank stare on Kitty's face lasted for a long moment, and then she swallowed visibly, and handed her son to Curiosity. She sat down heavily, and turned to Elizabeth with a questioning look.

"I might really go with them to England? To live?"

"The invitation was made," Elizabeth said.

Aunt Merriweather said: "We shall spend the winter visiting and we shall come back here before we sail—to greet the newest member of the family." She inclined her head slightly in Elizabeth's direction; the closest she would come to acknowledging her pregnancy in public. "Your son will be old enough to travel then, and you may sail with us. I hope you will."

"I had no idea," Kitty said.

"But now you do," aunt Merriweather said firmly.

The child in Curiosity's arms suddenly began to twist and arch as the small face screwed itself into a knot of misery to produce one long and plaintive wail. In response, two circles of moisture appeared on Kitty's bodice. She made a small distressed noise, glancing around herself in panic and embarrassment. Elizabeth felt a tugging in her own breast; whether out of sympathy with Kitty, or with the child's hunger, she was not quite sure.

Curiosity stood, making sympathetic noises. "No need to carry on, Kitty. Let's just get you to your room. He won't be satisfied with nothing but what you got to give him."

Kitty nodded. At the door, she turned back. Above the

baby's wails she said: "I understand that your concern is for the child, rather than for me. You think Richard would only want me because of Ethan, and the land . . ." She paused, and there was a fresh rush of color on her face. "Perhaps you are right about that, but perhaps you are not. I should still like to hear what Richard has to say."

"Of course, by all means," aunt Merriweather said. "It might be quite edifying."

Leaving the room behind Kitty, Curiosity paused at the door to throw Elizabeth a sour grin.

"Well, that was nicely done," said aunt Merriweather, sitting back with a satisfied expression. "Dr. Todd will have a harder time of it, anyway. You must be sure to keep her mind focused on the alternatives, Elizabeth, once he begins whispering in her ear."

"Richard is not the type to whisper in anyone's ear," Elizabeth said. "But I shall try to be the voice of reason. And there is Curiosity."

Aunt Merriweather seldom smiled very broadly, but a definite grin turned her face into a sea of fine wrinkles. "She is a treasure, that woman. I suppose there would be no chance of having her accompany Katherine—" In response to Elizabeth's frown, she inclined her head in surrender. "Your father does depend upon her. We mustn't take everything away from him."

Elizabeth was unwilling to bring up the subject of her father at the moment, in front of Hannah. But something else was weighing on her. "Aunt, had you thought—perhaps Richard does truly care for her."

"Hmmmpf." A gnarled hand waved away that possibility, diamonds flashing yellow and blue in the afternoon sunlight. "He hadn't thought of her for months, I'm sure. He's been overly occupied with the daughter of the lieutenant-governor —what was her name, Amanda?"

"Giselle."

"Very *French*," Aunt said, in the same tone she might have said *cannibal*.

"Her mother was Parisian, I believe," Amanda said. "But I observed Richard with Miss Somerville, and I don't think it was anything more than a flirtation. I doubt a marriage will come of it."

"I disagree," said Aunt, pressing her mouth into a thin line. "It would suit me very well if he should marry her. I do not like the idea of him snowed in here with Katherine for the entire winter."

"Usually we don't get snowed in for more than a few weeks at a time," suggested Hannah helpfully.

Aunt Merriweather's gaze turned toward her. "You have had a very instructive tea, Miss Hannah. But you look doubtful. Tell me what you are thinking."

With a small shrug, the girl put down her cake plate. "It wouldn't be polite."

"Would it not?" Aunt Merriweather raised one brow and tilted her head in Hannah's direction: an invitation, or perhaps a summons to be less than polite.

After only a short hesitation, Hannah said: "Hector and Blue went after the Hauptmanns' cat once. Got her cornered and that was that."

Amanda drew in a small sigh of dismay; Elizabeth did not know whether to laugh or cry. But Hannah's expression was serene, and she returned aunt Merriweather's sharpest scrutiny without a hint of anxiety. She wondered how Nathaniel could have ever doubted that this child was his: even the tilt of her head spoke of him.

"How old is this girl?" The question was directed to Elizabeth, but Hannah answered for herself.

"I'll be ten this winter, ma'am."

Aunt Merriweather stared, but Hannah never blinked. Suddenly the old woman's face lost its stony cast, and one corner of her mouth curled reluctantly upward.

"I understand you have a talent for medicine," she said. "Did you try to save the cat?"

"There wasn't anything to save once they got done with her, but I've got her skeleton. My father helped me wire it together. Do you want to see it?"

"Thank you most kindly for that generous offer," said aunt Merriweather. "Perhaps another time."

·   ·   ·

After another hour in her aunt's company, Elizabeth set off for home with Hannah. She wanted the exercise and the fresh air; she needed the time to organize her thoughts, and so she refused the company of Galileo which Aunt pressed on her so urgently.

They had just turned the path into the woods that took them out of view of the house when Amanda showed herself behind a pine tree, gesturing at them with frantic small motions of her pale hands.

"What is it?" Elizabeth asked, concerned. "Are you unwell? Shall we walk with you back to the house?"

Without a word, Amanda took her arm and pulled her off the path, through the jumble of foliage in reds and yellows and browns which crackled loudly underfoot. A grouse ruffled up indignantly from a meal of birch leaves and scurried off.

"Amanda, what is it?"

"There is nothing amiss with me, but I must have a word with you, and tomorrow there will be no time or opportunity."

"Hannah," said Elizabeth. "Could you please go on ahead? I will catch up with you."

"Can I call on Dolly?"

"Yes, I will come by and get you there. But I won't be long."

When the girl had disappeared down the path, Elizabeth turned to her cousin.

Amanda could barely meet her eye. "I have something I must confess to you. While we were in Montreal, Dr. Todd gave me a message for Kitty."

"For heaven's sake, Amanda. Why did you not say so?"

Amanda pressed her hands together in front of her face and closed her eyes. "Mother forbade me tell anyone, especially Kitty."

What Elizabeth wanted to do, if only she could, was to walk away from this information; she wanted to forget the harried and unhappy look on Amanda's face; she wanted never to hear Richard Todd's name again.

"I don't know, Amanda—"

"Oh, please, cousin. Please, I have no one else to turn to."

Elizabeth took a deep breath, and pushed it out again. "Go on, then."

In a rush, Amanda recited: "He said to tell Kitty that he would be back in Paradise before first snow, and that she should make her wedding clothes ready."

"I see." Elizabeth pressed a finger to the small ache that was blossoming between her brows. "And the young woman, Giselle?"

"I believe it was just a flirtation, although Mother does not. My mother does mean well, Elizabeth. She wants what is best for Kitty and the child."

"Yes," Elizabeth murmured. "I see that." A late oak leaf floated down to rest on the great drift of birch foliage, like a dull brown pebble on a beach of jewels. Overhead a kinglet called with a thin, high *seet-seet-seet*.

"Will you tell Kitty?"

"I think not, not right away. When he gave you that message Richard could not have known that Kitty would marry Julian. Perhaps he will see things differently when he arrives here, and it would be cruel to make Kitty hope."

"But I think he truly cares for her," Amanda said. "I believed his concern was real."

"Then why did he not send word all these long months?" Elizabeth shook her head. "He may be concerned for her welfare, but if he truly intends to marry her I fear it has more to do with other matters. Perhaps he is still under the impression that he needs her testimony against me. What a terrible muddle this is."

"It is most wickedly selfish of me, but I do so want Kitty to come to England with Ethan. It seems to me that it might be the right thing for them. If not for your father." Amanda averted her face as she said this, pale now, with so much of her earlier prettiness subdued.

"Amanda, you and I have had no time at all together in this brief visit. I wanted to talk to you, to know how you are. Do you—" She hesitated, looking for the right words. "Do you still have difficulty sleeping?"

"Do you mean, does the Green Man still come to me? I think I have finally outgrown him, Elizabeth. Or perhaps he has

found someone else more to his liking. There is no lack of
Green Men here, I think, if one wanted to seek me out."

Joe's face came to Elizabeth: and the hot, dry light in his eye
when he realized that night was falling. The fierce determination to protect himself, fear of one kind of death when another
sat breathing heavily on his chest.

"Here they are called stone men," Elizabeth said, and then, a
little breathlessly: "Have you seen them?"

Amanda turned her face up to the canopy of naked branches,
bony fingers against the sky. "I have seen men in the forest, but
they were all human enough. They smelled very human, at
least." She managed a smile. "No, Elizabeth. I have no need to
look for new ghosts."

Her eyes lowered to Elizabeth's waist and when she looked
up again there was the soft glittering of unshed tears in her eyes.
Amanda, pretty, quietly dependable, with a titled husband and
more land and money than she needed or cared about, was
without the children which had been her only ambition. And
unless she opened up the subject, Elizabeth could not talk to
her of that single, most important fact in her life.

"I must go," Amanda said hoarsely. "Mother will be looking
for me." And she squared her thin shoulders and turned back to
the house, pulling her cape around her.

At Lake in the Clouds they found Baldwin O'Brien firmly
settled into the best chair by the hearth. The high color in his
cheeks and nose might have been due to the cold, but Elizabeth
suspected a very different origin from the halo of scent that
surrounded him and made Hannah's nose wrinkle. He had
been interrogating Liam—that much was clear from the stony
look on the boy's face—and he squinted up at this interruption
as if Elizabeth were the interloper.

"Why are you alone, Liam?" she asked.

"I sent the Mohawk squaws away," O'Brien said. "Didn't
want them here."

Hannah quickly situated herself next to Liam, and scowled at
O'Brien.

"That is most abominably rude of you," Elizabeth said.

"Who are you to direct people in and out of my home? I must ask you to leave, and immediately."

Liam blinked at her thankfully, his mouth pressed hard together.

O'Brien scratched at his dusty beard and got up slowly. "I'm an agent of the state treasury," he said. "Got inquiries to make."

"Your role as an official of the government does not give you leave to harass us, or to trespass. If you had a passing acquaintance with your Constitution and Bill of Rights you would know that."

He narrowed his eyes at her. "I'm going," he said. "But if you folks got nothing to hide, then there's no reason to be so closemouthed."

"My husband has spoken to you at length."

"He'd make a good poker player. Don't give anything away."

"There is nothing to give away, as you put it."

"I don't know," he said slowly, looking around himself. "It's curious. You see this musket of mine? I had her thirty year—she went through the war with me. A fine gun, but wouldn't I like to have one of them expensive new rifles? You know I would. Like your man carries, and that big buck, too. The thing is, I ain't never come across Indians better outfitted, even the ones running furs out of Canada. Curious, like I said. Glass in the windows, there. And somebody's been burning wax candles."

Elizabeth forced herself to produce a grim smile. "What you see is nothing more than the fact that my husband married well. That is not a criminal offense, or even one to raise the interest of the treasury, as far as I understand it. Now," she said firmly. "I suggest that you leave before he finds you here and throws you out."

"I'm going." O'Brien threw up both hands in a gesture of surrender. "Don't want to give Bonner an excuse to toss another man off this mountain."

Liam's color came up in a rush. Elizabeth put a hand on his shoulder and pressed.

"He's going now," she said softly. "Steady on."

At the door, O'Brien pulled on his cap. "I'm heading home

to Albany, but I'll be back in the spring if that gold hasn't showed up in the meantime."

"Pray do what you must," Elizabeth said tightly. "And so shall we."

After a simple meal of stewed beans and squash, when the chores had been seen to, Elizabeth sat down to read aloud in the hope that it would calm them all after an eventful and emotional day. Falling-Day and Many-Doves joined them, bringing along the last of the corn for shucking and braiding.

Aunt Merriweather had brought Elizabeth a great many books, but when she suggested them one by one there was no particular excitement in the room.

"*Hamlet*," suggested Liam.

"Again? But we just finished it."

Falling-Day agreed with Liam. "It is not often we have tales of O'seronni ghosts."

Many-Doves and Hannah were quite willing to hear the same story again—Elizabeth thought that perhaps they could listen to it many times without tiring—and so she settled down near the hearth and began to read by the bright light of a pine knot, always with one ear turned toward the porch. Nathaniel and Runs-from-Bears had gone out to check trap lines and they had taken Will Spencer with them.

Full dark, and inside the cabin there was only the sound of the wood hissing softly in the hearth and the gentle crackling of corn husks. Elizabeth read the conversation between Hamlet and his father's ghost, and hands slowed at their work as they were caught up in the familiar story.

There was a step at the door. Elizabeth put down the book while her heart picked up an extra beat. It seemed to her, as it always did, that the men brought the forests in with them: the quiet room was transformed suddenly by the mere fact of their size, and the energy with which they moved. Everyone was up: there were traps to be put aside for cleaning and repair, a brace of fat snow geese and one of grouse to be hung, bowls of stew and rounds of corn bread to be provided, dry moccasins to fetch, damp heads to be toweled.

Will Spencer looked truly relaxed for the first time since he had come to Paradise, and he let himself be drawn into the normal flow of things without protest. While they ate, Nathaniel and Runs-from-Bears told of their day, and the things they had seen: a moose in rut; at dusk, a flock of ravens at roost that numbered in the hundreds; a single gyrfalcon on the cliffs above the falls. Falling-Day drew in air between her teeth at this last bit of information.

"Winter pushing hard from the north," was her explanation of such a rare sight.

"How was tea with your aunt?" Nathaniel asked Elizabeth, looking up from his bowl.

"Eventful," Elizabeth said. And seeing Hannah ready to tell all, from Kitty's story to what had passed with O'Brien, she said: "We have been reading this evening."

"Oh?" said Will. "Do you read aloud, then?"

Hannah brought him the worn volume, and he looked around the table with an expression of mild surprise.

"What do you think of the Danish prince?"

This question had been directed at Many-Doves, who sat to the side with her lap full of corncobs.

"Revenge is a bitter meal," Many-Doves said, without looking up from her work. "It is not one to linger over."

"He takes too long to get down to business," agreed Liam.

Falling-Day said: "He is like most of the O'seronni I have known."

"And how is that?" Will asked, looking distinctly unsettled.

"He thinks when he should act, and acts when he should think."

No one laughed at this, because Falling-Day did not mean it to be funny.

Nathaniel left a short time later with Will to show him the way down the mountainside to the judge's, and the rest of them returned to their work. Runs-from-Bears stretched expansively, working the muscles between his shoulders.

"How was Will in the forest?" Elizabeth asked, too curious to wait for Nathaniel's opinion.

"He moves like a cat," said Bears. "He knows how to listen."

"Ah," Elizabeth said, pleased with this, the highest of praise from Runs-from-Bears. "Nathaniel thinks him strange."

"Oh, he is strange," said Bears. "For an O'seronni."

Falling-Day said: "There is more than one kind of man in the world."

"And what kind of man is Will Spencer?" asked Elizabeth, intrigued.

"A rich one," said Liam.

"That is not what my grandmother means," Hannah chided him softly, and Liam dropped his gaze to the corn in his great red-raw hands.

"He is a dreamer," said Many-Doves for her mother. "He lives in other worlds and comes into this one only when he has some purpose to serve."

Falling-Day nodded. "Among the Kahnyen'kehàka he would become a shaman, if he survived at all."

Nathaniel walked Will Spencer as far as the village, and agreed to have a drink with him in the tavern. Axel had been dozing near the hearth while his customers served themselves, but he roused himself when he heard Nathaniel's voice.

"There's a rumor," he said, pouring their ale.

"There always is," Nathaniel agreed. "Do you mean the one about Todd heading back this way?"

Axel's teeth flashed in the lamplight. "I should have known it'd be no surprise to you, Nathaniel. His servant brought word down to Anna today, said she needed to get things in order for him. So it's true he's been up in Montreal all this time?"

"Actually, it was I who carried the message to his household staff," Will volunteered. "Dr. Todd was staying with a Mr. McTavish, in Montreal. A merchant."

Charlie LeBlanc turned from the drafts board. "The McTavish who started up the North West Company? By God, I'd like to make his acquaintance. There's a fortune to be made up in those parts."

"Which is exactly why Todd is spending time with him,"

suggested John Glove, chewing thoughtfully on his pipe. "He's got a keen eye for the right connection."

"Maybe Todd will move up that way, permanent. Leave us without a doctor." This from Ben Cameron, the brother-in-law of Asa Pierce.

Axel scratched his head thoughtfully. "Well, we done fine without him all summer. Those that passed on he couldn't have helped much, anyway."

There was a silence as they thought of the men they had buried in the past few months, Billy Kirby the most recent.

"We've had a bloody season, all right," said Axel. "Lost our heads, some of us. In more ways than one."

Nathaniel said: "Here's to a peaceful winter."

When they had raised their glasses together, Axel went off to see about a new keg, and the other men turned back to a game of draughts.

"At first I wondered what could possibly keep Elizabeth so far from civilization," Will Spencer said to Nathaniel. It was the longest sentence he had had from him all day, and the most curious. Will would not meet Nathaniel's eye, his gaze roaming instead over the room.

"I thought she might be disappointed in her plans to teach school. But this is a good place for her," he went on. "She always wanted adventure in her life."

"She's got more than enough of that," Nathaniel said. "Too much, maybe."

"You are a fortunate man," said Will Spencer.

On their way out, it occurred to Nathaniel that Spencer had made a confession of sorts, and that he would probably never hear such a personal statement again from him, should he see him every day for the rest of his life. The fact that he was setting off tomorrow loosened Nathaniel's tongue.

"In this part of the world, we think highly of men who know how to keep their peace," Nathaniel said to him as they stood in the small circle of lantern light at the door. "But you got most of them beat. I'll tell you, Spencer, I've got no idea what goes on in that head of yours. At first I thought you had a hole inside you, but now I'm wondering if it isn't just the eye of the storm."

That much earned him a flicker of a smile, and a flash from the mild eyes. "Elizabeth's imagination has found its equal," he said. "You see before you a rich man of little use to the world. Nothing more."

"Nothing more," Nathaniel echoed, laughing softly. It was their last exchange of the evening.

LX

While Nathaniel was gone to Albany to see aunt Merriweather settled in for another visit with the Schuylers, the winter seemed to give up its purpose and fall back. They were thrust into inordinately warm days: suddenly it was possible again to sit on the porch without a shawl, and to go bare-legged to fetch water. The sun shone on the harvested fields where crows hitched and hobbled after the overlooked kernel of corn. A flock of snow geese on their way south for the winter settled on Half Moon Lake as if the lack of cold stole from them their ability to fly, sending the villagers running for their muskets.

Runs-from-Bears took an immense bear already settled in for the winter, and there were days of rendering fat and storing it in lengths of washed and knotted deer intestines. The smells were so strong that Elizabeth found it hard to hide her reaction, and she was waved off, as she had been sent away during the setting of soap.

"Sooner or later I shall have to learn to do this, too," she said to Many-Doves, who only laughed at her.

"Why?" she asked. "Why should you do work that you were not raised to do, when we are here to do it?"

"Because I must do my share," Elizabeth protested.

"You do your share," she was told, and banished to the porch to sit in the warm sun and clean bushel after bushel of beans with Liam's help. A quiet work, a contemplative work, when what she wanted was to be up and active in these last days of freedom from the weather. She wished for Nathaniel, but was glad of Hannah, whom she would take with her into the woods to gather the last of the beechnuts, or just to explore the mountain. Although it meant leaving an unhappy Liam behind, Hannah was always pleased to have Elizabeth to herself.

In the fifth month of her pregnancy the curve of her belly was no longer possible to overlook. The child had recently become very active, rolling and kicking when she sat down to rest, as if to make her get up and go again. Elizabeth sometimes laughed out loud at the outrageousness of it. Leaning back with her weight on her hands, she let Hannah probe gently as she had seen her grandmother do. She called the small roundness *nihra'a ri'kenha*, Little Brother, and chided him indulgently for his exuberance.

"Four more months," Elizabeth said. "By then I will be waddling like a duck."

"You do that already, when you're tired." And Hannah screeched and rolled away from Elizabeth's tickling fingers.

They expected Nathaniel by the end of the week, calculating extra time for him to spend at the Schuylers' and for buying winter provisions and supplies for the schoolhouse. He was traveling by wagon, which would add an additional two days onto the journey or more, if it rained. The afternoon before the earliest day he might be expected to return, Elizabeth found herself agitated, unable to read or concentrate on any sedentary work. Liam hobbled out to the porch behind her with the help of a length of hickory that he had whittled into a rough cane.

"I always wanted to swim in that gorge," he told her, as they stared at the rushing water of the falls.

"Bears and Nathaniel swim in it every morning, summer and winter," Elizabeth told him. "They say it makes them resistant to the worst weather. You could join them, once your leg is healed."

"I can't imagine it," Liam said, his pale skin rising in sympathetic gooseflesh.

Hannah came shooting around the corner, her arms full of pelts.

"Where are you off to?" Liam asked, pulling her up short.

She looked back the way she had come, and Falling-Day and Many-Doves appeared leading the roan, his packsaddles piled high with provisions and small barrels strapped to either side. There was an awkward silence. It was not Elizabeth's place to tell Liam about the cave under the falls, but it would also be very hard to have him living at Lake in the Clouds and not share this knowledge. For the next few days they would be busy transporting supplies there, and he would soon figure out what they did not tell him.

Falling-Day said: "This is your home now."

"I got nowhere else to go," Liam said. "I don't want to go anywhere else."

There was a long pause while she examined him, and then she nodded.

"We store our provisions there—" She gestured with her chin over her shoulder.

In response to Liam's confused look, Many-Doves said: "Behind the falls."

Hannah hefted her load to a more comfortable position. "In case we get robbed again."

Liam dropped his head, but he could not hide the rush of color that moved up his neck and face and made the freckles on his forehead leap into relief. Elizabeth shook her head silently at the women, and they moved off into the forest to make their way around the shoulder of the mountain. It was many minutes before Liam found his voice again.

"They don't trust me," he said sorrowfully. "And they're right not to trust me. We did some terrible things, last year. It was a kind of fever in Billy, wanting them gone. It seemed important to me, too, I guess."

Elizabeth thought for a moment. She was both encouraged by the boy's willingness to take responsibility for actions he had known about and even participated in, and concerned that he took too much on his bony shoulders. For a moment she thought of his brother, and her anger caused her to lose focus of what Liam most needed.

When she could gather her thoughts again, she said: "I don't know many people who are as good a judge of character as Falling-Day. Do you?"

Liam shook his head, scuffing one bare foot back and forth on the smooth boards of the porch.

"She knows how to look inside a person's head, seems like."

"Yes, it does seem like that. She is slow to grant her trust, and loyal once she has done so."

He nodded again, and stole a sidelong glance at her from under the ragged fringe of russet hair. "You're saying?"

"I am saying that she has just shown a great deal of faith in you, Liam Kirby. She pointed out to you the cave where the winter provisions are stored, although it gives you power over us."

"I wouldn't do anything to hurt any of you—"

"I am glad to hear that," Elizabeth said, and she stood. "But I am not surprised. Come now, and I'll show you the cave."

Liam glanced doubtfully at his injured leg and the dingy wrappings that held the long splints in place.

"We shan't go far," Elizabeth said, already off the porch. "Just down there to where the gorge opens on the other side, at the base of the cliff. From there you can almost see the cave, if you know what you're looking for. Maybe Hannah will wave at us."

They crossed to the other side where the flow of water disappeared underground, and Elizabeth stopped as she often did to feel the earth vibrate through the padded soles of her moccasins. The water was still high from all the rain, marbled with foam and pushing hard on its way down the mountainside. As they walked along the lip of the gorge Elizabeth pointed out to Liam the natural stone steps that they used to go down to the water, covered with vibrant green moss.

"Looks deep," Liam said.

"Deep enough to dive in, here."

The sound of the water was louder now, and they gave up talking. Elizabeth lifted her skirts, wishing once again for the courage to give up European fashion once and for all for the practicality and comfort of Kahnyen'kehàka dress. She climbed carefully over the first few boulders at the bottom of the cliff face, turning to watch Liam make his way. When she was satisfied that he could manage, she sat down at a spot she liked to think of as her own, on a fine flat expanse of rock with a natural footrest that jutted out over the gorge. From here she had a view of her cabin, and if she craned her neck backward, a glimpse of the rock shelf where she had once stood while Nathaniel tipped her back into the rushing water. Elizabeth wished suddenly for her shawl, for it was cooler here than it had been in the sunshine on the porch, the damp rock a cold seat, indeed.

She pivoted, pointing the ledge and cave out to Liam, who peered upward with one hand cupped to his brow.

"I don't see anything!" he shouted.

Elizabeth caught a flash of movement from the corner of her eye that brought her up short: Dutch Ton was standing on her porch. In one hand he held a haunch of venison; in the other, a hunting knife.

She blinked to dislodge the mist of the falls from her lashes, and she blinked again. There was a pulse in her neck that was beating out of rhythm; she put one finger to it to still it. Liam was at her ear, but she could not understand him. She raised a hand and he fell silent, crouching down as if to hide. As if he saw the danger, or perhaps smelled the fear that rolled off her like sweat.

It was him. Dutch Ton stood there on her porch, squinting into the sun. He wore a patch over one eye now, but he was wrapped in the same mangy buffalo robe she had last seen him wear at the campfire where Jack Lingo had tried to burn her.

She thought that perhaps she might be able to breathe again if she could only stand, but all the muscles in her legs seemed to have gone to jelly. In some part of her mind she was thankful for the fact that Hannah was safe in the cave behind her. In another, she knew that if she could stay where she was, and be still, he might not see her. The angle of the sun was in her favor.

She saw the red slash of his mouth opening and closing, spraying bits of meat. He was talking. There was another man behind him, just out of view inside the cabin. The door began to swing inward.

He is dead. Jack Lingo is dead. She said the words out loud and firmly: an incantation, a prayer. But the door continued to swing in a clean arc. As clean as the trajectory of a bullet, or a rifle stock swung in anger.

Spit filled her mouth in a bitter rush, and in her head a simple refrain: *away away away*. Elizabeth came to her feet with a jerk, barely noting the slick surface of the rock beneath her. She felt her moccasins lose purchase; too late. She threw her arms up and pitched forward into the gorge just as the second man stepped out into the sun, his hair and beard catching the light in a red-gold flare: Richard Todd.

Falling seemed to take a very long time: long enough to hear Liam's high-pitched scream, loud enough to be heard over the falling water. His scream echoed, or perhaps that was another voice, from behind the falls. She twisted away to protect her belly, taking the slap of the water at an awkward angle and plunging down to the bottom. A flash of pain as she struck her head on a ledge of rock and then she was shooting up, vaguely aware that the water was hazy red with blood and that it must be her own. She broke the surface gasping, kicking against the heavy tangle of her skirts without effect. The force of the water tumbled her, once and then again.

Elizabeth thought of Nathaniel and of the child, and she went down in a great tide of sorrow and regret.

Liam would dream of it for years: Many-Doves coming through the falls as soon as Elizabeth hit the water, diving after her like a hawk after a trout. But Richard Todd was closer: he had already gone in from the other side, dragged Elizabeth up by her hair and flipped her over the edge of the gorge before Doves got there. Liam didn't see what happened then because he was on his way, pushing until his leg burned like hellfire. By the time he got to the other side, the two of them were already on their knees next to her.

He told himself that dead people didn't bleed like that. No matter how white and still, somebody pumping blood the way she was had to be alive. Many-Doves had her hand pressed to Elizabeth's head above the left ear. The blood welled up between her fingers and wound over her arm and wrist like snakes.

With a single jerk, Todd ripped the sleeve from his shirt and handed it to Doves. She took Elizabeth's head in her lap, the wet hair trailing over the rounded mound of her belly. The tendons on her forearm popped with the effort of pressing the linen to the wound.

Todd bent over to lift Elizabeth's lids one after the other. He studied her eyes closely, and finally sat back on his heels looking thoughtful. Then he made a fist and jammed two knuckles hard into Elizabeth's breastbone. Liam flinched, but Elizabeth's eyes only fluttered open. Her face contorted briefly and then her eyes closed again.

Hannah and Falling-Day came out of the woods. Hannah threw herself down next to Elizabeth and burst into noisy tears. Before Liam could get to her, Richard Todd leaned over and put a hand on her shoulder.

Liam had never heard him speak Mohawk before. Now he spoke to Hannah in that language, and the sound of it brought her wet face up in blank amazement. She turned to her grand-mother with a question. Falling-Day was bent over Elizabeth, and Liam could not see her face, but the answer she gave Han-nah seemed to calm her further. She got up, wobbling a little, and wiping her face with the back of her hand, ran off toward the cabin.

Hannah ran. She ran for blankets. She ran for water, for rags, for her grandmother's baskets of herbs and roots. She ran down to the village to deliver Falling-Day's message to Axel; she ran on to the judge.

There, she collapsed in Curiosity's arms and sobbed for ten minutes before she could find words, Mahican or Kah-nyen'kehàka or English, to describe what had happened at Lake in the Clouds.

For all its boniness, Curiosity's lap was made for little girls, even one with legs as long as Hannah's. Curiosity held on tight and listened while Hannah told her and told her again, drawing the picture with words and her hands and sudden short bursts of tears, pressing her hands to her face and her face to Curiosity's apron front. She smelled of yeast and roasting goose and lye soap. Comforting smells. She could have gone to sleep there on Curiosity's lap in the middle of the judge's kitchen.

But Curiosity was talking to her daughters, and it was their turn to run. Polly started throwing things into a basket at her mother's directions. Daisy opened the back door and shouted for Galileo, gave up and went out after him.

After a while Curiosity set Hannah down on a stool and smoothed her hair. Then she went off to tell the judge what had happened, and where she was going. Before the last of her skirts had disappeared through the door, Hannah was up again and off to finish her errands.

On the slope below Little Muddy, she heard a rifle shot. Hannah made herself stand still until the wind brought the acrid smell of the gunpowder to her, and then she set off again. She found Bears crouched next to his kill, reloading his gun.

Hannah loved Bears; she would have married him herself if she had been old enough. Whatever language came out when she opened her mouth, he understood; he understood even when she didn't talk. Curiosity knew how to hold little girls, but Runs-from-Bears had a different kind of comfort to offer. He slung the rifle around, lifted the doe over his shoulders, and they set off running together.

There was a comfort in running, when the rhythm was right. Hannah ran hard behind Bears, keeping her toes turned inward on the faint forest path, relieved to have him lead the way. She kept her eyes focused on the flashing heels of his moccasins, looking up every now and then, because she must, to the doe. Seeing the long, elegant arch of her neck and the dark eyes, glazed and lifeless.

They had no power to force Elizabeth back from the shadowlands until she was ready to come, but there were things they could do for her. The women stripped away the wet clothes and wound her like an infant in fur and doeskin. Falling-Day burned thistle and hawthorn to give strength to her heart and blood; she steeped little-man-root in corn water and dribbled it into her mouth, spoon by spoon. Richard Todd watched without comment. When Falling-Day began to sing a healing song to summon Bone-in-Her-Back home to them, he left quietly. Falling-Day watched him go. The gaunt lines of his face spoke of the injuries he had suffered, but there was something else: over the long summer some of the anger which had always burned so bright in him had gone out. She wondered what he knew of her youngest, her Otter. When there was time—when Bone-in-Her-Back had come back from the shadowlands—she thought she might be able to talk to Richard Todd about that.

While her mother mashed dried flag-lily root and precious sunflower oil into a poultice, Many-Doves washed the blood from Elizabeth's face and hair, working carefully around the dressing that bound the wound closed. When she had finished, she put her ear to Elizabeth's belly to try to hear the child's music: the beat of a strong heart. Her own child flexed and turned under her heart, as if he heard it too.

Liam had been watching from the corner, hoping for some work, some way to help. But the women did not need him, and he could not run errands as Hannah did. When the medicine smoke tickled his throat and made his eyes water, he finally got up and went out to the porch, where Richard Todd was drying out in the sun. Dutch Ton had disappeared, but Axel was there, wanting the story. Liam told it in a hoarse voice.

"By God Almighty," Axel said for the tenth time. "I wish Nathaniel was here."

At the thought of Nathaniel, Liam could barely swallow.

Axel was squinting at him. "You didn't push her in, did you, boy?"

"No!" His head came up and his color, too; he could feel himself burning like a torch.

"He didn't have anything to do with it. She saw somebody she didn't expect to see and she slipped, knocked her head, and went under. That's all." Todd had taken off what was left of his shirt and he wrung it with a twist.

"That's all it was," Liam echoed.

"What were you two doing up there, climbing around on the rocks—a breeding woman, and you with your leg the way it is?"

Liam felt Richard's sharp gaze on him, and his belly filled with dread. Had he seen Doves come through the falls? Did he know the secret of the cave? Dutch Ton might know, too, if he had caught sight of Many-Doves, and understood what he saw.

"She wanted to show me something," he mumbled. And, without meeting Todd's eye: "Where did Ton go to?"

"I passed him on my way here," Axel said. "He was headed down to the village, seemed like. Was he traveling with you, Todd?"

Richard shook his head. "I found him helping himself to the larder," he said. "I hadn't seen him since March, but Elizabeth had. He gave me these for her." He pulled a silver hair clasp and a ring out of his pocket. "Lingo took them off her, I guess."

There was a silence as they thought of Jack Lingo, and what Elizabeth had experienced at his hands.

"No wonder she started at the sight of Ton," said Axel.

Richard's head turned toward the forest and the sound of horses coming fast. "That'll be the judge."

"Not alone, sounds like."

The judge pulled up in front of the porch, with Galileo and Curiosity close behind. The men sat and stared at Richard Todd, but Curiosity slid down from behind Galileo's back in a flurry of bright skirts.

"I might've knowed that you and trouble would show up here together," she said. "Ain't you ever satisfied, Richard? What have you done to her now?"

Liam came to his feet to tell them the truth of it, but Axel had already stepped out, one hand raised in a peaceful gesture. "Hold up, now. Alfred, Curiosity. Galileo. First off, she's alive and it looks like there weren't no real damage—"

The judge's face contorted at this, but Curiosity's froze. "Since when you a doctor, Axel Metzler? Let me in there, I want to see that child for myself."

"Go on in," Axel said. "But you should know first that it was Richard here who pulled her out of the gorge."

Halfway up the step, Curiosity stopped. She pivoted toward Todd, her mouth as hard pressed and shiny as a knife. Her eyes traveled over his wet clothes and bare chest, and then she fixed on Richard's face.

"Close to a year now, I been wantin' to speak my mind to you and I guess the time has come. Money talk louder than truth in this world and I don't doubt you can still make folks see things your way by rattling the coin in your pockets. But not

me. No, sir. I got something for you, though: I got what you
need to hear."

Galileo made a soft sound, and she silenced him with a flash
of her eyes. Richard stood with his arms crossed, a vaguely
curious expression on his face.

"Go on, then," he said. "I suppose there's no stopping you."

"You sowed some seeds here last winter," she said, as if he
had not spoken. "Got men's minds all twisted up about these
people, about this mountain, and whose right it is to call the
Wolf home. Then you run off after a woman who didn't want
you and you didn't want, neither, thinking you could have your
way if you just grabbed hard enough. While you was gone,
things got nasty around here. We buried four men who would
be alive today if you hadn't put your greed to work on 'em. I
guess you probably know about Julian—I can see from your
face that you do."

She came closer, one long, bony finger poking at his chest.

"You pulled our Elizabeth out of the gorge today and saved
her life, that's a start. I guess you owe her that and more, the
way you been houndin' her. But I'm here to tell you, Richard
Todd, that what happened here don't put paid to everything
you got to answer for."

Liam felt slightly sick to his stomach, but Todd looked down
at her calmly.

"I am aware of all that."

"Are you?" she said, grimly. "We'll see, now won't we?"

And Curiosity turned on her heel and walked to the door,
where she stopped to stare back at the judge, one brow raised.
With his face averted from Richard Todd, he climbed the steps
and followed her inside.

Axel ran a hand over his face. "*Jesus nah,* that woman could
carve oak into toothpicks with that tongue of hers." Then,
reluctantly, he smiled. "And ain't she fine to listen to?"

Richard grunted, and pulled his mangled shirt back on. "If
you're not on the other end of it, I suppose. I expect Nathaniel
will have words for me, too. Tell him I'll come by as soon as
Elizabeth's on the mend. We've got things to discuss."

"Ja, if he can wait that long," Axel said. "Where can he find
you, if he can't?"

"If I'm not at home, I'll be calling on Kitty."

"Mrs. Middleton." Liam spoke up. "She's Mrs. Middleton now."

Richard nodded. "For the time being, at any rate."

It was terribly unfair, but Hannah had seen that look on her grandmother's face before and she knew that no argument would shift her purpose. Her eyes burning with exhaustion, she finally gave up her spot at the foot of Elizabeth's bed and climbed the ladder to the sleeping loft. But not before she had extracted a promise from Doves that she would come to fetch her when Elizabeth woke. She used those words, but her eyes said something else. Twelve hours after the accident, Elizabeth had still not broken through to them; Hannah did not need to be told that this was a bad sign.

The cabin seemed overcrowded with people: the women moving back and forth, always with something in their hands. Liam and the judge and Mr. Witherspoon sat at the hearth, talking little and dozing now and then. Other men from the village were out on the porch. Bears would have let her come and sit with him, but he was gone with Joshua Hench to find her father on the Albany road and bring him home. The only comfort about going to bed was that perhaps when she woke, they would have returned. Hannah wanted her father very badly. She pressed her face into her blanket, willing her tears not to come.

Elizabeth had never had a talent for colorful dreams. Perhaps, she had always thought, because her daydreams were so elaborate and carefully detailed that she had no imagination left when she finally went to sleep. But somewhere, somehow, she had learned the art of dreaming in color, for all around her was a deep hyacinth sea, a color she had never seen before her first voyage by ship, when she had left England for a new life with her brother at her side.

Julian stood beside her at the rail now, the wind ruffling his dark hair and his face shadowed with beard stubble.

"Watch the birds," he said, pointing. "They will show you the way."

"Come with me," she said, but he only smiled. There were wrinkles at the corners of his eyes. She saw too that there was white at his temples, and that the line of his jaw had softened with age in the month since he had traveled on ahead. He walked away from her now; his boots made no noise.

"Come with me," she called after him again, but he only waved his hand in salute, and walked on. There was no sound except the calls of the birds overhead: gulls, wheeling in rainbow colors against a stormy sky.

"I can't fly," she called after him, but he was suddenly gone, leaving her alone on this ship in the middle of an endless sea. "I cannot fly!"

She tried, then. Tried to follow the birds and got just far enough to catch a glimpse of her father's face: a blur of pale skin and the familiar features. She slipped away before she could hear what he had to say to her.

Hannah woke, as she had hoped she would, to the sound of her father's voice. What she heard now in his tone was not the rage she had half expected and might have welcomed, but something far more frightening. Despair had its own sound; it was one she had never imagined to hear from him. She looked down over the half wall that separated her sleeping space from the main room, and she caught just the flash of his profile as he disappeared into the bedroom. She had wanted more than anything to be with her father, but she did not want to follow him into that room. The thought of what he might have found there made her feel sleepy.

Hannah wound herself in her blanket, buried her head down deep in the bedding, and insisted on sleep.

She was on her back, her face turned toward him. The dressing on her head was scattered with traces of dried blood; her eyelashes were like bruised half moons against the milky white of her cheeks. He leaned toward her to call her name, and got no response.

Falling-Day put her hand on his arm. "Yonhkwihsrons." *She struggles.*

Nathaniel nodded to show that he had understood: it was not the best news, but there was reason to hope. Elizabeth was trying to find her way back to them. Falling-Day left the room and Nathaniel sat on the edge of the bed to watch her sleep. So many times he had reached out for her in this bed, and she had turned willingly to him. She had come to him with laughter or small sounds of sleepy welcome, in grand silence or with teasing words.

The smell of her could wake him from the dead; he knew this, he believed it absolutely. He hoped that the same was true for her, and so he stripped out of his buckskin and homespun and slipped naked into the cocoon of fur next to her. The corn husks in the mattress crackled as he moved closer to put his face to the slope of her shoulder where it met her neck, in that perfect curve that was now his solitary focus in the world. He rubbed his cheek against her skin and inhaled.

She smelled of herself, and nothing more. The relief of this loosened the tears from his eyes. Eventually, calmed by the smells of her, Nathaniel slept and hoped that she was aware of him.

The room was still dark when she woke him with an elbow and a mumbled curse. Unsure at first of what was real and what had been dream, he simply rolled away. Then Nathaniel sat up and leaned over her; he saw the meager light of the moon shining in her open eyes, her expression creased in confusion and irritation.

"Boots," he breathed.

"I cannot fly," she said, very clearly.

"But you can, lass. You're flying now. Don't give up."

She scowled at him even as her eyes fluttered shut and she fell away to sleep again, suspended in his arms above the world.

Elizabeth woke for short periods over the next day, sometimes talking or answering questions, sometimes without seeming to see any of them. When she began to turn her head and pluck at the furs in her struggle up toward the world again, Nathaniel fetched Hannah and kept her there.

"Can she hear me?"

"I think so. Talk to her."

Hannah's face contorted with the challenge of it. Then she leaned forward.

"Grandmother has been feeding you willow-bark tea," she said. "For the ache in your head."

"Tell her to make it stronger," Elizabeth muttered, one eye cracking open.

Hannah grinned broadly. "I will," she said. "I'll go now and fetch it for you."

"No," Elizabeth said, raising her hand an inch off the blanket. "Wait." Her tongue came out to trace her lower lip.

"What is it, Boots?" Nathaniel caught her hand.

"Tell me," she said. "Tell me about the baby."

He squeezed her hand. "The child is unharmed. We've been telling you so all along."

Elizabeth drew in one long, shuddering breath. "Good," she whispered. "Nathaniel, I saw, I think I saw—"

"Dutch Ton. Aye, he's in the village waiting to hear how you are. He brought you these."

From the table he took the gold band that had once been his mother's, and the silver hair clasp he had given Elizabeth as a wedding present. He put them in her hand. After a long moment, she looked up at him.

"He meant no harm?"

"It looks that way."

"Good," she said again, her eyes drifting shut. Then they struggled open again and she gestured him closer.

"That dream you had in Albany," she whispered. "I shouldn't have doubted you."

He put her hand to his cheek, and said nothing.

When she was sleeping soundly again, Nathaniel left her to Hannah's watch. The women gave him food, and then he went to clean up and see about fresh clothes. Most of the well-wishers and curious had drifted away when Elizabeth had first shown signs of waking, but he found Axel on the porch, nursing his pipe, and the judge.

"Tell me about Todd," Nathaniel said. He stood quietly until Axel had finished.

The judge was looking pale; he had lost some weight.

"Maybe you should go along home," Nathaniel suggested. "You need some sleep."

He shook his head. "Not until she's well again."

Nathaniel drew up, surprised. "That could take weeks, man. She knows you've been here and that you're worried. And there's Kitty and your grandson down there to look after."

The judge ran a trembling hand over his face. "I never spent enough time listening to her."

His agitation suddenly deflated, Nathaniel looked harder and saw clearly what he had missed, in his preoccupation with his own troubles. In the last month the judge had become an old man.

"She would send you home herself if she could," Axel said kindly. "She wouldn't want you to get sick, waiting here."

The judge looked up at Nathaniel, hopefully.

"That's true," Nathaniel said, and he saw the relief on the man's face.

"Maybe later today," he said thoughtfully.

Nathaniel nodded, and went off to find Liam, who was oiling traps in the other cabin for Runs-from-Bears. He asked the same question and got a longer, less-clear-but-more-detailed story of what had gone on at the gorge, and Richard Todd's role in it.

"I should have gone in after her," Liam concluded.

"Not with that leg," Nathaniel said, absently. "And Doves was there. If it weren't for the knock on the head, Elizabeth could have managed on her own anyway. But goddamn it, to be beholden to Richard Todd don't sit well. I guess I'll have to go look him up."

"He said to tell you that he'd be calling on Kitty."

"Did he? Looks like his judgment still ain't any better than his timing."

"I don't know what you mean."

Nathaniel shrugged. At the door, he turned back with a

thoughtful look. "It means he's still Richard Todd. It means, watch your back."

Elizabeth came fully awake to the first snow. Suddenly afraid that she had slept for weeks instead of days, she was distraught until Falling-Day told her that it was no more than mid-October, in spite of the waves of fine-grained snow which beat against the window.

"I might think I was still dreaming, if it weren't for the ache in my head," Elizabeth said, accepting a cup. When she had taken her willow-bark tea and some broth, Falling-Day helped her see to her needs, and then got Elizabeth settled against the bolsters, wrapped again in the blanket of pelts.

"How long will this dizziness last?"

Falling-Day lifted one shoulder and inclined her head. "Another week, perhaps until the next moon."

"Oh, dear." Elizabeth closed her eyes. "The children will be very disappointed to have school put off again."

"I think they're just glad to have you alive," Falling-Day said, sitting down to pick up a basket of sewing.

For a good while, Elizabeth was content to lie quietly and listen to the peaceful and familiar sounds of the fire in the hearth and the soft shuffle of moccasins in the other room. Nathaniel would be out hunting with Runs-from-Bears. She could hear Hannah and Liam talking; there was a rising tone of outrage and a small laugh in response.

"Did you think I was going to die?" The question had been asked before she fully knew her own intention, but Falling-Day did not seemed surprised. She looked up from the overdress she was piecing together.

"I worried, at first," she said finally. And then she put her sewing down and laid her hands flat on her knees. Her eyes were very dark when they settled on Elizabeth's.

"You have never asked me about my daughter."

Elizabeth felt herself flushing with surprise. "I did not wish to intrude on your memories."

Falling-Day turned her face toward the window. When she turned back, there was a remarkable disquiet to her expression.

"Sometimes, it seems to me that she cannot be very far off. That if I call to her, she will come. She has been very strong in my mind these last days. She died at the first snow, did Nathaniel ever tell you that?"

"No," Elizabeth said softly. "He has never told me about her death, except that she died in childbed, and the child with her. And that his mother and Curiosity were here."

"And Cat-Eater. You do not like to say his name."

Elizabeth shrugged, unable to deny that this was the truth.

Falling-Day said, "When I came out of the forest and saw him and Many-Doves bent over you, and the blood on his hands—I expected for a moment to see her there, on the ground. I was not with her when she walked the path, but I saw her go in my dreams."

Once Elizabeth would have had no response because the Kahnyen'kehàka reliance on dreams for information and understanding of the world had troubled her. Now her doubts were more about her own narrow view of things.

When Falling-Day saw the willingness to listen in Elizabeth's face, she nodded.

"Cat-Eater was at Sings-from-Books' side when she died. He could do nothing for her. But he could help you, and he did."

"You are trying to tell me something," Elizabeth said. "I don't understand."

"Then I will speak clearly. Perhaps it is time to make peace with him."

Elizabeth smoothed the pelt under her palm again and again. "Why do you say this to me instead of Nathaniel?"

Falling-Day raised a brow. "Because you might listen to me, and you might make your husband listen to you."

"Your opinion is very important to Nathaniel."

"Not in this matter," Falling-Day corrected her. "I did not stand up for him when my daughter turned to Cat-Eater, and he has never forgotten that."

Elizabeth had a question which she thought she must ask, or forever regret the lost opportunity.

"You encouraged Sarah to go to Richard? This is hard to

understand, given the role he played in the attack on your village, and the death of your husband and sons."

Falling-Day blinked at her. "Cat-Eater never raised his hand to any Kahnyen'kehàka."

"Nathaniel believes that he caused the attack."

"I know what Nathaniel believes," Falling-Day said. "But I was there, and he was not. Cat-Eater saved Sky-Wound-Round's life. He saved my life, and Otter's."

"Otter sees things differently."

"Men do, for the most part. Boys almost always see things as simple when they are not."

"Richard saw you bound like animals and marched down the road. And then he tried to have Nathaniel shot."

Falling-Day paused to gather her thoughts. "I do not deny that his hatred for Nathaniel was real and that he would have acted on it. You must ask Richard about these things if you want the whole truth—and I think that you should ask. I can only tell you about my daughter, who loved both of these men. I encouraged her to follow her heart."

"Follow her heart?" Elizabeth asked, almost bitterly. "I don't know what that means."

"I think that you do. Is this the life your family wanted for you, or the one you took for yourself?"

There was a small silence.

"And did Sarah take your advice?"

"Among our own people, it would not have been necessary for her to choose between these men. But they are neither of them true Kahnyen'kehàka, and they could neither of them bear the idea of the other, or believe that her heart was so large. So they made her choose. In the end she stayed with Nathaniel and bore him a daughter."

She bore him a daughter. Elizabeth wondered if she had misunderstood.

"Hannah is Nathaniel's child?"

The older woman lifted her chin, her dark eyes suddenly severe. "Hen'en." *Yes.*

"You know that Richard claims Hannah as his own. Why have you never told Nathaniel the truth?"

"My words cannot open his eyes. He must see this truth for himself."

Elizabeth sat back with a small gasp of surprise. "That is cruel."

Falling-Day spread her hands out in front of her. "Is it? Perhaps. Perhaps not."

"But you want me to encourage him to make peace with Richard."

"I think it is possible now, and it would be good. If we are to stay here."

"Perhaps we will not," Elizabeth said slowly. "You know that Nathaniel has told me it is my decision to stay or go and find another place to make a life for ourselves. Will you tell me too to follow my heart?"

"I will," said Falling-Day. "As you will one day tell Hannah, and the daughter you carry now."

Elizabeth's head snapped up, and Falling-Day laughed out loud.

"You are thinking of Chingachgook's dream of a great-grandson," she said. "But he did not look hard enough. He also did not feel what I feel. Here." She put the flat of her hand high on the left side of Elizabeth's stomach. "And here." She did the same on the other side, but lower. "Two heads, two heartbeats. A grandson for Hawkeye, and another granddaughter for Cora."

"Twins?" Elizabeth asked, staring at her own belly as if it might speak up. Then her expression of surprise faltered and was replaced by distress.

"Nathaniel will be out of his head with worry."

"Then do not tell him yet," Falling-Day said.

Elizabeth lay back, her palms resting lightly where Falling-Day had touched her. "I don't know if I should be overjoyed or just worried."

"The first will do for now," Falling-Day said. "You'll worry enough, in time. But listen now, for I will give you my best advice. Decide what kind of home you want for yourself, for your husband and your children, and if that means you must go away from here, then you must go."

"And take your granddaughter from your care?"

Falling-Day picked up her sewing again. "I will cope, as my mother did when I took my family and left her fire."

"You trust me with her." Elizabeth smiled, finally.

"Hen'en," said Falling-Day. "You have earned my trust."

Curled around the universe that was her children, Elizabeth wanted and needed to sleep, but found herself unable to calm her thoughts. She lay contemplating the view from the window: the shoulder of mountain crowded with fir and pine, somber green dusted now with white. Above that, a wedge of sky the color of old pewter. Another storm was coming.

What Falling-Day had told her of Richard and the raid on Barktown was almost more than she could reconcile with the tales she had heard from Nathaniel and Otter. The more she thought about it, the more confused she became: each of them told the story with complete conviction. In the end, she thought, perhaps they were all right. The stories of what had happened to each of them in those bloody days of the revolution were a web they wove together; the truth scuttled back and forth between the delicate strands of memory, and could not be pinned down. Where Richard fit into the whole was unclear; Elizabeth thought that she might never know, unless he himself told her. And it would be a long time before she was comfortable enough to have such a conversation with Richard Todd.

They might not even be here a year from now. Elizabeth lay back, and tried to imagine another life, a new start. A year ago she had been alone; now she had a husband; in another year she would have Hannah and two infants to care for.

Sarah had borne twins. Nathaniel had buried Hannah's brother with his own hands. She had tried again, and he had buried his second son in Sarah's arms.

Not this time. Elizabeth whispered it aloud in the empty room: it was a promise, and a vow.

LXI

By the end of October, Lake in the Clouds was adrift in snow; Elizabeth, healed enough to be bored but still unable to read or write for long periods, began to chafe at the narrow boundaries of the cabin; and Richard Todd had begun to court Kitty Middleton in earnest.

Nathaniel gave in gracefully on a clear afternoon and took her to the trading post. In the familiar cramped space filled with powerful smells of damp wool and burning tobacco and fermenting ale, Elizabeth heard the details of the courtship from Anna Hauptmann and Martha Southern as they measured great stacks of newly woven linen.

"Every day this week he's been up there in the parlor, driving Curiosity near out of her mind," Anna told her.

"She'll take the broom to the doctor one of these days," predicted Martha.

"Has Kitty spoken to you about Richard?"

"Kitty ain't been down here since the first snow," said Anna. "The child's got an appetite, and she can't get far away."

The perfectly round and bald head of Martha's youngest popped up out of the feed box where she had settled him, as if he had been called. He smiled at Elizabeth, displaying two tiny teeth.

"It's Daisy who comes by these days, most oft. On her way to the smithy, don't you know." This was accompanied by the grin and wink Anna reserved for matters of courtship. "Kitty herself don't go out much, as I understand it. Except for the occasional sleigh ride." The generous mouth twitched at the corner as Anna struggled with the urge to say more.

"The judge don't care for those sleigh rides much," said Martha. "If the sour look on his face is any indication."

From nearer the hearth, Charlie LeBlanc spoke up. "I think you women are being unfair," he said. "Richard ain't doing nothing wrong. If she don't want his sleigh rides, she'll send him on his way."

Anna dropped a bolt of cloth with a soft thud. "Some men don't budge so easy as you, Charlie."

Jed McGarrity coughed loudly into his fist. "Aw, Anna. The boy's got a point. Maybe Kitty likes Richard coming around. Maybe she's lonely."

"It is high time we called on her, in that case," said Elizabeth.

Dutch Ton was waiting for them in front of the trading post, swaddled in bearskin and his unmistakable smells. The shy, dark-toothed smile he gave her from under the brim of his old tricorn could not make him smell any better, but Elizabeth swallowed hard and tried to smile back.

"It were a bad fall," he said, as if he were picking up a conversation which had been interrupted just a few minutes before. "You better now?"

"Much better, thank you."

With fingers the color of charcoal he began to search through the sparse beard thoughtfully. Then he touched the patch over his eye.

"He's better off dead. Old Lingo were mean."

"Yes," Elizabeth agreed.

"I come to bring your pretties," he said, shuffling one boot against the frozen ground. "Did you get 'em?"

"My wedding ring, yes." Elizabeth held up her hand. "And the hair clasp. Thank you very much."

"I come to tell you about a man, too," he said. "But I forget his name. He's looking for you all."

Nathaniel seemed to come suddenly awake. "Was it my father? Did he have a message for me?"

"No." Dutch Ton shook his head. "Funny-talking man from across the water, asking about Hawkeye. Met him when I come through Fish House. He hired a scout and went off to find Robbie, see if he knew where your pa might be."

Elizabeth would have put her hand on Dutch Ton's sleeve if she could have forced herself past the smell. As it was, she tried to smile kindly.

"What did this man say that he wanted with Hawkeye?"

The big trapper shrugged. A blank look stole over his face, to be replaced suddenly by a guileless smile. "The Earl of Carrick," he announced.

"Who?" Elizabeth asked, dumbfounded.

"That were his name. The Earl of Carrick. And he were lookin' for Dan'l Bonner, or for somebody called Jamie Scott."

With a satisfied nod, his errand finally completed, the big man pulled his hat down firmly over his brow and muttered a farewell. He turned and shuffled off, without further discussion.

"He cannot have understood correctly," Elizabeth said, mostly to herself. "What would a Scots earl be doing in the bush, looking for your father? And how does he come to know of the name you use in the Albany bank?"

Nathaniel rubbed a finger over the bridge of his nose. "God knows," he said, looking distinctly uneasy. "Maybe this earl is looking for the gold, too."

Elizabeth stared after Dutch Ton, and as if he felt the weight of her gaze, he turned from the edge of the wood and waved.

"I wonder if we'll see him again."

"Oh, I expect so," Nathaniel said. Then he tugged lightly on her arm. "Are you still of a mind to call on Kitty today?"

"I am," she said, shaking herself slightly. "Perhaps my father will know something of this earl."

The path up through the woods toward the judge's had been broken, but the snow was still wet and heavy. After minutes, Nathaniel stopped to peer down into her flushed face.

"We should have ridden. We'll borrow a horse to get you home."

"Don't fuss, Nathaniel. The exercise does me good."

He made a sound in his throat that was somewhere between reluctant acknowledgment and reservation.

"Richard may well be there," she said. "It cannot be put off forever. I must thank him for his help."

Under her hand, Nathaniel's arm tensed. "I know what we owe him," he said. "What I don't know is how Kitty fits into his plans."

"Falling-Day thinks he has changed," Elizabeth said, watching his expression from the corner of her eye. "He spent time with his brother. Perhaps he has come to terms with some of what plagues him."

He laughed without a bit of humor. "Here he comes now," he said. "You can ask him."

Richard had appeared from around the very turn where, not so very long ago, his team had bolted with Elizabeth in his sleigh. Now he pointed his gelding's head toward them and approached at a walk.

Elizabeth felt Nathaniel go straight and silent, all of his energy flung forward. She knew if she looked at him she would find his expression wiped clear of all emotion, only his eyes flashing a warning. On Richard's face there was the same wariness and reserve: they faced each other over Elizabeth's head as tense and silent as wolves.

Richard slid down from his saddle and stood there, slapping one palm lightly with the reins.

"If you're on your way to see the judge, he's gone to call on Mr. Witherspoon," he said. He pulled his hat from his head and ran a freckled hand through the mane of hair. "If it's Kitty you're interested in, I'm told it's her rest time." He focused on Elizabeth. "You're better? The wound healed clean?"

"Thank you," Elizabeth said, not quite sure how to respond to this neutral tone.

"I've been by your place twice," said Nathaniel stiffly. "Didn't find you in. Came to thank you for your help."

"I am in your debt," Elizabeth added.

Richard raised a brow. Snow was settling on his hair; a rivulet of water ran over its brightness and down his forehead, but he did not move to brush it away. "You made me a promise once."

Until this moment, Elizabeth did not realize how much she had hoped Falling-Day had been right about Richard. Full of dread, she said: "I did as I promised. I appeared before the court, and answered the inquiries put to me. The court did not decide in your favor."

"I am aware of that," Richard said, one corner of the thin mouth turned downward.

"But you are determined still to try to take what is not yours," Elizabeth said.

Richard's head came up slowly. The frenzied anger that had been so much a part of him in the bush and at Good Pasture seemed to be gone. "The mountain is yours."

Nathaniel stilled beside her. "After all these years, it comes down to that? Why should we believe you?"

Richard only blinked, a decidedly Kahnyen'kehàka blink, the kind of blink she got from Runs-from-Bears.

"You said you'd bury me on the mountain, when my time comes."

Nathaniel's eyes were fever-bright. "I remember."

"That's all I'm asking. I won't go back to court on the mountain if you'll give me that much."

The column of muscles in Nathaniel's throat moved visibly. "Hannah is my daughter," he said. "I want to hear you say so."

Richard thrust out his chin, his head jerking back. His whole frame went still, and Elizabeth was overcome by a dread so palpable that she suddenly found it hard to stand. Nathaniel's hand steadied her, but his gaze never wavered from the man in front of him.

"Hannah is Sarah's daughter," Richard said. And then: "Hannah is your daughter."

Elizabeth leaned into Nathaniel and felt a tremor pass through him. On his face was the same disbelief and relief that must be on her own.

"In that case, if all you're asking is burial rights on the Wolf, then I'll give you that. And gladly." He was clenching and unclenching his right fist; Elizabeth wanted to grab it and thrust it toward Richard, to see their hands sealed around these words that had passed between them.

"That's all I'm asking of you," Richard said. "But I'll ask Elizabeth a favor in payment for the good turn I did her."

"Settle the business between you," Elizabeth said. "And then you and I can talk."

When Nathaniel put out his hand, Richard met it without hesitation. Elizabeth could not look away from the sight of two strong hands clasped. Whether he was to be trusted, that was still a question that could not be answered with any certainty. She was consumed with curiosity about what had transpired in Montreal between this man and his brother, but she thought she might never know. On an audible sigh, Elizabeth said: "This business you have with me. Is it about Kitty?"

Richard's gaze shifted away from Nathaniel. "Yes. I'd ask you to let her make up her own mind."

"Kitty is a mother and a widow," said Elizabeth. "Her view of the world has changed, I think, even without any help of mine."

"I noticed," said Richard. "But you managed to put the idea of going to England in her head, you and your aunt Merriweather."

Elizabeth crossed her arms in front of herself. She wanted to hold on to the excitement and relief of the past few minutes, but Richard could still agitate and irritate. She was tempted to give him what he promised without discussion, but then she feared also that to start off with less than honesty was to doom this uneasy truce.

"Pardon my confusion, but I cannot quite be sure who it is you are courting. Is it the Kitty you left alone and without word for the entire summer, or is it my brother's widow and the mother of my father's heir? Perhaps you have given up on the mountain to go after a bigger prize."

Richard's head snapped back and the color rose on his cheeks.

"Kitty has changed," he said. "But you haven't. If you were a man, I'd call you out for that."

Elizabeth grabbed Nathaniel's arm to keep him where he was.

"Do you mean to point out that I cannot be diverted from the issue at hand? Let me promise you this much: I will not exert undue influence on Kitty, or lie to her, if you will promise likewise. If in the end she decides to go to England, you will not hinder her. If she decides to stay, I will not try to change her mind. If your intentions are honorable, then I cannot see how this agreement could displease you."

Richard hesitated, the thoughts sparking vaguely behind his eyes. His gaze rested briefly on Nathaniel, and then shifted away.

"Done," he said hoarsely.

"We'll hold you to it," Nathaniel said.

Richard hefted himself back into the saddle. "It's not my half of the bargain that worries me," he said. "It's your wife's." And he wheeled his horse away, and was gone.

"He plans to marry Kitty before the year's out," Nathaniel said.

Elizabeth was not sure of that, but she thought it would not be wise to say so at this moment; Nathaniel's irritation was too close to the surface. "You may be right," she said. "But I think Kitty has a surprise or two in store for him."

Nathaniel grunted softly. "Let's hope she leads him on a chase out of Paradise."

Elizabeth picked up her skirts and took his arm once again. "That is one wish that you may actually see fulfilled."

They found Kitty not at rest, but in the kitchen with Curiosity and her daughters. The baby was in a cradle near the hearth burbling softly to himself, completely at ease with the great deal of noise and laughter that filled the room. Kitty stood at the long table, her arms elbow-deep in bread dough.

Curiosity put down her spoon with a thump and came toward them like a small storm. "You ain't got no more common sense than a home-struck cow, walkin' here in that snow. Sit down by the fire and I'll bring you some tea. Your head ache, don't it? Nathaniel, what was you thinking?"

"Short of trussing her like a calf, she couldn't be stopped, Curiosity."

"She is single-minded," Kitty supplied, wiping her hands on a piece of sackcloth.

"I hope that is sufficient discussion of my character deficiencies," said Elizabeth, taking the seat that was pressed upon her.

There was a great deal of rushing around and talk as the walkers were stripped of their wet shoes and garments. Curiosity presented them with toweling to dry themselves, tea and plates of cake, and bits of the day's news: Ethan had slept through the night for the second time in a row, which explained Kitty's clear eyes and high spirits at least in part. Manny had cut his hand at the mill, and would not be able to work for a week or more. Joshua Hench and Daisy would be married on New Year's Day, and the judge had offered them the parlor for the ceremony. There was a letter from aunt Merriweather which must be read aloud, as it was addressed to Elizabeth as well as Kitty. It included the story of her meeting with Abigail Adams, a woman Aunt found to be both overworked and overpraised.

The baby began to fuss, and Daisy swooped down to snatch him up and deliver him to his mother's lap. Kitty settled in a rocker on the far side of the hearth with the boy at her breast, carrying on an animated conversation with Polly about his recent growth of dark hair.

"Did you see, Elizabeth?" she called. "His eyes are such a bright blue now, and Curiosity says they will stay that way."

On her way out the door with a pile of laundry, Curiosity paused. "He got your mama's eyes, Elizabeth. Clear as the heavens."

The baby let out a belch many sizes too large for such a small person, and Kitty laughed out loud. "I hope he will have some of her delicacy of manner, too."

Elizabeth said, "I think motherhood agrees with you, Kitty."

"Yas'm, that it does." Curiosity winked at them, and then disappeared down the hall.

Flushing with pleasure at this praise, Kitty bent her blond head over her son's dark curls and looked up again only when Polly and Daisy sat down to their spinning nearby. Nathaniel leaned over to whisper in Elizabeth's ear.

"Richard has a battle before him," he said softly. "And he has none of the right weapons."

"Why do you say that?" she asked, truly amazed.

He gestured with his chin to the three young women, deep in a conversation that wove in and out of the rhythmic clatter and whirr of the spinning wheels.

"She's never had a home like this, with women around her. Do you think she'll give up Curiosity and this kitchen for Richard and feathered bonnets? Even your aunt might not be able to get her away, in the end."

"It is true I have never seen her so much at ease. Is it not strange, Nathaniel? A year ago I could not imagine ever leaving Paradise while Kitty could not wait to get out, and now—" She hesitated.

Nathaniel ran a thumb over her cheekbone. "Are we going, then?" His eyes with all their complexity of light and dark, and the greens and golds and browns of the great north woods. His gaze held her firmly bound to him, as firmly he had held her in his arms and would hold her again, in common purpose, in sorrow and joy.

"I don't know," she murmured, catching his hand against her face. "I truly do not know."

Whether they stayed in Paradise or went, it did not matter, not really. Not if she could look up and find him there. *Mine,* she thought simply. *Mine.*

LXII

Christmas, 1793

He was lost.

Not more than five miles north of Hidden Wolf on lands he had roamed and trapped and hunted all his life, Nathaniel couldn't deny that he had lost his way, and on Christmas Eve. At his feet there was a spattering of blood in the snow, and the glassy stare of the buck that had brought him so far afield. He had won the battle of wits and persistence, and he had lost: to pack the deer out he would need to butcher it first, and there was no time.

In the trees above and behind him he was vaguely aware of a restlessness. Drawn by the smell of blood, the wolves that often followed at a distance when he hunted without the dogs—as he did today—edged closer, eager enough that they might soon risk the rifle. Nathaniel neither feared the pack nor begrudged them the meal that he would have to leave behind; game was plentiful this season. His irritation was only with himself, for letting the chase get the better of him when he had come out with nothing more than a Christmas turkey in mind.

Out of habit and training, he reloaded his rifle and then he straddled the buck. With quick and economical movements of his knife he took the saddle to roast for tomorrow's dinner, his nostrils flaring at the coppery rush. The mist of his breath mixed with the steam from the open cavity.

The cloud cover that had swallowed the sun was moving

down the mountain slope, quietly devouring the snow-choked pine and white cedar so that even the constant chirp and fuss of the redpolls was dampened. Nathaniel swung his pack and rifle into place and began to climb upward anyway, the icy snow crackling underfoot. To walk hard was the only way to keep warm without building a fire, and to walk uphill toward the ridge was the only hope he had of getting his bearings. If the cloud cover broke. If the storm held off.

Elizabeth had taught school this afternoon, but she would be at home by now. Waiting for him. From up ahead Nathaniel heard a white owl call. Twilight on Christmas Eve, and time to be home.

Given the losses that both the Middleton and Bonner families had suffered in the past few months, it was only seemly that they keep a quiet Christmas. This was how her father had announced to Elizabeth that he and Kitty were accepting an invitation to spend the holidays with Mr. Bennett and his wife in Johnstown. Curiosity and Galileo were to go with them, because Kitty wished it so. Mr. Witherspoon would go too and would not be missed, he assured Elizabeth: it seemed that Christmas was the very worst time to try to preach Christ in Paradise.

Her curiosity aroused, Elizabeth asked her students about these vague reports of Christmas excesses. They were eager to tell her about the Kaes family's habit of a Christmas mummery, and Axel's love of fireworks, all of which she had missed the previous year because the judge had given a party of his own. She wondered if she should join in, given the recent loss of her brother, and found that even Martha, so recently widowed, was planning to take part. Christmas was a time of games and play-fulness, she told Elizabeth. It would sustain them in the long winter ahead. Elizabeth thought they could use a party; Falling-Day, Many-Doves, and Runs-from-Bears had left at the beginning of the month for a visit at Good Pasture, where Many-Doves' first child would come into the world early in the new year. Elizabeth missed their company very much.

But by dark Nathaniel had not yet come home, and Hannah

seesawed rapidly between resignation and disappointment. Liam, more stoic, sat quietly by the hearth cleaning traps. At eight, Elizabeth gave in and sent them down to the village.

"I want to wait for Nathaniel," she said. "And the walk is a bit much for me, in this snow."

With a significant look at the great mound of her middle, Hannah gave in with a grin.

Elizabeth followed the swing of the lantern until it disappeared into the wood, and then she closed the door firmly against the cold and turned back into the cabin. Only the dogs were left to her, and they slept in an untidy heap by the fire, uninterested in the fact that it was Christmas Eve. She made a tour of all three rooms, but as they had spent the late afternoon cleaning and making ready for the holiday, there was nothing left for her to do but to take up her book by the hearth.

At nine when the ache in the small of her back was no longer governable and a sharp kick to her liver set her teeth on edge, Elizabeth put down her book to pace the floor, noting as she did so that she had lost sight of her own feet. In the village more than one woman had taken silent measure of her girth and then raised a brow at the suggestion that the child was not due for another six weeks. But only Curiosity and Falling-Day had actually examined her, and as Elizabeth herself had not yet announced the fact that she carried twins, they too were silent.

She stopped before the hearth to examine the miniatures of Nathaniel's mother and her own. Recently Elizabeth had been thinking more and more often of her mother, understanding for the first time how difficult it must have been for her to leave her homeland and raise her children alone in another country. She had been only twenty-five when she left Paradise. Five years younger than Elizabeth was now, she had chosen to leave her husband and travel pregnant and alone to England. In the spring, Elizabeth thought she might have a conversation with aunt Merriweather in which difficult questions would be asked.

With a careful finger, Elizabeth touched her mother's likeness, tracing the brow and widow's peak which she had inherited. She was fortunate in the women she had around her, but she wondered about this woman who was both so familiar to her and a stranger. If she would have approved of the life Elizabeth had made for herself; how she would have greeted her grandchildren, held them and rocked them. If they would have the blue eyes she had passed on to Julian's son, or perhaps Nathaniel's hazel eyes.

He should have been back hours ago; she could not pretend anymore that she was not worried.

Elizabeth picked up the likeness of his mother to study the high forehead and calm expression in the dark eyes.

"Where is your son so late on Christmas Eve?" she asked out loud, and then jumped back, startled, at a pounding on the door.

They came in with a great rush of cold air and loud noise that set the dogs to barking: Jed McGarrity's fiddle arguing with the great variety of tin horns and penny whistles with which Elizabeth's students were armed. There were shouted greetings and a great deal of laughter: Axel and Anna, Martha and the McGarritys, the Kaes girls trailing beaux, and most of the children of the village, many of them masked.

Elizabeth forced herself to smile, swallowing her disappointment. Hannah and Liam had brought the revelry up the mountainside for her; she could do no less than be cheerful for them. Hannah fairly capered around the room, her plaits flying in an impromptu dance to the fiddle music.

"Is that you, Ephraim?" Elizabeth's laugh was genuine, now. It was not so much the mask that hid most of the pale little-boy face that shocked, but the fact that he wore an empty inkpot on the end of every finger of his left hand. These he waved and clattered in her face ferociously.

A volley of gunfire from the porch made her start up again and blanch, but Martha was at her elbow before she could even turn in that direction. "Just the Cameron boys," she said. "They like to waste their powder on Christmas Eve."

"You missed the fireworks!" Anna announced, pushing a bowl of doughnuts into Elizabeth's arms. "But they thought you might like the noise anyway."

"Ah," Elizabeth said. "How thoughtful."

There was a new round of shouting outside. She moved

toward the door with her heart high in her throat, hoping for the only Christmas surprise that seemed to matter now.

The door opened and the dogs took the opportunity to escape, howling into the night.

In the door frame was the large and familiar shape of Robbie MacLachlan, white-haired and blue-eyed, blushing the color of spring primroses. Beside him Treenie wagged her tail like a tattered flag.

The party turned in sudden silence to the door.

"Robbie MacLachlan," said Elizabeth, stunned.

"Oh, no, miss," breathed little Marie Dubonnet, her eyes wide with wonder. "That's Saint Nicholas."

When he had greeted everyone and convinced the younger children that he was not a Dutch saint, but only an old Scots soldier tired of his own company, Elizabeth drew Robbie into the workroom while the party carried on.

"What have ye done wi' Nathaniel?" he asked, his broad face creased with good humor. "Dinna tell me that ye've misplaced your guidman agin, and on the Yule?"

Then he looked closer at Elizabeth, and his expression sobered. He stood back, and pulled his hat from his head.

"What is it, lass?"

Determined not to ruin Hannah's Christmas Eve, Elizabeth pulled him farther away and into the shadows. Treenie followed, snuffling curiously at Elizabeth's stomach and rocking her back on her heels in her enthusiasm.

"He went out to get a turkey, very early this morning. I am worried, Robbie."

"Aye, and ye didna need tae tell me, for it's written clear on yer face, as much as ye wish tae hide it." He rubbed a hand over the white bristle on his cheeks, and then heaved a great sigh. "A few mair hours in the bush will no' harm me. I'll fetch him, aye?" He began to pull on his furs again, but then he stopped with a thoughtful look. "There's no' a chance o' foul play? Where is Richard Todd keepin' hisel', these days?"

Elizabeth shook her head. "There is so much to tell you, I don't know where to begin. Whatever is keeping Nathaniel,

Richard has nothing to do with it—he followed Kitty to Johns-town this morning."

"Did he? Luve-struck, is our Cat-Eater? Well. I'll have the whole o' the story later, lass. Let me be on ma way, sae much the sooner I'll be back."

"But you must be hungry." Elizabeth remembered her manners quite suddenly.

"It's no' sae bad. Thirsty, though."

"Robbie!" called Axel from the other room. "I've got the best of my schnapps here to warm your bones!"

The big man laughed out loud, with a half-apologetic glance toward Elizabeth.

"Aye, and wha' Scotsman wad turn that doon, on sic a nicht as this?"

Then with an encouraging wink to Elizabeth, he leaned over to talk into her ear. "Dinna fash yer bonny heid, lass. I willna be long." In three paces he had crossed the room to take the cup offered to him.

"Axel Metzler, ye're a rare mannie tae brew nectar such as this," he muttered, inhaling deeply.

The whole room seemed to shine with his energy, and Elizabeth was comforted although she could not say exactly why. He held the cup up to the room, and winked at her.

"Here's tae us," he bellowed. "Wha's like us? Gey few, and they're a' deid!" And he tipped back the cup with a neat movement of his wrist.

"Good Yule!" he finished, wiping his mouth with his hand.

"Good Yule!" echoed around the room.

Then he whistled to Treenie and strode to the door.

"But where are you going?" Hannah called.

"Dinna fear, lassie. I'm the ill shillin' ye heard aboot—ye canna be shut o' me. I'll soon be back."

"Robbie!"

He turned toward Elizabeth, one brow raised in question.

"Did you bring any word—"

"O' Hawkeye? Aye, lass. He's well. Do ye set doon and put up yer feet, and rest. I'll be back sae soon as I may."

.   .   .   .   .

It was another half hour before the Christmas mummers and revelers had been sent on their way to serenade the rest of Paradise, and Elizabeth could collapse into the rocker before the hearth. Hannah plopped down beside her, her face flushed still with excitement and pleasure.

"I'll make you some tea," Liam offered. It was a skill he had acquired after long tutoring, and one he was proud of. Elizabeth simply nodded.

"You're worried about Pa," observed Hannah. "He'll be back." She said this with such assurance and calm that Elizabeth had to smile. She was suddenly very tired, and content just to sit before the hearth and drink the tea that Liam pressed upon her. When they went off to their beds—Hannah to the sleeping loft, and Liam to his cot in the workroom—Elizabeth could not quite manage the energy to move. Although she did not mean to, she finally slept with the warmth of the fire on her face, and her hands spread protectively over her belly.

She did not hear the door open, some time later, nor did the familiar step wake her. Nathaniel stood looking down at her, wanting to touch the flushed curve of her cheek but loath to put even a finger on her, as cold as he was. She slept with her head bowed back. Her mouth was curved slightly in a near smile, so that he could see the glint of her teeth in the dim light of the dying fire. Her eyes moved rapidly behind lids as delicately colored as seashells. A good dream, then. One he did not want to disturb.

Nathaniel stoked the fire, and then he sat down in its warmth to watch his wife sleep. His stomach threatened loudly and his hands and feet had already begun to tingle painfully, but for the moment he could ignore all of that to study her in his own time.

There was a knock on the door and she started awake, her expression shifting from confusion and worry to joy as soon as she saw him. It was all the Christmas present he wanted or needed, to see how it pleased her to have him home. He brushed his mouth against her temple as he got to his feet.

"Nathaniel! What kept you so long?"

"I got disoriented." He grinned, moving toward the door.

"Thank God for Axel's fireworks. Now who could this be so late?"

"Robbie."

"You were dreaming of Robbie?" Nathaniel asked, surprised.

"I was not dreaming," she said, struggling up from the chair. "Robbie was here! He went out to look for you."

There was another muffled rattle at the door.

Nathaniel pulled up, suddenly uneasy.

"Who is it?" he called, reaching for his rifle.

From the corner of his eye he saw Hannah's head pop up over the rail of the sleeping loft. Liam had appeared in the shadows at the workroom door with a musket in his hands.

"Christ Almighty, man, will ye open the door afore I drop the bluidy great gomerel?"

Nathaniel threw up the bar and the door crashed open instantly to reveal Robbie strained forward, an unconscious man slung over his shoulder. He rushed into the room.

"Well, Robbie," said Nathaniel, laughing. "Brought us a Christmas present, have you?"

"Nathaniel," Elizabeth scolded softly, coming forward. But the corner of her mouth twitched.

"Is he dead?" called Hannah, already on her way down the ladder.

"Ach, no' a bit o' it. He's fu' o' drink." Robbie grunted as he deposited the limp form on the floor before the hearth.

The stranger was of middle age, dark haired and very lean of face, softly jowled. Nathaniel had never seen him before.

"—And p'rhaps froze a bit, forbye," conceded Robbie. "But he willna die, lass. It wad take mair than a cauld wind tae kill a Scotsman the likes o' this one."

Nathaniel and Elizabeth looked up at Robbie at the same moment.

"Do you know him?" Elizabeth asked.

"Aye, I do. It's no' sae proper as he wad have it, but I'll introduce him. This is Angus Moncrieff, factor and secretary to his lordship, Earl of Carrick. Or so he's tolt me."

He laughed in response to the blank look on their faces.

"We'll let him dry oot, shall we, and he can tell ye his own story. In the morning, I'm guessin', by the look o' him."

But Angus Moncrieff, factor and secretary to his lordship, Earl of Carrick, was producing a low moan, and he began to stir.

"Hannah, he'll want water," Elizabeth said, sending the little girl scuttling off to the drinking bucket. Liam went to get blankets, and in a few minutes they had the stranger sitting up before the hearth, blinking at them all groggily. Then his gaze fell on Robbie, and his dark eyes narrowed slightly. He rubbed his head with one trembling hand.

"I see ye beat me here, MacLachlan."

Elizabeth's head jerked up in surprise. Nathaniel could see the calculations going on behind her eyes, and the questions quickly multiplying, at odds with her impulse to be polite.

"Aye," said Robbie. "But no' by much. Yer scout will hae broucht ye down the Canada, and here was I, hopin' tae give these people some preparation for yer news."

Moncrieff had sat up, and he shook his head to clear it. "I must thank ye, man. The scout is still back in the village tavern drinking that devil's brew—"

"Schnapps, aye," Robbie agreed. "And ye decided tae come up here by yersel'. Ye're no' the first tae misjudge Axel's schnapps, Moncrieff."

"I fear I've come a long way to make a verra bad first impression," said the man gruffly. He looked around him, and started visibly at the sight of Nathaniel. "You'll be Daniel Bonner's son, Nathaniel?"

When this was confirmed, Moncrieff held out a hand. "I hope ye'll pardon the intrusion, so late and all. But I was anxious to make yer acquaintance."

"Maybe we should set at the table," Nathaniel suggested. "Before we get to the reason for your visit. I don't know about you, but I haven't eaten all day."

Elizabeth could not quite stop examining the stranger from Scotland, or wondering why a man of some means and education would have spent a year looking for Hawkeye. He had

started in New-York and worked his way upriver, looking for
clues but finding none until he came into the Albany area just
three months past. Elizabeth had a difficult time curbing her
curiosity while the men ate, filling themselves with huge
amounts of bread, leftover stew, Anna's Christmas doughnuts,
and the apple pie Elizabeth had made as a small present for
Nathaniel. He winked at her over his spoon, and she rubbed
her hand along the long line of his back as she went by.

They wanted Robbie's news of Hawkeye, but Nathaniel had
already silenced Hannah's questions on this with a small shake
of the head: not in front of the stranger. Not until they knew
his purpose. Moncrieff, on the other hand, could have talked
but seemed content to eat. He was of middle height with a
narrowness to him, from forehead to shoulders, but with strong
hands and dark eyes that were both keen and intelligent. Once,
Elizabeth thought, he had been a very handsome youth: even
now there was something about the way he held himself that set
him apart.

Moncrieff seemed to have recovered fully from his earlier
difficulties. Enough, at any rate, to ask about ale and to look
both surprised and disappointed to find there was none. Elizabeth filled his cup with cider as quickly as he could empty it, in
the hope of giving him reason to go out of doors so that they
might have a few minutes alone.

In the meantime they gave Robbie news of the village, and
the things that had passed over the summer and fall. Moncrieff
listened as closely as Robbie did, but his commentary was limited to an occasional raised brow.

"Had I known, Nathaniel, I wad hae stayed. Ye've had a hard
time o' it."

"We would have been glad of your help," Nathaniel conceded with a grim smile. "But we managed."

"Aye, ye always do." He cast a shy glance at Elizabeth's
shape, and smiled. "There's guid news, too, for which tae be
thankful on the Yule."

"That there is," Nathaniel agreed, following the line of his
gaze.

"Wait!" Hannah cried, jumping up so suddenly that she sent
her empty cup clattering to the floor. And then she disappeared

into the shadows underneath her sleeping loft, to appear again with her hands behind her back. She ran back to Robbie, and stood before him with a tremendous smile.

"Wha' have ye got there, lassie? A surprise?"

"Aye, a surrrrprise," she agreed, happily mimicking his burr. "Close your eyes and don't touch, please."

After a bit of teasing, he complied. Hannah produced one of the pairs of spectacles purchased in Albany, and with a conspiratorial grin in Elizabeth's direction, she slipped them carefully onto Robbie's face, hooked them gently behind his ears, and stood back with a triumphant cry.

Robbie touched his fingers carefully to the metal frames.

"Open your eyes!" Hannah demanded, thrusting a book into his chest.

The blue of his eyes blazed sharply, magnified by glass and perhaps by a little dampness. Elizabeth blinked hard, herself, seeing the look on his face.

Robbie lifted the book up and opened it.

"Holy Mary," he said reverently. "They work."

There was laughter all around, but Robbie kept his gaze fixed on the book in his hands, turning the pages with one great splayed thumb as if he thought that the clarity of the words, black on white, might turn out to be a trick of his mind.

"I dinna ken how tae thank ye for a generous act such as this," he said, looking up finally. Gently he took the spectacles from his face and held them on his open palm like a treasure.

"No thanks needed," Nathaniel said. "Not between us."

"Now you can read to us," Liam said hopefully, brushing the matted red hair out of his eyes and stifling a yawn.

"But not tonight," amended Elizabeth.

Moncrieff had been watching the conversation with some interest, but he stood now, clearing his throat quietly to get their attention.

"I ken it's late," he said. "But if I could have just a half hour o' your time, Mr. Bonner, I would be thankful. I've been a year looking for you, and it will be difficult to sleep if I dinna first say a few words. But if you'll excuse me for just a moment—"

And with the resigned look of anyone who had to leave the warm cabin for the realities of the Necessary, Moncrieff finally

went off to relieve himself of the effects of Elizabeth's generosity
with the cider.

Hannah fell on Robbie like a plague, fairly climbing up his
arm in her curiosity.

"Where's my grandfather?" she demanded, without niceties.
"And when is he coming home?"

Robbie laughed, shaking her off like a wet leaf. "When last I
saw him he was in guid health, and he bid me tell ye that when
next I came tae call. He doesna ken that Kirby's deid—" He
nodded to Liam, in acknowledgment of his loss. "And that
there's no sheriff tae put him back in gaol. Elizabeth, yer faither
is no' o' a mind tae see Hawkeye's sentence completed? Well,
then. I suspect he wad be here hisel' if he kent that. But he's in
Montreal, or should soon be."

"Montreal?" echoed Nathaniel, leaning forward. "Why?"

"Otter," said Robbie, simply.

Hannah was on her feet instantly, but Nathaniel caught her
up and kept her still.

"Yer faither went tae extricate him from some difficulties,"
Robbie continued. "We had word o' young Otter when Spotted-Fox came through ma part o' the bush."

"But he was supposed to be fighting with Little-Turtle,"
Hannah said. Liam started visibly at this, but Hannah's whole
attention was on Robbie.

The little girl's expression, half terror, half hope, made Elizabeth's heart clench. She went to her and put a hand on her
shoulder. "Well, at least we know where Otter is, and that your
grandfather is nearby." Elizabeth said this calmly, trying to
force the idea into Hannah's head, and her own.

Nathaniel rubbed a hand over his face, as if to wake himself
up. "What's this all about, Robbie?"

"It has tae do wi' a lass, as I understan' it." He grinned
lopsidedly. "As trouble oft does when a man is Otter's age."
But there was something uneasy about his smile, and Elizabeth
wished desperately to be alone with Nathaniel and Robbie so
that they might have the whole story.

There was the sound of a step on the porch, and Robbie
leaned toward Nathaniel with a sense of urgency. "Moncrieff
seems a guid mannie tae me," he said. "But the tale he has tae

tell ye is gey strange. I didna think I should tell him aboot yer faither, or where tae find him, wi'oot yer permission."

"What—" began Nathaniel, but Moncrieff was already half-way in the room, and the conversation turned back to less sensitive matters.

Hannah and Liam were sent back to bed, and the adults settled around the fire. In spite of the late hour, Elizabeth was curiously awake, and aware of the smallest details: the fact that Nathaniel had a cut on his thumb, the shape of the pine knot she had lit on the hearthstones for more light, and the large, neatly turned ears of Angus Moncrieff, still almost purple from the cold at their outer edges. Behind them the room was in shadows, but the fire glowed white and amber, pulsing slowly.

"We had some word of you from a trapper we know," Nathaniel began. "But he's simpleminded and he had things confused."

"A big man, in need of a wash?"

"Yes," Elizabeth confirmed. "He told us that *you* were the Earl of Carrick."

"No," said Moncrieff, his eyes narrowed slightly. "The Earl of Carrick would be Daniel Bonner's first cousin, Alasdair Scott."

There was a sudden silence. Beside Elizabeth, Nathaniel tensed as if he had heard a trigger cocked.

Robbie cleared his throat. "Speak plain, man. Spit it oot."

Moncrieff turned his hands over to stare at his own palms. Then he looked up steadily and met Nathaniel's gaze.

"I have verra strong reason to believe that your faither is the only son of James Scott, who was the younger brother of Roderick Scott, the last Earl of Carrick."

James Scott. Jamie Scott.

The hot August day in Albany; it seemed almost like a dream to Elizabeth.

Who is this James Scott?

I am. I do the banking for Bears. It's just a name, Boots.

Elizabeth was holding Nathaniel's hand; the tension humming in him said this was not a simple coincidence. She swallowed hard and tried to keep her face as expressionless as his, although she could not stop the color from rising on her neck and cheeks.

"I think you've got the wrong man," Nathaniel said. "But if you were right and you had proof, what of it, then? The younger brother of an earl has nothing to claim, as far as I understand it. His son even less."

Moncrieff grunted. "It's true, Jamie Scott came awa' to the New World with neither title nor lands. When he left, his brother Roderick already had a son and heir. That was Alasdair, the current earl, who is my employer. A man of eighty-two years, this summer past. In good health when last I saw him, but feeling his age."

Elizabeth squeezed Nathaniel's hand and he sat back to let her speak. "Why would his lordship send you so far to find a cousin he did not know existed? Unless the present Lord Carrick has no heir of his own?"

Moncrieff shifted in his chair. "You've got to the heart of it, Mrs. Bonner. The earl has no son, and so he sent me off to find Jamie Scott's son, or grandson. The last of the line, you see."

"And if Jamie Scott never had a son?" Nathaniel asked.

"But he did," said Moncrieff, taking a bundle of papers out of his vest and putting them on his knee. "There was nae trouble tracing Jamie Scott's movements. There are ship rosters, and land changed hands, after all. He took a guidwife, a young lady who emigrated from Edinburgh on the same ship as he. There's plentifu' information about his early dealings in the Colonies, including a letter hame to his brother announcing the birth o' a son, in 1718." The strong, slender hand rested on the papers. "But there's no detail at all about Jamie's death. Just a letter written by a priest in Albany to his lordship to notify him of the massacre, in '21, and the fact that a child had survived. A son called Daniel."

"It's a common enough name," said Nathaniel.

Robbie cleared his throat. "If the laird kent the lad had survived, why did they no' come tae find him then?"

Moncrieff leaned forward. "In fact, a great deal o' money was spent to find the child, wi'oot success."

"You've got no proof of any of this," Nathaniel said shortly.

The keen brown eyes turned to him, and examined Nathaniel's features closely and without apology. "There's proof," he said. "I see what I see. The lairds of Carrick have always marked their get, and you're the verra likeness of Jamie Scott."

"And how would you know that?" Nathaniel said testily. "You would not have been born when he set sail for the Americas."

Moncrieff seemed not at all perturbed by Nathaniel's irritation. From a purse he wore under his arm he drew a pendant which he opened with a small snap. Then he held it up by its chain so that it spun lazily, catching the light to cast it out again, before it came to a stop.

Elizabeth inhaled sharply, for it might as well have been Hawkeye as a young man: the same strong bones and coloring, piercing dark eyes under straight brows. And because it might have been Hawkeye, it was enough like Nathaniel to make him look away.

"James Scott?" She heard her voice crack.

"No," said Angus Moncrieff, snapping the pendant shut again to tuck it away. "Roderick, Earl of Carrick. Jamie's twin. They were born ten minutes apart."

"That proves nothing," Nathaniel said, the muscle in his cheek fluttering in a distinctly disturbing way.

"Let me ask you this, then. Have you nivver heard your grandfather's name spoke by your faither?"

"My grandfather's name was Chingachgook," said Nathaniel, his eyes flashing a warning that Elizabeth hoped Mr. Moncrieff could read. "We buried him on the rise at the back of the gorge in the late summer, near my mother."

There was a small silence.

"O' course. But have you no knowledge of your faither's natural parents?"

"They had a farm on the Hudson. They were killed in a raid, is all I know. A French trapper by the name of Bonner picked up my father wandering around afterward. Chingachgook offered to take the boy and raise him up, and the trapper was glad of it."

"He called himself Daniel when—Chingachgook, have I got that right?—when Chingachgook adopted him?" asked Moncrieff.

Nathaniel stood suddenly, and walked out of the light into the shadows, where he stood motionless.

"His name is Dan'l Bonner, called Hawkeye by the Mahican people who raised him. Longue Carabine by the French and the Huron. Those are the only names he has ever had or needed. Why worry him with lands and titles at this point in his life?"

Robbie had been quiet for all of this, but he spoke up, finally. "Because if he doesna find Laird Carrick's richtfu' heir, the title and the lands will revert to the English crown."

"And you're still enough of a Scot, after all these years here, to care?"

"Aye, and mair than that, laddie. There's muny a Scot who wad travel tae hell and dance wi' the de'il tae keep what's left of the border counties oot o' English hands."

"I want to talk to my wife," Nathaniel said from the shadows. "Alone."

She went to bed while Nathaniel showed the Scotsmen where they could sleep. For a long while Elizabeth lay with her head pillowed on her arm, listening to the murmur of his soft, low voice rising and falling in contrast to Robbie's. They were talking in the workroom; Moncrieff had been given a pallet under the sleeping loft.

In near full dark Elizabeth lay listening to that soothing music, and tracing the arc of the moon as it made ready to set. The confusion of thoughts in her head made it throb slightly—she was prone to headaches since her fall—and so she tried not to dwell on Angus Moncrieff, and the incredible but increasingly obvious fact that she had somehow managed to marry into a Scots earldom.

Aunt Merriweather would choke to hear it told. Elizabeth, who had scorned the very concept of a good match, had made the best match of all: if Moncrieff was right, Nathaniel would one day be the Earl of Carrick. It was almost enough to make her laugh out loud, the idea of it, but then Elizabeth remembered the tension in his face and the urge left her.

She sat up and lit a candle to brush her hair, afraid that otherwise she would fall asleep before he came in, and sleep uneasily for want of the rest of the news.

Nathaniel came in, and sat behind her on the bed to take the brush from her hands. The mattress crackled as he moved closer. With the steady movement of the brush over and over again through the length of her hair, she arched her back in pleasure.

"What of Otter?" she asked finally, when it seemed that he would never talk.

Nathaniel's voice at her ear, soft and close. "He got tangled up with the wrong woman. My father went to set him straight on the path home."

"What do you mean by 'wrong woman'?"

The movement of the brush paused, and he leaned forward to kiss her cheek. "One who doesn't want him."

"Ah. Otter may be of a different opinion. Do you think Hawkeye will have any success with a young man as strong-minded as he is?"

He went back to his work, drawing the brush down and down. "Aye, well. So was I at that age, and he managed to shift me out of Montreal, under pretty much the same circumstances."

"The same circumstances?" Elizabeth asked, all thought of Moncrieff and the Earl of Carrick suddenly eclipsed.

The steady motion of the brush never faltered, but Nathaniel cleared his throat. "The woman is not unknown to me. She collects backwoodsmen as a kind of hobby, I guess you might say, in international relations. I was one of her first trophies. This was before I knew Sarah," he added hastily.

A vague sense of familiarity with this story washed over Elizabeth. "Her name is not Giselle, by any chance?"

Nathaniel jerked in surprise, so that he dropped the brush and had to retrieve it. "What do you know of Giselle?" he asked, not quite managing to hide his surprise or discomfort.

"Oh, this and that," Elizabeth said, glad that her back was still to him and he could not see her face, for she feared she could not hide her scowl. "Richard apparently had a bit of an encounter with her this past summer, as well. Aunt Merriweather mentioned it to me. To think of Richard and Otter at odds over the same lady—it would explain Richard's long absence, in part. But I would have thought Otter far too young for her?"

"Then you don't understand the kind of woman we're talking about," Nathaniel said gruffly, taking up his brushing again. He worked in silence for a minute, one hand on her shoulder to hold her still. She had the urge to rub her cheek on his hand, but her bones were turning to liquid and she could do nothing but sit there and let him have his way.

"It explains Richard's sudden interest in Kitty," he said after some time. "After Giselle, he's got a better appreciation of a worthwhile girl." Before she could answer, he put his hand lightly over her mouth. "Never mind about Giselle," he said. "I got something else to say to you."

His whole posture changed.

"I'm sorry, Boots," he said quietly. "If I had known Moncrieff's purpose, I would never have let him in the door."

She turned to him awkwardly, taken by surprise. "But why?" she asked. "Nathaniel, I don't understand. Mr. Moncrieff's news is certainly a shock, but why this hostility?"

There was an unfamiliar uncertainty in his face, and worry. He leaned toward her and put his forehead on her shoulder, and her arms came up around him.

"I thought you would be angry," he said. "Back when you found out about the gold, you asked me if I had told you about everything. And I said I had."

She stifled an uneasy laugh. "But you didn't know about this. You could not have."

He shook his head. "No, I didn't know."

"You think that he is right, that James Scott was your grandfather."

He nodded wordlessly, and then turned from her to slip out of bed. From the small pile of things he kept on a shelf, he took a leather bag she had seen before, but never thought to ask about. Out of it he took a bound volume to put into her hands.

A Bible, well worn in bindings that crackled slightly when she opened it. And there, on the flyleaf:

James Scott and Margaret Montgomerie
Bound in Holy Matrimony on the sixteenth day of July, 1716

"The farm was burned in the raid," Nathaniel said. "The story goes, a trapper called Bonner found my father sitting next to the body of a woman. She was holding that Bible when she was struck down."

After a long while, Elizabeth said: "You did not show this to Mr. Moncrieff for a reason. Do you not wish your father to claim the title and lands?"

"Christ, Boots," he said, all of his exasperation and anxiety surfacing again. "Can you imagine my father an earl?"

"He has a greater acuity of mind than many I have heard of."

Nathaniel grasped her by the arms. She saw with some shock that he was on the edge of tears, a place she had seen him only one other time.

"Do you want him to sail off to Scotland? You haven't had enough of leave-takings?"

Elizabeth cursed herself for her shortsightedness, and put her hands on Nathaniel's face. "He need not go to Scotland," she whispered. "Neither need you."

He pulled away with a harsh laugh. "Moncrieff came all the way here to talk him into laying claim to the title, and he expects nothing in return? You heard them, they want us to go fight the English for them. As if we didn't have enough of fighting the damn English."

"There will be no more war between England and Scotland," Elizabeth said. "The country was razed so thoroughly after Culloden, Nathaniel, that there is no chance of it. And the war with France takes precedence right now. If there are battles to be fought over Scottish holdings, it would be in a court of law."

He grunted. "I ain't so sure you're right. You saw Robbie's face tonight; he'd pick up a musket and be on a ship tomorrow if he thought he could make a difference in throwing the English out of Scotland. But even if you're right, even if this is nothing more than a legal battle, it's one I want no part of. And neither should you."

Elizabeth sat quietly, thinking.

"You want to go," he said finally, in amazement and unease.

"Oh, no," she said, with a sharp shake of her head. "It is hard enough for me to think of leaving Lake in the Clouds at all. Scotland is not a temptation, Nathaniel."

He relaxed suddenly. "That's good to hear."

"Which part is good to hear?"

He blinked at her, confused and a little wary.

"Nathaniel," she said softly. "I think all this time you have asked me to make the decision about staying or going from here, and you have been struggling not to tell me what you want."

"I want you to be satisfied," he said, his breath stirring her hair. "That's all that concerns me."

"And you want to stay on Hidden Wolf," she said, pulling his face up to look into his eyes. "Wherever we might go, you will always want to come back home to Lake in the Clouds. This place is in your blood. Please just say so."

"I want to stay on Hidden Wolf," he parroted obediently. "If you'll be satisfied here."

"Nathaniel," she said, frowning.

He slid his arm around her and drew her down to lie beside him. The expression in his eyes stole her breath away.

"You want me to speak my mind. So then listen, listen to me." He paused to pull her closer.

"I'm happy with you here, Boots. Sometimes when I'm coming up the trail and I see the light in the window, I can't hardly move for fear that it's all been a dream, having you here in this place with me. I'm scairt of being without you. I never was easy to scare, even as a boy, but I've learned it now." His hand moved to the bulk of her belly and rested there. "All I want is to keep you safe, and to please you. So you'll stay with me. Tell me you'll stay with me."

"Oh, Nathaniel." She rubbed her cheek against his shoulder, held his face between her hands. "I am not going anywhere unless I go with you. I wouldn't be whole without you."

He let out a small sound from the back of his throat, and she saw the muscles in his cheek tremble. "You think you can be happy here, on the mountain?"

"I know I can," she said, and realized, suddenly, that it was the truth.

"Good," he said, the grip of his hands on her shoulders suddenly turning to a caress. "Good."

She held his gaze. "This is our place, Nathaniel, and Hannah's, and it will be our children's place. And I hope it will be your father's place, too. But first he must hear what Moncrieff has to say. If Hawkeye decides he needs to go to Scotland, then he will go. If he asks you to come along, and you decide to join him, then I will be there, too. But he deserves to know about his family."

Nathaniel pushed out his breath between his teeth. "I already told Moncrieff where to look for him in Montreal. He'll be off in the morning."

"Ah," she said, smiling.

On the table the candle sputtered, casting shadows over the ceiling. It was near dawn, and snow had begun to fall. For a long moment they were quiet together, listening to the muffled sounds of the waterfall. Elizabeth could have slept, but she fought it, not wanting to be drawn away from him now, even in sleep.

"Our first Christmas at Lake in the Clouds," she murmured. "But not the last."

His head came up, damp eyes glistening in the dim light. He looked at her hard. "Are you sure, Boots?"

"Yes," she said, lifting her face for his kiss. "There is nowhere else I want to be."

Sometime later he said, "You might be curious about that castle, in the end, or Montreal." A smile twitched at the corner of his mouth. "You may change your mind."

"Not about some things," Elizabeth said, spreading a hand on his cheek. "Not about this, not about you. Not the why or the wherefore, not the who."

"But the where, maybe. Someday."

His hands on her breasts, and a luxuriant stirring deep inside: the certainty of this, of his love and his desire, his protection and the life they shared. Elizabeth turned in his embrace and slid a leg over his hip, drew him closer. She let out a sound of welcome, and they came together gently, small movements that still drew from him a sigh of absolute surrender.

"Perhaps someday," she murmured against his mouth as she rose to meet him. "But for right now, Paradise is enough."

About the Author

SARA DONATI lives with her husband and daughter in the Pacific Northwest, where she teaches creative writing and linguistics at the university level.

Elizabeth and Nathaniel's epic story continues
in Sara Donati's next novel,
DAWN ON A DISTANT SHORE
to be published in spring 2000. Read on
for a preview . . .

The winter morning came with a pure, cold light, setting the ice and snow aflame with color and casting a rainbow across Hannah's face to wake her. She lay for a moment listening to the morning sounds: Liam was feeding the fire, humming to himself. The dogs whined at the door, and then a woman's voice: familiar and welcome, but unusual here, so early in the day.

The events of the previous night came to her in a rush and she stumbled out of her loft bed and down the ladder, pulling her quilt with her.

Liam held out a bowl. "Porridge," he said, without the least bit of enthusiasm. Since he had come to live with them Hannah had learned that Liam's first allegiance was always to his stomach, but she could not keep her gaze from moving toward the bedroom door. It stood slightly ajar.

Curiosity appeared as if Hannah had called for her.

"Miz Hannah," she said formally. "Let me shake your hand, child. Are we proud of you? I should say so."

Hannah found her voice. "She's all right?"

"She is. And those babies too." Curiosity laughed out loud. "If the Lord had made anything prettier He would have kept it for Hisself."

There was a feeble cry from the next room. Hannah stepped in that direction only to be caught up by Curiosity, who took her by the elbow and steered her back toward the table.

"Just set and eat, first. Pass some of that porridge over here, Liam, and stop pulling faces. It's honest food, after all."

"They are awful small," Hannah said, accepting the bowl and spoon automatically. "I was worried."

"Twins tend to be small," said Curiosity. "You were, when you come along. Nathaniel could just about hold you in one hand, and he did too. Carried you around tucked into his shirt for the longest time."

"He carried you up to bed last night too. Guess you didn't even notice," said Liam.

"Well, he's feeling perky, is Nathaniel." Anna put a cup of cider on the table in front of Hannah.

"A boy," said Liam. "Chingachgook was right. Nathaniel's got a son."

"So he does. And two fine daughters," added Curiosity. "Never can have enough daughters, is how I look at it."

Hannah's smile faded. "My grandfather should be here. He should know. I wish we had some word of him."

Curiosity sat down with a bowl of her own, and leaned toward the girl to pat her hand. "It looks like the good Lord is smiling on you today, Missy. Josiah Cameron brought a letter in from Johnstown just before the storm broke. Came all the way from Montreal."

"From my grandfather?" Hannah sat up straighter.

Curiosity pursed her mouth thoughtfully. "Don't think so. It was writ with a fancy hand, so I'd guess it was from that Scot—Moncrieff was his name, wasn't it? The one that come through here at Christmas. I'll wager he had some word of Hawkeye, though."

Outside the dogs began barking and Liam got up to see to them.

"That'll be the Judge," said Curiosity. "And half the village with him, by the sound of it. Ain't good news louder than Joshua's horn?"

"It is," said Nathaniel from the doorway. He looked tired, but there was an easiness to the line of his back that Hannah hadn't seen in a long time. She launched herself at her father; he caught her neatly, and bent over to whisper in her ear.

"Squirrel," he said in Kahnyen'kehàka, hugging her so hard that her ribs creaked. "I am mighty proud of you. Thank you."

"Is there word of Grandfather?" she whispered back.

A sudden wave of cold air and an eruption of voices at the door pulled Nathaniel's attention away. He patted her back as she let him go, but not before she saw the flash of worry move across his face, only to be carefully masked as he turned to greet his father-in-law.

Elizabeth Bonner believed herself to be a rational being, capable of logical thought and reasonable behavior, even in extreme circumstances. In the past year she had had opportunity enough to prove this to herself and to the world. But next to her, soundly asleep in the cradle beside the bed, were two tiny human beings: her children. She could not quite grasp it, in spite of all the evidence to hand.

Look, Curiosity had called, holding up first one and then the other child to examine by the light of the rising sun. *Look what you made!*

The day had been filled with visitors and good wishes, the demands of her own body, the simple needs of the infants. She was tired to the bone, but still Elizabeth looked. She lay on her side, watching the babies sleep. Her children, and Nathaniel's.

"Boots," Nathaniel said from the chair before the fire. "You think too hard."

"I can't help it," she said, stretching carefully. "Look at them."

He put down the knife he had been sharpening and came to her. She had seldom seen him look more weary, or more content. Crouched by the side of the cradle with his hands dangling over his knees, he studied the small forms.

"You did good, Boots, but you need your sleep. They'll be looking for you again before you know it."

She nodded, sliding down into the covers. "Yes, all right. But you're tired too. Come to bed."

Now Elizabeth's attention shifted to Nathaniel. She watched as he shed his buckskins, thinking what she always thought, and must always keep to herself: that he was as beautiful to her as these perfect children. The line of his back, the way his hair swung low over the wide span of his shoulders, the long tensed muscles in his thighs, even his scars, because they told his stories. When he lay down beside her she moved closer to his warmth instinctively. But instead of drifting to sleep, she was caught up in his wakefulness.

In the year they had been together she had at first been amazed and then slightly resentful of Nathaniel's ability to fall instantly to sleep—it was a hunter's trick, a warrior's skill as important as the ability to handle a gun. But not tonight.

"Now *you* are thinking too hard," she said to him, finally. "I can almost hear you."

He sought out her hand. "You knew about the twins. Why didn't you tell me?"

She hesitated. "Falling-Day thought you would worry overmuch. So did I. After what happened to Sarah—" Elizabeth looked into the cradle. Hannah's twin brother had died in Nathaniel's hands. Sarah had borne him one more child, a daughter, and he had buried her in her mother's arms on the same day. It was inevitable that he would think of those losses, even in his joy.

He said, "I should have been here."

"Nathaniel—"

"You must have been scared, when the storm came down."

He was determined to hear it, and so she told him.

"Yes," she said, finally. "But soon after, the pain started in earnest and I had little energy for anything else. And no choice, as you had no choice. But we managed, did we not?"

He made a sound in his throat that was less than total agreement. Elizabeth brought his hand up to rub against her cheek.

"Shall we name them for your father, and my mother? Daniel and Mathilde. Would that please you?"

"Aye, it would. And it will please Hawkeye." He turned to her, but his thoughts were far away. Gently, he fit his face to the curve of her neck and shoulder. He smelled of himself: honest sweat, leather and gunpowder, woodsmoke and the dried mint he liked to chew.

"You've been thinking of Hawkeye a lot today."

She felt the tension rise in him, coming to the surface of his skin like sweat.

"What is it? Tell me."

"There was a letter down at the tavern for me," he said, his voice muffled. "From Moncrieff. He's in Montreal."

She waited, slightly tensed now. "Moncrieff found your father?"

"Aye. In the garrison, under arrest."

Suddenly very much awake, Elizabeth sat up.

"Somerville's men took him for questioning," Nathaniel continued. "There's rumors about the Tory gold."

"Oh Lord." With a glance toward the cradle, Elizabeth folded her hands before her. "Tell me all of it."

Nathaniel recited the letter; he had had nothing to do in the long hours of the whiteout but to read it, again and again, and the words came to him easily.

When he had finished, she lay back down. "You'll have to go."

"You believe Moncrieff, then?"

She raised a brow. "I doubt he would make up such a thing. To what end, after all. It is true that we do not know him well, Nathaniel, but in this much I think he can be trusted." She paused. "We both know that you cannot leave Hawkeye locked up."

Nathaniel let out a hoarse laugh, but his look was troubled. "I can't leave him in gaol, and I can't leave you here alone. And you can't travel."

Elizabeth shifted to a more comfortable position. "It's true that I don't like the idea of you going so far, right now. But I don't see you have any choice."

In spite of the seriousness of their situation, Nathaniel grinned. He caught the plait that fell over her shoulder to her waist and gave it a good tug. "You're the one with the talent for breaking men out of gaol."

She flicked her fingers at him, but color rose on her cheeks. "Do you have any idea how we could possibly get Hawkeye out of a military garrison?"

"I'm sure something would come up," he said. "There's money enough, and money opens more locks than keys ever will. But I'm not about to leave you here alone with two new babies."

"Of course you must go. Moncrieff and Robbie cannot do it without you. Your father needs you."

"Boots," Nathaniel said wearily. "My ma always told me never to cross a woman in childbed, but—"

"A wise woman," interrupted Elizabeth. "Most excellent advice."

Deep in the night, Nathaniel brought first the girl child and then the boy to her for nursing as she could not yet manage them both at once. Curiosity had come to the door at the first hungry cries, but seeing that Nathaniel was attending to Elizabeth's needs, she nodded and slipped back to the bed she was sharing with Hannah in the sleeping loft.

Yawning widely, Elizabeth sat up against the bolsters and watched her son's small face. He tugged so enthusiastically that she winced. Nathaniel sat beside her, his gaze fixed on the boy. Mathilde was on his lap, newly wound and already asleep again.

Elizabeth said, "I wish that you did not have to go, Nathaniel. But I can not be so selfish. You will never rest easy here, knowing that your father needs your help. Some day you may call Daniel to you the same way, and I expect that he will do what he must to come. I trust that he will."

The candlelight lay like gold on the baby's cheek. Nathaniel touched the tender skin with one finger. "You need me too," he said, hoarsely. "It ain't right to leave you, Boots."

"You will come back to me, will you not? To us?"

"Aye," he said, his breath warm on her skin. "Never doubt it."

Romance Readers Never Go to Bed Alone!

SWEEPSTAKES

GREAT READING MEANS YOU NEVER GO TO BED ALONE AGAIN!

You could be one of 100 lucky readers to win this limited-edition "Romance Readers Never Go To Bed Alone!" nightshirt <u>ABSOLUTELY FREE</u> from Bantam Books!

To be eligible for a free nightshirt, submit your entry to:
ROMANCE READERS NEVER GO TO BED ALONE!
Sweepstakes,
2 Accradata Drive, P.O. Box 5812, Dept. IT, Unionville, CT 06085-5812

100 winners will be chosen in a random drawing from all eligible and completed entries. Your entry must be received by September 3, 1999.

How did you choose this book?
- ☐ Author
- ☐ Title
- ☐ Cover
- ☐ Advertisement
- ☐ Recommendation

How many books do you read a month?
- ☐ Less than one
- ☐ 1-2
- ☐ 3-5
- ☐ More than 5

How many of the books you read are romances?
- ☐ Less than one
- ☐ 1-2
- ☐ 3-5
- ☐ more than 5

Where did you buy this book? _____

_____

NAME _____ AGE _____

ADDRESS _____

CITY _____ STATE _____ ZIP _____

E-MAIL ADDRESS _____

NO PURCHASE NECESSARY.
Be sure to get your entry in by September 3, 1999!
See reverse for Official Entry Rules.

Bantam

Official Entry Rules:

1. NO PURCHASE NECESSARY.

2. Enter by completing the official entry coupon, or by printing your name, address, age, and answers to the questions on the previous page on a 3"x 5" card and mail the coupon or card to:

ROMANCE READERS NEVER GO TO BED ALONE! Sweepstakes,
2 Accradata Drive
P.O. Box 5812, Dept. IT
Unionville, CT 06085-5812

Entries must be received by September 3, 1999. No mechanically reproduced entries allowed. Entries are limited to one per person. Not responsible for late, lost, stolen, illegible, incomplete, postage due or misdirected entries or mail.

3. One Hundred (100) Prizes will be awarded: The Prize is a free "Romance Readers Never Go To Bed Alone" nightshirt (100% cotton; one size only). Estimated value of prize: Approximately $18.00. No transfer or substitution of the prize will be permitted, except by Bantam Books, a division of Random House, Inc. ("Sponsor") in its sole discretion, in which case a prize of equal or greater value will be awarded.

4. On or about September 17, 1999, the winners will be chosen in a random drawing conducted by Sponsor's marketing department from all eligible and completed entries received by the entry deadline, and the winners will receive their prizes by mail. Odds of winning depend upon the number of eligible entries received, which is anticipated to be approximately 10,000.

5. Entrants must be residents of the United States and Canada (excluding Quebec). Limit one entry per person. Void in Puerto Rico, Quebec and where otherwise prohibited or restricted by law. All federal, state and local regulations apply. Employees of Bantam Books, Random House, Inc., its parent, subsidiaries, affiliates, suppliers and agencies and their immediate family members and persons living in their household are not eligible to enter this sweepstakes. All federal and local taxes, if any, are the sole responsibility of the prize winner. By accepting the prize, winner releases Bantam Books, Random House, Inc., and their parent companies, subsidiaries, affiliates, suppliers and agents from any and all liability for any loss, harm, damages, cost or expense, including without limitation, property damages, personal injury and/or deaths arising out of participation in this sweepstakes or the acceptance and use of the prize.

6. By entering, entrants agree to abide by these Official Rules and the decision of the judges, which shall be final.

7. For the names of the prize winners, available after September 30, 1999, send a stamped, self-addressed envelope, separate from your entry, to Romance Readers Never Go To Bed Alone! Sweepstakes Winners, Bantam Books, Dept. DS2, 1540 Broadway, New York, New York, 10036 by December 31, 1999.

8. Sponsor: Bantam Books, a division of Random House, Inc., 1540 Broadway, New York, New York, 10036.